EDWARDIAN ENGLAND
1901–1914

I. Traffic at the Mansion House 1910

EDWARDIAN ENGLAND

1901–1914

—◆—

EDITED BY

SIMON NOWELL-SMITH

LONDON

OXFORD UNIVERSITY PRESS

NEW YORK   TORONTO

1964

Oxford University Press, Amen House, London E.C.4

GLASGOW NEW YORK TORONTO MELBOURNE WELLINGTON
BOMBAY CALCUTTA MADRAS KARACHI LAHORE DACCA
CAPE TOWN SALISBURY NAIROBI IBADAN ACCRA
KUALA LUMPUR HONG KONG

PRINTED IN GREAT BRITAIN

PREFACE

'AND so, poor wicked nineteenth century, farewell!' wrote Wilfred Scawen Blunt in his diary on the last day of 1900; and just over three weeks later, 'The queen is dead of an apoplectic stroke, and the great Victorian age is at an end. . . . This is notable news. It will mean great changes in the world.' It did.

The ordinary man, if not the professed historian, tends to think of history as falling tidily into centuries or reigns. History is seldom tidy. Shakespeare wrote under two sovereigns and in two centuries; the *Lyrical Ballads* are eighteenth-century verse by a Victorian laureate; Bernard Shaw's plays and political writings straddle four reigns (five, if uncrowned Edward VIII's 325 days are included). Politics and science know no chronological frontiers: Marconi did not delay his wireless-telegraphy patent, or R. W. Paul his first news-film, or Keir Hardie and John Burns their election as Labour's first M.P.s, for the few years that would have carried them into a twentieth-century almanac. According to an *obiter dictum* of Mr. William Plomer the Victorian age petered out towards the end of 1918—which leaves no room for an Edwardian (as Max Beerbohm would have said, an Edvardian) era. In some ways Mr. Plomer is right. In 1918 the leading figures in politics and the church, in industry, science, and the arts, were all Victorians. The prime minister had been in the Commons since 1890; the chief of the imperial general staff had seen service in Burma in 1885; the venerable president of the Royal Academy had been born before Victoria's accession, and the dynamic chief proprietor of *The Times* had founded the *Daily Mail* some years before her death. On the other hand the up-and-coming, forward-looking younger men—and women—in the early 1920's, who had grown to maturity under King Edward, did not see themselves as Edwardian. The greatest of the changes foreseen by Blunt, a great war, had cut them off from the days of their youth. They had a new world to build.

A great war—and this for the first time was a 'world' war—not only disrupts the lives of ordinary citizens. It stimulates new ways of thinking and releases new energies. It also accelerates progress, political, social, scientific. The battle for women's suffrage was finally won, not by militant Edwardian intellectuals skirmishing in Trafalgar Square, but by the girls in arms factories and field hospitals, the 'clippies' and 'nippies', the W.R.N.S., the W.A.A.C., and the W.R.A.F. So was the battle for short skirts and short hair. If state-sponsored science evolved poison-gas, it also encouraged the development of the motor-car (the wealthy Edwardian's toy), the caterpillar-tractor (the tank's legacy to agriculture) and the aeroplane. The need to restore

> shell shock cases
> To cannon-fodder status

was a potent force in undermining the British doctor's suspicion of Viennese theories of psychology, theories dating back—in Vienna— to the nineteenth century. Examples could be drawn from other spheres. The point to be made is that, in ringing in the new order, the first world war rang the knell of much, good and bad, of the old. When we speak of Edwardian England we usually mean a period ending, not when the king died on 6 May 1910, but when England declared war on Germany on 4 August 1914.

History, then, has provided the contributors to this volume with a tidy and convenient *terminus ad quem*. But several of them, as the reader will observe, have been exercised by the problem of a *terminus a quo*. Edwardian England came into being, according to the almanac, with the accession of King Edward VII on 22 January 1901. Neither that date, however, nor the turn of the century three weeks earlier is invested with the absolute quality of 4 August 1914—unless it be for the naval or military historian for whom, by chance, the Edwardian period coincides nearly enough with the lull between the Boer war and the world war. Commander Kemp and Professor Falls have had less need than other contributors to 'play themselves in' with descriptions of England in the later part of Victoria's long reign.

So long was that reign—the longest in English history—that it is illusory to regard 'the great Victorian age' as monolithic. If, as Mr. Howes says,[1] the spirit of the age is an elusive abstraction,

[1] *Infra*, chapter 11.

several elusive spirits presided over the years between 1837 and 1901, between the introduction of anaesthetics and the discovery of radium, between the opening of the London–Birmingham railway and the first London–Brighton motor-car rally, between the death of Lord Chancellor Eldon and the birth of Lord Chancellor Kilmuir, between *The Bohemian Girl* and *The Belle of Bohemia*, between *Pickwick Papers* and *Kim*. Stirrings of revolt against Victorianism had begun well before the reign was over. 'Had Queen Victoria died at seventy', Mr. Russell writes,[1] 'we should point with pride to the evidence in the eighteen-nineties of a youth and vigour altogether appropriate to a new reign.' Two of the foundation-stones of Edwardian thinking, as Mr. Quinton shows,[2] were laid by the Society for Psychical Research (1882) and the Fabian Society (1884). Mr. Howes quotes authority for the view that a renaissance of English music began about 1880. In a recent study of Edwardian literature Mr. Graham Hough has argued that both the Edwardians and 'the nineties' should submerge their identities in a period beginning about 1880, after the Victorian heyday, and ending in 1914—'a period distinct in spirit from what we usually think of as Victorianism, a period in which all the foundations of modern literature were being laid, but recognizably distinct from modern literature too'.[3] Likewise Mr. Bridges-Adams, with his communicable nostalgia for the Edwardian theatre in which he learnt his trade, insists that without the 'establishment', represented by Irving, there could have been no *avant-garde*, no Gordon Craig.[4] The Edwardians could not have flown aeroplanes, Professor Ubbelohde points out,[5] if the Victorians had not, in the eighties, evolved the petrol-driven motor-car. πάντα ῥεî. In the same progression of science, the contributors to some future volume on neo-Elizabethan England will date from the Edwardian era many of the constructive benefits and destructive horrors, in curative medicine and in atomic warfare, that seem to distinguish our present age.

Future historians, rejecting classification by sovereigns and centuries, may well isolate the period from 1880 to 1914 as an

[1] *Infra*, chapter 8.   [2] *Infra*, chapter 6.

[3] *Edwardians and Late Victorians: English Institute Essays*, edited by Richard Ellmann, Columbia University Press, 1961.

[4] *Infra*, chapter 10.

[5] *Infra*, chapter 5.

entity in its own right. Nevertheless the opening of a new century and a new reign in 1901 was a notable coincidence. The ordinary citizen, having celebrated both events with more than ordinary enthusiasm, looked forward to 'great changes' none the less hopefully because change had been, for a couple of decades, in the air. The intention of this volume is to show how, in the years 1901–14, the citizen fared. Was it all glitter for the rich, all tight-rope walking on the poverty-line for the poor? What did the upper class pay their servants, the middle class pay for their holidays, the working man's wife for his food or his children's shoes? What houses did they live in? What books and newspapers did they read—this first adult generation born since the passing of the first elementary education act? What plays and art exhibitions could they see, what concerts or sporting events attend? Did they go to church, or to the sea-side? How did they travel? What were their schools and their country pursuits, their conditions of employment in industry, of service in the armed forces? How did their elected representatives serve them, or their scientists, their prophets and priests, their king?

None of these questions is loaded with political or aesthetic implications, though contrasts of class and taste, both within the Edwardian period and between that period and what went before and came after, are implicit in many of the answers. It is impossible to read Miss Laski on working-class budgets and middle-class menus[1] without on the one hand recalling Mrs. Peel's chapter in *Early Victorian England*[2] and, on the other, drawing upon one's own experience of life under the welfare, and increasingly affluent, state. The mingled indignation and enthusiasm aroused by the post-impressionist exhibition in 1910 is almost exactly paralleled by the reception both of the preraphaelites in the 1850's and of the surrealists in the 1920's. Edward VII's relations with ministers, admirals, and generals, and his freedom to indulge in indiscretions, calculated or inadvertent, in foreign capitals, derive at least a part of their interest from comparison with the restraints that Victoria imposed upon herself and those which the development of constitutional monarchy has imposed upon later sovereigns. But the function of the contributors has been to record facts, not to point

[1] *Infra*, chapter 4.
[2] Edited by G. M. Young, two volumes, Oxford University Press, 1934.

morals, and the facts have been derived, wherever possible, from contemporary sources.

References to these sources, and to later authorities, have been kept to a minimum, in order that the reader should not be distracted by an over-abundance of footnotes. Blue-books and books of household management, newspapers and trade-catalogues, reports of sociological investigations and of scientific societies, these are among the primary sources, followed by memoirs, biographies, and histories. Even novelists are called in evidence. In no other period perhaps, certainly in England, has fiction been so true—often so drearily true—to fact. Several essentially Edwardian novelists, major or minor, and pre-eminently H. G. Wells and Arnold Bennett, described with photographic accuracy the physical surroundings of the middle- and lower-class characters in their books: these were the 'agglomerations' of detail that so offended Henry James but that can be so valuable to the social historian. One novel of a different kind, dealing with the period but written later, is drawn upon by several of the contributors—*The Edwardians*, by V. Sackville-West (1930). The validity of its witness to the mode of living of the aristocracy cannot be questioned.

Of the contributors, four were born under Victoria. Professor Falls was commissioned in a line regiment on the outbreak of the first world war; Mr. Bridges-Adams served his apprenticeship in the theatre under Irving, Poel, and Granville-Barker; Mr. Howes was a school-boy when Diaghilev first came to London; and Professor Blunden's memories of a country childhood compose the one avowedly autobiographical chapter of the book. The remaining contributors, whether Edwardian or Georgian by birth, are recognized authorities in their fields.

S. N. S.

CONTENTS

ILLUSTRATIONS

Acknowledgements are due in each case to those named, and in particular to H.M. the Queen for gracious permission to reproduce Plates II and III (*a*) and (*b*) from the Windsor Castle Library.

ILLUSTRATIONS IN THE TEXT

FOLK-SONGS IN THE TEXT

'The Seeds of Love' (Cecil Sharp) on page 422 is reproduced by permission of Novello and Company Limited and Dr. Maud Karpeles. 'Bushes and Briars' (R. Vaughan Williams) on page 423 is reproduced by permission of Novello and Company Limited and Mrs. Ralph Vaughan Williams.

CHRONOLOGICAL

NOTE. The *floruit* is the year the person reached the
in the *floruit* column give the date of death (twentieth
birth (nineteenth

Floruit	Obiit	Publications, Plays, Music
1895 J. M. Barrie[37] H. Bottomley[33] J. S. Haldane[36] Walter Sickert[42] Wilson Steer[42] G. F. Stout[44]	Randolph Churchill[49] Charles Hallé[19] T. H. Huxley[25]	Almayer's Folly; Amazing Marriage; Foundations of Belief; Golden Age; Jude the Obscure; Poems (Johnson, Yeats); Sister Songs; Time Machine. Guy Domville; Importance of Being Earnest; Notorious Mrs. Ebbsmith.
1896 Viscount Allenby[36] Earl Haig[28] Charles Holroyd[17] Nellie Melba[31] Rabindranath Tagore[41] A. N. Whitehead[47]	George du Maurier[34] Alfred Hunt[30] J. E. Millais[29] William Morris[34] Coventry Patmore[23]	*Daily Mail*; Greek View of Life; Love's Coming of Age; Shropshire Lad; Verses (Dowson); Weir of Hermiston; Works (Beerbohm). Prisoner of Zenda; Sign of the Cross.
1897 William Bragg[42] Frederick Delius[34] Viscount Grey[33] Aurel Stein[43] Henry Tonks[37]	Isaac Pitman[13]	Admirals All; Captains Courageous; Essay on Comedy; Liza of Lambeth; Nigger of the Narcissus; Spoils of Poynton; Studies in the Psychology of Sex.
1898 Austen Chamberlain[37] Earl Lloyd-George[45] J. Martin-Harvey[44] Lucien Pissarro[44] Charles Shannon[37] Alfred Sutro[33] Francis Younghusband[42]	Aubrey Beardsley[72] Henry Bessemer[13] E. Burne-Jones[33] 'Lewis Carroll'[32] W. E. Gladstone[09] Samuel Plimsoll[24]	Ballad of Reading Gaol; Elizabeth and her German Garden; Rupert of Hentzau; Plays Pleasant and Unpleasant; Turn of the Screw; Wessex Poems.
1899 Roger Casement[16] Stephen Phillips[15] F. C. S. Schiller[37] Marie Tempest[42]	Bernard Quaritch[19]	Awkward Age; Stalky and Co. Caesar and Cleopatra; Only Way. Enigma Variations.

TABLE

age of 35. The superscript figures following the names
century); those in the *obiit* column give the date of
century).

Art and Architecture	*Public Affairs*	
Westminster Cathedral	Salisbury, P.M.; Armenian atrocities; Jameson raid; Röntgen rays; Wood's first promenade concert.	1895
National Portrait Gallery; Glasgow School of Art; Poynter, P.R.A.	Kruger telegram; Marconi's wireless patent; Prince of Wales's Persimmon wins Derby; Derby Day filmed; Austin, poet laureate.	1896
Cardiff City Hall; Tate Gallery.	Royal Automobile Club founded.	1897
International Society; Sargent's 'Asher Wertheimer'.	Kitchener in Khartoum; Fashoda incident; imperial penny post; Folk Song Society.	1898
Victoria and Albert Museum.	Boer war; London Government Act.	1899

Floruit	Obiit	Publications, Plays, Music
1900 King George V[36]	R. D. Blackmore[25]	*Daily Express*; Lord Jim;
A. G. Gardiner[46]	Ernest Dowson[67]	Love and Mr. Lewisham;
Rudyard Kipling[36]	John Ruskin[19]	Oxford Book of English
Viscount Northcliffe[22]	Henry Sidgwick[38]	Verse; Philosophy of Leib-
Baroness Orczy[47]	Arthur Sullivan[42]	niz.
W. B. Yeats[39]	Oscar Wilde[56]	Dream of Gerontius; Hia-
		watha.
1901 Roger Fry[34]	Queen Victoria[19]	By the Ionian Sea; Hegelian
Ramsay MacDonald[37]	R. D'Oyly Carte[44]	Cosmology; Kim; Letters
J. E. McTaggart[25]	Kate Greenaway[46]	from John Chinaman;
Gilbert Murray[57]	F. W. H. Myers[43]	Poems of the Past and the
Arthur Pearson[21]	John Stainer[40]	Present; World's Classics.
Beatrix Potter[43]	Charlotte M. Yonge[23]	
James Pryde[41]		
Charles Ricketts[31]		
H G. Wells[46]		
1902 Earl Baldwin[47]	Samuel Butler[35]	Hound of the Baskervilles;
Arnold Bennett[31]	G. A. Henty[32]	Just So Stories; Path to
Frank Brangwyn[56]	Lionel Johnson[67]	Rome; Personal Idealism;
John Galsworthy[33]	Cecil Rhodes[53]	Peter Rabbit; Salt-Water
Arthur Rackham[39]	Frederick Temple[21]	Ballads; Songs of Child-
George Russell ('AE')[35]		hood; *Times Literary Sup-
		plement*; Wings of the
		Dove; Youth.
		Admirable Crichton; Paolo
		and Francesca; Quality
		Street.
		Witch of Atlas.
1903 George Arliss[46]	F. W. Farrar[31]	Ambassadors; *Burlington
Granville Bantock[46]	George Gissing[57]	Magazine*; *Daily Mirror*;
Gertrude Bell[26]	W. E. Henley[49]	Henry Ryecroft; Princi-
Charles Holmes[36]	W. E. H. Lecky[38]	pia Ethica; Principles of
H. H. Joachim[38]	Phil May[64]	Mathematics; Typhoon;
C. R. Mackintosh[28]	'H. S. Merriman'[62]	Way of All Flesh.
Lord Melchett[30]	Marquess of Salisbury[30]	Man of Honour.
Viscount Rothermere[40]	Herbert Spencer[20]	
	J. McN. Whistler[34]	
1904 Laurence Binyon[43]	William Harcourt[27]	Dynasts; Green Mansions;
Neville Chamberlain[40]	Paul Kruger[25]	Nostromo; Radio-activity.
Walford Davies[41]	F. Y. Powell[50]	Candida; Peter Pan; Pru-
Lord Duveen[39]	Val Prinsep[38]	nella.
Mahatma Gandhi[48]	Samuel Smiles[12]	
P. de Laszlo[37]	H. M. Stanley[41]	
Edwin Lutyens[44]	Leslie Stephen[32]	
R. W. Paul[43]	G. F. Watts[17]	
1905 Hilaire Belloc[53]	Henry Irving[38]	Biography for Beginners;
Alfred Douglas[45]	George Macdonald[24]	De Profundis; Golden
Harry Lauder[50]	William Sharp[55]	Bowl; Modern Symposium;
Marie Lloyd[22]	Alfred Waterhouse[30]	Modern Utopia; Return of
H. H. Munro[16]		Sherlock Holmes; Riches

Art and Architecture	*Public Affairs*	
Wallace Collection opened.	Commonwealth of Australia; relief of Mafeking; Labour Representation Committee; first Zeppelin flight; Quantum theory; Central London Railway ('tuppenny tube'); Boxer rising.	1900
Carfax Gallery.	Accession of Edward VII; President McKinley assassinated; Brodrick's army reforms.	1901
Deptford Town Hall; Horniman Museum; Old Bailey.	Boer war ends; Balfour, P.M.; Order of Merit; Elementary Education Act; Committee of Imperial Defence; Aswan Dam.	1902
Marischal College, Aberdeen; National Art-Collections Fund.	Irish Land Purchase Act; Joseph Chamberlain resigns; First Garden City Limited (Letchworth).	1903
City Hall, Belfast; Ritz Hotel, Piccadilly.	Russo-Japanese War (–05); Anglo-French entente; Licensing Act; Fisher, first sea lord; Ladies' Automobile Club; Motor Car Act; first London motor taxi-cab; Workers' Educational Association.	1904
Central Hall, Westminster; Durand-Ruel exhibition; Middlesex Guildhall; Piccadilly Hotel; Port Sunlight.	'Red Sunday' at St. Petersburg; Campbell-Bannerman, P.M.; Haldane at War Office; Anglo-Japanese alliance; Kaiser visits Tangier; Unemployed Workmen Act; militant suffragism; motor	1905

	Floruit	*Obiit*	*Publications, Plays, Music*
	Viscount Samuel[63] J. C. Smuts[50]		and Poverty; Scarlet Pimpernel. Man and Superman; Voysey Inheritance.
1906	Earl Beatty[36] W. H. Davies[40] Seymour Hicks[49] William McDougall[38] Harold Prichard[47] Lord Rutherford[37] Derwent Wood[26]	Dorothea Beale[31] Michael Davitt[46] 'John Oliver Hobbes'[67] G. J. Holyoake[17] F. W. Maitland[50]	Dawn in Britain; English Hymnal; Everyman's Library; Joseph Vance; King's English; Man of Property; Puck of Pook's Hill; Some Dogmas of Religion. Doctor's Dilemma; His House in Order; Nero; Silver Box. Omar Khayyám; Sea Drift.
1907	Norman Angell Max Beerbohm[56] Earl of Birkenhead[30] Ramsay Muir[41] William Nicholson[49] William Rothenstein[45] Bertrand Russell Vaughan Williams[58]	Viscount Goschen[31] Henry Kemble[48] Francis Thompson[59]	Father and Son; Jock of the Bushveldt; Lex Credendi; Longest Journey; *Nation*; *New Age*. Playboy of the Western World. Village Romeo and Juliet.
1908	Clara Butt[36] Walter de la Mare[56] Gerald du Maurier[34] F. M. (Hueffer) Ford[39] G. E. Moore[58] A. R. Orage[34]	Redvers Buller[39] Edward Caird[35] H. Campbell-Bannerman[36] Walter Headlam[66] 'Ouida'[39]	Autobiography of a Super-Tramp; *English Review*; Introduction to Social Psychology; Room with a View; Old Wives' Tale; Wind in the Willows. Passing of the Third Floor Back. First Symphony (Elgar).
1909	Lilian Baylis[37] G. K. Chesterton[36] Winston Churchill Gustav Holst[34] C. F. G. Masterman[27] W. Somerset Maugham Ernest Shackleton[22] B. H. Streeter[37]	H. O. Arnold-Forster[55] Charles Conder[68] John Davidson[57] W. P. Frith[19] George Meredith[28] A. C. Swinburne[37] J. M. Synge[71]	Ann Veronica; Condition of England; Oxford Lectures on Poetry; Personae; Prester John; Survival of Man; Time's Laughing-stocks; Unemployment. Blue Bird; Strife. Mass of Life.
1910	John Buchan[40] Lord Rayleigh[47] Forrest Reid[47] Donald Tovey[40] Edgar Wallace[32]	King Edward VII[41] Holman Hunt[27] George Newnes[51] Florence Nightingale[20] Goldwin Smith[23]	Clayhanger; Great Illusion; Howards End; Mr. Polly; Principia Mathematica; Thirty-six Poems (Flecker). Justice. Sea Symphony.

Art and Architecture	*Public Affairs*	
	omnibuses in London; Einstein's theory of relativity.	
National Museum of Wales.	Trade Disputes Act; Dreadnought, Lusitania and Mauretania launched; Bakerloo and Piccadilly tubes.	1906
Hampstead Garden Suburb; Royal Naval College, Dartmouth.	Dominion of New Zealand; Deceased Wife's Sister Act; Probation of Offenders Bill; Boy Scout Movement.	1907
Allied Artists; Epstein's Strand sculptures; Royal Liver Building, Liverpool; Selfridge's.	Asquith, P.M.; Lloyd George at Exchequer; Old Age Pensions Act; Coal Mines (Eight Hours) Act; Northcliffe acquires *The Times*.	1908
Buckfast Abbey; Orpen's 'Homage to Manet'.	Labour Exhanges Act; Trade Boards Act; Peary at North Pole; Union of South Africa; Blériot flies Channel; Edward VII's Minoru wins Derby.	1909
Adelphi Hotel, Liverpool; Contemporary Art Society; Post-impressionist exhibition; Shire Hall, Reading.	January and December General Elections; accession of George V; Churchill at Home Office; transatlantic wireless service; academic committee of Royal Society of Literature.	1910

Floruit	Obiit	Publications, Plays, Music
1911 Muirhead Bone[53] Gwen John[39]	E. A. Abbey[52] Charles Dilke[43] Passmore Edwards[23] Francis Galton[22] W. S. Gilbert[36]	Canzoni; Dolores; Everlasting Mercy; Hail and Farewell; Hilda Lessways; In a German Pension; Mr. Perrin and Mr. Traill; Poems (Brooke); Village Labourer; White Peacock; Zuleika Dobson. Fanny's First Play; Miracle.
1912 James Agate[47] H. Granville-Barker[46] James Jeans[46] Laura Knight Henry Ospovat[09] Frederick Soddy[56]	L. Alma-Tadema[36] General Booth[29] Octavia Hill[38] Andrew Lang[44] Lord Lister[27] Justin McCarthy[30] Captain Scott[68] Norman Shaw[31] W. T. Stead[49]	Crock of Gold; *Daily Herald*; Foundations; Georgian Poetry; Listeners; Poetical Works (Bridges). Oedipus Rex.
1913 Spencer Gore[14] Augustus John[61] John Masefield William Orpen[31] J. M. Thompson[56]	Alfred Austin[35] 'Baron Corvo'[60] Robinson Ellis[34] 'Mark Rutherford'[31]	Chance; *New Statesman*; Peacock Pie; Sinister Street; Sons and Lovers; World of Labour. Great Adventure.
1914 Henry Ainley[45] Vanessa Bell[61] E. M. Forster Hamilton Harty[41] Gerald Kelly Matthew Smith[59]	Ingram Bywater[40] Joseph Chamberlain[36] Hubert von Herkomer[49] Earl Roberts[32] John Tenniel[20] R. Y. Tyrrell[44]	Dubliners; Essays on Truth and Reality; Poems (Blunden). Pygmalion. London Symphony; Immortal Hour.

Art and Architecture	*Public Affairs*	
Admiralty Arch; Camden Town Group; Victoria Memorial; London County Hall.	Delhi Durbar; Agadir crisis; Parliament Act; National Insurance, Shops, Coal Mines (Minimum Wage), Official Secrets, Copyright, and Aerial Navigation Acts; Churchill at Admiralty; Amundsen at South Pole; first aerial post.	1911
	White Slave Traffic Act; Home Rule Bill; Ulster covenant; Titanic sunk; Royal Flying Corps; Marconi affair; National Union of Railwaymen.	1912
Sargent's 'Henry James'.	Franchise Bill; Welsh Church Disestablishment Bill; Panama Canal; Bridges, poet laureate.	1913
London Group.	First World War.	1914

1

THE KING

ROGER FULFORD

THE KING

THERE was a striking but innocent device, greatly enjoyed in the nineteenth century, known as the dissolving view. By a careful juxtaposition of magic lanterns one image was slowly faded out while the light from the other was intensified and a new picture was brilliantly revealed. There are only a few occasions in history when a nation is consciously aware that it is watching a dissolving view. One such occasion was the evening of 22 January 1901 when the British people heard that Queen Victoria, surrounded by her children and grandchildren, had died. The realization that the old image had dissolved was helped by the coincidence that the queen and the old century had come to an end together. No doubt the shock of realizing that something seemingly perpetual had dissolved was most keenly felt by those whose lives touched the queen and her court or by the business world which saw in her an assurance of imperial stability. But the impression was general, felt as keenly in Manchester or Newcastle as in the capital, as personally by the artisans as by the club-men and as solemnly by the board-school child as by the gaffer who could remember King William IV. Of course it is easy enough for posterity to interpret a single event as an end and a beginning. Many excellent films, plays, and books have done this—building up the significance of a great event as it appeared to those who lived afterwards. That is not necessarily what was felt at the time. But it was the realization of what was happening at that instant which makes that January day in 1901 rare and momentous for us. This is what Lady Battersea, a member of a leading Jewish family, wrote at the time:

Words seem to express less than facts in this case. Black, mourning London, black, mourning England, black, mourning Empire—those facts are text and sermon. The emptiness of the great city without the feeling of the Queen's living presence in her Empire, and the sensation of universal change haunted me more than any other sensations.[1]

[1] Lucy Cohen, *Lady de Rothschild and her Daughter*, 1935.

Lady Battersea here expresses the feeling of men and women at the time; they thought of the image which had dissolved: they could hardly direct their minds to the one which was emerging. Even at Osborne where the queen had died her family and personal servants could not speedily adjust themselves to the new order. Everything continued in the name of the dead queen; it was still the queen's dinner at night, though a king reigned; it was twenty-four hours before the family did homage to their new head—homage which generally takes place at the instant of the ruler's death. Such feelings—and they were general throughout the land—were an immediate test of the capacity, the personality, and the good feeling of King Edward VII. As the Irishman is supposed to have said, 'He won't be the king his mother was.'

And there is a little more force to that remark than the jest implies. King Edward had a longer apprenticeship to power than any sovereign in English history. He was 59 when he was proclaimed king, two years older than George IV when he came to the throne. For four decades, since he had reached maturity, he had been familiar to the public as the Prince of Wales. He had been popular—easily the most widely popular Prince of Wales in our history until that time. But it was the sense that the serene, dignified, and slightly mysterious Queen Victoria was dissolving to make way for this jaunty prince which made men wonder, and which explains the Irishman's remark.

Yet to his position King Edward brought solid advantages. These did not rest on his physical appearance, which was not altogether prepossessing. He was short and had grown stout. He had a very long nose—a reminder that through both his parents he inherited many personal characteristics of the house of Coburg. Though he was bald, his head was finely drawn and was to look splendid on coinage and postage stamps. His face was given strength, and its character set off, by a well-shaped beard. He loved dressing in ceremonial clothes, and he looked his best in the uniform of a field-marshal in the British army. In the short tunics of some foreign regiments he looked frightful. Although the king may not have been good-looking—he was at a disadvantage when seen against the sombre good looks of his brother, the Duke of Edinburgh, or the flamboyant appearance of his nephew the kaiser—he had an extraordinary sense of occasion, so that in any gathering, whether he was in uniform, or in a frock-coat, or in a short coat and wearing the familiar curly-brimmed top hat, he was immediately recognized, instantly conspicuous. His voice was very deep, which appeared to strengthen his slightly guttural speech; one of his friends, Lord Redesdale, has recalled the music of his voice and its perfect diction.

Perhaps the greatest advantage which in 1901 the king brought to his task was the width of his experience. He could say with Ulysses, looking back on a life of travel and variety,

'I am a part of all that I have met.'

He was the first English sovereign of whom it could fairly be said that he knew the world. King Edward had met the Americans in America, the Canadians in Canada, the Indians in India: he had travelled in Spain, Italy, and Russia: he was at home in Denmark and Germany: he especially enjoyed Austria and he loved Paris and the French. He was always loyal to the affections of his youth and he first fell under the charm of Paris when, as a boy, he visited the French emperor with his parents and asked his host whether he could not stay behind, adding that he would not be missed at home because he had so many brothers and sisters. Though this was not an accomplishment of his fellow countrymen or of his generation, he was a remarkable linguist. He spoke German almost interchangeably with English, and the statesman Haldane was greatly struck by his command of German slang. He had a good working knowledge of Italian and Spanish and he spoke French beautifully, showing himself a past master in the idiomatic subtlety of that language. This experience, this capacity through his knowledge of languages to sense something of contemporary feeling abroad, at once gave him authority. The majority of the aristocracy, of cabinet ministers, and of civil servants knew little enough of foreign lands: they travelled to Paris, or to that England by the Mediterranean discovered by Lord Brougham, and too often contented themselves, as did the Kickleburys on the Rhine, with the intelligence that tea abroad was made from boiled boots. Disraeli once complained that, owing to the insularity of English people, there was little real interchange of thought between England and foreign powers. He suggested that this was a principal defect of the Foreign Office and contrasted it with the personal knowledge of the Prince of Wales, derived from personal friendship with some of the leading men in the chief states of Europe. King Edward was perfectly capable, through private friendship, of assimilating the thought of foreign countries, though whether he was capable of transmitting, or wished to transmit, English thought is another matter. The great mistake, which was made at the time and has been senselessly repeated ever since, is in reading into the prince's travels far more than the facts warrant. Because he went to Russia to bury a tsar, to Germany to marry a niece, or to a spa for its purgative waters, he was not making the journey to exert influence or with designs in his heart. The most that can be said of these travels was that he enjoyed them and that they gave him knowledge and information. But a consequence of that knowledge was to increase the stature of the prince among his circle of English friends and in the world of government. Against his experience many politicians felt that inferiority which Dr. Johnson assures us is always felt by those who have never been to Italy. 'The country, and all of *us*, would like to see you a little more stationary', his mother had once written to him, when she complained that he was 'always running about'. But she was wrong. Travel and cosmopolitan life developed the king's mind which had remained completely dormant under the pressure of conventional education.

One other important advantage he carried with him. Leaving aside his personal friends he had a wider knowledge of many sections of the British people than any of his predecessors. In his generation people often thought that because they were on easy terms with the occupants of the pantry, kitchen, stable, garden, bothie, or keeper's cottage, they knew 'the people'. There are flaws in the argument. Certainly the king had an easy acquaintance-ship with the many types of human beings attached to a big house, inside and out. But in addition, as a London landlord and as a Norfolk landowner he had had the chance to meet working people and artisans in their own homes, on their own ground. He had been appointed to the royal commission on housing in 1884, and some of the questions which he put to the witnesses surprised listeners who did not know him, because they showed a real knowledge of working-class life. The essential frippery of Lloyd George's mind has never been more mercilessly exposed than when his biographer records how he explained to King Edward that 'the old folk depended on tea for one of their comforts'. The king might have retorted that the simple truths of life in the back streets of Caernarvon were not unfamiliar to one who knew the circumstances of existence in Kennington, where was a large part of the urban property of the duchy of Cornwall. 'Jupiter' was Campbell-Bannerman's private name for him, but in spite of investing him with the authority of the father of gods, he never failed to be impressed by the king's knowledge and grasp of conditions in the contemporary scene. A miner, who was a member of parliament, said at the time of the king's death, 'In the cottage homes throughout the empire the sorrow will be true and deep.'

Behind this knowledge and experience, which gave the king personal authority in addition to the authority of orb and sceptre, lay a question-mark about his private life. He had married in 1863 the lovely eldest daughter of King Christian IX of Denmark. As Princess of Wales and Queen Alexandra she won unbounded affection and admiration from all classes—a general popularity explained by a simplicity of character and warmth of heart which she was able to reveal on even the most formal occasions. She disliked the rigidity, the pomp, and the outward show of royalty, and in this respect was the exact opposite of King Edward. She was incurably unpunctual, and on many an occasion slid gracefully into the room with the inquiry, 'Am I late?' At such moments the king swallowed but did not speak. Though her rather haphazard ways may have been upsetting, her charm was captivating and was well expressed by A. E. Housman, the draftsman of the address on her death from the university of Cambridge, who said that she achieved in a day a second Danish Conquest more durable than the first.

As a young man the king undoubtedly treated Queen Alexandra with a marked lack of consideration: he led his own boisterous life, expecting to continue in Marlborough House and Sandringham the noisy companionship of bachelor days. In the 1860's and 1870's his association with other women is believed to have strained the marriage, but by degrees she centred her existence on Sandringham and her children and created an intensely affectionate family circle although the king was possibly somewhat on the perimeter of this.

In his maturity he enjoyed the society of a succession of brilliant women friends—friendships which were known to all the world and accepted by the queen with magnanimity. These included Lady

Paget (the American wife of the distinguished soldier afterwards discredited in the Curragh); Mrs. Greville (the hostess of Polesden Lacey); the Duchess of Marlborough (born a Vanderbilt); Lady Londonderry (a formidable *grande dame*); Mrs. Arthur Sassoon; Mrs. Willie James (daughter of a Scottish baronet whose entertainment of the king at West Dean Park prompted a familiar verse of Hilaire Belloc); Lady Troubridge, Lady Lonsdale, and Mrs. Cornwallis-West (the acknowledged beauties of the day); and the one to whom he was most constant, Mrs. George Keppel. Whether his association with any of these ladies developed into more than friendship, whether he treated them as Charles II or James II treated 'the beauties' of the Restoration court, will never be known. Perhaps it is not even of great importance. Here is what his intelligent and observant private secretary, Francis Knollys, has to say on this topic:

He is great friends with many women, and there are some women to whom it is impossible for the Prince to speak for five minutes without their imagining that he means much more than they thought of. He was only lamenting to me the other day that it was quite impossible for him to speak to a pretty woman without being accused of evil intent.

The somewhat guileless newspaper-man W. T. Stead, to whom Knollys said this, replied that the joy and brightness of life sprang from the freest possible intimacy between men and women 'if only it does not degenerate into adultery'.[1] The important point is that he loved feminine society. In 1906 as a mark of respect to his father-in-law, who had died that year, women were excluded from invitations to Windsor for Ascot. Ruefully the king observed, 'What tiresome evenings we shall have.'

Going back further in his life to his young manhood we can see that his choice of women friends then had been less discriminating. He belonged to a fast set, gay, reckless, and inclined to view women with the eye of possession. All this was clearly paraded before the public in the Mordaunt divorce case in 1870. Lady Mordaunt, a childhood friend of King Edward, confessed to her husband, a country baronet, that she had committed adultery with, among others, the then Prince of Wales. Whether she was in fact an adulteress or an imbecile is difficult to determine and really now is only of interest to a number of people long in their coffins. The interest, for those who study King Edward's character, lies in the publicity, in

---

[1] J. W. Robertson Scott, *Life and Death of a Newspaper*, 1952.

the fact that the case brought home to everyone the somewhat raffish circle of which the future king was a leader. Moreover, two rather suggestive points emerged.)The examination of the Prince of Wales, when he gave evidence, was formal except for this question: 'We have heard it stated in the course of this case that your Royal Highness is in the habit of using hansom-cabs. Is that so?' The Prince of Wales: 'It is.' Although there was no harm in 'London's gondolas' (it was only respectable ladies whom convention forbade to ride in them unchaperoned), there was something sly, 'incog.', and unpleasantly discreet about the prince using one.)

Public vehicles are not for royalty. When George IV's daughter, Princess Charlotte, ran away from her father's house, the part of the episode which most scandalized the public was that she had run from the house and engaged a hackney carriage. So the news that the heir to the throne used hansoms surprised the public, conjured up the vision of drives through gas-lit streets, and suggested improprieties. (Possibly more damaging for posterity were the prince's letters to Lady Mordaunt: these were not read in the proceedings but they were purloined by an enterprising journalist and published.) They reveal the less favourable side of the prince's character, which revelled in trivialities and personalities—neither a very respectable trait in a royal person. A representative specimen of this correspondence follows:

Marlborough House, Oct. 13. 1867

My dear Lady Mordaunt,

Many thanks for your kind letter, which I received just before we left Dunrobin,[1] and I have been so busy here that I have been unable to answer it before. I am glad to hear that you are flourishing at Walton,[2] and hope your husband has had good sport with the partridges. We had a charming stay at Dunrobin from the 19th of September to the 7th of this month. Our party consisted of the Sandwiches, Grosvenors (only for a few days), Summers,[3] Bakers,[4] F. Marshall, Alrud, Ronald Gower,[5] Sir H. Pilly Oliver (who did not look so bad in a kilt as you heard), Lascelles, Falconer and Sam Buckley, who looked first-rate in his kilt.[6]

[1] The Duke of Sutherland's house in the Highlands.
[2] Sir Charles Mordaunt's home in Warwickshire.
[3] Probably Lord and Lady Somers.   [4] Sir Samuel and Lady Baker.
[5] The Duke of Sutherland's son.
[6] Several of these names are obviously wrong: Alrud could be his brother Alfred. They are miscopied from the prince's handwriting. The published versions of the letters typographically sink to the level of a penny dreadful. It is clear that the prince wrote

I was also three or four days in the Reay forest with the Grosvenors.
I shot 4 stags. The total was 21. P. John thanks you very much for your
photo, and I received two very good ones, accompanied by a charming
epistle from your sister. We are all delighted with Hamilton's marriage,[1]
and I think you are rather hard on the young lady, as, although not
exactly pretty, she is very nice-looking, has charming manners, and is
very popular with everyone. From his letter he seems very much in love
(a rare occurrence now-a-days). I will see what I can do in getting a presentation for the son of Mrs. Bradshaw for the Royal Asylum of London
St. Ann's Society. Frances[2] will tell you the result. London is very empty,
but I have plenty to do, so time does not go slowly, and I go down shooting to Windsor and Richmond occasionally. On the 26th I shall shoot with
General Hall at Newmarket,[3] the following week at Knowsley and then at
Windsor and Sandringham before we go abroad. That will probably be on
the 18th or 19th of next month. You told me when I last saw you that you
have given it up. I saw in the papers that you were in London on
Saturday. I wish you had let me know, as I would have made a point of
calling. There are some good plays going on, and we are going the round
of them. My brother[4] is here, but at the end of the month he starts for
Plymouth, on his long cruise of nearly two years. . . . I remain.

Yours most sincerely

Albert Edward

Twenty years later the resounding Tranby Croft case startled the
nation. Here again, in the life story of the king it was not the verdict
that mattered, not whether Sir William Gordon-Cumming had
cheated at baccarat, but what did matter was the proof to the wide
world that the heir to the throne readily mixed with companions
where such things were possible. Just as the hansom-cab gave its
little twist to the Mordaunt case, so the information that the prince
travelled with his own set of crested dice gave its edge to Tranby
Croft. The Prince of Wales's motto 'Ich dien', it was whispered by
Victorian jesters, should henceforth give way to 'I deal'.

King Edward's reputation as a man of pleasure is perhaps the
first and most emphatic impression of him when he comes to mind.
We seem to hear the fat, deep chuckle; we seem to see the admiring

---

'Sir H. Pelly, Oliver'. The former was Sir Henry, the third baronet, and the latter is
Oliver Montagu, brother of Lord Sandwich.

[1] Presumably Lord Hamilton, afterwards second Duke of Abercorn.

[2] i.e. Francis Knollys, the prince's secretary.

[3] General Hall owned the famous shoot, Six Mile Bottom.

[4] The Duke of Edinburgh.

glance in the direction of a fashionable lady; we picture the sovereigns staked against those of his friends on the green baize table; we imagine him in Paris; we think of those cautious gentlemen at Coutts's bank paying his racing losses. Supposing it was all true and even supposing imagination wanders off to grosser pictures, do such things greatly matter? Does not Anthony Trollope put the matter fairly in his autobiography? 'If a rustle of a woman's petticoat has ever stirred my blood; if a cup of wine has been a joy to me; if I have thought of tobacco at midnight in pleasant company to be one of the elements of an earthly paradise; if now and again I have somewhat recklessly fluttered a £5 note over a card-table;—of what matter is that to any reader? We know that such were the tastes of King Edward, but the point is not the extent to which they were indulged but their impact and their influence on the age. The king never attempted to conceal his tastes, to hide his personal habits from the public. On one occasion, in Vienna, he had left a music-hall in the middle of the second act because he was bored. At once the newspapers proclaimed that he had left in order to show his disapproval of what was improper, and the Bishop of Ripon wrote a fulsome letter to him congratulating him on his splendid stand for morality. His private secretary inquired how he should reply to the bishop. 'Tell the bishop the exact truth', was the answer; and he added, 'I have no wish to pose as a protector of morals, especially abroad.' The result of this attitude coupled with the well-known cases to which allusion has been made meant that the whole world knew this side of his life. A pleasure-seeking prince may acquire a reputation: this may be well known to his aristocratic contemporaries, and some of it may trickle through to a wider public, but such things are soon forgotten, carried away by fresh atoms of gossip. But King Edward's reputation was removed by the Mordaunt and Tranby Croft cases from the world of gossip and speculation into the world of certainty. As the procession of all the King Edwards moved through the streets of London in the Lord Mayor's show soon after he came to the throne, the ethereal, saintly form of Edward the Confessor appeared; a cockney wit called out, ' 'Ello, Eddie. You don't seem to 'ave changed much.' His true character was known not only by the dukes but by the dustmen.

'The Prince of Wales is not respected.' The condemnation is formidable because it comes from Mr. Gladstone. Moreover, to be not respected in the nineteenth century was in itself one of the gravest charges. The strongest single influence in the nation at that time, and the prevailing thought of its finest minds, was religious. For example when a census of Sunday church attendance was made in the 1850's it was shown that $4\frac{1}{2}$ million people went to church in the morning, 3 million in the afternoon and 3 million in the evening. That was out of a total population in England and Wales of rather fewer than 18 million. The figure was impressive. To conduct life in defiance of that prevailing wind of thought was a great handicap comparable to the catholic leanings of the Stuart family against the protestant hurricanes of the seventeenth century. If King Edward's life had conformed to the doctrines listened to by more than 50 per cent. of the population in church he would have found many things easier. If he had behaved with the decorum of his younger brother, the Duke of Connaught, his in-fluence in the country would have been greater: his relations with his mother would have been more comfortable. This loss of respect was one of the penalties which he paid for his pleasures. But if he lost respect it is not wholly perverse to point out that his pleasures by no means diminished his authority. On the whole, official life in England—that is to say statesmen, church leaders, civil servants—had only a nodding acquaintance with those pleasures which the king enjoyed: it was a side of life to which they may have leaned in their youth, but of which they had little adult experience. Though it may have been rather disreputable to shine in dubious society, to know when to back one's judgement on the card table or at the race-course, such things win a measure of admiration from those who, from prudence, deny themselves these indulgences. The feelings of the conventional and respectable for the king are exactly summed up in some words of Wilfrid Blunt, who was himself by no means indifferent to the pleasures enjoyed by the king. He says that both King Edward and Solomon had 'that knowledge of women which, as we know, is the beginning of wisdom, or at least which teaches tolerance for the unwisdom of others'.[1] In spite, therefore, of many vicissitudes in his past career the predominant characteristic of the king when he ascended the throne was authority. It is perfectly true that Lord Esher, that shrewd and observant confidant, after attending the first meeting of the Privy Council following the death

[1] W. S. Blunt, *My Diaries*, 1920.

of Queen Victoria, wrote, 'I regret the mystery and awe of the Court.' Certainly authority can often lie in remoteness and seclusion, as it did with Queen Victoria, but though more accessible the personality of King Edward, direct and forthright, none the less imposed its sway on court and people.

No one has been very successful in showing us the true character of King Edward. The personality revealed to the public, to all brought into contact with him in public life, is familiar. What did his family and intimates find behind the image shown to the world? There are two principal reasons why no very clear picture emerges of the man behind the public face.

The first is that he was an appallingly dull letter-writer. A large mass of his correspondence exists, but he was one of those people who like to 'dash off' a letter and trust to its being acceptable through a few polite nothings and a pinch of gossip. Such dashed-off letters may have met the need of the moment, but for posterity they are almost as baffling as Joanna Southcott's empty box. Here is a typical example written to a close personal friend, Admiral Sir Henry Stephenson, who was in charge of the future George V when he was training with the Royal Navy and had just had to change ships.

Marlborough Club[1]
Pall Mall S.W. May 31 1887

My dear Harry,

I owe you my best thanks for 2 kind letters of 9th and 19th. It is certainly very unfortunate that the trip to Athens should not come off after all, but I trust it may in the Autumn. My son will I hope meet the King[2] here at the Queen's Jubilee.

My son was, I know, very sorry to leave you and his ship and comrades but I see there was no help for it and my brother[3] sent me a copy of his letter on the subject.

The Anglo-Turkish Convention having now been signed you will I suppose join the Squadron in Italian waters, but I fear there is no chance of seeing you come home as in my brother's absence the command of the Fleet will devolve upon you. Don't pin your faith in the newspapers, they are seldom right, and there is no foundation in the report that the Duchess of Cumberland[4] is going to Copenhagen in July. She is going on

---

[1] The club formed by King Edward when he took exception to the rules against smoking in White's.   [2] Of Greece.

[3] The Duke of Edinburgh.

[4] Queen Alexandra's sister, who had gone out of her mind.

as well as one can expect, but I fear it will be a long time before she recovers, alas!

We have been tremendously busy all this month and expect to be still more so the next two. We were going to Sandringham for Whitsuntide, wh. would have been very pleasant, but there were some cases of diphtheria amongst others Jackson (the head gardener) has got it but is going on well, so we had to give it up. All next week we shall be in the country for the Ascot Races and shall stay at old Mackenzie's house at Sunningdale.

The week before last I went to Gt. Yarmouth to inspect the Norfolk Artillery. Sir Harry [Keppel] was there and in great force, but soon after he lost his old friend Ld. Edward Russell and is terribly cut up about it. He never appeared at all at Epsom last week in consequence, but I hope he may go to Ascot with us.

I don't think I have any social news to give you, but gossip as you doubtless read in *Vanity Fair*, the *World* and *Truth* is rarely correct, and those charming Papers continue to be as spiteful and scurrilous as ever.

The great 'Early' [Lord Clonmell] has returned to London from his native Land, and his face is redder than ever. We always ask him why he is so sun burnt. . . .

Now I shall say goodbye, my dear Harry, and trusting that your shadow will never be less,

I am, Yours very sincerely

A. E.[1]

That long letter reveals with clarity the surface characteristics of the writer. There is concern for his son's disappointment over having to change his ship, there is an interest in what is happening and a marked accuracy of mind, there is a relish for tittle-tattle and a general, very pronounced, affability. The letter bears a great resemblance to those written in a gossipy mood by King George IV. But it is immature—the letter of an undergraduate to a friend, or a subaltern to his family. One of his biographers[2] tells us that like all polyglots the king was a dull letter-writer, but we are left wondering whether there was in fact anything deeper to his character.

The other reason why it is difficult for the inquirer to sense any clear picture of his character is that very little has come down to us from those who really knew him—members of his family and his circle of intimate friends. Queen Victoria's outbursts against him are familiar. When he was eight the diarist Charles Greville was told

---

[1] J. F. E. Stephenson, *A Royal Correspondence*, Macmillan, 1938.
[2] F. J. C. Hearnshaw.

that he was weaker and more timid than his sister, the Princess Royal, and that the queen thought him stupid and 'did not much care for the child'. These feelings were intensified as he grew older: they are to be found in some of the letters of Lord Clarendon— notably the book published in 1956, *My Dear Duchess*—in which Clarendon calls it 'an antipathy that is incurable'. But it is fair to remember that she outlived some of these prejudices, and that she was always touched by his kindness and affectionate nature. His father wrote of him: 'He has a strange nature. He has no interest for things but all the more for persons. This trait in his character, which is often found in the Royal Family, has made the family so popular.'[1] On another occasion his father wrote, 'since he has been here he has not read a single line, thought any thoughts or listened to a conversation. If he does read anything it is silly little novels (half farces) which he buys at the railway station.'[2] Such judgements do not perhaps cut very deep, and King George V tells us rather more when he writes in his diary on the night of his father's death, 'I have lost my best friend, and the best of fathers.' But the intimates of the king's young manhood—the Duke of St. Albans, the Duke of Hamilton, Lord Henniker, Lord Sandwich, and Lord Halifax—who really knew his character, were not the kind of men to write their recollections of these private matters. They were discreet men living in a more discreet age than ours. A contrast illustrates the point. When the official biography of King George V was being written by Mr. John Gore at the end of the 1930's several of King George's intimates were alive, and made their contribution to the picture. King Edward's official biography was not published until fifteen years after his death, when most of his close friends were old or dead.

Possibly the best account of King Edward, up to the time of writing, is to be found in the opening chapter by Professor Hearnshaw in the book which he edited in 1933, *Edwardian England*. He emphasizes the point which has been made above: 'What we still lack are the memoirs of several of his close personal friends. . . . One correspondent alone is supposed to possess nearly 3,000 of his letters; but access to them has been persistently refused.' He calls the official biography of King Edward 'the dry bones. The spirit of life does not move among them; the form of the man does not emerge.'

[1] *Letters of the Prince Consort*, edited by Hector Bolitho, 1933.
[2] Count Corti, *The English Empress*, 1957.

Dickens once said something of the same kind when he suggested by way of criticism that a character in a novel was drawn, not from inside his home, but from the house next door. Yet in the case of kings those who watch them from the house next door sometimes see them in relation to their official position more clearly than those who see them from inside. If therefore we attempt to sketch the outline of the king against his official work, and then fill in the political and social background, we may hope to catch a glimpse of the man, to estimate how far he moulded the decade known as Edwardian, and to determine whether he was a typical product of his generation who happened to be born to lead it.

'Has the prince got the mind, has he got the imagination capable of rising to his opportunities?' asked W. T. Stead. The answer to that question helps to explain why one way to approach, and understand, the Edwardian age is through the personality of the king. If Stead had in mind the practice of statecraft or the capacity at a dire moment to inspire the nation (as it could be argued that the king's son and grandson were to do) the answer would be uncertain. But if Stead meant the capacity to identify himself with the feeling of the time and to give that feeling coherence, then the answer could be 'yes'. For it was that easy kindliness, that absence of intellectual precociousness, and that attention to *les formes* which stamped both king and epoch.

The first thing to emphasize about King Edward as king was that he was a reforming king—not in the political sense of the word but with the meaning that he brought the monarchy up to date. Just as his father had reformed the domestic side of court life, so he let in colour and pageantry to that ceremonial side of the British monarchy on which for too long the widow's cap had been firmly placed. Like any other heir of a venerable relative he sorted possessions, burned papers, re-hung pictures, moved furniture, and opened rooms disused since his father's time forty years before. He had the somewhat unusual task, for a man of the world, of putting down excessive drinking at Balmoral. During her widowhood Queen Victoria had encouraged the highlanders to celebrate such anniversaries as the prince consort's birthday with copious libations of whisky: bottles of whisky were the stalkers' perquisite. All this was stopped. But although such changes were noticed, they are common to many on assuming an inheritance, and his claim to the title of

II. King Edward VII and Queen Alexandra

III (*a*). The Prince and Princess of Wales 1909
King George V and Queen Mary

III (*b*). The Royal Grandchildren 1902

The Princess Royal	King George VI	King Edward VIII
	The Duke of Gloucester	

reformer is wider. His reforms were outside—in the ceremonial presentation of himself to the people, in the reversion to those appearances in state which since her widowhood his mother had shunned. Less than a month after his mother's death he opened parliament in state, driving in George III's state coach. Such a spectacle had not been seen in Westminster since 5 February 1861 when parliament was opened with traditional splendour by the queen and the prince consort. To emphasize the character of the ceremony in 1901 King Edward expressed the hope that all peers who had them would drive in state coaches to the House of Lords. His particular innovation in ceremony was the substitution of evening courts for the afternoon drawing-rooms of his mother's day. Just as the evening is a more festive time of day than the afternoon, so it was possible, with artificial lighting and the formal dress which goes with it, to give these presentation occasions a new dignity, a revived splendour. The then news-editor of the *Daily Mail*, R. D. Blumenfeld, noticed, almost sadly, in his diary: 'Another of Queen Victoria's regulations is to go by the board. Drawing-rooms are to be turned into courts.' Many years previously Queen Victoria's uncle, King Leopold, had expressed his admiration of a fête organized at the queen's court. He added that there was hardly a country where so much magnificence existed as in England. The courts, organized personally by the king with some adaptations from similar continental ceremonies, were an effort to reflect in Buckingham Palace the varied dignity and magnificence of contemporary English life. They were held in the ball-room instead of the throne-room, and they were to last for half a century.

The king loved an excuse to dress up in uniform, inherited perhaps from the Hanoverian family, for it was a well-known characteristic of King George IV. He loved pageantry, and woe betide the courtier or lord who deviated by the position of even the obscurest star from what was correct. He gave the somewhat nonchalant Duke of Devonshire a piece of his mind for daring to appear wearing an order upside down, and the immaculate Rosebery was once reproved for appearing at a function looking like an American diplomat. A very true appraisement of this side of the king is again to be found in the diary of Wilfrid Blunt. The two men were contemporaries, though as Blunt says, 'I had never much to do with him directly.' But Blunt—the enemy of imperialism and of everything conventional in his native land (except perhaps the enjoyment of country-house life)—is a commentator whom we should heed. He writes on the day, 20 May 1910, when the king was buried:

He had a passion for pageantry and ceremonial and dressing-up, and he was never tired of putting on uniforms and taking them off, and receiving princes and ambassadors and opening museums and hospitals, and attending cattle shows and military shows and shows of every kind, while every night of his life he was to be seen at theatres and operas and music-halls.

The last is a slight exaggeration, though the novelist Robert Hichens, the author of *The Garden of Allah*, could write of the king in his reminiscences:

The Edwardian age through which I lived was certainly very attractive to me. Night after night as I sat in my stall at the opera and saw him coming into the omnibus box and taking up his opera glasses to survey the glittering women in the first and ground tier boxes I saw a man who looked, I thought, extremely genial and satisfied with his position in the scheme of the world.

He was like some splendidly plumed bird who seems to ask nothing more from existence than to be seen and admired, as he moved from London to Scotland, from Windsor to Portsmouth, from Sandringham to Yorkshire, from Goodwood to Doncaster. His mother moved almost furtively through the British Isles: about King Edward there was nothing furtive, all was open and publicity was welcomed. He liked all men to know where he was and what he was up to. That was one reason why journalists loved him. He was never the least 'stand-offish', and he thoroughly enjoyed being snapshot. He was an absolute contrast to his son. When King George went to stay with friends he never emerged except for the comparative privacy of a shoot. King Edward on the other hand was certain to show himself. After his operation, which had necessitated postponing the coronation, he went for a cruise in the royal yacht from Portsmouth round the west coast of Scotland. Although the doctors would have preferred him to remain quiet, nothing would do but he must land and see the Isle of Man. He was entertained by the novelist Hall Caine, who recorded what struck him— the simplicity of the king, 'just a gentleman in a lounge suit and two ladies [Queen Alexandra and Princess Victoria] wearing black sailor hats, driving in an ordinary hired landau, with a few friends and officials of the island in carriages and hackney cabs behind them, and three or four local journalists bicycling by their sides'. Here are some extracts from the official record in the *Annual Register* of the king's visit to Ireland in 1904. 'The king and queen and Princess Victoria [their unmarried daughter] arrived at Kingstown and had a very hearty greeting. They received addresses of welcome from various local bodies, to which the king replied, before proceeding to attend the Punchestown races.' Then three days later, when the royal party was staying at Lismore with the Duke of Devonshire: 'The king and queen attended Leopardstown races.' We are justified in picturing the king saying to his secretary beforehand, 'Fix the ceremonies to coincide with the races.'

Few men have ever in our history fitted the kingship more exactly than did King Edward. 'He gloried in the sceptre. He was fascinated by the orb', wrote E. T. Raymond.[1] But fascination went even further than that. He loved being in the centre of things, enjoying the feeling that men and women recognized the king. His triumph at the Derby in the closing months of his life shows this. In 1909 his horse Minoru won the race by a short head. A more cautious man would never have made the attempt to face the wildly enthusiastic crowd and lead in the winner. The police attempt to cordon the crowd was hopeless and he walked through the mass of people as they patted him on the back and called out 'Good old Teddie'. It was clearly an emotional strain, but he showed that he loved every moment of it. His enjoyment of the excitement of being king was well caught by Rudyard Kipling:

> The peculiar treasure of kings was his for the taking:
> All that men come to in dreams he inherited waking.

One of the shrewdest and most understanding of his contemporaries—the great Liberal editor A. G. Gardiner—could not imagine someone being king and not being bored to distraction by the experience. He drew a picture of a garden party on a sunny day at Windsor, with the king in the centre of the festivity, 'industriously smiling and gossiping'. The fashionable world presses round him, hungry for notice. Evidently Mr. Gardiner had been to one of these parties and with the independence and good manners of the true

[1] *Portraits of the New Century*, 1928.

Liberal he wandered off on his own, instead of hemming in the king, and listened to the rooks cawing in the elms. He then pictures the departure of the last guest, the lengthening of the shadows across the grass, and the emergence of King Edward, with his cigar, to take counsel with the rooks who know so well what is transitory and what is real.[1] Many human beings might have done that—but not King Edward. His critics might say that he lacked the imagination for such a consultation, but it would not have crossed his mind that there was anything insubstantial about his work, or that it was possible for him to be bored (as Mr. Gardiner hinted earlier) by what he so deeply enjoyed. Yet Mr. Gardiner was right in thinking that the king could and did experience boredom—but that was in the chances of social life, not in the discharge of his official duties. How well the courtiers knew the signs—the voice slower and a shade deeper in tone; the fingers drumming irritably on the furniture. The perceptive author of *The Edwardians*, Victoria Sackville-West, was speaking of what she knew when she wrote on this subject. At a court ball, the king catches sight of Lady Roehampton and beckons to her to relieve him from boredom. She was regarded by the respectable with not ill-founded suspicion, but as her critics watched her talking to the king and making him laugh they realized that they could not have acquitted themselves as she did. They would have been too conscious that the situation was deliriously exciting but at the same time too alarming; 'for the King, genial as he could be, was known to lose interest easily and to drum with irritable fingers upon the arm of his chair or upon the dinner-table. What a gulf there was between amusing the King and boring him! and for a woman, all depended upon which side of the gulf she occupied. Life and death were in it.' But the king was a curious mixture, for he was affectionate and kind-hearted—qualities which do not generally mark those who are easily bored. He thought nothing of travelling to Balmoral just to spend two days with his mother—'It was very dear and kind of him to come all that way to see me, for only two days, and gave me great pleasure.' He must have endured agonies when he visited Queen Alexandra's family in Denmark. Life was extremely formal, stiff, and old-fashioned, and the highlight of the day was a game of whist for low stakes. Sir Frederick Ponsonby[2]

---

[1] A. G. Gardiner, *Prophets, Priests and Kings*, 1908.
[2] *Recollections of Three Reigns*, 1951.

has left an amusing account of these excruciating days. He says: 'These evenings were a high trial to everyone, but the king behaved like an angel.' He endured these *longueurs* because he did not wish to hurt Queen Alexandra's feelings, and also perhaps because he felt that some self-sacrifice was becoming in the association of sovereigns. That was part of his work. In Disraeli's *Sybil* one of the characters laments the boredom and dullness of meeting country neighbours but she is corrected by Lady Marney who says, 'I am fond of work and I talk to them always about it.' So with the king: it was the interest of common responsibilities and duties which enabled him to bear the company of his fellow rulers, which of his own will he would not perhaps have chosen. But at home society and people were his recreation and he saw no reason why he should be obliged to pass time with those who bored him.

And there is one further point in all this. As a young man he had been given the impression, especially by Queen Victoria, that he was ill endowed by nature for the position he had one day to fill. Yet he was conscious that in one particular he far out-stripped all his family—in his understanding of human nature. He loved to show this off, to practise his art like any other *maestro*. In the chances of social life he could always make a contribution over and above the conventional palaver of royal persons. While it is true that he enjoyed banter in conversation, he was also very easy and made people forget that self-consciousness which is apt to assail those who talk to princes. When he saw Lord Rayleigh, the great authority on electromagnetism, at a social function he said, 'Well, Lord Rayleigh, discovering something I suppose?' Then he turned to the lady near him: 'He's always at it.' His remarks were often extremely personal: he could say for example to the Duchess of Rutland, 'You don't brush your hair.' No doubt some duchesses would have been greatly shocked by such an accusation from their sovereign. The point is that he knew the one to whom it was safe to say anything so personal. No doubt a king has great advantages over ordinary mortals in the opportunity for showing tact and good feeling. But it was his understanding of human beings and knowledge of individuals that enabled him to deal triumphantly with the kind of thing which must happen daily in court life. His son-in-law, the somewhat obtuse Duke of Fife, was understandably mortified at finding his splendid name omitted from the list of those staying at Windsor Castle for the funeral of Queen Victoria. The king was listening to the grumbles of his son-in-law when a courtier passed. The king proceeded to give this unhappy man a severe dressing-down. 'How can I have any confidence in you when you make omissions of this sort?' The duke was pleased to see the courtier reprimanded for this slight to his dignity. When the duke had gone the courtier apologized to the king who took him by the arm and said 'I know how difficult it has been for you and I think you did wonders. I had to say something strong, as Fife was so hurt that he came to me and said that he presumed he could go to London as he was apparently not wanted.'[1] When he was dying the king continued to work and see people: owing to some mistake he confused the identity of one of his official visitors so that they spoke at cross purposes. Perhaps in all his sixty-eight years he had scarcely done such a thing before and he was painfully mortified. Could there have been a clearer indication that his powers were gradually deserting him?

In exercising his social gifts the king was helped by his broad-mindedness and humanity. Admittedly he loved ceremony, but he seldom stood on it. Above everything else he could brave criticism—and he had had his fair share of this from Queen Victoria—without showing temper. Once the *Pall Mall Gazette* had caused great offence to the upper classes and was placed on the index of clubland for referring to the king (he was then Prince of Wales) as 'the little fat man in red'. The editor was somewhat tremulous at the prospect of meeting the prince after this escapade, but when they did meet he said he was afraid he had made some rather rough references to the prince in his paper. 'Don't think of it', was the answer; 'I am a liberal-minded man.'[2] But no one would pretend that King Edward, any more than any other human being, was for ever gracious and charming—a kind of perpetual fountain of amiability.

Just as he enjoyed display, showing himself off as the king, so he enjoyed asserting his personality by saying something sharp even to his closest friends. In the days of his youth this enjoyment took the form of practical joking—a little heavy and German and not always in good taste. The victim of many of such jests was Mr. Christopher Sykes, and his horrible experiences are told with delightful wit by his great-nephew in *Four Studies in Loyalty*. Some

---

[1] Sir Frederick Ponsonby, op. cit.   [2] J. W. Robertson Scott, op. cit.

readers might suspect a little collateral exaggeration in the account of this tomfoolery, but there is this confirmation in an anecdote of the prince's youth told by the prince consort to his eldest daughter. 'You would hardly believe it but . . . he tormented his new valet more than ever in every possible way, pouring wax on his livery, throwing water on his linen, rapping him on the nose, tearing his ties and other *gentilesses*.'[1] While no doubt such pleasantries were left behind with youth, there remained a certain fondness for making his friends feel uncomfortable. At a dinner at Windsor he turned to Haldane in front of several of his Liberal colleagues and said, 'Mr. Haldane, you are too fat.'[2] That philosopher-statesman loved the good things of life, yet it is questionable whether his sovereign, who shared his tastes and his corpulence, was the man to say this.

In Victorian times before mankind had become bemused by the intricacies of psycho-analysis some attention was paid to the mysteries of phrenology. When King Edward VII was a boy, his parents had had him examined by a fashionable phrenologist, who reported that the boy's self-esteem was very markedly developed. That was indubitably true, though it was possibly obvious without a too close examination of the bumps and contours of his head. Indeed this self-sufficiency was given impetus by the severity of his treatment in boyhood and by the constant snubbing from the queen which continued into his middle life. That form of vanity may well have partly explained why, in an age which was greatly governed by forms and ceremonies, he made such a conspicuous sovereign, such a natural leader of an epoch. But how would a man with that characteristic so pronouncedly developed, with the habit of self-assertion grown into his personality, manage the political duties of his position?

Queen Victoria's influence over the big issues of politics at the end of her reign was by no means negligible. Her long struggle with Gladstone, and Salisbury's remark, dragged from him in a moment of irritation, that the queen was as much trouble as a government department, are familiar and remind us that it was not always easy to convince the queen and perilously difficult to convert her. But if we except these great issues of policy, the minutiae of her relations

---

[1] Count Corti, op. cit.

[2] Overheard and repeated this remark sounds ruder than was intended. The king was solicitous about Haldane's health, and thought he took insufficient exercise.

with European reigning families, and church appointments, the queen's influence over the government was running down with her life. In part this was explained by her continued absence from Buckingham Palace, which cut her off from personal contact with Whitehall. King Edward immediately made his presence felt, for above all else he was a Londoner, a London king. At once there were signs of activity in the routine business of the crown. The signing of army commissions—partly owing to the failing powers of the queen and partly owing to the great increase through the war in South Africa—had fallen behind. More than 5,000 were waiting to be signed by the king. He arranged for a stamp of his signature to be made, 'which I shall keep myself'. In 1902 Mr. George Wyndham, the chief secretary for Ireland, appointed an under-secretary without telling the king. He was sternly rebuked and when he apologized for the oversight, explaining that it was due to over-work, the king remarked, 'Excuses of ministers are often as *gauche* as their omissions.' In his mother's day it had been customary to tell the newspapers the gist of the speech from the throne. The king strongly resisted this:

I am dead against any 'inspiration' being sent to the newspapers. It is done in no country, probably not even in America. The King's speech is drawn up by his ministers, but if the Press gets hold of it before it is made at the opening of Parliament from the Throne it becomes a perfect farce. Sandars[1] belongs evidently to a new régime. One has heard of the 'New Woman', but he is the 'New Man'.[2]

He differed completely from his mother in lacking the will or capacity to express himself on paper. His official letters, short but jejune, only differed in length from those to his private friends. Indeed the sight of these comments helps to explain why the writer of the article on the king in the *Dictionary of National Biography* decided that he was idle. Again unlike his mother, the king preferred to discuss official matters in an interview rather than by letter, though we may suppose that often his discussion did not go far beyond the kind of thing he said to Lang when he saw him on his appointment as Archbishop of York: 'Keep the parties in the church together—and prevent the clergy wearing moustaches.'

---

[1] J. S. Sandars was Balfour's confidential secretary. He had great power, and there was some criticism of his influence of which the king was doubtless aware. 'That Mr. Sandars is always interfering', complained a duchess.

[2] Sir Sidney Lee, *King Edward VII, a biography*, 2 vols., 1925–7.

He interfered much more vigorously than had his mother over the reprieve of criminals and the remission of their punishment. As was true of his great-uncle King George IV, he was inclined to greater leniency than his advisers at the Home Office recommended. For example, he urged clemency for Arthur Lynch, the Irishman who fought for the Boers. On the other hand he signed the pardon of the murderer of William Whiteley, 'the universal provider', with the proviso that as a constitutional monarch he was bound to do so, but he added:

The king is entirely averse to any form of punishment which errs on the side of severity, but he feels that as long as capital punishment is laid down as the penalty of murder, the commutation of that punishment should be based on legal or moral grounds, and that the tendency nowadays to regard a criminal as a martyr, and to raise an agitation on sentimental grounds in order to put pressure on the home secretary, is one which may eventually prove very inconvenient, if concessions are too readily made.[1]

Naturally on questions affecting the armed forces his interference was more direct. On appointments he had strong views which he expressed. When the Conservative government of Balfour was tottering to its fall the king had a talk with the Opposition leader, Campbell-Bannerman, at Marienbad where both men were taking the cure. In reporting this conversation to the Liberal chief whip, Campbell-Bannerman said that the king had said nothing against the government as a whole 'though freely criticizing departments'.[2] There can be little doubt that the service departments, with whose Conservative chiefs the king had had some passages, were here the targets for most of the attacks. When the Liberal government succeeded, the king found in Haldane, the new secretary of state for war—who was clever, a linguist, and abreast of the times—a man after his own heart. It is certainly true to say that without the king's support Haldane could never have carried the War Office with him in his sweeping army reforms. Here is a picture of the king at Taplow Court, the home of Lord Desborough, in a letter from Haldane to his mother:

He knew all about my difficulties with the Cabinet[3] and urged me not to give way. He is now really keen about the Territorial Army, and there are

[1] Sidney Lee, op. cit.
[2] J. A. Spender, *Sir Henry Campbell-Bannerman*, 2 vols., 1923.
[3] These came from Winston Churchill and Lloyd George.

few matters in which royal influence can be more effective. He had a photograph taken of himself and the house party on the lawn and insisted that I should be lying on the grass talking to him. He arranged the position of my feet so that they should not be out of focus and appear too big. It is a great comfort to have him behind me in my struggle.[1]

The king was no less adamant in his support of the Fisher reforms in the Royal Navy.

His hand was felt in many of those personal decisions which have to be made in Downing Street. He enjoyed twitting Lord Salisbury on the terrible appointment of Mr. Alfred Austin as poet laureate, and on one occasion sent him some verses so that the prime minister could see for himself 'the trash which the poet laureate writes'. He absolutely vetoed the appointment of Admiral Mahan to the regius chair of history at Cambridge on the fairly sensible ground that the appointment of a foreigner would be 'unpopular'.[2] Just before his coronation the king mooted the idea of the Order of Merit—'a decoration entirely vested in the sovereign's hands'. Without much enthusiasm Salisbury agreed to this, but the order survives today an untarnished dignity among the dubious trifles shovelled out from Downing Street. King Edward always kept the choice of members in his own hands.

These with many other examples which can be easily culled from his biographies show the range of the king's interest in government and they were supplemented by considerable activity in other spheres.

In the celebrated article in the *Dictionary of National Biography* on King Edward (which gave great offence to the king's family and friends) there occurred the phrase that in home politics 'he was content with the role of onlooker'. That was unfair, as is clear from what has been written above. The article also contained the statement that 'he was too old to repair the neglect of a political training'. But although that has been generally accepted by historians and they have concluded that the king's political importance was negligible, it rests in fact on a misconception. The political influence of the crown is not necessarily exercised in opposition to the government—though in history it often has been. The sovereign can play an important part in putting his influence and authority behind the

---

[1] Dudley Sommer, *Haldane of Cloan*, 1960.

[2] The king put forward Morley, but in the result, and happily, J. B. Bury was chosen. See Lee, op. cit.

government, which is exactly what King Edward did, especially when the Liberal party was in office.

He liked to do things himself. While he naturally kept Whitehall informed of what he was doing he liked to make his arrangements independently. In 1903 when he made the round of European visits which culminated in Paris and the speech which was supposed to have initiated the *entente cordiale*, he kept all the arrangements in his own hands. His private secretary tells us that most of the suite had no idea where they were going, and he suggests that the king may have kept his own counsel for fear of opposition from Whitehall.

If he disapproved of someone he would never display civilities even though they were demanded by the protocols and conventions of Whitehall. There are two examples of this. The first was Lloyd George. Although Mr. George was chancellor of the exchequer he resolutely refused ever to have him as minister in attendance. In 1908 he wrote to the prime minister, 'I shall have no more to do with him than what is absolutely necessary.' The other was King Leopold of the Belgians, to whom he was closely related. The Belgian government was distressed that King Edward neither visited their king nor invited him to England. But Edward made it plain that he shared enlightened opinion in England over Leopold's régime in the Congo, and that he would never relent.

Perhaps the best account of the king in his official life is to be found in a letter from George Wyndham, who was chief secretary for Ireland when the king paid an official visit there in the summer of 1903. When the royal yacht arrived at Kingstown Wyndham had breakfast with the king and his entourage; he narrowly escaped the mistake of seizing one of the three covered dishes placed for the king's personal consumption. Everyone was on edge: the ministers had from the start been dubious of the wisdom of the visit, and the news had come in through the night that Pope Leo XIII had chosen that moment to die. The king came in. In the interval of asking for a boiled egg and some more bacon he said: 'The pope's dead—of course we had expected it.' After breakfast, with only twenty minutes before he had to land, he settled down with Wyndham to send a message of sympathy to the Vatican, to alter some of the arrangements, and change the wording of the reply which he had to make at Kingstown. The two men smoked cigarettes and, in

Wyndham's words, the king showed 'the greatest good sense and calm, monumental confidence that all would go right'. The king was given a tremendous, jubilant welcome for the whole of the journey from Kingstown to Dublin: he was perfectly composed and as unhurried at the end as he had been on board the yacht. On 22 July he received eighty-two addresses from various public bodies—though not from Dublin Corporation which, by three votes, had declined to present one. As may be imagined, the Irish contrived to make everyone a little anxious how the ceremonial would be observed. One man shot his address straight into the waste-paper basket. The king was perfectly cool. 'Hand me the address', he said in his fat, cosy whisper, and then in returning thanks contrived to give the impression that he was surprised to find the Irish such adepts in court etiquette. On the following day the king rode to a review. On the way back, although he was immediately protected by his brother the Duke of Connaught and the Master of the Horse, he was in danger from the exceptional noise and cheering which made the horses lining the route extremely restive. Unmoved, the king rode on, bowing and smiling and waving his hand to the ragamuffins who had climbed into the branches of the trees. In spite of being in uniform he allowed himself a cigarette. When he got back he thanked those who had ridden with him and, as Wyndham said, 'beamed enough to melt an iceberg'. He left Ireland after a visit which authority had dreaded, with the cry echoing in his ears, 'Come back! Ah, ye will come back.'[1]

The issues of King Edward's reign were protection, education, liquor, the budget of 1909, and the threat to the House of Lords. He was too inexperienced—and perhaps had no occasion—to interfere with Balfour's government though he was irritated by their feebleness. He went some way with the Liberal government on the questions of protection, education, and liquor: he was apprehensive of the budget, and greatly distressed by the attacks on the Lords. Here it is important to distinguish between the situation in the king's reign and in the reign of his mother. She disapproved violently of Gladstone's foreign policy and Irish policy, and she did what she could to throw the power of the crown against him. Until the last year of his reign the king, though critical in details, was not

---

[1] *Letters of George Wyndham*, privately printed, 1915, and R. Fulford, *Hanover to Windsor*, 1960.

violently opposed to what his governments were doing. We should not, therefore, expect a great display of political influence by the king. Even when, after the beginning of 1909, he became most apprehensive of Liberal measures he was not so much concerned to thwart them as to bring them to accommodation with the Opposition. The Licensing Bill of 1908 proposed a reduction of 'on' licences by roughly one-third with the provision that compensation was to be paid by a levy on the trade. The Lords, encouraged by the malt-liquor men, determined to do battle with the Commons by summarily rejecting the bill. The king saw the leader of the Conservatives in the House of Lords and urged him not to reject but amend: he expressed the fear that if 'the attitude of the Peers was such as to suggest the idea that they were obstructing an attempt to deal with the evils of intemperance then the House of Lords would suffer seriously in popularity'. He also did what was possible in the closing months of the last winter of his life to prevent the Lords from rejecting the budget of 1909. Although he privately disliked some of the proposals in the budget he would have entirely agreed with Rosebery that it was the height of madness 'to stake the existence of the House of Lords on its rejection'.

There is one important point—and it has perhaps been insufficiently stressed—in attempting to estimate the position of the crown in King Edward's reign. Political measures in the decade were of less importance than political feeling. By its end political feeling had risen to a higher pitch than ever before in English history, or at any rate since the violent days of the seventeenth century. This explosive animosity at Westminster was a reflection of the indignation between classes and between the sexes as the century developed and drew the nation away from the more orderly march of the nineteenth century. Now the king plainly felt that it was the duty of the crown to attempt to assuage these passions—he showed this over the Liquor Bill and over the House of Lords. Whether as the last issue developed his authority might have wholly or partially successfully brought the parties to a compromise is impossible to say because he died as the storm was mounting. We can certainly say that he would have tried. And we can also say that he had one advantage over his successor King George—namely that he was instinctively more in sympathy with liberal aspirations than his son, who was by nature a conservative. Wilfrid Blunt, who was staying with one of the leaders of the Conservative party when the king died, wrote in his diary: 'All the same I can see that the prospect of a new and more Conservative King is welcome in this house.'[1]

Moreover King Edward was always conscious of the importance of liberalizing the court. According to Sir Frederick Ponsonby, in the *Dictionary of National Biography*, the instincts of the king's private secretary, Francis Knollys, were 'wholly liberal'. His politics came under fire from the Conservatives, but it is possible that the authority of King Edward, even though he was recognized as 'tainted with liberalism', might have persuaded the Conservative lords to a course of moderation and sense. Seeing in George V a politically more sympathetic person they hardened their hearts, hoping that they might carry the day with the support of the occupier of the palace. King Edward had always dreaded the weakening of the power of the House of Lords because he felt that if the peers were docked of their power they would leave the crown exposed. He held this view although he felt it was indefensible for the House of Lords to be in the hands of the Conservative party. Possibly he was right in his apprehensions over House of Lords reform, because when the Parliament Act became law in 1911 half of the fury of the Conservative party is explained by their feeling that Ireland was to be coerced into home rule by the vote of a single chamber. They were determined to drag in the crown to their rescue. To an extent they were successful. At a dinner party at Buckingham Palace the Conservative leader Bonar Law lectured King George V, and told him that if he agreed to the Home Rule Bill half his subjects would think 'you have acted against them. Have you ever thought of that, sir ?'[2] It is inconceivable that even a New Brunswicker could have spoken in such terms to King Edward.

And in justice King Edward must be credited with the foresight of sensing the danger developing to the British empire from Europe. He did not hope to moderate party warfare in order to satisfy his own political partialities, still less because it was more comfortable when politicians were not throwing 'Billingsgate' at one another—to use the king's phrase. He saw the folly of stirring up passions at home in the face of a future which he could only interpret as dark and terrible. His comment on the budget of 1909 was

---

[1] W. S. Blunt, op. cit.
[2] Robert Blake, *The Unknown Prime Minister*, 1955.

perceptive: he asked Asquith whether the cabinet, in considering the proposals, had taken into account the possibility of having to finance a European war.

That particular horror and the possibility of avoiding it occupied the forefront of his mind. When Asquith saw him just before he became prime minister he told his wife, 'He talked a little all over the place, smoking a cigar, about Roosevelt, Macedonia, Congo, &c.' What was going on abroad came naturally and instinctively to his mind: to that, problems at home were subordinate. No king in English history (not even the crusading Richard) travelled in Europe with the persistence of King Edward. His journeys as Prince of Wales were continued as king. But they took on a new importance. What had been unofficial became official: what had been private became political: while the Baron Renfrew or the Earl of Chester might escape publicity the Duke of Lancaster could not. There were relatives to see in Portugal, in Spain, in Germany, in Russia, and in Scandinavia: there were, in early autumn, the purgative waters of Marienbad to endure and then the spring to greet in Biarritz. He was a good listener,[1] and no doubt absorbed a great deal of information, not much of which he passed on to the Foreign Office. On these excursions the king repeatedly saw his fellow sovereigns, their heirs, and ministers. But it is a great mistake to suppose that such meetings were designed to further a particular policy or were indeed political in any sense. At their most serious they could perhaps be called, in the language of the twentieth century, 'fact-finding missions'. We see the king during the famous meeting with the tsar at Reval mirrored for us and all posterity in the vivid and masterly picture by Sir Harold Nicolson.[2] The king is being briefed by the author's father before meeting the emperor. What were the agricultural prospects? How did the empress get on with the ministers? What were the exact terms of the Anglo-Russian convention? What were Russian railways like? Would it be wise to mention the Duma? Who were the leading Russian scientists and men of letters?

[1] Sir Frederick Ponsonby has given one example of this. In 1904 the king went to Portsmouth where submarines were just coming into service. The theory of their working was explained to the king by Fisher, who was commander-in-chief at Portsmouth at the time. Captain Reginald Bacon then came to dinner and repeated Fisher's explanation. An enthusiastic young officer, on the following day, showed the king over a submarine repeating everything which the king had already heard. To Bacon and the young officer the king listened with rapt attention.

[2] *Sir Arthur Nicolson, Bart., First Lord Carnock*, 1930.

These were the king's questions, interlarded with such topics as 'Will the czar be wearing the Scots Greys uniform? What decorations will he be wearing?' It is obvious that the king asked these questions so as to be able to carry on an intelligent conversation with his host. He did not want the visit to consist of family trifles and find himself embroiled in little Tatiana's attack of whooping-cough. He wished above all else to make himself agreeable—to make a good impression and to show that his country was interested in Europe. No doubt at the time newspapers and others were searching for deeper motives—for what, even then, was called 'the story behind the story'. But was there one? Possibly the most effective answer to this was given by Sir Henry Campbell-Bannerman. He and the king were photographed in close colloquy at Marienbad above the caption 'Is it peace or war?' Sir Henry drily remarked to a friend, 'The king actually wanted my opinion as to whether halibut is better baked or boiled.'

No doubt the particular gifts of the king no less than his particular opportunities enabled him to supplement the policy and views of his government, and on one occasion to crown them. That occasion was in Paris in the spring of 1903, where by the kind of personal success which he deeply enjoyed he was able to improve the feeling between Great Britain and France. Sir Frederick Ponsonby, who was with him, gives a large part of the credit to his gift for public speaking—first the impromptu speech at the Hôtel de Ville ('Paris, où je me trouve toujours comme si j'étais chez moi'), and then the famous speech at the banquet without notes and in French. There are few people, as Ponsonby remarked, who can make a telling speech in a foreign language. The king could do this in both French and German.

If the king had been asked what was the purpose of his foreign peregrinations and consultations he would probably have replied that he was hoping to dispel ancient prejudices and suspicions against his own country which had been dominant in Europe for decades; for geographically as well as dynastically Great Britain had been on the perimeter of Europe. At least his efforts were designed to bring the English off the boundary and closer to the centre. Forty years earlier, in 1866, he had gone to Russia—probably the first member of the British royal family to go there—in the hope of fostering what he then called an *entente cordiale* and of stamping

Metropolitan & District Railways.

CORONATION DAY. 26TH JUNE, 1902.

The Metropolitan and District Railways will arrange for a Special Train for Members of Parliament and their friends, to leave the under-mentioned Stations for Westminster, at the following times, on Thursday, 26th June, 1902, viz.—

STATION.				A.M.
Kings Cross	...	...	Dep.	7.12
Gower Street	...	...	...	7.15
Portland Road	...	...	...	7.17
Baker Street	...	...	...	7.19
Edgware Road	...	...	...	7.22
Praed Street (Paddington)		...	...	7.25
Bayswater	...	...	...	7.28
Notting Hill Gate		...	...	7.30
High Street (Kensington)		...	...	7.33
Gloucester Road		...	...	7.35
South Kensington		...	...	7.37
Sloane Square	...	...	...	7.41
Victoria	...	...	...	7.44
St. James' Park	...	...	...	7.46

Arriving at Westminster at 7.48 a.m.

Members of Parliament intending to make use of this Train should make application, before 10 a.m. on 23rd inst., to the :—

General Manager, Metropolitan Railway, 32, Westbourne Terrace, W.,
or the
Manager, District Railway, St. James' Park Station. S.W.,

stating number of Passengers travelling, so that the necessary Permit Cards may be forwarded.

Passengers travelling by this Train must purchase Ordinary Tickets for the Railway journey at the Booking Offices in the usual way, and show them, together with the Permit Cards, to the Ticket Examiners when passing on to the Station Platforms.

14th June, 1902.

IV. A hand-bill

(Address only to be written here.)

J. C. B. Millar Esq

21. Evelyn Rd

Wimbledon

B. W.

A·D· Coronation·1911
FIRST U·K·AERIAL POST
By Sanction of H·M·Postmaster General

For conveyance by AEROPLANE from LONDON
to WINDSOR. No responsibility in respect
of loss, damage, or delay is undertaken
by the Postmaster General

Copyright   D.L.P.Jno

V. A postcard

out the embers of anti-British feeling caused by the Crimean war. And in this connexion we should do well to heed some words of Sir Edward Grey. He dismisses the accusation that the king gave British policy a bias against Germany. He emphasizes that when the king went to Berlin in 1909 he enjoyed making himself popular there (as he did) just as much as making himself liked in Paris, Rome, or Lisbon. Grey, who never looked favourably on exaggeration, says that something in the nature of genius is required to account for the king's remarkable power of projecting his personality over a crowd. And enough has been said to show that in this display of genius (if we care to call it that) there was something singularly gratifying to the nature of the king.

It has of course been said—and it can be argued—that King Edward did harm by his personal interventions abroad. In support of this there is the weight of beliefs (which cannot just be dismissed as propaganda) in Germany that he was working to encircle that country, to satisfy a long-standing personal vendetta against his nephew, the kaiser, and an even older resentment against Prussia, which dated back to that country's mutilation of Denmark in 1864 and its absorption of Hanover in 1866. (Queen Alexandra was daughter of the king of Denmark and sister of the *de jure* queen of Hanover.) He is 'a Satan', wrote the kaiser, and in his correspondence with the tsar the king was referred to as 'the greatest mischief-maker and the most deceitful and dangerous intriguer in the world'. Therefore in assessing the benign results of King Edward's interference in Europe—notably the better understanding of England in certain countries—we should heed the malign results of that interference. Although it is fair to notice that the relations of uncle and nephew vastly improved towards the end of the king's reign, we could argue that if the king had stayed at home, occasionally inviting his nephew to shoot the pheasants at Sandringham, the *rapprochement* with France might have gone ahead without the exacerbation of Anglo-German relations. We have seen, as is true of all people who are by nature easy-going, that the king enjoyed being liked. Popularity was to him peculiarly sweet. Yet his ancestress Queen Caroline said a very true thing about the efforts of her eldest son to make himself liked. 'My God, popularity always makes me sick, but Fritz's popularity makes me vomit.' In international relationships popularity has especial dangers.

People have been too ready to dismiss the king as a *flâneur*
because the policy for which he worked at home of conciliation
between parties was smashed on the rocks and the policy for which
he worked abroad of pacification perished with the outbreak of war
between Russia and Germany on 1 August 1914. We should not
minimize an individual's sway over his age because events after
his death moved in a headlong rush otherwise than he wished. If
we judge Cromwell in 1660 by Charles II's triumphant entry to
London, Gladstone by the Dublin rising of 1916, Disraeli by the
Suez crisis of 1956, or Lenin by Stalin's butcheries in 1938, we
should dismiss the policies of these world leaders as of slender
ultimate importance. Though the king was of course a pigmy
compared with these giants he deserves to be judged by the same
standards as they—his contribution to his age.

King Edward's influence abroad, his position as a leader of social
life, and his authority behind the scenes of government single him
out as one of our powerful kings. It was Leonard Hobhouse, no
friend to royal personages but a far-sighted observer of public life,
who wrote in 1904 that 'The Monarchy has vastly increased its
prestige—a change which can only be viewed by men of popular
sympathies with grave concern.'[1] But as we learn from the author of
the Acts of the Apostles there is a tribute of praise and gratitude in
those simple words, 'He served his own generation.'

Then comes this cry from the critics of Edwardian times—their
appetite for savagery sharpened by two world wars: Was the
generation worth serving? And to answer that question we want
to look closely and without liverish indignation at that strange,
long-dead society of which the king can fairly be called the fugle-
man. One word of caution is fair. The severest and most amusing
critics of Edwardian society are those who have been part of it.
They give us a picture of endless profusion, of unrelenting self-
indulgence. Here is Sir Osbert Sitwell on the London season before
1914:

> Never had there been such a display of flowers . . . a profusion of full-
> blooded blossoms, of lolling roses and malmaisons, of gilded, musical-
> comedy baskets of carnations and sweet-peas, while huge bunches of
> orchids, bowls of gardenias and flat trays of stephanotis lent to some
> houses an air of exoticism. Never had Europe seen such mounds of

[1] *Democracy and Reaction*, 1904.

peaches, figs, nectarines and strawberries at all seasons, brought from their steamy tents of glass. Champagne bottles stood stacked on the sideboards. . . . And to the rich, the show was free.

That is a fine passage from a fine book.[1] Mr. John Gore, in his fascinating *Edwardian Scrapbook* (1951) has described how he and his neighbour, at a dinner party for 24, counted the plates and glasses. They found that 362 plates and dishes had to be washed with 72 wine-glasses. No wonder that the junior fry below stairs, as Mr. Gore called them, swam away for ever to less steamy waters. Here is Miss Sackville-West on the same subject:

> Those meals! Those endless, extravagant meals in which they all indulged all the year round! Sebastian wondered how their constitutions and figures could stand it; then he remembered that in the summer they went as a matter of course to Homburg or Marienbad. . . . Really there was very little difference, essentially, between Marienbad and the vomitorium of the Romans. How strange that eating should play so important a part in social life!

Perhaps it is fair to comment that most of the evidence for these gargantuan feasts comes from the younger generation just old enough to fill a place but young enough to pine for the moment of 'getting down' when they could join their friends on tennis-court or ballroom-floor. The 'endless' dishes were proffered though not all of them were accepted, and we know that once when guests were squeezed at a dinner-table, without much room for trencher-work, a lady and her neighbour agreed to eat only alternate courses. By a natural, kaleidoscopic process of reasoning people have heaped all the indulgence of the age on to the king. He was the head of it all, therefore he was greedy. There is no evidence for this: he was certainly interested in food, as are many people—even in the present, abstemious age. His conversation with Campbell-Bannerman showed as much; so did his remark to Haldane when they were motoring on the borders of Germany and Austria: 'You always know when you are in Austria because the coffee is so good.'

August 1914 put an end to the Edwardian age with the same sudden finality as did the disorders in Paris in July 1789 to aristocratic life in France or the October revolution in St. Petersburg to the wayward existence of *The Cherry Orchard*. There was no gradual

[1] *Great Morning*, 1948.

blending of Edwardian and Georgian, no slow development of
'gracious living' into the cocktail and the *thé-dansant*. But like
everything whose end is abrupt and terrible, like the *Titanic* or
Pompeii, the catastrophe focuses attention on the change. Superficially of course, Edwardian society was totally at variance with
what was to follow in the twentieth century, but whether it was
fundamentally different has perhaps been insufficiently pondered.

To begin with, the country was immensely rich, and dominant
throughout the world. In a letter written at the close of the year in
which Queen Victoria had died, the kaiser wrote to King Edward,
'I thank God that I could be in time to see dear Grandmama once
more. . . . What a magnificent realm she has left you, and what a
fine position in the world. In fact the first "World Empire" since the
Roman Empire.'[1] From the impoverishment of the later decades of
the twentieth century we should not make the common mistake of
looking back too censoriously at that enjoyment of solid wealth
which we cannot share. The Edwardians are the rich prebends and
canons: we are merely the church mice. But to picture the Edwardians as given over to a parade of riches—a mere swagger of plate
and mahogany—indifferent to the poor without and the starving
on the confines of their empire is a travesty of truth. Our generation may have cured or may hope to cure such evils: theirs discovered them. And they were not discovered by the politicians, the
economists, or the sociologists: they were first detected and publicized by the churches. The familiar picture of the Edwardian age
riding to disaster, preoccupied with 'fun' and unconcerned with the
misfortunes of others is not borne out by a shrewd American observer, Mr. Price Collier, whose book *England and the English* was
published in 1909. He writes:

> The enormous amount of unpaid and voluntary service to the state, and
> to one's neighbours, in England, results in the solution of one of the most
> harassing problems of every wealthy nation: it arms the leisured classes
> with something worthy, something important to do. . . . When a man
> has made wealth and leisure for himself, or inherited them from others,
> he is deemed a renegade if he does not promptly offer them as a willing
> sacrifice upon the altar of his country's welfare.

That is not universally true or absolutely true of 'society', but there
is much truth in it. Moreover there is important testimony in support

---

[1] Lee, op. cit.

of this from Bryce who in 1909 published *Hindrances to Good Citizenship* while he was serving as British ambassador to the United States:

We all know about the luxury and extravagance but let us note the diffusion among the richer and educated classes of a warmer feeling of sympathy and a stronger feeling of responsibility for the less fortunate sections of the community: the altruistic spirit, now everywhere visible in the field of private, philanthropic work seems likely to spread into the field of civic action.

Individuals in all walks of life were no doubt as selfish and as indifferent to these things as they have ever been, but what Bryce was saying was true of a large proportion of that affluent society. With Charles Masterman they saw that they were 'passing into an age governed by the demands of incapacity to share in the benefits created by the competent'. Moreover, just as Edwardians were conscious of what was wrong and unjust around them, they were by no means unconscious of the doom to their way of life which was lying just ahead. There are many proofs that this was so. A year after King Edward's death Mr. R. S. A. Palmer, who was killed in the war, wrote to his family of his conviction that the British empire had reached its apex in 1897: 'The descent lies before us.' Many of his generation and of his seniors would have echoed that prophecy. Indeed their sense of what was coming, their feeling of apprehension, gives the Edwardians their particular fascination. This can be sensed by any perceptive observer of the past. The superficial and those who glory in the harsher realities of the later years of the twentieth century may say that such fears did not disturb that land of make-believe which the Edwardians created for themselves. With Lewis Carroll they might say:

> And though the shadow of a sigh
> May tremble through the story,
> It shall not touch with breath of bale
> The pleasance of our fairy-tale.

The king himself was acutely conscious of the accumulation of anxieties both at home and abroad. From 1907 onwards he was often depressed—noticeable in a man of his normally sanguine temperament—and more and more frequently entertained the idea of abdication from which he was dissuaded only with difficulty·

And was it not also true of society, just as it was true of Kipling's empire, that 'the descent lies before us'? We can easily enough conjure up, with the help of Sir Osbert Sitwell and Mr. Gore, a nostalgic picture of Edwardian society, the smell of tuberoses drenching the atmosphere, the strain of the *Merry Widow* beating in the mind. Here is Mr. Gore's recipe for a west-end dance in the season:

Take a large square room. Heat to 120 Fahr. Smear the sides with hothouse exotics. Take 100 best young persons of both sexes. Mix well and stir round quickly. Strain Blue Danube *ad lib*. Keep pouring the contents out and filling again at fifteen minute intervals. . . . Strain more Blue Danube and keep on stirring, emptying and filling till the mixture melt or boil and serve them . . . jolly well right.

Then there were the men for whom, as Mr. Price Collier suggests, society was chiefly designed. We see them in the pages of Daisy, Princess of Pless—Tippy Rocksavage, Bumbles Roxburgh, or Creepy de Crespigny. All was caught most admirably for us in Mr. Sandy Wilson's version of *Valmouth*:

> Do you remember Coko Ffoulkes,
> Flossie St. Vincent and Bimbo Stookes,
> Twirly Rogers and Bushy Ames?
> They all of them had such expressive names,
> And Monkey Trotter in guardsman's rig
> Doing a rather suggestive jig.

And the song is introduced with the plaintive lines—

> The men we loved have all passed on
> Like the world we knew they are dead and gone.

But these illustrious names did not make the Edwardian world: they did not even make Edwardian society. They were a memorable fragment of it. King Edward and 'Monkey Trotter' were as remote from one another as Lord Curzon from Keir Hardie. The truth was that during the king's maturity, from 1870 onwards, society had changed at a rapid rate. He had played some part in starting the change till, by the time of his reign, society had become as various in its origins and traditions as a random selection of African chieftains. The change from Victorian times was absolute. But it was much more than mere enlargement, for English society had never been rigidly exclusive. The Miss Berrys, Lady Waldegrave, or Beau Brummell were all ornaments of English society in their day: by any test of birth or quarterings they could never have been admitted to a continental aristocracy. Society in the early days of the nineteenth century was a unit, and it represented political power. It is believed that in those days a hostess giving a party did not invite men. The news that it was being given was spread, and the men within the charmed circle appeared. There was no need in those exclusive days for the formidable *grandes dames* to welcome their guests with the frosty challenge of King Edward's day, 'And who nominated you, young man?'[1] A perceptive contemporary observer, Mr. G. S. Street,[2] thought that by the time of King Edward society meant nothing at all, for he makes the excellent point that it was not just the old politico-aristocratic society diluted by vulgarians and financial magnates but that society had split into numerous sets. Admission to one set certainly did not mean admission to all. He notes first of all, in a class almost to itself, the society frequented by the king. One of his endearing traits—rare in kings—was constancy to old friends, and his round of English visits remained very much as king what it had been as prince—the Duke of Devonshire at Chatsworth, the Duke of Richmond at Goodwood, Lord Savile at Rufford, Lord Carrington, Lord Crewe, Lord Rosebery, Mr. 'Lulu' Harcourt,[3] Lord Iveagh, and Lord Londonderry. They could be regarded as the rump of the old political aristocracy. In addition there was an exclusive set based on birth and tradition. These were perhaps more to be found in the country than in London. Possibly to illustrate this point we might say that Sir George Sitwell was a member of this set, and while it would be insulting to Sir Osbert to say that he belonged to the smart set, it was some of the characteristics of that set to which his father took vigorous and amusing exception. 'Such a mistake to have friends, dear boy.' The members of this exclusive set were really antagonistic to the admission of wealth to the drawing-rooms of London. In a curious anonymous book called *Society in the New Reign, by A Foreign Resident* (1904), this distinction was emphasized. The author draws attention to the traditional set 'preserving an independent social existence of their own. Thus the Spencers, in Lady Spencer's lifetime, were entirely outside smartness.

---

[1] Many similar subtleties of Edwardian life are to be found in Sir Lawrence Jones's admirable book *An Edwardian Youth*, 1956.   [2] *People and Questions*, 1910.

[3] It was after the king had been the guest of Mr. Harcourt that his host in a public speech on the House of Lords unwisely referred to 'the black hand of the peerage' which had assassinated many fair measures desired by the people. King Edward strongly disapproved of such a speech following his visit.

So at first were the Cadogans.' But it is inevitably the smart set which has caught the fancy of posterity, has been regarded as the only society, and been attached to King Edward as though it were his creation. Mr. Street went so far as to say that the smart set was only a welter of people whose claim to social importance was in the possession of titles or the association with them or, directly, the possession of money. 'They fill the paragraphs of fashionable intelligence,' he goes on, adding that it is they who are attacked 'with so much fury and exaggeration by lady novelists'. The last is a palpable if ungallant blow at Elinor Glyn. But he is surely right when he says that while compilers of newspaper paragraphs were busy with countless functions and with the season, 'the powerful people follow their own tastes and are apt to stay away'.

Certainly King Edward gave unity to these confusions and distinctions of Edwardian society. He belonged in a sense to them all, just as he had belonged to White's, the Turf, the Marlborough, the Cosmopolitan, and was patron of the Garrick and attended gatherings of the Savage Club. As king and by nature he was no doubt most at home with the old, more exclusive, politico-aristocracy, but he would have been quite at home with the smart set. Had not *The Times*, thinking perhaps of his friendship for Lipton the grocer, said that if King Edward had been born in a humbler station he would have made a successful business man? But the point is not that King Edward dominated society by belonging to it—for as king he was much withdrawn from social circles both by his absences abroad and by the claims of private friendship. Rather it was his personality —'so strong and direct', as Haldane once happily defined it—which seemed to catch not only the various social groups but a far wider circle and give them that unity which we loosely call Edwardian. If we were to attempt to carry the point further and define the word, we might say that it stood perhaps for gaiety—'fun', if the reader so wishes it—in the smarter orders of social life and high spirits throughout all walks of life.

> Life's a game of see-saw
> Many the ups and downs,
> Sometimes you're counting your five pound notes
> And others you're counting your 'browns'!

There was a lightness of heart in England. How else, we may be tempted to ask from the cosiness of life in the 1960's, could the country have endured the misery which hovered around the cottage and dwelling-place of the working-classes? But with these high spirits there went, in all classes, a marked attention to behaviour. Miss Sackville-West, with unerring precision, strikes the difference between the age which came in with George V and 1914, and that which went out with King Edward. Two girls are discussing contemporary life and, speaking of her lover, one says: 'Adrian says that love is the only thing which matters. Father and mother say behaviour is the only thing which matters.' High spirits and behaviour mark the age of King Edward. No doubt it was partly chance that those two things were also distinctively the king's. From his youth men had marvelled at his spirit—'vigour seemingly inexhaustible', Gladstone had once called it. His attention to behaviour is sufficiently obvious. Mr. H. J. Bruce, in his book *Silken Dalliance* (1946), tells how as a junior Foreign Office man he served the king at Marienbad. The king's only explosion of anger was when he found that Bruce had kept a young lady waiting for a game of golf: 'When I was a young man I was taught never to keep a lady waiting.' But if high spirits and behaviour identified the king with his people that does not mean that King Edward moulded the decade in the sense that perhaps King Louis XIV, Queen Elizabeth I, or Lorenzo de' Medici stamped the age with their relentless image in the way that butter takes the impression of the pats which beat it. Rather would it be true to say—and this is also true of King George IV during the Regency—that the king's personality and temperament caught and reflected some broad image of the generation which came to maturity with him. For is it not true that Edwardianism died with King Edward? In his 'Portrait of an Age'[1] Mr. G. M. Young calls this decade 'the flash Edwardian epilogue' to Victorianism, though with equal justice it might be regarded as a stylish send-off to the hard journey down 'the descent which lies before us'. So far as the credit for that fair start can belong to an individual it belongs to the king. As the Archbishop of Canterbury stood by the death-bed of King Edward on 6 May 1910 he thought that he had seldom seen 'a quieter crossing of the river'. And many of his contemporaries were not wholly wrong when they felt that he was also a spectator of the passing of the last of the kings.

[1] The final chapter in *Early Victorian England* (*supra*), separately published as *Victorian England, Portrait of an Age*, 1936.

2

THE POLITICAL SCENE

ASA BRIGGS

Professor of History in the University of Sussex

THE POLITICAL SCENE

'WHAT a series of changes political and social this event will produce!' Lord Esher noted in his journal on the accession of Edward
VII in January 1901. 'It is like beginning to live again in a new
world.' This reaction was widely shared. Similar feelings were
expressed by many people who, unlike Esher, had no access either
to court or cabinet. An old queen had died and a long age had ended.
To that age the queen had given her name. Without her the country
suddenly seemed strange and forlorn. Yet there was as much relief as
regret in 1901, and the adjective 'Edwardian' was coined at once to
proclaim not continuity but contrast. The 'Uncle of Europe' seemed
a less remote figure than the aged 'Mother of her People'. The new
reign promised both more colour and more contact, more extravagance and a great deal less restraint. Some hoped that it would
promise more happiness. 'There is an avuncular benevolence about
the king which is irresistible', wrote the distinguished Liberal
journalist, A. G. Gardiner; 'he likes to be happy himself, and he
likes to see the world happy.'

The happy image persists after more than half a century. The
response to what is called Victorian has shifted and fluctuated: the
appeal of the Edwardian has remained curiously fixed. Preceded by
the long reign of Victoria, the Edwardian age was followed by the
cataclysmic experiences of the first world war. What happened
between 1901 and 1914, therefore, seems to have a kind of frozen
unity, the unity of 'the dear dead days beyond recall'. The Edwardian age has been compared, therefore, with those other ages in the
past which seem 'to detach themselves from the general stream of
events, to be, as it were, islands in time, countries of the imagination, to which we would, if we could, escape'.[1]

However persistent, this image is distorted. Edwardian society
was picturesquely but perilously divided, and the greatest of the

[1] J. Laver, Introduction to *The Age of Extravagance*, 1955.

many contrasts of the age was not that with what had gone before but that between the divergent outlooks and fortunes of different groups within the same community. The implications of the clash of out-looks, fortunes, and tactics could seldom be completely evaded, and during certain years of the Edwardian period, if more particularly during the four years after the king's death in 1910, there was open and violent internal conflict. Will transcended both law and con-vention. The greater international violence of 1914 was a culmina-tion as well as an historical divide. Moreover, throughout almost the whole period and most obviously after the coming into power of the Liberal government in 1905, the happiness of the few was tempered by the misery of the many—a better documented, more vocal, and more active misery than ever before—and by nagging and frustra-ting doubts and anxieties concerning both ends and means. There was more probing and more publicity, more searching after facts, official and unofficial, massive and trivial, and more speculation on the proper relationship between private action and public good.

The argument and the conflict, the introspection and the uncer-tainty, were not restricted to the sphere of economic or industrial relations. Questions of sex were sometimes more prominent than questions of class: sometimes the two were associated. The law as interpreted by the courts was as suspect as the laws passed (or rejected) by Parliament. While novelists and dramatists were treating these problems as themes, a number of thinkers and writers were challenging underlying intellectualist assumptions about 'human nature in politics'. Graham Wallas in his book with that title (1908) turned for his explanations to memory, instinct, and habit, while the young Bertrand Russell wrote a little later of the 'barbaric substratum of human nature, unsatisfied in action', finding 'an outlet in imagination'. The verbal violence of the para-dox ruffled even polite literature. Behind the surface of Edwardian Britain there was little complacency. 'New winds' were known to be 'blowing hard through society'.[1] 'It was not death which gave imperial England such a disturbing appearance in the spring and summer of 1914: it was life.'[2]

The country-house, the continental hotel, the long week-end, the

---

[1] The phrase comes from a letter of Lady Frances Balfour, quoted by R. Fulford, *Votes for Women*, 1957.

[2] G. Dangerfield, *The Strange Death of Liberal England*, 1936.

pull of exuberant fashion, the speculation in South African shares, even the sense of social superiority itself were in their different but related ways means of escape. Whether or not Edwardian Britain is an island in time to which we would, if we could, escape, it always demanded its own islands. It paid for them without being too concerned about the cost, and often, particularly in retrospect, they were islands in the sun. The golden summer of 1911, with its sunshades, straw hats, and record temperatures, has cast its spell on historians. (Yet the heat of the summer could be blamed for the large number of industrial disputes and even for the 'nastiness' of politicians.) In moments of release and withdrawal, when pressures were relaxed and doubts were stilled, there was peace and pleasure, as well for the 'underprivileged' (precariously pursuing their own ways of life, influenced but not broken by 'mass culture') as for the successful. Edwardian Britain, like Sebastian, the young Duke of Chevron in V. Sackville-West's novel *The Edwardians*, could best come to terms with itself when it kept its divided selves separate. 'Then', Miss Sackville-West writes of Sebastian, 'he could manage to sustain himself by thinking that one self redeemed the other.' Perhaps it was better not to think at all. There was no guarantee of redemption, of security—which in retrospect seems to have been so great—or of happiness. 'When every man of a certain income has purchased a motor car', wrote C. F. G. Masterman, a very distinguished and still provocative Liberal social critic in 1910, 'that definite increase of expenditure will be accepted as normal. But life will be no happier and no richer for such an acceptance; it will merely have become more impossible for those who are unequal to the demands of such a standard.'

Motor cars were the newest symbols of speed and status—in Masterman's vision 'wandering machines racing with incredible velocity and no apparent aim' down the country lanes of England. They were not, as the railways had been in the previous transport revolution, an instrument of democracy, but rather a perquisite of private ostentation in an age of public penury. (Their value at elections was recognized as early as January 1906. 'The motor car is everywhere', noted *The Times*, 'and there are few candidates who do not appreciate its advantages and invoke its aid.') There were only about 8,500 motor cars in the country in 1904 when compulsory registration was introduced. Yet, like so much else in Edwardian

Britain, the motor car was a product of the late nineteenth century. So too was the *Daily Mail* (1896). The year 1901 was far less of a break in economic, social, or political history than at first sight and still in current legend it appears to be. Long before Lord Esher wrote of 'entering a new world' there had been waves of talk of this kind. A new century preceded a new reign: it encouraged as much assessment and anticipation as the accession of the new king. During the last decade of the nineteenth century the adjective 'new' shared with *fin-de-siècle* a modishness which is still reflected in terms like *Art nouveau*, the New Woman, or even the New Liberalism.

If there was much that was 'new' before 1901, more that was old survived the queen. There were, indeed, few problems, or ways of approaching them, which seemed really new when Edward VII, himself a middle-aged man with a far longer past than a future, ascended the throne. It is true that in July 1902 the Marquess of Salisbury, who had been prime minister, with a short break of three years, since 1886, was succeeded by A. J. Balfour, but there was nothing surprising or ominous about the succession. Balfour, born in 1848, had been leader of the Conservatives in the House of Commons since 1891; he was Salisbury's nephew; and he was the last man to wish to follow a 'new course'. 'Mr. Balfour', J. L. Garvin commented in an article called 'From Amurath to Amurath', 'is made prime minister precisely because it is desired by the ruling families that the minimum of change should be made.' It was as clear to the Conservatives of 1902 as it had been to the Liberals of 1885 that if the 'maximum of change' were to be made by the party, it would be at the behest of Joseph Chamberlain, yet Chamberlain ungrudgingly accepted Balfour as leader in 1902 in the knowledge that this was the way things were done in a patrician democracy. 'To entrust Mr. Balfour with the formation of the Cabinet', wrote T. H. S. Escott, 'was to adopt an expedient which would gratify the orthodox tradition by keeping the premiership in the hands of a great family, which would also humour the democracy by giving its chief, Mr. Chamberlain, plenary authority over the whole combination.'

The politics of the first two years of Edward's reign thus follow naturally from the politics of the last six years of Queen Victoria's. The empire was at the centre of them. The Boer war did not end until May 1902, and that war was the climax of late Victorian

VI (b). Mr. A. J. Balfour and a 24-h.p. Daimler

VI (a). Lord Salisbury on his Locomobile

THE PEOPLE'S RIGHTS

Russell & Son Photo

BY
THE RIGHT HONOURABLE
WINSTON S. CHURCHILL, M.P.
HODDER AND STOUGHTON · LONDON
ONE SHILLING net

VII. A pamphlet of 1910

imperialism, an imperialism 'where much was exalted and much corrupt, and where much, perhaps the greatest part, was no more than adventurous'.[1] The general election of 1900 which gave Balfour and Chamberlain their substantial majority of 128 was a 'khaki election' fought, at least from the Unionist side, on the sole issue of the war, 'the waving of the flag and the cry of khaki'. The tone of politics in the first years of the new reign was not dissimilar from that of the 1890's, although the demand for 'efficiency', which was a product of the Boer war as it had been of the Crimean war, encouraged a keener debate and a greater seriousness. Élie Halévy chose 1895, not 1901, as the date of resumption of his masterly *History of the English People*. He detected no significant change in 1901, although he saw the period after the Unionist victory of 1895 as the prologue of the new century, as a period which did 'not belong to the British nineteenth century' as he saw it. The unstable mixture of caution and stridency, high-minded talk and brash vulgarity, of hidden influence and shrill public argument, was as much a feature of the first years of the new reign as it had been of the last years of the old. Even Balfour himself, the prime minister famous for never reading newspapers, was in harmony with the times when in his last month of office in 1905 he recommended a peerage for Sir Alfred Harmsworth, the pioneer of popular journalism. He is said to have put his arm round the new Lord Northcliffe's shoulder and to have told him 'I am very proud of you.'

Chamberlain and Tariff Reform

There was a real sense, however, in which Joseph Chamberlain's decision in 1903 to leave Balfour's cabinet and to lead a 'raging, tearing campaign' for tariff reform marked the beginning of a new phase in British politics. It was not that Chamberlain's behaviour was surprising. He had always shown exceptional vigour and resource in taking up new issues when old ones proved exhausted or of too narrow an appeal. Furthermore this particular issue could be deduced logically from the particular kind of aggressive economic imperialism of which he had been for long the most eloquent and forceful advocate. 'Protection will not be Protection', wrote J. A. Hobson in 1901, 'but Free Trade within the Empire.' This was the central thesis of Chamberlain and of the Birmingham men who

[1] G. M. Young, *Victorian England, Portrait of an Age*, 1936.

directed the protectionist movement through the committees of the Tariff Reform League, as much a Birmingham product as the Liberal caucus which had been manufactured thirty years before. In accepting the merits of this thesis Chamberlain was merely reaching the same conclusion (and a new point of political departure) as many business men in his own city had reached before. They led: he followed. This was an old pattern which goes far towards explaining Chamberlain's popularity in Birmingham, his great and always invulnerable bastion. Yet as soon as Chamberlain himself decided to seek to lead the nation, politics were galvanized. There was a 'new fever in the blood'. 'You can burn all your political leaflets and literature', he told Herbert Gladstone, the Liberal whip, in the lobby of the House of Commons. 'We are going to talk about something else.' That 'something else' reshaped national history.

In the first place it split the Unionist cabinet, which had survived earlier differences on the Education Bill of 1902, and threatened the unity of the Unionist party, which had been in almost uninterrupted power since the home rule crisis of 1886. Not only did Chamberlain resign when he decided to make his appeal to the country, but his resignation in September 1903 was accompanied by the resignations of three Unionist free-traders, including C. T. Ritchie, the chancellor of the exchequer. It was a confusing moment. 'It would appear', one back-bench Liberal commented, 'that we have now arrived at a Government in which there is no room for any convictions. Mess and muddle have had their day: now is the day of make-believe. We are to have a ministry of balance, a government of philosophic doubt.'[1] He went on to add, as most political commentators would have added, that this 'appearance' was misleading: the substitution at the exchequer of Chamberlain's son Austen for Ritchie would prove that free trade was not safe in Unionist hands. Nor was it. The Unionist free-traders, some of them pre-eminently safe and respectable men who had opposed Chamberlain in the distant 1880's before he joined hands with Salisbury and were now only too willing to oppose him again, also included brilliant young men like Lord Hugh Cecil and Winston Churchill. They also included 'imperialists' who refused to believe that protection was a necessary consequence of 'imperialist policies'. Whatever their gifts,

[1] *Halifax Courier*, 15 September 1903. The back-bencher was J. H. Whitley, the future whip and eventually speaker of the House of Commons.

they found it difficult as Unionists to retain the confidence either of their colleagues or their constituents. Their position appeared to be and was anomalous. Cecil might pour aristocratic scorn on the imperialism 'which thinks of nothing but trade returns', and the aged Goschen, who had coined the slogan 'unauthorized programme' to describe Chamberlain's radical manifesto of 1885, might add to the political phrase-book 'gamble with the food of the people'; but what they said strengthened liberalism rather than suggested that conservatism would remain true to free trade. Balfour, who, in a well-known phrase, was 'hampered by no passionate convictions', and who now found himself with few lieutenants of capacity or authority, very cleverly held his party together for far longer than even his admirers thought possible. Yet his skill was evident only in his tactics: his own limited and highly sophisticated acceptance of tariffs as means of retaliation was far removed from Chamberlain's bold and essentially constructive attitude towards the question.

To Chamberlain, the introduction of a new tariff system would not only protect British business men and bring the widely separated colonies into closer economic and spiritual union, but it would be of direct benefit to working men. It would link the two causes of empire and social reform. It was thus the question of questions. Just as the militant free-traders of the Anti-Corn Law League had argued sixty years earlier that repeal of the corn laws would improve the condition both of the business man by opening up new markets and of the working man by cutting the cost of living, so the Tariff Reform League, under the able direction of Professor W. A. S. Hewins, first director of the London School of Economics, argued that protection would not only guarantee employment for working men but would provide sufficient revenue to permit the government to introduce useful measures of social reform. Chamberlain had always professed a keen interest in social reform from his radical days onwards: he had been the first front-bench politician to sponsor the idea of old age pensions in 1892. During the Boer war, however, and particularly at the time of the khaki election, he had devoted all his energies to more immediate causes, and in 1902 he virtually abandoned his leadership on the old age pensions issue. Perhaps the main reason was the refusal of successive Unionist chancellors of the exchequer to consider heavier direct taxation:

they were as wedded as Gladstone had been to peace-time 'retrenchment', and they recognized that only the imposition of revenue
duties, of which they disapproved, would offer any flexibility in
embarking upon new projects, domestic or imperial. Chamberlain
was dissatisfied, but had to accept their logic in 1901 and 1902. They
in turn were increasingly disturbed by the demands which were
being made upon them. 'There is no party or section of party',
Hicks Beach, the Unionist chancellor of the exchequer, complained
in April 1901, 'that is in favour of economy for economy's sake.'
In 1903 Chamberlain came out boldly for a new system which he
believed would make it possible for the country to spend more on
social reform and on defence. Britain would be richer through increased employment, the unorganized empire would be developed
through increased investment and growing trade. When Chamberlain discussed these questions in private as in public, 'he spoke like
a seer—as one quietly, unemotionally, slowly describing a vision as
it unfolded itself to him.'[1] He was a shrewd enough politician to
know that 'only a great cause could capture the democracy', and he
plunged himself into it with great exuberance. Yet he was also
shrewd enough to say in private that not one general election would
be required to convert people to a new tariff policy, but several.
'Two or three, perhaps more. It will take years.' There was no break
with Balfour, yet Chamberlain must have known that Balfour was
hardly the man to convert the country to anything.

A majority of the politically active nation accepted free trade,
most of them conventionally. For some, however, free trade was
still a religion. The principles behind it were eternal: its revelation
was the greatest triumph of the nineteenth century. Enough Liberals
were so sure in this faith that Chamberlain's attempt to subvert it
gave them a greater sense of righteous unity than they had felt
since the golden age of Gladstone. While the tariff controversy split
or confused the Unionists, it rallied the Liberals. They had been so
divided on issues and personalities both before and during the Boer
war that they seemed to be disintegrating into a party of 'sections'.
The name 'Liberal' not only meant different things in different parts
of the country according to the structure of local society and the
forms of local leadership, but it provided no real unity at the centre.

[1] The words are Sir Percy Fitzpatrick's. He took part in a memorable tea-party with
Chamberlain and Milner in Johannesburg on Chamberlain's visit to South Africa, 1902–3.

Imperialism, which consolidated the Unionists behind the banner of the flag, fragmented the Liberals into groups. Ambition as well as opinion then led the groups to move in different directions through the political wilderness.

Diversity of Liberals

The most influential group consisted of Liberal imperialists, many of whom had formed and clarified their imperialist convictions even while Gladstone was still party leader. For long their most lively personality was Lord Rosebery, the one surviving Liberal ex-prime minister. No one doubted Rosebery's brilliance: many envied his experience. Winston Churchill said of him, 'I feel that if I had his brain I would move mountains.' No one doubted also Rosebery's intense belief in empire: he conceived of it both as a necessary condition of Britain's power and as an expression of Britain's 'mission'. He had opposed the evacuation of Egypt at a time when many Liberals, however unrealistically, were insisting on withdrawal, and he had succeeded in retaining Uganda when a powerful Liberal section opposed it. During the Boer war he demanded a more vigorous deployment of national resources and a more militant leadership. He was not only an ex-prime minister, but a possible alternative prime minister. Just as the Crimean war had focused attention on the need for 'efficiency', so the Boer war, with all its disappointments and disasters, gave critics of the government ample opportunities to demand a complete 'overhaul' of politics and administration. Rosebery suffered from the disadvantage of being in the House of Lords, a difficult position from which to direct the forces of democratic protest, but he tried to appeal to the patriotic crowds as well as to the Unionist peers on the opposition benches. He had, after all, established himself as a local politician in democratic London, and he knew how to sway an audience of shopkeepers and working men. In a much-noticed London speech of July 1901 he claimed that no government within living memory had 'crowded such a frightful assembly of errors, of weaknesses, and of wholesale blunders into its history'. He demanded, as Chamberlain also demanded in different language, a programme based on support of the empire coupled with social reform at home. He talked of education 'co-ordinated and systematized'—(characteristic words)—of old age pensions, housing, and temperance. For him, the link between social reform and empire was the conviction that only a better housed, better fed, and better educated people could fulfil its imperial destinies. He urged the Liberal party to abandon some of its old 'cumbersome programmes' (home rule, not specified, was one of these), to 'wipe the slate clean' of the errors of the past, and to purge itself of all 'anti-national elements'.

Rosebery won the support of a number of extremely able Liberals, and his Liberal League, founded in 1902, had among its vice-presidents Herbert Asquith, the future prime minister, Sir Edward Grey, the future foreign secretary, and R. B. Haldane, the future secretary of state for war and lord chancellor. Increasingly, however, Rosebery himself lost ground in the Liberal party after 1902, and figured more as a brilliant and knowledgeable critic than as an active politician. Already by 1903 when Chamberlain raised the cry of tariff reform, Rosebery's section of the Liberal party was more significant than Rosebery himself. Asquith followed Chamberlain round the country, assailing his fiscal theories in what Rosebery described as 'clinching, convincing speeches': Rosebery himself stayed in his tent, seldom making any 'clinching' utterance. He was known to adhere to free trade, but there was something chillingly equivocal about such comments as 'Free Trade was not in the Sermon on the Mount'. He did not, therefore, contribute to or benefit from the drive towards Liberal unity which followed Chamberlain's new departure. Many Liberals disliked him intensely. The other leaders of the Liberal League had watched both their enmities and their friendships more carefully. When the controversies over South Africa became faint and imperial questions no longer divided the party, no personal feelings prevented their collaboration with Liberals whose views had once been radically different from their own.

At the opposite end of the party there had been the Liberal anti-imperialists, men who disliked all imperial connexions and were not ashamed to be called 'Little Englanders'. They were extremely unpopular during the Boer war when they were dubbed 'pro-Boers' or, in Rosebery's equally unflattering phrase, 'anti-national elements'. John Morley, who had been an early critic of 'imperialism' in the 1880's, when Professor J. R. Seeley's *The Expansion of England* was published, summed up more clearly than most of them a philosophy of liberalism which left no place at all for 'imperialism'. 'Had they thought of the relationship between imperialism and social reform?' he asked the members of the Palmerston Club in Oxford nearly three years before Chamberlain launched tariff reform. 'What we wanted was resolute and sustained attention to strengthening our industrial position. What was the use of conquering new markets when it was as much as we could do to hold the markets which we had already?'

Morley represented residual Gladstonianism. David Lloyd George, the youngest and most detested of the leading 'pro-Boers', scathingly attacked specific instances of 'recklessness' and 'inhumanity' associated with the Unionist government's conduct of the war: in more general terms he considered the war 'an outrage perpetrated in the name of human freedom'. He made himself as unpopular with many of his fellow Liberals as with the Unionists, and on one celebrated occasion taunted the middle-of-the-way Liberal leader Henry Campbell-Bannerman with having been captured, stripped of his principles, and left on the veld. At least one discerning observer saw a curious affinity between the young Lloyd George and Joseph Chamberlain, the man he hated most. He called Lloyd George 'the very reincarnation of the present colonial secretary in his younger days', and asked pertinently: 'Will time work . . . a similar change in the virulent Little Englander? Will he a score of years hence be the tower of strength of the Imperial or of the Parochial party?' His answer was more cautious. 'None can say now, but that he will be by then one of the foremost men in the nation's Parliament is beyond question.'[1]

Between the Liberal imperialists (or 'Limps') and the 'pro-Boers', a large number of whom were 'radical' in their approach to domestic policy, were the Liberals with neither prefix nor suffix. Their leader was Campbell-Bannerman, who after 'creeping to the front inch by inch, no one exactly knows how', had been unanimously elected leader of the Liberal opposition in the House of Commons on Harcourt's resignation in 1898. The post was not attractive. In a *Punch* cartoon the departing butler, Harcourt, is saying to the new man, 'Well, 'Enery Bannerman, so you've took the place, 'ave you? I wish you joy! She used to be a Liberal Old Party, but now she's that contrairy there's no living with her.' The Boer war made the post even less attractive, but Campbell-Bannerman stuck to it with tenacity and courage. He supported the war, but did not hold the

[1] E. T. Raymond, *Mr. Lloyd George*, 1922.

government free from responsibility for having started it. He refused to be called a 'Little Englander', but he indulged in no patriotic claptrap about the Boers. He demanded 'efficiency', but he also asked for 'justice'. His criticism of the Unionist government for employing 'methods of barbarism' in South Africa, particularly by burning farms and building concentration camps, was held against him at the time, but was quoted in his favour when the wave of jingoistic imperialism had subsided. His middle-of-the-way followers were wont to distinguish between two kinds of imperialism, the one 'false', based on military power, the other 'true', based on strict standards of national morality. 'They believed that the greatness of Empire did not depend upon area or territory, but upon the quality of the men and women whom they were rearing at home to carry on the command of the Empire.'[1]

The Boer war seemed to teach lessons which reinforced these distinctions. It cost Britain £270 million, and by forcing the British to use 400,000 troops to dispose of the greatly outnumbered Boers revealed to the rest of Europe the blatant weaknesses of British military power. 'The truth is', wrote Campbell-Bannerman to a friend in 1903, 'we cannot provide for a fighting Empire and nothing will give us the power.' But he added—and it was an addition which demonstrates where and how precariously he stood— 'a peaceful Empire of the old type we are quite fit for'.

Between the end of the war and Chamberlain's call for tariff reform, Campbell-Bannerman consolidated his position as party leader. Rosebery remained outside his 'tabernacle', but Liberal imperialists, pro-Boers, and plain Liberals co-operated encouragingly and often fiercely in the fight against the Education Bill of 1902. The Nonconformists, in particular, were roused on this occasion to a scathing denunciation of all that the government stood for. This last great nonconformist political demonstration, during which all the old nineteenth-century war cries were heard, even caused some dissension in government ranks, especially among the Liberal Unionists. It certainly played its part in convincing Chamberlain that, unless some new and exciting cause were taken up, a Liberal victory at the next general election would be probable. Yet Chamberlain's demand for tariff reform and the introduction by the Unionist cabinet of a new Licensing Bill in 1904, another measure

[1] *Halifax Courier*, 21 September 1900.

calculated to alienate Nonconformists, guaranteed that the Liberal revival would continue.

At this point, however, there was still no guarantee of complete Liberal unity. The days of 'war to the knife and fork' at competing Liberal banquets were over. So too were the days of devastatingly revealing Liberal split votes in the House of Commons. Yet there was intrigue behind the scenes concerning both personalities, including the personality of the leader, and policies. The most encouraging sign was a marked swing of opinion at by-elections. The government won the last few by-elections of 1903, but there were high Liberal polls in constituencies which they had not bothered to contest in 1900. In January 1904 the Unionist run was at last broken at Norwich. The constituency had returned two Conservatives unopposed in 1900, but on this occasion the Conservative candidate, very moderate in his views on tariff reform, was opposed by a Liberal and a Labour candidate. The Liberal candidate was returned with a majority of nearly 2,000.[1]

Liberal enthusiasm was based not only on a sense of rediscovered if still incomplete unity but on deep convictions grounded in the history of the party. Belief in free trade in goods was a philosophy of life even when it was not a religion. Protection was thought to be more rather than less wicked if the poor were to be tempted to vote for it by 'promise of old age pensions, to be paid out of their own earnings and the restriction of their children's food'. Once again it was Chamberlain whom Liberals considered the chief agent of destruction. The 'humbug' he talked deserved to suffer 'crushing defeat from a thoughtful democracy, determined to be free'. Distaste for the protection of the Church of England was part of the same philosophy. So too was a refusal 'further to endow the brewers'. All these were historic Liberal causes. Cobden and Bright were still abroad in the land. Indeed Cobden, the centenary of whose birth was celebrated on 3 June 1904, was perhaps the most widely quoted politician on the Liberal side. New causes were always directly related to old ones. Most Liberal social reform manifestoes, for example, gave at least as prominent a place to temperance reform as to old age pensions. The evils of poverty, malnutrition, bad housing, and illiteracy were all associated with 'the drink problem', despite the young Liberal Seebohm Rowntree's painstaking demonstration

[1] Liberal 8,576; Conservative 6,756; Labour 2,444.

in *Poverty, a Study of Town Life* (1901) that primary poverty had nothing to do with the way the poor spent their incomes. 'Privilege' on the part of the rich and 'lack of responsibility' on the part of the poor were still the main targets of criticism. Even among the 'new Liberals' who advocated increased state intervention and waved Rowntree's book on their platforms as a new testament, there were many, like J. A. Hobson, who were prepared to argue that had Cobden lived he would have been a 'new Liberal' himself. Since he had eventually come to accept the need for legal restrictions on child labour on the ground that the employer and the child were unequal in bargaining strength, he would have been compelled, so the argument ran, to accept legal restrictions elsewhere. Given time, 'the difference between a true, consistent, public-spirited liberalism and a rational collectivism' would disappear.

A 'new Liberal' left wing was very active in Edwardian Britain, publishing facts and exploring values. The facts related to poverty, to wealth, to land, to a lesser degree to industry, to domestic issues, and, not least, to imperialism. Symposia, the first of which was *The Heart of Empire* (1902), led the way: they contrasted the pomp of empire with the squalor of working-class life in Britain. They directed attention to the distribution of national wealth and the rewards of foreign investment. Books on these subjects, the most influential of which was L. G. Chiozza Money's *Riches and Poverty* (1905), ran into many editions, as many as ten in five years. Articles by outstanding writers like C. F. G. Masterman, H. W. Massingham, H. N. Brailsford, and E. D. Morel exposed conditions not only in Britain and the British empire but in other people's empires. Morel's *Red Rubber* (1905) and Brailsford's *The War of Steel and Gold* (1914) were manuals of exposure of 'exploitation'. Periodicals, notably the *Nation* (1907),[1] pulled all the issues together and underlined their urgency.

The facts were disturbing. Half the total national income of Britain accrued to one-ninth of the population, one-third to one-thirtieth: half the national capital belonged to one-seventh of the population. This was said to be the root explanation of poverty, the poverty which had been statistically demonstrated and measured by Charles Booth and Seebohm Rowntree. Official investigation

[1] The periodical was really older. In 1899 a group of young Liberals acquired the *Speaker*. This became the *Nation* after a financial re-arrangement.

during and after the Boer war had revealed some of the social products of this poverty—'physical deterioration' among youth, for example, and inadequate education. The 'physical deterioration' was no more serious, the left-wing Liberals argued, than moral deterioration: 'imperialism' distorted values, encouraged 'a kind of intellectual dry rot', and upset social priorities. It had become a necessary part of a vicious and corrupting system. It was in the material interests of only a few, and was itself responsible for the debasing contrast between talk of the empire on which the sun never set and the grim facts of the slums over which the sun never rose.

The Idea of Empire

Yet the 'new Liberal' left wing did not have a monopoly of enthusiasm or of dedication in the years which followed the political crisis of 1903. L. S. Amery, the chief correspondent of *The Times* during the Boer war, called Chamberlain's Birmingham speech of May 1903 'a challenge to free thought as direct and provocative as the theses which Luther nailed to the Church door at Wittenberg. Men who . . . would have resented being described as anything but Free Traders found themselves hating Free Trade with all the intensity with which any Calvinist had ever hated the Church of Rome.' Amery was a disciple of Alfred Milner, the British high commissioner for South Africa during the decisive years from 1897 to 1905. Milner's famous *Kindergarten* stamped on all its scholars a profound attachment to the cause of empire as a fulfilment of individual and national duty. Like his fellow proconsul Lord Curzon, who was viceroy of India from 1898 to 1905, Milner believed that 'in Empire we have found not merely the key to glory and wealth, but the call to duty and the means of service to mankind'. Milner was by origin a Liberal; Curzon both by origin and by temperament was a high Tory; yet they were at one in pointing to imperial responsibility as the crowning glory of British politics. 'The Empire is with us. It is part of us. It is bone of our bone and flesh of our flesh.' A little island had been transformed by a 'great idea': little men could also be transformed into far greater men if they made the empire their ideal. British possessions were not merely 'a great historical and political and sociological fact' but a field of enterprise and service, calling Englishmen to 'a personal as well as a national duty, more inspiring than had ever before been sounded in the ears of a dominant people'.[1]

The idea of a developing empire thus had the power of an ideal. The ideal was proclaimed in the public schools and maintained in a tangled network of clubs and societies, many of them drawing deliberately on members of more than one political persuasion. London was honeycombed with such societies. However much the 'new Liberal' left wing might expose the grimmer facts of empire and seek to disseminate them among 'the voting multitude', the imperialists drew strength from their private loyalties, associations, and means of influence. Behind the façade of Edwardian democracy the interlocking influence of these smaller and more intimate groupings was always considerable.

For many 'imperialists' social reform was as necessary a panacea as it was for the Liberal left wing. It would eliminate national divisions and augment national strength. Milner, for example, held that just because 'the maintenance and consolidation' of the British empire was 'the first and highest of all political objects for every subject of the Crown', so 'social reform' was the key to its domestic policy. 'A nobler socialism' could take the place of socialism based on class warfare. If the British nation was weak and impoverished it would be incapable of maintaining and developing its empire. Its international success depended on an incessant struggle against 'irregular employment and unhealthy conditions of life'. Cobdenism, with its stress on 'unfettered competition' and 'cheapness', was a crude philosophy resting on sectional and short-term interests. Not all 'rational Imperialists' were tariff reformers, but those tariff reformers, in particular, who upheld 'an imperial conception of trade' explicitly refused to believe that 'the mere blind struggle for individual gain' would 'produce the most beneficent results'.[2]

In fact, both Cobdenism and militant protectionism rested on structures of interest as well as on opinions and ideals. Some

[1] G. N. Curzon, *Subjects of the Day*, 1915. Lord Cromer, the third of the great proconsuls and a confirmed Liberal, wrote an introduction to this volume in which he called Curzon 'the most able, as he certainly is the most eloquent exponent of that sane Imperialism to which this country is wedded as a necessity of its existence'. The first of Curzon's speeches printed in this volume had been delivered at an Empire Day dinner given to Milner in 1906.

[2] A. Milner, *The Nation and the Empire*, 1913. A. P. Thornton distinguishes brilliantly between 'a commercial conception of empire' and 'an imperial conception of trade'. *The Imperial Idea and Its Enemies*, 1959.

interests continued to support free trade as the most prudent and effective policy: shipbuilders and cotton manufacturers, for example, joined with import merchants and city financiers in allegiance to the old, tried system. Metal manufacturers and industrialists producing chemicals, glass, and building materials were the backbone of the Tariff Reform League. The old rivalry between Manchester and Birmingham was re-enacted once more in Edwardian Britain with the City of London continuing to support Manchester in a great triangle of economic orthodoxy. Chamberlain's lieutenants and Chamberlain himself in his moments of vision might talk in eloquent language of the claims of empire and the necessity for social reform, but the League made most of its appeals *ad hominem* and *ad locum*, ingeniously varying its statistical information and its propaganda to suit the background and needs of industrialists in different parts of the country. Its propaganda suffered from the critical fact that it was not very well timed in terms of the business situation. There was a slight upward move in British exports in 1903 and 1904 and a considerable upward move in 1905. British industry continued to suffer from serious structural problems, but the movement of the trade cycle in the crucial months before the general election of 1906 favoured the Liberals rather than the protectionists.

Because Britain was a democracy, a fact which Milner at least often regretted, the imminent general election was of major importance in determining the direction of Edwardian politics. Both parties realized that, however forcefully they could appeal to particular interests or to particular intellectuals, they would have to depend for votes on the working classes, the great majority of the all-male electorate. Free trade could be preached as a working-class creed: the symbolism of the big and small loaf which had been so effective during the 'hungry forties' was still as effective as any verbal message. Could protectionism also be preached successfully as a working men's creed? This was the biggest of all the questions which the tariff reformers had to consider. 'Unless I have the support of the working people,' Chamberlain asserted in May 1905, 'clearly my movement is already condemned and utterly a failure.' Chamberlain relied on three planks of argument. First, the empire was in the interests of working men. It provided the best market for British goods and the best guarantee of employment. As Arthur Pearson's *Daily Express* put it day by day on its front page with planned reiteration, 'Tariff reform means work for all.' Chamberlain hoped that the British working man had woken up to the fact, as Cecil Rhodes had once expressed it, that unless he kept the markets of the world he would be starved. The 'three-acres-and-a-cow idea', Rhodes had said, 'had been found to be humbug, and the working man has found out that he must keep the world and the trade of the world if he is to live, and if the world is shut to him he is done'. 'Remember', Chamberlain added, 'that the colonial does a great deal for you, the foreigner does nothing.' Second, the working man was by nature 'patriotic', as patriotic as any proconsul. He was not just concerned with pennies. 'England without an empire' was beyond his comprehension. 'England in that case would not be the England we love.' The empire belonged to the working classes as much as to any other class; indeed, it was their grandsires who had spilt their blood to gain and to hold it. Third, tariff reform would prepare the way for social reform. In his first speech after the election Chamberlain told the Commons that he doubted whether the chancellor of the exchequer would ever find the money for a policy of social reform unless he was able 'to widen very much more than I think he will be under the present system the basis of taxation'. Social reform, as conceived before and after 1906, was remedial reform designed to meet the needs, assessed from outside, of that section of the working-class community which was least well-off.

By concentrating on the first plank of the protectionist argument, taking the second too much for granted, and neglecting the third, Chamberlain failed to win the battle for working-class votes in 1905 and 1906. The appeal of cheap food and the fear of a 'stomach tax' proved stronger than the vague hope of increased employment, even though there was severe 'winter distress', particularly in London, in the months preceding the opening of parliament in February 1905. Throughout the whole Edwardian period the pressure on real wages was the main fact of working-class existence: the unevenness of wage rates entailed that large numbers of people would be living in poverty even when fully employed. As for Chamberlain's second argument, the 'patriotism' of the working man, as of other sections of the community, did not survive the Boer war unscathed. 'Imperialism' was sharply criticized, particularly after the Unionist government had accepted the principle of importing indentured Chinese labour to work the South African mines. The government showed itself completely insensitive to Liberal and Labour criticism of this policy, which Milner inconsistently and mistakenly decided to follow. By the end of 1904, 20,000 Chinese were at work in the Rand mines, and nine months later there were 47,000. No trade unionist could approve of this policy. Nor could any genuine philanthropist. Labour was being treated as a commodity in a fashion of which neither Cobden nor Bright, let alone Keir Hardie, could ever have approved. 'Chinese slavery' thus became a valuable electoral asset to the Liberals. It united middle-class and working-class critics of the government, and threw into dramatic relief the whole sequence of events in South Africa since the Jameson raid. It made it easy to depict Chamberlain not as the maker of events and policies but as the 'tool of financiers'. It made much of the older language of imperialism sound like cant: 'the imperial idea had suffered a contraction, a loss of moral content from which it never completely recovered'.[1]

As far as social reform was concerned, Chamberlain could offer far less than most of his political opponents. He shared the doubts of his colleagues as to whether social reform could be paid for within the existing fiscal system, but not all of them shared his belief that it was worth while paying for it. He could not be specific even had he wished to be so, yet the only chance of winning working-class votes—and it was a slender chance—would have been to be very specific indeed. As it was, the Unionist government's Unemployed Workmen Bill of 1905, authorizing the setting up of local distress committees to provide temporary work, labour bureaux, and schemes to encourage mobility, won little working-class support. It was generally thought of as an 'economy' measure, and since the treasury refused to place any funds at the disposal of the distress committees, it depended on an obsolete appeal to charity. Balfour's decision at the close of the session of 1905 to appoint a large and representative commission to inquire into the working of the poor laws was of strategic importance in relation to the whole twentieth-century history of social policy, but it was of no electoral advantage at the time.

Labour Representation

Chamberlain's failure, and the failure of the Unionists, to convince or to rouse the working classes derived in the last resort,

[1] Thornton, op. cit.

however, from far deeper causes. His Tariff Reform League had a trade-union branch, but the Unionist government had quarrelled with the trade unionists and had shown no signs of seeking to heal the breach. It was clear in 1903 and 1904 that 'organized labour', still a minority movement among working men, had no confidence in either Balfour or Chamberlain. Indeed, a powerful section of organized labour had been pledged since the formation of the Labour representation committee in February 1900 to work for the election of independent Labour candidates to parliament. One of the few independent members already there, Keir Hardie, had made his reputation as 'member for the unemployed', and he did not believe that protection was even capable of relieving unemployment. He attacked both main parties as parties of capital, and, for all his infectious idealism, saw parliamentary politics primarily as 'a method of protecting or advancing certain interests'. 'The House is still without its clearly defined Labour group,' he wrote in 1902, 'but that is coming.'

Hardie was a socialist and one of the founders of the Independent Labour party which had been set up in Bradford in 1893. Many of the trade unionists were not socialists, however, and it was for pragmatic reasons that they gave their support to the Labour Representation Committee. The famous Taff Vale judgment of July 1901 threatened the whole existence of trade unions as bargaining bodies, and the urgent desire of trade unionists to reaffirm the special position of the unions under the law and to have recognized their right of picketing forced them further into politics. Even an old 'Lib–Lab' trade unionist, Henry Broadhurst, who was strongly anti-socialist, demanded in August 1901 that efforts should be made to return a hundred Independent Labour members to the next House of Commons. Balfour offered nothing to the trade unionists, although it had been Disraeli, his greatest predecessor as a Conservative prime minister, who had introduced the legislation of 1875 on which the rights of trade unionists before Taff Vale had been thought to be securely based. Balfour's supporters were even less generous. *The Times*, which had greeted the Taff Vale judgment with unrestrained enthusiasm, improved the occasion by attributing the comparative inefficiency and rigidity of British industry to the existence of trade unions. The Unionist majority in the House of Commons voted resolutely not to interfere with the judicial decision.

VIII (*a*). Suffragettes on the march 1908

Mrs. Pethick-Lawrence, Miss Christabel Pankhurst, Miss Sylvia Pankhurst, Dr. Garrett Anderson

VIII (*b*). A Christmas card of 1901

IX. Fire Brigade at Port Sunlight

There were only two million trade unionists in Britain, one in six of British wage-earners, yet trade union resistance to the Taff Vale judgment and desire to have it repealed as quickly as possible were key factors in British politics between 1901 and 1906. Within one year of Taff Vale the affiliated membership of the Labour Representation Committee had risen from 356,000 to 861,000. In February 1903 the important decision was taken to create a parliamentary fund for Labour candidates, the fund to be raised by contributions from affiliated societies at the annual rate of one penny a member. Trade union funds were henceforth to assist directly the growth of an independent political party. The exact measure of the party's independence has been a matter of dispute. It was proudly proclaimed and zealously defended, yet in 1903 the leaders of the Labour Representation Committee and the Liberal chief whip, Herbert Gladstone, agreed at the national level upon a pact of accommodation which would give the new party a free hand in thirty constituencies. The pact was not a formal alliance, it was for one election only, and it in no way controlled what the Labour leaders would or should say. On the Liberal side it was valuable in that it permitted Liberal funds to be saved and that it offered the prospect of defeating a number of Conservative candidates whom Liberals alone or Liberals in competition with Labour candidates might not have been able to beat. On the side of Labour it was a guarantee of a quota of Independent Labour candidates for the next House of Commons who would not be opposed by Liberals.[1]

Had Chamberlain known of the 'pact', his strictly limited hopes of winning the next election would have been further reduced. What he did know was that both the Labour Representation Committee and the socialist parties were opposed to his policies. Philip Snowden's pamphlet, *The Chamberlain Bubble*, published late in 1903, had sold nearly 40,000 copies by April 1904. Ramsay MacDonald, the secretary of the Labour Representation Committee, also published a booklet, *The German Zollverein and British Industry*, which was a manual of anti-Chamberlainite statistics. Many of the local Labour leaders, like David Shackleton of the Darwen weavers, who won Clitheroe unopposed in August 1902, had much in common with Liberals in their sturdy nonconformity and their 'strong leaning

[1] For details of the background and nature of the pact, see F. Bealey and H. Pelling, *Labour and Politics, 1900–1906*, 1958.

towards the temperance party'. Others, however, looked forward eagerly to the eclipse of the Liberal party as a new age of democracy dawned. Ramsay MacDonald himself wrote of socialism taking the place of liberalism in a process of evolution. 'Each new stage in evolution retains all that was vital in the old and.sheds all that was dead.... Socialism, the stage which follows Liberalism, retains everything of permanent value that was in Liberalism by virtue of its being the hereditary heir of Liberalism.' In Hyndman's Social Democratic Federation such talk was dangerous heresy, and among convinced socialists of different schools from the Fabian Society across the political spectrum there were many whose whole approach to politics was anti-Liberal. They were in the minority, however. In the Liberal revival of 1903 to 1906 Labour was one current, albeit a very powerful one and one which would in time become a new river. Even Hardie often thought of the issues in terms of 'People versus Privilege'.

There were Liberal successes at several by-elections after the Norwich victory of January 1904. At the first three by-elections of 1905 two constituencies were lost by the government and in the third, a London seat, a close contest ended in a remarkable reduction in the large Unionist majority. During the early summer of 1905 an opposition candidate won Whitby, though no Liberal candidate had stood there at all in 1900. These by-election results confronted Balfour with some difficult decisions. He had made a great success of holding together his own party in parliament: his only hopes of avoiding defeat at the forthcoming election seemed to rest on his exploiting remaining splits among his opponents. This hope was the basis of his tactics in 1905 and 1906. It proved delusive, and his tactics may well have had the opposite effect of further increasing the size of the Liberal party in the House of Commons.

There were three 'splits' which gave him his opportunity. The first was the most theoretical, that between 'Liberals of the old school' and 'socialists'. Balfour knew more about 'socialism' than most Unionists: later on he was to see his heavy defeat at the polls in 1906 as part of a European and possibly a world-wide swing to the left. He could hardly exploit fears of 'socialism', however, until the 'socialists' became a party 'of some obvious strength' in parliament. The second split was more apparent, that between 'home rulers' and the rest. Unionism had been founded on the exploitation of this split in the past, just as Unionism of a new kind in the future was to be founded on fear of 'socialism'. The traditional split assumed immediate significance in November 1905 when Campbell-Bannerman made a speech on Ireland at Stirling, which Rosebery immediately challenged. Campbell-Bannerman spoke of Irish home rule being achieved not by one single measure but by instalments: he advised the Irish to accept the instalments provided that they were 'consistent with and led up to the larger policy'. This very moderate statement provoked Rosebery, who had for long been lukewarm about home rule and as prime minister had accepted the doctrine that before home rule could be adopted England as the 'predominant partner' should be convinced of its justice. He now claimed that Campbell-Bannerman had hoisted the flag of home rule and declared 'emphatically, explicitly and once for all' that he could not 'serve under that banner'. What he did not know was that Asquith and Grey, his two Liberal–Imperialist allies in the Liberal League, had approved of Campbell-Bannerman's speech before it was delivered. Rosebery's ignorance, the price of his aloofness, and his candour, a testimony to his character, ruined his chances of asserting claims to Liberal leadership which were already tenuous. Balfour, seeking to profit from the 'slip', strengthened Campbell-Bannerman. It was Rosebery who was placed in an awkward position, not the Liberal party.

The third split was intimately bound up with the second. Indeed, historically, it derived from the same source. Balfour knew from private gossip how unwilling were Asquith, Grey, and Haldane to serve in a Liberal government under Campbell-Bannerman's leadership. There was much talk in political circles of Campbell-Bannerman being relegated to the House of Lords or even being fobbed off with a minor post. Asquith was thought of as the 'natural' leader in the House of Commons. The gossip was substantially true. In September 1905 Asquith, Grey, and Haldane reached an agreement, sometimes known as the 'Relugas compact', that if and when Campbell-Bannerman asked them to join a Liberal government they would do so only on their own terms. Campbell-Bannerman was to go to the Lords, Asquith was to lead the Commons and to hold the office of chancellor of the exchequer, Grey was to be foreign secretary, and Haldane, who had never yet held any office, was to be lord chancellor. If this compact had been observed, Campbell-Bannerman's cabinet-making would have been very difficult indeed. A Liberal government, pledged to the extension of democracy, would have been bound by the private decisions of a small private clique, a clique of men of great ability but also of great pretensions. It was also a clique of men of great influence. Haldane wrote to Lord Knollys, the king's secretary, informing him of the compact. Knollys showed the king Haldane's letter, and the king, who approved of the idea, went on to discuss the matter with Haldane. It is difficult to believe that Balfour himself did not know what was going on. Lord Esher, from the vantage point of the court, knew about 'the likely cabinet arrangements': he also knew of the arguments for and against resignation which Balfour was examining. 'I had several hours with A. J. B.', he wrote on 20 November, three days before Campbell-Bannerman's Stirling speech. 'He went through "the change of Government" papers 1873–4, which the King told me to show him.'

Campbell-Bannerman in Office

Given this background—and the illness and resignation of Earl Spencer, 'the Red Earl', the Liberal leader in the House of Lords since 1902—Balfour decided to profit from the occasion to resign rather than to ask the king to dissolve parliament. He expected that Campbell-Bannerman would find it difficult to form a strong cabinet and that a Liberal government split into 'factions', with some of the factions 'unpatriotic', would be bound to make a poor showing before the nation. A general election in 1906 following a period of Liberal 'rule' would be far more likely to favour the Unionists than a general election in 1905 following a long period of Unionist rule. Balfour doubtless found the precedents of 1873—and of 1885—interesting if not encouraging. He might even have hoped that Campbell-Bannerman would be unable or unwilling to form a cabinet at all, and that the Unionists could then have posed as 'the party of government'. He had his own worries too within his own party. The cabinet was divided on tactics and policies, and Chamberlain had publicly disapproved of a Unionist walk-out from the House of Commons which Balfour had staged when the Liberals introduced a motion on the fiscal question. In the autumn of 1905 the National Union of Conservative Associations supported Chamberlainite policies. There was a measure of relief in Balfour's act of resignation as well as of tactical anticipation.

He resigned on 4 December 1905. A day later Campbell-Bannerman took office. This was the great turning point in Edwardian
politics, although it was not clearly recognized at the time. In
December 1905 a number of timid Liberals looked back to 1873 and
remembered that in similar circumstances Disraeli had refused to
take office. As usual Campbell-Bannerman's common sense and
resolution stood him in good stead. *The Times* might suggest that
there was 'a general feeling that Sir Henry Campbell-Bannerman is
hardly the kind of Prime Minister to make a successful fight against
Mr. Balfour and Mr. Chamberlain', and the king and the public
might speculate ominously on the state of his health, but Campbell-
Bannerman, well advised by Morley and others, saw at once that
firmness was the best policy. He went on to form a surprisingly
powerful cabinet. Balfour's would-be adroit tactical resignation was
the prelude to a major shift in democratic politics. The Unionists
did not regain power until the 1920's.

The 'Relugas compact' did not survive the excitement of Liberal
cabinet-making. Grey, the aristocrat of the group—a man who dis-
trusted public opinion and was described by A. G. Gardiner as 'the
least democratic, as he is the least demonstrative of men'—tried to
stand by it and immediately made it clear to Campbell-Bannerman
that he would not accept office unless Asquith was leader in the
House of Commons. Asquith, however, gave way. It was a sign of
the social consensus behind the political conflicts of Edwardian
Britain that Asquith was staying with Lord Salisbury at Hatfield
when the crisis came. When Campbell-Bannerman offered him the
chancellorship of the exchequer, he accepted it. The compact was
broken. Somewhat lamely Asquith argued that it had been made
at a time when the conspirators had envisaged a Liberal ministry
being formed after, and not before, a Liberal victory at a general
election: he rightly maintained that the need to demonstrate Liberal
unity was greater than the claims of the compact. Grey and Haldane
yielded more reluctantly, the former becoming foreign secretary as
he had wished, the latter becoming secretary for war. In neither
case did Campbell-Bannerman falter in his statesmanship. He ruled
out all talk of self-abdication. He was correct with Grey and firm
with Haldane, who had wanted the lord chancellorship. Had
Balfour's tactics been different and had Liberal cabinet-making
followed rather than preceded an election, it would have been far

less easy to contain the Liberal League, as Campbell-Bannerman did, or to avoid recrimination and resentment. Rosebery, of course, was out, but his son-in-law, Lord Crewe, became lord president of the Council.

Some famous names were symbols of Liberal continuity. Lord Ripon, aged 78, was lord privy seal; Sir Henry Fowler, aged 75, was chancellor of the duchy of Lancaster; Herbert Gladstone was home secretary. A place was found within the ministry also for the sons of Harcourt and Spencer. Some less famous names were a guarantee of the Liberal party's future. Among the junior ministers were Herbert Samuel, Reginald McKenna, and Walter Runciman, all of whom were to play an important part in twentieth-century politics. Winston Churchill, the controversial convert to liberalism, became colonial under-secretary at the age of 31. Two former proconsuls added strength in the House of Lords, where it was notably absent. Lord Elgin, the new colonial secretary, was an ex-viceroy of India: Lord Aberdeen, an ex-governor-general of Canada, became lord-lieutenant of Ireland. There was little that was proconsular, how-ever, about Morley's appointment to the India Office ('banishment to the Brahmaputra') or Bryce's appointment as Irish secretary, and the 'right-wing' flavour of the cabinet was qualified conspicu-ously by the choice of Lloyd George, 'the leader of the militant spirits below the gangway', as president of the board of trade and John Burns as president of the Local Government Board. Burns was no longer 'the man with the red flag' he had been in the 1880's. His links with organized labour were, by his own choice, weak, and he has passed into history as the man who told Campbell-Bannerman, 'I congratulate you, sir. It will be the most popular appointment you have made.' In fact, however, as W. T. Stead noted at the time, Burns's preferment was 'hailed with more enthusiasm than that evoked by the appointment of all the rest of his colleagues'. He was the first working man who had won his way to cabinet rank, and there was 'not a man of the whole nineteen cabinet ministers' who did not feel 'that the ministry is stronger, more popular, and more efficient because the Battersea engineer is sitting cheek by jowl with marquises and belted knights in the inner councils of the king'.

This extravagant language was more in keeping with the public mood of the times, the mood of the by-elections, than the proud, private language of the makers of the 'Relugas compact'. Yet public

and private language expressed different facets of Edwardian politics—the democratic surface and the private core, the People and
the people who counted. Campbell-Bannerman knew something of
both. He had reminded the Unionists in the House of Commons in
the 1905 debate on the Address that 'behind any parliament or any
majority in parliament' was 'the public conscience' from which both
parliament and the majority derived their power. He was telling
Esher a few days after taking office that 'criticism in opposition was
one thing; accomplished fact another'.

Campbell-Bannerman spoke with confident authority and with
customary moderation when he made his first big speech as prime
minister in the Albert Hall on 21 December 1905. Free trade would
be defended: the import of Chinese labour had been stopped. 'Those
domestic questions which concern the Irish people only and not
ourselves should, as and when opportunity offers, be left in their
hands.' He announced no great changes in foreign policy, and remarked that on Indian questions it would be a 'wise rule' to keep
matters of internal administration outside British party politics.
On foreign questions generally there was room for 'substantial
continuity of policy'. He went into no detail about proposals for
domestic social reform, but promised that the law relating to trade
unions would be amended, that there would be changes in the poor
law and the rating system, and that efforts would be made to study
'with advantage . . . how best to mitigate the evils of non-employ-
ment'. There was little that was bold about his programme, although
The Times on the eve of Christmas reported that there was alarm in
the city that the future held possibilities of 'the robbery of anyone
that has anything to be robbed of'.

The 1906 Election

The appeal to the country which followed in January 1906 was
far more interesting than Campbell-Bannerman's Albert Hall speech.
The election lasted for nearly three weeks, and everyone agreed with
Morley that it was 'the most exciting general election for years'.
Local issues were still inextricably bound up with national issues,
and there was scope not only for a great variety of programmes but
for a great variety of ways of advertising them. The popular national
press vulgarized the issues, Campbell-Bannerman himself complaining that it had fallen into the hands of 'capitalists and others',

but the competitive local press enjoyed one of its last great campaigns. Old and new weapons of propaganda were employed side by side. Bury's Liberal candidate had a picture of Sir Robert Peel on the cover of his election manifesto: at near-by Bolton Labour posters were described as 'pantomime in character, depicting the working man in shackles with plutocratic capitalists lording it over him'. At Thirsk the nonconformist Liberal candidate was reminded by hecklers:

> This is the truth that I'll maintain
> Until I'm old and hoary
> That whatsoever party reigns
> Old Thirsk returns a Tory.

At Newark, which the Liberals had contested only once since 1885, the *Advertiser*, fighting a keen battle against the Liberal *Herald*, appealed to electors:

> Ye burgesses of Newark,
> The parrot cry ignore,
> The shout so false which Rads repeat—
> Your food will cost you more.
> Can you forget the unemployed,
> The injured trades around?
> No! Newark's voice for fair play cries
> With no uncertain sound.

In an attempt to inject local interest into the fiscal question, the Unionist candidate at Newark reminded his hearers that they had to pay a toll if they wished to set up a stall in Newark market. 'Why should not the foreigner also pay a toll for the use of the finest market in the world—a market he cannot possibly do without?' City campaigns were often far more sophisticated, although local candidates often had to fend for themselves with no help from prominent national personalities.

In such a setting there were as many unauthorized programmes as there were enthusiastic candidates. 'Motives are very mixed at all elections', *The Times* commented, 'even when those who speculate upon such matters are most convinced that they know the governing factor. They will be more mixed than usual on this occasion, because the issues are more than usually numerous and ill-defined. Party speakers on either side may pretend to rule out this or that issue,

but they are only expressing their own desires.' Many Unionists
would have liked to rule out 'Chinese labour' completely: some
Liberals would certainly have liked to rule out home rule. Candidates on both sides talked of the need for greater 'efficiency', the
Liberals berating, as John Burns did, 'the administrative blunders,
departmental scandals, appalling waste and political evasion and
dishonesty' of the Unionists, the Unionists accusing the Liberals of
preaching 'vague and conflicting generalities' and failing to see the
need for a new fiscal system which would provide the only escape
from 'stagnation'. The Independent Labour party put both Unionists and Liberals in the same category. 'The main reason for the
existence of Liberals and Conservatives is to protect the interests
of the rich and keep you divided. . . . Create and finance and control
a party of your own, and thus prove democracy is a reality.' Such
a party would begin by dealing drastically with unemployment,
bad housing, and malnutrition: school meals and old age pensions
should be in the forefront of any Labour programme.

There was much talk of democracy at the election. The Unionists
tried to read the democratic portents, the Liberals to capture
the democratic slogans, and the socialists (of all persuasions) to
identify democracy with socialism. Even anti-socialists were compelled to talk of social reform, 'securing social and economic reform
which had been too long delayed'. Left-wing Liberals agreed with
socialists that 'the only real alternative to protection is a large and
vigorous policy of social reform'. There was plenty of talk about
empire too, much of it unflattering. 'Chinese labour' was the main
controversial issue in many constituencies: the mine-owners, more
than one candidate claimed, had been the only real beneficiaries of
the Boer war. 'Yellow labour' was even keeping 'English labour'
out of jobs:

> No savvy Trade Union, no wantee that vote.
> You wantee cheap labour? You sendee big boat!
> Suppose no more fightee—you sojer go home;
> When dollars can catchee, let Chinaman come.[1]

The Times noted with some alarm that 'we have had many indica-
tions of the anxiety felt in the Colonies concerning the line that will
be taken by a party which has too often treated the Colonies as

[1] *Chester Chronicle*, 6 January 1906.

disagreeable incumbrances'. Overshadowing all other issues, however, was the issue of free trade. Liberals made the best of it, but Unionist free-traders were in a very difficult position. They were hounded by Chamberlain's supporters, and they could get no help from Balfour. Few of them were prepared to go to the lengths of an independent Unionist free-trader at King's Lynn who told the local inhabitants that to vote for a tariff reform candidate would be to make King's Lynn 'a suburb of Birmingham'.

There were no psephologists in 1906 to predict the course of the election. The swing to the Liberal party in the by-elections was under-estimated or discounted by some observers, as was the eagerness of the party to contest seats which had been uncontested in 1900 and in some cases since the 1880's. The long period of Unionist rule had made most observers cautious. So too had the size of Balfour's majority. To secure a majority of 40 over the Unionist and Irish members, Campbell-Bannerman's party had to win 137 Unionist seats: in 'the great revulsion of 1895', which transformed Rosebery's majority of 31 into a Unionist majority of 153, there had been only 92 changes of seat. John Morley on the eve of the first poll suggested three alternative outcomes of the election. First, the Liberals would be equal to the Unionists and the Irish put together: this would give the Irish Nationalists power to call the tune. Second, there would be a Liberal majority of about 80 over the other parties. Third, there would be a Liberal majority of between 30 and 40. The *Daily Mail* predicted something like the first outcome: Lord Hugh Cecil something like the third. The first was a forecast not of 1906 but of 1910. The second seemed very optimistic. Some tariff reformers were very hopeful about their prospects. The result of the election was 'a terrible disappointment' to Hewins, for example: 'it never occurred to him that the reaction might be so complete as to keep the Tories out for six years'.

As the results were announced—*Daily Mail* magic lanterns screened them in Trafalgar Square and on the Embankment—it became clear almost at once that there had been a Unionist débâcle. The very first result, Ipswich, was a Liberal gain. The next ten results, all coming from Lancashire, were dramatic. All ten constituencies had been Unionist in 1900: they now returned among their members six Liberal and four Labour candidates. Balfour himself was defeated by a young Liberal lawyer in Manchester: 'this was the first occasion', wrote Lord Newton, 'on which I had seen him seriously upset'. Churchill, whom the Unionists had attacked without mercy as a 'ratter', was returned by another Manchester constituency. These and other northern results were so decisive and so numerous that they surprised the Liberals themselves. There were more surprises to come. London, which had returned 51 Unionists and 8 Liberals in 1900, returned only 19 Unionists with 40 Liberal and Labour candidates in 1906. In the remaining English boroughs Unionist and Liberal victories in 1900 were reversed. The 1906 election was the first since 1886 at which the Liberals captured a majority of the English constituencies. The Celtic fringe remained a Liberal stronghold. All the representatives of the Welsh boroughs were Liberals: in Lloyd George's phrase not a 'single tribe' had been left behind to disturb the progress of the Israelites. In Scotland 25 Liberals were returned as against 6 Unionists, compared with 15 and 16 respectively in 1900. When the final reckoning was made, there were only 157 Unionists in the new House of Commons as compared with 402 in the old. There were 401 Liberals, including 24 Lib–Labs, 83 Irish Nationalists, and 29 'Labour party' candidates, backed by the Labour Representation Committee.

This was an electoral 'revolution' which gave the Liberal government a majority of 357, a preponderance unequalled since the first election which followed the Great Reform Bill of 1832: moreover, the strength of the Liberal party in 1906 was more broadly based geographically than Labour party strength after the remarkable victory of 1945.[1] It is scarcely surprising that contemporaries and historians alike have sought to discover the 'deeper causes' of this great manifestation of democratic change, which robbed the Unionists of most of their power outside the universities, the richer parts of London, the Chamberlainite citadel of Birmingham, which remained impregnable, the socially (and ecclesiastically) exceptional city of Liverpool, and the agricultural counties of Kent and Sussex. Balfour was the first of the analysts. In a number of letters written to friends and acquaintances after the event, he detected 'a faint echo of the same movement which has produced massacres in St. Petersburg, riots in Vienna, and Socialist processions in Berlin', described Campbell-Bannerman as 'a mere cork, dancing on a

---

[1] For a valuable comparison of 1906 and 1945 see R. Jenkins, *Mr. Balfour's Poodle*, 1954.

torrent which he cannot control', and concluded that what had happened had 'nothing whatever to do with any of the things we have been squabbling over the last few years'. He was fascinated by the twenty-nine Labour victories, which gave working men fifty-three places in the House of Commons. He wrote to the governor-general of Australia, for example, asking for advice on a subject with which Australians, he said, were already familiar—the rise of labour.

It is impossible as yet to say what perturbations this new planet, suddenly introduced into our political heavens, will cause in existing orbits, but certainly it is curious that while *you* are writing to me about your hopes of getting rid of the 'third' Party system in Australia, *we* should suddenly find ourselves, for the first time, with a 'fourth' Party system in Great Britain.[1]

Other commentators also were more interested in the new Labour minority than in the huge Liberal majority. A 'Liberal voter', for example, wrote to *The Times*,

hazarding the prediction that the Labour party has introduced into the organism of middle-class liberalism now perhaps for the last time triumphant, the seeds of inevitable disintegration. . . .

The parties of the future [he went on] will not be Free-Traders and Tariff Reformers, nor Home Rulers and Unionists. The settlement of these questions, in one sense or the other, will be by-products of the great struggles, of which the new Parliament will probably witness many a sharp preliminary skirmish, between those who are willing to march, through the wilderness of acute and bitter controversy, towards the promised land of a new and nobler social order, and those who see nothing in the enterprise but the sordid struggle of the poor for the vanished heritage of the rich.

The New Parliament

The Times itself, in one of a number of leaders on the subject (30 January), described the Labour victories as 'the most significant outcome of the present election' and argued that they 'lifted the occasion out of the groove of domestic politics'. It was at pains to add that not all the new Labour men were socialists: indeed it claimed that socialism had 'no chance in this country' if the Labour movement were treated in the right way. The *Edinburgh Review*, the organ of orthodox and traditional whiggery, was more gloomy and

[1] B. E. C. Dugdale, *Arthur James Balfour*, 1936. See also K. Young, *Arthur James Balfour*, 1963.

discerned tendencies towards socialism even in the Liberal majority: 'what may be called the spirit of socialism pervades the whole House'.

Such memorable verdicts displayed more foresight than insight. Labour questions were assuming a new significance in politics, and the demand for direct working-class representation was central to the newest statements of democracy. Yet fears of socialism had been expressed since the 1880's, and it was the fiscal issue which had been the main propaganda issue of the 1906 election. Many of the 220 new Liberal members of the House of Commons in 1906 (a very high proportion of 'new men') had felt far more strongly about this issue than anything else. Their strong feelings were shared on the other side of the House. The large group of Chamberlainites, over 100, among the Unionist minority had tried, not without success, to make the election into a referendum on tariff reform. For many of the Liberal victors, particularly the small business men, barristers, solicitors, journalists, and writers, who gave a new flavour to the House of Commons, individualism was far more meaningful than socialism. Free trade and nonconformity dictated their attitudes to all branches of politics. They themselves saw their victory in terms of the 'sweeping away of the last relics of feudalism': their rhetoric was the rhetoric of 'the People'. They believed, as Halévy put it, that the reforms of the franchise effected as long ago as 1867 and 1884 were at last bearing fruit. Anti-Irish panics, waves of imperialism, and the artificial 'khaki election' of 1900 had delayed the advent of democracy, but they had not been able to destroy it. 'The conscience of the nation' had at last made itself clear.

The Labour members came from a different section of the population—all the Labour Representation candidates were of working-class origins—yet many of them shared this approach. They were as proud as the Liberals of their heritage of nonconformity and just as anxious to preserve it. Some of them were members of socialist societies and groups as well as of trade unions, and their excitement at winning so many victories was infectious enough to impress even Hyndman, the leader of the left-wing Social Democratic Federation, who had himself been beaten in a 'class war' contest at Burnley. The more practical among them, however, were very practical indeed, guided by real if limited conceptions of 'fairness' and 'justice' rather than by treatises on socialist principles. *The Times* was right to draw a distinction between 'labourism' and 'socialism'. The *Manchester Guardian* went further. If 'the good people' who were afraid of socialism 'knew how much more serious a respect for property and society is to be learnt in the offices of a great trade union than in the fifth form of a public school and at a second-rate Oxford college they would not vex their hearts with these dim fancies'.

It is hardly surprising that disgruntled Fabians pointed to what they thought was the 'hollowness' both of the Liberal and the Labour victors. 'We do not deceive ourselves by the notion that this wave of liberalism is wholly progressive in character,' wrote Beatrice Webb, 'much of its bulk is made up of sheer conservatism aroused by the revolutionary tariff policy of Chamberlain.' The socialist and Independent Labour candidates, George Bernard Shaw believed, were 'more dependent on Liberal votes than ever'. 'I apologize to the Universe', he concluded, 'for any connection with such a party.'[1]

He had far less reason to apologize than he believed. The new parliament was far 'newer' than the new reign or the new century had been. 'There is a great change in this parliament', a Westminster policeman told Philip Snowden, one of the most dedicated of the newly elected Labour members. The remark was echoed by many of Snowden's older parliamentary colleagues who confessed, whatever their politics, that 'they did not expect things to go on as before' and exclaimed that 'for weal or woe we are beginning a new era in Parliamentary history'. The presence of the little band of Labour members with their own officials and their own whips was the most obvious sign of change: they chose to sit on the opposition side of the House. The appearance of the large numbers of new Liberal members was another obvious sign of change. 'Elected to do great deeds, they intended and hoped to democratize the institutions of the country, break the privileges of the aristocracy, destroy the land monopoly and bring comfort and happiness to the manual workers and the poor.'[2] Equally new was the thinness of the Unionist benches. Not since the middle years of the century had the Conservative benches been so deserted. Balfour himself was absent from the first session until the City of London obligingly returned him.

---

[1] *Clarion*, 2 February 1906. Quoted by Bealey and Pelling, op. cit., p. 278. On reading this article 'Baron Corvo', Frederick Rolfe, sent a subscription of five shillings to the Fabian Society.

[2] A. Mackintosh, *From Gladstone to Lloyd George*, 1921.

His detachment from democracy was almost complete. He faced the biggest electoral majority since 1832, yet he planned from the start to check its operations by relying on the House of Lords. His social views were equally undemocratic. 'His vision of society', wrote a hostile journalist, 'is of a refined company, dowered with delicate appetites and gracious sentiments and protected from the raging mob without by a moral police that is crumbling away and by the more material defence of ancient privilege sustained by the authority of law.' Neither his constitutional nor his social defences proved adequate in the period of Liberal rule which lasted until after the outbreak of the first world war. The most that could be hoped for was deadlock and crisis, and the nation had to pass through both before Balfour, by then unpopular with his own party, resigned in November 1911 the leadership which he had held in the House of Commons for twenty years.

Balfour, of course, was not personally responsible. Prolonged Liberal rule in the parliamentary, social, and international circumstances of Edwardian Britain involved the likelihood of three kinds of deadlock or crisis. The first was constitutional, the second, in the broadest sense, social, and the third was bound up with defence and foreign policy. All three kinds of crisis were crises of democracy. The constitutional question turned on the powers of the House of Lords: the powers of the Lords were in question, however, because the Liberal government, fresh from its great electoral triumph, wished to carry out legislation of which the Lords disapproved. The social question turned on the ability of the Liberal government to direct and control the forces of discontent in society. Many of the discontented groups, notably the suffragettes and the militant trade unionists, claimed that their causes were the true 'democratic' causes which in the short run should be advanced by 'any means' and which in the long run, like all democratic causes, would be bound to triumph. How would 'Liberal democracy', resting upon a belief in free discussion, peaceful persuasion, and tolerance for all opinions, react to the 'militant democracy' of irreconcilable sectional groups? The international question was as likely to provoke differences of opinion among Liberals as conflicts between Liberals and their opponents. Given that 1906 was a victory for 'democracy', how would the new democracy deal with the problems of power? What would be its response, for example, to the building of a great German navy or to the responsibilities of empire? Would public opinion be brought to bear more directly than it ever had been hitherto on matters of imperial and foreign policy? Given that crises in international relations might begin abroad, what would be the reaction to them in Britain? The critical element in all these questions was magnified on many occasions by the continued existence of 'the Irish question' which could not indefinitely be kept on ice. Particularly between 1911 and 1914 the Irish problem 'engulfed and embittered all the feuds of Britain'.[1]

Asquith and Lloyd George

An analysis of these three crises of democracy must follow rather than precede a statement of the record of achievement of the Liberal governments, which were confirmed in office with greatly reduced majorities at two general elections in 1910. Campbell-Bannerman disappeared from the stage in April 1908: 'a better Radical than Asquith, a better Liberal than Lloyd George', he was succeeded inevitably by Asquith just as Asquith was succeeded, perhaps less inevitably, by Lloyd George. The first change of prime ministership brought no great change of political balance. The contrast between Asquith's *gravitas* and Lloyd George's impatience provoked both argument and action after 1914: before 1914 the two qualities were complementary, not incompatible. Indeed, the continued power of a united Liberal party depended on this combination of gifts. Asquith had what all his contemporaries recognized to be, in Lord Esher's words, 'a keen delving mind, with incisive powers of speech'.[2] He was as concise as he was incisive. He was tolerant inside his cabinet and authoritative in the House of Commons. Sir Charles Dilke, who had long experience of parliament and was no mean judge, thought that Asquith was a greater parliamentarian than Gladstone. Lloyd George was a political genius who cast spells rather than won debates. His mind moved fast and daringly rather than probed deep. He made no effort to limit his exuberant rhetoric unless there was a good political reason for doing so. His jauntiness kept politics perpetually exciting. Asquith hardly ever, in Lord Curzon's

---

[1] K. Feiling, *A History of England*, 1952.

[2] Esher had a low opinion of Campbell-Bannerman whom he dismissed as 'amiable'. He judged him 'possibly below the calibre of his predecessors, with the exception of Perceval, Addington, Goderich and Liverpool'.

words, 'kindled an audience into flame': Lloyd George was always
doing it both in parliament and on the platform. He could kindle
Lord Curzon too. On one occasion he told him that he did not mind
him 'as long as he kept to his bombastic commonplaces which had
been his stock-in-trade through life, but if he were going to try here
that arrogance which was too much even for the gentle Hindu, they
would just tell him they would have none of his Oriental manners'.[1]

Lloyd George supplied Liberalism with driving force: Asquith
kept it controlled and intelligent. He also during his short spell as
chancellor of the exchequer linked the old liberalism with the new.
He practised economy, the supreme Gladstonian virtue, and prepared a scheme of old age pensions, a test of the 'new liberalism'.
Lloyd George, who succeeded him as chancellor, introduced 'People's
budgets' which were deliberate exercises in a highly pragmatic 'new
liberalism' which did not shirk from 'robbing the hen roosts'. He
proudly proclaimed his purpose of 'raising money to wage implacable warfare against poverty and squalidness'. *The Times* might
dismiss his 1909 proposals as a chaotic 'welter of half-ascertained
facts, half-thought out arguments and half-sincere sentimentalism',
but he had made his budget meaningful to the democracy. 'When
you find the House of Commons is lifeless and apathetic,' he argued,
'you must stir public opinion by violent means, so that the public
will react upon the legislation.' Public opinion was violently stirred
—on both sides. The budget was the first chain in a sequence of
events which carried Britain through a major constitutional crisis
which only ended with the passing of the Parliament Act in August
1911. It was carried on a day when the temperature in London stood
at ninety-seven degrees in the shade.

The sequence of events included two general elections, in January
1910 and in December 1910. In neither case was the campaign as
exciting as the issues which Lloyd George and his colleagues had
raised. The electorate refused to treat the elections simply as
referendums, where the merits of the House of Lords were to be
decided democratically in the name of democracy. There was
as much talk about tariff reform at the first of the two elections
as there had been in 1906, although Chamberlain himself had
been forced out of politics by illness in July 1906—a tragic loss to
the protectionist cause—and business men had even less reason for

---

[1] Quoted by Mackintosh, op. cit.

being united on the merits of tariff reform than they had been earlier in the decade. As Asquith put it, 'after seven years of controversy the world is strewn with the wreckage of Mr. Chamberlain's prophecies on tariff reform. Our overseas trade has expanded beyond expectation; the census of production has shown that we are more than holding our own, and that the "injury" of dumped goods is imaginary.' The great burst of late Edwardian foreign investment developed enterprises outside the boundaries of the formal empire. Although the Unionists regained a number of seats in January 1910 which they had lost in 1906 and returned 273 members to parliament, they did far less well than they had anticipated—on the basis of by-election results—before the budget crisis began. The Liberals returned 275 members as against the 401 of 1906, a large drop, and they were now dependent on the support of Labour with 40 members and the Irish Nationalists with 82. Labour itself did far less well than it had hoped: the 40 included a number of miners' representatives who in 1906 had not been associated with the Labour Representation Committee. The Irish Nationalists were now in a key position.

Between the first and second general elections of 1910, a period of intense backstairs political activity in a variety of efforts to resolve the constitutional crisis, the Unionists themselves became more and more uneasy about the merits of tariff reform as an election issue. Great pressure was put upon Balfour, particularly by a group of influential Unionist journalists led by J. L. Garvin of *The Observer*, not to drop the 'food taxes' altogether but to announce that he would not impose a new food duty without first making an appeal to the country. In other words he was being advised to promise yet another referendum, this time with the Unionists themselves fighting on the democratic slogan 'Trust the People—rather than the autocracy of [the] Cabinet.'[1] At a crowded Albert Hall meeting on 29 November Balfour announced his willingness to submit tariff reform to a referendum, a promise which inspired one member of his enthusiastic audience to call out 'that's won the election'. It did not. The election, wrote Sir Sidney Low, proved 'the most apathetic in living memory', and the total poll fell by a million votes. A considerable number of seats changed hands, but the over-all result did

---

[1] A. M. Gollin, *The Observer and J. L. Garvin*, 1960. Garvin's influence on the Unionist party at this time was such as no journalist had ever exercised before.

not radically alter the parliamentary situation. One fewer Unionist and three fewer Liberals were returned than in January and the Labour party and the Irish Nationalists each gained two seats. The Liberals had achieved the feat, unprecedented since 1832, of winning three general elections in a row: the Unionists were forced, in consequence, to reconsider their whole plan of strategy. The main casualty in their reconsideration was tariff reform, a result which Joseph Chamberlain's son Austen had predicted even before the election was fought. After the second defeat of December 1910 contributions to the Tariff Reform League dwindled to a trickle: the number of its propaganda publications dwindled also. As soon as Bonar Law replaced Balfour as Conservative leader, he was bombarded with requests to drop the 'food taxes' completely, and this was done in January 1913. The preferential aspects of tariff reform were shelved far less dramatically than they had been introduced nearly ten years before. 'We are beaten,' wrote Austen Chamberlain, 'and the cause for which father sacrificed more than life itself is abandoned.'[1]

Ireland and South Africa

Ireland provided a new cause for both Liberals and Unionists. The Liberals decided that the time for compromise and delay was past and that Ireland was ripe for home rule: the Unionists, thwarted in England, decided to commit themselves to the cause of Ulster. In both cases the decisions were based on something more than expediency. The Liberals were influenced not only by their reliance upon Irish votes at Westminster, but on their traditional principles and their recent experience: the Unionists believed that the break-up of the United Kingdom would be the first stage in the break-up of the empire as a whole. Passions were roused, particularly among the 'insiders' of politics, which split influential families and threatened civil war. 'Even on the neutral territory of an Embassy', wrote the German ambassador, 'one did not venture to mingle the two parties.' The parliamentary machine almost cracked under the strain of the Irish question. So too did the unity and loyalty of the army.

The recent experience which influenced Liberal opinion related to South Africa. Campbell-Bannerman's policy of granting complete

---

[1] A. Chamberlain, *Politics from Inside*, 1936. He could not foresee, of course, that his brother Neville was to redress the defect twenty years later.

self-government to the white population of the Transvaal and the
Orange River Colony so soon after the end of the Boer war was an
example of what he meant by 'true imperialism', the imperialism
which ended in the transfer of responsibility: the new constitution
of South Africa, designed in Durban in 1908 and ratified in London
in 1909, was regarded by Liberals as the great culmination of this
achievement. Old adversaries were converted into new friends just
as old colonies had been converted into new 'dominions' at the fifth
colonial conference of 1907. What the Liberals either did not foresee
or refused to consider in the debates of 1909 was that the new constitution would prevent the emancipation of black Africans which
missionaries and administrators in other parts of Africa had proclaimed as an objective. Only Dilke, an old though unorthodox
Liberal imperialist, and the Labour members of parliament argued,
cogently but to no effect, that if an empire was to be maintained at
all, it had a duty to safeguard native interests. Was it simply the
duty of parliament at Westminster, MacDonald asked, to rubber-
stamp colonial bills? Asquith replied that union in South Africa
would be impossible if the British government were to be given the
right to intervene in native affairs, while Balfour went further and
claimed that to give black Africans equal rights with white South
Africans would be to threaten the whole fabric of white civilization.
This interesting debate, the importance of which was appreciated
by only a small number of members of parliament, stands out in
retrospect as a critical debate on the meaning and future of empire.
It was more important than the Morley–Minto reforms in India
which marked a cautious step towards the acceptance of elections
in Indian government. The old Liberal case for self-government,
which was rooted in nineteenth-century argument, was exposed at
its weakest point in Africa: new arguments were advanced which
were to echo in mid-twentieth-century politics.

　　Yet the lessons drawn from the latest chapter of events in South
Africa were simple ones, and they were applied, without over-much
thought, to the complex situation in Ireland. Liberals believed that
John Redmond, the leader of the Irish Nationalists at Westminster,
could become an 'Irish Botha'. His anglophile views and his enthusiasm for Liberal principles were guarantees of future co-operation
between a self-governing Ireland and the rest of Britain. In April
1912 Asquith introduced the third Liberal Home Rule Bill: its fate

dictated the pattern of British politics between then and 1914. Private parleys and public debates were accompanied by mass covenants and drilling of troops. The excitement was maintained until the outbreak of war. The same day in July 1914 that a constitutional conference on Ireland called by George V broke down, news reached the cabinet of an ultimatum sent by Austria-Hungary to Serbia; a few days later, with European war still nearer, there were serious disturbances in Dublin; and although later in 1914 the Home Rule Bill in amended form was finally carried under the Parliament Act without the consent of the peers,[1] the Irish question was far from solved. It was abundantly clear that Redmond no longer spoke in the name of the Irish Nationalists in Ireland.

Redmond's consistent and ultimately unpopular pursuit of a liberal line of conduct contrasted with the militant and revolutionary tactics employed by Unionists in Northern Ireland with the strong support of Unionists in England, particularly their 'meekly ambitious' new leader, Bonar Law, and of proud old imperialists like Milner. In February 1910 Sir Edward Carson had become leader of the Ulster group of members of parliament at Westminster: he played an outstanding part in mobilizing the energy and enthusiasm of Unionists as a whole.

> One Law, one Land, one Throne.
> If England drive us forth
> We shall not fall alone.

Bonar Law stated publicly in Belfast in April 1912 that Ulster 'held the pass for the Empire', and a few months later, in July, made his famous 'Blenheim pledge' in which he declared that he could 'imagine no length of resistance to which Ulster will go' which he would not be ready to support 'and in which they will not be supported by the overwhelming majority of the British people'. Bonar Law was certainly supported by the overwhelming majority of Unionists, and there were many young Unionist members of parliament who were both 'ready to support Ulster in a physical sense' and had taken 'effective means to that end'.[2] Milner, who believed that the coercion

---

[1] Despite the mood of 'national unity' which the war fostered, radical and Liberal members of parliament, 'in defiance of propriety', cheered when the clerk in the House of Lords called 'Le Roy le veult' and the Government of Ireland Act became law in September 1914.

[2] Lord Winterton, *Orders of the Day*, 1953.

of Ulster by military force in the name of home rule would have
been 'an act of revolutionary illegality', was prepared to serve as
'the real leader of resistance' if all attempts at compromise broke
down.

The embroilment of the Liberal government in this long and
bitter struggle tested to the full both the ability and the character
of the Liberal leaders: it did not succeed, however, in capturing the
whole-hearted interest of the majority of the British population.
Halévy has written that as parliament ploughed through the weary
formalities of passing the Home Rule Bill three times to defeat the
Lords' obstruction, the public viewed the controversy with boredom.
The comment is exaggerated, but it is certainly true that there was
far greater public interest in the programme of social reforms which
the Liberal government carried before and after the constitutional
crisis of 1909 to 1911. Asquith might have raised the temperature
of domestic politics had he tried in 1913 and 1914 to make an appeal
to the English population to support by all means the government
of the day in their battle with factions, minorities, and illiberal elements within the armed forces. He was temperamentally averse to
all such appeals, however, and he believed that such a line of action
would do infinite harm. It is notable that in 1913 and 1914 the kind
of appeal his most dynamic minister, Lloyd George, chose to make was
not on Ireland—an issue on which he was ready to seek compromises
—but on a comprehensive measure of 'land reform' which would
entail another long and noisy battle with the British aristocracy.
Lloyd George planned to fight the next general election on this
issue. He never failed to appreciate the need for 'kindling the public' with big schemes of social reform. He was far less successful with
his 'land plan' proposals of 1913—based on a statistical inquiry in
which Seebohm Rowntree, the investigator of poverty, took a
leading part—than he had been in the 1909 budget crisis. Fervent
Liberal audiences might sing lustily that the land belonged to the
People, but the Land League was less effective in its propaganda
than the Budget League had been. This does not imply that Lloyd
George had not selected the land issue with care. It was close to his
heart, but, just as relevant, he saw clearly that the Liberal party was
by its social composition and traditional outlook far more capable
of reaching a new 'land settlement' than of dealing expeditiously
and comprehensively with the more thorny problems of industry.

Social Reforms

Social reform in more general terms was perhaps the greatest achievement of the Liberal government, and the years from 1906 to 1914 are usually associated with the origins of the mid-twentieth-century 'welfare state'. Campbell-Bannerman had promised in 1906 that England would become 'less of a pleasure ground for the rich and more of a treasure house for the nation': on taking over from him in 1908, Asquith told the Commons that it was his view also that 'property must be associated in the minds of the masses of the people with the ideas of reason and justice'. The Old Age Pensions Act of 1908, which introduced non-contributory pensions 'as of right', though on a test of means, and the Mines (Eight Hours) Act of the same year were early instalments of this programme. The first act laid down the important principle that the strictly limited sections of the aged population who were entitled to pensions were not to be treated as paupers or deprived of any franchise, right, or privilege: this principle was in marked contrast to the principles of the 1834 poor law, which treated the claims of the poor 'not as an integral part of the rights of the citizen but as an alternative to them'.[1] The second act marked a sharp break with the nineteenth-century factory acts, which had been consolidated in a great codifying act of 1901: the 1908 act was the first definite statutory regulation of the hours of work for adult males, as distinct from children or women.

In 1909, 'the year of the budget', the Trade Boards Act established in certain 'plague spot' industries boards with power to fix the minimum wage for workers. The Board of Trade was given the authority to extend the act by provisional order when it was satisfied that the rate of wages in a particular trade were 'exceptionally low' or where 'other circumstances' of the trade were deemed to make government intervention necessary. In the same year the Labour Exchanges Act gave the Board of Trade the task of setting up and supervising labour exchanges which would provide unemployed workers with the chance of finding out locally the state of the labour market. The first of these important acts accepted the principle of government intervention to fix a legal minimum wage: the same principle was applied more controversially in 1912 when,

---

[1] T. H. Marshall, *Citizenship and Social Class*, 1950.

in a crisis situation, the Coal Mines (Minimum Wage) Act laid down a minimum wage not for a badly organized but for a well organized industry. The second act did not imply a policy for alleviating unemployment, but without such an act no future employment policy could have been developed. For the two acts of 1909 Churchill, as president of the board of trade, took the responsibility. A year earlier Lloyd George had told Masterman that if he was to take the field for 'a real democratic policy' Churchill would have to be 'converted'. In 1909 Churchill showed how far his conversion had gone. He pledged the government to an insurance scheme which would safeguard the citizen against the perils of unemployment, and looked forward to 'the universal establishment of minimum standards of life and labour, and their progressive elevation as the increasing energies of production may permit'. Of Lloyd George's budget he said, ' it involves all other questions; it has brought all other issues to a decisive test'.[1]

It was Lloyd George who introduced insurance when the budget crisis was over. As early as 1908 he had visited Germany to study the social insurance scheme in operation there, and in his 1909 budget speech he had discussed the outlines of a future programme. He continued to brood on the question during the constitutional crisis, assisted by memoranda from young civil servants, William Beveridge and Llewellyn Smith guiding him in the details of unemployment insurance[2] and W. J. Braithwaite in the problems of health insurance. In 1911 the speech from the throne promised not only measures 'for settling the relations between the two Houses' and for 'extending self-government to Ireland' but for 'providing for the insurance of the industrial population against sickness and invalidity and for the insurance against unemployment of those engaged in trades especially liable to it'. The promise of insurance legislation was fulfilled in May 1911 when Lloyd George introduced his proposals for a contributory insurance scheme. With a number of amendments the bill became law in December 1911, and after six months' hectic work—compared with the twenty-five years the Germans had had to perfect their scheme—the law was put into operation in July

---

[1] W. Churchill, *Liberalism and the Social Problem*, 1909.

[2] Beveridge, whose book on *Unemployment* (1909) had great influence, was responsible for the idea of labour exchanges. For his part in developing social policy during this period, see *Power and Influence*, 1953.

1912. Even then it was not until January 1913 that the full 'system' began to work. It was not at all like a 'continental system'. C. F. G. Masterman, who was called in to help with the working of the scheme, described it in 1913 as being 'not a classical but a gothic building'. It had a large number of blemishes but it was at least capable of extension. As Masterman recognized, the alteration of one pillar or the addition of one wing would not destroy symmetry if there was no symmetry there. The purpose of the building would in the broadest sense dictate its future development, and the purpose was clearly stated by Sydney Buxton, a 'new Liberal' and president of the board of trade, in 1911. The bill was based on the premise, Buxton said when he moved the second reading, that 'the employer and the State should enter into a partnership with the working man in order as far as possible to mitigate the severity of the burden which falls upon him'.

The distinction between the contributory basis of insurance and the non-contributory basis of the Old Age Pensions Act of 1908 is socially and historically significant. Non-contributory aid to the sick and the unemployed, what Mrs. Webb called the provision of 'an enforced minimum of civilized life', had been advocated in 1909 by the signatories of the minority report of the royal commission on the Poor Law, appointed in 1905 on the eve of the fall of Balfour's government. Neither Liberals nor Unionists were prepared in the fiscal circumstances of 1911 and 1912 to finance welfare out of general taxation. Insurance seemed the answer to their problems. They could buttress their fiscal preference by extolling the merits of the voluntary system of thrift which they sought to extend rather than to suppress and by attacking 'bureaucracy'. Austen Chamberlain, for example, called what Mrs. Webb described as 'an enforced minimum of civilized life' 'establishing an intolerable bureaucratic tyranny'. Yet Lloyd George himself ranged further than most of his colleagues in his speculations on the significance of his own proposals. A note in his papers, dated 7 March 1911, reads:

Insurance necessary temporary expedient. At no distant date hope State will acknowledge a full responsibility in the matter of making provision for sickness, breakdown and unemployment. It really does so now, through Poor Law: but conditions under which this system had hitherto worked have been so harsh and humiliating that working-class pride revolts against accepting so degrading and doubtful a boon. Gradually the obligation of the State to find labour or sustenance will be realised and honourably interpreted.

This note is certainly a key document in the history of the 'welfare state'.

In introducing his legislation Lloyd George boldly claimed that he was turning from controversial questions to a question which had 'never been the subject of controversy between the parties in the state'. This was historically inaccurate, but broadly true of the previous ten years when 'insurance' was generally approved on both sides of the House and there were many signs that nineteenth-century concern for public health, 'the health of towns', was giving way to twentieth-century concern for personal health, 'the health of people', particularly women and children. The century had been ushered in with a Midwives Act, and during and after the Boer war spokesmen of both parties had admitted how much needed to be done if 'the health of the People' was to be improved as a matter of urgency. Lloyd George's hopes seemed to be justified in the light of the first reception of his bill. 'Tories almost as enthusiastic as the Radicals', wrote George Riddell in his diary, 'treating Lloyd George as if he was a saviour of society . . . Balfour all smiles and cordiality.' *Punch* depicted the chancellor of the exchequer standing in evening dress on a platform stage and acknowledging the applause of the audience with the words, 'Never known the haloes to come so thick before. Pit and gallery I'm used to, but now the stalls and dress circle have broken out.'

Despite this initial enthusiasm, there was prolonged controversy before the bill became law and further controversy before the law could be put into practice. The opposition came from many sides and for many reasons. Some Labour members of parliament and politically active working men considered the introduction of the contributory principle as a 'set-back' to social reform: so too did the socialist intellectuals of the Fabian Society, led by the Webbs, who wanted to alleviate social 'injustice' by using the re-distributive mechanisms of state finance. At the other end of the social scale there was a 'revolt of the duchesses', backed by domestic servants and popular newspapers, including the *Daily Mail* and *The Times*, both of which were controlled by Lord Northcliffe.[1] Some of the

---

[1] *The Times* welcomed the bill at first (5 May 1911) while stressing that it would cost money and need modifications.

'duchesses' held mass meetings in the Albert Hall to exhort the public not to 'lick' stamps on the new 'bureaucratic' and 'German' insurance cards. 'It is not only 3*d*. a week we shall lose', the servants cried, 'but our independence, self-respect and character.'[1] There was also bitter opposition to the bill from a section of the doctors. The opposition was virulent and sustained, but its causes and its consequences were far from simple. The opinions of general practitioners and their dissatisfaction with their incomes, status, and limitations on their professional freedom under the pre-1911 'contract medical practice' or 'club system' had encouraged them to look to the state to help them solve their problems. Their first reaction to the bill was ambivalent.[2] Opinion hardened, however, in the late spring of 1911, and there was a tough battle to ensure that doctors should not be directly dependent on the 'approved societies' which were to administer insurance benefits. This battle was won by the doctors, with Lloyd George supporting them, but the British Medical Association continued to oppose the amended measure mainly on the grounds that rates of remuneration would be inadequate. It attempted to lead doctors in a concerted refusal to participate in the scheme once the law was passed—a kind of doctors' strike—but it failed in this endeavour. At the appointed time, January 1913, the full scheme came into force.

In its final form, the National Insurance Act provided compulsory contributory health insurance for all manual workers, male and female, between the ages of sixteen and seventy who were employed under contract of service. Other persons earning less than £160 a year could insure themselves voluntarily and become 'panel patients'. Their own contributions were to be backed by contributions from employers and the state. The scheme was to be controlled from above by national insurance commissioners: Lloyd George turned for assistance in this connexion to Sir Robert Morant, according to the Webbs 'the one man of genius in the Civil Service', 'a strange mortal, not altogether sane', whose reorganization of education after the passing of the Education Act of 1902 had greatly impressed

---

[1] *Daily Mail*, 18 November 1911.

[2] There were several letters in the *British Medical Journal* on the subject of a state service before Lloyd George's bill was announced. A special committee of the British Medical Association had also been considering the subject. The *British Medical Journal* described the bill in its first leader as 'in its conception one of the greatest attempts at social legislation which the present generation has known'.

Lloyd George, the chief opponent of the measure. Morant proved bureaucratic, a grim guardian of the gothic castle, who cared little for its labyrinths. He showed little interest in or understanding of the 'voluntary agencies' which stood between himself and the ordinary insured person. The sickness benefits under the National Insurance Act, which were to be 'reasonably adequate' rather than generous, were to be administered by 'approved societies'. After considerable business pressure it had been decided in May 1911 that these societies should include not only trade unions and friendly societies but commercial insurance companies. Medical benefits, as a result of doctors' pressure, were to be supervised by local committees in each county and county borough. Unemployment insurance, the benefits from which were to be 'narrowly cut' and strictly limited in duration, was conceived of only in selective and experimental terms. Only workers in a limited number of trades, including building, shipbuilding, and engineering were included, two and a quarter million workers in all.

It is sometimes argued that the programme of Liberal social reform legislation which culminated in the National Insurance Act was mainly the product of Labour pressure. Such an argument is over-simplified. There was strong Labour support for certain of the Liberal measures, on occasion sustained Labour pressure, and sometimes, as in the case of the Education (Provision of Meals) Act of 1906, direct Labour initiative, but Liberal interest in social reform was more than derivative or tactical. Of course, some Liberals were more keen than others. Conspicuous among the less keen, because of or despite his past, was John Burns. Conspicuous among the more keen were junior ministers like Masterman and Buxton and backbenchers like Edward Pickersgill and Percy Alden. Liberals had long been prominent in the agitation against 'sweating' which was the prelude to the Trade Boards Act: indeed it was John Stuart Mill who had first pointed to the problem in a chapter in his *Political Economy* 'On Popular Remedies for Low Wages'. A large number of bills on the subject were introduced before 1909 by Liberal private members, and it was a Liberal newspaper, the *Daily News*, which organized an extremely popular 'anti-sweating exhibition' in 1906. There was also a well-rooted Liberal interest in the idea of a 'minimum wage', and the subject was canvassed vigorously in Edwardian Britain not only by trade unionists but by Seebohm Rowntree. Up to a point, thoughtful Liberals recognized, they could move step by step with socialists. As L. T. Hobhouse, one of the most thoughtful, put it, 'individualism when it grapples with the facts, is driven no small distance along Socialist lines'. On where the point of divergence was to be placed Liberals disagreed. Churchill, who did not hesitate to say that in the main the lines of difference between parties were 'increasingly becoming the lines of cleavage between the rich and the poor', perhaps stated the difference between liberalism and socialism more strikingly than most of his contemporaries.

Liberalism has its own history and its own traditions. Socialism has its own formulas and its own aims. Socialism seeks to pull down wealth: Liberalism seeks to raise up poverty. Socialism would destroy private interests; Liberalism would preserve private interests in the only way in which they can be safely and justly preserved, namely by reconciling them with public right. Socialism would kill enterprise: Liberalism would rescue enterprise from the trammels of privilege and preference.

On questions where there was a clash of mood and outlook between Liberal upholders of 'individualism' and trade-union supporters of 'solidarity' there was the biggest difference between the two views of life and politics. Yet Campbell-Bannerman yielded to the Labour view in carrying the Trade Disputes Act of 1906 which rectified the Taff Vale judgment. The Liberal response to the Osborne judgment of 1908—a judgment which restrained unions from spending their funds on the maintenance of political parties— was slower and more reserved, and when at last in 1913 a Liberal bill was passed the Labour members recognized it only as 'an instalment, and not the final settlement of Labour's demands'. There were more basic differences between liberalism and socialism which can be traced in the pattern of amendments and modifications which Liberals introduced into Labour proposals and in the hedges of moral qualifications which surrounded such 'progressive' measures as the Old Age Pensions Act of 1908.[1] In much of this beneficent legislation the Liberals saw working-class life from outside: they applied norms of behaviour derived from one class to another. Their zeal was often and quite inevitably greater than their insight.[2]

[1] According to the act pensions were to be withheld from those 'who had habitually failed to work according to ability and need and those who had failed to save money regularly'.

[2] R. Titmuss, 'Social Administration in a Changing Society' in *Essays on the Welfare State*, 1958.

The Constitutional Crisis

The Unionists did not frontally oppose much of this Liberal social welfare policy. A section of backbencher Unionists led by Sir Frederick Banbury, Harold Cox, and Lord Robert Cecil were always vociferous in their complaints about 'socialism', but they were in a minority. Banbury might argue that the Education (Provision of Meals) Act 'put a premium on idleness' or Cox grumble that the Old Age Pensions Act meant that 'all drunkards, wife-deserters, pimps, procurers and criminals in the country were to get pensions at the expense of honest men', but both men were recognized to be extremists, 'anarchist leaders' Lloyd George called them.[1] Official Unionist opposition to the Old Age Pensions Act was, as Halévy writes, timid and feeble, and the National Insurance Act, despite the public clamour outside, was subjected to only one major delaying amendment in the House of Commons and passed its second reading in the Lords without a debate. The House of Lords was particularly careful not to appear to be holding up labour legislation. Favourite Liberal proposals, such as a new education act, were treated savagely by the Lords, but the Trade Disputes Act went through without a division. When the Liberals began to realise almost from the start of their ministry that they would have to face implacable opposition in the House of Lords and started to consider constitutional measures to circumvent it, the Unionists even tried to split Liberals and Labour representatives by drawing an over-neat distinction between social and constitutional reform. In 1907, for instance, Balfour complained in the House that 'social reform was now going to be shelved in order to modify the constitution', and a Unionist amendment to the Address expressed regret that 'social legislation should be postponed for the purpose of effecting revolutionary changes in the powers exercised by parliament over the affairs of the United Kingdom'.

In fact, the Liberals could not avoid the three kinds of deadlock and crisis which disturbed their long régime. The constitutional crisis was not simply a contest of abstractions: it was a struggle for political power and social policies. MacDonald saw this as clearly as

---

[1] Lord Rosebery's rhetoric concerning his former colleagues was equally exaggerated. He called the old age pensions scheme 'prodigal of expenditure' and said that it might 'deal a blow at the empire which could be almost mortal'. The 1909 budget, he exclaimed, 'threatens to poison the very sources of our national supremacy'.

Asquith or Lloyd George. Weak in the Commons, the Unionists were overwhelmingly strong in the Lords. Of the 602 peers only 88 described themselves as Liberal. Nor was there much hope of a 'non-political' group among the rest: 355 were Conservative Unionists and 124 Liberal Unionists. During the long period of Unionist rule before 1906 this great majority had been inert or impassive, but as soon as the 1906 election was over Balfour and the leader of the Unionists in the Lords, the fifth Marquess of Lansdowne, took immediate steps to concert activities as 'two separate armies . . . in a common plan of campaign': the result was the rejection of a Liberal Education Bill in December 1906. This was a major bill, a touchstone of Liberal philosophy, which all Liberals had been pledged to support at the general election. If Parliament had not been in session for such a short time there might well have been a dissolution in 1906 and a new appeal to the people. The ultimate constitutional crisis of 1909–11 was implicit in the electoral revolution of 1906. Lloyd George saw the true nature of the problem. 'If they tamely allow the House of Lords to extract all the virtue out of their bills so that when the Liberal statute book is produced it is simply a collection of sapless legislative faggots fit only for the fire, then a real cry will arise in this land for a new party.'

Given the strength of the forces of opposition inside the House of Lords and behind the scenes, it was certain that the way of the Liberals would be hard and perilous. They were also threatened from the start from a different direction. Discontented groups which could not get what they wanted from the Liberal government would either suffer frustration or consider direct action. In either case there would be a heightening of social tension. The very extent of the Liberal victory in 1906 was an indication that the country had swung as far to the left in electoral terms as it could do. Any sectional demands which the Liberal government failed to satisfy, whether they were moderate or extremist—opinions about what constituted 'moderation' or 'extremism' varied—might well generate un-parliamentary or even anti-parliamentary activity. If such demands were passionately pressed, like the demand for votes for women, they would be bound to make traditional political methods difficult to pursue. The leaders of such groups might go on to argue that their failure to get what they wanted was due not only to the immobility of parliament, the 'conservatism' of the judges, or

Asquith's 'lawyer's mind' but to weaknesses within liberalism itself
—the incompleteness of its philosophy of progress, the 'caution' and
'timidity' of its leadership and tactics, or even—and it was a popular
explanation—the 'collusion' between front-bench Liberal leaders and
their Unionist opponents.[1] Such 'explanations' of Liberal 'weakness'
were usually associated with appeals to 'true democracy': there
were other explanations, however, which attached no virtues to
democracy and rested on more or less frank appeals to authoritarian
creeds, old and new. Whatever counter-action the Liberals took
against their critics would be bound to excite controversy. If they
were too 'weak', they would be in danger of alienating some of their
friends, who would find it all too easy to accuse them of abandoning
Liberal principles. If they were too 'firm', their enemies and a number of their 'friends' would deem it natural to seek a 'safer' and more
truly 'conservative' government. The solicitude for safety could
even be measured statistically from the evidence of by-election
results.

The Social Crisis

All reforming ministries are confronted with problems of this kind
within the framework of democracy. There were, however, three
special features of the social, economic, and cultural background of
late Edwardian Britain which gave exceptional encouragement to
advocates of direct action. First the economic situation remained
difficult for the least well-off sections of the community. In 1908,
for example, there was a higher proportion of unemployment among
the wage-earning population than there had been since 1886, the
year of Bloody Sunday in Trafalgar Square. Significantly more days
were lost in labour stoppages in 1908 than during any year out of
the previous ten. The gloom of 1908 was caused by cyclical movements in the international economy, but structural factors within
the national economy perpetuated working men's difficulties. Most

---

[1] One of the main attacks on 'collusion' came from Hilaire Belloc and Cecil
Chesterton. Belloc's *Mr. Clutterbuck's Election* may be compared with the message
of *The Party System* (1911) and *The Servile State* (1912). It is also interesting to compare
these writings with the talk of a coalition in 1910 composed of the 'moderate' wings of
the Liberal and Unionist parties, pledged to government in the 'national interest'.
See D. Lloyd George, *War Memoirs*, vol. i, 1933, pp. 32–41; A. Chamberlain, op. cit.,
pp. 191–3, 283–94, 576–7; and the Earl of Birkenhead, *Frederick Edwin, Earl of
Birkenhead*, vol. i, 1933, pp. 203–9.

important, the pressure on real wages continued and increased. Between 1902 and 1909 the cost of living had risen by 4 or 5 per cent.: between 1909 and 1913 it rose again by nearly 9 per cent. Money wages responded unevenly and with great strain. There was fierce discontent particularly among unskilled workers, whose wages were already very low, often below the poverty line, and workers in the coal and transport industries, who were becoming far more highly organized and militant. Even in the cotton industry, however, the Cotton Spinners' Amalgamation was so dissatisfied that in 1913 it terminated the Brooklands agreement by which the industry had been regulated for twenty years. Trade unions grew rapidly in numbers and strength against this background. Membership rose by two-thirds between 1910 and 1913, and some of the new unions, notably the National Union of Railwaymen founded in 1912, were of a very different stamp from the old craft unions of the nineteenth century. One section of trade-union opinion, certainly the most articulate, was determined to use union bargaining power to improve labour's position. Parliamentary methods, as followed by the Liberal party and the Labour party alike, were judged to be slow and ineffective, and far more, it was thought, could be gained from well directed and concerted strikes than from the quest for greater political power. The report of the parliamentary committee to the Trades Union Congress had argued in 1907 that it was 'overwhelmingly within the competence of labour to alter the unequal state of society': the more militant trade unionists of 1910 to 1914 were openly sceptical about parliament ever being able to accomplish 'a democratic revolution in the name of labour'.[1] They knew that it could not deal with their immediate grievances: how, then, could it deal with long-term aims? The result was a period of 'industrial warfare', 'a great upsurge of elemental forces' during which it appeared for a time as if 'the dispossessed and disinherited classes in various parts of the country were all simultaneously moved to assert their claims upon society'. The peak points of this period were the dock and railway strikes of 1911, the year of George V's coronation, the coal strike of 1912, and the Port of London strike of the same year. In 1914 a plan for a Triple Alliance of miners, railwaymen, and

---

[1] 'We have grown too smug, too respectable', a miners' federation delegate told the Trades Union Congress in 1913. 'There are too many of our people in the House of Commons, and too many J.P.s in our midst!' (*T.U.C. Annual Report*, 1913).

transport workers was drafted, and long before this there was much talk, some of it highly colourful, of a civil war between labour and capital. *The Times*, for example, warned the public in January 1912 that it must be prepared for a conflict between labour and capital 'on a scale such as has never occurred before'. Old-fashioned labour leaders were almost as unpopular among the new unionists as capitalists. The secretary of the Locomotive Engineers, for instance, found the Triple Alliance conference door literally shut in his face.

Battles between capital and labour posed peculiarly awkward problems for a Liberal party which included a large number of employers and spoke in the name of a large number of working men: there were always contradictory voices in the party's counsels just as there were contradictory elements in its philosophy. A second feature of later Edwardian Britain made this economic battle far more noisy. Discontented labour was not the only group to resort to direct action in an attempt to overcome its difficulties. The advocates of direct action within its ranks could always point to the example of other people. There was a kind of contagion in society and politics, what has recently been called a 'factor of reverberation'. The 'duchesses'' opposition to the National Insurance Act, for instance, entailed a direct threat to disobey the law, a serious enough threat to goad Lloyd George into framing a number of colourful social homilies. 'Were there now to be *two* classes of citizens in the land—*one* class which could obey the laws if they liked; the *other* which must obey whether they liked it or not? . . . A Law to ensure people against poverty and misery . . . was to be optional. Was the law for the preservation of game to be optional? Was the payment of rent to be optional?' This was a practical extension of the theme of Galsworthy's *The Silver Box*. A greater inspiration to militant labour came from the tactics of the suffragettes, a much smaller but a more consistently militant minority. The Women's Social and Political Union had been founded in October 1903 by Mrs. Emmeline Pankhurst. 'We did not begin to fight, however,' wrote Mrs. Pankhurst, 'until we had given the new Liberal government every chance to give us the pledge we wanted.' The government would not give the pledge, and suffragette tactics developed accordingly. The Liberal government faced a persistently nagging agitation which went on until the outbreak of war. Society was disturbed by policies which involved a complete lack of respect for any institution except human life: 'nothing', wrote the Speaker in 1913, 'is safe from their attacks'. Even the empire seemed to be shaking: Lords Curzon and Cromer were prominent in 1909 in the foundation of an Anti-suffrage League. Yet there were enough supporters of the suffragettes within the Liberal party to make repression difficult. Brailsford and H. W. Nevinson, for example, resigned their position as leader-writers on the Liberal *Daily News* in 1909, on the grounds that 'we cannot denounce torture in Russia and support it in England, nor can we advocate democratic principles in the name of a party which confines them to a single sex'.

The third factor in the late Edwardian situation was the outlook and policies of the Unionist party. Sectional discontents could be nourished both by 'tactical necessity' and by philosophies of direct action—the syndicalist message of *The Miners' Next Step* (1912), for example, the guild ideas of A. R. Orage's *New Age*, founded in 1907, or foreign doctrines like those of de Leon or Sorel. One of the most powerful incentives to think and act sectionally, however, was provided by the example of the Unionist party both in Ulster and in Britain. The Conservatives were so desperate in their struggle to conserve that they threatened to destroy. They were the biggest of the discontented groups in Britain after their failure to oust the Liberals from power at the two successive general elections of 1910. They could win by-elections but not general elections. They were a constitutional party, but they declared themselves ready to use 'all means which may be found necessary to maintain our claims'. It is scarcely surprising that J. H. Thomas of the National Union of Railwaymen asked the House of Commons why if Ulster could arm with impunity, his union should not spend its half million on arms too.

International Crisis

The talk and use of force presented the biggest of all the threats to Liberal democracy, and force in the form of national power was, of course, the chief element in the third kind of crisis which disturbed and finally shattered Edwardian Britain—international crisis. The Liberal party included a pacifist left and a large number of radicals, old and new, who were in sympathy with pacifist policies. It was seldom difficult, even in the early months of 1914 itself, to win public

applause by contrasting war expenditure with social service expenditure, battles against foreign enemies with battles against poverty
and disease, and dreadnoughts with schools and hospitals. Within
the cabinet itself there were many struggles about priorities. There
was strong and almost unanimous opposition to plans for conscription of the kind put forward by Lord Roberts, and the opposition
was on democratic grounds. Other countries might maintain conscription in the name of democratic equality: the British Liberals
resisted it consistently in the name of democratic freedom. Yet the
Liberal government could not help considering questions of defence
and of national power betwen 1906 and 1914, and Haldane's
schemes of army reform, while little appreciated by the generals
or the politicians, were of the utmost immediate value when war
broke out in 1914.[1]

Liberals had always been more tender towards the navy than
towards the army. Between 1907–8 and 1913–14 naval estimates
rose by 50 per cent. This was the period of the 'naval race', which did
much to exacerbate public feelings against Germany: the race followed the launching by the British in 1906 of the first all-big-gun
ship, the *Dreadnought*, a ship which made all existing battleships
obsolete. Two years later fear of 'acceleration' of the German naval
programme, a fear stimulated by the newspapers, stirred thousands
of British people and forced the Liberal government to review its
earlier plans for cutting naval expenditure. The *Dreadnought* agitation was forced on the government by a curious but not unusual
coalition of democratic opinion, newspaper pressure, and backstairs
manœuvres of a powerful oligarchic triumvirate behind the scenes
consisting of Admiral Sir John Fisher, first sea lord, Lord Knollys,
the king's private secretary, and Lord Esher, who among his many
official and unofficial duties served as a member of the committee of
imperial defence. The Admiralty itself was torn by feuds, but the
Liberal government pushed on with the naval building programme.
A new note of truculence followed the appointment of Churchill to
the Admiralty in place of McKenna in 1911: with all the enthusiasm
of a convert, he proved as zealous in supporting naval expenditure as
he had been hitherto in supporting social reform. 'His old connection
with the Army and now with the Navy', wrote Wilfrid Scawen Blunt,

---

[1] 'Serve him right', said Campbell-Bannerman on sending Haldane to the War
Office in 1905.

'has turned his mind back into an ultra Imperialist groove.' Not all supporters of a 'Big Navy' were open imperialists. Battleships were regarded as symbols of comparative power by the people who were suspicious of Germany, but they were also regarded as the means of safeguarding peaceful commerce by the people who were suspicious of nobody. One of the reasons why battleships were 'the most formidable weapon in the imperialist armoury' was because the opponents of imperialism seldom saw them as instruments of imperialism at all.

There was more public concern for the symbols of power in the years before 1914 than for the policies which were to determine how power was to be employed. The press was full of talk, much of it melodramatic, about 'the German menace', spies, imaginary invasions, even real crises. But the conduct of foreign affairs was not thought, even under a Liberal government, to be a proper sphere of daily concern for a democracy. Eyre Crowe at the Foreign Office 'deplored all public speeches on foreign affairs': Grey as foreign secretary agreed with him. Even the cabinet itself had no clear idea of the extent to which the country was committed in foreign affairs, and there were genuine divisions in it on the eve of war. The country as a whole—with the suffragettes in the vanguard—was quickly converted to the war not by arguments about the maintenance or restoration of the balance of power but by the facts of the German invasion of 'little neutral Belgium'. Grey recognized more deeply than most that the war would put out the lights of liberalism at home and overseas, but he also believed—and the shades of empire gathered round his remark—that if Britain did not go to war 'we should be isolated, discredited and hated: and there would be before us nothing but a miserable and ignoble future'.

3

THE ECONOMY

ARTHUR J. TAYLOR

*Professor of Modern History in the
University of Leeds*

THE ECONOMY

Surely there never was a time in the life of the world when it was so
good, in the way of obvious material comfort, to be alive and fairly
well-to-do as it was before the war.

c. e. montague, *Disenchantment*

Viewed across half a century of war and economic crisis the
England of Edward VII stands out in the mind of a later generation
as an era of peace and prosperity—a brief Indian summer at the
close of a century of British political and economic pre-eminence.
Distance may lend enchantment to a view and time enhance the
glories of a season; in the colder light of the statistician's analysis
Edwardian prosperity loses something of its depth if little of its
glitter. Yet the aura of well-being remains, surviving even the
memory of the stormy years of Irish rebellion, suffragette disturbance, and, not least, labour unrest amid which the era approached
its end.

The Edwardians, for their part, saw themselves not at the end of
an old era but at the beginning of a new century of promise. The
inheritance into which they entered was a mixed one. Thirty years
earlier, in 1870, Britain had held an undisputed supremacy among
the nations. Her ships carried the world's goods, her factories filled
its markets; from her pits and furnaces came half its coal and iron.
During the course of the next three decades, however, this proud
supremacy was steadily eroded. By 1900 Britain had been surpassed
in output of coal and iron by the United States, in steel by both
the United States and Germany. Though she remained the world's
greatest exporter of manufactured goods, her position in foreign
markets was increasingly challenged by American and European
competitors. Still worse, her farmers, long reconciled to dependence
on a restricted home demand, now found even this market slipping
away from them as grain in ever-growing quantity poured into
British ports across the oceans of the world.

Increased competition for limited markets had brought with it lower prices, smaller profit-margins, and years of severe and often prolonged depression. Between 1855 and 1875 the volume of British exports had doubled and their value had increased to an even greater extent. Over the next twenty years, while outgoing cargoes continued to increase in volume—though at a slower rate—their value showed no similar appreciation. It was little consolation to merchants or industrialists to be told that their order-books were lengthening, if their incomes showed no rise in consequence. Not surprisingly men spoke of a 'great depression' and, faced with declining share-values and rising unemployment, evinced little inclination to count what blessings their changed fortunes had to offer. Yet there were compensations. Cheap food, which brought distress to the farmer, was a boon to the industrial worker, enabling him to eat more plentifully and leaving a larger margin for the purchase of the lesser necessities and simpler luxuries of life. Even the propertied classes had perhaps more to gain than to lose from the general price decline. Yet to the industrialist, who remembered the golden years of the early seventies, the succeeding quarter-century of falling prices and mounting working-class truculence seemed burdened with disappointment and depression. In the dark days of 1893 and 1894, with their record of commercial stagnation, industrial depression and labour unrest, the talk was no longer of free trade and expansion but of protection and retrenchment.

Notwithstanding these disappointments and forebodings the long reign of Queen Victoria had come to its end in a blaze of economic prosperity. The revival, at first hesitant, had by 1899 clearly assumed boom proportions. The following year saw trade at record heights, industry stretched to near capacity, and employment, especially in heavy industry, plentiful and remunerative. The economic omens for a new century and a new reign could hardly have been more propitious.

To the more cautious, however, this early promise seemed too good to last. The pessimists were already tightening their belts and preparing for the inevitable slump. Even before the end of 1901 these fears had received a measure of confirmation. There was a slight decline in exports, a check to expanding coal output, a slackening in the demand for cotton. For three further years the symptoms of incipient decline persisted. In 1904 the economic Jeremiahs were more vocal than ever. The cotton industry by this time was showing more serious signs of disturbance; wool was little better placed; and, even more ominously, the heavy industries were languishing. Yet the depression never became severe or general. Export values moved obstinately upward, and the carrying trade by land and sea was more active than it had ever been.

In the event, the year of crisis, as much expected as it was confidently predicted, failed to materialize. By 1905 the patient had turned the corner; two years later he was back almost to the rude health of 1900. This time, however, the boom collapsed more sharply. Though Britain rode the American crisis of 1907 with little financial difficulty, her economy was not allowed to escape wholly unscathed. Depression took hold of industry in 1908 and maintained its grip into the following year. Thereafter, however, the upward trend was resumed and the economy knew no further severe or extended crisis before the cataclysm of 1914. If the era had an unquiet end, its troubles were less those of economic depression than of a prosperity unevenly shared.

Foreign Trade

The key to Edwardian prosperity lies in trade. At the ebb tide of their fortune in 1894 Britain's exports, including her re-exports of imported produce, had been valued at £284 million. The late Victorian upsurge had already carried this total to £354 million by 1900 but this was only the beginning of a continuing upward movement. By 1913 the figure had reached £635 million, of which all but £110 million represented home-produced goods. Even when allowance has been made for rising prices, this was an expansion twice as vigorous as that of the preceding twenty years.

Behind these bare but eloquent figures lies a vast pattern of energetic activity—the activity of merchant seamen and captains, dockers and tallymen, shippers and clerks in city offices, railwaymen and carriers, and, not least, mill-owners and factory-hands in towns and cities throughout the British Isles. Since the middle ages textiles—first wool and later cotton—had held pride of place among Britain's export industries. This pre-eminence survived unbroken until the first world war. In spite of the rapid expansion in foreign demand for British rails, machinery, and coal, textiles still claimed one-third and the products of heavy industry no more than one-quarter of Britain's home-produced exports in 1913. But the gap was narrowing every year. The overseas customer still came to Britain for his clothing and his household goods, but he also came increasingly to seek the coal and machinery with which he might manufacture these essential commodities for himself.

These changes in emphasis among the leading export commodities, though significant, were in no sense peculiar to the Edwardian economy. The trend against textiles was already well established before the end of the nineteenth century, and the cotton trade showed, if anything, greater resilience after 1900 than in the preceding two decades. Nor was the pattern of Britain's export trade as yet greatly affected by the appearance of such commodities as the motor-car and the products of the rubber and electrical engineering industries. Within fifty years these would have come to loom large in Britain's commercial landscape. As late as 1913, however, they comprised in total no more than 3 per cent. of her exports, a proportion three times as great as in 1900, but as yet significant rather as a pointer to future growth than as a mark of present achievement. The export of chemicals, another characteristic material of the new age, was by 1913 worth more than £20 million, but its recent growth had been surprisingly slow—slower indeed than that of the export trade as a whole. British commercial achievement in the new century was based firmly—some were already inclined to say too firmly—on those established commodities which every nation demanded but which an increasing number were now well able to supply for themselves.

Though Britain's trade was world-wide, her merchants had always found their best markets near home. At the end of the nineteenth century fully one-third of the exports of her own products were still sent across the narrow seas to Europe. Asia took rather more, and the Americas rather less, than one-fifth, and the remainder was shared almost equally between Africa and Australia. Over the next decade and a half this broad pattern showed little variation, but within it there were significant changes of detail. In the Americas, for example, the relative downward trend in exports to the United States continued, but British firms found compensation in the demands of the newly invigorated economies of Canada, Argentina, and Brazil. Likewise, although Britain's principal European customers remained consistently faithful to her—with

Germany to the last the best customer of all—they took less of her consumer-goods and more of her machinery and coal.

Throughout the nineteenth century the ships which carried the products of Britain's factories to her markets overseas had brought back essential supplies of food and raw materials. Since the 1870's they had also carried growing cargoes of manufactured goods— optical instruments and toys from Germany, watches from Switzerland, silks from France, and machinery from the United States. For a decade after 1900 the relative importance of these manufactured imports declined, only to rise again with renewed vigour in the last four years of peace: but even in 1913 less than one-quarter of Britain's retained imports consisted of manufactured goods. The geographical pattern of Britain's import trade followed closely that of her exports; her merchants bought most readily where they could also sell. But there were exceptions to this rule. Since the American civil war, the United States had commanded an increasing share in the British market, whereas American buyers had become of increasingly less importance to the British manufacturer; and in consequence by 1900 Britain's adverse balance of trade with the United States was already in excess of £100 million and rising every year. Between 1900 and 1914 Britain lessened her dependence on American wheat and meat and turned instead to Argentina, Russia, and Australia. This shift of emphasis was dictated solely by price movements favourable to the new suppliers; but it helped Britain to reduce her adverse trade balance with the United States by almost one-third. In Europe there were similar changes. The tide of change was running against the countries of the Mediterranean and in favour of those of the north-west. Englishmen apparently preferred butter on their breakfast tables to port at the other end of the day: more directly and significantly they were choosing to buy cheap German steel rather than to make their own from the ores of Spain.

Fast as Britain's export trade had grown over the second half of the nineteenth century it had signally failed to keep pace with the rising tide of her imports. A trade deficit of some £25 million in 1850 became one of £160 million in the course of the next half-century. In most of these years the enterprise of British shippers and insurance brokers had brought a harvest of invisible exports more than sufficient to make good this deficiency; but after 1890 only the

dividends arising from her overseas investments stood between
Britain and a deficit on her current account. The Edwardians
checked this rake's progress. For the first time in half a century
exports grew more rapidly than imports and by 1913 a modest
annual balance had been achieved on the exchange of goods and
services. At the same time the rapid increase in British capital
holdings overseas was yielding returns which in 1913 fell only
narrowly short of £200 million and gave the over-all balance of payments a decidedly wholesome aspect. To a nation which since the
days of Samuel Smiles had set thrift and solvency high in the
calendar of human virtues this was achievement indeed.

Industry

The fluctuating fortunes of British merchants are eloquent of the
changing fortunes of the British economy as a whole. One-third of
the produce of Edwardian industry, it has been estimated, went
overseas, and the rise and fall of foreign demand exercised a decisive
influence on the country's prosperity. Yet the pattern of a nation's
trade is in many ways a distorted reflection of its more general
economic life. Britain, for example, spent more on imported food
than she received for all her exports of manufactured goods, yet
her farms employed more labourers than either her mines or her
textile factories; and more men and women were engaged in paid
domestic service than in all the metallurgical industries—from pin-
making to shipbuilding—put together. Trade, in short, though its
influence was widely pervasive, touched directly only the higher
peaks of industrial activity: to view the wider economic landscape
we must look beyond the returns of the customs officers to the no
less illuminating calculations of the compilers of the census.

Among the principal occupational groupings into which the
census-takers divided the British population agriculture long held
pride of place, not only as the nation's oldest industry but by
simple weight of number. Throughout the nineteenth century,
however, the land had been slowly losing its hold in face of the
insistent claims of industry and the towns. Until the 1860's this
decline had been only relative but thenceforward the farming
population fell absolutely as the town-dweller looked increasingly
overseas for supplies of cheaper bread and meat. By 1880 the protective dykes of distance behind which the grain-farmer had hitherto

successfully sheltered had been finally broken: the railway and the
steamship were bringing the products of the prairies to the homes
of the industrial classes, undercutting the British farmer and driving
the labourer from the countryside into mine and factory. In the last
thirty years of the nineteenth century agricultural employment and
rents alike fell by one-quarter and wheat acreage by one-half; and
in 1894, with wheat prices at their lowest point for more than
a century and a half, the outlook for the grain-farmer seemed black
to the point of despair.

By 1900 agriculture's tide had at last passed its lowest ebb.
Recovery thereafter was, however, slow and chequered. Though
food prices increased, the advantage fell more to the overseas than
to the home producer; and the gains of the farmer stemmed less
from higher prices than from more efficient and rational production.
The wheat acreage was stabilized at the low levels of the nineties
and a fuller emphasis placed on dairying and horticulture. An east-
ward migration of farmers from the hard-farmed west to the arable
south-east brought cost-reducing practices to holdings which the
pressure of foreign competition had made increasingly unprofitable.
These improvements in returns and prospects stiffened morale and
brought a measure of tangible reward to those who had endured the
worst years of depression. Profits began to recover, more particularly after 1910, and the retreat from the land was first checked and
then turned. For the first time in half a century the census in 1911
recorded an increase in the total of farm labourers. Progress was,
however, still limited. Consolidation of holdings continued to thin
the ranks of occupying farmers. Though his outlook had brightened,
the farmer's lot still compared unfavourably with that of the cotton
spinner or the coal-owner, and agriculture in 1914 was an industry
little equipped to meet the demands of an economy at war.

The decline of agriculture after 1880 had brought with it a demand, in part practical, in part sentimental, for the return of the
small farmer, driven from the land, according to popular tradition,
by the enclosure movement of an earlier era. Victorian governments
had given their blessing to the smallholdings movement, but their
legislation, permitting local councils to create holdings, was too
tentative to produce much of practical consequence. Among the first
fruits of the Liberal victory of 1906 was a measure designed to prod
reluctant local authorities into more purposeful activity. By 1914

some 14,000 holdings covering 200,000 acres had been created under the act of 1907, but this modest achievement left little mark on the general pattern of English rural life. Indeed the limited character of this piece of legislation and its comparative ineffectiveness show only too clearly how little prepared was even the most radical of British governments to influence the process of economic adjustment and to arrest the course of agricultural decline.

In the closing years of the nineteenth century the textile industries, like agriculture, had frequently found themselves becalmed in the doldrums of economic recession. The census of 1901 had, for the first time, shown an actual decline in factory employment in both the cotton and the woollen industries. During the nineties cotton manufacturers had lacked both the resources and the incentive to re-equip their mills beyond the point of making essential replacements of worn-out machinery; and in the woollen districts of the West Riding the signs of depression were even more evident. Over the next decade all this was changed. In cotton expansion went forward cautiously before 1905. Then, in the brief span of four years, the industry's spinning capacity was increased by more than one-quarter and the gains in weaving, though less immediately striking, were in the long run equally notable. This revived growth brought new prosperity to Lancashire. Dividends which had averaged less than $3\frac{1}{2}$ per cent. in the nineties only once fell below 5 per cent. in the decade after 1905, while wages moved upwards in 1906 and again, though only temporarily, in 1907. Across the Pennines the revival was no less marked and the woollen industry reached notable heights of prosperity in 1911 and 1912. Yet there remained some disquieting features in this general record of expansion and well-being, more especially in the case of cotton. The transfusion of new capital into the industry had not by 1914 resulted in a commensurate rise in output, though there had been some improvement in labour efficiency. Mill-owners were reluctant to discard old equipment and to concentrate production on new machines and in newer and more efficient mills. A preference for the mule as against the more efficient ring spindle died hard in Lancashire. In 1913, when in the United States ring spindles outnumbered mules by eight to one, in Britain the mule still retained a four to one superiority. Though the mule produced a better yarn, this advantage in quality could only be achieved at the cost of a loss of output so considerable as to make the sacrifice of doubtful wisdom in the increasingly competitive world of the twentieth century.

The check which, in differing degrees, had come to both agriculture and the textile industries in the twenty years after 1875, was less severely felt by coal. The opening up of export markets had done much to mitigate a reduction in the rate of growth of home demand. But though output continued to rise unevenly, coal prices were generally too low for the comfort and well-being of either mine-owner or collier. From 1895, however, the pressure of demand tended to increase and prices moved sharply upward. Output rose by almost one-half in less than twenty years, reaching its highest point at 287 million tons in 1913.

For thirty years before 1900 the balance of activity in the industry had been shifting from older worked districts, like Northumberland, Lancashire, and the Black Country, to areas of more recent development such as south Yorkshire, the east midlands, and south Wales. This trend continued into the new century, yet so buoyant was the demand for fuel that only Lancashire among the major coalfields showed any symptoms of absolute decline before 1914: even at its lowest ebb in 1905 the industry was enjoying prices and profits which had been exceeded only in the very best years of the preceding quarter-century. Between 1900 and 1914, as the returns to the tax inspectors clearly indicate, coal was experiencing a run of prosperity of a degree and length scarcely precedented even in the most abundant years of its nineteenth-century past.

To meet the increasing demands made upon them coal-owners had sunk new pits and lengthened their pay rolls. The 'famine' prices which prevailed in the coal market throughout 1900, and to a lesser extent in 1901, encouraged investment and led to important developments particularly in the south Yorkshire and east midland coalfields. At the same time labour recruitment was intensified. In the twenty years before 1914 employment in coal-mining rose by almost two-thirds at a time when the working population as a whole was increasing at only a quarter of that rate.

The contribution which this rapidly expanding and profitable industry made to Edwardian prosperity cannot easily be overstated. The net value of the industry's output, as measured by the census of production in 1907, was more than double that of the cotton industry and three and a half times as great as that of the

primary iron and steel industry. Moreover, by providing bulk outward cargoes in place of ballast, British coal-exporters helped to
reduce freight rates to the general benefit of the nation's commerce.
Yet, as in the case of cotton, it is possible to paint too bright
a picture of the industry's well-being. The gains which came with
high prices were offset in part by rising costs, the result not only of
justifiable wage increases but also of declining labour-productivity.
Output per miner, which between 1896 and 1900 had always
exceeded 290 tons a year, never rose above 260 tons between 1910
and 1914. This decline was in the first instance a consequence of the
losing battle which the miner was always waging with his environ-
ment; but, though the increasingly difficult conditions of mine-
working offer a partial explanation of the industry's diminishing
returns, those engaged in the industry cannot themselves escape all
responsibility for its shortcomings. Coal-owners might, not un-
justifiably, plead that, so long as labour remained cheap and plentiful, there was neither the necessity nor the incentive for them to
resort to the use of such devices as the coal-cutter and conveyor,
which were both costly to introduce and difficult to apply; and the
miners, for their part, could counter charges of absenteeism and
idleness by pointing to the increasing arduousness of their work.
Yet had the Edwardians been more given to self-criticism they
might have expressed greater concern that an industry, which was
growing daily more significant in the nation's economy and claiming
an increasing share of its manpower, had become so prodigal of the
resources in its hands.

Coal, however, had as yet little cause to fear the competition of the
foreigner; but this was far from the case with iron and steel. The
challenge which American and German producers had mounted to
the British steel industry before 1900 increased rather than diminished with the coming of the new century. Between 1900 and 1910
Germany's steel output doubled, and that of the United States rose
by no less than 150 per cent. In Britain production increased by no
more than one-fifth; and, as the war of 1914–18 was so soon to
demonstrate, steel-making was one aspect of industrial activity in
which economic pride and prestige went hand in hand with political
power.

Seen in the narrow context of the Edwardian economy, the relative
failure of British steel-producers was less culpable than it came to

appear in 1916, the year of the Somme and the shell crisis. If, as some observers believed, American and German superiority arose primarily from cost advantages beyond the control of the British steelmaker, it was both expedient and profitable for British firms to concentrate their efforts on more remunerative sectors of heavy industry than primary steel production. The influx of cheap con-- tinental steel might cause anxiety to far-sighted politicians, but it enabled Britain's yards to maintain their dominant place in world shipbuilding and her engineering shops to expand their remunera- tive activities. Nevertheless the suspicion was growing that British steel was dearer than it need have been; that, when every allow- ance had been made for the undoubted handicaps under which the industry laboured through the depletion of native ore supplies and the growth of foreign tariff barriers, there remained a cost differen- tial only ascribable to the industry's inefficiency and its conservative attitude to its problems of innovation and organization.

That sections of the steel industry could and did overcome the seemingly insuperable obstacle of discriminatory foreign competi- tion is made evident by the experience of the south Wales tinplate industry. As late as 1891 almost three-fifths of British tinplate had been exported to the United States. But in that year, at a single stroke, exports to this highly profitable market were reduced to a mere trickle by the enactment of the McKinley tariff. The energetic efforts of British merchants, and still more the virtues of the com- modity itself, decisively made good this loss. By 1914 Britain was producing almost half as much tinplate again as in 1891, and over half of this increased output was being dispatched to markets widely dispersed among the five continents. Even in tinplate-making, how- ever, the initiative of the merchant was hardly matched by that of the manufacturer. Here, as in the major steel industry, there is evidence of a failure to adopt new techniques and new forms of organization, which, if it can be explained, can scarcely be excused by the widening profit margins which the new markets brought.

The relative inefficiency of steel-making, like that of Britain's coal and cotton industries, caused some disquiet among thoughtful Edwardians; but the shortcomings of the primary industry could be readily forgotten in the achievements of the engineer. By 1911 the mechanical and electrical engineering industries, in their various branches, were employing two and a half times as many men as iron and steel; and it was in these industries, growing rapidly even in the years of the Great Depression, that the forward thrust of Edwardian economic expansion was most heavily concentrated. The major activities of the British engineering industry in 1914, as for half a century earlier, lay in the making of power-engines and industrial machinery and of ships and railway materials. In these fields the Edwardians were important innovators. What has been characterized as a 'minor revolution' was taking place in the industry in the quarter-century before 1914. Its roots lay overseas, but the changes, once brought to Britain, were extensively adopted. In the machine-shop, for example, a wide range of new and more specialized tools replaced the long-dominant centre lathe. These innovations deman-ded a new organization and discipline in the workshop. Emphasis came to rest increasingly on planned specialization: long-established skills were challenged, old routines shaken, and new patterns of authority established, with significant consequences both for the relationship between master and man and for the attitudes and policies of employers' organizations and trade unions.

No less important developments were occurring in shipbuilding. The reciprocating engine gave way to the more efficient turbine, and more specialized types of vessel—the refrigeration-ship and the oil-tanker, in particular—were developed to carry the new commodi-ties of international trade. Britain was in the forefront of these developments; and although in shipbuilding, as elsewhere, foreign competition was increasing in intensity, three-fifths of the world's ships were still being built in British yards in 1914. In popular estimation these innovations were eclipsed by the new emphasis on the building of large ocean-going liners, a development which reached its culmination in the laying-down of the ill-fated *Titanic*. Another luckless ship, the *Lusitania*, and the far more fortunate *Mauretania* owed their existence to an unprecedented governmental incursion into the economic field. Out of considerations of national prestige—in part to recapture the Atlantic blue riband from Germany, in part to forestall the threatened transfer of a major British shipping company into American hands—the Balfour administration in 1903 granted a loan and annual subsidy to the Cunard Line to finance the building and operation of these two transatlantic vessels. By 1907 the *Mauretania* was in service, the blue riband regained, and a precedent established which, at intervals of a generation, was to help justify similar state assistance over the next fifty years.

Important as were these developments in general engineering and shipbuilding, they were no more significant than the emergence and growth of new forms of engineering enterprise, more particularly the activities of the electrical engineer and the motor-car manufacturer. The electrical industry in Britain can trace its beginnings to the early 1880's. By 1882 a number of public buildings—the House of Commons, the British Museum, and the Savoy Theatre among them—as well as a Scottish coal-pit were lit by incandescent lamps; and in the same year water was being pumped by electric power in the Trafalgar pit on the Forest of Dean coalfield. In the course of the next few years the first private houses, in Kensington, were also lit by electricity. After these promising beginnings, progress for twenty years was disappointingly slow. The obstacles to growth were less technical than legislative and administrative, and when, towards the end of the century, the worst of these barriers were removed, the pace of development quickened appreciably; yet even in 1914 electricity's achievement fell far short of its already accepted potentialities. In street and domestic lighting, as in industrial power-supply, inroads had been made in territories where gas and steam had hitherto been dominant, but at no point had electricity gained a decisive upper hand. With transport the case was somewhat different. The long-distance conveyance of goods and passengers remained a monopoly of the steam-railway, but in towns and cities the electric tram had established a hold which, in its turn, it was already being compelled to defend against the competition of the motor-bus. Edwardian city-dwellers, like their fathers before them, might well travel home through gas-lit streets to coal-heated homes, but many of them at least could make the journey in the modern comfort of the electric tram.

In the use of electricity, as in the making of steel, Britain lagged behind both Germany and the United States, and this tardy progress was reflected in the relatively slow growth of the electrical engineering industry. After 1900, however, the tempo of activity increased. By 1911 employment in electrical engineering was approaching 100,000, while the export of electrical machinery and equipment had passed £6 million and was still growing fast. The foundations had been laid of the great companies which, in the course of a generation, were to come to positions of dominance in British industry. By 1914, for example, the General Electric Company was firmly established in London and the great steel concern of Vickers had moved into the electrical field. Vickers' acquisition of the American-established British Westinghouse Company did something to bolster British pride in an industry in which a significant proportion of the emergent enterprise was founded on American capital and to which German companies still offered formidable and successful competition overseas.

The record of the motor-car industry offers close parallels to that of electrical engineering. Though its beginnings lay in the nineteenth century, the motor-car industry in Britain was essentially an Edwardian creation. In part it was the offspring of an already flourishing pedal-cycle industry; but by 1911 the child had clearly outgrown the man. Employment in car-manufacturing had then come to outnumber that in the parent industry by three to two. After 1900 the industry's progress had been rapid; yet as late as 1913 Britain remained on balance an importer rather than exporter of motor-cars and motor-car parts. In the making of cars British manufacturers had not surprisingly conceded a long lead to the United States, with its larger population and greater transport problems. Less decisively but more surprisingly they had also fallen behind the French; and this inferiority in private car manufacture was only partially redressed by the relative success of British manufacturers in the building of public service vehicles.

The inability of Britain to lead Europe in either electrical or motor-car engineering was disquieting to observant contemporaries; so too was her relative failure in many fields of chemical manufacture. This was a long-standing weakness, but its significance seemed to grow in proportion as the twentieth-century demands on the chemical industry increased. The failings were more evident in some directions than others. In the making of synthetic dyestuffs, for example, British inferiority was such that by 1914 all but one-tenth of the dyestuffs used in this country were of German origin. In the heavy chemical industry, on the other hand, Britain was more advantageously placed, though even here ground was lost after 1900, more particularly as the electrolytic process made rapid headway in Germany and the United States.

Dismay at the inability of Britain to establish or maintain a lead

in such key industries as steel and chemicals was understandable
in a nation which had been long accustomed to an undisturbed
economic predominance; but the evidence of this comparative
failure should not be allowed to obscure the magnitude of the growth
which these industries were in fact experiencing in the early years of
the new century. Between 1901 and 1911 each of the great producer-
goods industries—coal, iron and steel, engineering, and chemicals—
increased its labour force by at least one-third. This was a rate of
expansion more than twice that of cotton and one comparing even
more advantageously with the increases in the clothing and boot and
shoe industries (5 per cent.), in furniture-making (8 per cent.), in
earthenware (10 per cent.), and glass manufacture (3 per cent.). In
building these years saw an actual decline in employment of 15 per
cent., and not surprisingly this regression was no less marked in the
associated brick-making industry.

The changing size of an industry's labour force, however, is apt to
be a misleading guide to its growth and prosperity. An industry may
increase in numbers but decline in efficiency. On the other hand
a relative decline in manpower may be not only offset by improved
efficiency but positively compelled by it. This was the case with the
boot and shoe and the clothing industries. Each had long resisted
the forces of mechanization and technological change. In both, however, at the end of the nineteenth century the machine was making
increasingly rapid headway. Change came most quickly in the
Northamptonshire boot and shoe industry, where, in little more
than a decade after 1890, shoe-making was transformed from
a thriving village industry into a monopoly of the factory-towns of
Northampton and Kettering. In tailoring and dressmaking the
economies of factory industry were less pronounced, and despite
a continued concentration of production in factories at Leeds and
elsewhere, there remained substantial pockets of shop-workers
awaiting the attentions of the Trade Boards Act of 1909, as well as
large numbers of seamstresses employed on a piece-work basis in
their own homes. No such developments in technique or organization had occurred to offset the decline of employment in the building trades. House-building, which accounted for fully six-sevenths
of the nation's building activity in 1907, was carried on in the early
years of the twentieth century with the same materials and by the
same labour-consuming techniques which had satisfied builders for

generations. The decline in building employment was no more than
a reflection of an equal recession in building activity. The 1890's
had been boom years for private building and this prosperity persisted into the new decade. By 1905, however, some decline was
apparent and the depression which gradually developed outlasted
the years of peace.

When every allowance has been made for such changes in labour
efficiency, there remains a notable contrast between the rates of
growth of those industries which principally served the industrial
producer and those which catered more directly for the needs of the
individual consumer, a contrast essentially disadvantageous to the
latter. There were exceptions to this trend. Tobacco manufacturing
was growing rapidly, as were industries concerned with food preparation; but these exceptions, though important, at best only serve to
modify the general picture. In part this emphasis on the making of
producer-goods reflected the changing requirements of the foreign
consumer, but it was also one indication among many of the way in
which, in the short run at least, the Edwardian economy was geared
to satisfy the demands of the capitalist entrepreneur rather than of
the industrial labourer.

Transport

An economy is not compounded simply of pits and mills, of
artisans and machinery. Its effective functioning demands the
services not only of factory-owners and machine-hands but of clerks,
administrators, and accountants, and no less of transport workers
and distributors. The ranks of the white-collared workers were
growing rapidly in Edwardian England. Employment in the public
services was half as large again in 1911 as it had been only ten years
earlier, while over the same brief period employment in commercial
occupations had risen by one-third and in the professions by one-
sixth; and at almost every point these increases were even greater
in the case of women than of men. The age of the typewriter and the
telephone had arrived, and in the vast reorientation of women's
work which was now in train the claims of domestic service were
already giving ground before the more persuasive attractions of the
office.

Significant as were such changes, not least for their wider social
implications, they were equalled in economic consequence by

developments in the field of transport. For over half a century the railway had monopolized all but the local carriage of passengers and goods. This monopoly remained virtually unimpaired even in 1914. From year to year, almost without interruption, railway traffic increased. There was even a modest growth in the mileage of railway track, though this was a consequence of efforts to tidy up rather than to expand the existing system. Throughout the Edwardian years dividends on ordinary railway stock fluctuated little, moving on average between 3 and $3\frac{1}{2}$ per cent. and never seriously threatening to quicken the pulse or to disturb the sleep of the cautious investor. But to those who could read the lessons of the past and the signs of the present the outlook was less certain. The road had given way to the canal, and the canal in its turn to the railway. Now, with the advent of the motor-car, the wheel was coming full circle and road transport would come into its own again.

The power-driven road vehicle has an existence almost as long as the railway engine itself. A year after the Liverpool–Manchester railway was opened in 1830 a railless steam-carriage had been put into service between Gloucester and Cheltenham; but another half-century was to pass before the internal-combustion engine could be applied to road transport. The development of motoring, like the use of electricity, was hampered in Britain by legislative restrictions, though the most irksome of these had been removed by 1900. A speed limit of fourteen miles an hour was, however, still enforced and even in 1903 this was only raised to twenty miles an hour. Yet in spite of these early discouragements the number of motor vehicles in Britain had reached 23,000 by the end of 1904. The greater proportion of these were private cars, principally of foreign manufacture; and one-third of them were registered in the London area. The motor taxi had only just made its appearance and as yet there were few motor-buses. In the course of the next few years the number of vehicles steadily increased and by 1910 the total had passed 100,000. Private motoring, however, remained the preserve of the wealthy few. Cars were expensive to buy and no less so to maintain. Doctors made increasing use of them, though many country doctors remained faithful to the horse and trap even into the inter-war years. Outside the medical profession the car tended to remain a symbol of prestige and a source of pleasure rather than the servant of business. The thin trickle of cheaper Fords which began to arrive from America in 1908 was no more than a portent of a later age of more popular motoring.

From an economic standpoint the progress of private motoring was in many respects less significant than the emergence of the motor-bus and the taxi-cab. Between 1905 and 1910 the aspect of London's streets was radically changed, not primarily through the growth of private motoring—the motorist tended to seek his amusement elsewhere—but as a consequence of the advent of the public service vehicle. At the end of 1904, 11,000 licensed hansom-cabs were sharing the London streets with two upstart motor-taxis. Six years later, the number of motor-taxis had grown to over 6,300 and there were now fewer than 5,000 horse-cabs. The victory of the motor- over the horse-bus came almost as quickly. At the beginning of 1905 only a score of motor-buses were operating in London; three years later there were a thousand, and by 1913 three times that number.

The bloodless victory of the motor-bus was not achieved, however, without at least a show of opposition. Early in 1907, for example, the motoring correspondent of *The Times* felt compelled to defend the new vehicle against its more severe detractors. He conceded that motor-buses added unpleasantly to the noise and smell of London's streets and that the mere pedestrian went in constant peril of a liberal mud-drenching. 'But', he added, 'it must be noted for the motor-omnibus that, if it distributes a thicker stream of mud laterally than do the old fashioned omnibus and its horses, the trajectory of that mud is lower and more regular than that of mud cast up by the hoofs of horses.' The motor-bus, however, had to fight more than a verbal battle. The tramcar was in its heyday. With the growth of the electric power industry it had entered the third and most vigorous phase of its brief existence. Between 1900 and 1907 the nation's tramway mileage was doubled, so that by the time the motor-bus was making its appearance in London and elsewhere, the new electric tramcars had already firmly established themselves in the streets and on the balance sheets of almost every sizeable municipality. The tramcar's struggle against the motor-bus was destined to be a losing one. The speed and flexibility of motor-bus transport would in the long run outweigh such modest, if solid, advantages as the tramcar could offer. But for a generation the tram was able to enjoy a precarious security. Local authorities who had sunk capital into cars and tram-tracks were not prepared to give them less than their full lease of effective life.

Whether in the form of tram or bus, or of the London tube—experiencing in these years its most rapid period of development—local transport made substantial headway in scope and efficiency during the Edwardian era. The consequences were far-reaching. The expansion of urban areas went forward with growing vigour. The residential central districts of Britain's towns were turned over increasingly to commerce and administration. The wealthy now sought the surrounding countryside, the poorer simply moved on to take more crowded possession of the inner suburbs. What the nineteenth-century railroad had achieved for Illinois, Minnesota, and the American territories further west, the tramway now accomplished for the more modest pioneers of Golders Green, Finchley, and Hendon. Here, as in a widening ring to the south as well as the north of the Thames, colonies of the prosperous London middle class took root and settled. At the same time areas of older development like Hammersmith and Willesden—the latter itself a creation of the transport revolution of the previous century—were increasingly given over to working-class occupation; and while these boroughs continued to grow, population decline began in the more central area. In Middlesex and Surrey the census-takers found more than one-third as many inhabitants in 1901 as they had done a decade earlier; in the county of London, on the other hand, they registered a slight decline. Similarly, while Birmingham's population grew only slowly after 1891 and ceased altogether to increase in the next decade, that of neighbouring King's Norton and Handsworth—soon to be absorbed by their predatory neighbour—more than doubled in the course of twenty years. Overcrowding, daily becoming more acute, had been among the most intractable of the problems faced by the later Victorians. Whatever their failings might be in other directions, the Edwardians had here at least laboured to good purpose. The noisy tram was the unsuspected bearer of light and health to many otherwise condemned to lives of increasing urban drabness and squalor.

If before 1914 the motor-car could still be regarded as a rich man's toy, the aeroplane was even more evidently a young man's folly. But young Englishmen were seemingly less foolhardy than their contemporaries across the Channel. The distinction of making, in

1903, the first flight in a heavier-than-air machine belonged to the Wright brothers; but after this initial American achievement, the initiative in the new world of aeronautics passed to the French. Blériot's channel crossing in 1909 shook English pride and encouraged emulation. In 1910 the *Daily Mail* offered—and duly awarded—a prize of £10,000 for a flight between London and Manchester. Though Britain in the air, as in so much else, had made a discouraging start, the leeway could readily be made good. As yet the aeroplane had no economic significance and even its military potentialities were appreciated only by the few. Aircraft were small in number and so simple in design that the cost of building a machine was no greater than that of making a motor-car. Yet, for all its crudity, the aeroplane, with the wireless telegraph, provides perhaps the most tangible evidence that this was a generation standing on the threshold of a new era, an era as rich in present promise as it was to prove pregnant with future disaster.

The State and the Economy

Such economic success as was achieved by the Edwardians owed little if anything to the promptings of central authority. Edwardian governments neither claimed nor acknowledged responsibility for the short-term prosperity or the long-term growth of the nation's economy. At its heart Edwardian England remained unrepentantly *laissez-faire* in the crucial sense that industry and trade were left to take their own course unhelped and unhindered by the ministering power of a beneficent state.

The ark of the *laissez-faire* covenant was free trade. In the increasingly competitive world of the late nineteenth century the principle and practice of free trade had more than once been put to serious question, most notably in the activities of the Fair Trade League and in the clamour for imperial preference. Yet, notwithstanding the vigorous advocacy of Joseph Chamberlain, the most the tariff reformers could achieve was the imposition in 1901 of 1s. tonnage duty on the export of coal; and even this impiety was not allowed to survive the return of a Liberal administration by more than six months. As the value of exports fell in the years before 1895, so the hopes of the reformers had mounted; but thereafter the sustained buoyancy of overseas demand cooled the expectations of even the most ardent protectionist.

As with the tariff, so with financial policy in general, the aims and attitudes of Edwardian governments differed little in their essentials from those which had dominated the nation's economic thinking since the days of Peel and Gladstone. Edwardian chancellors of the exchequer had no greater ambition than to balance their annual budgets, intent above all on avoiding deficits but equally zealously guarding against the achievement of anything more than a nominal surplus. From this standpoint one budget was very much like another. The government had no aspiration to use its spending to influence the level of investment or employment, to check a boom, or to forestall a slump. With the advent of Lloyd George it is possible to see a more conscious attempt to redistribute the wealth of the nation to the advantage of the wage-earning classes, but, for all the bitterness which it aroused, the budget of 1909 was severely limited both in purpose and effect. Though Edwardian governments were becoming increasingly spendthrift by Gladstonian standards, with first defence and then social welfare making new demands upon the public purse, their expenditure never represented more than a tithe of the nation's total outlay. Even in 1914, with the welfare state initiated and the demands of defence becoming daily more pressing, Britain was spending more on alcohol than on all the services of central government combined. Under these conditions the influence which government spending exerted on the general level of investment and consumption and on the rise and fall of business activity was bound to be limited in significance; but such as it was, it was unwilled and haphazard. It is only in so far as a persistence in free-trade attitudes and practices may itself be held to constitute a deliberate and beneficent act of policy towards the economy that British governments in these years can be said to have adopted any positive attitude towards the wider problems of the nation's economic growth and prosperity.

To speak thus of the activities of government is not to suggest the total absence of an economic policy, but rather to indicate the limitation of its objectives. And limited as were such aims, their consequences should not be underrated. Between 1900 and 1914 the scope of government legislation and activity steadily widened, touching provision for advanced education, regulation of hours and conditions of work, and, most adventurously of all, national insurance against sickness and unemployment. In general, the objects of social policy were palliative rather than preventative, but they were none the less welcome on that account. In any balance sheet of Edwardian achievement, the welfare activities of its reforming administrations must take an honoured place, even if their future promise was greater than their present attainment.

Living Standards

A modern government is expected to direct the nation's economic energies in three related directions: to the preservation of national solvency by the maintenance of a favourable balance of payments; to the promotion of long-term economic growth through the encouragement of profitable investment; and to the achievement, side by side with these, of a continuously rising standard of life equitably shared by all sections of the population. In recent years British governments have rarely found it possible to meet all these demands concurrently with equal effectiveness. By contrast the Victorians, without the benefits of central planning and direction, were able in their most prosperous years between 1850 and 1875 to achieve this combination of ends through the sheer dynamism of their economic activity. How, by such standards, is the achievement of the Edwardians to be measured?

To a generation inured by hard experience to recurrent balance of payment crises and conditioned by the exhortations of its leaders to the belief that the attainment of a favourable foreign balance is the *summum bonum* of economic existence, the Edwardian achievement may seem to fall little short of the miraculous. Only in their most golden decades had the Victorians succeeded in expanding their export trade as rapidly as did the Edwardians, and the combination of such a degree of growth with the achievement of a narrowing trade deficit was a feat which proved beyond even their vigorous capacity. Judged by the standing of her currency and the strength of her position as the world's creditor Britain's economic prestige was never higher than at the close of the Edwardian era, and the uninterrupted growth of her investments overseas gave promise of a continuing reward in days of peace and a valuable reserve against the exigencies of war.

The evidence of Edwardian achievement in relation to economic growth and rising living standards is, however, less immediately convincing and necessitates closer scrutiny. To take first the question of living standards. During the second half of the nineteenth century, and more particularly in its later decades, the standard of life of the British people had been rising steadily and appreciably. In the twenty years after 1875, notwithstanding the country's growing economic difficulties, the purchasing power of the working classes had increased by an estimated 40 per cent. This marked upward tendency was fundamentally the outcome of mounting industrial efficiency, but at the last it was more directly influenced by the cheap food which reached England in ever-growing quantities from every corner of the globe. The standard of life of the middle classes grew less rapidly than that of the workers after 1875: not only was food of more limited significance in middle-class budgets, but there was also a tendency for wages to increase more rapidly than profits and salaries. Even this difference, however, was only one of degree. If the business man never tired of complaining about hard times and declining share prices, the keeper of his household purse was happy to find her money spreading further, her larder better filled, and her home more comfortably furnished than ever before. There was, of course, poverty amidst this growing plenty, as the investigations of Charles Booth and Seebohm Rowntree made abundantly clear, and the tide of depression left its flotsam of bankrupts as well as of unemployed; but, for all the justifiable alarms which attended the years of trade depression, it was only the unfortunate few who were not appreciably better off in 1895 than they had been twenty years earlier.

During the next twenty years the advance in general living standards was at many points more restricted; between 1900 and 1910 indeed levels of consumption rose little if at all. By 1914 the average family was spending a rather greater proportion of its income on food than it had done at the beginning of the century. Englishmen were now eating more wisely, if in some respects less well, than in the recent past. They ate slightly less meat, particularly pork and bacon, but rather more dairy products, sugar, fruit, and vegetables. Such advances, however, affected the population unevenly. Food prices were rising fast, faster indeed than the incomes of the majority of the people, and the growth of the nation's food bill was as much a result of increasing prices as of improving standards of diet.

The price of coal, like that of food, was high by late Victorian standards. Coal was never dearer than in the abnormal conditions of 1900, but even at its cheapest in 1905 it was dear enough to discomfort the poorer consumer. Yet if both food and fuel were dear by the measure of the recent past, housing was relatively cheap. The building activity of the years round the turn of the century had helped to hold rents in check. In some fast-growing centres like Hull, Chatham, and above all the motor-manufacturing town of Coventry, rents did in fact rise sharply—in Coventry by as much as 18 per cent. between 1905 and 1912. But such increases were exceptional. In the larger towns, and more particularly in London, the extensive building of the years before 1905 was sufficient to hold rents firm in a period of generally rising prices: and in the smaller urban areas increases between 1905 and 1912 averaged less than 2 per cent. Homes also tended to be better furnished and equipped, though the gains—and this was equally true of clothing—were modest, and largely concentrated in the years after 1910.

For the bulk of the population the purchase of these essentials exhausted the greater part of the family income. Tobacco and alcohol—usually in the form of beer—took much of what remained, though proportionately less in 1913 than twenty years earlier. The Englishman had rarely indulged his traditional taste for beer more thoroughly than in the prosperous summer of 1899, but the Boer war and its early reverses induced a measure of sobriety which affected more than the temper of the nation. Henceforward beer consumption fell uninterruptedly until 1910 to the satisfaction of the advocates of temperance and the discomfiture of brewers, already harassed by renewed proposals for licensing reform. The decline in beer-drinking owed less to economic circumstance—though it was no doubt influenced by it—than to changing social habit. Drunkenness remained to the last a problem of the age, but the tide had turned perceptibly, if not decisively, in favour of temperance. The rich as well as the poor were becoming more abstemious and the demand for wines and spirits fell even more rapidly than that for beer. As one habit was discarded, however, another was quickly found to take its place. What they saved on beer and wine, the Edwardians spent at least in part on tea and tobacco; and the exchequer recouped from these weaknesses what it had lost to the persuasive propaganda of the temperance reformers. The cigarette came into its own. As late as 1895 little more than 5 per cent. of the nation's tobacco imports had

The Lover's Lament

AT THE LOSS OF THE

Old Steam Trams,

Electrocuted Dec. 31st. 1906.

Twas NOT SWEET OF OLD, as our love we told
On the top of the Old Steam Car,
When a wand'ring breeze, made us cough and sneeze,
With a smell, like rotten eggs and Tar!

But the lights were low, and the pace was slow,
And the corner seats were cosy,
And many a Miss has received a kiss
On the top of the Car
From Perry Barr
Or the Tram that came from Moseley!

Yes, the Electric Car, can go very far,
In a very short space of time
But that dazzling light, is FAR too bright
So each loving pair, have a stony air
Of not being aware, that each other is there
And gone are their joys sublime!

No, the fact that these Cars are painted blue
And are awfully, terribly, painfully new,
And the fact there is plenty of elbow room,
Will never make up for that friendly gloom
And the joys so sweet,
Of the corner seat
ON THE TOP OF THE OLD STEAM CAR.   F.S.R.

SCOTT RUSSELL & Co., B'HAM. SCOTT SERIES.

X. A postcard of 1906

XI. A poster of about 1910

gone into cigarette-manufacture; by 1914 this proportion had risen to 40 per cent. and it was still rising.

Whether the change from beer to tea and tobacco should be regarded as evidence of a rising or of a declining standard of life is a moot point, unresolvable by the economist, and perhaps no less by the student of ethics. But there were other, more certain, signs of an improving material existence in these years. Englishmen travelled more, not only by car but by train and bicycle, and spent more on their health and enjoyment. Southend and Blackpool—no less than Bournemouth—were expanding rapidly to meet the demands of excursionists and holidaymakers from London's east end and the industrial north-west. The music-hall, growing in popularity at the close of the Victorian era, increased its hold on popular affection; and the new cheap newspapers were in ever-widening demand. Yet significant as these changes might be, they touched only the margin of general expenditure. Over the wider areas of demand the picture which the statistics present, particularly for the years between 1900 and 1910, is of a growth in consumption disappointing in its slowness. This bleak conclusion is reinforced by the estimates of real wages which suggest that the working man could command no more goods and services in 1913 than he had done in 1895 and that his purchasing power had actually declined in the course of the Edwardian decade itself.

Statistics are fallible and those of real wages in particular may be all too easily distorted by a variety of errors and misjudgments in compilation and interpretation; but the cumulative evidence which the statisticians present is too overwhelming for its trend to be ignored. What then becomes of the notion of Edwardian prosperity, of that 'thrice happy first decade' of good living and extravagance? Did it exist merely in the imagination of those who, facing the uncertainties of a later era, exaggerated every symptom of well-being in a vanished world? Or is it rather that, with the Edwardians, riches and poverty went hand in hand, the rich becoming wealthier as the poor became more numerous? Expert witnesses can be called to support both points of view. Charles Masterman in 1909 condemned the growth of extravagance in a society where poverty was still so tragically evident. 'Public penury, private ostentation,' he declared, 'that, perhaps, is the heart of the complaint.'[1] A decade

---

[1] C. F. G. Masterman, *The Condition of England*, 1909.

later Arthur Bowley, himself a young Edwardian as well as an eminent statistician, expressed a different opinion. 'I think', he wrote, 'that the increase of luxury and the abundance of wealth which many people believed they observed before the war were illusions, fostered by the newspapers.'[1]

The working classes for their part were not unaware that the world's increasing riches were passing them by. Though as yet denied the sophisticated evidence of the cost-of-living index, they were reminded daily that prices were rising and that wages at best were struggling to keep them company. But the bare equation of earnings and living costs, whether crudely effected in the mind of the wage-earner or more carefully assessed by the statistician, needs some modification if it is to do full justice to the facts of the worker's existence. Account must be taken of variations in employment opportunity, of changes in hours and conditions of work, and of the influence on living standards of public measures for the advancement of social welfare. At all these points the Edwardian wage-earner was better placed than his Victorian father had been. In neither of the two most serious years of industrial stagnation—1908 and 1909—was unemployment as severe as in 1879 or as in the long depression between 1884 and 1887; hours of work were in general reduced—in coal-mining by legislation, and elsewhere, as in cotton, by negotiation—and conditions of employment were improved, not least as a result of the passing of the Trade Boards Act of 1909; while the National Insurance Act gave limited but valued benefits to wide sections of the working community.

More fundamentally, the crude index of real wages misleads in so far as it gives no weight to changes in the balance of occupations within the economy—to the trend from lower to higher paid industrial occupations and from manual to office employment. In the problems which came with stagnant wage-rates and lack of employment the bricklayer might find some compensation in seeing his children established in an engineering shop or, even more desirably, in an office. But such consolations were not for all. The first decade of the twentieth century was no time to be old and caught in a declining or unfashionable trade; or yet to be employed in an occupation, such as railway-working, where custom and industrial

[1] A. L. Bowley, *The Change in the Distribution of the National Income, 1880–1913*, 1920.

discipline had tended to fossilize earnings. If some groups, like the miners, were appreciably better placed in 1914 than they had been twenty years earlier, and others had succeeded in holding their own in face of price inflation, there were many whose lot had been less fortunately cast. With all its measure of increased opportunity and leisure, the Edwardian economy wore only a thin veneer of prosperity in the eyes of large numbers of the wage-earning class.

Declining though they might be in proportion to the size of the general population, the industrial working class remained much the largest and yet the most cohesive of the nation's major groupings. The minority—perhaps one-quarter—of the population who earned their living other than by their hands included not only the employers of labour in town and country, from small farmer to business tycoon, but also tradesmen, lawyers, teachers, clerks, and typists, as well as a small company of rentiers, maintaining themselves by rents, dividends, or pensions. The fortunes of this multifarious assortment of the great and little were as varied as were the upper and middle classes themselves. For those with fixed incomes—landowners with land let on long leases, holders of consols and railway stocks, and some professional men and pensioners—the rising cost of living meant increasing economic difficulty: but inflation, which dealt harshly with the less fortunate, also brought opportunity and profit to the industrialist and the investor.

In little more than a decade before 1914 the share of the national income accruing to the profit-earning classes increased by more than 15 per cent. This advance was most apparent in the case of overseas investment, which grew both in size and profitability and which, however much it might ultimately benefit the economy as a whole, gave its most immediate and spectacular returns to a city minority. The experience of the investor at home was more varied. After the lean years of the early nineties, holders of industrial shares had received a welcome fillip in the renewal of prosperity after 1895. By 1900 many share values had appreciated by as much as 50 per cent., and though the trend over the next decade was on balance towards recession rather than further advance, these limited losses had largely disappeared by 1913. Even when allowance had been made for changing money values, the industrial investor had every reason to feel in better heart in 1913 than he had done two short decades earlier. If the high hopes of 1900 had scarcely been realized, at least the fears bred of the bitter experience of 1886 and 1893 had proved equally without justification. The economy, as seen through the weather eye of the stockbroker, was notably resilient, offering less than the expected quota of upsets and showing at the last a welcome capacity for expansive growth.

Not all industrialists and investors, however, shared equally in the fruits of rising prosperity. In cotton the trend to higher returns was unmistakable. The industry's tide of fortune had finally turned in 1898; dividends in spinning were consistently attractive for the next fifteen years, and never more so than in 1907 and 1908. 'At this time', it has been said, 'a man who couldn't make cotton pay had to be in some way mentally deficient.' Investment in coal-mining was no less rewarding. Between 1899 and 1913 coal was yielding a profit of 1s. a ton, the equivalent, so it was estimated, of a return of 10 per cent. on the capital employed in the industry. During the previous quarter-century coal-owners had had to content themselves with no more than half that amount. Coal and cotton were no doubt among the more prosperous sections of the economy, but their achievement was exceptional only in degree. There were some, nevertheless, to whom the benefits of prosperity came both less profusely and with less consistency, and some for whom the note of prosperity had a wholly hollow ring. Of these last the most conspicuous were the builders and those with whom their fortunes were inevitably linked. But such unfortunates were a minority in a nation where by 1913 the investor could face the future with an expectation borne high by the reality of present success.

The appearance of middle-class prosperity was accentuated by two further features of Edwardian society, whose pervasive influence was to deepen as the new century unfolded itself. The one was a falling birth-rate, the other a growing tendency for wealth to concentrate itself in the nation's capital. Between 1901 and 1911 the population of Great Britain increased from 36 to 41 million.[1] This rate of growth, though rapid by the standards of subsequent decades, compared unfavourably not only with that of contemporary Germany and the United States but also with Britain's own past rate of increase. The cause of the decline is evident enough. Though the death-rate was falling more rapidly than it had ever done in the

---

[1] These figures apply only to England, Wales, and Scotland. The figures for Ireland are 4·45 and 4·4 millions.

past, the birth-rate was also dropping sharply. Between 1900 and 1914 the crude birth-rate fell by no less than 10 per cent., a decline attributable in part at least to the spread of birth-control. It was among the middle classes that the practice of family limitation took earliest and firmest root. In the endless struggle to keep up appearances, made more difficult by the growing scarcity of cheap domestic labour, the middle-class family made a virtue of smallness. The traditionally large Victorian household gave place to the small family, frequently of two children or less. The house itself might now be more modest but the possibility of higher living within its walls was enhanced, and this was especially the case in the first generation when the advantage of fewer mouths to feed, and of fewer children to educate, was felt more strongly and immediately than any prospective loss of family earning power.

At the same time, the appearance of prosperity was also magnified in the public eye by the increasing wealth of London. In part this wealth was an outcome of new industrial development on the city's outskirts, but it arose far more from the nature of Edwardian prosperity with its emphasis on trade, shipping, and overseas investment. The lion's share of the profits in all these fields fell to city men and it was the wealth of the city that made possible the good living of London's outer suburbs and the extravagant gaiety of her west end.

This brief and inevitably limited survey of the changing kaleidoscope of her people's experience provides clues to many Edwardian problems, not least to the paradoxical existence of an outward show of high prosperity and the concomitant prevalence of smouldering discontent. The bias in income distribution in favour of the employing classes was less pronounced than some contemporaries believed, but it was real enough. The disparity between the fortunes of capital and labour became more apparent after 1910 when general prosperity and the ostentatious luxury of the few made the relative poverty of the many at once more conspicuous and more galling; and it was in these years of rising national wealth that discontent flared into open revolt. The roots of the bitter strife which now overtook wide sections of industry went deep, and more than the standard of life was in question. In the conflict the prosperous miner found himself no less involved than the depressed railway-worker; for if the railwayman had seen his earnings outstripped by the upward movement of prices, the miner was no less conscious that his wages had failed to keep pace with the rising tide of profit. Beneath the immediate economic controversy lay a deeper issue of which it was part cause, part consequence, the problem of a society not only 'fissured into an unnatural plenitude on the one hand and ... an unnatural privation on the other',[1] but divided no less in sympathy and feeling. Class divisions were never so acutely felt as by the Edwardians: the world of Forsyte comfort was also that of *Strife* and *The Silver Box*.

The Edwardian failure to raise general living standards was, however, as much a failure in accumulation as in distribution, a failure to create wealth as well as to exercise an effective stewardship over it. In one respect the Edwardians might claim that the times were against them. Their immediate predecessors had improved the standard of life less through any positive efforts of their own than through a windfall cheapening in the price of the commodities which they obtained from overseas. This uncovenanted benefit slipped away from the Edwardians to the particular disadvantage of those classes for whom cheap food was the first essential of comfortable existence. Rising commodity prices, however, brought gain as well as loss. If they increased costs, they also quickened overseas demand; and the evidence of this is plain in the soaring total of British exports. The demands upon her export industries might have been expected to revitalize the whole of Britain's industrial economy, but in the event production rose no more rapidly after 1900 than in the preceding two decades. In the conditions of a sellers' market which obtained in the early years of the new century it is difficult to see how a greater increase in productivity could have failed to bring forth its answering demand; but so long as production lagged, so long also would a latent consuming power lie unawakened. If, therefore, the key to Edwardian prosperity lies in trade, the clue to its limitations must be sought in industry.

The reasons for this shortcoming in industrial efficiency, the most fundamental of all Edwardian economic weaknesses, are complex, but sufficient has already been said to suggest their nature. To criticize industrialists for their failure to maintain Britain's nineteenth-century supremacy in the world of nations is to ignore the basic facts of economic life: to criticize them, on the other hand, for

[1] Masterman, op. cit.

failure to make full use of the resources still at their command is at once more justifiable and more pertinent. The relative failure to increase the productivity of British industry derived in part from a shift of emphasis in the direction of industries with little or no scope for increasing returns—most notably coal—and in part from past neglect; but it was also a consequence of present conservatism and complacency. The Edwardians were not unaware of these failings. Fact-finding missions went to the United States—not for the first or last time—and returned to emphasize British shortcomings in management and enterprise, more particularly the unwillingness of employers and employed to experiment with new methods and machinery and the tendency for industrial control to settle in the hands of family dynasties and of the elderly. Not all these lessons went unlearned, but the mood of self-criticism was short-lived. In an era of expanding trade it was all too easy to be complacent and forget the lessons of the past. Thus, although the Victorians, for example, had come to accept, in practice if not in theory, the view that economic success flows most readily to the big battalions, the trend towards large-scale enterprise and industrial combination, which had gathered pace in the years of stagnant trade, lost ground after 1900, and the rationalization of industry was checked rather than accelerated.

Investment

If the Edwardians were less successful in increasing their creature comforts than in paying their way in the world, how successful were they in providing for their successors? This was not a thriftless generation, judged at least by the standards of the immediate past. Edwardian investment was widely spread. It built not only factories and shipyards but houses, schools, and tramways, and these not in Britain alone but in every continent. Yet this very diversity prompts its own questions. Was too much capital sent abroad? Was that at home employed as well as it might have been?

Throughout the nineteenth century British foreign lending had not only benefited both borrower and lender but contributed indispensably to the growth of that international economy on which the nation's general prosperity so much depended. With the growth of new industrial nations no less well equipped to play the role of international creditor doubts arose about the wisdom of these extending commitments. 'Great Britain', it was said, 'was fast equipping less developed countries with instruments of production which would enable their cheaper labour to be used in competition with that of British workers';[1] and in the process her own industries were being deprived of the resources which would have improved their own competitive efficiency.

How justifiable were such criticisms? The facts, at least, are hardly in dispute. The closing years of the Victorian era had been distinguished by large-scale investment at home and by a relatively low level of capital export. Home investment continued to dominate the financial picture, though each year to a lessening degree, until in 1907 it was finally overtaken by investment overseas. Thereafter, though the extent of domestic investment was in no sense negligible—its relative decline may be attributed at least in part to the ending of the building boom—overseas lending remained in the ascendant until 1914. It was this late burst of foreign lending, in seven years exceeding £1,000 million, which raised a fierce and continuing controversy.

Capital invested abroad by the mid-Victorians had produced a threefold return. Most obviously it had brought back dividends; but it had also meant orders for British goods, and in due course cheaper materials and food for British industry and its workers. This multiplication of bounty was no longer assured in the changed world of the twentieth century. Though dividends were no less abundant, orders might well go not to Britain's manufacturers but to her competitors; and these same competitors shared to the full in the benefits of an increased supply of cheaper food and raw material.

The Liberal answer to such arguments was at once simple and classical. To buy in the cheapest and sell in the dearest market was an axiom justified as much by experience as by logic. As custom went to the cheapest producer, so capital should be allowed to flow to the highest bidder, whether he be at home or overseas. But even if this principle is accepted, its practice in the conditions of the Edwardian era seems of doubtful wisdom. The Liberal argument rested at the last on the assumed existence of a free market. But Britain after 1900, as for a generation before, was facing competition not from open but from protected economies; and, even within Britain itself, it is doubtful whether the channels of enterprise were as untrammelled as the *laissez-faire* argument presumed.

---

[1] G. D. H. Cole and R. Postgate, *The Common People, 1746–1946*, 1946.

British industrialists had traditionally supplied much of their own capital needs by ploughing back profits and by short-term borrowing. The London capital market had bent its major energies to satisfying the wants of government, of public authority, and of the overseas borrower: its services to industry were of recent date and as yet limited in scope. In consequence, while established industries like coal and cotton had little difficulty in meeting their requirements, free money seeking profitable investment was all too easily attracted overseas. There was as yet no obvious place in this scheme of things for those new industrial enterprises on which the nation's rapid economic growth so largely depended. It was, therefore, perhaps a failure of institutions as much as of enterprise itself which accounted for Britain's laggardly performance in the industries of a new age.

If the conditions of a free economy tended to make British investment less effective than it might otherwise have been, a similar criticism may not unjustly be levelled at her governments' doctrinaire persistence in policies of free trade. The arguments which the electors so resoundingly endorsed in 1905 have, in more sophisticated form, been re-endorsed by latter-day commentators. Free trade and all that went with it made the wheels of commerce move the faster to the benefit of the world in general and of Britain in particular. Yet it is at least arguable that, by the end of the nineteenth century, a selective tariff, designed solely to protect rising industries, would have brought substantial benefits to the British economy. British car-manufacturers, for example, could then have faced their French competitors on equal terms. Instead they found themselves back-markers in the industrial race, frustrated by foreign tariffs from effective competition in European markets yet themselves without benefit of comparable protection at home. Such conditions inhibited that full growth of diversity and flexibility in the nation's economy on which its success in the highly competitive world of the twentieth century was so largely to depend.

Conclusion

The indictment of Edwardian economic achievement is thus a formidable one. Beneath a society glittering in its surface splendour lay an economy in which wealth was becoming not less but more unevenly divided and in which the forces of economic growth

themselves seemed unnecessarily held in check. Even if it be conceded that many of the ills of the Edwardian economy were inherited
— that the decline in industrial investment and productivity, for
example, had set in a generation before—it is hard to deny that the
Edwardians were slow to adjust themselves to the conditions of a
more favourable era. Yet justice perhaps as much as charity demands
that the final word should be of achievement rather than of failure,
of the reality of Edwardian prosperity rather than of its limitations.

These were not wholly locust years. It was no fault of the Edwardians that their most substantial achievement, the amassment of vast
reserves of credit overseas by the vigorous pursuit of foreign trade,
was so largely dissipated in four years of war. The surplus had been
bought at a price—the narrowing trade gap was as much a reflection
of a failure to consume as of a capacity to sell—but its gains, realized
and prospective, were none the less considerable. At home the two
decades before 1914 saw a notable extension in the amenities of
urban life. Not all such advances left their mark on the nation's
income statistics, but they added materially to the well-being and
comfort of its citizens. Edwardian prosperity itself, with all its
limitations, had also its own advantageous qualities. If the tide of
prosperity ran slowly—too slowly for many—its course at least was
generally smooth. Those who had known the wilder fluctuations and
the deeper depressions of the last quarter of the nineteenth century
could be thankful even for so small a mercy. And if the Edwardians
displayed a greater tendency than their Victorian forefathers to set
leisure above wealth in their calendar of values, is this wholly to be
held to their discredit?

At the last, moreover, the Edwardians revealed an unwonted
capacity for grappling with their most fundamental difficulties.
Between 1909 and 1914 the level of general investment and industrial activity—outside building—was rising as rapidly as at any
time since 1875; and though the major problem of economic justice
loomed large and unresolved, its settlement had at last been brought
within the frame of government policy. A generation like the present
which, no less than the Edwardians, faces its own problem of reconciling economic growth and solvency with an improving standard of
life, and which stands with them under the same judgment of
complacency, should not perhaps weigh even these limited achievements too lightly.

4

DOMESTIC LIFE

MARGHANITA LASKI

DOMESTIC LIFE

In so far as any single group in a community imposes a popular image of its domestic life on an age, for Edwardian England that group was the very rich. From a variety of popular media the simplest among us has at least a crude impression of an aristocracy and a plutocracy whose gay and often gaudy glitter was maintained by hierarchies of submissive servants, of homes adorned—as George Duke of York wrote to his wife in 1901—'with all that Art and Science can afford', the backgrounds for gargantuan dinner parties and gorgeous balls in the metropolis, and for week-end parties of near-feudal splendour in the country. Because it is the rich who impose this image and because it is the rich who can take fullest advantage of the new range of choices—social, technological, aesthetic—that an age has to offer, any account of Edwardian domestic life must give to the rich more attention than their numbers might seem to warrant.

But if the popular image is that of the glitter and gaiety of birth and wealth, novel readers have rather found their characteristic pictures of domestic Edwardian England in the drabber lives of different sections of the middle classes. Wells has provided many of them: Ann Veronica struggling to free herself from the cramping respectability of the suburban home; Joan and Peter, children of the intelligentsia, brought up to awareness of high thinking and freedom and beauty; and, lower down the social scale, poor Mr. Lewisham with his futile hopes of living the life of an educated man on an income of a pound a week, and Mr. Polly's melancholy ill-fed life among the smaller shopkeepers. Galsworthy uncovers the moral weaknesses of the solidly established professional classes, Bennett's Vera tries to enliven provincial business life with dainty and daring touches, and Mr. J. B. Priestley, looking back on his boyhood, recalls the merriment, the innocence, and the aspirations of the small business and professional families of Yorkshire. There were so many kinds of middle-class domestic life in Edwardian England that no general picture can serve.

For the domestic lives of the upper working classes, the skilled craftsmen and artisans, little material exists and no general picture emerges. For some, we know, domestic life must have expanded and improved with higher wages and increased amenities; for others, as branches of skilled hand-work fell into desuetude, there must have been degradation and loss. But the few details that emerge, mostly from autobiographies, justify few general statements about lives that must often have varied greatly from region to region and even from trade to trade. Finally, if we turn to the reports and social polemics of the period, we come to the domestic lives of the poor, the overcrowded, underpaid, underfed lives of ugly, stunted, unhealthy people among whom, says J. C. Drummond, 'malnutrition [was] more rife . . . than it had been since the great dearths of mediaeval and Tudor times'.[1] The Edwardian poor have attracted strangely little attention in imaginative literature and play almost no part in commonly held images of Edwardian England. But to look at the domestic lives of the poor, both urban and rural, is to shadow our pictures of upper and middle-class life with horror and dismay.

Numerically the demand on our attention of the rich or even of the middle classes as a whole is slight. In 1901 there were seven million households in England and Wales. Only 400,000 people declared their income for tax purposes at more than £400 a year, and income tax, which started on incomes of £160 a year, was paid by fewer than a million people. As Peter Laslett[2] puts it, 'the famous middle class of literature and reminiscence turns out to be largely a matter of aspiration, imitation and snobbery. A third of the population was trying to live in a way that only a seventeenth of the population could live.' Another third of the population was living in penury, on incomes too low for the maintenance of working efficiency. 'It has been hazarded as a guess', says Laslett, that the distribution of incomes in Edwardian England was just about as unequal as it has ever been anywhere.'

Domestic Service

Never again would the pleasures of domestic life be sustained

---

[1] J. C. Drummond and A. Wilbraham, *The Englishman's Food*, 1939.
[2] *The Listener*, 28 December, 1961.

by the labours of so many people who themselves enjoyed few
if any of them. In 1901, of four million women in employment,
one and a half million, that is, nearly half, were in domestic
service. The 1901 census had coined the phrase 'standard of
comfort', this standard being the number of domestic servants per
hundred separate occupiers or families (excluding hotels). Not
surprisingly, in different parts of the country the standard varied
greatly. In Hampstead there were eighty female domestics to every
hundred occupiers, in Rochdale only seven. In Westminster, to
every hundred occupiers there were twelve menservants. Ten years
earlier, in 1891, of London families who kept servants, not quite
half had more than one servant and nearly one-tenth had more than
three; by 1951, only 178,000 women and men together were in
domestic service, employed in only 1 per cent. of households including institutions and hotels. Certainly the period up to the first
world war was the last in which servants formed a stable and
formally hierarchical society, probably the most stable and
formally hierarchical of those years. But this is to speak only of
the servants of the rich. In the middle classes the usual grumbles
about the difficulties of finding servants and their misdemeanours
when found—grumbles as perennial as those at the uncouth behaviour of the younger generation—had begun to strike a new note.
Already in 1895 the *Quarterly Review* had written, 'London servant
girls of fair intelligence will not for long consent to spend their days
in cellar chambers and their nights in inhuman attics. . . . Women
of the middle class, who need domestic servants, had better therefore become wise in time.' But signs of growing wisdom did not
appear. Mrs. C. S. Peel, writing in 1902, explained, 'The young
working-girl of today prefers to become a Board School mistress, a
post-office clerk, a typewriter, a shop girl, or a worker in a factory—
anything rather than enter domestic service.'[1] Like the earlier
writer, Mrs. Peel did not blame the girls. Their choice was made, she
says, not so much for lighter work or better pay, but because 'in
these professions she has the full use of her hours of liberty, and,
more important reason than all, she enjoys a higher social position:
she is in point of fact a "young lady"'. Mistresses, Mrs. Peel com-
plains, are no longer interested in their craft. They despise and
know nothing of housekeeping and fail to train their daughters to

[1] *How to Keep House*, 1902.

run a home. The remedy for the servant problem, she suggests, is to make housework 'more fashionable'; but it is a remedy that was not applied.

In any genteel home there was plenty of work to keep the servants fully occupied from about 6.30 in the morning till 10.30 at night or even later, for personal servants at least must wait up until their masters and mistresses chose to go to bed. In some measure the great amount of work to be done derived from the nature of the equipment still generally in use—the coal fires, the oil lamps, the inadequate hot-water and sanitary systems—and as modern equipment was installed the labour required dropped. Not only, for instance, did it take less time to switch on and off a radiator or electric light than to lay, light, and feed coal fires, trim lamps, and often clean up the ravages they made when they smoked, but with the new fuels the rooms and their furnishings kept appreciably cleaner and the actual amount of housework needed was substantially reduced. But at least as potent a demand for servants' labour arose from the formality of the lives lived. To take only one example, if the family was of the class that made and received calls, some servant must be on duty at the front door all afternoon and some servant must be available to bring up the tea. Even if only one general servant is kept who shares the housework with the mistress, that servant must still, by 3 o'clock, have finished all her heavy work and be ready, properly dressed, to do both these tasks.

But though increase in domestic conveniences and decrease in formality would gradually reduce the number of servants needed, it would never again do so to the point where the supply exceeded the demand, and, as the writers quoted have indicated, it was already more difficult to find new servants than it had been a generation earlier. There was an increasing disinclination to employ menservants, who were more expensive, less biddable, and needed a licence costing 15s., but this hardly helped. Such a great country-house as Chevron, in V. Sackville-West's novel *The Edwardians*, where service was hereditary, would still have few difficulties, though even there young Frank, the son of the estate carpenter, disturbs tradition by choosing to work in a garage rather than serve the great house. Registry offices abounded, but for really high-class servants the best method was thought to be use of the advertisement columns of the *Morning Post*. At a pinch, job servants could

XII (*a*). Boy Scouts 1909

XII (*b*). Girl Guides 1910

XIII (*a*). Vacuum Cleaner at Work

XIII (*b*). A Gentleman's Bathroom

be found, but these came expensive; a cook, for instance, would receive between 10s. and £1 a week with her food, washing, and beer, a housemaid between 10s. 6d. and 15s. Of more regularly employed job servants, a washerwoman would get between 2s. 6d. and 3s. 6d. a day and a charwoman 2s. 6d. a day, both with food, beer, and sometimes fares included.

The servant-keeping class, however, was not co-terminous with the rich or even with the comparatively well-to-do. All upper and middle-class people kept servants, but servants were often kept in at least the upper working classes as well, here not so much to maintain the pattern of a formal and complicated way of living as for needed assistance in the often painfully hard task of maintaining even a poor Edwardian home. Jack London,[1] in his first peregrination into what he calls the Abyss, London's east end, was startled to have a working-class door opened to him by a servant, a 'very frowzy' slavey who might well have been one of those half-timers or 'partial exemption scholars' the Fabian reformers were so vehement about, a child over 12 who was allowed by law, after attending school for half the day, to work for not more than $27\frac{1}{2}$ hours a week. Even in a middle-class home such a girl need be paid only 3s. a week; in poor districts she might get half a crown, but where regulations were not strictly enforced it was possible to find children of more tender years working for far less: we hear of a girl of 6 who acted as nurse-maid for 29 hours a week at a wage of 2d. and her food.

These poor drudges have little in common with the boys and girls who, at the age of 14, entered service as a profession where there was a settled hierarchy of advancement, and prospects far above the common lot of the working classes: from hall-boy (or, in an old-fashioned house, from page-boy or 'buttons') at between £8 and £16 a year, through under-footman (£20 to £35) and upper-footman (up to £50) and so on to butler with a possible top wage of as much as £100 a year; from between-maid (or 'tweenie') at between £10 and £18 a year, through under-housemaid (£16 to £20) and upper-housemaid (£18 to £22) to head-housemaid at between £24 and £30 a year; or from scullery-maid at £12 to £18 a year through kitchen-maid and all the ascending varieties of cook—plain cook, good cook, professed cook—right up to cook-housekeeper who, at the top of her profession, might earn £80 a year.

[1] *The People of the Abyss*, 1903.

Clearly the patterned and often comparatively well-paid lives of such servants supported a considerable industry devoted to their needs, as we may see if we consider the servant in her bedroom in

Servants' Press Bedsteads.

No. 79.—**Low Press Bedstead,** painted Oak, with iron lath bottom,
3 ft. 3 in. high.

3 ft. 3 in. by 6 ft.............................. £3   3   0

If with sacking bottom in iron frame, 10s. extra.

The Bedding measurement for this is 3 ft. by 6 ft.

From a Heal & Son catalogue

a wealthy Edwardian home at about 6 o'clock in the morning. The servant—assuming, for the moment, that admonitory image, the good mistress—sleeps on a servant's bed, often 2 feet 6 inches wide as against the more usual 3 feet. By 1901 even a servant's bed might be made of wood instead of iron, and cost, with wood lath spring bottom, about 25s. A 'Plain Woollen Flock Mattress for Servants' Beds' could be bought for 10s. with a feather bolster for 4s. 6d. and

a grey goose-feather pillow for 3*s*. 9*d*. A pair of York blankets—all
blankets were sold in pairs—cost 6*s*. 6*d*. and cotton pillowcases
about 1*s*. 9*d*. each. Sheets might be bought by the pair (between
about 5*s*. 9*d*. and 6*s*. 6*d*. for plain Bolton sheets), or, more economically, unbleached calico sheeting costing from 10*d*. to 1*s*. 4*d*. a
yard could be made up into sheets at home. The bed itself, to save
space, might be made to fold into a 'press'.

A suite for a servant's bedroom, consisting of toilet table, wash-
stand, chest of drawers, towel-horse, and chair, could be bought for
between three and four pounds, the floor covered with oilcloth or
rush matting and the windows hung with casement cloth, perhaps
the most popular fabric of the period for cheap clothes as well as for
furnishings, available for as little as 4¾*d*. a yard. The good mistress
or housekeeper would insist on the importance of keeping bedroom
windows open; servants often came from unhygienic conditions and
their rooms must be ventilated, if necessary against their will. But it
would be foolish to assume that all mistresses visited their servants'
rooms or gave them such equipment as that described. There were
many 'inhuman attics', as the writer in the *Quarterly Review* called
them, and Mrs. Hodgson Burnett, in *A Little Princess* (1905),
describes one such:

This was another world. The room had a slanting roof and was whitewashed. The whitewash was dingy and had fallen off in places. There was
a rusty grate, an old iron bedstead, and a hard bed covered with a faded
coverlet. Some pieces of furniture too much worn to be used downstairs
had been sent up. Under the skylight in the roof, which showed nothing
but an oblong piece of dull grey sky, there stood an old battered red
footstool.

Even if the fireplace had been in good condition, it is unlikely that
a fire would have been laid there. Only top servants and visiting
ladies' maids had this privilege, and it is improbable that the central
heating, if this had been installed, would have extended so far. In
winter the servant must gain what warmth she can by dressing
quickly in the clothes she had bought at one of the many local Bon
Marchés which specialize in her needs: in ribbed vest at 3¾*d*. or
'combies' at 10¾*d*., in *broché* corsets at 2*s*. 11*d*., in stockinette
directoire knickers which new would have cost 3*s*. 11*d*. but were
reduced, slightly soiled, in the autumn sales to 1*s*. 6¾*d*. which
brought them nearly down to the price of casement cloth knickers at

1s. 0¼d.; in a moirette skirt (petticoat) at 1s. 6¾d., in cashmere hose at 1s. 9d. for two pairs (in summer, lisle), and then servants' special non-creaking shoes, spring (i.e. elastic) sided at 2s. 11d. All these would, of course, be provided by the servant herself, and so would her morning print dress and apron and cap, unless her mistress required her to wear uniform. The lady's maid did not wear uniform, but a black or dark skirt and blouse over which she might, in the course of her work, don a dark apron. The butler wore dark trousers, a dark tailcoat, and a white shirt and collar, and the footmen would be similarly dressed unless in livery; for the footmen the morning toilet must include shaving, since only a soldier servant might wear a moustache.

Almost all day and almost every day the servants worked. In a large household the young maids might get a sit-down in the afternoons while they mended the household linen, but they must soon be on their feet again to prepare tea for the servants' hall, though the good mistress will see that the youngest of them are in bed soon after ten. Only the butler was allowed, as a matter of prerogative, to go out for an hour or so before luncheon or dinner, and sometimes both, though the good mistress with a good cook was advised to be lenient on this point. For the others, one free day monthly, a half day on Sunday, and one free evening a week was a generous allowance of free time, and possible only where a considerable staff was kept. A fortnight's holiday a year was usual. To detail the servant's labours would require (and in the period often received) a substantial chapter. We can do no more than glimpse them now and again at one or other of their tasks.

Dwelling-Houses and Accommodation

Between 1 April 1901 and 31 March 1911 approximately 981,000 dwellings were built. No figures are available to show how these new houses and flats were distributed among the different classes; but the usually execrable housing conditions of the poor, both in town and country, and the many complaints that the Local Government Act of 1894 which instituted parish councils had not been used, as it could have been, to implement the building of cottages for agricultural labourers, suggest that the proportion of new upper- and middle-class houses to those for the working classes did not correspond to numerical representation or to most urgent needs.

'It is the day of the smallish country house', wrote the architect Ernest Newton, commenting that country seats and noblemen's mansions were no longer built. To build a smallish house was reckoned in 1906 to cost about 8*d*. a cubic foot in the country, about 10*d*. a cubic foot nearer London. Many fanciful plans exist for houses that architects hoped might prove tempting to clients, but it is safer to examine those that were built, and such is 'The Haven', designed for a site in Surrey by the progressive architect M. H. Baillie Scott. 'The Haven' cost £2,300 to build, including stables and outbuildings, with all structural work in English oak and with floors of oak and maple throughout. The accommodation consisted of drawing-room, dining-room, boudoir, studio, and billiard room; eight bedrooms (of which two were servants' bedrooms) and two bathrooms, one being a downstairs bathroom that also served as a cloakroom; a kitchen with pantry, larder, and servants' w.c.; and, in outhouses, a cycle-shed, a wash-house, a coal-shed, stables, harness-room and coach-house. This bare description does not convey that 'The Haven' was a House Beautiful indeed. (The sequent 'Beautiful'—we find House Beautiful, Garden Beautiful, even God's Acre Beautiful—was much used by those whose visions rested rather on a hierarchical medieval utopia than a socialist and egalitarian one.) It was built round a central courtyard to give 'the suggestion of a little inland haven enclosed and sheltered'. Half-timbering and leaded glass windows adorned the garden front. The billiard room and the 'dining-hall' were in the Tudor style with exposed beams, deep fireplaces, and heavily latched doors. It is almost a surprise to learn that the architect has remembered practical needs to the extent of placing under the bathrooms a heating chamber 'which is utilized for heating generally and also the hot water for the baths'.

'The typical Garden City house is a small one', wrote C. B. Purdom of Letchworth,[1] where the first residents were mostly business and professional men, and a typical house at Letchworth will serve as a model for the suburban dream-house of the period. It contained on the ground floor a living-room with built-in window-seat and inglenook, a kitchen and larder, and, reached from the outside, a coal-shed and earth closet; and on the first floor three bedrooms, bathroom, and separate w.c. Such houses, deliberately and nostalgically

[1] *The Garden City, a Study*, 1913.

looking back to the cottages of William Morris's dream of John Ball's England, would be the chosen dwellings of those who shared what R. C. K. Ensor[1] has called 'a generous and Utopian atmosphere of socialist enthusiasm'. Those who did not, still looked back, but to periods of greater pretensions: to Queen Anne or Georgian for the 'smallish country-house' and to those confused and grandiose dreams which lay behind the semi-detached villadom that in the Edwardian period, as before and after, extended the towns further and further into the countryside.

Only a few fortunate working-class families might hope to enjoy the amenities of new model cottages. £150 was reckoned to be the most a landlord could be expected to pay to provide often desperately needed rural housing, and the Country Cottages Exhibition of 1905, sponsored by the *Spectator* and the *Country Gentleman* at Letchworth, showed what could be done for this sum—though it was feared that most of the visitors were gentry, looking for cheap week-end cottages. At a capital cost of £150 or a little more and an inclusive rental of 5s. a week, a cottage could contain a living room, scullery, and three bedrooms of adequate dimensions. A few cottages might have bathrooms or a fixed bath in the scullery, and these were said to be popular. The notion that the working classes should have bathrooms was beginning to take root, though with many reservations.

It must be frankly admitted that the average cottager would have little use for it, and in such families it is often only the children who enjoy a weekly 'tub'. A recent inspection of some model cottages in which the greater part of the scullery floor-space was taken up by a full-sized bath left one wondering as to the probable uses to which it would be put—whether the cottager would find it a handy place for storing potatoes, for instance.

Thus Mr. Baillie Scott,[2] as architects go progressive and even utopian. The most usual reaction is probably typified by the response of the landowner to the delegation of farmworkers asking for a rise: 'You'll be asking for bathrooms next.'

But with or without baths model cottages were few. Those dreadful insanitary cottages which, in Victorian novels, provided justification for the hero and repentance for the squire, persisted

[1] *England, 1870–1914*, 1936.
[2] *Houses and Gardens*, 1906.

into the Edwardian era, despite the efforts of many real-life Louis Fitzjocelyns, Robert Elsmeres, and Little Lord Fauntleroys. In most villages labourers' cottages were overcrowded and in deplorably poor condition. The average family of an agricultural labourer was one of four to six children and the average cottage contained only two bedrooms. The admirable social researches of the period have provided many descriptions of rural living-conditions: for instance six people in a two-bedroomed cottage in Oxfordshire, rented at £2. 10s. a year, where only one bedroom could be used in winter because of the cold, and the two beds had only one pair of thin blankets between them; a two-room cottage in Yorkshire, rented at 1s. 11d. a week, inhabited by man and wife and five daughters, the bedroom filled by two large bedsteads with father, mother, and baby in one, the next two girls in the other, and the two oldest girls sleeping in a rough loft—the only other bedroom furniture is a chest of drawers and there is no carpet or rug on the red-brick floor. In Somerset, where overcrowding was especially gross, in 1913 the medical officer of health found one two-bedroomed cottage where three boys and two girls slept in one room, and the mother with three other children in the second; in another cottage, two boys of 16 and 19 and two girls of 14 and 19 all shared a room. Most cottage bedrooms were so small that the volume of air per person was grossly insufficient. In one bedroom of 700 cubic feet slept three people of both sexes aged 15, 20, and 21; in two bedrooms of 660 and 480 cubic feet slept a mother and eight children. Even common lodging-houses had to allow 300 cubic feet for each adult, 150 cubic feet for each child under 12; and the eighth annual conference of the Independent Labour Party, held in Glasgow in April 1900, recommended that this minimum should be doubled in each case. Indeed the late Professor Huxley had reckoned that 'to be supplied with respiratory air in a fair state of purity, every man ought to have at least 800 cubic feet of space to himself'.

According to the registrar-general's definition, overcrowding was said to exist when the average number of people per room (not per bedroom) was more than two. Bad as were the conditions in the country, they were inevitably worse in the towns. The 1891 census, that available to Rowntree when he wrote his classic study of conditions in York,[1] showed that in Glasgow, the worst

---

[1] B. Seebohm Rowntree, *Poverty, a Study of Town Life*, 1901.

town in the kingdom, 59 per cent. of the population was over-crowded by this standard. In London the figure was 19 per cent., though it must be remembered that there the figures for, say, Bethnal Green, with 315 inhabitants to the acre, were balanced by those for, say, Mayfair. In the east end of London overcrowding often meant beds let on the three-relay system—three tenants to a bed, each occupying it for eight hours, and the floor space below the bed similarly let. Some cases cited include a room with cubic capacity of 1,000 feet, three adult females in the bed and two adult females under the bed; and a room of 1,650 cubic feet with one adult male and two children in the bed, and two adult females under the bed. In York only 6·4 per cent. of the population was technically overcrowded, but what this meant in terms of accommodation is shown by some of the cases investigated by Rowntree. The official designation of overcrowding, he points out, ignores the fact that in overcrowded homes the actual number of persons per bed-room exceeds four; the average air space available is less than 300 cubic feet per person. On a September evening in 1900, with the outside temperature at 50° Fahrenheit, Rowntree investigated the condition of bedroom windows in York. In the highest type of working-class houses, those of the well-to-do artisans, he found 10 per cent. of the windows open; in the lowest, the typical slum dwellings, only 3 per cent. of the windows were open. Both in town and country many working-class people must have woken up with severe headaches, and indeed the report of H.M. commissioners for inquiring into the conditions of the working classes stated that overcrowding was a greater cause of deterioration in health than were infectious diseases.

Decoration and Furnishing

In Edwardian England, for people who decorated their homes consciously rather than accidentally, there were two basic styles to choose from, as there had been since William Morris's work first became known. One style sought to create an impression of wealth, the other, of a special kind of poverty. The wealthy style, which is always expressed in terms of dark shiny woods, rich colours and fabrics, curves, gilding, and elaborate ornamentation, at this date leant on the antique rather than on the contemporary and admitted a wide range of periods: Tudor, Jacobean, Queen

Anne, and Chippendale pieces, sometimes genuine and sometimes not, often jostled each other in the same room, and antique collecting was a fashionable pastime. (Durlacher, in Bond Street, was a favourite dealer.) But inevitably, as in every period, there might be a considerable variance between the smartest rooms and those that would later be influenced by them. Miss Sackville-West describes the drawing-room of some old-fashioned aristocrats as it appeared to a fashionable lady:

The very rooms in which they dwelt differed from Sylvia's rooms or the rooms of her friends. There a certain fashion of expensive simplicity was beginning to make itself felt; a certain taste was arising, which tended to eliminate unnecessary objects. Here, the overcrowded rooms preserved the unhappy confusion of an earlier day. Little silver models of carriages and sedan-chairs, silver vinaigrettes, and diminutive silver fans, tiny baskets in silver filigree, littered the tables under the presiding rotundity of the lamp-shade. (Sylvia noticed, with amusement, that no ash-trays were included among this rubbish.) Palms stood in each corner of the room, and among the branches of the palms nestled family photographs, unframed, but mounted upon a cardboard of imperishable stiffness. . . .

Yes, certainly the room was overcrowded, There were too many chairs, too many hassocks, too many small tables, too much pampas grass in crane-necked vases, too many blinds and curtains looped and festooned about the windows. . . . Everything had something else superimposed upon it; the overmantel bore its load of ornaments on each bracket, the mantel-shelf itself was decked with a strip of damask heavily fringed, the piano was covered over by a square of Damascus velvet, on which more photographs and more ornaments were insecurely balanced. In the centre of the room stood a sociable. . . .

It was after this model that what H. G. Wells calls 'an ordinary English living-room' in a lower-middle-class home was constructed:

It was a small, oblong room with a faint projection towards the street, as if it had attempted to develop a bow window and had lacked the strength to do so. On one side was a fireplace surmounted by a mantel-shelf and an 'overmantel', an affair of walnut-wood with a number of patches of looking-glass and small brackets and niches on which were displayed an array of worthless objects made to suggest ornaments, small sham bronzes, shepherdesses, sham Japanese fans, a disjointed German pipe and the like. In the midst of the mantelshelf stood a black marble clock. . . . The mantelshelf itself and the fireplace were 'draped' with a very cheap figured muslin. . . . The walls were papered with a florid pink wallpaper, and all the woodwork was painted a dirty brownish-yellow colour and 'grained' so as to render the detection of dirt impossible. . . . There were flimsy things called whatnots in two of its corners, there was a bulky veneered mahogany chiffonier opposite the fireplace, and in the window two ferns and a rubber-plant in wool-adorned pots died slowly upon a rickety table of bamboo. . . . There was a steel engraving of Queen Victoria giving the Bible to a dusky potentate as the secret of England's greatness; there was 'The Soul's Awakening', two portraits of George and May, and a large but faded photograph of the sea front at Scarborough in an Oxford frame. A gas 'chandelier' descended into the midst of this apartment . . . and the obliteration of the floor space was completed by a number of black horsehair chairs and a large table, now 'laid' with a worn and greyish-white cloth for a meal.

The second style, though tinged now with the eccentricities of *art nouveau* and sometimes, at its worst, known as 'Quaint', derived directly from the work of William Morris, and was characterized, then as later, by the use of light-coloured natural woods, waxed rather than polished, fabrics of wool or cotton rather than silk with a strong bent towards the apparently hand-woven or hand-painted, and clear bright colours. The dream it enshrined was not that of wealth or noble ancestry but rather of an egalitarian peasant utopia, a synthesis of Morris's postulated future world of Nowhere and his postulated medieval world of John Ball. At its worst the dream became enshrouded in an escapist mysticism of castle rather than cottage. A living-room was called a hall, a lady's bedroom a bower, small windows made of tinted glass were recommended so that the harsh intrusion of reality might be avoided, and one architect, proposing inscribed mottos for beams and walls, suggested that 'to still further conceal the heart of our mystery it may be well that they should not only be written somewhat illegibly but also in a foreign tongue'.

But these were ephemeral excesses. Characteristically this style was simple, clear, and open, and moreover was now for the first time available at reasonable cost. Where Morris's own furniture was hand-made and therefore expensive (as indeed the furniture of Voysey, Lethaby, Barnsley, and Gimson continued to be in our period), Mr. Ambrose Heal, who entered his family's old-established upholstery business in 1893, set about producing well-designed, machine-made furniture at moderate cost and, what was more, with far greater attention paid to comfort than had been usual in this style. Settles were still made. A settle in an ingle-nook might be considered the typical furnishing of an Edwardian Home Beautiful. But now it would have cushions on it. Heal's oak 'country cottage' furniture—windsor chairs, gate-leg tables, dressers, bookcases— were of designs that have retained their capacity to please. His carpets designed by Voysey were often of a beauty that makes one regret their disappearance, and the rush mattings at 2s. 3d. a square yard ('very "cottagey" and inexpensive') have held their popularity to the time of writing. As always with this style of furnishing there is a moral undertone of protest, and Heal's catalogue of 1909 describes the interior it is designed to supplant:

In the 'cottage of gentility', that of the weekender, instead of a homely and comfortable simplicity, we find all the pretentious stuffiness of the suburban villa, the 'new art' overmantel smothered in rococo photograph frames, ineffable green grotesques of cats and other depressing forms of pottery.

Inevitably, in view of its origins, this style was also recommended for the artisan instead of 'the unserviceable inanities of the ordinary artisan's cottage parlour, the "suite" in imitation "saddlebags", the stained and sticky table which affords a ricketty [sic] stand for the glass case of waxed fruits'.

But many cottage sitting-rooms had less, aesthetically and physically, than this. Here, from Rowntree and Kendall's *How the Labourer Lives* (1913) is the room of a farm-labourer earning 17s. a week, the only sitting-room for father, mother, and five children:

There is a bright fire in the living-room, but it is very obviously the abode of poverty. There is no carpet on the stone floor, but a good-sized hearthrug and a smaller rug, both of them made out of clippings by Mrs. Arthur, and two small bits of sacking. The place is clean and fresh. The wall would do with a new paper—the last, as Mrs. Arthur explains, having been put on when 'there weren't so many of 'em'. But it is not likely to get it. Four or five almanacs are hung up, and on the mantelpiece are two gaudy advertisements, duplicates of 'Price's Child's Night Lights', two old vases, a clock, and various tins. There are five wooden chairs, including a small high-chair, a stool, and a wooden table.

But though poor, this room is, as the authors say, 'clean and fresh' and there is house-proudness in the attempts at decoration. None of this can be said of many urban slums. Here is Rowntree in his earlier book, reporting on a house in York:

Two rooms. Seven inmates. Walls, ceiling, and furniture filthy. Dirty flock bedding in living-room placed on a box and two chairs. Smell of room from dirt and bad air unbearable, and windows and door closed. There is no through ventilation in this house. Children pale, starved-looking and only half clothed. One boy with hip disease, another with sores over face.

Finally, a room in the east end of London, described by Jack London:

It was not a room. . . . It was a den, a lair. Seven feet by eight were its dimensions, and the ceiling was so low as not to give the cubic airspace required by a British soldier in barracks. A crazy couch, with ragged coverlets, occupied nearly half the room. A rickety table, a chair, and a couple of boxes left little space in which to turn around. . . . The floor was bare, while the walls and ceilings were literally covered with blood marks and splotches. Each mark represented a violent death—of an insect, for the place swarmed with vermin.

Hygiene and Sanitation

Among the extremely poor, as for many years before and after our period, there was no knowledge of hygiene and few opportunities for its practice if known. In poorer districts many houses all over the kingdom were without water taps or any form of sanitary accommodation. A typical description of such conditions comes from Dr. Alfred Salter when he visited a maternity case in Bermondsey at the turn of the century:

It was a cold day, but the family was so poor that they had not even a penny to put into the meter for heat. The house was one up, one down, with a small scullery and no backyard except for a shut-in paved area, three feet deep. Drying and washing were done in the front court, where, at the other end, there was *one* stand-pipe for twenty-five houses, with the water 'on' for two hours daily—though never on Sundays. There was no place to wash in—no other water to wash with. There was no modern sanitation. There was *one* water-closet for the twenty-five houses and a cesspool. Queues lined up outside that water-closet, men, women and children, every morning before they went to work. . . . There was no possibility of decency, modesty or health for these people. . . . The conditions of thousands of homes were the same.[1]

[1] A. F. Brockway, *Bermondsey Story, the Life of Alfred Salter*, 1949.

And not only in Bermondsey, but all over the country. In York, for instance, in 1899, 15 per cent. of all the houses in the city were without separate water supplies and here, too, as many as twenty-five houses shared a single tap. In such conditions a mother is not likely to squander $1\frac{1}{4}d$. on a cake of toilet soap, $1\frac{3}{4}d$. on a toothbrush, nor can she inculcate regular hygienic habits of any kind, even if she knows what these are.

Yet whether with main drainage in the towns or a septic tank in the country, there was now no technical reason for the water-closet situation to be other than satisfactory. The comparatively new wash-down closets, some with high cisterns, some of the 'low-down suite' type, adequately disposed of detritus and no longer presented a danger to health. But these were far from universal. Many older closets of the pull-up handle type were still in use, and of these many, as those of the earlier flushing kind, could exude miasmic odours into the house. Memories of illnesses caused by inadequate sanitary systems were still lively among upper-class housewives, who were advised to keep a look-out for sore throats in the servants whose duty it was to empty slops. These, and other more utopian considerations, often dictated the use of an earth-closet rather than a water-closet in country houses, sometimes even where main water and drainage were available. The earth-closet had been invented in 1860 by the Rev. Henry Maule; an improved model, that of Dr. Poore, was installed in many houses in Letchworth, and as late as 1900 portable earth-closets and commodes were being advertised for use in bedrooms, sickrooms, and nurseries. Only the largest houses would be likely to contain more than two water-closets, one in the downstairs cloakroom and one in, or more usually adjacent to, the single bathroom: the chamber-pot, usually sold as part of a toilet set, was in constant use, slops being emptied, if necessary, three or more times a day.

These toilet sets are worth a moment's consideration, for many of them were extremely pretty. A simple set in willow-pattern or plain cream Wedgwood could be bought for 7s. 6d., the basic set consisting of basin, ewer, soap dish, brush jar, and one chamber-pot; toilet pails and sponge-bowls were extra. But more fanciful sets were available: in Old Staffordshire style at 9s. 6d., in Spode at between 25s. and 32s., and, oddly, in plain clear glass at 21s. Especially suitable for the week-end cottage or garden-city house were sets in 'the rougher hand-made pottery, thrown on the wheel, [which] will appeal to those who prefer to retain the mark of "the potter's thumb"'. But the potter's thumb always comes expensive in an industrial age, and Heal's asked between 15s. and 22s. 6d. for these.

At the beginning of our period the making of toilet sets must have represented a not inconsiderable industry, for even by 1900 the water-closet system had not reached many towns and was far from common in many more. At Liverpool and Coventry, for instance, most houses had water-closets by the beginning of the century, but in Blackburn and Wigan fewer than half. Water-closets began to be introduced into Manchester only in 1898, and the pail system, in which large pails supplied by the municipality were more or less regularly emptied, was at that date still in force in many other Lancashire towns. As Dr. Salter indicated, in poorer districts water-closets were rare indeed and other arrangements usually inadequate. In York most closets in working-class districts were midden privies in which closet and ashpit were combined, the refuse from both accumulating in a brick-lined pit. Until 1901 the corporation made a charge of a shilling every time a midden privy or ashpit was cleared, thus, as Rowntree drily remarks, 'giving a householder a strong inducement to allow refuse to accumulate for as long as possible'. Yet in York, as in many other cities, an association between inadequate sanitation and such almost endemic diseases as enteric and typhoid had been unassailably established.

But even supposing that the slum dweller could endure the outrageous stench of the midden privies, many of which leaked and distributed filth all over their own and adjacent floors, these were not often readily available. Out of 11,560 houses investigated by Rowntree, 3,130 or 27 per cent. (over 20 per cent. of all houses in York), had no separate closet accommodation, and in some cases one closet served 15 houses; in Bermondsey, as we have seen, it might be one closet to 25 houses. Here, certainly, the conditions of the rural labourer were an improvement on those in the poorer districts of the towns.

Yet, at least when out of England, the rich had at this date something of the reputation for an obsession with plumbing that the Americans were later to acquire. In Dinard, in Pau, and all along the Riviera coast, only those hotels with *l'installation hygiénique* could hope for English patronage, and, wrote C. F. G. Masterman:[1] 'At Biarritz to-day, the villas which are not entirely sanitary do not let.' No doubt, as is not uncommon, the travellers demanded more abroad than they expected at home, for in an English upper-class home after the servants' breakfast a typical hub of activity would be that around the housemaids' closet where the maids would be filling the hot-water cans, cans of polished brass or enamel ware or painted to resemble grained wood, each covered, when filled, with a folded towel or perhaps a beribboned cosy from a charity bazaar. In few bedrooms were there fitted basins, and in very few houses more than one bathroom. An English architect, commenting on an American house-plan, remarks, 'American characteristics will be recognized in the ample cupboard-space provided in the bedrooms and the servants' bathroom'; and Mrs. Peel, writing in 1933 of the house in Brompton Square that she modernized in 1900, says, 'Neither architect nor builder suggested central heating, a second bathroom, or, indeed, any labour-saving arrangements.'[2]

In a rich home it was perhaps in the bathroom that art and science were most happily combined. The most expensive fixed baths were of porcelain crockery, made in one piece, standing on four complicated legs and elaborately decorated on the outsides; but cast-iron baths were coming in, and by 1910 were widely available at popular prices. The more expensive baths often had elaborate shower arrangements enclosed in glass or curtains at the tap end; or a separate shower might stand in a corner of the room. A heated towel-rail was already a pleasant luxury; so were the metal fitments for tooth-glass, tooth-brushes, sponge, and soap affixed to the wall, and the convenient looking-glass hung over the pedestal wash-basin. At best, walls and floor might be of marble; more often, the walls would be tiled or half-tiled in white, and the floor covered with linoleum or the new cork carpet. Windows, again at best, could be of stained glass; or they might be frosted, or merely covered with a fancy opaque paper. Where there was no separate housemaid's closet, the hot-water cans would have to be filled at the bath, which would soon gather some ugly marks from the unavoidable knocking.

With a week-end house-party the single bathroom would be

---

[1] *The Condition of England*, 1909.
[2] Mrs. C. S. Peel, *Life's Enchanted Cup*, 1933.

reserved for the ladies, and possibly only for the lady of the house. For the visitors, and certainly for the gentleman visitors, portable baths would be available, morning or evening or possibly both. After the maid had come in with the early-morning tea and biscuits (Osbornes, 7*d*. a lb., Thin Arrowroots, 8*d*., Digestives, 9*d*.), had drawn the curtains and lit the fire, the bath, which had been standing out of the way against a wall or under the bed, would be set on its bath-sheet before the fire. Several shapes were available, the hip, the saucer, and, often used for children, an egg-shaped bath with a lid which could be packed full of clothes when the family went on holiday. As in later periods towels ranged from the exiguous to the ample, and soap from a plain coal-tar or brown windsor to Floris's Carnation soap at 4*s*. 6*d*. or even their Royal Violet at 6*s*.; a honeycomb sponge of good quality could cost 30*s*. or more.

Heating, Lighting, and Housework

The use of fuels, whether for lighting, cooking, or heating rooms or hot water, was very much in a transition stage. A new house of any size would almost certainly be lit by electric light, whether from the mains in town or from an electric-light plant in the country; or a new or newly done-up country-house might be lit by acetylene or air-gas. But in older houses, and even in houses where electric light had been partially installed, the back quarters might for some time yet be lit by gas or oil lamps or, in the servants' bedrooms, candles; one candle a week per servant was considered a fair allowance for this purpose.

In only a very few houses would a kitchen fire not need to be lit first thing each morning. In these a gas cooker might have been hired from one of the gas companies who supplied gas at prices ranging from 2*s*. 10*d*. to 6*s*. per cubic foot. In a small flat the washing-up water was sometimes heated on a gas cooker and the bathroom served by a gas geyser; or, in a larger establishment, a multi-point pressure heater (the first, the Ewart 'Califont', came on the market in 1899) could heat water for every tap on the circuit, with the single disadvantage that hot water drawn at one point entailed only cold water from another. Or—rarely in 1901 but increasingly through the years—cooking could be done by electricity, whether on an electric stove or by means of separate pieces of electric equipment, such as stewpans and kettles; by 1906 the

XIV. Teddy Bear and Bassinette 1911

XV. Works Canteen 1908

king's yacht had been fitted up with 'a complete electric outfit, including soup and coffee boilers, hot-plates, oven, grills and hot-closets'. But though the probable future of electricity as a means of cooking was well recognized, its costs were hard to reckon and most people were still chary of installing it for this purpose. In 1902 the cost per board of trade unit was between 4d. and 6d., with lower daytime charges to encourage use; by 1906 it had in some places come down to as low as 2d. a unit. Writers on domestic crafts extolled electricity's advantages of cleanliness and the economy of being able to turn it on or off at will; a house fully equipped with gas and electricity could, it was fairly said, dispense with the services of at least one servant. But so far as cooking, warming, and water-heating went, solid fuel still overwhelmingly held the field.

So it was almost certainly a solid-fuel stove that cook-general or kitchenmaid must light as soon as she came down in the morning, whether a range, fixed in place with brickwork, or a kitchener, standing on four legs and potentially if not actually movable. If the cook was fortunate, the old-fashioned type of cooker, in which control of dampers provided hot water or a hot oven but seldom both, had been replaced by one in which the hot-water boiler was directly over the fire and no heat need specifically be diverted to it. But for a large house, and especially where there were central-heating radiators, an independent boiler would almost certainly have been installed. A modern, moderate-sized cooking stove would need its chimney sweeping every six weeks or so, and would burn about a ton of coal in forty days. On an average the price of coal could be reckoned at about £1 a ton, but the variations were great, depending not only on quality, but also on district and on quantity bought. As with many other commodities, the poor, buying in small quantities, paid the most; a hundredweight of coal seldom cost as little as 1s. and might be as much as 1s. 6d. On the other hand, coal bought in or near the collieries might cost only 14s. a ton, and even in London five tons of coal bought at a time could come at the rate of 15s. the ton.

Fireplaces burning coal were responsible for a great deal of domestic work, both indirectly in the amount of dirt they caused and, more obviously, directly. Before a family came down to breakfast all fireplaces must be tended and this could not but take

M

some time, even if the fireplace was a modern one, built to throw out the utmost amount of heat and with an aperture then thought to be the probable minimum of 1½ feet high by 2½ feet broad. A coarse cloth is laid on the rug before the fireplace and on this is placed the housemaid's box containing black-lead, brushes, leathers, emery paper, cloths, and utensils for cleaning the grate; beside or beneath the receptacle for these utensils is the cinder-pail for the ashes, a japanned pail with a wire-sifter inside. The ashes, swept up, are deposited here, the cinders being reserved for use in the kitchen or under the copper. The black-lead is laid on with a soft brush, then brushed in with another, and then polished. The new fire is laid—first paper, then dry kindling, then coal—and the polished parts of the grate rubbed up with the leather. The fire is lit and, at intervals throughout the day, looked in on and when necessary replenished. If the fireplace is in constant use, the chimney will need sweeping every quarter; if a chimney should catch fire and prove not to have been swept for three months, the householder is liable to a fine.

The labour involved in tending grates made for eager exploration of new methods of room heating. Some favoured slow-combustion stoves, burning only about a scuttle of coal a day, or a ton in four months; or anthracite stoves which, although they tended to give off noxious fumes, had the not inconsiderable advantage in soot-laden air of burning smokeless fuel—it was reckoned that six tons of solid matter, consisting of soot and tarry carbohydrates, were deposited every week on every quarter of a square mile in and about London; or gas fires; or, most convenient of all, electric radiators which could be moved about at will.

The actual housework, like the fuel situation, was in something of a transition stage. The importance of labour-saving devices was now widely recognized by progressive housewives if not yet by builders. Gadgets for the cook were nothing new, but a sink in the kitchen rather than the scullery was still something of an innovation. Books of domestic instruction still contained receipts for making polishes for furniture, silver, brass, and boots, but proprietary goods, many of them still known at the time of writing, were already widely available—Ronuk or Johnson's furniture polishes, Bluebell metal polish, Goddard's plate powder, Nugget boot polish, and Meltonian cream. Carpets might still be swept with a broom after tea-leaves had been strewn to lay the dust and to give a pleasant aroma, but they might equally be swept now with a patent carpet-sweeper (in 1906 Bissell's cyclo-bearing carpet-sweepers were advertised in five sizes costing from 9s. 9d. to 17s. 3d.), or with that new English invention of 1901, the vacuum-cleaner. The earliest vacuum-cleaners consisted of machines on wheels, drawn up outside a house and inserting their nozzles therein. Soon portable domestic models were available. The first of these, costing, in 1905, between twelve and fifteen guineas, were hand-driven and ponderous, needing one servant to push the machine along and another to turn the handle; by 1906 an electrically operated vacuum-cleaner, costing about £35, could be operated by one servant.

The vacuum-cleaner will not yet help with the dusting and this, in an Edwardian drawing-room filled with knick-knacks, was a necessarily slow task, demanding much care. A patent knife-machine may be available to help the hall-boy or under-footman to clean the knives, but there are no machines to help clean the boots and shoes, to fill the scuttles, or to trim and fill the oil lamps. And there will be few, if any, labour-saving devices to help the 'tweeny' or 'up-and-down girl' who belongs to the housemaid in the morning and to the cook in the afternoons.

Electricity was already lightening the task of the lady's maid with electric irons, curling-tongs, driers for use after shampooing— for the lady's maid must be a skilled hairdresser. But only hand labour will suffice to clean the $2\frac{1}{2}$ yards of brush-braid sewn round the inside hem of her mistress's skirt to catch the mud, and this could be a good hour's work. The valet, too, must spend considerable time first thing in the morning brushing the master's clothes which he has brought down the evening before and then taking them up to the dressing-room after a housemaid has cleaned and dusted it and lit the fire. Then he must air the body-linen before the fire, lay out the clothes for the day, and set and strop the razors, and be capable, if need be, of shaving his master. The safety-razor had been on sale since the 1880's, but its use was still looked upon as somewhat unmanly.

Where means allowed, no small part of the Edwardian servants' time was taken up with the preparation and service of meals, of which a country-house breakfast may serve as an extended example. With the reception-rooms cleaned, the fires laid and lit, the newly pressed clothes taken up to the bedrooms (where a valet or footman is not kept, a parlourmaid will leave the clothes of gentlemen guests on a chair outside their room), the inkwells filled, sometimes the newspapers ironed and the mistress's small change washed, the servants will have sat down to their own breakfast at about 8 o'clock, the valets and ladies' maids in the steward's room (if such there be), the housekeeper in her own room, and the other servants in the servants' hall; though in some homes, it need hardly be said, the servants or even a single servant must eat at the kitchen table. After this breakfast, while the ladies and gentlemen were making their toilettes, the dining-room would be prepared for breakfast which would not be served until 9 o'clock or even 9.30.

A plain damask cloth is laid over the baize on the dining-room table and a sideboard cloth on the sideboard. 'A touch of refinement', said Mrs. Beeton,[1] 'is added by plants and flowers', but despite the new enthusiasm for cut flowers in the house, some people considered greenery on the breakfast table a little genteel. Where several dishes are to be served, the table will be laid with three knives and two forks for each person, a small plate for bread and butter, and a serviette (so-called) between the knives and forks. Some symetrical order should be maintained in the placing of salts and peppers, butter, toast, marmalade and, sometimes, fruit. The tea and coffee equipages may stand either at one end of the table or on the sideboard with the cups and saucers, the bread, and the fruit-plates. Cold dishes (ham, tongue, potted meats, sardines, &c.) may be placed on either table or sideboard and so may the hot dishes, kept warm by spirit-lamps. At this meal it is more usual for guests to help themselves than for the servants to stay and serve them. In some houses the lady guests are not expected down to breakfast and may not descend until half-past twelve. In very few houses now are guests expected to attend family prayers before breakfast or, indeed, are family prayers held at all.

But the body is amply sustained. Two 'simple' breakfasts (the epithet is Mrs. Beeton's) suitable for large parties are as follows:

Winter	*Summer*
Oatmeal Porridge	Wholewheat Porridge
Kidney Omelet	Ham Omelet
Baked Eggs (*au gratin*)	Poached Eggs on Toast

[1] *Mrs. Beeton's Book of Household Management*, edition of 1906.

Fried Cod	Fried Whiting
Grilled Ham	Grilled Kidneys
Potted Game	Potted Beef
Veal Cake	Galantine of Chicken
Stewed Prunes and Cream	Strawberries
Scones, Rolls, Toast, Bread	Scones, Rolls, Toast, Bread
Butter, Marmalade, Jam	Butter, Marmalade, Jam
Tea, Coffee, Cream, Milk.	Tea, Coffee, Cream, Milk.

The distinction between the seasons seems fine indeed.

Upper- and Middle-class Housekeeping

Clearly a substantial Edwardian home required considerable organization, and the housekeeper's job or, in her absence, the mistress's, was no sinecure. Ideally the good mistress should be in the kitchen quarters before 10 in the morning, inspecting the contents of the larder, making lists for the tradespeople, seeing that the back-premises are clean and in order. Even the best of cooks must be closely supervised to prevent her taking advantage of the many possible ways of cheating, and to forbid all perquisites was not to ensure that they were not taken. Many cooks assumed they had rights in all dripping, bones, jars, and bottles,[1] and it was the good mistress's duty to see that if dripping was sold, lard and cooking-butter were bought with the proceeds, and that the rag-and-bone man should not be allowed to call, for bones should be used for stock, and jars and bottles returned to the purveyor. Then the milkman, unwatched, would often give short measure, paying the cook a small fee not to notice and so gaining a few pints to sell for his own benefit. But not enough mistresses were good mistresses, not enough housekeepers reliable housekeepers, and in some households waste, improvidence, and virtual embezzlement prevailed.

Extravagance among the very rich was often gross, and not only among the typical *nouveaux riches* of the period, the colonial millionaires who had made their piles in South African diamonds or Australian gold. The perquisite system among the servants often amounted to theft, and in taking no steps to check it the rich were accused of creating plague-spots of corruption. There were great

[1] It will be remembered that some ten years earlier there had been a disturbance in the Pooter household, when the charwoman was accused of taking 'some kitchen fat and leavings' home with her.

houses of which it was said that not only was every boy and girl
who took service there corrupted, but neighbouring villages as well.
Mrs. Peel writes of one household of thirty persons, excluding all
guests, where the expenditure per head per week on food and cleaning materials came to £4, though all mutton, game, rabbits, garden
produce, milk, cream, butter, and eggs came from the estate; and to
eat £4 of food a week was virtually impossible. One ducal establishment had three turtles, costing £20 each, sent down from London
every week-end in case they should be wanted; usually they were
thrown out to rot. In another house the chef never taught his under-
lings to examine eggs before mixing them, so if one egg was tainted
in a basinful of thirty or forty, the whole lot was thrown away.
Though the number of households in which such excesses took place
must have been, in numbers, comparatively few, the anecdotes
circulated and were admired rather than deplored. The tone was set
for a desired atmosphere of careless extravagance, and the conspicuous display of the period was apparent rather in waste than in
good housekeeping.

But to achieve this effect, even in moderated form, good housekeeping was in most households essential, and the mistress must
make a serious approach to the duty of budgeting her household
allowance. Mrs. Peel reckoned at the beginning of the period, that
8s. 6d. a head per week would suffice for 'plain but sufficient living',
10s. for 'nice living', 15s. for 'good living', and between 17s. 6d. and
£1 for 'very good living'.[1] Middle-class budgets are generally
estimated on an annual basis, and here, to start with, is the budget
of a well-to-do middle-class family, living near London. The family
consists of husband, wife, three daughters (aged 14, 16, and 18) and
two grown-up sons who are already in business and so need only
small allowances. The family income is £2,000 a year.

	£
Rent, rates, and taxes	300
Boys' allowances @ £50 each	100
Governess and classes for girls	100
Dress and personal allowances of husband and wife @ £100 each	200
Wine	50
Coal and light	45

[1] Almost identical estimates were made by middle-class domestic advisers in the
1930's.

Wages (manservant £50, cook £30, kitchenmaid £16, 2 house-
    maids @ £20 and £16, sewing-maid £25)   .   .   .   157
Washing @ £2 per week   104
Housebills for 14 people @ about 12s. per head, not including
    garden produce, flowers, and some eggs and poultry, but
    including occasional dinner-parties   437
Garden and stable expenses, including wages of 2 men and 1
    boy and keep of 2 cobs   300

                                      Total   £1,793

leaving £207 for doctors, holidays, &c.

From such a budget much can be inferred. More than a quarter of
the total income is spent on servants, whose numbers exceed
those of the family. Apart from the amount of service provided,
no very extravagant living is possible. The family holidays, with the
servants on board wages (between 10s. 6d. and 15s. 6d. a week,
exclusive of firing and light) can hardly amount to much more than
a brief period at a seaside resort—perhaps Bexhill where mixed
bathing has just been introduced, though the custom will quickly
spread. The girls and the governess, it might be felt, come off
meagrely, and certainly the sum provided would have been insufficient to send the girls to one of the good new boarding-schools
like Roedean where, in the uniform jibbahs and cloaks, they could
enjoy such amenities as the swimming-pool, the carpentry shop, the
domestic science wing, and the splendid playing fields for hockey
and lacrosse, cricket and tennis. Nor would the wife have much
opportunity to set up as a local leader of fashion, though no doubt
the sewing-maid was a great help.

    Meals would undoubtedly be satisfying but not, except for parties,
'fancy'. Edwardian recipe-books give the impression that middle-
and upper-class meals tended to consist of elaborately decorated
constructions for the purposes of entertaining, and sufficient but
gastronomically dull food for purely domestic purposes; as compared with cookery-books of the first half of the nineteenth century,
a deterioration in the quality of recipes is marked. In the light
of later knowledge, some of the culinary practices seem distressing:
thus the cook was advised, if she suspected the meat might be going
'off', to half-cook it, in which state it would keep better, and the
practice of putting meat to be boiled in hot, not cold, water was still
not general. True, Liebig, some fifty years earlier, had said that hot

water was the better method, but Escoffier had said that it was not, and 'in these matters', as a late-Victorian cookery-book had complacently remarked, 'we prefer the chef to the chemist'.

For likely meals for a family such as this Mrs. Beeton is a helpful guide. As compared with her 'simple' country-house breakfast, a suitable breakfast for this family would seem almost spartan; say, porridge, poached eggs on toast, sausages, marmalade, toast, scones, bread and butter, tea or coffee; or, more economically still, only one main dish such as boiled eggs, finnan haddock, or brawn, with a choice of only bread and butter or toast. In summer the porridge might now be replaced by one of the new breakfast cereals from America, such as shredded wheat or those cornflakes which the law of England forbade to be registered under their original name of Elijah's Manna[1] and which therefore came to England in 1908 as Post Toasties.

Searching Mrs. Beeton's pages for a winter family luncheon to present as a suggested menu to her mistress, the cook of such a family might have proposed veal cutlets, cold roast beef with baked potatoes, apple-tart with custard, beetroot, pickles, butter, cheese, biscuits, and fruit; and for summer, salmon mayonnaise, grilled cutlets with potatoes, cottage pudding, and again butter, cheese, biscuits, and fruit. For dinner the family would eat formally, even without guests, though a four-course—as opposed to a possible five- or even six-course—meal may suffice, say, haricot bean soup, braised sweetbreads, roast fillet of beef (roasted, probably, in a patent bottle-jack roasting-screen which needs winding up only twice during cooking for the meat to be sufficiently turned) with cauliflowers and mashed potatoes, a choice of apricots condé or soft roes on toast, and then cheese and dessert. The servants will, at least officially, eat more simply: a suggested day's menu for the servants consists of cold lamb, salad, stewed fruit, and rice pudding for midday dinner, and for supper, cold meat and pickles.

But if meals on this budget must be rather economical than lavish, the allowance for wines can be considered at least adequate at a time when whisky was available at between 37s. and 66s., hock at from 24s. to 126s., claret at from 12s. (ordinary) to 400s. (Château Lafite), and champagne, the most widely drunk of

---

[1] Breakfast cereals had originally been developed as a suitably pure food for Seventh Day Adventists awaiting the Second Coming.

all wines, at between 66s. and 156s. The prices are for a dozen bottles.

Some allowance for alcoholic drinks is found in almost all middle-class budgets. Thus, two ladies living in a country town on £500 a year spend £18 on wines and aerated waters (soda-water costs about 1s. 3d. per dozen bottles), and even on as little as £200 a year, £5 is allowed for wines. At least where a manservant is kept, household beer is still provided, and a barrel of beer is often kept in such working-class homes as can afford it. If bought in smaller quantities, a pint of beer will cost a working man between 2d. and 3d.; the cheaper 'dinner ale' costs 1½d. a pint.

But there were large tracts of teetotalism, and not only among the many chapel-goers who had inherited this tradition. No licensed public house was allowed at Letchworth, and in many a high-minded family water-drinking and vegetarianism (and perhaps earth-closets and hand-weaving) seemed unquestionably linked. Let us dream, writes Baillie Scott, of a dining room table in the future 'no longer disfigured by the family joint' but adorned, instead, with 'piles of luscious fruit and nuts'. And since vegetarianism knows no income limits (though one might guess it to be commonest in the middle ranges), here is a suggested menu for a far from simple vegetarian luncheon: *Purée de Céleri à la crème, Omelettes aux tomates, Œufs durs au gratin, Risotto milanaise, Asperges, Sauce hollandaise, Salade de légumes, Crème caramel renversée, Pommes à la royale, Fromage.* One may suspect that it was not only the carnivores who needed the yearly purge at Homburg or Marienbad or Baden-Baden, or, if financially less well endowed, at a British hydro.

The budget just discussed does not suggest that this family's way of living differs materially from what it might have been even fifty years earlier, and this, of course, was true of the lives of many such families. The next budget seems rather more specifically a product of its own time. It is that of a young husband and wife, living in a London flat, with an income of £700 a year.

	£	s.
Rent, including rates and taxes	100	0
Wages of two maids (£22 and £20)	42	0
Food and cleaning materials for 4 people @ 10s. a head, less lunch for husband 6 days a week	104	0

	£	s.
Washing @ 10s. a week (rubbers are washed at home and servants' washing is charged at the rate of 1s. 3d. per week)	26	0
Coal, 1 ton a month @ £1	12	0
Electric light	8	0
Wood, 1s. per week on average	2	10
Wine	10	0
Repairs and replacements	10	0
Office expenses, train fares, and lunches @ 12s. per week	30	0
Life, fire, and accident insurances	25	0
Savings	50	0
Dress @ £40 each	80	0
Total	£499	10

leaving £200 10s. for all other expenses.

Obviously the young couple can live, if they choose, far more luxuriously than the country family. In such circumstances a young couple could take a full part in social life, repaying richer, more lavish hospitality with charming little dinner-parties, and able (after Saturday lunch) to pay country-house visits with none of that embarrassment that frequently afflicted indigent bachelors and young girls when faced with the often substantial tips then expected; in a large house, and without their own valet and maid, the young couple might be expected to give £1 to the butler, the same or a little less to the footman who valeted the husband, 5s. to the head housemaid, and, if extra services were proferred—say, horses ridden or bicycles cleaned—extra tips would be expected. For shooting and fishing holidays the outside servants must, of course, be tipped. For three or four days' grouse driving, the game-keeper would expect up to £2, the loader 5s. a day, and the cartridge carrier 2s. a day. For heavy bags, heavier tips were given. 'The custom of tipping in private houses is one which most people deplore', said Mrs. Peel, but the custom persisted and was indeed worsened by the tendency of the *nouveaux riches* to push up the standard with tips of as much as £2 or £3 to a footman and £5 or even £10 to a butler.

£200 a year was probably the least on which true middle-class gentility could be maintained with comfort. On this sum a single lady could live in a small labour-saving flat equipped with gas

and electric light and manage with only one servant. But she would
have to make many small economies, such as washing 'vests, hand-
kerchiefs and all kitchen cloths and dusters at home'.

Lower-Middle- and Working-Class Urban Housekeeping

It was, however, possible to eat an adequate amount of food at
a cost of less than 8s. 6d. a head. Rowntree, in his survey of York,
gives half a dozen budgets from what he calls the 'servant-keeping
class'. The amounts spent on food range from 8s. 10d. a week per
head down to about 5s. a head for a family of three adults and
three children. The actual quantities bought by this last family
are of interest in the general picture they give of the prices of
common food-stuffs. In the week ending 24 May 1901 this family
bought:

1 st. flour, 1s. 5d.; 1½ lb. self-raising flour, 3d.; 1 oz. yeast, 1d.; 1 lb. lard,
6d.; 2 lb. jam, 9d.; 3 lb. oatmeal, 7½d.; 2½ lb. butter, 2s. 11d.; ½ pt. cream,
10d.; cream cheese, 5d.; ½ lb. tea, 1s.; 3 lb. treacle, 9d.; 2 lb. beefsteak,
2s.; 1 st. potatoes, 8d.; cauliflower, 4d.; rhubarb, 6d.; 3½ galls. milk,
3s. 6d.; ½ lb. marmalade, 2½d.; asparagus, 6d.; 1 lb. 2 oz. beefsteak,
1s. 1½d.; ½ lb. currants, 3d.; ½ pt. vinegar, 1d.; lettuce, 2d.; 4 lb. sugar,
3d.; ½ lb. bacon, 3½d.; 3 lb. apples, 1s. 6d.; 6 oranges, 6d.; 1 lb. nuts, 5d.;
4½ lb. beef, 3s. 4½d.; 17 eggs, 1s.; ¼ lb. potted shrimps, 6d.; ½ lb. mutton,
4d.; 6 bananas, 6d.; 2 lb. halibut, 1s. 1d.; 12 oz. rice, 2d.; 2 oz. cornflour,
1½d.; 4½ oz. Benger's food, 7½d.; ¼ lb. cocoa, 6d.

These prices are fairly average. Both the beef and the mutton
would be English; chilled beef and mutton, now widely available,
cost only about half as much, though with the disadvantage,
especially for the poor, of seldom providing bones for soup. The
sugar bought was cheap; often this cost as much as 2d. or 2½d. a lb.,
though a reduction was usually given for buying in bulk. The eggs
were distinctly cheap, and the treacle may well have been fetched in
the customer's own jug. This family obviously made its bread at
home, a custom still common in the north but becoming rare in the
south. If bought, the average price for a quartern loaf was 5d.
Mrs. Beeton thought that 1 lb. of bread per head per day was a proper
allowance; in 1878 a cookery-book recommended 8 lb. a week for
a woman, 16 lb. a week for a man or boy, and in 1960 the average
weight of bread eaten weekly by each person in England was 3 lb.

From these ingredients, the meals for Friday, the first day of the week in question, were as follows:

Breakfast: Porridge, eggs, bread, butter, toast, boiled milk, tea.
Dinner: Beefsteak, potatoes, cauliflower, sponge pudding, stewed rhubarb, cream, dates.
Tea: Bread, butter, tea-cake, pastry, tea.
Supper: Bread, butter, tea-cake, Benger's food, cocoa.

In the York study Rowntree examined the budgets of four upper-working-class families whose incomes were over 26s. a week—a clerk earning 35s. (5 in family), a foreman earning 38s. (8 in family), a foreman earning 27s. (4 in family), and a railway employee earning about 44s. (4 in family) with other small additions to his income. Only one family, the second, has by Rowntree's standards an adequate diet and this family spends 3s. 2¼d. a head for a week's food, the lowest weekly average of this group. They pay 4s. rent for a four-roomed house with a shared yard and an outside lavatory, but they have the convenience of a tap in the kitchen. Their meals, on the first day of the week examined, are as follows:

Breakfast: Toast, tea.
Dinner: Soup, dumplings, meat, bread, tea.
Tea: Sardines, bread, milk, tea.
Supper: Bread, cheese, cocoa.

The tea drunk with almost every meal cannot have been freshly made each time, for this family, like the last, bought only half a pound a week, paying 1s. 2d. for it. Tea could, however, be bought for as little as 1s. 6d. a pound; the average national consumption at this time was 6 lb. a head a year. This family, said Rowntree, had an excess of 18 per cent. in the case of the protein they ate and an excess of no less than 30 per cent. in energy value.

Rowntree's standards of judgment must have consideration, for they were closely re-examined and accepted by other social investigators throughout this period. They were based on what was then known of food requirements in terms of proteins and calories. It is important to remember that vitamins were not discovered until 1912; that the composition of proteins, and hence the different food-values of different types of proteins, were discovered in the same year; that it was not until the first world war that the relation of calcium and phosphorus to the causation of rickets was investigated.

More, it was believed that growing children of whatever age needed less food than adults; thus a boy of 14–16 years was estimated to need only eight-tenths of the food of a man at moderate muscular labour, such a man (typically a house-painter) being said to need 125 grammes of protein a day and the fuel value of 3,500 calories.

On this basis Rowntree drew up some standard dietaries, for men, for women, and for older and younger children. The standard adopted, which included no butcher's meat, was less generous than that required by local government boards for workhouses. The minimum necessary weekly expenditure on food proved to be 3s. 3d. for a man, 2s. 9d. for a woman, 2s. 7d. for children aged between 8 and 16, 2s. 1d. for children between 3 and 8 and the same, because of the cost of milk, for children under 3. To provide a nutritious diet for these prices, which do not include costs of fuel, utensils, &c., would require, says Rowntree, more knowledge than the poor possess and an unlikely willingness to alter established eating habits.[1]

To these costs for food alone Rowntree adds estimated minimum costs of rent (at between 1s. 6d. for a single man and 5s. 6d. for a family of man and wife with four to eight children), household sundries including clothing at 6d. a week for each adult, 5d. a week for each child, with fuel at 4d. and other sundries at 2d. a week per head. Nothing is allowed for travelling, for recreation, for luxuries of any kind—a glass of beer, a halfpenny newspaper—or for insurance, sick benefit, or union dues. The basic minima for food, rent, and sundries Rowntree finally reckons at 7s. a week for a single man, 21s. 8d. for a family of husband, wife, and three children, 37s. 4d. for a family of husband, wife, and eight children.

These figures represent Rowntree's famous poverty line. Any family with less than these required amounts is said to be living in primary poverty, that is to say, in conditions where the family income, given the utmost knowledge and economy, is insufficient to maintain health and working efficiency. In addition Rowntree developed a concept of 'secondary poverty', in which the total family income would be sufficient for the maintenance of mere physical efficiency, were not some portion of it absorbed in other expenditure, either useful or wasteful—for instance, in paying fares

---

[1] In the spring of 1960 it was reckoned that an old-age pensioner could live adequately on a 'very simple but nutritious diet' for the sum of 25s. per week.

or debts or where the father drank or the mother was an inefficient housekeeper. Rowntree reckoned that 43·4 per cent. of the wage-earning class in York and 27·8 per cent. of the city's whole population was living in poverty; and similar proportions would, he and other investigators believed, hold good throughout the country.

The diets of people living at or below the poverty line were of course execrable. 'The gravely deficient "poverty diet" of England which persisted throughout the thirties dated from about 1890', said Drummond, and during the Edwardian period the position was one of deterioration rather than improvement. Between 1870 and 1900 the wholesale prices of commodities had fallen by about 40 per cent.; between 1880 and 1890 wages had risen by 11 per cent., and between 1890 and 1900 by another 11 per cent. But in the decade 1900 to 1910, wholesale prices rose by 13·4 per cent. and retail prices showed a similar increase; between 1900 and 1912 wages rose on the average by $2\frac{1}{4}d.$; the real wages of workers declined by more than 13 per cent. A concrete example of the price-rise in terms of foodstuffs is shown by the housekeeping books of a Birmingham boys' home in 1903 and in 1911. Amounts of groceries (7 lb. jam, 14 lb. sugar, 1 lb. currants, &c.) totalling 12s. $10\frac{1}{2}d.$ in 1903 cost 17s. $11\frac{1}{2}d.$ in 1911, an increase of 40 per cent. But not only did the value of the sovereign decline by about 2s. 6d. during this period; the standard of living of the poor declined in quite another way too. As Philip Snowden pointed out in his book *The Living Wage* (1912), new expenses had fairly come into the category of necessities through 'the development of tramways, the coming of the halfpenny newspaper, the cheap but better-class music hall and the picture palace, the cheap periodicals and books'. People, as he says, cannot see these things without wishing to partake, and to be deprived not only of basic necessities but also of new luxuries, intended specifically for your kind, is penury indeed. Professional football was increasingly attracting working-class crowds on Saturday afternoons; but for a man living at the poverty line, the price of a ticket was prohibitive. He himself proposed, in this book, 'a universal minimum wage of 30s. a week'.

Two budgets, one urban and one rural, will suffice to show how families live below the poverty line. For the urban budget we cannot do better than take the first in Rowntree's book, that of a labourer with 17s. 6d. a week. He has a wife who is 'a good manager' and five children; the eldest is deformed and threatened with tuberculosis, the others show plain marks of deprivation. For the week ending 30 June, 1899, the family purchases were as follows:

Friday: 1½ st. flour, 1*s*. 10½*d*.; ¼ st. wheatmeal, 4*d*.; yeast, 1*d*.; 1 lb. butter, 10*d*.; 2½ lb. bacon, 1*s*.; 6 oz. tea, 6*d*.; 1 lb. currants, 3*d*.; 1 lb. lard, 4*d*.; 1¼ lb. fish, 4*d*.; 1 tin condensed milk, 5½*d*.; onions, 1*d*.

Saturday: Bag of coal, 1*s*. 3*d*.; 4 lb. beef, 1*s*. 7½*d*.; 5 lb. sugar, 9*d*.; ½ lb. dripping, 2½*d*.; ½ st. potatoes, 2*d*.; 8 eggs, 6*d*.; baking powder, 1*d*.; literature, 2*d*.; 1 oz. tobacco, 3*d*.; black lead, 1*d*.; lemons, 2*d*.; cabbage, 2*d*.; insurance, 5*d*.

Sunday: Milk, 1*d*.

Monday: Stamp, 1*d*.; stationery, 1*d*.; sewing-cotton, 2*d*.; glycerine, 2*d*.; pair of slippers, 1*s*. 1½*d*.; rent, 3*s*. 3*d*.

Tuesday: Yeast, 1*d*.; 1 lb. soap, 2½*d*.; starch, 1*d*.; blacking, 1*d*.; scrubbing brush, 3½*d*.

Thursday: Lettuce, 1*d*.

The diet provided by these purchases is, says Rowntree, 'very inadequate'. On the first day of the week in question, the meals were as follows:

Breakfast: Brown and white bread, butter, tea.
Dinner: Fish, bread, tea.
Tea: Bread, butter, onions, tea.
Supper: None.

The diet is, of course, far worse than any day's menu might suggest in that the quantities available for each person are so small. Seven people took their dinner off 1¼ lb. of fish—about 2½ oz. for each person including a father who does manual labour and three boys over the age of 7. One tin of condensed milk and a pennyworth of fresh suffice the family for the week, although the other two children are aged 4 and 2. And though the joint may seem comparatively large, the children are said to have only a small piece each on Sunday, since meals for the father to take to work with him must be provided out of it for the rest of the week.

But this northern family is better off than many a southern one in that its bread, which includes wheatmeal, is home-made, and it eats butter, not margarine. In the south of England there is an increasing tendency to buy margarine, or 'overweight butter' as it was sometimes called, for this cost only 6*d*. to 9*d*. a pound as compared with 1*s*. to 2*s*. for butter. But in these cases the diet is, of course, appreciably worse, as it is worse where white bread is eaten and not brown, condensed milk drunk and not fresh. The new refinements, conveniences, and inventions in foodstuffs tended to be disastrous to the health of the Edwardian poor.

Rural Poverty Housekeeping

It is commonly supposed that in times of dearth the rural labourer is far better off than the urban one, but in our period this is often not the case. In 1907 the weekly earnings of labourers in England averaged 17*s*. 6*d*., including extra payments and payments in kind, such as harvest money, rent of cottage, and cheap milk, usually at 1½*d*. a pint all year, but sometimes, in summer, at 1*d*. a pint. This average wage represented a rise of 3 per cent. over the preceding ten years, but in the same period the cost of living had risen by 10 per cent. In many counties earnings were far below the national average; Oxfordshire was lowest with an average total weekly wage of 14*s*. 6*d*., the average cash payment being only 12*s*.

Several villages were, during this period, investigated in some detail. For instance on the Ridgmont estate of the Duke of Bedford, reputedly one of the best of England's landowners, Mann[1] found that 34·3 per cent. of the inhabitants—41 per cent. of the working-class inhabitants—were living below the poverty line. Of 220 households in Corsley, Wilts., Miss Davies[2] found 28 families in primary poverty, 37 in secondary poverty; that is, about a third of all families were living below the poverty line. The prime cause of poverty, everyone agreed, was children, and on the average the number of children per married woman in the country was five as against the townswoman's four. Moreover, more children were born in poorer than in richer families. In Corsley Miss Davies found that from the families living in primary poverty in the village—one-eighth of the total number of families—nearly half of all the children in the parish were drawn; only one-third of all the children in Corsley lived above the line of secondary poverty.

From Corsley, then, we may take a sample rural poverty diet, that of a labourer with wife and five children. He earns 15*s*. a week, pays 1*s*. 6*d*. rent for his cottage, 5*s*. a year rent for an allotment of 20

---

[1] H. H. Mann, *Life in an Agricultural Village*, 1905.
[2] Maud F. Davies, *Life in an English Village*, 1909.

XVI. 'A House for the Art Lover' 1906

XVII. Millinery at the Bon Marché

poles, and 2s. 5d. a month to his Friendly Society. His deficiency of necessary income Miss Davies reckons at 7s. 6d. a week. This is what the family bought during a week in January 1906.

½ lb. tea, 8d.; 3 lb. sugar, 5½d.; 1½ lb. butter, 1s. 6d.; bacon, 1s. 4d.; Quaker oats, 5½d.; 2 oz. tobacco, 6d.; cheese, 9d.; ½ lb. lard, 2½d.; ¼ lb. suet, 2d.; baking powder, 1d.; papers, 2d.; 1 lb. soap, 3d.; oranges, 2d.; ½ lb. currants, 1½d.; 1 pt. beer, 2d.; coal, 1s. 2½d.; loaf, 2¼d.; milk, 6½d.; butter, 4d.; sugar, 2¼d.; loaf, 2¼d.; oil, 2½d.; stockings, 6½d.; bread bill, 3s. Total: 13s. 4¾d.

The week's diet which these purchases provided may be given in full. It is similar to many millions such, and better, no doubt, than many:

Breakfast	Dinner	Tea	Supper
Saturday Father: fried potato, bacon, tea. Mother and children: potatoes, bacon, tea.	Bread, butter, tea.	Bread, butter, tea.	..
Sunday Parents: bacon, tea. Children: porridge.	Potatoes, cabbage, boiled bacon, currant and suet pudding.	Bread, butter, cake, tea.	Mother: porridge.
Monday Father: fried potato, bacon, tea. Mother and children: toast, tea.	Father: bread, cheese. Schoolchildren: bread, butter, tea. At home: fried potato, bacon, tea.	Toast, tea.	Potatoes, greens, bacon.
Tuesday Father: fried potato, bacon. Others: porridge.	Father: bread, cheese. Schoolchildren: bread, butter. At home: porridge.	Toast, tea.	Potatoes, greens, bacon, suet pudding.
Wednesday Father: fried potato, bacon, tea. Others: toast, tea.	Father: bread, cheese. Others: bread, butter, suet pudding.	Toast, tea.	Potatoes, greens, bacon, tea.

Breakfast	Dinner	Tea	Supper
Thursday Father: fried potato, bacon, tea. Others: broth.	Potatoes, bacon.	Toast, tea.	Potatoes, greens, bacon, tea.
Friday Father: fried potato, bacon, tea. Others: toast, tea.	Father: bread, cheese. Schoolchildren: bread, lard. At home: soup (a present).	Toast, tea.	Potatoes, greens.

The broth, which constitutes the sole breakfast for everyone but the father on Thursday, is butter, milk, and water. The mother is nursing the youngest child, which presumably explains her indulgence in supper on Sunday. Supper, incidentally, is taken by the whole family at 6 p.m.; tea is at 4.15 p.m. when the children, who, like the husband, have taken dinner with them, return from school.

It must be admitted that this budget contains many luxuries, or what Rowntree says must be considered luxuries on minimum incomes. Such are the papers, the beer, the oil if it should be used to light more than a single room at a time, and certainly the oranges, for Rowntree says—and later knowledge gives tragic irony—that primary poverty means that if a mother wants to spend twopence on oranges, she must deny her children that treat and buy bread instead. Not that she can buy much bread: one mother is quoted as saying that she gives her children bread and margarine, not bread and jam, because then they don't so often come back for more.

Though, in the case of this family, possession of an allotment obviously helped considerably, the various Allotment Acts gave less relief to the rural labourer than had been hoped. A man working eleven to twelve hours a day including Saturdays has little energy to spare to till an allotment, even if he can find the money for its rent. Many county councils made it a rule not to approve applicants with less capital than £10 an acre, and the new allotments tended to go not to labourers but to tradesmen, often simply for the grazing of a pony. Then many employers disapproved of their workmen renting allotments, and many allotments were ravaged by the protected game-birds of the big estates. As for pig-keeping, the tenants of tied cottages had to obtain permission from the employer to keep a pig and this was often withheld; more, as one working woman said to the social investigator, 'What's the use of hungering ourselves to feed a pig?'

As rural life progressively decayed, as rural depopulation increased, it became steadily easier for the rural housewife to obtain an ever greater choice of goods, even if shoddy fabrics and sophisticated foodstuffs often replaced what formerly had been of better quality. Though less bread was baked at home, often, in the south, because cottage ovens had fallen into disrepair, in many villages the baker now called regularly with loaves far whiter than the housewife used to bake. So did the butcher with cheap frozen meat from Australia and the Argentine, at about 4*d.* a pound as compared with 7*d.* or 8*d.* for fresh; 4*d.* or 5*d.* a pound for frozen meat sausages as against 6*d.* for fresh beef sausages, 8*d.* for fresh pork. Miss Davies comments on a great increase in grocery consumption by the country housewife over the past forty years. Where formerly she might have bought an ounce of tea or coffee and a pound of sugar a week, she will now take a quarter of a pound of tea and three pounds of sugar. In many country budgets now tinned foods often appear. Almost if not quite as wide a range of tinned foods was available as existed some forty years later. But where the rich might indulge in, say, tinned asparagus tips or *fonds d'artichauts*, the poor generally confined themselves to tinned milk, fish (mostly salmon and sardines), and fruit. Their use of these new packaged foodstuffs often brought recriminations for their extravagance; the poor, said one critic, could manage perfectly well if they confined themselves to the good old-fashioned oatmeal (2*d.* to 3*d.* a pound) instead of lazily buying the new patent groats (2½*d.* to 3*d.*). But patent groats, in addition to saving fuel, had acquired some reputation as of value to the nursing mother, and where there is an infant in the house a pitiably small expenditure on patent groats is liable, as in the budget given above, to appear.

Not only groceries but all forms of household goods now tempted the housewife on her doorstep. Commercial salesmen constantly appeared to offer clothes, hardware, and furnishings on the instalment system, and often the housewife bought when she would have been wiser to avail herself of the clothing club run by the vicar's wife for something like 6*d.* a week.

Below the poverty line clothes must be bought sparingly indeed

and often they were bought second-hand or, in the country,
obtained through charity from better-off relations or local gentry.
Even among the very poor convention demanded certain expen-
ditures that later generations would consider unnecessary; a
constantly worn white apron, costing between 4½d. and 6d. was
obligatory for the housewife, and a constantly worn head-covering,
costing about 6d. to 1s., for her husband and sons. The minimum
annual budgets for necessary clothing given by Rowntree for various
members of a family are as follows:

Man

	s.	d.
Boots (1 pr. 5s., repairs 2s.)	7	0
Socks (4 prs. @ 6d.)	2	0
Coat (1 second-hand)	3	6
Vest (1 second-hand)	1	6
Trousers (1 pr. second-hand)	3	0
Shirts (2 new ones @ 2s.)	4	0
Cap and scarf, say	1	0
Total	22	0

Woman

	s.	d.
Boots (1 pr. 2s. 11d., repairs 1s. husband does repairs)	3	11
Slippers (wear old boots)		
Dress (second-hand)	5	0
Aprons (2 @ 6d.)	1	0
Skirt (go without)		
Stockings (2 prs. @ 6½d.)	1	1
Underclothing (1 of each article)	2	11
Stays (1 pr.)	2	11
Hat (a new one lasts several years), say	1	0
Jacket (ditto)	1	6
Shawl (ditto)	1	0
Total	20	4

Boy of 12 years

	s.	d.
Boots (2 prs. @ 3s. 11d.; repairs 2s. 2d.)	10	0
Suit (8s., extra trousers 2s.)	10	0
Shirt (one)	1	3
Stockings (2 pairs @ 1s.)	2	0
Caps, &c.	1	6
Overcoat (do without)		
Total	24	9

XVIII (a). 'Ladies' Knickerbockers for walking, golf, tennis, riding and cycling' 1906

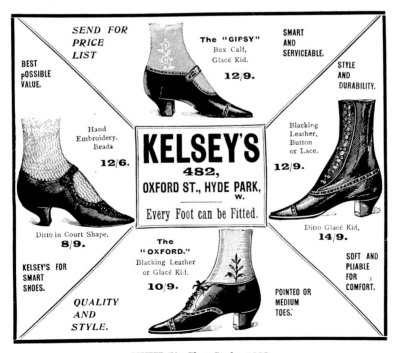

XVIII (b). Shoe Styles 1903

Child of 2 years

	s.	d.
Boots or shoes (1 pr.)	2	11
Dresses (2 @ 1s. 6d.)	3	0
Underclothes (2 of each article)	1	11½
Night-dresses (none)		
Pinafores (3 @ 6½d.)	1	7½
Socks (2 prs. @ 4d.)		8
Hat (one)	1	0
Coat (one)	2	0
Total	13	2

In some northern towns wooden clogs were still worn, and in almost all towns there were bare-footed children. For the country labourer's family, and especially for the wage-earner, boots, which must be something better than shoddy, were a constant expense:

There's two pairs for my husband at 5s. each. These last him a bit over a year, with mending. The eldest boy buys his own shoes out of his pocket money. Herbert has to have two 4s. pairs. Then Violet has to have two pairs every year—that's 6s. And Bobbie has had three pairs, and the last is just worn out. They were 3s. 6½d., 2s. 11d., and 3s. 11d. Oh, and the mending won't come to less than 10s. a year. Then—I forgot myself—sometimes my sister sends me her old ones, but I got one pair this year at 4s. 6d. And the youngest . . . he's cost 5s. for shoes.

The speaker is the wife of an Oxfordshire farm labourer, with four sons and a daughter. The father earns 13s. 6d. a week, the wife 1s. 6d. for looking after the house next door, and the 16-year-old son earns 8s. a week. There is a 27 per cent. protein deficiency in this family's diet although they have an allotment and one-twelfth of the food eaten is home-produced.

With such wages and such dietaries it follows that the health of the Edwardian poor was appalling. At the very beginning of the period some public unease had arisen over the low standard of recruits for the army. Of those who offered themselves in 1900, the health and physical development of one-half was below the comparatively lax standard required by the authorities who had, in any case, already taken the practical ameliorative step of lowering the required standard; the required height, which in 1883 had been 5 ft. 3 in. was brought down in 1900 to 5 ft. In the poorest districts of York at the beginning of the period the death-rate was 27·8 a year per 1,000 of the population; in the richest districts it was 13·49. In London, which held one-seventh of the population of England, the average age of death was in the west end 55 years and in the east end 30 years. One adult in every four in London died on public charity. To go from the west to the east end, said Jack London, was to encounter 'a new and different race of people, short of stature, and of wretched and beer-sodden appearance'. Miss Davies describes the typical marks of deprivation among the rural poor: dullness, nervousness, laziness, 'strangeness' or 'peculiarity' of disposition, dirtiness, and a general air of neglect.

Then as later the upper working class and lower middle classes were ignored by social investigators, but for many people in these groups conditions during the period must have improved. The small overall rise in wages masks the not inconsiderable gains made by the workers in certain industries through the new conciliation boards and notably in the mining, steel-working, and textile industries. Here we may assume that advantage was taken of the rapidly multiplying mass-produced aids to a higher standard of living, though it is to be doubted whether a healthier as opposed to a more ample diet was among them. Except among 'simple-lifers' brown bread was still tainted with the stigma of poverty; and so few vegetables and such small amounts of fruit were eaten that neither appears in the 1904 cost-of-living index. Mr. Polly's gastric condition was probably far from uncommon:

There had been the cold pork from Sunday, and some nice cold potatoes and Rashdall's Mixed Pickles, of which he was inordinately fond. He had eaten three gherkins, two onions, a small cauliflower head, and several capers with every appearance of appetite, and indeed with avidity; and then there had been cold suet pudding to follow, with treacle, and then a nice bit of cheese. It was the pale, hard sort of cheese he liked; red cheese, he declared, was indigestible. He had also had three big slices of greyish baker's bread, and had drunk the best part of the jugful of beer. . . . So on nearly every day in his life Mr. Polly fell into a violent rage and hatred against the outer world in the afternoon, and never suspected that it was this inner world . . . that was thus reflecting its sinister disorder upon the things without.

Hospitality and Charity

Keeping oneself to oneself was a prized characteristic of people of Mr. Polly's kind and entertaining, on the rare occasions when it took place, was apt to be formal, awkward, and pretentious. But in the north of England, where conviviality has traditionally triumphed over formality, manners were generally more free and easy, social life jollier, and the food better. Throughout the north, middle-class high tea, taken at about 5.30 p.m., was usual, as it was to be for many years to come. At the least there would be some savoury relish and plenty of more or less rich cakes and bread and butter. At the high tea for a betrothal party, such as the one Arnold Bennett describes in *Anna of the Five Towns*, a well-to-do hostess would really spread herself:

At one end of the table, which glittered with silver, glass, and Longshaw china, was a fowl which had been boiled for four hours; at the other a hot pork-pie, islanded in liquor, which might have satisfied a regiment. Between these two dishes were all the delicacies which differentiate high tea from tea, and on which the success of the meal really depends; hot pikelets, hot crumpets, hot toast, sardines with tomatoes, raisin-bread, currant-bread, seed-cake, lettuce, home-made marmalade, and home-made jams. The repast occupied over an hour, and even then not a quarter of the food was consumed.

After a high tea, even a lesser one than this, a full supper was seldom eaten, and the evening meal was likely to consist of bread and butter and cakes with perhaps cocoa or Benger's food.

Among the smart folk of the metropolis, meals were, as always, focuses for entertaining, and luncheon was often a social meal. Where many people were invited a new chic custom had arisen of seating the guests at small tables, four or six at each, though the single table was more usual. At smart tables, dishes were now handed by the servants—service *à la russe*, as it was called—though old-fashioned people deplored the elaborate ritual entailed, the consequent delays. At an informal luncheon one wine only would be served, but at a more formal one, claret or hock would be served with the meal, port and sherry to follow, and, if men guests were present, liqueurs with the coffee. Mrs. Beeton provides several recipes for American cocktails—the Manhattan, the Martini,[1] the Brain Duster, the Yankee Invigorator; in some cosmopolitan homes apéritifs were now served before dinner.

[1] *Ingredients.* Half a wineglassful of good unsweetened gin, half a wineglassful of Italian vermouth, 6 drops of rock candy syrup, 12 drops of orange bitters, 1 small piece of lemon peel, crushed ice.

Method. Half fill a tumbler with crushed ice, pour over it all the liquids, then strain into a glass, and serve with a small piece of lemon peel floating on the surface.

After luncheon new avocations had arisen for leisured women, of which the foremost was auction bridge. For many women bridge had become an almost single-minded devotion, and in the afternoons it might be played not only in private houses but also in the new women's clubs—the Ladies' Army and Navy at the corner of Cork Street, the Empress run by Miss Helen Henniker in Dover Street, and, also in Dover Street, the Empire, patronized by Lady Jersey. A new type of woman, said that caustic commentator who called himself 'A Foreign Resident',[1] had arisen with the new century, 'the married bachelor of the fair sex', living and entertaining in a little bandbox of a Mayfair house. Her husband might be a country squire engaged on his estates or she might be, now, the increasingly acceptable divorcée, legally assisted through her difficult ordeal by Sir George Lewis of Ely Place. Attendance at Sir Francis Jeune's divorce court was one way that fashionable ladies killed time; others were palmistry, necromancy, crystal-gazing, and betting on horses. These, says the Foreign Resident dourly, had taken the place of charity and good works.

Some ladies, mostly of the educated classes and not only from politically progressive groups, still took an active interest in the conditions of the poor and gave regular hours to working in clinics and crèches. But good works undertaken solely from a sense of moral obligation had undoubtedly diminished. Store catalogues still advertised 'rugs and blankets for charitable purposes' and in some villages a good lady, often the clergyman's wife, would lend charity blankets for winter use or maintain a layette that could be borrowed at need. Often in the budgetary arrangements of poor country dwellers, though seldom of town ones, we hear of gifts of old clothes or shoes, and sometimes the kitchen waste of a great house would be handed out to the needy, though in one case at least all mixed together, hard and soft, sweet and savoury, in a nauseous mess. Jack London tells of a London hospital that, with a strange disregard for hygiene, did the same:

The hospital scraps . . . were heaped high on a huge platter in an indescribable mess—pieces of bread, chunks of grease and fat pork, the burnt skin from the outside of roasted joints, bones, in short, all the leavings from the fingers and mouths of the sick ones suffering from all manner of diseases. Into this mess the men plunged their hands, digging,

---

[1] *Society in the New Reign*, 1904.

pawing, turning over, examining, rejecting, and scrambling for. It wasn't pretty. Pigs couldn't have done worse. But the poor devils were hungry.

When Charlotte Yonge had started writing, in the middle of the nineteenth century, her objections to bazaars as a means of raising money for charity had been shared by many. Already, by the nineties, only the old-fashioned characters in her novels still lamented this improper juxtaposition and by the Edwardian period all such objections had been forgotten. Not only bazaars now but jumble-sales, whist-drives, and ping-pong tournaments brought conviviality to the leisured and benefits to the poor, and no one mentioned the propriety of keeping alms-giving under a bushel. The patronage of royalty, as in the smart League of Mercy presided over by Princess Alice of Albany, effectively disposed of any such arguments. But some difficult social problems did arise. At the beginning of the period, retail trade, no matter how wealthy, was unacceptable in society. 'Were a person actually engaged in retail trade to obtain a presentation', says the contemporary volume of the *Manners and Rules of Good Society*, 'his presentation would be cancelled as soon as the Lord Chamberlain was made aware of the nature of his occupation', and snubs to aspiring tradesmen of substantial property were anecdotal small talk. Peers might marry chorus-girls—and why they *married* them is, as Peter Laslett points out, one of the fascinating unanswered questions of the period; they might marry the daughters of wealthy Americans whose fortunes had been made in ways at least as socially, and often far more morally, reprehensible. Rough diamonds might be accepted and so, notoriously, were the Jews who none the less provided, says the Foreign Resident, 'the only humanizing influences that leaven London society to-day'. It was difficult indeed, as Miss Sackville-West explains, to define just what made *entrée* possible:

So this is the great world, thought Anquetil; the world of the élite; and he began to wonder what qualities gave admission to it. . . . He could perceive no common factor between all these people; neither high birth nor wealth nor brains seemed to be essential . . . for though Sir Adam was fabulously rich, Tommy Brand was correspondingly poor; and though the Duchess of Hull was a duchess, Mrs. Levison was by birth and marriage a nobody; and though Lord Robert Gore was a clever, ambitious young man, Sir Harry Tremaine was undeniably a ninny. Yet they all took their places with the same assurance, and upon the same footing. Anquetil knew that they and their friends formed a phalanx from which intruders were rigorously excluded; but why some people qualified and others did not, he could not determine.

It would not be possible for very much longer to exclude the rich shopocracy. Once the king had accepted Sir Thomas Lipton, what could possibly be said against people like Mr. Harrod, whose shoot-ing-box on Exmoor was visited by 'academicians and parliamen-tarians', Sir Blundell Maple who, just like his betters, formed part of the glittering audience in the boxes at the Covent Garden Opera House, Colonel F. Dickins (of Dickins and Jones), a dashing officer of the Victoria Rifle Volunteers, and philanthropic employers like Mr. Debenham and Mr. Derry who had abolished the detested system of having their shop-assistant employees 'live-in' ? It was noticeably advantageous to invite the wives of the shopocracy to take a stall at the bazaar; and their daughters were often discovered to be pleasantly, even unusually, domesticated.

But if charity sometimes played a usefully leavening part in Edwardian society, it cannot in general be said that the plight of the less fortunate was actively present to the Edwardian rich. 'Nothing is so out of fashion to-day as genuine emotion of any kind', said the Foreign Resident; and Sir Lawrence Jones,[1] recalling the country-house parties of his youth, writes: 'All was friendliness and gaiety and "sun-burnt mirth"; no sound or rumour from the neighbouring countryside, where men and women were presumably living labori-ous lives, ever penetrated that self-sufficient enclave.'

The Condition-of-Women Question

Looking back it seems surprising if not shocking that the most ardently supported cause of the period eventually proved to be votes for women and not the condition of the poor. In view of current needs, the choice seems almost frivolously irresponsible, parti-cularly when we consider that for many Edwardian women con-ditions of life were steadily improving. As we have seen, new choices were opening for working-class women who formerly could hope, at best, only to become domestic servants. Women's labour was far cheaper than men's, and in some trades, such as watch-making at Coventry, girls were increasingly taken on as apprentices while the

[1] L. E. Jones, *An Edwardian Youth*, 1956.

boys went off to earn higher wages in the bicycle works. There were already three women school-teachers to every man and openings in clerical work were rapidly widening. In the last decade of the nineteenth century the proportion of female clerks had risen from 8 to 18 in every 100 and, by 1911, to 32 in every 100. For middle-class girls, several forms of superior training were leading to superior jobs. Already by 1901 there were 212 women doctors, 140 women dentists, and even two women accountants. Girls of less capacity became private secretaries or often lady photographers. Photography was, as for many years previously, a popular hobby. Second-hand Brownie and 'Nipper' cameras at about 3s. 6d. were on regular offer in the advertisement columns of *Little Folks*, and a hobby formed in the nursery might lead to a profession for life, or at least for a pre-marital working life. Electric lighting now enabled dark rooms to be kept free from excessive heat and carbonic acid gas, and where the rich were constantly being photographed by Bassano, Alice Hughes, or Lafayette, the not-so-rich would attend nearly as often at the studios of the suburban or provincial lady photographer. Even some upper-class ladies worked, and for these, strangely, retail trade was not only permissible but fashionable. Several ladies ran clothing establishments. Lady Duff-Gordon had founded the exclusive 'Lucile' in the early nineties, Mrs. Cyril Drummond the high-class 'Mascotte' in 1906, and the Countess of Warwick had a ladies' underwear shop in Bond Street with 'Countess of Warwick' in large letters on the window. Lady Angela Forbes had a flower-shop—'My Shop'—in George Street, Lady Auckland a millinery shop, Lady Rachel Byng an 'artistic needlework' shop. Authorship and journalism had long been open to women, and in 1911 there were as many women authors and journalists as in 1931.

It has often been said that revolutions occur not when conditions are intolerable but when they show signs of improvement, and this may be true for the women's emancipation movement of the Edwardian era. In any case the improvement, though apparently irreversible, was limited in scope, and probably the majority of women were barely touched by it. Masterman, writing in 1909, suggests that the agitation for the vote represented for the women 'an outlet for suppressed energy and proffered devotion', and the obviously unsatisfactory lives of many Edwardian women gives the suggestion some plausibility. Of most rich women, 'What did they

find to do with their time?' is the first question on the lips of
anyone who contemplates the domestic help available to them;
and the pastimes they found, from rigid time-consuming formality
to bridge and the petting of pugs and pekingese, seem, as a way of
life, fretfully unsatisfactory. In less exalted circles, what was later
to be known as 'suburban neurosis' was already developing. Masterman writes: 'The women, with their single domestic servants, now
so difficult to get, and so exacting when found, find time hang
rather heavy on their hands.' For the younger suburban women,
Wells's Ann Veronica stands as the exemplar:

> 'Then I suppose when I have graduated I am to come home?'
> 'It seems the natural course.'
> 'And do nothing?'
> 'There are plenty of things a girl can find to do at home.'

If in the upper and middle classes the women were bored, in the
working classes they were often debased. Rowntree comments:

> No one can fail to be struck by the monotony which characterizes the
> life of most married women of the working class. Probably this monotony
> is least marked in the slum districts, where life is lived more in common.
> ... But with advance in the social scale, family life becomes more private,
> and the women, left in the house all day whilst their husbands are at work,
> are largely thrown upon their own resources. These, as a rule, are sadly
> limited, and in the deadening monotony of their lives these women too
> often become mere hopeless drudges ... the conditions which govern the
> life of the women are gravely unsatisfactory, and are the more serious
> in their consequences since the character and attractive power of the
> family life are principally dependent upon her.

Formal Living

If essentially time-consuming rather than stimulating, the range
of afternoon avocations for a lady of leisure was great. Sometimes
an afternoon might be devoted to personal or household shopping.
Stocking the linen-cupboard was a substantial task seriously undertaken, each item bought needing to be marked in red cross-stitch
(whether by the shop or by a maid at home) with the mistress's initial,
the destined purpose (nursery or maid's or spare-room, &c.), the
date bought, and the number of each piece in its set; thus 3/6 on
a sheet or towel would indicate that it was number three of a set of
six. For the extended labour that this form of shopping would entail

an appointment would probably be made; for shorter calls, the frock-coated manager would himself cross the pavement to the carriage or electric brougham to serve the customer at her minimum inconvenience.

On a fine summer day in the country there would be tennis-parties and garden-parties or, at least, tea in the garden with straw-berries and cream and elaborate tea-equipages carried out to rustic or wickerwork tables, made, after 1908, at the new Dryad workshop in Leicester after the Austrian model. On Fridays or Saturdays many would start off for their week-ends, some to country-houses by motor-car or train, these latter met at the station where the express made a request stop by a victoria or a dog-cart with a wagonette for the luggage or, by about 1908, by a Darracq or a Wolseley. But not all Edwardian week-enders left for sumptuous country-houses. Many—notably business people—went regularly to the new luxurious hotels that were being built round the coasts, and some rented furnished houses on the Thames for the summer months. Others built 'holiday homes' where, to quote one architect, 'the formal routine conventionalities which have to some extent domi-nated the permanent home can be set aside for a freer and less re-stricted existence'. The accommodation, he recommends, should include 'at least one large sitting-room, as well as four or five bed-rooms, bathroom, and the usual kitchen premises, reduced to their simplest form, while a veranda or garden-room is an important feature'. But often the holiday home was a converted railway carriage, or a tin bungalow lined with matchboarding and costing about £230 or a little more with finials to the roof. And the con-version of former labourers' cottages by the gentry was proceeding apace.

But apart from the week-end exodus, perhaps the most typical afternoon activity of the upper classes was leaving cards and paying calls. Though these customs existed well before this period and lingered, in attenuated form, for some time afterwards, it was now that they achieved their most developed patterns. They amounted, in effect, to a series of coded communications where to know or not to know the code was tantamount to inclusion or exclusion.

The first desideratum was to obtain cards, engraved in small copper-plate (*not* old English). For a lady they should be thickish, about $3\frac{1}{3}$ in. by $2\frac{1}{2}$ in., and for a gentleman small and thin. It must have been during this period that the inconvenient decision arose (rather than was taken) not to put telephone numbers on cards; the telephone, usually inconveniently situated in the flower-room, in a corner of the hall, or in a lobby between the smoking-room and the gentlemen's lavatory, was seldom used for chats and never for more formal social intercourse such as the giving or accepting of invitations. Then a cardcase was needed, often a very pretty cardcase in ivory or silver or gold, sometimes with a thin washable ivory sheet for notes and a pencil included (cardcases lingered vestigially as part of the fittings of expensive limousines until the 1930's). The hostess at home, with whom we are principally concerned, must possess a silver salver for the hall-table on which cards could rest, though it was not correct for a servant to receive cards on a salver; they must be taken with the hand.

The strict rules as to who left cards on whom and when and how and why would demand more space than can here be spared. To instance a few at random: A lady who has met another lady at a dinner-party or at afternoon tea should not leave cards until further meetings have enabled her to feel sure that her acquaintance is desired; residents call on newcomers, not vice versa, the lady resident of highest social standing usually taking the initiative; a gentleman should not leave his card on a young lady but on her mother. 'The etiquette of card-leaving is a privilege which society places in the hands of ladies to govern and determine their acquaintanceships and intimacies', and this privilege could as well be used for snubs as for acceptance. Thus if a lady of higher rank returns a call by a card only, without asking if the mistress of the house is at home, 'it should be understood that she wished the acquaintance to be of the slightest'; and should a lady of lower rank return a card-leaving with a call, this would be a serious breach of etiquette. Ladies having a large acquaintance are advised to keep a visiting-book in which to enter cards left and due; but ladies who know fewer people can make do by ruling a line down the middle of a memorandum book.

Calling, by this period, was almost entirely confined to afternoon calls (still often known as morning calls) made between 3 and 6 p.m. The lady or gentleman making the call—or, if the arrival is by carriage, the servant—asks if the lady of the house is at home. If the answer is no, the visiting lady leaves three cards, one of her own and two of her husband's, for *he* calls on both the master and the mistress, *she* only on the latter. If the mistress is at home, no cards are given. Instead the servant precedes the visitor to the drawing-room and announces the caller formally. A gentleman carries his hat, stick, and gloves upstairs with him, laying them tidily on the floor beside him as he sits down. He would, of course, be wearing morning dress. Though a young man might stroll about town in a dark suit and a bowler hat, he would not dream of doing so in Pall Mall or Piccadilly or Bond Street, where ladies might be met.

A purely ceremonious call should last only a quarter of an hour and take place before 4.30 when tea is brought in. Conversation should be lightly sustained on topics of the hour. More intimate acquaintances may come later and stay longer, expecting to partici-pate in the tea poured by the tea-gowned hostess from a silver tea-pot on a silver tray replenished from a silver kettle over a silver spirit-lamp; and to partake of thin bread-and-butter and small cakes proffered by the assiduous young men who had been invited to a dinner or a dance the previous week, for *their* post-entertainment calls were obligatory. But they may, if the degree of acquaintance justifies it, call on a Sunday when friends, not mere acquaintances, are expected and longer stays permissible. When, finally, the visitor rises to go, the hostess will ring the bell to indicate to the servant below that the door should be opened and the carriage called. If the hostess feels especially gracious or if her lady visitor is of higher rank, the hostess may accompany her to the head of the stairs; or the host right down to the hall.

Evening Amusements

At the time of day when formal calling was ending, some evening entertainments had already begun. In many convivial districts in the north, neighbours—perhaps a group based on church or chapel attendance—would meet weekly at one or other home, and after the high tea settle down to an evening's whist-playing or (as both Bennett and Mr. Priestley have described) an evening of home-made music. The gramophone or phonograph was rather for the young and even fast; although, on the wax cylinders or single-sided disks, many operatic arias and other reproductions of serious music were available, we find a certain disapprobation of gramophones in homes that did not possess them, a cultural snobbishness similar to that expressed towards television in the 1950's. There were still many homes in which, when asked for the evening, you might take your music in the reasonable expectation that you would be asked to play or sing. If asked by the young people you might take your ukelele or banjo, but in the drawing-room the piano was the chosen instrument.

In this period the piano was an essential status-symbol of refinement. In the Staffordshire drawing-room of the hostess who provided the Lucullan high tea described a few pages back the piano, artistically turned away from the wall, was 'adorned with carelessly flung silks and photographs'. When Mrs. Chepstow, the evil heroine of Robert Hichens's *Bella Donna*, sought to give impressively spiritual touches to her room at the Savoy Hotel, she concealed the racing paper in the waste-paper basket and scattered about the room *The Nineteenth Century and After*, the *Quarterly Review*, *The Times*, and several books—D'Annunzio, Hawthorne, Emerson, Goethe's *Faust*—and placed Elgar's *Dream of Gerontius* open on the music-stand of the rosewood piano. Grand pianos stood in specially designed alcoves in new Homes Beautiful, and uprights in most suburban parlours. Since Sir Edward Burne-Jones, in 1880, had decided that the ordinary grand piano was ugly and had designed his celebrated 'Orpheus' piano, elaborately painted on all possible surfaces, the decorative treatment of pianos had proceeded apace. Edwardian England provided a great variety of pianos, suitable for any of the rooms designed in what were now beginning to be called 'schemes of colour' or 'colour schemes'— painted pianos, pianos in the Chippendale style, pianos after Elizabethan virginals, and even a piano by Mr. Lutyens in the Gothic manner to suit a similarly decorated room.

There were few evening pleasures to be found at home for the very poor, and in the towns their major consolation was, almost inevitably, drink. Drink, wrote William James in 1902, stands to the poor and unlettered in the place of symphony concerts and literature, and in lieu of other amusements the Edwardian working classes often drank to excess. Women, it was noticed, were drinking more than they had been, and street-fights between women, conducted with fisticuffs or with the ubiquitous and potentially dangerous hat-pins, were a not uncommon sight. The urban public houses were generally open from about 6 in the morning until at least 11 at night, and, on an average, every working-class family spent 6s. a

week on intoxicants, a terrifying figure in view of the general level of
working-class incomes. But with homes that could of their nature
provide no pleasure or relaxation, there was little else for the poor
to do. During the period the new cinematograph entertainments,
often held, to start with, in empty shops, increased their attendance
until it was worth the exhibitors' while to build special edifices known
as 'picture-palaces'—a name that 'took' in a way that earlier
attempts to assimilate gin-palaces to do-gooding coffee-palaces had
not. Philanthropic attempts at entertainment had dwindled almost
to a few east-end clubs run as much for the moral benefit of the
public schoolboys and undergraduates who gave their services as
for the delight of those who came. Occasionally, in a village here
and there, an active rector or squiress would encourage use of
a reading room or village hall, or arrange a magic-lantern lecture;
one or two enterprising villages took advantage of the Parish
Councils Act to fit up bathing pools, which must have been a godsend to the young people on summer evenings.

But for the most part, village life was increasingly moribund.
With the new manufactured goods coming in from outside, the
diversity of village crafts had dwindled. The old village festivals and
customs were dying or had died away. The public houses, no longer,
since the coming of railways, able to depend on the patronage of
passing carters, were dreary places, and the old church orchestras
had been replaced by at least a harmonium. Even the villagers'
clothes were now uniformly dark and drab in place of the brighter
colours previously worn. With the widespread replacement of arable
by dairy-farming and the breaking up of estates into market
gardens, local jobs for young girls had almost disappeared. The girls
left the villages to seek employment in the towns, followed inevitably by the young men. There can be small doubt that for the
most part the lives of Hodge and Mrs. Hodge, as they were often
referred to, were even more lacking in gaiety, colour, and variety
than those of the slum-dwellers in the towns.

But some other country or quasi-country dwellers had their
evenings filled with diversity and interest. In some more formal
suburbs and in provincial towns the 'Cinderella' dance had arisen,
public Cinderellas being held in town halls for charitable purposes,
small Cinderellas in private houses, and subscription Cinderellas
arranged under the aegis of ladies of local standing who kept the

disposal of tickets in their own hands. These Cinderellas were usually small and early, ending, as their name indicated, at midnight, with light refreshments, not a supper, and only a professional piano-player to dance to. But they had their disadvantages. It was found that young ladies were always in the majority, and that the males who took tickets were usually very young men with their way in the world still to make.

Those who lived in the rural Arcadias of the garden suburbs and, indeed, in some other suburbs too, had a wide choice of more or less improving evening occupations. Small cultural societies proliferated—societies for drama, for madrigal-singing, for dancing the newly revived country-dances or singing decently bowdlerized versions of recently rediscovered folk-songs, and for listening to lecturers of all kinds. The university extension lecture movement, started some thirty years earlier to bring the universities to the people, had soon been captured by the middle classes, but in 1903 a new attempt was made with the Workers' Educational Association, based on an alliance between the universities, the co-operatives, and the trade unions. By 1910 the W.E.A. had only 5,800 members, but these were still genuinely working-class; it was not until much later that the W.E.A., like the earlier movement, came in some districts at least to provide middle-class diversion rather than working-class education.

For summer evenings in the suburbs there were clubs for golf, for cricket, for tennis, and throughout the year there were many more or less impromptu parties and 'hops'. Although an Ann Veronica might feel her freedom was unreasonably curtailed, in one important respect it was substantial as compared with older generations, and this was in her freedom to woo. In contrast with the upper-class girl who, even when safely engaged, would not be allowed to drive alone in a carriage with her fiancé, the middle-class girl in a lively suburb would have ample opportunities for meeting eligible young men in conditions that allowed a final choice to be more or less freely made.

All gentlefolk changed for dinner, if only for a suburban evening at home reading the *Strand Magazine* or a nice new novel by E. Temple Thurston or Anthony Hope or W. J. Locke. At Crossways or Glaed Haem, Three Gables or Le Nid, the change might be only into a *demi-toilette* evening blouse of chiffon with lace insertions, but for the country-house party—indeed for any even quite small party

—the change was into full evening dress. Here is Miss Sackville-West's description of the duchess's evening toilette as seen by her daughter:

Her mother was seated, poking at her hair meanwhile with fretful but experienced fingers, while Button [the maid] knelt before her, carefully drawing the silk stockings on to the feet and smoothing them nicely up the leg. Then her mother would rise, and, standing in her chemise, would allow the maid to fit the long stays of pink coutil, heavily boned, round her hips and slender figure, fastening the busk down the front, after many adjustments; then the suspenders would be clipped to the stockings; then the lacing would follow, beginning at the waist and travelling gradually up and down, until the necessary proportions had been achieved. The silk laces and their tags would fly out, under the maid's deft fingers, with the flick of a skilled worker mending a net. Then the pads of pink satin would be brought, and fastened into place on the hips and under the arms, still further to accentuate the smallness of the waist. Then the drawers; and then the petticoat would be spread into a ring on the floor, and Lucy would step into it on her high-heeled shoes, allowing Button to draw it up and tie the tapes. . . . Button, gathering up the lovely mass of taffeta and tulle, held the bodice open while the Duchess flung off her wrap and dived gingerly into the billows of her dress. . . . [She reached] down stiffly for the largest of her rubies, which she tried first against her shoulder, but finally pinned into a knot at her waist. Then she encircled her throat with the high dog-collar of rubies and diamonds, tied with a large bow of white tulle at the back [and] slipped an ear-ring into its place.

Then bracelets, then fan (probably an ostrich-feather fan), then gloves, and the duchess was ready to descend to her guests for a rich formal meal of at least eight courses, served on a damask cloth heavily laden with silver, glass, flowers including, probably, trails of smilax, innumerable bon-bon dishes and table napkins folded into cunningly convoluted shapes, each shape having its name—the Fleur de Lis, the Rose and Star, the Sachet, the Slipper, and many others. The actual food for a formal dinner for eight persons should cost between about 30s. and £2. 10s., but, as we have seen, the prices paid for food in great houses were very often not fair ones.

After dinner, when coffee (usually French but sometimes Turkish) had been served in the drawing-room and the gentlemen had rejoined the ladies, both might settle down to tables of bridge, the

ladies, probably, with more enthusiasm than the gentlemen who
might well drift off to the billiard room, a *sine qua non* in respectable homes of the period. There they might smoke their pipes, which
was not done in the drawing-room. Indeed, it was only in rather
smart drawing-rooms that anyone smoked, and a lady who had
adopted the habit—usually with Turkish or Egyptian cigarettes—
would generally confine it to the privacy of the boudoir or the company of her own sex only, unless, of course, she belonged to a fast
Bohemian set, what Maurice Baring had called the *haute Bohème*.

Another favourite country-house after-dinner pastime was paper-
games. Some houses were famous for their paper-games and, of these,
some notorious for the horrors they held for guests unable to respond
eagerly to, say, 'Styles', which might involve writing an essay on
a given subject in the manner of, say, Ruskin or Stevenson, or
'Epigrams', whose name is sufficiently descriptive of its possible
terrors, or 'Consequences' or 'Qualities'. The language in which some
conversations took place was often a jargon such as all exclusive
societies periodically adopt. At the beginning of the period fashionable ladies might speak of a 'teagie' (a teagown) and a 'nightie',
approve this or that with 'deevie' (divine) and disapprobate with
'diskie' (disgusting); borrowing money from one's friends, a not
uncommon need, was 'lootin' one's pals'—no smart person ever
pronounced a final *g*. Later, as Miss Sackville-West has recorded,
the fashion was for Italianate endings: 'And after dinn-are, we might
have a little dans-are'. . . . 'I'm sure Mrs. Spedding dans-ares like
a ballerina. And anyway, if you won't let Sebastian bring you as
a partnerina, I shall ask you to bring Sebastian as a partnerino.'

Even with a little dans-are after dinner, the country-house party
was unlikely to sit up late. At about half-past 10 whisky would be
brought in or, in old-fashioned houses, tea, and by 11 the house-
party would be on the way to bed, leaving the butler to lock up. But
not necessarily each to his own bed: morals were often less than
stringent, and the good hostess was expected to arrange sleeping
accommodation according to currently desired proximities. Such
arrangements are said to be the usual consequence of formally
organized marriages, and in the highest circles little more than the
appearance of free choice, and sometimes barely that, was given to
marriageable girls.

Yet it is hardly possible to meet an upper-class Edwardian who

was young in those days and does not now maintain that the
social life of the London season represented an epitome of
pleasure never since equalled; and if in essence a marriage market,
it was a marriage market adorned with all that luxury could provide and took place in an ebullition of gaiety. Concerts, theatres,
and operas will be considered elsewhere, but dances can fairly count
as domestic entertainment, and to be invited to enough dances the
first necessity for a young man was to get on to the hostesses'
lists. Thereafter invitations would shower in from ladies whose
acquaintance he had never made, and needing to be repaid only by
the due returning of calls. During the season a young man need never
dine at home. With spare white gloves and a spare collar in his
pocket he would be off almost every evening to the dinner-party
where he would meet a selection of the young women who had been
presented that year at the evening courts introduced by King
Edward to replace the former afternoon presentations. And after
dinner he and they, and of course their chaperones, would go off to
the ball which would start, if it was a really smart one, at about 10
o'clock.

Outside, the houses would announce the ball with red carpets and
striped awning. Inside, they would be elaborately decorated, not
least with the cut flowers which were increasingly replacing the
former pot-plants and 'artificials'. These last, made of satin or
taffeta, dexterously shaped and folded, had rather made their way
to the ladies' dresses where they vied with real roses and carnations
and, above all, Parma violets, the chosen flower of the period.
Dance programmes might be waiting on a table, but more probably,
now, in Kensington than in Mayfair. The dances in which the young
ladies, seated by their chaperones, were invited to partake were
almost all waltzes, and though 'Do you reverse?' was sometimes
heard, to do so was rather fast and not permitted at court balls. An
occasional two-step might be introduced, an occasional polka, and
always there was a set of lancers; some favourite tunes of the
period, apart from those that derived from the currently popular
musical play, were the *Valse Bleu*, the *Sourire d'Avril*, the *Choristers'
Waltz*, and the *Machiche*—'the most wonderful tune in the world'—
which persisted for three seasons. At a small dance a buffet would
be provided, at a large one an elaborate ball supper; a typical
menu includes three *plats chauds*—soup, cutlets, and quails—and

a plethora of *plats froids* with three fish dishes (salmon, lobster, and prawns), six meat and poultry dishes including *médaillons de foie gras*, salads, sandwiches, and eight different kinds of sweet. The menu would sometimes be written on whimsical cards—on the sail of a boat, the petal of a lily—and champagne, that favourite drink of the Edwardians, would flow profusely. After supper, dancing continued until about three in the morning when the party would end with a furious *galope* and a burst of hunting-horns. And though, after each dance, it was proper to return a young lady to her chaperone, it was still possible that an interval might have been found—perhaps in the conservatory, perhaps on a sofa in a dark nook under the stairs—when *he* had spoken and *she* accepted.

However strictly the young lady had been brought up before marriage, given wealth and a liking for luxury her marital bedroom might well present the appearance of such a bower of bliss as in earlier periods would have been thought proper only for a professional courtesan. Underclothes, like nightgowns, could be exquisite froths of fine lawn and embroidery and lace, increasingly exiguous as the period wore on. Corsets, perhaps in a delicate Parma violet shade, could be enticingly pretty, and the new bust bodices, if bags rather than supports, provided a new focus of excitement. When the bride slips into bed, it is between fine French or Irish linen sheets, monogrammed and threaded with ribbons, her head on a goose-feather pillow covered with a frilled embroidered pillowcase. Her soft mattress, now perhaps on one of two 'twin' beds, is stuffed with extra quality hair and French wool, and her blankets are of merino edged with silk ribbon. Fitted cupboards conceal her often enormous variety of clothes, and her dressing-table is decked with a set of brushes and combs, hand-glass, clothes-brushes, trinket trays in precious metal or enamel work, and with cut glass or Venetian glass scent-sprays; and soon, if not yet, it will also carry the cosmetics that older women semi-secretly used, lip-salve and rouge, papier-poudre, and loose face-powder to replenish the swansdown puff sewn to a handkerchief and tucked away in the gold-mesh purse-bag or the Dorothy bag.

But the promise must often have belied the performance. It was usual to bring up girls in complete biological ignorance, and the knowledge picked up by boys was often surprisingly incomplete. Sir Lawrence Jones recalls a group of Oxford undergraduates asking a doctor whether women ever enjoyed sexual intercourse. The answer was: 'Nine out of ten women are indifferent to or actively dislike it; the tenth, who enjoys it, will always be a harlot.' This attitude and this ignorance make it perhaps not surprising that throughout the period the illegitimacy rates in the west end of London were consistently higher than in the east end. What does seem surprising, in view of the notorious rakishness of some sections of the upper classes, the diminishing force of religion, the scanty amusements of the poor, and the still limited though spreading knowledge of birth control, is that between 1901 and 1903 and again in 1907, the illegitimacy rates for England and Wales were the lowest ever recorded—3·9 per 100 live births.

The Fortunate Children

The accommodation of most homes ensured that parents and children led a common life. The institution of the 'children's hour' between afternoon tea and dressing for dinner was obviously needed only in those homes where a formal life and a sufficiency of servants kept mother and children apart unless special arrangements were made for their meeting, and writers on the care of children are emphatic that such arrangements should be made, even at the cost of inconvenience or sacrifice. Although the repressive discipline of earlier periods still held wide sway, newer ideas were tending to make the lives of some fortunate children, in everything except diet, probably pleasanter than children's lives had ever been before. These newer ideas were in fact of now fairly ancient lineage. As Peter Coveney has shown in his book *Poor Monkey*,[1] the weakening of the concept of original sin had led, towards the end of the eighteenth century, to a new use of the concept of the child as a symbol of innocence, a virtual replacement of the prelapsarian Adam in that role. The unspotted world of the child came to stand in contrast with the world's slow stain on maturity. Mawkishness inevitably set in. Already in Victorian times it was, at least fictionally, a happier lot to die than to grow up, and the attitude reached its apotheosis in 1904 with Barrie's creation of Peter Pan, the boy who chose never to grow up because adult life was so repulsive.

But many Victorian parents were virtually unaffected by these

[1] *Poor Monkey, the Child in Literature*, 1957.

newly developing views, and Edwardian attitudes to the child varied greatly. Patches of savage repressiveness still persisted, even among the educated upper classes. But more generally in the upper and upper-middle classes the child was king, the heir of the ages, whether cosseted as a plaything for its putative innocence, or laden, as in many high-minded intellectual families, with the burden of creating a new, clear-eyed, uncorrupted world because itself reared in a new, clear-eyed, uncorrupted freedom among beautiful thoughts and beautiful things. The school of St. George and the Venerable Bede which Wells depicts in *Joan and Peter* is a very fair example of a new progressive school; that novel also gives some useful pictures of older, more conventional educational establishments.

Edwardian children, like Edwardian servants, often helped to sustain a very substantial industry. For one thing, upper-class children were likely themselves to have a great many servants exclusively devoted to their well-being, and of these the most important was the nanny or nurse. This might be a nanny of the old-fashioned kind who had worked up through the proper hierarchy of service and earned between £30 and £50 a year, or it might be one of the new Norland nurses, trained at the Norland Institute and wearing its special uniform. The latter could certainly be trusted not to drug the infant with laudanum or gin, in the first place, probably, to keep it quiet during the christening ceremony when a placid baby might be expected to extract bigger tips from the godparents, and since these might vary between £1 and £5, the temptation was not unsubstantial. The Norland nurse might also be expected to make more sensible use of the family medicine cupboard with its bottle of iodine for the reduction of chronic swellings (but not for open wounds), its castor-oil for a mild purgative and epsom salts for a severe one, its ergot, said to be valuable for blood-spitting, and its eucalyptus and camphorated oil for colds; aspirin, though recently invented, was not yet usual in domestic use. When infectious diseases struck the nursery, the Norland nurse could be expected to know all the current precautionary measures, such as wringing out a sheet in carbolic solution and hanging it before the bedroom door to catch the germs. But this is not to denigrate all nannies, for many of them were excellent and felt by many parents to bring to the child a loving understanding that formal training could not give.

It was, of course, possible to keep a single-handed children's nurse (£20 to £25 p.a.), but both a Norland nurse and a highly trained nanny would expect some help, and in a really substantial family this could consist of a second nurse or even two, paid, according to responsibility, between £20 and £30 a year; an under-nurse at between £20 and £25; and, at the bottom of the ladder, a nursery-maid (£10 to £18 a year), probably a 14-year-old in her first job. Then there might be a schoolroom maid and a young ladies' maid, both hoping to become proper lady's maids one day, but meantime doing such work as their titles suggest, including looking after clothes and hair and going out with their young mistresses as required. But it was probably the head nurse who accompanied the children to the weekly dancing-classes with dancing-shoes in a stuff bag and, for the boys, white cotton gloves; for dancing-class, like Kensington Gardens in London, was where nurses could meet their colleagues to take proper competitive pride in the turn-out of their young charges and, in the park, of the mail-carts or bassinettes in which they were pushed. 'Bassinette', though originally referring to wickerwork baskets on wheels, was now generically used for perambulators of all materials. A superior coach-built bassinette of dark green or dark blue embossed with the family crest above its penny-farthing wheels would cost upwards of four pounds without the almost obligatory frills of white button-in hood-linings and canopies of white *piqué* edged with *broderie anglaise* or lace. Cheaper perambulators costing about 39s. 11d. sold in large quantities, and during this period the folding push-chair, with a square of carpet tacked to its seat and costing only a few shillings, became popular.

There were new ideas about the proper accommodation for children. We all have a nostalgic picture of the dark, cosy Victorian nursery, its cast-off shabby furniture brightened by the varnished scrap-screen, but for the tended Edwardian child only the new, and that of a special child-oriented kind, was good enough. It was not uncommon for an entire nursery suite to be provided at the top of the house with day-nursery, night-nursery, other bedrooms, playroom, bathroom, and pantry fitted with the means of simple cooking. Where there was no service-lift this meant, of course, a great deal of carrying up and down stairs for the nurserymaid. But some journeys might be spared if the system of communicating tubes had been installed or, better still, if the house had its own internal telephone switchboard, wired to the nursery as well as to garages and service-cottages. Special children's furnishings, especially sets of low tables and chairs, were extensively made, whether in simple woods or painted in pastel colours with whimsical pictorial transfer decoration—Dutch scenes were much favoured. A playroom was often fitted with a complete set of gymnastic apparatus—ropes, swings, trapezes, parallel bars—and big enough to give floor space to a large number of big expensive toys such as see-saws, rocking

'A very smartly-dressed doll, price 3s. 6d., the pretty sunshade costing 1s. 0½d. extra'

horses (whether the older kind on rockers or, towards the end of the period, the newer ones on swing-irons), big push animals on wheels, and doll's prams.

For toys this was a golden era. It was after about 1900 that the English toy industry began to make headway against former German predominance, and a new variety of splendid and ingenious toys had begun to come on the market. Dolls, at this period, were often exquisitely dressed and provided with lavishly over-sufficient wardrobes and accessories; and baby dolls, which some now considered psychologically more desirable, rapidly gained popularity. Since about 1880 the English toy soldiers made by the firm of W. Britain & Sons had deservedly been world-famous and long continued to be, but now new kinds of toys were being invented. In 1901 appeared the first quality toy steam locomotive, built by Bassett-Lowke to scale proportions to run on standard gauges, and in the same year Mr. Frank Hornby took out a patent for a new toy called 'Mechanics made Easy' which in 1907 was renamed Meccano. By the end of the period an almost limitless range of toy vehicles could be bought, motivated by clockwork, by steam, and by electricity, together with all the appropriate accessories for realism such as signals and station-sets. The best-known toyshop in England was probably Hamley's, but for simpler pleasures a child might go to Ellisdon's for novelties and for magic to Davenport's which had opened in 1898 in the Mile End Road.

The named soft toy was now starting its long run of popularity. Probably the first was the Golliwog, named for the hero of Miss Upton's book, *The Adventures of Two Dutch Dolls and a Golliwog*, first published in 1895; Golliwog also gave his name to a card game. Then came Teddy Bear, said—but the claims of origin are various— to have been derived by an American toy-buyer from a cartoon of a bear shot by Teddy Roosevelt and first shown by the German toy-maker Marguerite Steiff at the Leipzig toy fair in 1903. However that may be, before long Teddy Bears were being made in England, short plump bears as compared with their long thin German ancestors and fitted, after 1908, with a device that made them growl when tilted backwards. Then, in 1910, came a toy dog with a label round his neck reading 'I am Caesar: I belong to the King', for *his* model was Edward VII's dog Caesar who had marched in his master's funeral procession. There was also a wide variety of educational toys on sale—card games, not only frivolous like 'Pit' but also instructive (like sets of famous Frenchmen and masterpieces of art), the old dissected maps now renamed 'jig-saws', glove puppets providing opportunities for self-expression, and many kindergarten devices of German origin involving plaiting and weaving and threading.

But children have other ploys than playing with toys designed for the purpose, and collecting was not only enthusiastically pursued but could be, as the advertisement columns of *Little Folks* showed, a highly organized avocation. Favoured fields included crests, printed addresses (1*d.* per dozen), coloured advertisements (2*d.* per dozen), postmarks and postcards (Raphael Tuck's were in especial demand and the rate of exchange was 10 postmarks for 1 postcard) and, right from the beginning of the period, cigarette-cards from Wills, Players, Salmon & Gluckstein (who did a much sought-after set of famous generals), and Ogden's Guinea Gold. Other favourite swops and sales included sets of children's magazines (*Chums, Girl's Own Paper, Chatterbox, Young England, Captain, Girls' Realm, Every Boy's Annual, Rosebud Annual*, &c.) and books, especially the coloured fairy-books of Andrew Lang, Kipling's *Jungle Books*, and the girls' novels by L. T. Meade and

E. Everett Green. Girls also collected entries for their elegantly leather-bound gold-edged albums with pastel shiny pages for poems and quips and occasional leaves of rougher paper for drawings and paintings.

The upper-class children's magazines of the period were far from being as self-centred as they later became, and while providing plenty of light entertainment, including versions of the currently popular riddles (Why did the coal scuttle, the bull rush?), also showed a wider concern for the less fortunate than was then generally visible in adult life. *Little Folks*'s readers maintained a cot at a children's hospital, and many of the swops and sales advertised were for its benefit. Nor was the magazine chary of drawing attention to the actual conditions of the poor; we read of mothers who drink, of children who die or, living, are dirty, half-starved, and shoeless.

Clothes, for upper-class children, were in something of a transition between formality and ease. Some boys, for everyday, still wore Norfolk suits with knickerbockers, stockings (Norfolk hose), boots, and cloth caps; others wore flannel shorts, half hose, and school-caps. For parties, sailor-suits were *de rigueur*. These, worn by the king's grandchildren, caught on with lightning speed and were soon available in the Bon Marchés for as little as 2s. 4½d. (special sale price), but snobbish little boys were well aware of the difference between these, with their single band of braid on the collar, and their own from Rowe's of Gosport in the proper three-banded tradition. Girls too wore sailor-tops with pleated skirts over black stockings; but for parties they wore white dresses with sashes—these, which could be of greater or lesser expense and beauty, were a focal point of conspicuous display—topped, for transit, by a red velvet Red Riding Hood cloak. But some little girls, and the reader can guess which families *these* came from, wore jibbahs and sandals for everyday and liberty silks or smocked velvets for best. For bedwear, pyjamas—'pie-jim-jams'—were recommended for boys and girls alike, though most girls still wore nightgowns. When considering girls' clothes we should not omit mention of the famous 'Liberty bodice', intended to replace the too common demand for corsets at a too early age; but, in all but the most progressive families, girls laced into corsets all too soon, and did not think to take them off even for Swedish exercises or hockey.

The limits of children's freedom varied greatly. E. Nesbit's novels show how wide sensible parents could safely make them, in town as in country, but on a higher social rung many a girl might reach marriageable age without ever having left her home unaccompanied, if only by a maid.

Taking all in all and comparing our period with those that preceded it, the life of an Edwardian child whose parents were financially secure was idyllic in all save diet. There, current ignorance virtually ensured that no child of whatever class could be healthily fed. In the diets of even the wealthiest nurseries stodge prevailed and fresh fruit played little licit part. Acidosis was not a recognized condition, and a thin, nervy, easily nauseated child was likely to be 'fed up' on cream and thick slices of bread and butter. A baby, unless it was a breast-fed baby, would come off worst of all, for it was the better educated parents who were most likely to destroy the infant's only source of vitamin C by boiling the milk.[1] It was also the richer parents who were more likely to feed the infant on one of the many patent foods which were predominantly farinaceous and deficient in proteins, fats, and most vitamins. The poor condition of babies so fed was often masked by their deceptive readiness to put on weight; but they were pale, fat, flabby, tended to develop more or less mild rickets, and in later life to have poor teeth.

Children of the Poor

Even allowing for the dietary deficiencies imposed by ignorance, the differences between the physical conditions of rich and poor children were gross, as a few statistics show. The average height of working-class schoolboys was five inches below that of public schoolboys, and the average weight of working-class boys at the age of 13 was eleven pounds less than that of boys from wealthier families. At the beginning of the period, 18 per cent. of children born in the west end of London died before the age of 5; in the east end, 55 per cent. did so. Though the infant mortality rate fell by one-third between 1900 and 1910, it remained largely unchanged in poverty areas. In Blackburn, for instance, in 1911, the infantile death-rate in the wealthier area was 96 per 1,000, in the poorer areas 315 per 1,000. In institutions the death rates for infants were often terrifyingly

---

[1] Somewhat surprisingly, Mrs. Peel wrote in 1902: 'Milk keeps better when boiled, but ... many doctors consider that milk subjected to boiling heat is lacking in nourishment.'

high. In 1907, in the poorer districts of West Ham, 15 in every 1,000 infants died in the first week of life; in four large London voluntary hospitals the rate was 30 per 1,000, and in London Poor Law institutions 47 per 1,000. Generally speaking, infant mortality in Poor Law institutions (many of which had not yet put into effect the recommendations of the 1834 Poor Law report) was two to three times as great as in the population as a whole, something like a third of all children born and staying there (in Scotland, a half) dying within their first year. But at least, if the child died in the workhouse, the workhouse buried it. If it died in a poor home where the parents had been unable to pay or to keep up the payments to a burial club, the body might, as Jack London describes, be kept in the home for some time while efforts were made to collect the money for something more than a pauper's funeral:

During the day [the body] lies on the bed; during the night, when the living take the bed, the dead occupies the table, from which, in the morning, when the dead is put back into the bed, they eat their breakfast. Sometimes the body is placed on the shelf which serves as a pantry for their food. Only a couple of weeks ago [in 1902] an East End woman was in trouble, because, in this fashion, being unable to bury it, she had kept her dead child for three weeks.

Wealthy babies were born at home with the attendance of family doctor and monthly nurse, and home birth was still the general practice. For artisans some provident societies paid lying-in benefits to members' wives, but for the poor, conditions of birth, like all others, were difficult. To employ a midwife of minimal qualifications cost at least 5s. and home facilities were often non-existent. Occasionally an expectant mother could obtain a card for admission to a hospital, but it was not unknown for a husband officially to desert his wife before the birth so that she could bear her child in the workhouse in better and cheaper conditions than at home.

The subsequent feeding of the infant was an appalling problem. Breast feeding among the poor was rapidly declining because of the mother's inability, on her poverty diet, to produce a sufficient flow of milk; as it was, the cost of child-bearing for poor women was usually chronic ill-health over and above that usual in their class—digestive troubles, bad teeth, anaemia, general debility. The most usual substitute for mother's milk was sweetened condensed skimmed milk at about 5d. a 6-oz. tin. This was excessively rich in sugar and deficient in fats: after the report of the select committee on food adulteration in 1894, it had been required to carry a label stating that it was unsuitable for the feeding of infants and young children, but it was still extensively used. Poor mothers often proved unable to understand the warning label, and even Mrs. Beeton, citing an unnamed authority, says 'it may be broadly asserted that a healthy child would do well on condensed milk alone for the first few months'. But many mothers could not afford even this, and reared or attempted to rear their babies on flour and water.

From the turn of the century there had been efforts to make clean milk available for nursing mothers, for analysis had shown that much of the milk sold was filthy, germ-laden, watered, and doctored with dangerous preservatives. The first English milk dispensary had been opened in 1899 in St. Helen's. In 1901 Liverpool established milk depots for infants whose mothers were unable to feed them, and in the same year Battersea's municipal milk depot sold sterilized 'humanized' milk to mothers for about 1s. 6d. to 1s. 9d. a week (fresh milk in towns cost about 2d. a pint, and skimmed milk 1d.); some other municipalities issued certificates to producers of clean milk, but it was found that in most places the price of 'certified' milk was one the public would not pay. This did not obtain everywhere: in York the demand for clean milk was so great that the dairy farmer supplying it had to put up the prices to reduce demand.

It is already clear that in the families of that third of the population living below the poverty line, the children had no chance of a diet adequate even in quantity. Those who came off best were often the youngest members of large families at the period when the family income was being supplemented by the earnings of the older ones. But this period was likely to be brief, and, generally speaking, working-class children (apart from Jewish children who even in the poorest districts tended to be much better fed) were usually hungry and showed all the recognized signs of malnutrition, from rickets and stunted growth to grossly carious teeth. The L.C.C. medical examiners charted as normal any child with three decayed teeth, slight eye defects, and many slight abnormalities due to malnutrition. Ills of ear, nose, and throat abounded.

The general conditions of the care of poor urban children were equally unsatisfactory. Social workers pleaded for crèches, day nurseries, clinics, school dinners; the Destitute Children's Dinner

Society, formed in 1864, had 58 dining-rooms, and the London School Dinner Association ran soup kitchens, but their efforts were insufficient. Inquiries had shown that meals were required at 393 schools in the London area for 44,320 children, and that charitable agencies had been able to provide meals at only 214 of these schools and for only 17,162 children. Despite these figures the L.C.C. in 1907 declined to operate the Education (Provision of Meals) Act of 1906 which allowed meals to be provided for necessitous schoolchildren, claiming that voluntary agencies met the need. Yet of one of these schools, the Chaucer School in Bermondsey, H.M. Inspector had written, 'Most of the children are small for their age. A large number show signs of insufficient feeding. Mentally they are very slow and appear to have so little power of memory that a day's holiday wipes away the knowledge previously obtained. . . . They are, in a large number of cases, in chronic want of food.'

Gradually, however, the act was implemented and school care committees set up. In 1907 the first infant welfare centre was opened in St. Pancras, and in the same year Birmingham ran a poster campaign with directions for mothers, in an effort to 'combat the mortality among infants in hot weather'. But for many years to come all such ameliorative efforts were to be far from adequate. A Fabian tract of 1909 described our schoolchildren as 'the most ragged and filthy in Europe', and pointed out that where, in 1904, France, excluding Paris, had 322 crèches, England, excluding London, had 19. Another Fabian tract, this time of 1911, putting the case for school clinics, describes the background of a London working-class child:

The advent of a typical slum (poverty spot) mother increases the doctor's feeling of hopelessness. . . . Take a concrete case, that of a child with discharge from the ears. The mother . . . is a person with tattered, frowsy, and safety-pinned raiment, conforming generally to the blouse and skirt type; the sleeves are torn to a conveniently free length, the waist is commodiously ample. Neither face nor hands are especially clean, the face is coarse in feature and grinningly amiable. Conversation reveals much surface plausibility, with much genuine and deep-laid sloth and inertia. The home is in two or three dark, semi-basement rooms, low, hung with lines on which hang flapping clothes, cumbered with backless chairs, decayed tables, peeling veneer chests of drawers and iron bedsteads heaped with brownish coverings. . . . To expostulate with such a woman for sewing her child's clothing tightly upon its back is to get a glib explanation (glaringly denied by the conditions) that this is done regularly every night after the equally regular bath.[1]

And unless we must assume a startling decline of social habits over the next thirty years, to this we can fairly add information gleaned from *Our Towns*, the 1943 report on the condition of many slum homes in which no meal is ever cooked or sat down to, where defaecation and micturition take place on the floor with, at most, a piece of newspaper laid down, and where no provision of any kind is made by girls and women for periods of menstrual flow.[2]

In such conditions it seems futile to discuss any children's toys or amusements that cost money. Dolls were made, as they always have been, from a rag, a bone, a hank of hair, though if a penny did become available, it could be profitably laid out at one of the many penny bazaars with their splendid range of penny tin models—steam-rollers, hansom-cabs, locomotives, fire-engines, models of different motor-cars and, in the latter part of our period, of motor-buses. The various organizations such as the Boys' Brigade, whose basis was church membership, and from about 1907 the Boy Scouts, could not on the whole recruit from the lowest levels. Though the original tests for first class scouts revealingly demanded that a boy should be able to read and write and have at least 6*d.* in the savings bank, the cost of the uniform was often prohibitive at about 15*s.* Similar considerations applied to the Girl Guide movement which got going, as a result of popular demand, in 1909. The amusements of slum children were generally of an older kind—skipping, hopscotch, 'alleys', begging for the guy, in the north 'mischief night' (30 April or 4 November) and in London making shell grottoes for St. James's day (25 July).

There was, said Jack London, 'one beautiful sight in the east end, and only one' and this was the little girls dancing as the organ-grinder went his rounds. It was a sight that moved many writers. There are Laurence Binyon's lines about the dark city street, lit only by the glow from a tavern window:

there, to the brisk measure
Of an organ that down in an alley merrily plays,

---

[1] Mrs. Townsend, *The Case for School Nurseries*, Fabian Tract 145, 1909; L. Haden Guest, *The Case for School Clinics*, Fabian Tract 154, 1911.

[2] In Edwardian England disposable sanitary towels were on sale at between 1*s.* and 2*s.* a dozen; but the more usual protection was still folded linen or cotton towels, washed out after use.

Two children, all alone and no one by,
Holding their tattered frocks, through an airy maze
Of motion, lightly threaded with nimble feet,
Dance sedately: face to face they gaze,
Their eyes shining, grave with a perfect pleasure.

And Max Beerbohm, in his essay 'A Morris for May-Day' (1907):

Often, in London, passing through some slum where a tune was
being ground from an organ, I have paused to watch the little girls
dancing. In the swaying dances of these wan, dishevelled, dim little
girls I have discerned authentic beauty.

Domestic Religion

Whether with plenty or in poverty Edwardian life was essentially
one based on material values, and if religion played in several
groups an important social part, there were few in which it was
cherished as of spiritual value. Religion still played its conventional role in the ceremonies for passage rites in all groups, for
birth, confirmation, marriage, and death, though even here many
progressive people dispensed with them. The upper classes were, as
always, among religion's most stalwart supporters in outward and
visible signs. Though, as has been pointed out, few households now
started the day with family prayers, most upper-class families in
the country would think it proper to go to church on Sundays, and
most of the guests at a country-house party would think it proper
to accompany their hostess there, even though this meant, for the
women, changing from the tweeds into which they had changed
after breakfast into their dress again—and then back into tweeds
and then back to a dress for luncheon. Religion would certainly be
expected of the servants, and Miss Sackville-West has charmingly
described the black-clad procession of the Chevron maids to church.
In towns, too, upper-class people would go to church, and then, in
London, to the church parade in Hyde Park which was a social
event not to be missed.

But newer habits, especially those of week-ends at lower social
levels than the country-house parties, were eating into church-
going habits, and the Anglican churches especially were beginning
to feel the effects of a steadily declining recruitment into the ranks
of the clergy. Nonconformity held its adherents better than the
Church of England did, but even so the rising labour movement

was, as Ensor points out, largely recruited from the ranks of non-conformity and now providing in the secular field opportunities hitherto available only through the chapel. As to the working class, says Masterman, 'This class—in the cities—cannot be accused of losing its religion . . . because it had never gained a religion.' In London in 1902 a little over two in every eleven people attended a place of worship, a noticeable drop from a previous count made in 1886, though nothing like as steep as it later became. But it must not be supposed that even the rural labourers were devoted church-goers. In Corsley, the Wiltshire village investigated in commendable detail by Maud Davies in 1909, only about 100 people out of a population of 824 attended morning service, and this included the children in the choir. Rowntree, investigating village life a little later, found that 'the feeling of the poorer people towards the churches seemed to be one of indifference, if not of half-resentful scorn'. He comments that for many even a halfpenny for the collecting-box may be too much to spare, and concludes that 'the full enjoyment of the social aspects of Christian fellowship, whether in church or chapel, the tea meeting, the harvest thanksgiving, the missionary meeting, is not for the very poor, but for whose who can co-operate actively by gifts of money or of kind'.

In the middle classes even social custom often proved insufficient to maintain earlier religious habits. 'It is the middle class which is losing its religion,' wrote Masterman, 'which is slowly or suddenly discovering that it no longer believes in the existence of the God of its fathers, or a life beyond the grave.' In some parts of the community, and notably among the intelligentsia, religion had either been replaced by an active agnosticism or had simply withered away. H. G. Wells's Peter in *Joan and Peter* was perhaps a little unusual among children in being so far distanced from religion that he had never heard of grace after meals; but the parents of such a boy as he would, on Sunday mornings, be likely to seek something they thought of in terms similar to religious ones by swinging over the downs in hairy tweeds, a book of verse in their pockets, believing communion with Nature and Beauty to be a more valuable spiritual experience than church-going. Many socialist parents believed that socialism would prove a spring of action even more potent than religion had been and some hopefully sent their children to the socialist Sunday schools. And though many a more conventional

Edwardian mother would dutifully repair to the night-nursery each evening to hear the children's prayers, there were few children who had any reason to believe that personal prayer played any part in adult life.

It is often said of the Edwardian period—as, indeed, of others—that it was one in which we see the break-up of family life. There does not seem to be evidence to support this view. Though religion could no longer be relied on as a cohesive force and the power of socialism to replace it had not yet been tested, the Edwardian family showed no less stability as a social unit than families had done in the past, whether sustained by the bonds of formality among the rich, amid the broadening opportunities enjoyed by the middle classes and by the upper working classes, or in the intolerable surroundings of urban and rural slums.

5

SCIENCE

A. R. UBBELOHDE, F.R.S.

*Professor of Thermodynamics in the
University of London (Imperial College)*

SCIENCE

The Social Background

THREE general comments can be made about those aspects of science and technology whose germination or whose contemporary influence were of importance to Edwardian England.

First, largely because of its educational background, society was almost wholly unpenetrated by and impenetrable to the importance of science in national affairs. Leaders of British science were probably as eminent and as far-seeing as in other eras, but their valiant struggles with the inherited consequence of public neglect of science had to be followed by the painful lessons of the first world war before new measures could bear fruit abundantly. The beginnings of modern practice with regard to scientific and technical education, and in the spending of public moneys on scientific research, were disappointingly slow; this was an undoubted element of weakness in the rivalry between Britain and younger industrial nations such as Germany.

A second general comment refers to applications of science to meet various human needs. In the broadening flow of technological victories, the Edwardians witnessed some highly important *premières*. As in other eras, a host of minor triumphs of applied science came their way, but commercialized wireless telegraphy, successful flight in machines heavier than air, the mass production of motor-cars, and the bulk production of synthetic fertilizers (and, incidentally, of explosives) were quite out of the common, and must be included among those technical innovations whose scope was wide and whose impact is still growing. Other major developments of applied science that can also be placed in the Edwardian era (though probably somewhat less precisely) include the potential conquest of tropical diseases such as malaria and sleeping sickness through the mastery of the life cycles of the insects which carry them. In this era, too, massive research was begun on therapeutic chemicals to replace drugs of natural origin and other cruder remedies. Planned tests were made systematically on a long sequence of chemically related substances. Such programmes of research led, for example, to the successful medical treatment of syphilis with 'salvarsan 606' and pointed the way to the subsequent mastering of many other diseases.

A third striking feature was the emergence of revolutionary innovations in modern physics, briefly designated as the quantum theory, the relativity theory, and the study of nuclear energy in terms of the disintegration of atoms. Their revolutionary character lay in their undermining the structure of classical physics, which had been confidently built up since Galileo and Newton in terms of precise mathematical concepts of motions and forces attributed to indestructible atoms. Some of the most far-reaching consequences of abandoning the classical attempt to define the motion of small particles with mathematical determinism, and of recognizing the disintegration of atomic nuclei, are still being worked out. It was not to be expected that these developments, which affect the whole of the metrical description of nature, could be fully appreciated at their very beginnings. Contemporary Edwardians may more readily be excused for not grasping the importance of such revolutionary discoveries in fundamental science, than for their laggard response to national needs in scientific education and research.

Albert and Edward

Social incentives for the growth of pure and applied science in Britain suffered a grave setback with the death of the Prince Consort in 1861. Because of efforts made and stimuli provided by governments of the younger industrial nations, some relative decline in Britain's leadership was only to be expected from the high summit of 1851, when the world came to Britain to see the marvels of the new wealth generated by industrialism displayed in a Great Exhibition. Had Albert lived longer the social incentives for the continued growth of pure and applied science might well have been kept strong in Britain. Albert's education and temperament nourished his German attitude towards *Kultur und Wissenschaft*. The habit of patronizing scientists and philosophers was probably as well developed by various German princelings as anywhere in Europe, at a time when such patronage gave vital social and financial incentives for their work. The court of Weimar is a well-known instance. In some of the German states, particularly in Prussia, this habit of patronage evolved without any real break into government support for science and learning throughout the eighteenth and nineteenth centuries. In Britain, the development of pure and even more of applied science during the nineteenth century followed a much less deliberate plan of growth in a pattern that can be observed again and again—brilliant beginnings followed by a baffling transfer of initiative to less original but more tenacious peoples. Possibly the very success and economic advantage obtained by developing an early start must needs obstruct later and more intricate elaborations of applied science in any nation, not just in Britain. This pattern of brilliant start and disappointing follow-through was described in clear but somewhat dispirited terms in 1902 by the president of the British Association for that year, Professor (later Sir) James Dewar:

Heredity imposes obligations and also confers aptitude for their discharge. If His Majesty's royal mother throughout her long and beneficent reign set him a splendid example of devotion to the burdensome labours of state which must necessarily absorb the chief part of his energies, his father no less clearly indicated the great part he may play in the encouragement of science. Intelligent appreciation of scientific work and needs is not less but more necessary in the highest quarters to-day than it was forty-three years ago, when His Royal Highness the Prince Consort brought the matter before this Association . . . in his presidential address, . . . hoping that by gradual diffusion of science and its increasing recognition as a principal part of our national education . . . the claims of science may no longer require the begging box . . . and the State will recognize in science one of its elements of strength and prosperity, to protect which the clearest dictates of self interest demand. Had this advice been seriously taken to heart and acted upon by the rulers of the nation at the time, what splendid results would have accrued to this country. We should not now be groping in the dark after a system of national education. We should not be wasting money, and time more valuable than money, in building imitations of foreign educational superstructures before having put in solid foundations. We should not be hurriedly and distractedly casting about for a system of tactics after confrontation with the disciplined and co-ordinated forces of industry and science led by the rulers of powerful states. . . . As it is, we have lost ground which it will tax even this nation's splendid reserves of individual initiative to recover.

Despite such prodding, Edward was to show himself a characteristic Edwardian in his attitude towards science, which can be charitably described as benevolent impenetrability. One of the last privileges of royalty to be surrendered is the exposure to new inventions, and the opportunity to sample them. One early use of Marconi's development of wireless telegraphy has a delicious flavour of the wonders of science applied to domestic happiness in the royal family. When Albert Edward was recuperating from an injured knee on board the royal yacht at Cowes, he was apparently fascinated by the tapping out of wireless messages. Up to 150 were sent across the water to his mamma at Osborne, most of them variants of the comfortable theme 'H.R.H. the Prince of Wales has passed another good night and the knee is in good condition'. But apart from such instances of the royal pleasure in the novelties of applied science, the evidence is that social incentives for the development of science came primarily from other directions, not from the ruling classes.

Private Laboratories

Allowing for local adaptations, social fashions in the western family of peoples are largely imitative. This was certainly true about the patronage of artists, and, in a similar but much less prominent way, the patronage of natural philosophers by various courts of Europe can be traced through several centuries. It is not perhaps surprising that some English noblemen, whose estates might be equated in terms of power and wealth with some of the smaller European principalities, were keen amateur scientists. One well-known precursor in Britain was Sir Walter Ralegh, who when imprisoned in the Tower in 1607 found twin solace in writing his *History of the World* and in converting a henhouse into a laboratory for the distillation of cordials. An interest in science and personal practice of experiments became highly fashionable in the seventeenth century, about the time the Royal Society was founded.

In the eighteenth century Lord Shelburne supported some important and original work by Priestley (1733–1804). Discoveries that are still famous were made by Cavendish (1731–1810) in his own private laboratory. Among the middle classes it is pleasing to remember that even Dr. Johnson reserved one of the garrets in his chambers for his books and for the pursuit of Chymistry. But by the mid-nineteenth century this tradition of scientific work as a hobby of individuals was dying out. It is true that Lord Salisbury (d. 1903) found recreation and refreshment from public duties in the practice of chemistry and photography in his private laboratory at Hatfield. The third Lord Rayleigh (d. 1919), a much more eminent scientist and one of the leaders of Victorian physics, had his laboratory at his family home at Terling in Essex. This laboratory was also used by the fourth Lord Rayleigh (1875–1947). But such activities would be regarded by contemporaries as merely one of the many forms of eccentric behaviour that were the peculiar privilege and characteristic of wealthy English noblemen. No evidence suggests that private laboratories had much influence in disseminating ideas about the national importance of science, any more than Gladstone's 'Homer Table' helped to sustain Greek culture among those less fortunately placed in their access to the Greek heritage. This lack of support from the ruling classes for the national pursuit of pure and applied science during the nineteenth century had become sufficiently serious in its consequences by 1900 to give special significance to any kind of support from other sources.

In this respect, probably the most important public platform was provided by the yearly meetings of the British Association. A study of the contemporary fellows of the Royal Society also gives valuable information about what scientists of influence and importance were doing for Edwardian England outside their own specialist fields.

The British Association

The British Association for the Advancement of Science was founded in 1831 with the objects: 'To give a stronger impulse and more systematic direction to scientific inquiry; to promote the intercourse of those who cultivate science in different parts of the British empire, with one another and with foreign philosophers; to obtain a more general attention to the objects of science, and a removal of any disadvantages of a public kind which impede its progress.' Charles Babbage's *Observations on the Decline of Science in England* (1830) and the inspiration derived by Babbage and his collaborators from the *Deutsches Naturforschers Versammlung*, are said to have contributed largely to the foundation of the association.

To be fruitful in yielding new knowledge, scientific research demands a high degree of abstraction from the everyday world. But

to be fruitful in leading to new applications of science, this knowledge must be communicated throughout the nation as a whole. In
our own time, means of communication between scientists working
in different directions and between scientists and other members of
the community have been developed in various ways. Although
problems of communication lead even now to recurrent grumbles,
on the whole contemporary needs are provided for effectively. But
in Victorian and Edwardian times problems of effective communication of science were greatly aggravated by the inadequate educational background of most of the public, whose interests were
nevertheless vitally concerned. This enhanced the relative importance of the reports and of the president's address at the yearly
meetings of the British Association. To spread the public interest
in science, these annual meetings were held in rotation at various
large towns in Britain or, in some years, in cities of the empire
outside the British Isles. Large numbers of the public were thus
exposed to one week's stocktaking every year of the scientific state
of the nation. At one time, man's place in nature had attracted
tremendous public interest to the meetings of the association, but the
passionate controversies of the Victorian sixties about evolution and
about natural selection as one of its mechanisms had died down by
Edwardian times. Metrical sciences such as physics and chemistry,
though of much more immediate importance for Britain's industrial
welfare, never attracted the same interest from the general public.

Speakers at the British Association had plenty of scope for
grumbling about the lack of public recognition of science in Britain.
Remarks made by various presidents help to throw light on the
general social background to science. The president for 1902,
Professor Dewar, part of whose address to King Edward was quoted
earlier, also voiced complaints about the meagre public expenditure
on scientific research in Britain. He pointed to the fact that Germany
had 4,500 works-chemists more highly trained than England's
1,500–2,000, and considered that the German development of British
inventions and discoveries was primarily due to want in Britain of
diffused education in science even for the so-called educated classes.
In 1903 the president, Norman Lockyer, examined even more
fully the reasons for the inadequate application of science to industry. He stressed that the need to organize science in Britain was
quite as urgent as any need to organize a navy in Germany, and

pleaded that it was far better to spend state money on brains to promote trade than on a navy to protect it. Professor E. Ray Lankester, the president for 1906, in his address to the annual meeting held at York, included a particularly bitter complaint about the impenetrability of the governing classes to the importance of science for the nation's welfare:

It is, unfortunately, true that the successive political administrators of the affairs of this country, as well as the permanent officials, are altogether unaware today, as they were twenty-five years ago, of the vital importance of that knowledge which we call science, and the urgent need for making use of it in a variety of public affairs. Whole departments of government in which scientific knowledge is the one thing needful are carried on by ministers, permanent secretaries, assistant secretaries, and clerks who are wholly ignorant of science, and naturally enough dislike it since it cannot be used by them, and is in many cases the condemnation of their official employment. Such officials are, of course, not to be blamed, but rather the general indifference of the public to the unreasonable way in which its interests are neglected. A difficult feature in treating of this subject is that when one mentions the fact that ministers of state and the officials of the public service are not acquainted with science, and do not even profess to understand the results or their importance, one's statement of this very obvious and notorious fact is apt to be regarded as a personal offence. It is difficult to see wherein the offence lies, for no one seeks to blame these officials for a condition of things which is traditional and frankly admitted. . . . The reason is, I think, to be found in the defective education, both at school and university, of our governing class, as well as in a radical dislike among all classes to the establishment and support by public funds of posts which the average man may not expect to succeed by popular clamour or class privilege in gaining for himself— posts which must be held by men of special training and mental gifts. Whatever the reason for the neglect, the only remedy which we can possibly apply is that of improved education for the upper classes, and the continued effort to spread a knowledge of the results of science and a love for it amongst all the members of the community. . . . Members of the British Association . . . might do a great deal by insisting that their sons, and their daughters too, should have reasonable instruction in science both at school and college. . . . The trifling with classical literature and the absorption in athletics . . . is considered by too many school-masters as that which the British parent desires as the education of his children.

In relation to the function of the British Association as a platform for drawing attention to public aspects of the advancement of science, it is interesting to note that its annual meeting was held in South Africa in 1905, in Dublin in 1908, in Canada in 1909, and in Australia in 1914. Lord Salisbury was its president in 1894 and A. J. Balfour in 1904.

The Royal Society

Fellows of the Royal Society may be regarded as including practically all British scientists of recognized leadership in some special field. At the end of Edward's reign, in 1910, names of fellows who would still now be widely recognized for their contributions to knowledge included the following:[1] in chemistry, H. E. Armstrong (1876) and Sir William Crookes (1863); in physics, W. H. Bragg (1907), Sir James Dewar (1877), J. Ewing (1877), J. H. Jeans (1906), Sir Joseph Larmor (1892), Lord Rayleigh (1873), Ernest Rutherford (1903), and J. J. Thomson (1884); in anthropology, Sir Francis Galton (1860); with the physiologist C. Sherrington (1893), the surgeon Lord Lister (1860), and the engineer C. A. Parsons (1898), professing branches of science less fully represented amongst the Edwardian fellows. Those familiar with the detailed history of the science of the end of the nineteenth century will recognize from this short list that the Royal Society had some volcanoes that were far from extinct in the Edwardian era, particularly in physics where the experimentalists Bragg and Rutherford were to prove themselves world leaders before their stint was done, Bragg with his work on X-ray diffraction and Rutherford with his researches on the disintegration of atoms. Fellows elected for their public services included Sir William Abney (education, 1876), Asquith (1908), Balfour (1888), Lord Curzon (1898), and Lord Rosebery (1886). Members in the Dominions included Adami (pathology, Canada 1905), Adams (geology, Canada 1907), and Alcock (zoology, India 1901). Foreign members included Bryce who became Ambassador to U.S.A. (1893) and world famous names such as Amagat (1897, physics, French), von Baeyer (1885, chemistry, German), Cannizzaro (1889, chemistry, Italian), Emil Fischer (1889, chemistry, German), H. A. Lorentz (1905, mathematical physics, Dutch), A. A. Michelson (1902, physics, U.S.A.), and I. Pavlov (1907, physiology, Russian). Other famous names of foreign members who were fellows in 1900 but who died before 1910 included J. Willard Gibbs (1897, thermodynamics,

---

[1] The year in brackets is that of election to fellowship of the Royal Society.

U.S.A.), J. H. van't Hoff (1897, thermodynamics, Dutch), F. Kohlrausch (1885, chemistry, German), and D. I. Mendeleev (1892, chemistry, Russian).

This list makes it clear that the Royal Society was in a healthy and active state; it was fulfilling its functions both in the promotion of natural knowledge in Britain and in fostering relations with scientists overseas. Edwardian science was only socially weak, and its shortcomings did not lie in the quality of its top scientists. But their communication was faulty, and their influence in the nation inadequate. There was also a lack of well trained and plentiful rank and file, partly stemming from a lack of demand. This situation must be mainly attributed to the educational background, still to be examined.

The proportion of fellows of the society who were academic scientists had been growing notably. Lay fellows, elected for their general and social interest in the sciences, were diminishing in numbers. An outcome of this gradual change in character was that the society probably contained a greater number of distinguished scientists; but the transformation can hardly have helped the dissemination of science in public life.

Fellowship of the Royal Society[1]

	1881	1914
Academic scientists	134	289
Applied scientists	62	79
Distinguished laymen	54	38
Sailors	13	6
Soldiers	26	6
Clergymen	14	4
Medical men	55	11
Other fellows	120	40

Science Fiction

Edwardians who were effectively sheltered from any appreciation of the national importance of science were not in any way slow to show interest when it could contribute to their entertainment. If they had had more tenacity in the pursuit of abstract ideas, ways to scientific knowledge might no doubt have been found through the fashionable sport of ballooning. The motor-car, and its humbler

[1] D. S. L. Cardwell, *The Organization of Science in England*, 1957.

kinsman the bicycle, might have led onwards to bold and adventurous speculations in engineering science. But for the majority of Edwardians the evidence is that the pursuit stopped short where the sporting interest ended.

Science fiction might be thought to have been a more alluring means of access for the Edwardian public to the potentialities of science, but this view does not bear close examination. At least four authors whose writings were very popular might have prompted some filling up of the gaps left by a non-scientific schooling. Even if Jules Verne failed to attract or convince English readers as much as he did his compatriots, he was publishing new books almost up to the end of his life (1828–1905). By their emphasis on sport and travel, and on the scientific eccentricities of men sufficiently wealthy to be indifferent to average behaviour, some of his works ought to have stimulated the Edwardian imagination. The hard work put in by Sherlock Holmes to make himself the premier scientific criminologist of his age was handicapped by the limited scientific knowledge which his creator, Conan Doyle (1859–1930), had picked up in the course of a medical training for general practice. Most of this must be described as elementary, and certainly failed to communicate the national importance of science to a public whose scientific knowledge was even more rudimentary. One suspects, for example, that despite his furious industry, Holmes's practical training in chemistry did not extend much beyond the use of litmus. On one occasion at least ('The Naval Treaty') this simple and traditional test for acids and alkalis appears to have been sufficient basis for the dispatch of several telegrams and the arrest of a murderer. Rudyard Kipling (1856–1936), whose sensitive apprehension extended to most things that would have concerned and interested his contemporaries, makes only a few references to scientific matters, but those few are characteristic and generally highly perspicacious. Thus the recent intrusion of chemistry amongst subjects taught at schools is noticed with benevolent sarcasm in the story 'Regulus' in *A Diversity of Creatures* (1908). His famous tale 'Wireless' in *Traffics and Discoveries* (1904) shows that he appreciated the extra dimension it had introduced into human communication much more keenly than his king. In Kipling's story, 'With the Night Mail' (1904), about an airship with gas turbines which was navigated on light beams, the astonishingly detailed foresight of modern technological

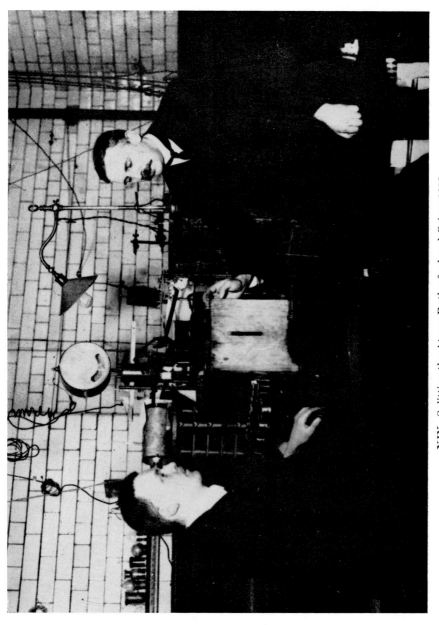

XIX. Splitting the Atom: Rutherford and Geiger 1912

XX. Professor Ray Lankester 1905

developments was in true filiation with the visionary projects of Roger Bacon and Leonardo da Vinci. Prophecy depends on vision, and prophets of technology appear to have been universally more successful in foreseeing the physical artefacts to come than in elucidating the scientific principles upon which they are founded.

Both in bulk and in quality the science fiction of H. G. Wells (1866–1946) was remarkable. When making excursions into imaginary byways of evolution, the stories of Wells—though thrilling to read even now—tended to concentrate on producing the *frisson* dear to all romantics. Wells was in this respect a lineal descendant of Horace Walpole. The jargon and idiom of many of his science stories reflect contemporary ideas about natural history, but they gave the Edwardians no more access to scientific realities than was given by *The Castle of Otranto* to medieval ways of life. On the other hand, when foreseeing mechanical inventions of the future, Wells, like Kipling, made some astonishingly accurate prophecies. Probably the most famous is his vision of 'land-cruisers', to be familiarly described as 'tanks' in the first world war.

Science in Schools

As Norman Lockyer said in his presidential address to the British Association in 1903, the main cause of Edwardian impenetrability to science was rooted in the ideas and practice of leading schools in the late nineteenth century. Leaders in various walks of life were insulated from scientific knowledge. Because of similar deficiencies in education, their fathers had been many of them incapable of making the necessary adaptations of public policy and public expenditure to provide for education and research in various branches of science of national importance. In this respect education in Restoration England had probably been less narrow. The divergence of the main current of English school learning towards the 'trifling with classical literature' about which Ray Lankester complained, had already attracted comment in the late eighteenth century when Dr. Johnson, in his *Lives of the Poets*, felt it worth while to point a contrast with Milton's purpose as a schoolmaster which, he said, was:

to teach something more solid than the common literature of Schools, by reading those authors that treat of physical subjects; such as the Georgick, and astronomical treatises of the ancients. This was a scheme of improvement which seems to have busied many literary projectors of that age.

Cowley, who had more means than Milton of knowing what was wanting to the embellishments of life, formed the same plan of education in his imaginary college.

But like Milton, Dr. Johnson had tried schoolmastering as a way of life, and he leaves no doubt about his own very different judgement:

The truth is, that knowledge of external nature, and the sciences which that knowledge requires or includes, are not the great or the frequent business of the human mind. Whether we provide for action or conversation, whether we wish to be useful or pleasing, the first requisite is the religious and moral knowledge of right and wrong; the next is an acquaintance with the history of mankind, and with those examples which may be said to embody truth, and prove by events the reasonableness of opinions. Prudence and Justice are virtues and excellencies of all times and of all places; we are perpetually moralists, but we are geometricians only by chance. Our intercourse with intellectual nature is necessary; our speculations upon matter are voluntary and at leisure. Physiological learning is of such rare emergence, that one may know another half his life, without being able to estimate his skill in hydrostatics or astronomy: but his moral and prudential character immediately appears.

Those authors therefore are to be read at schools that supply most axioms of prudence, most principles of moral truth, and most materials for conversation; and these purposes are best served by poets, orators and historians.

Such a philosophy of education made fine empire builders, as it would have done two thousand years earlier. But its deficiencies of access to science and technology became increasingly dangerous as technological progress increasingly permeated the civilized world. As one example, compared with many things Britain has contributed to modern India, the training of her scientists and especially her technologists does not rank very high.

Thomas Arnold and other leaders of English public school education at the beginning of the nineteenth century would have agreed almost without demur with Dr. Johnson. By the time he was well established at Rugby, Arnold 'somewhat improved' the status of mathematics, but the degree of improvement was notable only because the subject had been completely neglected by previous headmasters. Arnold died in 1842. In 1859 Rugby had a laboratory and lecture room built for science, which was an option alternative to

modern languages. Of the 128 schools examined by the Public
Schools Commission (1861–4) and the Schools Inquiry Commission
(1864–8) only 15 had room set apart for practical work; only 18
devoted as much as four hours a week to science teaching, and many
gave it no time at all. Even the Greeks of the fifth century B.C.
appear to have achieved a better educational balance. For many
needs, at home and in the empire, the educational programme of
the schoolmasters who taught the leaders of Edwardian England
gave excellent results, but it left those leaders impervious to national
implications of the advancement of science and technology. Undoubtedly this weakness enhanced the perils and the sacrifices of
1914–18.

Despite the contemporary statements already quoted, it might
perhaps be argued that gaps in the school education of Edwardian
leaders must have been made good subsequently, at the universities, or in the course of other kinds of training for the professions.
One objective way of testing such a view is to examine the educational background of those who were fellows of the Royal Society
in 1905, taking that year as the middle of the era under discussion.
Although it would be foolish to equate too closely any awareness of
national impacts of science and technology with fellowship of this
learned body, the history of the Royal Society and the broad
national interests of its founders make it significant to find out how
many of the Edwardian fellows were taught at public or grammar
schools. Collation of the year book of the Royal Society for 1905,
and of obituary notices, yields the following information:[1]

Educational Background of Fellows of the Royal Society (1905)

(For the explanation of the terms A and B see page 245)

University or other higher education	A	B	Totals
Oxford	11	13	24
Cambridge	45	22	67
London (including hospital schools)	38	42	80
Scottish universities (mainly Edinburgh) . . .	29	33	62
Irish universities (mainly Trinity College, Dublin) . .	16	4	20
Other universities (16 home—mainly Owens College, Man-chester—remainder abroad)	18	11	29
Self-taught (e.g. as engineering apprentices) . . .	23	11	34

[1] Thanks are due to the librarian of the Royal Society for lightening the statistical
search.

Nine out of the 24 Oxford fellows had been to well-known public schools, but for the other universities the proportion is minimal. Graduates of London and of Scottish universities frequently moved to other universities for further training after graduation. From London 28, and from Scotland 20, built up their higher education either by proceeding to Cambridge (23) or Oxford (5) or to universities abroad, chiefly in Germany (20).

There were also 10 fellows who began in the navy at 14, nine from military sources, and 10 grown up in the museums, at Kew, or at similar official centres. (110 names not included above are of fellows whose educational background was not recorded in the information studied, or who were elected for non-scientific eminence, such as politicians and judges.) Though the information is necessarily incomplete, in the main this analysis bears out other evidence which goes to show to what extent Edwardian schooling deflected the future leaders of England from the need to come to terms with the advancement of science. It also gives a clear picture of the relative strength of the British universities in educating specialists in their chosen scientific fields.

University and Technical Education

From the grumbles and complaints of contemporary scientists no very gratifying account can be expected of British university and technical education in science in Edwardian times. Certain vital struggles can be recognized. Although various efforts that were being made were mostly not consolidated into firm advances until after the first world war, they formed an important background to Edwardian science. By their very nature these struggles were not at that time closely co-ordinated, which makes any brief account of them seem rather scrappy.

In education, it is characteristic of British ways that new ventures have been begun predominantly by private or local effort. Universities at Oxford and Cambridge, and in Scotland, had centuries of traditions of corporate existence largely independent of central financial support. There had been a royal commission in 1872 to inquire into the relationships of the state to science, and regional colleges of higher education were founded at Newcastle in 1871, at Leeds in 1874, at Bristol in 1876, Sheffield 1879, Birmingham 1880, Nottingham 1881, and Liverpool 1881. Charters to transform and promote some of these regional colleges into state universities with civic support were being actively granted in Edwardian times, to Birmingham in 1900, Liverpool in 1903, Leeds 1904, Sheffield 1905, and Bristol 1909. The Imperial College of Science and Technology received its charter in 1908 to join together the City and Guilds College, the Royal School of Mines, and the Royal College of Science into a single foundation. But British ways of thinking have never worked at their best when beginning to implement rather abstract conceptions such as state-administered aid. Indeed there has always been a lurking and probably salutary fear of some of the consequences of such abstractions. In the newer universities a highly cherished status of independence did but reflect the long familiar enjoyment of academic independence at Oxford and Cambridge, and by the Scottish and Irish colleges. Even in our own times when the sums provided by the state have taken a preponderant role in university finances, independence from excessive subjection to central control is still regarded as a primary condition for healthy university life.

Although few would doubt that a large measure of academic independence can promote flexible adaptation to new conditions in a way impossible for unwieldy national administrations, the past history of older, wealthier academic bodies shows that independence from central control can undoubtedly help to shelter the slothful from the light of inquiry and the fearful from the winds of change. This aim to preserve academic independence was especially harmful in Edwardian times for the advancement of science. Claims for large monetary aids from the state particularly for the newer universities could not easily be pressed or be made politically acceptable simultaneously with the insistence on university independence. By now we are familiar with the curious combination of spiky independence and insatiable demands for help shown by the have-nots of all kinds in a world of technological wealth. But in the beginnings of the civic universities it was precisely the newest requirements for practical training in science and for the financing of research whose satisfaction was most retarded, because they were the most expensive. Practical response to the growing awareness of the need for more science teaching was slowed up in a way that is now easy to understand. When Norman Lockyer made the public complaint at the British Association meeting in 1903 that Germany had 22 universities, and gave more state aid to one of them than was received by all the 13 universities in Britain, his statements illustrate how far British public provisions for higher education had fallen behind those of other nations. At that time figures for the number of universities were—United States 134, Germany 22, Italy 21, France 15, Britain 13. Probably this relative decline reached an extreme limit just at the end of the Edwardian era.

Wars have often stimulated intense technological development. The Ecole Polytechnique in Paris, the first college of applied science in the world, was born of the French Revolution in 1794. Some of its early contributions are still of major importance. Germany after the defeat of Jena and France after the defeat of Sedan founded new state universities to foster and to focus efforts of national recovery. But as it happened, Britain's wars in the nineteenth century involved neither a terrain nor enemies that might not have been encountered five hundred years earlier, and gave little or no impetus to new applications of science. The trials and sufferings of the first world war had very different consequences for a vigorous advancement of science in Britain, but the blood-bath of 1914–18 was part of the price to be paid for the ground lost since 1851. At the outbreak of the war it has been estimated that the total public aid (including municipal support) given to the English universities was around a quarter of a million pounds, about one-third that given in Prussian Germany.[1]

At levels less advanced than university teaching British technical and scientific education was promoted by private effort in numerous small institutes, far too numerous and mostly too small for real effectiveness. In the report of the royal commission of 1881–4 to investigate technical education at home and overseas, Huxley had already noted the peculiarity of English science that 'its army has been all officers. Until the last quarter of a century there has been no rank and file.' Though the urge and effort throughout the nineteenth century can be described as vigorous, the outcome at that time for technical education was unavoidably more parochial than would have been achieved in a programme with more central sources of financial support. Technical education was still too much like England before the Norman conquest, full of small and sometimes vivid kingdoms and principalities, but not economically or efficiently

[1] Cardwell, op. cit.

administered in relation to foreign rivals. Evidence that the state of scientific and technical education in Britain's chief competitors was being anxiously studied, with the sense that time was running out to develop counterparts suited to Britain's needs and ways, has already been mentioned. In Germany the technical colleges origi- nally founded to inject science into the workshops showed a much more positive growth than in Britain. Many of them were raised to the status of technical high schools between 1860 and 1890, and in 1899 the kaiser raised them all to degree-awarding universities.

Applied Science in Britain and the Empire

One achievement in providing adequate public support for science was the foundation of the National Physical Laboratory in 1900. For more than ten years previously the Royal Society and the British Association had been pressing that Britain should have a laboratory comparable with the Berlin Physikalisch-technische Reichsanstalt, founded about 1886 by the famous German physicist Helmholtz. In a somewhat verbose address to the British Associa- tion in 1891 Sir Oliver Lodge had said:

> But what I want to see is a much larger establishment [than the Board of Trade laboratory] erected in the most suitable site, limited by no speciality of aim nor by the demands of the commercial world, furnished with all appropriate appliances, to be amended and added to as time goes on and experience grows, invested with all the dignity and permanence of a national institution, a physical laboratory in fact comparable with Greenwich Observatory and aiming at the highest quantitative work in all departments of physical science.

In view of the rapid development of applications of physics to technology, a time lag of even fourteen years behind the Reichs- anstalt was serious. The original terms of reference of the National Physical Laboratory, 'for standardizing and verifying instruments and for the determination of physical constants', were rather aus- tere, but since its foundation its activities have been enriched and it has amply fulfilled the purpose described by the Prince of Wales (later George V) at the official opening in 1902. 'The object of the scheme is, I understand, to bring scientific knowledge to bear practically upon our everyday industrial and commercial life, to break down the barrier between theory and practice, to effect a union between science and commerce.' For the Edwardians this marked a real beginning in national measures to support applied science. Even so, government funds in support of its own national laboratory were obviously found to be quite inadequate by those who were waiting to use the results to be obtained. Evidence for this niggardliness of public expenditure is to be found in the gifts accepted by the national laboratory from wealthy individuals. In 1909 these included £10,000 from Sir Julius Wernher to enable extensions to be made to the metallurgical laboratory. In the same year £20,000 was received from Sir Alfred Yarrow to endow a test tank for model ship constructions which was to bring much fame to the national laboratory.

It must be remembered that Britain's constructive effort was spread over an enormous geographical area, which in itself made intensive developments relatively less attractive. An important part of Britain's technological achievement lay in efforts overseas, within the empire and outside it. Important examples included the completion of the Aswan Dam in Egypt in 1902 and the initiation in 1905 of the first oilfields concession in Persia to ensure fuel for the Royal Navy. Success in these wider fields helped to compensate for uneasiness felt at the growing competition nearer home, particularly in branches of industry and commerce most closely tied to scientific research and development, such as the chemical industry. In the fine chemicals group of industries the predominant position attained by German dyestuffs organizations by 1900 was particularly galling, since the key invention which was ultimately to replace all natural by synthetic dyestuffs had been made by W. Perkin in England in 1858. Perkin was a pupil of A. W. Hofmann, the German professor who was chosen to start the first British centre for training in practical chemistry and research at the Royal College of Science in South Kensington in 1845. Hofmann is said to have reproached his pupil for leaving pure research to exploit the discovery of the synthesis of rosaniline, which brought much wealth to Perkin. In fact, one outcome of this early economic success appears to have been that further research was neglected in Britain. The decline from early leadership can be dated quite closely. Even after the 1862 exhibition in London it was still possible for Hofmann to write, 'The contributions of the United Kingdom and in particular the splendid chemical display . . . prove the British not only to have maintained their pre-eminence among the chemical manufacturers of the world, but to have outdone their own admitted superiority . . . in 1851.'[1] But at the 1867 exhibition in Paris this lead had been reversed, and this could be attributed particularly to the facilities provided by the Prussian government at Bonn and Berlin for educating masters and managers of industry in advanced chemistry, in large and well-equipped laboratories. It is estimated that by 1901 between 80 and 90 per cent. of dyestuffs used in Britain were made in Germany. During an active period of development from 1886 to 1900 the six largest chemical firms in Germany originated 948 patents for wool and cotton dyestuffs, compared with 86 patents from the six largest British firms.

Even in the empire the lack of adequate scientific education was beginning to have most serious consequences. The difference between the impressive British responsiveness to opportunities for engineering projects in the empire, and the neglect of newer even more far-reaching ways in which applied science could serve imperial needs, is brought out by the tenacious struggles of Sir Ronald Ross (1857–1932) to establish really effective measures for the prevention of malaria. Ross had received a classical education and migrated to scientific studies by way of medicine. His critical discoveries about the life cycle of the malaria parasite were perfected between 1895 and 1899 in India, where he was seriously handicapped by lack of books and research facilities, and by the demands of a government service unsympathetic to this work. In the hope that he might induce the Indian government to second Ross for special duty on malaria investigations, Sir Patrick Manson wrote to the India Office in the summer of 1897, in a vein unfortunately all too familiar:

To our national shame be it said that few, very few of the wonderful advances in the science of the healing art which have signalised recent years have been made by our countrymen. This is particularly apparent in the matter of tropical diseases in which we should, in virtue of our exceptional opportunities, be *facile princeps*. But even in tropical diseases Frenchmen, Italians, Germans, and Americans and even Japanese are shooting ahead of us. We have to get a Koch to find for us the cholera germ, and a Haffkine to protect us from it, a Laveran to teach us what malaria is. . . .

Ross was eventually appointed to special duty by the government of India in January 1898 and was given a laboratory consisting of

[1] Quoted by Cardwell, op. cit.

two rooms, an office, and a veranda. The first meeting of a tropical medicine section of the British Medical Association was held at Edinburgh in July 1898. At this meeting Ross's work was described by Manson, in particular the mode of infection by the mosquito. Practical measures to apply the new knowledge about the life cycle of the malaria parasite began on an extremely modest scale, at Freetown in Sierra Leone, where Ross and a small handful of colleagues studied the breeding grounds of mosquitoes and successfully organized ways of suppressing them. Dramatic success was obtained in 1902 at Ismailia, where Ross for a derisory fee showed the administrators of the Suez canal how to stamp out the spread of malaria locally. In 1903 follow-through work by W. C. Gorgas at Colon first made possible the building of the Panama canal. Consequences of this backroom work have been particularly great for world population and cannot even yet be fully appreciated.

Other aspects of British applied science of importance to trade and commerce, which warrant special mention even in a brief survey, refer to wireless, to aviation, to the cinema, to mass-produced motor-cars, and to large-scale industry in synthetic chemicals, which gave major support to Germany's needs of fertilizers and explosives for the first world war.

Wireless Telegraphy and Electronics

Though it only began at the turn of the century, wireless telegraphy passed by such vigorous stages into world service that it must rightly be regarded as an Edwardian growth. Of course, as in practically all successful applications of science, many precursors might be named. Properties of electromagnetic waves with wavelengths millions of times longer than those of visible light were scientifically well understood from theoretical work (1864) by a Cambridge professor, Clerk-Maxwell (1831–79) and from experiments (1887) contrived by Hertz (1857–94) to test these theories. Application of these abstract scientific concepts to the practical transmission of messages over long distances at first depended on the use of extremely crude spark generators to produce electromagnetic waves which could then be made to carry messages in Morse code. At the receiving end such waves were first detected by a 'coherer'. This was a glass capsule containing filings of nickel, whose electrical resistance changed when the electromagnetic waves passed over them. A clear line of practical development was first established by the tenacious and far-seeing work of the Irish-Italian Marconi.

Dating the real beginnings of a man's scientific work can be somewhat arbitrary; prominent incidents mentioned below merely mark convenient turning points. The first of all patents in wireless telegraphy was granted in England, in 1896, to Marconi at the age of 22. Marconi received early and most valuable public support from Sir William Preece, chief engineer of the Post Office, who arranged for demonstrations to his colleagues. Preece also gave these demonstrations influential publicity in lectures on 'telegraphy without wires' in December 1896 and again in June 1897 at the Royal Institution. Those whom we would now term British communication engineers were ready to take effective interest in this aspect of applied electromagnetism. Telegraphy 'across the wires' had reached great importance for the British empire since the laying of the first transatlantic cable by a British company in 1857–8. For Marconi, a significant step forward was the outcome of his determination to send wireless messages across the sea. This possibility had already received some attention even before 1900 when the Marconi Wireless Telegraph Company began its commercial life with a capital of £100,000 by a transformation of the Wireless Telegraph and Signal Company, itself recently formed. There is some dispute whether the first passenger liner that had wireless installed was the U.S.S. *St. Paul* (1899) or the German *Kaiser Wilhelm der Grosse* (1900). Whatever the truth may be about these more humdrum applications, it is pleasing to record the characteristic Edwardian flavour of many of the earliest uses of the new means for sending messages. The flashing to London of results of yacht races at the Kingstown regatta, and loyal messages to royal personages, were only to be expected. Albert Edward and his injured knee have already been referred to. Theodore Roosevelt could not resist a new opportunity of exercising the American urge to spread the sense of fellowship. To Edward VII in January 1903: 'In taking advantage of the wonderful triumph of scientific research and ingenuity which has been achieved in perfecting a system of wireless telegraphy I extend on behalf of the American people most cordial greetings and good wishes to you and all the people of the British Empire.'

The Royal Navy first asked for a demonstration at its spring manœuvres in 1899. Patent conflicts soon became active, and it seems possible that Kaiser Wilhelm secretly supported the German Professor Sleby in stratagems not wholly worthy of the imperial integrity, to deprive Marconi of patent rights in Germany and to 'break the Marconi monopoly'. A second major advance in wireless also reached clear success when Ambrose Fleming, professor of electrical engineering at University College, London, filed a patent in November 1904 for his invention of the thermionic 'valve'. Though his prototype 'valves' were shaky things—dragon-flies with their wings not yet dried—they permitted emancipation from the clumsy coherer-detector and the spark transmitter of radio waves. The Fleming valve thus marks the beginning of the modern era of electronics, and soon led to striking developments of more accurate and powerful emitters and receivers of wireless messages.

Aviation

Edwardians might fairly claim man's mastery of the air as a triumph of their own times, though the evidence suggests that most of them were quite unaware of it. To achieve a viable aircraft so many problems of applied science needed to be solved that the time and place of indisputable success were to some extent like winning at horse racing—skill and a good lineage are essential, but even then the winner is favoured by luck. Significant contributions were being made to the problems of controlled flight well over a century before actual triumph was made sure. When it came, definitive success attracted surprisingly little attention, possibly because of the long-drawn-out efforts.

One means of 'lifting' the aircraft from the ground involves Archimedes' principle, which requires that to impart the necessary buoyancy to aircraft, large volumes of air must be displaced by something whose density is even lower than that of air. In France in 1783 the Montgolfier brothers achieved this by using heated air to fill the balloons; however, the low density of hydrogen, discovered by Cavendish in 1766, made this gas a much more manageable filling than hot air for balloons. The buoyancy method of lifting aircraft was 'news' in 1784 when Dr. Johnson (*aet.* 75) petulantly refused to discuss ballooning with any more of his correspondents. Flight in balloons is hampered by great difficulties of controlling the direction of travel of a spherical object. Some attempt to improve dirigibility was made by Santos-Dumont in France in 1898, by the contrivance of an elliptical balloon 825 feet long and 11½ feet in diameter. This was powered with two small motors driving a single shaft and propeller. In Germany Count Zeppelin had a long innings with buoyant aircraft whose dirigibility was greatly improved by building them with a rigid instead of a flexible envelope. The first 'Zeppelin' made its first flight in 1900; by the time the fourth was due to be built in 1908, public interest in Germany was so great that six million marks were raised by public subscription. Up to the first world war 25 Zeppelin airships had been constructed or nearly completed; 88 more were built for scouting and aerial bombing during the war.[1]

A second way of providing 'air-lift' does not involve the use of buoyancy and thus avoids the bulkiness of aircraft depending on Archimedes' principle. It involves using the aerodynamic thrust created by relative movements of air over an aircraft in directions which will lift it upwards. Ways of applying such a thrust have been played with for centuries in various forms of kite; purposive experiments using manned gliders fitted with rigid or flexible wings to 'glide' on air currents yielded important contributions to the final solution.

Successful flights by Wilbur and Orville Wright were first made in what was essentially a large box kite, whose construction had been tested in many gliding trials. So far from making news headlines, these early flights at Kitty Hawk in North Carolina in 1903 and at Dayton in 1904 were carried out in comparative secrecy. Real publicity was not given to their success until 1908, when Wilbur Wright came to Europe. Partly because of this secrecy, parallel progress in various European centres was made without full knowledge of the American work. For Britons, 'crossing the channel' is symbolic, with overtones and echoes right back through history. If only for this reason, the first flight across the channel, by the Frenchman Blériot on 25 July 1909, impressed the Edwardians probably more than the earlier flights by the Wright brothers; but neither achievement appears to have raised as much ripple on the surface of society as many other contemporary political or sporting events whose memory has now passed into oblivion.

For controlled flight another essential is to contrive a source of

[1] M. J. B. Davy, *Interpretive History of Flight*, 1948.

power with high power-to-weight ratio; adult humans can develop about $\frac{1}{10}$ horse-power and since they weigh about 140 lb. the power-to-weight ratio of even the most cunningly contrived 'flying man' cannot rise much above 1/1,500. This limitation appears to be the main reason why earlier designs for human flight such as those of Leonardo da Vinci were doomed to failure. The simple pair of tricycle petrol engines fitted to a flexible balloon by Santos-Dumont in 1898 developed 3·5 horse-power for a weight of only 66 lb., bringing the power-to-weight ratio down to about 1/20. The Wright aeroplane was fitted with a propeller driven by a 12-h.p. 4-cylinder petrol engine, with a power-to-weight ratio of 1/15. Modern aircraft are fitted with much more powerful engines which provide really strong aerodynamic lifting thrusts; their power-to-weight ratio is kept as low as possible, so that much additional weight can be packed into the aircraft and be lifted into the air.

The Cinema

In its technological development and in its social functions the cinema was a highly characteristic Edwardian growth. Most of the scientific problems to be solved in making and showing cinematograph films were attacked and mastered during this era. Even colour films of a sort were being shown at the Royal Institution of Great Britain in 1906.[1] What started as a mere seepage into music-hall entertainment at the beginning of Edward's reign had become a rising tide at its end. As is well known, eventually the cinema practically overwhelmed the music hall. Among the early records of national occasions displayed in moving pictures by R. W. Paul, Derby Day (1896) was noteworthy. This was the first to be projected on to the screen at the Alhambra Theatre, London, only twenty-four hours after the race had been run on Epsom Downs. Royalty was good film. Queen Victoria's Diamond Jubilee (1897), her funeral (1901), and the coronation of Edward VII in 1902 were fully filmed. In 1907 four companies filmed the arrival of Kaiser Wilhelm at Southampton and the films were shown the same evening at the Empire, Alhambra, Hippodrome, and Palace theatres in London.[2] Edward's own funeral was very properly given the solemnity of

[1] F. A. Talbot, *Moving Pictures*, 1923.
[2] R. Low, *The History of the British Film, 1906–1914*, 1949.

a cinematograph record, followed by prompt display before hundreds of thousands of people.

From the special standpoint of this history three things need to be said about applied science in the cinematograph industry in the Edwardian era. The first echoes what has already been said about the growth of so much British applied science. British pioneers were brilliant in this field of application, as in many others; but compared with American, French, Italian, and other nations the British follow-through in no way corresponded with the promise of the earliest days. In the beginnings of commercialization numerous small producers 'built' films, rather like Morris building bicycles. A few happen to have been more businesslike, though not necessarily more creative, than their fellows; among these R. W. Paul (1869–1943), a scientific instrument-maker of Hatton Garden, is generally recognized to have been the first to bring cinematography into the commercial field. A show given at Olympia in 1896 appears to have been the first projection of motion pictures on to a screen for which an admission fee was charged. Between 1898 and 1906 the duration of films rapidly lengthened, as is shown by extracts from Paul's catalogue:

> 1898 average film length 40–80 ft.
> 1902   ,,   ,,   ,,   100 ft.
> 1906   ,,   ,,   ,,   650 ft. (11 min.)

A second comment is that the growth achieved in the film industry came from the demand of the masses, not the leadership of the upper classes. It is on record, for example, that Asquith did not visit a picture palace until 1911, on which occasion he laughed heartily and continually made witty comments anent the pictures— no doubt to the great annoyance of humbler patrons.

A third comment illustrates the curious forms in which a latent urge towards refinement becomes expressed in mass production. The earliest infiltration of the cinema into Victorian and Edwardian music hall was merely as one of the 'turns'. But when the supply and demand for moving pictures had grown so that displays could be profitably organized in their own right, the 'picture palaces' aimed to provide all kinds of material refinements for a surprisingly low price of admission, including plush carpets, bevelled mirrors, soft lights, and 'usherettes'. The first theatre in Britain entirely devoted to films seems to have been the Balham Empire. There was unconscious irony, in view of the Edwardian opportunities for comfortable enjoyment and for slumber, in the caption: 'Wake up, John Bull, excellent pictures in the Balham Empire.' Even the names of early cinemas display the effort to achieve a somewhat meretricious distinction, apparently regarded as having sales appeal. Names such as the Olympia, Bijou, Empire, Jewel, Gem, Mirror, Picturedrome, Pallasino, and Palaceadium contain detritus from more than one civilization composed into a romantic mosaic, like the eighteenth-century synthetic hermits' grottoes built from all kinds of glittering fragments both truly ancient and bogus. Board of Trade figures for the capital of companies in Britain engaged in film exhibition illustrate the rapidly growing mass appeal of the cinema. In 1908 there were three companies with a capital of about £100,000, in 1909 103 companies with a capital of about £1·4 million, and in 1912 205 companies with a capital of about £3 million. There were fierce international conflicts over patent rights, especially between British pioneers and the supporters of American inventions by Edison. After intervening struggles characteristic of technological development in an age of *laissez-faire*, attempts at creating an American monopoly were eventually frustrated. By 1914 all the large towns in Britain had many picture theatres; in the six largest towns outside London, Manchester held the lead with one cinema seat for eight inhabitants and Liverpool lagged with only one cinema seat for fifty-two inhabitants. Clearly cinemas had become firmly established in Edwardian times in a way that doubting contemporaries had been afraid to forecast at the beginning of this new development of applied science.

Motor-cars and Mass Production

Early forms of the motor-car were in direct and quite obvious craft sequence with horse-drawn coaches and private carriages. Five motorized omnibuses were touting for customers in 1897; by 1906 their number had grown to 700.[1] The first motor-driven taxi-cab began to compete with the horse in 1904. Like their French and German rivals, designers and constructors of British craft-built motor-cars produced some very practical, long-lasting models. Kipling hired a typical gentleman's car from a Brighton firm in

[1] S. Desmond, *The Edwardian Story*, 1949.

XXI. 'Progressive Woman: Lady Chemists in the University at Leeds' 1908

"GO TO SLEEP, MY DARLING, MOTHER'S WATCHING NEAR."

ANOTHER TRIUMPH OF SCIENCE. 1910.

XXII

1899, together with an engineer, at $3\frac{1}{2}$ guineas a week. This was 'Victoria hooded, carriage sprung, carriage braked, single cylinder, belt driven, fixed ignition'. At times this embryo could cover eight miles in an hour, but by 1902 Kipling decided that a single-cylinder engine was too easily defeated by the Sussex hills and bought a Lanchester car.[1]

The design by Henry Ford of a motor-car for mass production was a clear break in this craft sequence. Ford's first assembly line was set up at Detroit, U.S.A., around 1903. Mass-production methods avoided much of the delays and expense of craft building, but the automobile which resulted can be charitably described as a maid of all work, serviceable rather than attractive. Mass-produced cars were to serve demands much more varied than any mere need for omnibuses or for rich men's carriages. 20,877 Ford cars were assembled in Britain in the period 1910–14, in rapidly growing numbers as the following figures show:

1910	1911	1912	1913	1914
570	1,458	3,187	7,310	8,352

These mass-produced cars formed part of a population of about 132,000 private motor-cars in Britain in 1914.[2]

Synthetic Chemistry

By Edwardian times their well devised training and native industriousness had given German scientists something like world leadership in the production of fine chemicals, as well as in the production of synthetic dyestuffs. A new development, originating from the leadership of Paul Ehrlich, involved a massive and systematic effort to synthesize drugs for chemotherapy. Since the lead given by the British surgeon, Lister, powerful disinfectants have been used in medicine to kill bacteria and other micro-organisms. But their action on most other living cells is likewise lethal, so that such crude disinfectants could not be used within the body to attack deep seated invasions by foreign micro-organisms. The new plan of research in chemotherapy aimed to find chemicals with strong but

[1] R. Kipling, *Something of Myself*, 1937.

[2] I am indebted to Dr. F. Llewellyn Smith, of Rolls-Royce Ltd., for obtaining this information. Records of sales of Ford cars before 1910 have not been obtainable.

highly specific bactericidal action, so that they could be used without hurt to the living cells of an infected body. Great patience and tenacity were required in this research, as is recorded by the number 606 given to 'salvarsan' or arsphenamine, an organic drug containing arsenic introduced by Ehrlich and Hata in 1910. Its number tells the sequence of organic chemicals that were synthesized and tested before a clinically satisfactory drug was found for the treatment of syphilis. Since this pioneering success chemotherapy has ramified in many directions and is now supplied by a highly prosperous drug-making industry.

'Heavy' chemical industry had been developed on a large scale in Britain at least since the eighteenth century. As economists are by now well aware, its growth in modern industrial communities parallels and often outstrips economic growth as a whole. The Edwardian era was no exception to this general trend which would not call for special mention in regard either to Britain or to her chief trade rivals. Reference should, however, be made to a new chemical industry, the production of synthetic fertilizers by the fixation of atmospheric nitrogen. Sir William Crookes at the 1898 meeting of the British Association had proclaimed in a dramatic way how the growth of populations made demands on food-producing land that could only be met in an acceptable way by the production of synthetic fertilizers. Many of the soil's requirements are restored by good systems of agriculture. Components such as potash or lime which are removed by the crops can be restored in the form of mineral fertilizers, but even the most conservative use of manures and organic waste matter does not adequately restore nitrogen compounds in forms that plants can assimilate.

Only three solutions could be seen by Crookes—to accept a diminishing supply of foodstuffs and progressively lower the standard of nutrition, which would not be acceptable in technologically advanced communities; to import most of the country's main food requirements from countries with abundant land, which was the solution adopted in the latter half of the nineteenth century by Britain, like ancient Rome in this respect; or to supplement any natural manure returned to the fields with other readily assimilated nitrogen compounds added to the soil after each crop. In the main, this third solution was adopted by Germany and other countries of western Europe. Enormous deposits of sodium nitrate had been discovered in Chile; exports (of which over 80 per cent. went to Germany) totalled 1,350,000 tons in 1900. But this economic situation was unstable and unsatisfactory. It left a staple requirement of life at the mercy of a foreign country, Chile. Germany's sensitiveness to naval interference with her trade would have probably added that it left a staple requirement of life exposed to attack by a strong rival nation, Britain.

There are enormous amounts of free nitrogen in the atmosphere but only very restricted forms of plant life, such as the legumes, can assimilate it by means of symbiotic bacteria grown in their root nodules. The technological problem was to convert free atmospheric nitrogen into a compound assimilable by plants. It was solved mainly through the leadership of the German chemist Fritz Haber. Working in conjunction with his brother-in-law, C. Bosch, Haber devised practicable methods for converting atmospheric nitrogen into ammonia. Many entirely new applications of chemistry to industry were involved, which have since had ramifications in numerous directions.

In Germany a working process was established by about 1905; this was taken up and perfected in 1910 by the Badische Anilin- und Soda-Fabrik. Its importance for German war-needs may be gauged by the opening of the huge Leuna works in 1917; by 1918 over 200,000 tons of ammonia per year were being synthesized in Germany alone. Britain and other technologically advanced countries did not acquire effective industrial plants for the fixation of atmospheric nitrogen until after the first world war. In attacking and solving the technical problems involved, Haber and his colleagues were supported by the strong contemporary development of chemical thermodynamics in various German universities. The Dutch chemist van't Hoff (1852–1911), who was a professor at Berlin university, made vital contributions to this branch of science. The school of Walther Nernst (1864–1941) at Göttingen and later in Berlin strengthened and extended the foundations of this science in ways which have had extremely far-reaching results for pure science as well as for the scientific development of industrial processes. Effective approach towards the absolute zero of temperature, of particular importance for thermodynamic research, was made in 1907 when the Dutch physicist, H. K. Kamerlingh Onnes, first liquefied the inert gas helium which boils at 4 degrees above absolute zero.

Quite in keeping with many other applications of science, that which gave means for supporting life in one direction by providing more food also gave new means for killing by providing synthetic explosives in bulk. Ammonia is readily converted into nitric acid by oxidation with atmospheric air over a catalyst. Patents for this process were taken out in 1902 and the first technical plant was erected in Germany in 1909. The process was in full operation there in 1914, turning out some 250 tons of nitric acid daily. Nitric acid was an irreplaceable requirement in the manufacture of high explosives for filling shells and bombs as well as for the production of gun cotton and other propellents to project them from guns. Before the industrial synthesis of ammonia was achieved the main sources of nitrates had been natural deposits, access to which was protected by adequate sea power. It is not too much to say that successful industrial processes for synthesizing ammonia and nitric acid freed Germany during the first world war from one of the worst strangleholds a strong Royal Navy could have made effective. In 1916 the allies used nearly 3,000,000 tons of Chilean sodium nitrate. Norman Lockyer's prophetic remark to the British Association in 1903 that state aid for science could be much more profitable than more money for the navy was beginning to be justified. Further ironic demonstration of this dictum became evident in 1917, when the German submarine attack almost cut off the supply of natural nitrates from Chile, and seriously threatened England's supplies of high explosives.

Among other developments in industrial chemistry originated or strikingly developed in the period, threads made from nitrocellulose had been exhibited in Paris in 1899 and artificial silk was being made by the cuprammonium process before 1909.[1] The first plastic to set under the influence of heat was a phenol-formaldehyde composition 'bakelite', patented by Leo Baekeland in 1907. Improvements in motor-cars called for hydrocarbon fuels with carefully controlled properties, demand for which transformed the petroleum industry. Large refineries were developed to deal with complex transformation processes, and world-wide exploration for oil was begun.

[1] E. J. Solvay, *The Evolution of the Chemical Industry*, 1960.

Advances in Pure Science

Scientists often make a convenient division between two main branches of natural knowledge, those that can ultimately be referred wholly to applied mathematics and those for which there is not even a distant hope of reducing all the observables to mathematically satisfactory models. Physics is the leading example of mathematics applied to the world of experience. From the time of Isaac Newton observables have been treated as relevant in physics only if they can be wholly reduced to mathematically definable operations such as measurement or enumeration. Chemistry, geology, meteorology, and kindred sciences have made successful use of many non-mathematical concepts for classifying natural knowledge, but increasing experience suggests that ultimately all these concepts will likewise be expressible in mathematical models. To follow the domestic usage of the Royal Society, all the foregoing are termed *A* sciences. According to the same usage the *B* sciences include biology, zoology, and botany, in which the observables are not primarily measurable though increasing use of physics and chemistry is being made to elucidate various aspects of them.

As late as 1900 experience of the previous 150 years would have encouraged the expectation of steady future development and the hope of continued clarification of both the main branches of natural knowledge. Throughout the Edwardian era this expectation was in fact fulfilled for the *B* sciences; the Victorian fires of fierce controversies associated with Charles Darwin had largely burnt out; many of those sciences were awaiting the development of more exact methods of observation before they could make a new leap forward. Brief mention may be made of biochemical studies of substances which have profound physiological effects even when present in minute quantities in the body. The first adrenal hormone, epinephrin, was isolated in 1901, and was later synthesized. Vitamins were still only partially identified, but their role in various deficiency diseases was being actively studied during this period by workers such as Sir Frederick Gowland Hopkins.

Psychologists may dispute the scientific worth of Edwardian developments. However this may be, books such as Freud's *Interpretation of Dreams*, published in 1900 and translated into English in 1913, began to spread novel ideas about the subconscious outside specialist circles.

The Metrical Sciences

By contrast with the orderly growth of the B sciences, revolutionary changes in physics emerged during Edward's reign. At the start of the era, physical studies of atoms were still in a rudimentary state, so much so that the president of the British Association for 1901 attributed real news value to the applications of the atomic theory to interpret the physical properties of matter. Research to arrive at trustworthy counts of the number (known as Avogadro's number) of atoms or molecules in a given quantity of matter, received widespread attention, but various independent ways of making such counts did not reach final agreement till 1908–10. X-rays had been discovered in 1895 by Röntgen; although they were applied for clinical uses as early as 1896, their use in elucidating the structure of matter was not begun until 1912–13.

Side by side with these normal developments three upsetting innovations in physics had become well established by the end of the Edwardian decade. Ultimately, each of them was to displace the very foundations of mathematical theory applied to describe observable nature, though some of the more profound implications were not understood until much nearer our own time. Two of these revolutionary departures from Newtonian physics originated in Germany; the quantum theory of radiation was first published in 1900 and the theory of relativity in 1905. Both these theories had foundations that were almost philosophical in nature, although the consequences were given precise mathematical form. The third completely novel theory which dealt with the disintegration of atoms was arrived at more directly on the basis of experiments. Perhaps characteristically, this more empirical innovation originated from British workers, Rutherford and Soddy, whose first theory of the atomic disintegration of matter was published in 1902.

Any complete account of these three theories would involve a survey of most of modern physics, which has been completely transformed by them. Only a skeleton outline will be given, to indicate their time and place in Edwardian science.

The Quantum Theory and Relativity

Early in the nineteenth century it had been discovered that 'empty space' in the neighbourhood of matter was not in fact wholly

XXIII. A poster of 1914

XXIV (*a*). The Cinema's first Studio Stage 1902

XXIV (*b*). Open-air Cinema on Hampstead Heath

empty. By simple tests it could be shown to contain something called 'radiant heat' or 'radiant energy'. Subsequent experiments showed that the quantity of radiant energy in unit volume of empty space, termed the density of radiant energy, was controlled by the temperature of material objects in its immediate neighbourhood. Within a space enclosed between walls at uniform temperature, it was shown that the quantity of radiant energy was perfectly definite and constant. Both theory and experiment confirmed that radiant energy flows freely from one part of empty space to another with the velocity of light; but that it exerts a slight pressure upon matter. Stefan's law (1879) showed that the density of energy in enclosed space is proportional to the fourth power of the temperature, when in equilibrium with matter. But contemporary physics could only give an inadequate account of the colour or, expressed more scientifically, of the partition of energy among the various wavelengths that constitute the spectrum of electromagnetic radiation in equilibrium with matter. Victorian scientists were particularly concerned at this lack of success, because they thought they knew all about the ether which was believed to fill empty space. Various attempts were made to calculate the partition of radiant energy in terms of supposed properties of the ether, regarded as undergoing electromagnetic oscillations with a range of wavelengths. Despite a suggestive theory by Lord Rayleigh, it proved impossible to reconcile the colour spectrum of radiant energy observed experimentally, particularly in the ultraviolet, with any properties that could reasonably be attributed to the ether in classical physics. At that time the fundamental inadequacy of contemporary models of the ether was sometimes described as the 'ultraviolet catastrophe'. In 1900 Max Planck published a formula which fitted the observed distribution of energies in the radiation spectrum extremely well. But Planck's formula was derived by abandoning one of the fundamental properties till then attributed to the ether. Instead of following the general assumption that the ether behaves like a continuum, Planck introduced the notion—at that time with very little justification—that the quantity of radiant energy of any wavelength in enclosed space could increase or decrease only by finite amounts, termed quanta. In Planck's theory, filling an enclosed space with radiant energy was like filling a bucket with peas instead of water. In place of the classical conception of a continuous flow of energy, Planck's hypothesis meant that an elastic oscillator can only change its energy by a succession of discrete amounts, termed quanta. This assumption at once gave the correct answer for the partition of radiant energy in enclosed space, though its full elaboration into quantum mechanics which is now used to describe the modern physics of small particles was not worked out until well after the Edwardian era.

With characteristic penetration and boldness Albert Einstein made use of Planck's basic assumption, that an oscillator can only take up a succession of quanta of energy, to formulate the first successful theory (1907) which gave the heat content of solids at low temperatures. In physics, solids had long been regarded as elastic bodies, capable of oscillations of various wavelengths; in this respect they showed mechanical analogies with properties attributed to the ether. As the temperature of a solid rises there is an increase of its energy content associated with atomic oscillations. By assuming that these oscillations can only increase or decrease their energy by discrete quanta, exactly like Planck's ether, the falling off in specific heat which is observed experimentally with solids at very low temperatures can readily be explained. Einstein's successful development of quantum physics gave strong support to extensions in other directions, and also stimulated advances in the thermodynamics of solids. Measurements of specific heats down to very low temperatures had been started by Sir James Dewar at the Royal Institution. They were greatly developed in Germany by the school of Walther Nernst, and led to the enunciation of a third law of thermodynamics known at the time as the 'Nernst heat theorem' (1906). The new quantum physics was apparently highly abstract in nature, but some of its consequences probably influenced contemporary applications of thermodynamics such as Haber's industrial synthesis of ammonia.

In 1912 Einstein extended quantum physics still further by pointing out that the energy in a beam of light must behave as if subdivided into quantum packets, or photons, instead of being distributed continuously in space. This change of viewpoint at once explained why light of a given wavelength falling on a metal surface causes the emission of electrons of definite energy. Earlier theories of continuous radiation led to the expectation of the emission of electrons with a range of energies. Quantum theory was placed on an even wider basis in 1913 by Niels Bohr, who first showed how it could account for the electronic structure of matter.

A second break with inherited mathematical theories of physical phenomena was made by Einstein (1905) by formally abandoning the hypothesis that 'motion' relative to the 'ether' could be observed and could thus be given physical meaning. Einstein's special theory of relativity can be expressed in a variety of ways, depending to some extent on the philosophical inclinations of the enunciator. Mathematically, the theory explains the failure to detect any 'motion' of our earth relative to the 'ether' of space, in the Michelson–Morley experiment (1881). In view of subsequent developments of nuclear energy, a more upsetting conclusion was that kinetic energy and mass are interchangeable.[1] This could not be directly verified at the time, but has been fully confirmed as a result of subsequent studies of atomic disintegration.

The Disintegration of Matter

The peculiar 'radiation' spontaneously emitted by uranium and its compounds was discovered by Henri Becquerel in 1896. Monsieur and Madame Pierre Curie were able to isolate a highly concentrated fraction, radium, by chemical means in 1898. Rutherford and Soddy (1902–3) separated a whole sequence of different radioactive substances with sufficient clarity and certainty to support their disintegration theory. (This was one of the very few Edwardian advances in science to receive notice by *Punch*.) Until that time, concepts inherited from ancient Greece had prevailed; it had been assumed that atoms were indestructible and eternally unchanging constituents of matter. Rutherford discovered that when they disintegrate, atoms evolve considerable quantities of energy. The possibilities of one day harnessing the energy of atomic disintegration had already attracted the far-seeing eye of Sir William Ramsay, who was well known as one of the discoverers of the gaseous inert elements (1894–1902). In his address as president of the British Association in 1911, Ramsay estimated that through various applications of inanimate energy each British family by then had an average of twenty 'helots' in its service. He stressed that stores of energy known at that time were not unlimited. The tides, the winds, the internal heat of the

---

[1] In addition to familiar terms dependent on velocity, the kinetic energy E was shown to contain a 'rest mass' term mc^2, where c is the velocity of light, and m is the mass.

earth, the heat of the sun, the power stored with water, or in coal, in peat, and in the forests all have their foreseeable limits as sources of energy to be harnessed by man. Ramsay's hope was to find catalysts for the exceedingly slow radioactive disintegrations which

had been observed in naturally occurring elements, with a view to liberating their stored-up energy at a rate that could be utilized. We are the somewhat apprehensive inheritors of this Edwardian hope. Its realization in terms of the atom bomb and in terms of nuclear power stations has been accomplished in a way characteristic of so much technological aspiration and prophecy. For mankind scientific achievement brings constantly widening demands, and new problems in the conflict between good and evil to replace the old. One cannot help thinking that life was more restful in the days of Albert Edward.

6

THOUGHT

ANTHONY QUINTON

Fellow and Tutor of New College, Oxford

THOUGHT

THE thought of the first fourteen years of the present century shows more inner coherence than might have been expected. In part, no doubt, this is due to the definite boundaries set to the period by the close of a long reign at one end and the outbreak of war at the other. In philosophy these years saw the collapse of the imposing system of absolute idealism. For all its philosophical novelty, as far as it concerned religion and society it was fundamentally a compromise. It offered a middle path, between religious dogmatism, whether traditionally orthodox or tractarian, and materialistic infidelity. It asserted the ultimate truth of Christian belief on the condition that the more questionably concrete and historical elements in the faith were metaphysically etherealized and understood as symbolic in intent. Without the encumbrances of literal-minded belief, Christianity could float up out of the reach of scientific criticism. In much the same way idealism endorsed loyalty to the established social order, not on the grounds of any divine prerogatives of its actual constituents but because it represented the highest achievement possible to the common spirit of the community in its current historical situation. Idealism seemed to have set up effective defences against religious unbelief and political radicalism by making judicious concessions to them, to have vindicated God and the state by disembarrassing them of superstitious accretions.

The Edwardian period saw idealism defeated on all three fronts: as a metaphysical system, as a theology, and as a social doctrine. A new generation of realists, led by Russell and Moore, attacked it at its intellectual heart by showing its logic to be an elaborately deceptive technique for having things both ways. In theology modernism came close to abandoning all claims about supernatural existence and to interpreting Christianity simply as a system of moral demands. In the realm of social thought one group of critics repudiated the intellectualism inherited by the idealists from the

Enlightenment and a broad movement of libertarian protest condemned their obsession with the majesty of the state.

Some of these counter-currents, in particular modernist theology and the various forms of pluralist social theory, could be seen as further developments of the original idealist initiative. The opposing movements that were to survive the first world war with their vitality unimpaired were not. The realism of Russell and Moore turned into a philosophy of analysis and rejoined the tradition of Hume and Mill which had been the main object of idealist criticism. In the religious domain liberalism was swept away by the horrors of war and supplanted by the theology of crisis. In politics the needs of the times established the supremacy of the state over all other forms of human association more firmly than ever. The idealist compromise had failed to obliterate the contingency of the world, the remoteness of God, and the confined rationality of man as a social being.

IDEALISTS: ABSOLUTE AND PERSONAL

At the outset of the twentieth century absolute idealism was the dominant body of philosophical ideas in Great Britain, and F. H. Bradley was the commanding personality of the school. Few were prepared to accept his uncompromisingly Parmenidean convictions undiluted. The older idealistic professors generally watered down his scepticism in order to find a secure place in their systems for such traditional sanctities as God, human personality, and the state. Compared to the broad orthodox mass of philosophers he was an extremist, but he was certainly the most admired philosopher of the time. Russell and Moore, at the beginning of the decade in which they were to revolutionize philosophy together, were just emerging from close and devoted discipleship to him. Similarly McTaggart, the most brilliant innovator within the general framework of idealism, had the highest respect for Bradley and, submitting his first essay on 'the further determination of the Absolute' to him in 1893, was gratified by the favourable response it evoked.

Hegelian idealism came late to this country. In 1865, thirty-four years after Hegel's death and the beginning of a long decline in his European reputation, an enthusiastic medical man, J. H. Stirling, published a long, rapturous book called *The Secret of Hegel*, believing, not altogether wrongly, that in Hegelianism he had found

a powerful philosophical ally for the defenders of Christian orthodoxy against evolutionary biologists, geologists, and biblical critics.
To Stirling's literary influence was added the teaching of Jowett at
Balliol. Hegel's metaphysical etherealization of religion, his view
that dogma was a first, crude, pictorial version of metaphysical
truth, was congenial to Jowett. It provided principles for his practice of taking large, interpretative liberties with scripture and the
creeds. It was in Jowett's Balliol that T. H. Green, the first substantial theorist of British idealism, emerged with his doctrine of
the world as an eternal consciousness of which minds and objects
were only unstable and impermanent fragments, of mind as the
constructor, not the evolutionary by-product of nature, of self-
realization not pleasure as the moral end, and of the claims of the
state as overriding the interests and conscience of the individual.

Idealism in Green's presentation of it was an earnest, fumbling,
and somewhat disjointed affair. But by the turn of the century
Bradley and others had produced a body of doctrine that was
articulated and logically well knit. The central principle was essentially logical in character. It distinguished two ways of regarding
any whole: the way of understanding which saw the world analy-
tically as an aggregate of independent and externally related
entities, and the way of reason which saw things in their true unity
and interconnectedness as internally related. The analytic understanding of natural science and empiricist philosophy was a useful,
practical device; but by carving the world up for its own convenience into externally related elements it was abstract and
falsifying. True knowledge was only to be attained by the apprehension of things in their systematic internal relatedness.

This schematic conviction had impressively numerous and detailed applications. The first was a monism which held the apparent
plurality and independence of things to be merely apparent, a
function of our limited grasp of the world. The next was an epistemological idealism that affirmed the homogeneity of subject
and object in knowledge. Nothing could exist that was not present to
a mind and only ideas were present to minds. Self-subsistent natural
existences were unintelligible. A further consequence was the coherence theory of truth which replaced the commonsensical view
that truth lay in some correspondence of proposition and fact by
the contention that the truth of a thought consisted in its fitting

coherently into an all-inclusive system of thoughts. In Bradley's view discursive thought and the language in which it was expressed were abstract and selective in the account they gave of the world. They could report mutilated aspects of things but not the things themselves in their individuality. The world, then, could only be truly grasped by a kind of intuitive identification with it.

The idealist principles had appropriate consequences in the more peripheral regions of philosophy. Morality was neither the pursuit of an unending series of momentary satisfactions nor obedience to some fixed, externally imposed rule, but rather the systematic fulfilment and development of the self, a process whose final outcome was self-transcendence and immersion in the absolute. In politics the problem of the relations of state and individual was dismissed as a product of vicious abstraction. Obedience to the state was justified neither by the value of its effects nor by the intrinsic character of the state itself, but by the fact that in obeying the state one was obeying one's more realized and so more real self. History was no random sequence of unpredictable contingencies but a necessary and rational process of development. Religion, finally, was regarded as a graphic, imaginative anticipation of true philosophy. The concept of God was an anthropomorphic notion of the absolute, but the absolute was above personality and, as fully real, beyond morality. Within it, furthermore, the apparent division of mind into separate personal unities disappeared.

Bradley and his School

Most of these views are to be found in Bradley's imposing set of treatises and essays. By the beginning of the century his philosophy was complete in its main outlines and his chief occupation during its first decade was the composition of the essays, largely concerned with the elaboration and defence of his position, which were later brought together in 1914 as *Essays on Truth and Reality*. Their main message, expressed in a more amorphous and conciliatory way than in his earlier writings, is that nothing short of the all-inclusive and harmonious whole is real. Truth lies in the coherence of a system; our intellectual constructions possess truth in varying degrees but, because of thought's inevitably selective and abstracting mode of operation, never completely. Much of Bradley's attention is devoted to pragmatism, which had urged against him the man-made,

conventional nature of truth, its changeable, provisional, and relative
character. As Schiller, the leading English pragmatist, saw, Bradley
had made large concessions to his opponents. In these essays it is
not coherence alone, the satisfaction of the intellect's demand for
absence of contradiction, that is the criterion of truth; but rather
the satisfaction of the whole of man's nature, including the demands
of the moral and religious consciousness. The head-on collision
between Bradley, proclaiming the demands of the intellect, and
William James and his followers, champions of the will, seemed to
be resolved by an expansion of the former attitude to include the
latter within itself, the possibility of carrying out such an incor-
poration harmoniously being only the last, if most extensive, of
Bradley's many philosophical acts of faith.

Bradley's leading philosophical ally, Bernard Bosanquet, had
never been as lonely or as combative a defender of idealism. He
began in the eighties as a friendly critic and developer of Bradley's
logical theories. Bosanquet was even more definite than Bradley
about the difference between a metaphysically well-grounded logic,
which took inference to be the movement in all directions towards a
coherent system, and traditional formal logic, deductive and induc-
tive, which took inference to be a mechanical, linear process. At the
end of the century he returned to a fully-articulated exposition, in
The Philosophical Theory of the State, of a Hegelian political theory
with extensive liberal modifications. Although the community is
rated as higher than the individual, its task being the realization
of our true selves by any means to hand, there is no identification
of true community with historical nationality. Bosanquet was prepared to envisage an international state. The individual human
being fared no better in his two major metaphysical treatises of
1912 and 1913. The only true individual is the absolute, the one
harmonious and truly all-comprehending 'concrete universal'. As
with Bradley, the absolute was beyond personality and the proper
aim of personal life was self-transcendence, a realization of one's
place in the whole which involved the forfeiture of personal identity.
Yet for all their similarity of content the metaphysical systems
of Bradley and Bosanquet have a very different flavour. Where
Bradley emphasizes the enormity of the gulf between reality
and appearance, between the whole and its partial manifestations, Bosanquet insists that the various levels of appearance are

approximations, of varying degrees of closeness, to reality. If the absolute is the only true concrete universal, a human community, for example, is still a very fair draft of a coherent system. For Bradley, appearance was a dispensable ladder on which to mount to a more or less mystical apprehension of reality in its harmonious wholeness; for Bosanquet, on the other hand, the conception of reality as a coherent system was a vantage-point from which to obtain a clear and adequate understanding of appearance. A single view of the nature of things led in Bradley to a renunciation of the common world, in Bosanquet to an acceptance of it that was broadminded to the point of indiscriminateness.

Bradley's other leading disciple, H. H. Joachim, published his first and most interesting work, *The Nature of Truth*, in 1906. A finely written book, it exhibited a mournfulness which was symptomatic of the decrepitude of the absolute idealism it expressed. First of all, the theories which see truth as a correspondence of abstract proposition and concrete fact and as an intrinsic quality of independent logical entities are dispatched. The former is held to be unintelligible on account of the extreme logical heterogeneity of its two poles, the latter on account of the pluralistic isolation it ascribes to propositions. Judgements, for Joachim, possess neither meaning nor truth in isolation. The systematic practice of science reveals empirically that beliefs can only be understood and verified against a massive background of other cohering beliefs. But for the finite and fallible human mind the notion of a fully coherent system of judgements is always an unreachable ideal. Joachim was oppressed by the logical analogue of the religious problem of evil, what he called the negative element in reality, displaying itself in the fact of error. Reality, which should be perfect and coherent, obstinately manifests itself in a fragmentary and incoherent form. How can this 'self-estrangement' of reality be explained in idealist terms? If reality is what Bradleyan metaphysics takes it to be, how could it have presented itself in the mutilated form of appearances to finite minds?

Absolute idealism was essentially an Oxford product. Idealists in other places were less affected by Bradley's radical scepticism and so were unwilling to abandon the reality of the finite human mind or admit the less-than-absolute truth of moral and religious convictions. Many philosophers of a generally idealist persuasion stopped short of the full rigours of idealism, following in the steps of the copious Pringle-Pattison who had protested against the implications of Hegelianism for God and personality before Bradley explicitly drew them in *Appearance and Reality*. One outcome of this internal disquiet in the school was a kind of edifying eclecticism which argued on idealist principles, not to establish hard and painful truths, but rather to express common beliefs about men and the world in a cheerful, boneless idiom in which all conflicts were ultimately resolved, all apparent set-backs and disasters seen as merely circuitous paths to final perfection. For the most part these good-natured spiritualizers, such as J. S. Mackenzie and Sir Henry Jones, were disciples of Jowett's successor as Master of Balliol, Edward Caird. For them as for him idealism was a technique rather than a body of truths, one that by taking a very distant and optimistic look at the world saw all its oppositions reconciled and harmonized in a developing and spiritual unity. Jones's book of 1909, *Idealism as a Practical Creed*, provided in its title a convenient name for their standpoint.

Cambridge Idealism

Two forms of personal idealism, however, emphasizing the indestructible reality of the individual human mind, were of a much more clear-cut variety. One was the Cambridge idealism, if two such unique and idiosyncratic thinkers can be brought under a common designation, of McTaggart and James Ward; the other was the pragmatism of a group of philosophers at Oxford under the leadership of F. C. S. Schiller, who introduced themselves in the composite manifesto *Personal Idealism*[1] in 1902. McTaggart and Ward were still clearly idealists, to the extent that the metaphysical priority of mind to nature was fundamental to their thinking. So also were some of Schiller's early associates: Rashdall, for example, was a Berkeleyan. But with G. F. Stout the outermost possible limit of idealism was reached and Schiller himself, with his constant invocation of Protagoras and his loyal adherence to William James, cannot properly be described as an idealist at all.

Although McTaggart's great metaphysical system, *The Nature of Existence*, did not appear until the 1920's, the main lines of his

---

[1] *Personal Idealism, Philosophical Essays by Eight Members of the University of Oxford*, edited by Henry Sturt, 1902.

thought were evident in the three books he published in the first decade of the century. The final picture of the world that he sought to establish is clear enough for all its peculiarity. For him the world is a society of minds, enjoying eternal, or rather timeless, existence, and related to one another by love. Nothing exists but these minds and their ideas. There is no God and no matter, space and particularly time are illusions. An essential point is the mutual independence of the minds who, with their ideas, are all that exists. Minds can perceive one another but they cannot overlap, cannot literally share one another's ideas. Their relations are uncompromisingly external. The absolute is a society and not an all-engulfing personality, as with Green's eternal consciousness, or an impersonal tissue of coherent experience in which all distinction of persons is confounded, as with Bradley. In one important sense of the word, then, McTaggart was not a monist. Everything in the world was of the same kind, it was all mental, but it was not all one thing. Like Berkeley he accepted the doctrine of internal relations as applied to the knowledge of objects by subjects. The only possible objects of knowledge must have a community of nature with their subjects, must be ideas and so constituent parts of those subjects. But he was not prepared to apply it to all apparent pluralities. McTaggart's method was superbly and arrogantly deductive. He starts from the modest empirical assumption that something exists, and the two principles that everything is infinitely divisible and also dissimilar in some respect from everything else. From these he deduces the 'principle of determining correspondence' which specifies the systematic character which must be possessed by anything that really exists. Applying this principle to the apparent contents of the world he finds that only minds are in conformity with it. Nothing but minds, therefore, and their states can exist. Minds possess eternal existence in both directions, are pre-existent as well as immortal. There is no reason to suppose that God, a specially important or influential mind, exists. McTaggart's main conclusions were published in more or less popular form in 1906 in *Some Dogmas of Religion*. This marvellously lucid book both calls for and triumphantly exemplifies its author's special brand of unswerving rationalism. Religion must rest on dogma as well as emotion, and dogma needs proof. McTaggart was a magnificent writer and took immense pains with his writing. This literary tactic expressed his determination, entirely opposed to the woolly edification of most idealists, that philosophy should be absolutely clear and definite. Few people, perhaps, have been convinced by McTaggart's arguments, yet his influence has been of considerable, if unrecognized, importance. The revolution inaugurated by Russell and Moore from 1903 onwards was even more a revolution in philosophical style than in doctrinal substance and the new plain style was something they owed to a large extent to McTaggart.

James Ward, the other leading Cambridge idealist, is a less striking figure. Like Bradley, he owed a good deal to Lotze and was a strenuous opponent of the native British tradition of associationism in psychology. In place of James Mill's theory of mental chemistry, which saw the life of the mind as a mechanically constituted succession of atomic sensory elements, he argued for a continuous flux of experience, a 'presentational continuum', comparable to William James's 'stream of thought'. He was particularly emphatic in his opposition to Hume's view of the self as reducible to the complex totality of its own ideas. Experience was inconceivable without both subject and object, the two terms in the relation being necessarily distinct from one another. Ward's defence of personality rested on this comparatively formal foundation. The chief task of the subject self is to distil clear ideas from the amorphous flux of the presentational continuum by an active process of selective attention. The products of this activity are abstractions; in particular the world of discrete substances assumed and developed by natural science is not a true account of the facts but a conceptual convenience. In reality the world is, like the mind, a continuum, its content not sharply divided into active mind and passive matter. Active mentality permeates the whole of existence even if often in a rudimentary and habit-bound fashion. His final picture of the world was more or less Leibnizian in its main lines. It is a vast system of mind-like striving entities at various stages of development. Ward extended Darwin's idea of the evolutionary continuity of men and other living things to take in the whole contents of the world. But at the upper limit of the scale of being he hesitated. He did not think that the existence of God could be proved. At best it was a conjecture for which there were various good theoretical and practical reasons.

Pragmatism

The varieties of personal idealism so far considered were all heresies within the body of the idealist church. More sympathetic than absolutist orthodoxy to new movements of thought in the United States and France, they were still well within the main tradition of classical rationalism. They still held the world to be a spiritual unity of some sort, even if not as close-knit and undifferentiated a unity as Bradley's absolute, and they insisted, with varying degrees of firmness, on the metaphysical priority of mind, conceived as reason or intellect, to nature. But with the collaborative volume *Personal Idealism* in 1902 a radically anti-intellectualistic philosophy makes its first appearance in Britain. For Schiller and his associates mind still made nature, but it was the ordinary concrete human mind in its daily business of living that they were concerned with and its crucial attribute from their point of view was the will. Schiller and his pragmatist allies were reacting to Bradley much as the great German irrationalists had reacted to Hegel. But the immediate parent of British pragmatism was, of course, William James. His essential doctrine was that we need to believe more than we can possibly know. Intellectualists, the descendants of Descartes, whether idealist or empiricist, all refused to believe what could not be rationally proved. But thought, James held, is for the sake of action and action cannot wait on proof. A belief is justified by its contribution to practice, not by its rigid conformity to the intellectualist's abstract canons of evidence. What James wanted to believe—that the world was full of novelty, spontaneity, and chance—Bergson, by his critique of the abstracting intellect, made it possible for him to believe. The human intellect, according to Bergson, inevitably distorts the living and continuous flux of reality whose nature can only be truly grasped by intuition. For voluntarism in general, then, reality is no timelessly perfect system of forms, it is a living, plastic, developing plurality. Within it are minds, whose concern is not passively to reflect their surroundings but rather to satisfy their impulses by voluntary action. The truth for which these agents seek is neither pictorial correspondence nor abstract formal coherence; it attaches to those ideas, rather, which it is valuable for the will to have in its struggle for existence.

Schiller and his allies, then, associated the emphasis on the irreducible nature of personality, from which their joint volume took its name and which was already widespread in British philo-sophy, with an insistence on the fundamentally active and volitional character of the mind which had been anticipated by the post-Hegelian irrationalists and was now fully explicit in the work of James and Bergson. Schiller called his own philosophy humanism and took for its motto the dictum of Protagoras that man is the measure of all things. The proper starting-point for philosophy is the concrete, striving, human mind. To take this as the basic type of existence is to adopt pluralism. The world is seen first and fore-most as a multitude of voluntary pursuers of purposes. Thinking is a practical activity; the beliefs which it produces are instruments for the practical conduct of life; the truth at which they aim is their capacity for satisfying actual human purposes. Consistently enough Schiller was prepared to extend his Protagoreanism to reality itself which he saw as plastic, subservient to human purposes, and taking its form from the active, human point of view from which it was considered. Schiller's essay 'Axioms as Postulates' in *Personal Idealism* was the first of a long series of works in which he mounted an onslaught on formal logic as the idol of intellectualism. There are no eternal or *a priori* truths for all truth is dependent on prac-tical utility. The evolution of knowledge rules out eternal verities for each new discovery reacts to some degree on the meaning and truth of what has been discovered before. But truth is not a merely subjective feature of beliefs; though relative it is inevitably social. The task of logic is not the sterile extraction from assumed premises of what is already contained in them. There are no such things as the timeless meanings of the formal logician. We must concern ourselves with what words are intended to mean by a particular person in a particular concrete situation. The proper role of logic is to aid discovery by the critical evaluation of claims to truth and this is a more or less ethical affair. Truth is a species of value, it is the theoretically useful. It is acquired by adventurous exploration, by the speculative assumption of hypotheses, not by mechanical operation in accordance with inflexible rules.

More general consequences of this line of thought were the falsity of determinism and the concept of a finite God. Determinism con-flicted with the idea of the human mind as essentially active, and it presupposed the impossible—complete knowledge. In his first work, *Riddles of the Sphinx*, Schiller had written sympathetically of the conception of a limited, personal God put forward in John Stuart Mill's late essays on religion. Rashdall argued for the same view in his *Personal Idealism* essay on 'Personality; Human and Divine'. A person, Rashdall said, 'is a conscious, permanent, self-distinguishing, individual, active being'. That God exists as a personality follows, in a Berkeleyan manner, from the systematic unity of the natural world; he is the mind for whom that world exists. But minds, although created by God, are not, once created, dependent on him in the same way as natural objects. God limits himself by the creation of minds and the all-inclusive absolute is not to be identified with God but is rather a society of minds presided over by God. In this idea of God as a self-limiting creator Rashdall saw the beginnings of a solution to the problem of evil. We shall see later how these speculative defences of God as personal and moral led to theological heterodoxy. Rashdall's rejection of absolutism was to prove insufficiently radical for more conservative theologians.

Three of the original personal idealists went on to do significant work in philosophy: Schiller, Rashdall, and Stout. Rashdall directed his attention to theology and ethics, becoming the intellectual leader of modernist theology and producing in his *Theory of Good and Evil*, published in 1907, a form of idealistic utilitarianism which persuasively combined the main ideas of the two philosophies, absolutist and naturalist, against which the pragmatic manifesto had originally set itself. Stout went on to construct a cumbrous, circumspect system of philosophy in which a firmly realistic theory of knowledge was loosely contained in an idealist metaphysics. Only Schiller remained loyal to the original pragmatist creed and immune to the attractions of any sort of intellectualism. His strenuous insistence on novelty, adventure, and experiment, his belief that mind was fundamentally will aiming at satisfaction through practical activity, was the only pure philosophical expression of an important feature of the Edwardian mental atmosphere, that hearty self-confidence which saw nothing as impossible to man and envisaged history as an evolutionary advance into an unprecedentedly better state of affairs. It is significant that H. G. Wells's only contribution to *Mind*, the philosophers' professional journal, his article 'Scepticism of the Instrument' of 1904, was a piece of orthodox pragmatism.

The first decade of the century saw both the formation and the dissolution of the first main attack on the orthodox absolute idealism that was dominant at its beginning. Long before the outbreak of the war it was clear that the attack had failed. Most of its supporters had drifted away to other interests or to other philosophical points of view. Idealism was not to fall to the champions of practice but to an intellectualism much more rigorous than its own. And it was not the high-handed treatment of personality meted out by idealism that proved its downfall, but rather its blithe subjectivization of physical nature. Personal idealism had too much in common with its absolute counterpart: not just a belief in the metaphysical priority of some sort of mind but more fundamentally a looseness of argumentative style, a reliance on rhetoric where convincing proof was needed. The victory of realism was due in the end more to its enforcement of an altogether higher standard of intellectual discipline than either of its predecessors had exhibited than to its originally revolutionary but soon much qualified idea that the object of knowledge was wholly independent of the fact of its being known.

REALISTS ON KNOWLEDGE, LOGIC, AND ETHICS

It is not difficult to pick out the year in which the new logical realism, and indeed modern analytic philosophy in general, of which realism was the first phase, appeared on the scene. In 1903 G. E. Moore published both his revolutionary article 'The Refutation of Idealism'[1] and his immensely influential *Principia Ethica*, while Russell published his magnificent *Principles of Mathematics*, the prose anticipation of his greatest achievement, *Principia Mathematica*.[2] Moore and Russell have had long and distinguished philosophical careers. Yet if they had both given up the subject at the outbreak of the first world war, when they were both in their early forties, their strictly philosophical reputations would not have been substantially impaired. We should have been deprived of Moore's great work as a teacher of philosophy but practically nothing was added by him later to the doctrines and arguments contained in *Some Main Problems of Philosophy* which, though only published in 1953,

[1] Reprinted in his *Philosophical Studies*, 1922.

[2] Alfred Norton Whitehead and Bertrand Russell, *Principia Mathematica*, 3 vols., 1910–13.

was written in 1909–10. Russell's much more mobile and receptive intelligence has expressed itself in all sorts of directions since 1914 but never, perhaps, to more purpose than in the fifteen years between his *Philosophy of Leibniz* in 1900 and his *Our Knowledge of the External World* in 1914.

Friends and colleagues at Trinity, Cambridge, Moore and Russell came to philosophy from different directions, from classics and mathematics respectively. Their differing backgrounds correspond to very differing points of view. Moore is a conservative analyst of thinking, stimulated by the speculative excesses of philosophy to a tenacious defence of common knowledge and a devotedly accurate obsession with the precise meaning of common language. Russell, however, has always been a constructive analyst, aiming to extract from common belief the hard core of logically and empirically justified matter in it and to express this result in a language adequate by the standards of his own great systematic presentation of formal logic. In the first decade of the century, however, these important differences were still only implicit. The general standpoint of Russell's *Problems of Philosophy* (1912) is much the same as that of Moore's lectures of 1909–10.

Both began their philosophical careers as disciples of Bradley, an understandable allegiance for pupils of predominantly idealist teachers. Moore's first essays were written in the prevailing neo-Kantian jargon and Russell's first substantial work, *Foundations of Geometry* (1897), sought to deduce the basic principles of geometry from a subjective, Kantian concept of space. But they soon broke with idealism and supported each other in the work of demolition. Their disenchantment, however, for all its coincidence in detail, arose from different sources. Moore rejected idealism because it was simply incredible, in blatant conflict with obvious facts: Russell rejected it as inadequate to the nature of mathematical truth.

The Critique of Idealism

The first line of attack, initiated by Moore, was directed against epistemological idealism, against the more or less Berkeleyan view that the only possible objects of knowledge for the mind were its own ideas. Admitting that there was more to idealism than the belief that to be is to be perceived, Moore insisted that this belief was an essential presupposition of the total idealist doctrine. His refutation was disarmingly simple, resting on a distinction between the act of awareness and its object. Such phrases as 'the sensation of green' are ambiguous, for they can refer either to the mental activity of sensing green or to the green thing sensed. Idealists had consistently confused the whole, the awareness of the object, with one of its parts, the object itself. But act and object are clearly distinguishable, there is no necessity for the properties of the one to be possessed by the other. In particular it does not follow from the unquestionably mental character of the act of awareness that its object must be mental as well. Admittedly the act on its own is elusive and, in Moore's phrase, 'diaphanous', but nonetheless the object is neither a part nor a quality of it, it is something quite distinct. Moore concluded his 'Refutation of Idealism' by insisting that in perception we are commonly aware of the independent existence of material things in space. There is no problem of getting outside the circle of our own sensations since we emerge from it with every sensation we have. The boldness of this conclusion was soon considerably modified. Moore was soon saying that colours and shapes rather than material things were the direct objects of perception and next that sense-data, the elements common to sensations, dreams, imaginings, hallucinations, and the having of after-images, were what we strictly perceived. Even so the act–object distinction was firmly retained.

With this modification the scene was set for Moore's main and continuing problem about perception: what is the relation between sense-data and material objects? They are not parts of the surfaces of such objects since a sense-datum of one side of an object will change in size as we move away from it while the size of the object remains unchanged. Russell argued in 1912 that the conception of a world of independent material things was the simplest hypothesis capable of accounting for the regularities in our experience of sense-data. Moore was attracted towards this Lockean view but recognized the difficulties it contained. How could rational grounds be provided for preferring it to the theory that an object is nothing more than an orderly collection of sense-data? In *Our Knowledge of the External World* in 1914 Russell presented a fully worked-out version of this latter doctrine. 'The thing', he said, 'is the class of its appearances.' A material object is an extensive, orderly system of *sensibilia* converging on a centre which is conventionally taken to be the literal place of that object. But a *sensibile*, or appearance, is not a mental, subjective entity. Where the appearance of a thing from a certain position is experienced by some mind there is an actual *sensum* which does involve a subjective element, the act of awareness, but the *sensibile* exists whether any mind experiences it or not. At this point Moore's original realism about perception has undergone its furthest possible dilution. Nothing but idiom seems to separate the assertion that a *sensibile* does exist at this place from the assertion that if anyone were to occupy this position he would have a certain sensation. And with this final, phenomenalist, transition a doctrine envisaged by Berkeley and not far from his final position is attained.

More fundamental, if less immediately striking and effective, as an undermining of idealism was Russell's attack on the coherence theory of truth and, through it, on the basic principle of internal relations. His style of argument here is characteristic of the difference between his method and Moore's. Its rapid sequence of ingenious arguments is directed towards the exposure of internal inconsistencies in the idealist position. Moore, by contrast, patiently and laboriously accumulates the full detail of the conflict between existing philosophical theories and the massive certitudes of common sense. For him no philosophical argument is likely to attain the degree of obvious validity required to overturn the deep-seated and universal convictions of the human race. Against the coherence theory Russell argues that, as a proposition affirming that no proposition is wholly true, it refutes itself. Again, if the truth of a belief depends on its coherence with other beliefs there must be some initial supply of accepted beliefs to start from. Finally the principles of coherence must themselves be true in some other way than through their coherence since until they are accepted as true no question of coherence can be settled. At best coherence can be a limitedly useful test of truth and ultimately the truth or falsity of beliefs must rest on their relation to independent facts.

Both Russell and Moore made short work of the other alternative, James's pragmatist one, to their own correspondence theory. Nevertheless the correspondence theory was not without difficulties. It seemed to account for true beliefs well enough, but Russell was concerned about its account of false belief. Must we admit 'objective falsehoods' for them to correspond to ? He was unwilling to interpret non-correspondence with fact as anything but correspondence with a non-fact.

Moore had directed a few parenthetical blows at the doctrine of internal relations in his 'Refutation of Idealism', but it was not until 1916 that he set about it systematically with a delicate but devastating argument. Russell's criticism was based in part on his belief in the irreducibility of relations to qualities, a thesis presupposed by his developments of formal logic. Defenders of internal relations, by taking the relations of things to be grounded in their qualities, had been led to treat the totality of a thing's relations as essential to it, as constitutive of its nature. But the idea of 'the nature of a thing' is ambiguous. It could mean the properties a thing logically must possess to be identified as of a given kind or as satisfying a given description; but it could also mean all the properties and relations that the thing possesses. To know what a thing is to know the former narrower set of properties and thus to be able to identify it. The further knowledge that we then accumulate does not alter or subvert the original identification, and unless that identification is somehow made there is no starting-point for the accumulation of knowledge at all. With internal relations refuted there was once more a place for contingency and plurality in the world, for brute facts and mutually independent things.

The third main aspect of idealism to be dismantled by Russell and Moore was its critique of abstractions. Moore's initial break with idealism was made in his essay on 'The Nature of Judgment' in 1899 where he attacked Bradley's failure to accord to the objects of thought an existence truly independent of the minds that are aware of them in thinking. In *Problems of Philosophy* Russell advanced a thoroughgoing Platonism which was opposed both to the Bradleyan idea and to the image of empiricist tradition. *A priori* knowledge in general and mathematical knowledge in particular relate to a timeless, intellectually inspectable world of independent essences. Necessary truths describe the immutable relations of these essences. Inference or reasoning, it follows, is neither, as the idealists believed, a process of mental construction nor is it any kind of associative habit. It is rather an application of our knowledge of the eternal geography of the world of essence.

The broad outlines of the realism of Russell and Moore were clearly established by the end of the Edwardian period. It saw the world as an infinity of particular things, externally related to one another and of radically different kinds. There were material objects in space, minds aware, in a somewhat complicated fashion, of those objects, and logical essences inspectable by minds but independent of them. Truth consisted in the correspondence of propositions and independent facts, whether the propositions were perceptual, recording an awareness of the material world, introspective, recording an awareness of one's own mental states, or abstract, recording intellectual apprehension of the world of timeless universals. Set beside Bradley's featureless absolute the universe of the realists was a complex and variegated affair, containing a plurality of things and a plurality of kinds of things. It is worth noticing that despite Moore's reverence for common sense and common language and Russell's concern for strict logical rigour the outcome of their joint efforts was unquestionably a metaphysical system.

Russell's Logic

Kant's view that Aristotle had brought the science of logic to its perfect completion prevailed in England until the middle of the nineteenth century. But in the 1840's Augustus de Morgan and George Boole initiated the revolution in the subject that was to culminate in Whitehead and Russell's *Principia Mathematica*. The innovations of Russell's nineteenth-century predecessors affected both the structure and the scope of the discipline. From a collection of rules of thumb the new logicians turned it into a species of algebra. The goal of this process was a unitary deductive system in which all the laws of logic could be derived from a minimum set of intuitively obvious axioms. Second only to this in importance was the enlargement of scope. De Morgan had sketched a logic of relations and others, notably the great American C. S. Peirce, had developed and generalized his idea, making possible the formalization of a host of logical connexions which the Aristotelian insistence that every proposition must have one subject and one predicate had obliterated. Another enlargement was the rediscovery of the logic of compound propositions which had been discovered by the Stoics but largely neglected for the ensuing two thousand years. While logic was becoming more mathematical, mathematics itself was increasingly in need of assistance from logic. Non-Euclidean geometry and Cantor's transfinite arithmetic were salient instances of mathematical theorizing that had lost all apparent contact with the observable, empirical world.

The culmination of these various lines of development was the logistic hypothesis, independently arrived at by Frege and Russell, and the main topic of the latter's *Principles of Mathematics*. It stated that the fundamental concepts of systematized mathematics were all definable in purely logical terms and that its fundamental propositions were, given these definitions, wholly deducible from the principles of logic. *Principia Mathematica* presented the fully elaborated vindication of this hypothesis. At the base of the system are five primitive propositions (pretty evident truths of the logic of compound propositions or propositional calculus) and a handful of undefined notions. The immediate yield of these exiguous data is the propositional calculus itself and from this is derived the functional calculus, embodying the logic of relations and, deeply embedded within it, a version of the traditional logic of Aristotle. The concept of a class is defined in the terms of the functional calculus and with this the construction is in principle complete; for natural numbers are defined as classes of classes whose members pair off with one another and Peano had shown how the whole of mathematics could be deduced from the theory of natural numbers. More recent developments in logic have cast doubt on the feasibility of Russell's logistic project: logicians have shifted their interest from his kind of comprehensive system-building to the theory of proof, to the formal investigation rather than the construction of deductive systems. But *Principia Mathematica* is still recognized as the greatest single achievement of modern formal logic, an Old Testament, so to speak, preparing the way for Gödel and the meta-mathematicians.

Its effects on subsequent philosophy, in the English-speaking world at any rate, have been very large. Some of these arise from the details of the construction, others from Russell's philosophical discussions in the second and third chapters of the introduction, others again from the exemplary character of the work as a whole. As for the first: no one realized more clearly than Russell the philosophical significance of the distinctions and clarifications of terminology from which the system started. They added up to a systematic ordering of the forms of discourse that was richer and clearer than anything provided by Aristotle or Mill. To start with there were

simple attributive or relational propositions ascribing a property
to a given individual or asserting a relation to hold between a group
of individuals. Such atomic propositions could be combined by the
conjunctions *and, or,* and *if . . . then* to form molecular propositions.
General propositions—whether universal, *all F are G,* or existential,
some F are G—could be conceived as limiting cases of molecular ones,
as very long conjunctions and disjunctions respectively. Russell's
definition of *if. . . then* bequeathed a mass of problems to his successors. His interpretation of *if p then q* as *it is not the case that both p
and not q,* though it vastly simplified the computational treatment
of inferences with hypothetical elements in them, led to paradoxes,
for example that *if p then q* is true, whatever *p* and *q* may be,
provided that *p* is false or *q* is true. Secondly, Russell's theory of
descriptions and his theory of types profoundly influenced the course
of later thinking. The theory of descriptions offered an analysis
of sentences whose subjects did or could fail to refer to anything.
Russell offered a technique for translating such sentences which
was of interest on its own account and also served, in Ramsey's
words, as a paradigm for philosophical analysis in general. Sentences containing puzzling elements were replaced by sentences
of a much more logically complex variety from which the per-
plexity was absent. The implication was that common language
was misleading as to the true logical form of the facts it reported,
and it was also implied that a formally perfect and non-misleading
form of expression could be arrived at by logical analysis. A similar
point against common language was made by the theory of types.
Russell discovered that there were grammatically well-formed sentences which were logically absurd, in that their truth entailed their
falsity and their falsity their truth. Therefore logical as well as
grammatical limitations had to be imposed on the formulation of
discourse. Together these two doctrines encouraged suspicion of
ordinary grammatical speech. A sentence's grammar was no safe
guide to its meaning and it could be grammatical without having
any meaning at all. The natural inference was that a logically
ideal or perfect language should be constructed around the logic
of *Principia Mathematica.* This was the project of Russell's and
Wittgenstein's logical atomism worked out in the years just before
1914 and most fully developed in the latter's *Tractatus Logico-
Philosophicus* (1922).

Moore's Ethics

The doctrine expounded in Moore's *Principia Ethica* conformed both in content and in method with his theory of knowledge. In the first place it was an uncompromisingly realistic theory. It saw goodness or intrinsic value as being as much a self-subsistent part of the universe as minds, material objects, or universals and as being irreducibly distinct from any of these. It established this point by the exact and painstaking demolition of all attempts to deny the uniqueness of intrinsic value by identifying it with something else, whether human experiences of pleasure or the evolutionary survival of the race or the self-realization of the individual.

His chief opponents in this field were not the idealists so much as the moral philosophers of the empiricist tradition. The most influential feature of his ethical theory was his negative criticism of their common endeavours to find some empirically observable kind of circumstance in terms of which the concepts of morals could be defined. Moore accused this line of thought of committing the 'naturalistic fallacy' and the conviction that naturalism is indeed fallacious has governed the thinking of subsequent moral philosophers in this country with amazing tenacity. The uniqueness and consequent indefinability of intrinsic value was something that Moore simply asserted rather than argued for. In effect his procedure was to challenge anyone to compare the concepts present to his mind when he thought of goodness and of any kind of empirical state of affairs proposed as identical with it and to see if he could honestly maintain that they were not quite different. More persuasive, perhaps, were the shrewd and detailed objections to the positive arguments of such naturalists as Mill and Sidgwick for their accounts of goodness in terms of pleasure. Bradley had attacked the doctrine of pleasure for pleasure's sake as morally squalid and with a somewhat abstract and elusive argument about the logical incoherence of its concept of the ultimate moral end. Moore, in a more determined and pedestrian fashion, set about the precise detail of the naturalists' reasoning and urged the unacceptability of their conclusions to logical intuition.

Moore's own positive views were not at all definite except in their broadest outlines. Our moral convictions, in his opinion, are pieces of knowledge based in the end on our capacity for being directly aware of the goodness of states of affairs. Our moral faculty yields self-evident moral axioms, in particular that the only intrinsically good states of affairs are human states of mind, above all the contemplation of beauty and 'personal relations'. As ethics this theory had little influence but as moral advocacy it had some importance in constituting the creed of the remarkable group of Cambridge intellectuals later known collectively as 'Bloomsbury', including Keynes, Clive Bell, Roger Fry, and Virginia Woolf. It was a doctrine of cultivated and contemplative enjoyment, in which rules of conduct had an insignificant place, and was far removed from the social concern of the idealists and their utilitarian predecessors. Its acceptance was probably due more to the exemplary force and purity of Moore's character than to the philosophical considerations on which he based it.

Oxford Realism

A movement of thought, parallel to that of Russell and Moore, was developing during the same period at Oxford. But it turned out to be far less influential, principally because its leading exponents were far less impressive men than their Cambridge counterparts. John Cook Wilson, who became professor of logic at Oxford in 1899, and his ablest disciple H. A. Prichard, who gave an extended account of their common convictions in 1909 in his *Kant's Theory of Knowledge*, were both slightly absurd figures: Cook Wilson for his pugnacious eccentricity and long-windedness, Prichard for his leathery and obdurate dogmatism. They, and their less talented ally H. W. B. Joseph, took donnishness to its comical extreme, above all in the complacency with which they played Canute to the advances of mathematical and scientific knowledge. Cook Wilson's blustering against non-Euclidean geometry and Russell's logic, and Joseph's assaults on Einsteinian physics and Freudian psychology, are in the same pathetic tradition as Hobbes's struggle with Wallis or the confidence of the Christ Church 'wits' in the genuineness of the *Letters of Phalaris*. Practising critical philosophy in its most bleakly negative form, they elaborated an essentially intuitionist doctrine. According to them, knowledge was the intuitive apprehension of logically independent objects, reasoning the intuitive apprehension of the timeless connexions between universals, moral consciousness the intuitive apprehension of necessary principles of conduct.

An important feature of Cook Wilson's procedure was his concern with the ordinary meaning of words. In him, as in many other Oxford philosophers, this predilection arose from a background of classical studies and it has remained the most conspicuous inheritance of later philosophers from Oxford realism. It underlay Cook Wilson's critique of Bradley. For the idealists thought and reality consisted in the end of judgements, the acts of mind which issued in the making of statements. Cook Wilson argued that a judgement, as ordinarily understood, was the conclusion of a more or less precarious inference. Judgements in this sense might well all be less than wholly true and owe what truth they did possess to their coherence with other beliefs. But not all acts of thought were judgements, and to treat them as if they were was simply to confuse entirely distinct things. In particular it was to fail to recognize the uniqueness and indefinability of knowledge (regarded by Cook Wilson and Prichard much as Moore regarded goodness). There could be no definition of knowledge, let alone a justification of it. It could only be exemplified, as by the elementary propositions of mathematics. Such exemplification showed knowledge to be the intuitive and incorrigible awareness of something independent of the act of knowing itself. Prichard argued that idealists from Berkeley onwards had made a play on the phrase *in the mind*. Something known was in the mind to the extent that it was known, but it was not necessarily a mental state in the way that the act of knowing logically had to be. With this muddle dispelled there was no solid ground for doubting that many objects of knowledge were entirely non-mental, as they appeared to be. Knowledge was not only unique among acts of thought, it was also fundamental. Believing, wondering, being under the impression that, had all to be explained in terms of it. Both Cook Wilson and Prichard began as uncompromising realists about perception, just as Moore had. To perceive something was to find it, not to make or construct it. This led them into criticism of the traditional doctrine of appearances as the immediate objects of perception. An appearance was not a self-subsistent thing in its own right; to talk about it was to talk about real things from a particular point of view. But the hold of the argument from illusion was tenacious. Cook Wilson admitted that the secondary qualities of material objects were not immediately perceived but inferred, while Prichard was led on to the extraordinary view that in every perception we mistake the extended colours we actually perceive for material things.

This realism covered the objects of thought as well as the objects of perception, conceiving them as timeless universals whose relationships were open to inspection by the intellect. But while going thus far with the early Russell, Cook Wilson had only contempt for the formal logic with which Russell's realism about universals was associated. His concern with the ordinary meaning of words led to an insistence on the absolute distinctness of grammar and logic that was very different from Russell's, one which hinged on the intentions of the speaker as revealed in such features of utterance as emphasis. Both distinguished the logical from the grammatical subject of a sentence. But while for Russell it was the irreducible residue of a theoretically motivated analysis, for Cook Wilson it was that aspect of the state of affairs being described which the speaker took for granted. Some of Cook Wilson's criticisms of idealist logic had a bearing on Russell as well. Both Russell and Bradley took universal propositions such as 'All men are mortal' to be hypothetical. Against this Cook Wilson maintained that such propositions were genuine, categorical, assertions while hypothetical statements were not, being employed rather to state that the solution to one problem was conditional upon the solution of another. Half a century later other Oxford philosophers were to use arguments very like Cook Wilson's in a much more powerful criticism of the pretensions of formal logic to represent the real nature of thought.

The ethical consequences of Cook Wilson's philosophy were worked out in a brilliant and influential essay of Prichard's, 'Does Moral Philosophy rest on a Mistake', published in *Mind* in 1912. Just as Cook Wilson rejected traditional epistemology as an attempt to define and justify the unique and indefinable concept of knowledge, so Prichard saw traditional ethics as a radically misguided attempt to define the indefinable concept of obligation and to give reasons for the self-evident principles of conduct in which it figured. In Prichard's opinion the wrongness of lying was something we just know, like the fundamental truths of mathematics. To attempt to justify ultimate principles of conduct leads inevitably to their deplorable conversion into counsels of prudence. Most moral philosophers have tried, unconvincingly, to show that to act in accordance with the generally accepted principles of conduct will lead to happiness. Even if this were true, which is doubtful, it would be irrelevant. Not only is the intuitively obvious obligatoriness of an action an entirely sufficient moral reason for doing it, it is the only genuinely *moral* reason there could be for doing it. Those moral philosophers who try to derive the rightness of actions from the consequences they produce are in fact destroying morality, properly so called, altogether and substituting for it the reflective pursuit of personal advantage. Almost as important as this rigorous doctrine of *fiat justitia, ruat coelum* was Prichard's distinction of the rightness of actions, which is determined by the form of the action itself and the principles specifying the forms of obligatory action, from their moral goodness, which depends rather on the intention with which they are performed. The main theories of the Oxford moralists, which constituted orthodox academic moral philosophy until the second world war, are all derived from Prichard's first essay on the subject.

RELIGIOUS THOUGHT

The German Influence

The Edwardian period saw the full accommodation within British theology of the results of German biblical criticism. In the nineteenth century religious thought in this country had been comparatively isolated from what had been going on abroad. Tractarianism, to take the most important strand, was an entirely native phenomenon. But while the Church of England was occupied with adjusting itself to the aftermath of the Oxford Movement, reinterpretations of Christian doctrine had been taking place on a large scale in Germany. The final outcome of the Tübingen school's historical criticism of the Bible was the liberal protestantism of Ritschl and Harnack. Baur, the leader of the Tübingen school, had been a disciple of Hegel, and the Hegelian view of religious dogma as a more or less symbolic representation, in a concrete and historically conditioned form, of the timeless truths of idealist metaphysics constituted a framework of general ideas for the work of the biblical critics. The idealist philosophy has been described as a philosophical broad church movement—an apt enough description of Jowett's latitudinarianism and the ethical strenuousness of T. H. Green. But as expounded by

Bradley it reached a degree of broadness which made it impossible to call it a church movement at all. At this point, as we have seen, it called forth the reaction towards orthodoxy of the personal idealists.

Bradley's immanentist theory of an absolute that was neither personal nor moral represented the extreme limit to which abstract metaphysical rationalization could go in finding some sort of place for religion in the universe. As a purely intellectual approach to religious dogma it emptied the traditional beliefs of their familiar, literal sense but provided nothing in their place for religious emotion to attach itself to. Ritschl and his followers, while accepting the negative consequences for theology of this line of thought, shifted the focus of religious interest from the general character of the universe to the historical personality of Christ. Agreeing that dogmatic theology was only acceptable in the form of a somewhat boneless speculative philosophy, they were not prepared to regard that philosophy as the purified essence of Christian faith. What really mattered was the ethical aspect of Christ's life, the moral example provided by his deeds and words. Christ was seen as an enlightened ethical teacher, expressing for all men and all times the most elevated principles of nineteenth-century liberal morality. Faith was the outcome not of metaphysical argument but of the subjective impression produced by the contemplation of his life and sayings. Miracles were discounted. In Harnack's case this highly personal interpretation of Christianity had destructive implications for the idea of the church as the authoritative interpreter and developer of the faith as well as for the dogmatic elements of the faith itself.

At this point liberal protestantism came into open conflict with the crucial emphasis of Tractarianism. The Oxford Movement had resisted the claims of the individual, whether as a rational interpreter of scripture or as an emotional responder to religious experience, and had insisted on the authority of the church as an historically developing institution. From this it followed that the essential feature of Christian life was participation in the sacraments administered by that church rather than in good works or the contemplation of religious truth or private religious emotion. There was less at issue between the Tractarian tradition and the Catholic modernism of Loisy and Tyrrell than there was between it and Harnack's liberal protestantism with its exclusively ethical and individualistic prepossession. Loisy was not concerned with Christ's

actual words and acts but saw his chief service to the world as lying
in the foundation of the developing church. Christ's work only came
to fruition after his death. In this doctrine what was only a prominent feature of Tractarianism became the central core of the faith.
The Catholic modernists had no use for the kindly, enlightened
Christ of the liberal protestants. They saw him much as Schweitzer
was later to do in his *Quest of the Historical Jesus,* that is as very
much a man of his time, convinced of the imminence of the second
coming and the end of the world.

Gore: Kenosis and Miracles

The two leading personalities in English theology in the first
decade of the century were Charles Gore, bishop of Oxford, and
Hastings Rashdall, dean of Carlisle. Gore was an Anglo-Catholic,
considerably influenced by the teaching of Green who had been his
tutor at Oxford and particularly concerned with the social implications of Christianity. With his friend Scott Holland he was prominent in the Christian Social Union and an active critic of the
economic institutions of contemporary society. Their form of
Christian socialism was as much the outcome of the radical rejection
of *laissez-faire* in Green's political philosophy as it was of the
Tractarian conception of the church as the authoritative moral
arbiter of society. At the beginning of his career Gore combined his
Anglo-Catholic view of the religious significance of the church and
his moral repugnance for the contemporary economic order with a
fair measure of theological liberalism. In the most disturbing contribution to *Lux Mundi,* a collection of essays published in 1887, he
argued that the biblical critics' view of the Old Testament must be
accepted. Though in some sense true as a whole it could not reasonably be taken as literally inspired throughout. It was the story of
the education of a race, imperfect in being made up of writings of
very different kinds and of very different degrees of reliability. Only
the New Testament could be regarded as authoritative for the
Christian believer and even it was not immune from critical reinter-
pretation. Gore's most extreme step was his conception of kenosis,
the view that God, in taking on humanity in the Incarnation,
divested himself of divine omniscience and retained only the
knowledge appropriate to a man living at his time. It followed that
his words, and in particular his references to the fulfilment of the

Old Testament prophecies, must be understood as the words of an actual human being living in the first century A.D. and not as the unalterably authoritative words of God.

By the turn of the century, however, Gore, originally execrated by orthodox theologians, had come to be the leader of resistance to the encroachments of a liberalism much more adventurous than his own. His long conflict with Rashdall began in the 1890's with a dispute about the ethics of religious conformity, set off by an essay of Sidgwick's on the subject. Rashdall rejected as unduly stringent the conditions for honest subscription to the credal formulae of the church laid down by the unbelieving Sidgwick and supported from the other side by the devout Gore. He wanted to treat the creeds in the same way as the Thirty-nine Articles, in other words as formulae to which one could honestly and candidly subscribe while making fairly substantial reinterpretations of their literal sense. To Rashdall three beliefs alone were essential to genuine Christian faith: the existence of God, the immortality of the soul, and Christ's being the son of God. Neither miracles nor the virgin birth need be accepted literally. Gore was prepared to go as far as the kenosis and no further. Rashdall could not see why one who was willing to go that far was not willing to take further liberties of interpretation. Thus in 1903 when a clergyman called Beeby was deprived of his licence by Gore for expressing his disbelief in miracles and the virgin birth Rashdall went pugnaciously into battle for him against his bishop. In 1911 a young Oxford theologian, J. M. Thompson, was deprived of his licence for publishing a book[1] denying the veracity of the Gospel accounts of miracles, and soon afterwards the veteran conservative theologian William Sanday admitted that he could not accept the occurrence of miracles if these were held to be *contra naturam*, in conflict with the general laws of nature.

Yet this tendency against which Gore strove was one that if not exactly initiated by *Lux Mundi* was entirely continuous with the theory of miracles advanced in that book. The *Lux Mundi* essayists had cheerfully accepted the doctrine of biological evolution and abandoned the special creation view with its idea of a singular divine intrusion, and had seen in the mechanism of evolution God's way of working out his purposes in the world. Furthermore they had denied miracles any value as evidence for Christ's claims to divinity though

---

[1] *Miracles in the New Testament.*

they had not doubted their genuineness. At best, in their view, miracles were coherent with Christ's being the son of God. Hegelian philosophers of religion attempted to dissolve the problem by maintaining that the truly miraculous thing was the existence of the world as a whole and that particular events were only miraculous as elements in that whole. But to say that everything was miraculous seemed merely an evasive way of saying that nothing was. Rashdall's own position was quite explicit. In the first place revelation was 'quite independent of what are commonly called miracles'. As far as acceptance of the truth of Christian faith was concerned they were neither here nor there. Secondly, while holding that suspensions of natural law were not *a priori* incredible, Rashdall thought it would be 'practically impossible to get sufficient evidence for the occurrence of such an event in the distant past'.

Rashdall and Modernism

The modernist movement in the Church of England, of which Rashdall was the most distinguished and active member, stood closer to the liberal protestantism of Ritschl and Harnack than to the catholic modernism of Loisy and Tyrrell, though it owed something to both. 'The true foundation', Rashdall said, 'not merely for belief in the teaching of Christ, but also for the Christian's reverence for his Person, must, as it seems to me, be found in the appeal which his words and his character still make to the Conscience and Reason of mankind.' It was only in Rashdall's emphasis on the appeal of Christ to man's reason that this position differed from that of Harnack. He could not admit that a judgement of value about the character of the historical Christ was a sufficient basis for the whole structure of the Christian faith and he deplored the liberal protestants' disregard of philosophy. His own philosophy of religion was, as he realized, very close to Berkeley's. He saw theism, and also Christianity, its highest particular exemplification, as best supported by a version of idealism in which spirits were ultimately distinct from one another, even if not as strictly presupposing such a theory. Matter is only intelligible if understood as existing for mind. Its content is conceivable only as it is given in feelings, and its relations, in particular its spatial structure, presuppose a relating intellect. But the natural world does not exist only for me, so there must be another universal mind for which nature in its systematic wholeness

exists. Nature is not only an object of thought for this mind, it is also
an object of will. Genuine causality, as opposed to mere correlation,
can only be conceived by us as a kind of volition; so, since every
event must have a cause, there must be a unitary will behind nature.
To these idealistic and causal arguments for theism Rashdall added
an argument from man's moral consciousness. We recognize the
objective validity of our moral judgements and this logically implies
a divine mind to affirm the objective moral law. There could be no
such law in a purely material universe. The world, then, is the
thought or experience of the divine mind; it is also the effect of the
divine will. Finite minds are products but not parts of the divine
mind. 'Reality is the system or society of minds and their experience.' Rashdall was essentially an intellectualist. He denied the
existence of any intuitive faculty for religious knowledge. Such
knowledge must come from rational inference. There is no opposition
between reason and revelation. Religious experience is of no cog-
nitive value and has a merely psychological interest until it has
been submitted to rational criticism. The claims of specifically
Christian theism do not rest on miracles but on the appeal of Christ,
as embodying the highest ethical idea in its fullest perfection, to the
individual conscience. But this revelation is not a unique, closed
historical event; revelation is continuous and the function of the
church as a developing institution is to give it the appropriate
doctrinal expression for its time.

With Rashdall modernism reached its lucid and reasonable
consummation. He provided an optimistic, conciliatory, and easily
acceptable version of Christian doctrine from which its more
paradoxical elements were eliminated. The only admissible miracles
are those, such as Christ's healings, which exemplify little known or
unknown laws of the effect of mind. The incarnation was seen rather
as a case of man's approaching as near as humanly possible to being
God, rather than of God's literally taking on the body of a man.
Christ, Rashdall insisted, had the soul as well as the body of a man.
The atonement he interpreted in the manner of Abelard, not as a
sacrifice or a vicarious assumption of guilt, but as a moral example
of humility before God. In this theology the attempt to reconcile
Christian doctrine with the general current of secular thought,
initiated by the *Lux Mundi* essayists, with their endorsement of
evolutionary theory, of historical criticism of scripture, and of the

idea of Christ's human self-limitation, is fully carried out. The modernists' aim was to deprive Christian doctrine of any tincture of intellectual offensiveness. How much, Ronald Knox saw them as asking, will Jones swallow? More politely put, they sought to make Christianity attractive to the modern cultivated man. Knox's conservative protest was made in an entertaining book, *Some Loose Stones* (1913), which set out in detail the criticism satirically expressed in his imitation of Dryden, 'Absolute and Abitofhell'. Its immediate object was a collective volume, *Foundations*,[1] put out by a group of Oxford theologians in 1912. In this volume the modernist technique of mollification was applied to the detail of Christian dogma. One contributor saw the Bible not as an historical record so much as a classic of religious experience, important for its spiritual power as the standard expression of the religious life. Another presented a liberal doctrine of authority in which neither the church nor the individual witness of the spirit was seen as intrinsically authoritative but only the spiritual experience of the saints as a whole, the character of their lives testifying to its validity. H. H. Moberly attempted to lead modernism towards a closer alliance with absolute idealism, arguing that the personal idealists' reaction was the result of an insufficiently penetrating and coherent conception of personality. B. H. Streeter agreed with other essayists in accepting the eschatological Christ of Schweitzer (who had been translated into English in 1910[2]) rather than the sentimental, liberal Christ of Harnack. To say that God was in Christ was to say that in order to see God one must look at the life and character of Christ in which it was most fully revealed. His boldest assertion was that the Resurrection and Christ's appearances to the apostles thereafter must be understood in a special sense, not quite as 'objective visions', that is, as mental states brought about by God's will, but as something very similar, namely awareness of the glorified and incorruptible body of the risen Christ and not of his actual physical body.

Outside the Church of England modernism went even further than Rashdall and the essayists of *Foundations*. The most extreme

---

[1] *Foundations, a Statement of Christian Belief in terms of Modern Thought, by Seven Oxford Men.*

[2] Albert Schweitzer, *The Quest of the Historical Jesus*, translated by W. Montgomery, preface by F. C. Burkitt.

version perhaps appears in the *New Theology* (1907) of R. J. Campbell, a nonconformist minister, where an exclusively immanentist
view of God is put forward and the unreality of evil proclaimed.
('Sin', Campbell wrote, 'is a blundering quest for God.') Rashdall
was always clearly opposed to any sort of pantheism, indeed his
distinctly metaphorical conception of the divinity of Christ was
largely the result of his determination to ensure the transcendence
of a personal God. He also opposed it on moral grounds, rejecting
the Panglossian implication of the unreality of evil which Campbell blithely accepted. In this extreme form modernism was most
exposed to the emotional revulsion brought about by the catastrophe of 1914. In the first essay of *Foundations* Christianity had
been recommended as a specific for post-Victorian 'cosmic weari-
ness'. A few years later the spiritual sickness of the world was very
different, calling forth the Kierkegaardian theology of crisis of Karl
Barth and others whose domination of modern religious thought
gives Edwardian modernism such a remote appearance today.

Religious Experience and Mysticism

In one respect Rashdall was unrepresentative of his time: in his
failure to ascribe importance to, and in what was perhaps his
distaste for, religious and particularly mystical experience. Two
very different influences worked to bring this into the centre of
interest: the generous, muddled, and shapeless reflections of William
James in his Gifford lectures of 1901–2, *The Varieties of Religious
Experience*, and the scholarly studies in the mystical philosophy of
Plotinus of that most un-Edwardian figure W. R. Inge. James had
always been well-disposed towards religious belief; it could be said
that his pragmatic theory of truth was a device for giving people
the right to believe what they liked in the non-empirical realm. In
general his pragmatism regarded the emotional satisfaction of a
belief as evidential. Religion was vindicated to the extent that it
worked in making for more effectiveness in the business of living.
He had a lifelong interest in psychical research and was scornful
of those narrowly and conventionally scientific persons who refused
to pay any attention to anything at all out of the ordinary in
mental life. His work in and around psychical research led him to
F. W. H. Myers and it is Myers's theory of the subliminal self which
James relies upon to extract some general conclusion from the great

mass of evidence accumulated in his *Varieties*. After unrolling his great panorama of particular recorded religious experiences James concludes that religion is no anachronistic survival of primitive thought, since the concrete experiences which are its true foundation continue unabated. All religious experience involves a sense of uneasiness, of 'something wrong about us as we naturally stand', and a compensating solution, 'a sense that we are saved from the wrongness by making proper connection with the higher powers'. Some shape is given to this nebulous conception by James's theory that 'whatever it may be on its *farther* side, the "more" with which in religious experience we feel ourselves connected is on its *hither* side the subconscious continuation of our conscious life'. About the 'farther side' James is not very explicit, though he is prepared to call it God, and 'God is real since he produces real effects', by which James means that our highest ideals have some influence on us and the observable world. For all his pragmatism James was cautious in stating his own beliefs and the only deity that he was prepared to endorse was a thin, amorphous, and only mildly consoling affair.

More orthodox students of mystical experience were prepared to go a good deal further. Inge believed that by returning to the fountainhead of Hellenistic philosophy from which early Christian doctrine had taken so much of its form the conflicts of liberals and conservatives could be avoided. Inge resembled the modernists in his open-mindedness about science and in his disregard for miracles. But he could allow science a free hand in its own domain just because he was convinced by the evidence of mystics that there was a transcendental domain to which science did not apply. He was thus no sort of immanentist and his general emotional bias was as far removed as it could be from the earnest meliorism of the modernists. Inge was an extreme conservative in politics, a disbeliever in secular progress, and an opponent of democracy. Furthermore he had no use for the ethical emphasis of Harnack and his English followers. Inge accepted a more or less Augustinian dualism. On the one hand was heaven, the timeless, mystically accessible realm of eternal values, and on the other earth, explicable by science and peopled by radically sinful men needing firm authority. The entire modernist project of making theology palatable to men influenced by secular thought was quite unnecessary; theology and science were autonomous disciplines and concerned with realms that did not overlap. Above all Inge differed from the modernists in his resolute theocentrism; the world, in his view, was in no sense necessary to God but simply an emanation from him, a free overflow of his perfection.

An interest in religious experience is obviously closely connected with psychical research. In the early years after its foundation in 1882 the Society for Psychical Research was principally concerned with the scrupulous investigation of claims about human survival of death. The chief theoretical outcome of this theologically relevant inquiry was F. W. H. Myers's substantial treatise *Human Personality and its Survival of Bodily Death,* published posthumously in 1903. Myers's main theoretical construction is the idea of the subliminal self, conceived as a vast submerged structure of mental activity underlying and in various ways connected with the ordinary conscious self. Myers puts forward the subliminal self to account for three main kinds of mental phenomenon and to relate them to one another. First are unconscious mental events or situations, exemplified at one extreme by sensations too weak to catch or be subjected to attention, at the other by the more or less systematic mental structures implied by the fact of hypnotism or, even more strikingly, by instances of divided personality. Secondly, the subliminal self is held to contain the causes of ordinary conscious occurrences which have no straightforward physical or psychological explanation, such as hallucinations or the original intuitions of men of genius. Finally and crucially there are supernormal phenomena, in particular of telepathy and multiple apparition. Myers's book is more remarkable for its wealth of illustrative examples and for its colourful and persuasive rhetoric than for solid argument. It remains important as the first full-dress attempt to draw systematic theoretical conclusions from the carefully authenticated concrete findings of the Society for Psychical Research. Myers did not convincingly justify the common allocation of his three classes of puzzling phenomena to the subliminal self. Though it was appropriate enough as a general name for the first class of straightforwardly subconscious occurrences it seemed to add little to our understanding of the other two classes. To many it appeared to be no more than a convenient but undiscriminating repository for all the psychologically perplexing elements of mental life.

SOCIAL THOUGHT

It is a measure of the authority and pervasiveness of the idealism of Green and Bradley that the two really substantial new departures in the social thought of the Edwardian period were as much reactions to it as were the new personal idealist and realist tendencies in philosophy and the development of an ethical modernism in religion. The first of these new departures was the resolute adoption of a scientifically neutral attitude to the moral and political aspects of society. The intellectualism that was explicitly repudiated by McDougall and Graham Wallas and rather less deliberately undermined by the researches of Westermarck was a comprehensive affair: it included the whole method of social thought of the Enlightenment, and in particular Bentham's psychological hedonism, as well as idealist social theory. But the ultimate sympathies of anti-intellectualists were more with the utilitarians than with the idealists. They believed, with the utilitarians, in an empirical science of society even if they rejected as an over-simplification the utilitarian view of human nature and the fundamental springs of human action. The second new departure was a widespread hostility to the absolute claims of the state and a corresponding emphasis on the reality and desirability of other, more or less non-political, forms of human association. These pluralistic ideas found a concrete expression in guild socialism, a reaction of somewhat syndicalist inspiration to the state-socialist proposals of the Fabians, and in the distributivism of Hilaire Belloc. Although the Fabians had repudiated the eschatological features of Marxian socialism they shared Marx's view that it was in the economic life of society that its determining factors and the ultimate source of its ills were to be found. The guild socalists re-established the aesthetic tradition of English socialism initiated by Ruskin and Morris, objecting to the ugliness and spiritual sterility of capitalism rather than to its wastefulness and economic injustice. Here, in direct contrast to the social scientists, the method of idealism was not disowned—it was, rather, more perseveringly applied—but the basic tenet of idealist social theory was repudiated.

The Science of Society

The most comprehensive, if in the end least fertile and valuable, of Edwardian contributions to the natural science of society was the doctrine advanced by W. McDougall in his widely read *Intro-duction to Social Psychology* (1908). He was in no doubt as to the importance of his subject, holding that social psychology was the fundamental and unifying discipline for the whole of social science. Like Schiller, James, and Bergson he was a declared enemy of intellectualism, whether with Bentham it represented men as engaged in the enlightened pursuit of self-interest, or with the idealists as preoccupied with the rational search for some more elevated form of self-realization. The real prime movers of human action, in his view, were constitutionally innate instincts, purposive tendencies to perceive, attend to, respond emotionally to, and act upon various objects. Where Bentham had placed man under two sovereign masters, pleasure and pain, McDougall saw him as the subject of a large and heterogeneous assembly of rulers: his ten primary instincts. Much of his work was given over to the analysis of the developed forms of human feeling and action in terms of his theory's initial outfit of instincts. This analysis was pretty much a matter of *a priori* classification, reminiscent in its general lines of the mental chemistry of associationists like James Mill, and even closer to the only faintly empirical theories of the passions advanced by Descartes and Hume.

McDougall was concerned to rebut the simplifications of the hedonist tradition in psychology. But his insistence on the purposive nature of human activity, on its plastic responsiveness to experience, and on its irreducibility to mechanical categories of explanation, was not undertaken in the interests of the usual anti-hedonist con-ception of man as a twofold being, driven by natural inclinations on the one hand and by a rational faculty of conscience on the other. Against this Kantian type of view he affirmed that moral dis-positions, the psychological precondition of man's social existence, were not innate but must be explained in terms of the primary instincts. His derivation of moral capacity was a cumbrous and involved business, occupying a good deal of the book. Human moral conduct presents the misleading appearance of uncaused activity. It certainly involves the voluntary control of primary instinct by the idea or ideal of the self and by the self-regarding sentiment, but this controlling agency is itself a late and complicated causal develop-ment. At first social control of behaviour operates through the agent's anticipation of reward and punishment, then by way of these sanctions' symbolic equivalents—praise and blame. This movement is brought about by men's recognition of the power of society as a whole and by the feelings of humility that this induces. Full moral agency is attained with the formation of a controlling ideal of the self when the sanction is internalized.

A blunter and less complicated account of morality in naturalistic terms is to be found in the more theoretical parts of Westermarck's enormous encyclopedia of moral anthropology, *The Origin and Development of Moral Ideas* (1906–8). Westermarck took the only sensible task of ethical science to be a description of the empirical facts of human moral consciousness. Its upshot was not the rational justification of men's ordinary moral beliefs, and even less the proposal of new ones: it was rather the provision of a deterministic explanation of actual moral belief in all its variety. That there was a fair measure of agreement between the codes of different societies, which was the only sort of objectivity Westermarck was prepared to recognize, could be attributed to the comparative uniformity of human nature and circumstances. Moral judgements arise from moral emotions and moral emotion is a species of retributive emotion, kindly when approving, hostile when disapproving. The species is differentiated by the disinterestedness and apparent impartiality of the emotions falling within it. The cause of disin-terestedness Westermarck saw, following Hume, in natural sym-pathy, the tendency to it being enforced and rendered habitual by custom and society. In copious detail he reviewed the moral attitudes of varying societies towards the welfare of others, the welfare of the agent, sexual conduct, animals, the dead, and super-natural beings. The substantial differences of moral opinion that prevail among men he attributed to some extent to the different conditions in which they live, but more especially to the different beliefs held by men about the consequences of action, and above all to their different beliefs about the desires and interests of super-natural beings. His self-consciously ponderous insistence on scientific neutrality obscured from him the existence of a problem about the comparative rationality of conflicting moral beliefs, though a mildly humanitarian bias emerged in the closing pages of his book.

A more articulate awareness of the distinction between the causal explanation of human beliefs and their subjection to rational criticism is to be found in the very much subtler application of psychological realism in Graham Wallas's *Human Nature in Politics* (1908). Wallas starts from the contrast between the general acceptance of representative democracy as the ideal form for political institutions and its failures in practice, with the consequent apprehensions about its further extension to which these failures give rise. He saw in this disappointment a result of the reluctance of students of politics to pay sufficient attention to actual human nature. Intellectualists, they fail to take account of the part played by non-rational impulses and instincts in the formation of political loyalties and purposes. The political realm offers particular invitations to irrationality because of the special nature of the entities which populate it and which form the topics of political discourse. Political entities—nations, classes, and parties—are abstract and symbolic in character, conceptual devices whose manageable simplicity for thought is bought at the price of very limited correspondence to the complex areas of fact to which they refer. Because of this pervasive oversimplification politics is preeminently a field for non-rational inference. The art of the professional politician, as a result, is not to produce rational convictions in the voting populace but rather to operate on its non-rational political impulses, to exploit and manipulate his audience in precisely the same fashion as the commercial advertiser. But Wallas, one of the original Fabian essayists and an active social reformer, did not stop here. His interest in drawing attention to the non-rational nature of ordinary political thought and behaviour was to make democratic institutions more effective, and he thought there was no more dangerous obstacle to this aim than the belief that, as they stood, they gave expression to the real and rationally arrived at wishes of the general public. In particular he was critical of the democratic metaphysics which, following Rousseau, supposed a formed popular will to underlie the workings of electoral institutions. The electoral process should be conceived as a mechanism for creating rather than simply finding public opinion. Wallas was also critical of the accepted Platonic conception of the civil service, remote as it was from democratic orthodoxy, and explored the possibility of finding some safer basis for political solidarity than the sense of common nationality.

The Attack on the State

European political philosophy, considered as an inquiry into the proper limits to the action of the state, has, through the centuries, oscillated from one extreme to the other. In the high middle ages the orthodox theory was that the state's authority was wholly derived from and thus circumscribed by the church; its demands were held to have no moral claim over the individual without the church's ratification. At the close of the middle ages such thinkers as Ockham and Marsilio of Padua developed a kind of political equivalent of Averroism in which all heavenly matters were remitted to the church while the state was held to be supreme on earth. The real import of this polite but fictitious dualism emerged in the absolutism of the renaissance with Machiavelli's purely secular politics, Bodin's theory of sovereignty and, at a simpler level, the doctrine of the divine right of kings. A new limit to the state was propounded by the natural law theorists of the seventeenth and eighteenth centuries. For them the moral consensus of mankind took the place of an institutionalized church as the moral controller and critic of the state. With the period of the French Revolution explicit absolutism returned, first in the democratically mystical form given to it by Rousseau and then in the authoritarian nationalism of Hegel. At the same time the natural law tradition was weakened from inside by the utilitarian critique of its supposedly self-evident first principles of social justice. At the end of the Victorian age, for all the tenacity of classic natural-law liberalism, active political thinking at all levels was dominated by the presumption of the omnicompetence of the state. In the first place idealist social theory asserted the moral supremacy of the state over its citizens, as the incarnation of their best selves, and, following T. H. Green, called for large-scale state intervention, in fields hitherto protected by doctrines of *laissez-faire* and freedom of contract, to secure society's moral improvement. Secondly, the Fabian socialists, the liveliest source of reforming opinions, brought together Marx's theory of the economic foundations of society, the utilitarian doctrine of legislation, and Green's belief in intervention to produce a theory of bureaucratic statism in which the demands of rational economic efficiency overrode all traditional rights and limitations on government. At a more popular level two independent movements of opinion combined to enhance unreserved admiration for the state. On the one hand the successful carrying out of liberal constitutional reform seemed, by rendering the state truly democratic, to remove all need for its limitation, and, on the other, patriotic enthusiasm, nourished by imperial expansion, weakened older and more particular loyalties than that of devotion to the national state.

The chief theoretical resistance to this combination of absolutist tendencies was the doctrine of pluralism, which held the state to be just one among many forms of communal organization. The only pre-eminence that the pluralists would allow to the state was as a final arbiter between the claims of other associations. It cannot rightly be regarded as their creator or authorizer. Families, churches, trade unions, and professional associations are as much independent social realities as the state. It is significant that the ultimate origin of this mode of thought was in the scholarly study of medieval institutions. In his great *Deutsche Genossenschaftsrecht* Otto von Gierke had argued that Teutonic, as against Roman, law had always, even if only instinctively, recognized the real personality of other forms of corporate life than the state. In 1900 F. W. Maitland, another student of medieval law, published a translation of some parts of Gierke with an important introduction. Pluralism was not, then, any sort of reversion to natural-law doctrine; it went back rather to the medieval view that the factor limiting the operations of the state is institutional not moral, and not just the church, as in explicit medieval theorizing, but the whole complex tissue of corporate human life, whose real self-subsistent personality is implicitly recognized in legal practice. The direct object of pluralist criticism was, as J. N. Figgis put it in his *Churches in the Modern State* (1913), the theory that

all and every right is the creation of the one and indivisible sovereign. . . . No prescription, no conscience, no corporate life can be pleaded against its authority, which is without legal limitation. In every state there must be some power entirely above the law, because it can alter the law. To talk of rights against it is to talk nonsense.

Beside this attack on the pre-eminence and absolute authority of the state on the level of theory there were two movements parallel to it on the level of practice. The more substantial of these was the guild socialist movement, initiated by A. J. Penty's book

The Restoration of the Gild System (1906), which was the mild English counterpart of continental syndicalism. Penty's horizon was rather small: his idea was to remove the degrading unpleasantness of industrial work and the related shoddiness of its products by organizing producers into small self-governing organizations of craftsmen. He and other guild socialists drew their inspiration from the middle ages, as the pluralists had. A more immediate influence was the visionary socialism of Ruskin and Morris which saw as the greatest evil of industrial capitalism not poverty and economic injustice so much as the moral and aesthetic impoverishment that it caused. The contribution of guild socialism was to provide a concrete programme for this form of discontent with the quality of capitalist culture. For others soon appeared to generalize Penty's relatively small-scale proposals. At first the chief source for guild socialist ideas was the *New Age*, a weekly review edited by that somewhat mysterious figure A. R. Orage. Arriving in London in 1905 from an obscure career as a schoolmaster in Leeds, Orage had already taken up Nietzsche's philosophy, the first of the protracted series of intellectual fashions he was to follow. His form of Nietzscheanism held that the creative self-assertion of the pre-eminent individual could only be made effective by a cultural revolution against plutocracy. So sharp an opposition to the liberal idea of inevitable progress towards rational enlightenment necessarily ruled out any endorsement of Fabianism. Orage believed that guild socialist ideas should be propagated by a small group of leaders, but with the accession of the young G. D. H. Cole to the group guild socialism was soon reconstituted on the lines of a mass movement.

Two main features of contemporary society were attacked by guild socialists: its economic structure and its bureaucratically centralized political institutions. As a recipient of wages the worker is degraded; his labour, his most valuable possession, is treated as a mere commodity; he has no security of employment and no control over the productive uses to which his labour is put. He is a victim of 'wagery', deprived of freedom, security, and democratic rights. What is needed is a form of economic organization which, by bringing democracy into industry, will restore meaning and dignity to his productive work. The capitalist state is only superficially democratic. Its mechanically territorial system of election is incapable of representing men's real interests; for that a functional or occupational system is required. Furthermore the state is ineffective, since it leaves the decisions about what most matters to men to a handful of profit-minded owners and managers. The economy should be reorganized in the form of producers' guilds, holding the capital and equipment of their industries on trust for the community as a whole and arriving at economic decisions about production and selling by methods of democratic self-government. In view of the ineffectiveness of straightforward political action this change should be brought about by way of the trade unions, the existing nucleus of the future guilds. The state would continue, its place in the scheme being to represent the interests of men as consumers, but guild socialists incorporated in their own doctrine the pluralist rejection of the unique sovereignty of the state.

A concern with the spiritual impoverishment of the industrial proletariat also inspired the distributivism of Belloc and Chesterton. Like the guild socialists they sought for institutional devices to protect the labouring man from the plutocratic controllers of the economy and from the centralized state. The institution they favoured was peasant proprietorship or, more generally, a wide distribution of land and capital in order to satisfy the universal human desire for property and, even more important, the indispensable human need for it as a condition of security and self-respect. Belloc rejected socialism. Defining it as the ownership by the government of all the means of production, he believed that not even the maintenance of democratic political institutions under such an arrangement would be able to preserve personal freedom.

Liberals, Fabians, Sexual Reformers

Anti-intellectualism in sociology has continued to prosper, indeed it has become a movement of international scope. Reinforced by such influential allies as Freud and Pareto it has come to be the prevailing atmosphere of all reasonably informed consideration of social problems, though often with pessimistically authoritarian implications that would have been most uncongenial to its founders. The defence of extra-political associations as protectors of freedom, on the other hand, has largely disappeared as a coherent movement of thought, presumably because of the political upheavals that have brought political systems into existence beside which the confident, bureaucratically-centralized nation-states of the nineteenth century have a utopianly liberal appearance. Both of these currents of social thought were original contributions of the Edwardian period and as such are more characteristic of it than the vigorously persisting survivals of older movements. At the time, however, these older movements secured the greater measure of attention.

Victorian liberalism had been given its classical form by Mill's three great treatises: *Liberty, Representative Government,* and *The Subjection of Women.* The doctrines expressed in them had become almost second nature to the majority of reflective people by the end of the century, and the task for succeeding liberals was simply to implement them in practice. The distinguished line of Victorian critics of democracy came to an end with W. E. H. Lecky, who published his defence of hereditary aristocracy as a condition of personal freedom, *Democracy and Liberty,* in 1896. The reactionaries of the Edwardian age were lonely figures with little intellectual influence, even if welcomed by the holders of established interests. W. H. Mallock is a representative example. In a series of books he argued for the fostering of the natural aristocracy of talent, believing the rewards provided by a capitalist economy to be a good indication of the whereabouts of ability. Economic progress is due to the ideas and the energy of the 'inventive classes' and hardly at all to labour, whose productivity remains much what it has always been. A small minority of the population has conceived and realized the ingenious new forms of productive capital. In his *Critical Examination of Socialism* Mallock applied his argument to the ideas of Marx which, he held, were only true of the most primitive sort of society. Marx simply refuses to admit the pre-eminent contribution of ability to social welfare: Fabians admit it but propose to set up a system which, while leaving the able in control, deprives them of any reason for exerting their ability. Moral arguments for equality reveal a sentimental incapacity to understand the facts of economic life. Nor can equality of opportunity be uncritically endorsed: the provision of opportunities is expensive and they should not be wasted on the unpromising.

Compared to the lively and malicious satirist of the *New Republic* the later Mallock was a ponderous old fogey. The most important effect of his examination of socialism, perhaps, was the vigorous pamphlet, *Socialism and Superior Brains,* that it evoked from

Bernard Shaw in 1910. Shaw described Mallock's view that the inventive should reap the whole benefit of their abilities as 'abandoned blackguardism' and pointed out that in the current scheme of things it is not the inventors who get the profit of their inventions. How, he asked, could railway shareholders claim George Stephenson's ability as their own? The plain fact is that the proprietary class which reaps the rewards and the productive class which provides the services are quite distinct. An equally uncompromising version of conservatism, but more traditional than Mallock's gospel for the suburban rentier, was advanced by Lord Hugh Cecil in his *Conservatism* in 1912. He bluntly expressed the convictions of an important if largely inarticulate class of conventionally minded people.

Traditional liberal ideas were pleasantly put forward, at the level of belles-lettres, by that somewhat Silver Age figure Goldsworthy Lowes Dickinson. In *Letters of John Chinaman* (1901) he borrowed a literary device from the eighteenth century to depreciate contemporary civilization. He contrasted the realities of modern European life—the barbaric pursuit of economic interests and the fetishism of wealth—with the unconvincing pretensions of conventional moral and religious piety. European religion is an otherworldly superstition, ideally suited, by its utter impracticability, to afford some slight decorative concealment to what its professed adherents take to be the real business of life. Continuing this side of the attack in his *Religion, A Criticism and a Forecast* (1905) Lowes Dickinson argued that men should try to preserve the ethical values of religion without its exploded metaphysics. They should confine it to the practice of looking at the empirically given nature of things from the point of view of ideals. Lowes Dickinson's liberal attitude towards moral and social institutions derived ultimately from reverence for a sweetened, 'ethical' Plato who had as much historical warrant and as much serious appeal to the emotions as Harnack's modernized Christ.

A somewhat similar hostility to economic criteria of value, but in this case inspired by Ruskin rather than Plato, underlay the much solider assault of J. A. Hobson on the contemporary economic order. The pure theory of a competitive economic system had been the most impressive intellectual product of early utilitarian liberalism. Hobson, although a dedicated liberal, traced the morally repugnant consequences of *laissez-faire* capitalism, its inequality and its radical insecurity, to a deep theoretical defect in the system. Classical economics justifies a competitive economy as the best way of utilizing resources. Hobson rejected its reliance on effective demand as a measure of social value, for effective demand is determined as much by the advantage of possessing economic pull as by real economic services rendered. In a way that anticipated Keynes, he argued that a competitive economy is inherently unstable: not all of the surpluses acquired by producers over and above their costs are productively used for investment. The unproductive surplus leads to under-consumption and thus to economic depression. The state should tax this mass of attempted and deleterious saving to finance projects for the common good. This attack on orthodox economics, not unlike Veblen's but intellectually superior to it, was most fully developed in Hobson's *Industrial System* (1909). In his *Imperialism* (1902) he had carried the argument further, interpreting the struggle of European nations for African colonies as a search for outlets for the products of the glutted home market, a doctrine that was to catch the attention of Lenin.

An application of economic theory to general problems of social policy that has stood the test of time a good deal less successfully than Hobson's was Norman Angell's attempt to demonstrate in *The Great Illusion* (1910) the economic absurdity of war. Angell urged that there is no connexion between military power and prosperity; the Norwegian standard of life is higher than the Russian. It is economically impossible to expropriate the possessions of a conquered enemy: what could be removed would only dislocate the victor's own economy; the skill of the conquered population and the natural resources of the land they occupied, the really important things, cannot be removed at all. Finally the international system of credit is so closely interlocked that everyone must suffer from its dislocation, victors and vanquished alike.

The most interesting liberal thinkers of the period wrote very much as individuals. To the left of them the liveliest and much the most widely read political theorists were the Fabians, who were members of a thoroughly organized movement. Yet the Fabians were represented in the public mind by Shaw and Wells, who were far too individual for their ideas to be neatly contained within the doctrinal boundaries of an organized group. Fabianism had begun in

the eighties, emerging from the somewhat quaintly idealistic Fellowship of the New Life founded by Thomas Davidson. The fellowship's
ideals of open-air fraternity were soon replaced by a self-
consciously hard-headed emphasis on exact knowledge and coldly
rational calculation. Agreeing with Marx about the natural tendency of the times towards economic concentration, the Fabians
believed that revolution was not necessary to bring about the
transfer to the community as a whole of those elements of capital
that could usefully be managed by it. Their goal was a democratic
political system which, having found landlords and capitalists
superfluous, itself controlled and planned the economy. The theoretical foundation of their position was a highly generalized form of
Ricardo's theory of rent. Regarding the rent of ability as well as
the rent of land as a reward arising from the accidental advantage
of ownership and not from actual services rendered, they contended
that all rent belonged to the community as a whole and thus should
be appropriated by the state. To prepare for this consummation
what is needed is, first, a careful accumulation of the relevant facts
and then their widespread dissemination in order to prepare the way
for the democratically constitutional changes required. In particular the Fabians were in favour of a gradual movement towards
the socialization of rent by the development of economic activities
at the municipal level. Their socialism was resolutely practical:
disdainful of all forms of ethical romanticism, it stressed the greater
efficiency to be expected from publicly owned economic under-
takings. This emphasis expressed their belief in rationally and
skilfully conducted administration, based on extensive factual
research. In the Webbs this belief led to the production of an
imposing mass of empirical studies and the consequent proposal of
detailed reforms, most notably their minority report on the poor
law which proposed a comprehensive scheme of social security to
be financed out of general taxation. But in Shaw and Wells the
administrative doctrine took on a more grandiose form: both were
concerned with the problems of leadership, of establishing a Platonic class of high administrators. This search was to lead Shaw into
the specification of a superior type of human being and Wells into
the imaginative construction of ideal communities authoritatively
ruled by scientists and exploiting to the full all possibilities of
technical progress. For all their differences—and Shaw's intellectual

asceticism was diametrically opposed to Wells's indulgent fondness for the most ordinary tastes of ordinary men—both came to believe in rule by experts, though where Shaw's aristocracy was conceived in somewhat Nietzschean and mystical terms, Wells's Samurai were thought of as the scientifically informed and qualified minority of the population.

Shaw's position is most humorously expressed in *Man and Superman* (1903), whose title reveals his fundamental preoccupation. In the prefatory 'Letter to A. B. Walkley' Shaw writes that the point of his modern version of the Don Juan theme is to show how women, using the middle-class conscience for their own biological purposes, attempt to tame men, to bring down their Promethean energies to the humdrum task of providing for the family. The man of genius, the truly positive man, because he is driven by an impersonal concern for society as a whole as strong as the maternal instinct of women, is inevitably unscrupulous to them. Where women triumph the positive man is curbed, breeding for excellence is ignored, and the outcome is democracy, the rule of a promiscuously-led multitude. Shaw's theme is even more explicit in the 'Revolutionist's Handbook' attached to the play. Here John Tanner is made to say that the important revolution must take place in the species, not in forms of social organization; its issue must be the superman. If man is to make himself God he must change his breeding habits and come to think of his position as husband as being that of a public functionary. Proletarian democracy can only lead to rule by demagogues. Reform and progress are illusory if man remains as he is, and he must be changed by selective breeding. In these gleeful exaggerations, where Shaw half-seriously carries his line of argument to the limit, he in effect confronts the paradox of a fully consistent Fabianism. The rational and efficient ordering of society requires good administration, there can be no good administration without a pre-eminently qualified class of administrators and, since these administrators are not to be found amongst men as they are, a new type of man must be made. A proposal for improving the social arrangements of men as they are turns into a scheme for creating a kind of man for whom no social problems would arise.

Wells's conception of the ideal social order paid little attention to the character of the ruling class on which Shaw had concentrated, and emphasized the concrete results of rational government, whose positive aspects Shaw had almost completely ignored. In 1902 in *Anticipations* Wells offered a prophetic sketch of probable effects of mechanical and scientific progress on the conditions of human life. Improved means of transport and communication will alter the distribution of population, the city will give way to the urban region, the world-state become a practical possibility. The traditional class structure will be replaced by an inevitable waste-basket of urban poor, a large intermediate mass of mechanics and engineers and, at the top, a class of skilled experts. Family life will be rationalized and simplified, personal and sexual relations become informal and more various. Democracy will give way to rational rule by the expert. In *Mankind in the Making* (1903), which he was later to describe as 'woolly revivalism', Wells addressed himself to Shaw's problem of creating a new ruling class. But he rejected eugenic policies on the ground that we do not know what qualities to breed for. In *A Modern Utopia* (1905) the desired outcome is presented in a superficially narrative form: it is a society constructed on Baconian principles with every inducement to activity and creativeness, a determined disregard for habit and tradition, and a kindly ruthlessness towards human deficiency, for example by exiling drunkards to islands. Progress and political stability are reconciled by the rule of the Samurai, the dedicated and self-sacrificing intellectual nobility, who neither inherit nor are elected to their positions, but qualify for them. In a phrase of which he was fond Wells asserted that this could only come about through an 'open conspiracy', the co-operative endeavour of all those who wanted to clear the way to a rational future of the accumulated rubbish of the past. In *New Worlds for Old* (1908) Wells represented his plans for the deliberate and radical reshaping of society as socialism since they regarded collective effort as superior to individual dilettantism. Parenthood must not be left in its haphazard condition but be considered as a public service. The economic system is wasteful and unproductive, private property should comprise only intimate and personal things, all else should belong to the community. Society should seek to make use of the spirit of service which already contributes much more to general well-being than the spirit of gain.

The Fabian Society was not the only influential by-product of the Fellowship of the New Life. It was at a meeting of the fellowship that the two principal sexual reformers of the epoch, Havelock Ellis and Edward Carpenter, first met. Both, as might conventionally be expected, were extraordinary men. Ellis was shy, sensitive, and thoroughly incapable in the practical affairs of life. Yet his literary output was enormous in extent, even if it now appears rather hollow in substance, and seems to have been sufficient to support him in a style of life which, though frugal enough in detail, must have involved much expense on account of travel, frequent changes of residence, and his wife's debts. Carpenter was at the enthusiastic opposite extreme to Ellis's sibylline reclusion. A fervent disciple of Whitman, he put his egalitarian ideals into practice in his life after a brief period as a clergyman. Neither Ellis nor Carpenter now appears a very substantial figure. Ellis is only read for the attractively dated illustrative material in the six heroically laborious volumes of *Studies in the Psychology of Sex* published between 1897 and 1910 (he added a seventh in 1928), while Carpenter's gigantic free verse poem *Towards Democracy* (1883–1905) has sunk into a deserved oblivion. To the extent that the large changes of modern times in the more personal side of life, in the patterns of sexual, matrimonial, and parental relationships, are due to intellectual rather than economic causes, the influence of Freud has plainly been paramount. Yet Ellis, at any rate, certainly did a great deal to make the conventional forms and ideal possibilities of sexual conduct discussible. He was much more of a compiler than a theoretician and it is in the level, unexcited, quietly determined tone in which he recounts the explosive material he has collected that the explanation of his principal service to the human race is to be found. Not only did he establish a tolerable alternative to total concealment of facts about sexual behaviour: he also, by his undeviating insistence on the potential richness and spirituality of sexual satisfaction, helped to replace the prevailing attitude of horror and disgust by one of inquiring respect. His theoretical conclusions on detailed matters were generally vague and tentative, but in one case at least, his questionable view that homosexuality was as congenital as colour-blindness, it helped to diminish the dismal superstition that inversion is always a moral crime.

Ellis, for all his conscious determination to be scientific about sexuality, was fundamentally a moral advocate. With Carpenter the advocacy was explicit. Himself a homosexual, he argued in such works as *The Intermediate Sex* and *Love's Coming of Age* for a more liberal attitude towards sexual deviants and for greater sexual freedom and openness generally. The earlier book makes many bold claims for what Carpenter called 'urnings': they are actively idealistic, more sentimental than sensual, a progressive force in moderating the clash between extremes of sex differentiation, healthy, well-behaved, fond of the opposite sex, not the products of 'nervous degeneration', publicly useful in their freedom from family ties and only the source of social evils in so far as they are suppressed. The law, he concluded, should not try to regulate the voluntary private conduct of adults. In *Love's Coming of Age* he called for people to think openly about what was in their minds a great deal anyway. Without denying the value of sexual restraint and even, as an exercise, of asceticism, he urged the need for sexual instruction for children in order to heal the evil dissociation of sexuality from love. The emotionally immature Englishman of the public school variety has never come of age. With unintentional callousness the immature man divides women into ladies, drudges, and prostitutes, evoking from them the undesirable defence of craftiness. Finally, some recognition of the diversity of men's needs in the form of a more flexible idea of the marriage-relation is needed, one in which the union is neither exclusive nor irrevocable.

Whatever their limitations Ellis and Carpenter set on foot a movement that was to prove much more resilient than the other liberal initiatives of their age. With the first world war pragmatism in philosophy sank almost without a trace, modernism gave way to an eschatological emphasis in religious thought, guild socialism vanished while socialism of a centralizing kind, whether Fabian or Marxist, prospered. But one piece of progressive optimism that the war's revelation of the folly or wickedness or impotence of man was unable to stifle was the belief in the redeeming possibilities of a liberalized personal life.

7

READING

DEREK HUDSON

READING

ALTHOUGH the Edwardian years coincided with a steady expansion of British reading habits, and saw the publication of much good literature, the start of the century did not prove particularly encouraging to the book trade. In August 1900 the London correspondent of the *New York Evening Post* reported that the British bookseller was almost as great a grumbler as the British farmer and that in any bookshop he was liable to tell a tale of woe: 'The trade is not what it was once, you know, sir, and what with the war and sixpenny reprints, some of us are pretty well at the end of our tether.' And the bookseller would 'proceed to show you shelf after shelf of war-books which are not selling, and shelf after shelf of spring fiction which we hoped to get rid of, but which is now so much old stock'.[1] Yet the South African war, despite its damping effect on creative publishing, gave opportunities to adventurous writers like Winston Churchill, who was made to speak prophetically as 'a certain youthful war-correspondent' in a contemporary poem by Cotsford Dick:

> I have published a romance,
> Have escaped from vile durance,
> Have done all I can to make myself a name;
> And it will not be my fault
> If some social somersault
> Does not land me on the pinnacle of fame.[2]

The war was still dragging on when Queen Victoria's death provided publishers with a chance of showing their loyalty and enterprise. The biographical literature in the opening months of 1901 ranged from Mrs. Gurney's *The Childhood of Queen Victoria*,

---

[1] *New York Evening Post*, 8 August 1900, quoted in *Sell's Dictionary of the World Press*, 1901.

[2] *The World*, 18 April 1900.

Francis Aitken's *Victoria: The Well-Beloved*, G. A. Henty's paper-covered *Queen Victoria*, and a new edition of Richard Holmes's biography ('the whole of the text, except the last chapter, was read to H.M. Queen Victoria, and was approved and authorized by her') to Cassell's *Life and Times* in sixpenny weekly parts, Mrs. O. F. Walton's *Pictures and Stories from Queen Victoria's Life*, an anonymous *Private Life of Queen Victoria* 'by One of Her Majesty's Servants' (a bad omen this), and a penny pamphlet in the Religious Tract Society's 'Excellent Women Series'. As early as March 1901 Arthur Mee was ready with *King and Emperor, The Life History of Edward VII* at 1s. 6d. ('At the present moment King Edward VII is the most striking personality in the World. His loyal subjects are longing to read all about their King. This book will give its readers information—Fresh, Interesting, and Up-to-date. God save the King!') In September Skeffington announced that the king had accepted a copy of *The Coronation Service*, in royal cloth, 2s. net. By February 1902 John Long was offering at three guineas Edward Spencer's *The King's Race-horses: A History of the Connection of H.M. King Edward VII with the National Sport*; and Newnes *From Cradle to Crown*, a biography in twenty sixpenny weekly parts.

The advertisements in the *Bookseller* for 1901–2 not only furnish this and other evidence of an absorbing public interest in the royal family, but they also convey a confused yet intriguing impression of the spate of miscellaneous books flooding the shops at the beginning of the Edwardian era. In March 1901 the new books included Laurence Binyon's *Odes*, Jowett's *Sermons on Faith and Doctrine*, and *Daddy's Girl* by Mrs. L. T. Meade. In April Macmillan declared that 58,000 copies of *Elizabeth and her German Garden* had been sold, and John Long was publishing novels with titles like *Once Too Often, Bitter Fruit, Women Must Weep*. In June came Gissing's *By the Ionian Sea* from Chapman & Hall and P. F. Warner's *Cricket in Many Climes* from Heinemann. In November Macmillan offered Kipling's *Kim*, already serialized in *Cassell's Magazine*. December brought the choice of Chatto's *The Grand Babylon Hotel* by Arnold Bennett or Heinemann's *A Little Tour in France* by Henry James, with ninety-four illustrations by Joseph Pennell. Around these names played a variegated stream of novelists of all shades of popularity—Anthony Hope, Hall Caine, Marion Crawford, G. A. Henty, Stanley Weyman, Conan Doyle, Elinor Glyn, Mrs. Humphry

Ward, Guy Boothby, E. Phillips Oppenheim, Nat Gould, Rita, and many more. In the same month it was possible both to hear the steady heart-beat of the Oxford University Press as it announced *The Structure and Life History of the Harlequin Fly* and to be told that Ella Wheeler Wilcox's *Poems of Passion* and *Poems of Pleasure* were 'favourites with all cultured persons'. And which of these publications of November 1901 was the more typical of Edwardian England—*Louis Wain's Annual* or FitzGerald's *Rubáiyát of Omar Khayyám* in an *édition de luxe* on Japanese vellum?

It is a rhetorical question: but, to answer it seriously, the Fitz-Gerald *Rubáiyát* was the more typical publication of a period delighting in fine printing and illustration, much of which has seemed mannered and overwrought to posterity. Let us give credit, however, to an age that could recognize genuine talent, that commissioned such an artist as young Henry Ospovat to illustrate *The Poems of Matthew Arnold* (1900) and *Shakespeare's Songs* (1901), and, when he died at thirty-one, kept his memory alive until a memorial volume introduced by Oliver Onions appeared from the Saint Catherine Press in 1911. Ospovat awaits re-discovery, but he was honoured, and rightly, by Edwardians.

Amy Cruse, in a study of the Edwardians and their literature,[1] contended with some truth that two qualities must be especially looked for in their writings—realism and cleverness, 'or, more properly, smartness'; the first deriving from a reaction to Victorian fastidiousness and sentimentality, the second from the strained ideals of high society which had been imitated by the middle classes. Intellectually and artistically there was perhaps a slight decline from the finest achievements of the nineties. The realistic novel was, indeed, the dominant literary form and encouraged an abundance of popular trash by writers like Elinor Glyn and Rita; yet there existed in all classes a large body of serious readers who enjoyed the classics, the better contemporary novelists, and the agreeable essays of E. V. Lucas, G. K. Chesterton, Hilaire Belloc, and Alice Meynell. In the essay, which was the second most characteristic literary form, cleverness and gentleness met, and nothing more strongly conveys the sense of peaceful leisure that possessed the reading classes than the collections of essays and society memoirs surviving on the library shelves of a later age. A sunny world, by turns gracious,

---

[1] *After the Victorians*, by Amy Cruse, Allen & Unwin, 1938.

complacent, and witty, is reflected in their pages and in the fluent stanzas of contemporary light verse. The names of Lucas, Chesterton, and Belloc sufficiently indicate that the entertainment value of Edwardian literature was remarkably high, and it extended to the level of political propaganda, particularly when Bernard Shaw was the writer. The attitude to change was generally hopeful. A contemporary poetry reviewer could write: 'Though the wild words of the father, on seeing his little son apparently slain by a motor, are natural enough, we cannot help feeling that the attributes of motoring are not wholly Satanic'; and in its guarded optimism the sentence is characteristically Edwardian.[1]

The period was not, in general, notable for poetry, yet care and enthusiasm were lavished both on the writing and reading of verse of all kinds. When the poet laureate of Edwardian England—Alfred Austin, a nonentity sandwiched between Tennyson and Bridges—died in 1913, the *Observer* published (8 June) the views of many well-known writers, scholars, and publishers on the choice of a new laureate. This canvass indicated some of the Edwardian poets who were taken seriously by their literary contemporaries. The voting went in favour of Rudyard Kipling, with William Watson coming second. Robert Bridges, Henry Newbolt, and Alice Meynell found strong support. Among the other poets mentioned for consideration were Thomas Hardy, Laurence Binyon, Alfred Noyes, Owen Seaman, Austin Dobson, and Stephen Phillips.

At the outset of Edward's reign the reading matter provided for his subjects was, at least, vigorous and varied. As the reign proceeded the quality of the serious writing advanced. But works of real literary or artistic merit remained in a small minority, a fact which is the more surprising to posterity because of the high survival value of a handful of outstanding authors. Too often the books of the period were characterized in some degree by vulgarity, prolixity, or pomposity. Little sound guidance could be expected from society at the highest level. The duchess in V. Sackville-West's *The Edwardians* 'never opened a book', and there were many like her. It is the glory of the period that a relatively small circle of connoisseurs was as much alive to the merits of Max Beerbohm, Saki, or Ernest Bramah, as it was to those of Joseph Conrad and

---

[1] *The Eagle*, a magazine of St. John's College, Cambridge, March 1910, reviewing *Cornish Breakers and other poems* by C. E. Byles, 1909.

1907

CHAMBER
MUSIC

BY

JAMES JOYCE

ELKIN MATHEWS
VIGO STREET, LONDON

XXV. A decorative title-page 1907

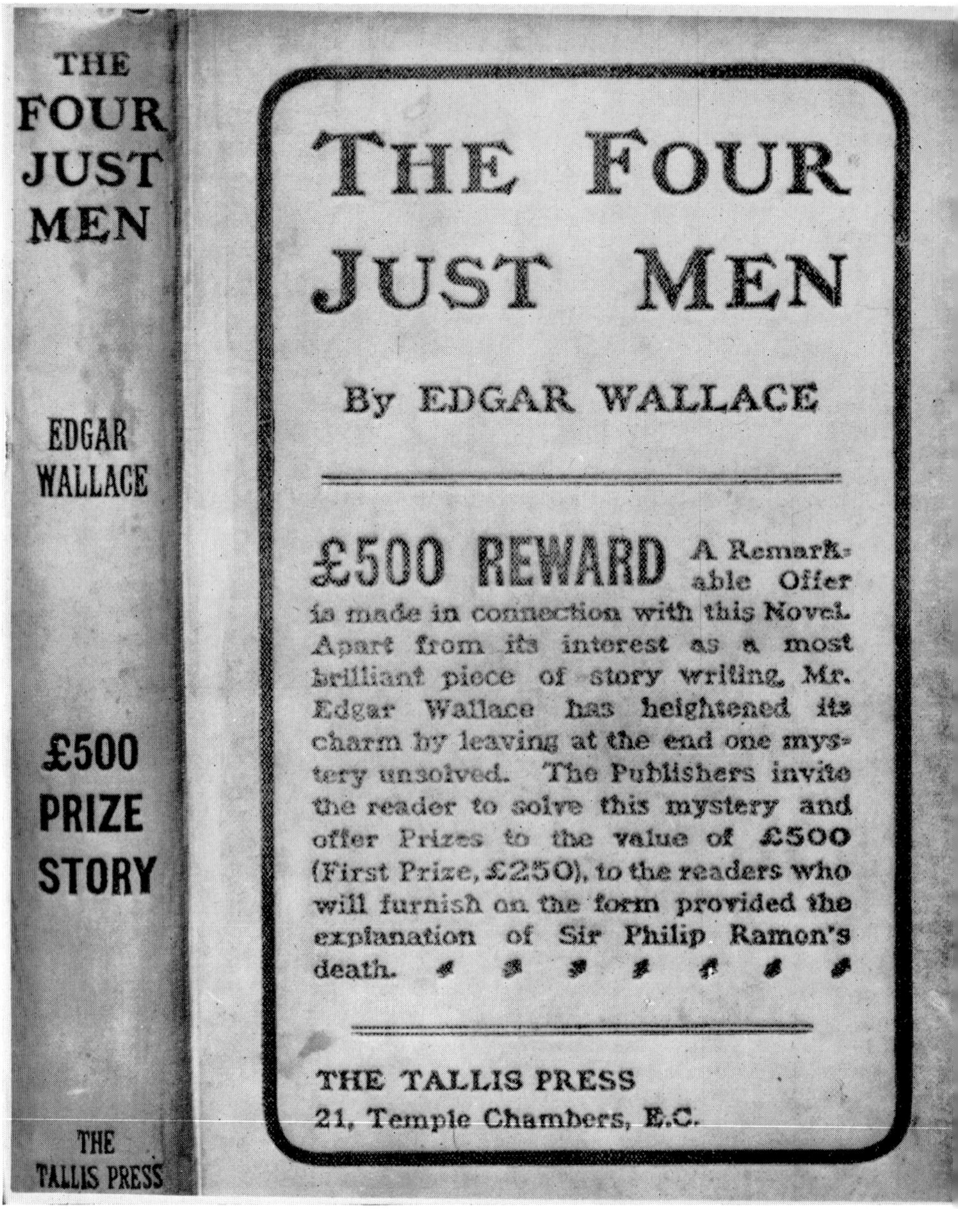

THE
FOUR
JUST
MEN

EDGAR
WALLACE

£500
PRIZE
STORY

THE
TALLIS PRESS

THE FOUR JUST MEN

By EDGAR WALLACE

£500 REWARD A Remark-
able Offer
is made in connection with this Novel.
Apart from its interest as a most
brilliant piece of story writing, Mr.
Edgar Wallace has heightened its
charm by leaving at the end one mystery unsolved. The Publishers invite
the reader to solve this mystery and
offer Prizes to the value of £500
(First Prize, £250), to the readers who
will furnish on the form provided the
explanation of Sir Philip Ramon's
death.

THE TALLIS PRESS
21, Temple Chambers, E.C.

XXVI. A best-selling thriller 1905

Henry James; and that many a good middle-class household heard the novels and poems of the Victorian giants read aloud of an evening.

In quantity, the number of books published and the facilities for library reading both showed remarkable advances during the Edwardian years. In 1901 the number of new publications totalled 6,044, a figure which had more than doubled by 1913, when the total was 12,379.[1] Behind this trend lay an improvement in family incomes and an ever-increasing attention to education, which accelerated the decline of illiteracy. The history of the public library movement is an illuminating guide to this progress. The number of borrowers' tickets in force at Croydon public libraries went up by an average of a thousand a year in 1902–4.[2] In 1880 there had been 95 British library authorities; in 1900 there were 352; and in 1920 there were 551. The libraries issuing books, or 'service points', in 1896 were 480; these had grown to 920 by 1911. The books in stock in 1911 were 10,874,066, as against 4,450,000 in 1896. Books issued advanced from 26 millions in 1896 to 54 millions in 1911. Most revealing of all, public expenditure on the libraries jumped from £286,000 in 1896 to £805,445 in 1911.[3]

More books were published and made available, then, to readers in Edwardian England than ever before. And an incomplete list chosen at random will remind us that many fine books and writers shed lustre on this brief reign. They were notable years in English literary history that saw the appearance of Conrad's *Nostromo*, Galsworthy's *The Man of Property*, Bennett's *The Old Wives' Tale*, Wells's *Kipps* and *Mr. Polly*, Kipling's *Kim* and *Puck of Pook's Hill*, Gosse's *Father and Son*, W. H. Hudson's *Green Mansions*, Henry James's *The Golden Bowl*, Hardy's *The Dynasts*, Gissing's *The Private Papers of Henry Ryecroft*, Belloc's *The Path to Rome* and *Cautionary Tales*, Walter de la Mare's *Songs of Childhood*, Kenneth Grahame's *The Wind in the Willows*, Masefield's *Salt-water Ballads*, and many of the translations of Gilbert Murray. A pronounced trend to social realism, a love of romantic adventure and the outdoor life, a reaction to Victorian parental authority, a wistful preoccupation with fantasy and the spirit of childhood, a renewed interest in the

[1] *The English Book Trade*, by Marjorie Plant, Allen & Unwin, 1939.

[2] *The Reader's Index: the Bi-monthly Magazine of the Croydon Public Libraries*, vol. vi, 1904.

[3] *A Century of Public Library Service*, Library Association, 1950.

classics, are all represented here. Comparative literary merit may be debated, but for the social life of the time the student must read Wells, Bennett, and Galsworthy. Mr. Polly, the shopkeeper, was not only a great lover of the classics, but he also acquired, it will be remembered, a second-hand copy of *The Path to Rome*.

Mr. Polly was, of course, an enlightened man. When the historian turns to consider which works of fiction were actually most in demand, the picture is hardly flattering. Ernest A. Baker, the librarian of Woolwich public libraries, made an interesting experiment.[1] He sent out a circular to twenty-one of the largest public libraries in the country, including a number of representative London libraries, asking them how many copies they had of books by certain specified novelists. The writers were divided into three classes; the first class contained authors deserving, in Mr. Baker's view, to be well represented in every public library; the second class consisted of what he termed popular mediocrities and doubtful cases; the third class contained novelists who were, in his opinion, 'decidedly below the standard admissible in a rate-supported library'.

In Class I of Mr. Baker's list we find Balzac, Meredith, Henry James, Conrad, and Turgenev, established in that order of popularity. The aggregate number of copies of works by Balzac in the selected libraries was 426, and the average per library 20. The figures for the other novelists in Class I were Meredith, 390 and 19; Henry James, 353 and 17; Conrad, 153 and 7; Turgenev, 109 and 5. It is an interesting result, though the absence of other eminent novelists such as Dickens from the list has no significance, for Mr. Baker's choice of runners was decidedly arbitrary.

Much more interesting are the comparative findings in the next two classes. Several lengths ahead of Balzac, and well in the lead among the 'popular mediocrities and doubtful cases', is M. E. Braddon with an aggregate of 2,296 and an average per library of 109. Mrs. Henry Wood (1,903 and 91) is close behind her, followed by Emma Jane Worboise (1,617 and 77), Marie Corelli (822 and 39), Mrs. M. W. Hungerford (785 and 37), and Ouida (721 and 33). These are the 'queens of the circulating libraries', and, quantitatively, they have a commanding place in a survey of Edwardian reading habits, although their reputations had all been firmly

[1] 'The Standard of Fiction in Public Libraries', by Ernest A. Baker, *The Library Association Record*, vol. ix, 1907.

established long before the close of the nineteenth century, and two of their most famous books, Miss Braddon's *Lady Audley's Secret* and Mrs. Henry Wood's *East Lynne*, had been published in the early 1860's. Male competitors are outdistanced. In Class II Fergus Hume, Frank Barrett, E. Phillips Oppenheim, and C. J. Cutcliffe Hyne come pounding behind. The leader in Class III, consisting of authors who, in Mr. Baker's view, ought not to be found in any 'rate-supported library', is Guy Boothby, with an aggregate of 899 copies and an average per library of 45; his nearest rivals are Rita, William Le Queux, and Florence Marryat.

Surprising as it may be to find so many Edwardians absorbed in the popular fiction of the preceding generation, these samples do not really tell us anything unexpected, and they tend to bear out Mrs. Leavis's contention 'that the general reading public of the twentieth century is no longer in touch with the best literature of its own day or of the past. . . . It is almost impossible for the novel which is an aesthetic experience to become popular, and, on the other hand, popular fiction cannot now contain, even unwittingly, the qualities which have made the work of Defoe, Dickens, and Smollett something more than popular fiction.' Earlier than Lytton, as she points out, fiction did not invite uncritical reading or encourage self-dramatization.[1]

Mrs. Leavis was writing in the 1930's, before the general deluge of 'paperbacks' had put much of the best literature into many more hands; but, whatever Mr. Baker's survey of the public libraries in 1907 may say, the Edwardians must be given credit for a determined and successful attempt to give the classics wider circulation. Collections of reprints such as the Chandos Classics, Macmillan's Globe Series, and Morley's Library were all useful, if limited in scope. The first titles in the World's Classics were published by Grant Richards in 1901, and by 1909 the Oxford University Press, which had taken over this series, was advertising 150 volumes at prices ranging (according to the elegance of the binding) from 1s. to 5s. 6d. The first ten volumes of Collins's Classics, published in 1903, sold 80,000 copies at a shilling each within six months.[2] The triumph of Dent's ambitious, carefully planned Everyman's Library,[3] of

[1] *Fiction and the Reading Public*, by Q. D. Leavis, Chatto & Windus, 1932.
[2] *The House of Collins*, by David Keir, Collins, 1952.
[3] See *The House of Dent 1888–1938*, Dent, 1938.

which the first fifty volumes were published *en bloc* in February 1906, was greater still, and by the time the second fifty had been produced Dent's were unable to cope with the demand. The success of Everyman had a far-reaching effect on the firm of Dent, which began building a new factory at Letchworth in August 1906, and on British publishing generally. In 1906 alone 152 volumes of Everyman were published; and by 1909 Cassell's, taking advantage of the trend, were able to announce that they had sold 900,000 copies of the 85 titles in their People's Library of classics.[1]

The popularizing of the classics on this extensive scale was perhaps the most remarkable achievement of Edwardian publishing, but there is another important feature that deserves to be mentioned—the growth of educational reading among the working classes. The newly founded Workers' Educational Association stood witness to a stir in our society; and an article by Henry Clay in its journal *The Highway* (September 1909) afforded an insight into 'What Workpeople Read'. The inquiry covered the reading of thirty-four working people, in social, economic, and historical subjects only (but these, and especially economics, were the chief interests of the worker-student). 'At the head of the list, with nine readers, was Blatchford's *Merrie England*. George's *Progress and Poverty* was second with seven. Toynbee's *Industrial Revolution*, Ruskin's *Unto this Last*, and Blatchford's *Britain for the British* had six each. Green's *Short History* and Kropotkin's *Fields, Factories, and Workshops* had five, and the same number had read parts of Adam Smith's *Wealth of Nations*.' Only one reader had tackled Marx. Many of the books read were works of socialist propaganda, easily accessible, but while it is no surprise to find Robert Blatchford and Henry George well represented, it is an encouraging portent for the future of democracy to see that workers could appreciate the virtues of detachment and scholarship, and that they were also reading Arnold Toynbee the economist (uncle of the historian), J. R. Green, and Adam Smith; these authors, together with Ruskin, Carlyle, Mill, H. G. Wells, Bernard Shaw, and the Webbs, have been among the chief influences on socialist thought from Edwardian days onwards. In this connexion, too, Williams and Norgate's excellent Home University Library, whose first volumes appeared in 1911 under the auspices of such editors as Gilbert Murray and H. A. L. Fisher,

---

[1] *The House of Cassell 1848–1958*, by Simon Nowell-Smith, Cassell, 1958.

deserves honourable mention for its clear intention to cater for the new reading public created by adult education.

When we shift from adult to juvenile educational attitudes, the broad contrast lies between the economic and the whimsical. During Edward's reign, *Alice's Adventures in Wonderland* was perhaps more popular as a vehicle for political parody than as a national classic; its revival in the first world war was to confirm its permanent status. Rudyard Kipling, having already written *Stalky*, gave Edwardian boys and girls the avuncular *Just-So Stories*, the wisdom of *Kim*, and the charm of *Puck of Pook's Hill*; G. A. Henty was staple reading for the boys, but the fancy and sentiment of J. M. Barrie, whose masterpiece *Peter Pan* was first performed in 1904, more nearly typify the literary Edwardian's attitude to his children— deprecated later, but a revolution in imagination at that time—and made easy the delighted acceptance of Kenneth Grahame's *The Wind in the Willows* (1908). Barrie, again, was partly responsible for forwarding the vogue for richly illustrated Christmas books—to be admired by children with very clean hands—which received a great impetus from the appearance of his *Peter Pan in Kensington Gardens* (1906) illustrated by Arthur Rackham. The same artist, who had already decorated Grimm's *Fairy Tales* and *Rip Van Winkle*, went on to illustrate Shakespeare, *Undine*, and Wagner, and to identify himself lastingly with those lavish Edwardian gift-books, in the making of which his nearest competitor was Edmund Dulac. From the first the expensive *de luxe* editions, with their book-markers, tissue fly-leaves, and prints mounted on brown paper, found ready buyers among the more prosperous members of the upper and middle class.

It was, indeed, a rich period for the children of the middle and upper classes, when they could turn from the tough wit of Belloc's *Cautionary Tales* and the delicate humour and pure water-colours of the growing sequence of Beatrix Potter's animal fantasies to Arthur Mee's beloved *Children's Encyclopaedia* (first published in 1907). Children were being increasingly and thoughtfully studied in these years. A writer like Algernon Blackwood progressed from stories of the ghostly and macabre —another Edwardian obsession, evidenced by the books of Charles Whibley and Arthur Morrison (Black-wood's psychologist-detective John Silence was a truly Edwardian conception)—to fantastic novels about childhood, which showed considerable understanding of child psychology and were no doubt influenced by the enormous success of Maeterlinck's *The Blue Bird* (1909). One could indeed say of Edward's reign, as Johnson said of Shakespeare, that 'fairies in his time were much in fashion'. Theosophists, mystics, and occult philosophers abounded, from Mrs. Besant to 'A. E'.

And what, after all, was that famous contemporary Sherlock Holmes, with his uncanny talent for self-disguise, but a full-size fairy or wizard who could take what human shape he pleased? Holmes was principally a creation of the 1880's and 1890's, but his place in the Edwardian period is assured by the appearance in the *Strand Magazine* in 1901–2 of perhaps his most famous adventure, *The Hound of the Baskervilles*, issued in book form in the latter year, and by the publication of *The Return of Sherlock Holmes* in 1905. The sales of Conan Doyle's books in the Edwardian years were, by the way, relatively modest compared with the enormous demand for them that developed later. Between 1908 and 1914 the *Return* sold an average of 750 copies a year at 3*s.* 6*d. Sir Nigel*, after a spectacular start, averaged 200 copies a year between 1907 and 1914, while the collected edition of Conan Doyle in twelve volumes had an average sale of no more than 40 sets between 1903 and 1914. The great days for Conan Doyle were yet to come. The same may be said of P. G. Wodehouse, who between 1902 and 1910 was writing only stories for boys which did not sell particularly well in those years; his first title outside this sphere, *Psmith in the City*, had a first printing of 2,000 in 1910 and was not reprinted until 1919. The late Victorian romantic Anthony Hope was more completely a man of this time; between 1901 and 1906 his *Tristram of Blent* sold 28,150 at 6*s.*[1]

We have seen that the majority of Edwardian library readers were happily content with the works of Victorian ladies, like M. E. Braddon and Mrs. Henry Wood, of long-established fame; moreover, books by many famous authors first published in Edwardian years sold better later on. Which, however, were the original best-sellers of Edwardian England? Mr. Desmond Flower conducted a valuable investigation into the best-sellers of 1830–1930, defining 'best-sellers' as works of fiction that 'not only have reached six figures in a fairly short time, but which, during the long or the

[1] Information by courtesy of John Murray (Publishers) Ltd. and A. & C. Black Ltd.

short life that fate allowed them, took the country by storm and, in many instances, affected the reading tastes of the British public'. His list is confined to one work of each author, and a selection from that part of it which covers the Edwardian period, restricted to English authors, is relevant to this essay:

1901 *Anna Lombard*, by Victoria Cross.
    The History of Sir Richard Calmady, by Lucas Malet.
1902 *The Four Feathers*, by A. E. W. Mason.
1903 *When It Was Dark*, by Guy Thorne.
1904 *Baccarat*, by Frank Danby.
    The Garden of Allah, by Robert Hichens.
1905 *The Boy in Green*, by Nat Gould.
    The Morals of Marcus Ordeyne, by W. J. Locke.
    The Scarlet Pimpernel, by Baroness Orczy.
    The Four Just Men, by Edgar Wallace.
1907 *Three Weeks*, by Elinor Glyn.
1908 *The Blue Lagoon*, by H. de Vere Stacpoole.
1909 *The Rosary*, by Florence Barclay.
1910 *The Broad Highway*, by Jeffery Farnol.[1]

The survey suggests that the Edwardians were not remarkable for widespread literary taste. Yet Desmond Flower's list is not entirely representative; Galsworthy's *The Man of Property*, for example, which appeared in 1906—the same year as his successful play *The Silver Box*—is not mentioned, though it is true that Galsworthy's sales did not rise spectacularly until the first world war induced a mood of nostalgia for the past. Conrad's Edwardian novels, including some of his finest works, sold notoriously badly when they first appeared. Another most distinguished writer, E. M. Forster, had little immediate commercial success; in the years 1908–13 his novels *A Room with a View* (1908) and *Howards End* (1910) sold only 2,312 and 9,959 copies respectively.[2] The Edwardians gave massive support, however, to that ponderous classic of biography, Morley's *Life of Gladstone* (1903) which sold 25,041 copies in its first year, was issued in fifteen sixpenny parts and in two volumes at 5*s.* (1906), and had a further large sale in three volumes of Macmillan's

---

[1] *A Century of Best Sellers 1830–1930*, compiled with an introduction by Desmond Flower, National Book Council, 1934. Incidentally, Farnol's *The Broad Highway* was the 'top-seller' of 1911 in U.S.A.; see *Sixty Years of Best Sellers: 1895–1955*, by Alice Payne Hackett, New York, 1956.

[2] Information by courtesy of Edward Arnold (Publishers) Ltd.

shilling library (1911–12).[1] Still more prosaically, and perhaps
snobbishly, they bought 10,000 copies of another valuable informative work, *Who's Who*, in 1901 (price 5*s*.), and 12,000 copies in 1910,
when the price had doubled.[2]

But for an impression of the great mass of Edwardian publishing
towards the end of the reign, the student with time to spare cannot
do better than turn the advertisement pages of the *Bookseller* of
1909. . . . 'The sales of Nat Gould's Novels exceed 6,000,000 (Six
Million) copies.' 'Any edition of my books, prose or verse, published
by any firm except Messrs. Gay & Handcock is pirated and not
authentic. Ella Wheeler Wilcox' (you could buy them in limp white
cloth, in limp lambskin, or 7 volumes in leather, in case to match).
How to Skate on Rollers by 'Rinker'—'*The* Book of the moment on
The Craze of the moment.' Such ephemera were, however, inter-
spersed with reminders of the prosperity of light literature: 'The
Success of 1908 was undoubtedly the work of a new Author in the
person of Mr. A. S. M. Hutchinson, whose clever humorous novel
entitled *Once Aboard the Lugger* brought forth unanimous praise
from the critics. Please order it today. Third Impression. 6*s*.' And
there is much to be said for a time in which one could buy Walter
Raleigh's *Shakespeare* for 4*s*., Eric Parker's *Highways and Byways in
Surrey*, with Hugh Thomson's drawings, for 6*s*., J. Meade Falkner's
Moonfleet for 7*d*., and novels by Conan Doyle, F. Anstey, W. W.
Jacobs, Somerset Maugham, and A. E. W. Mason in Newnes's sixpenny series.

Although several highly gifted Edwardian authors were less well
supported in their own era than they deserved, most talents of any
note were at least recognized by a section of their contemporaries,
who had as a whole a considerable thirst for knowledge and at the
end of the reign had lost part of their dangerous satisfaction with the
status quo. To sum up, the period showed a great advance in book-
reading habits, in publishing enterprise, and in the circulation of the
classics. Before the newspapers and periodicals of the Edwardians
come under review, let us briefly consider two matters in which
books and newspapers were closely linked.

On 17 January 1902 there occurred an event as important to
literature as to journalism, the first publication of the *Times Literary*

---

[1] *The House of Macmillan*, by Charles Morgan, Macmillan, 1943.
[2] Information by courtesy of A. & C. Black Ltd.

XXVII. *Art nouveau* from the Guild of Women Binders 1903

XXVIII. Illustration by Arthur Rackham from *Peter Pan in Kensington Gardens* 1906

Supplement, which has admirably fulfilled ever since its aim of providing a detached and informed criticism of books (it then included notices of art, theatre, and music as well as book reviews). The *T.L.S.* devoted a leading article in its second number (24 January 1902) to a department of the literary scene, the art of railway reading, which was relatively under a cloud in Edwardian times. 'Real books', declared the writer, 'are seldom read nowadays in railway compartments. Occasionally a trashy novel may be seen; but more often than not your fellow-passenger will be content with one of those amazing publications—*Comic Cagmag* or *Hoity-Toity Bits*—which joke with difficulty, retail fibs about nobodies, and minister to the ancient and inbred love of the acrostic in the Anglo-Saxon race.' Things had been very different in the 1850's and 1860's, when an earlier *Times* article had inspired Murray's notable series 'Reading for the Rail'; they were to improve again later; but in Edwardian England railway bookstalls were not at their best. Even at Euston, where the bookstall had once had a good reputation, 'one or two "novels of the hour" at six shillings stand all forlorn amid a wilderness of trash at sixpence; and in an obscure corner are huddled a few fly-blown "remainders" of Pictorial Albums and works of unpopularly "popular" Entomology.'

It seems that the rates demanded for railway bookstalls were excessive, for in 1905 W. H. Smith & Son found it impossible to renew their contracts with the L.N.W.R. and G.W.R., which affected 200 bookstalls. In every important town on these lines W. H. Smith now opened shops instead of bookstalls, a change which extended to stationery and soon revolutionized the business of the firm.[1] It was a trifle unscrupulous of the leader-writer in the *T.L.S.* to hint that King Edward set a bad example by being preoccupied with railway eating rather than with railway reading: 'Every one will have noted that on the King's journey the other day from Sandringham to London so soon as the train had started luncheon was served.'[2]

Another episode involving *The Times* makes, at a distance of years, an impression as curious as the story of the railway bookstalls

---

[1] See *The History of W. H. Smith & Son*, printed for private circulation, 1921.

[2] Sir Harold Nicolson has confessed his admiration of the ingenious way Sir Sidney Lee in his biography contrived to convey that the king was a voracious eater. ' "He had", wrote Sir Sidney, "a splendid appetite at all times, and never toyed with his food".' (*Biography as an Art*, ed. James L. Clifford, O.U.P., 1962.)

—the conflict between the publishers and *The Times* Book Club in 1906–8. The proprietors of *The Times* had established the Book Club in 1905 in an attempt to improve the low fortunes of the newspaper. By way of inducement annual subscribers were offered membership of the club, which would not only lend books as soon as they were asked for but also sell recent books 'virtually as good as new' at a greatly reduced price. Winston Churchill's life of his father *Lord Randolph Churchill* was, for example, advertised in 1906 for seven shillings instead of thirty-six. The Publishers' Association drew up a revised net book agreement, binding on its members, which stipulated that a net book should not be sold as 'second-hand' within six months, and refused to supply the Book Club except at the full price. *The Times*'s definition of a second-hand book as 'one which has been used by more than two subscribers, and is returned in such a state that it cannot be sold as a new book' proved unacceptable to the publishers.

A battle was now joined, in which the publishers withdrew their advertisements from *The Times*, and the newspaper's subscribers were urged to boycott the publications of Messrs. Macmillan, who had taken a lead in the dispute, and of several other publishers. *The Times* was not without supporters ready to agree that the price of net books was exorbitant—Bernard Shaw made an edition of *John Bull's Other Island* and other of his plays exclusively available to the Book Club—and reviews in the *T.L.S.* of books issued by offending publishers were prefaced by a minatory notice inviting subscribers to 'abstain from ordering the book so far as possible'. The end came in 1908 when John Murray was awarded £7,500 in an action for libel against *The Times*, which had printed letters accusing him of 'simple extortion' in pricing the three-volume edition of *The Letters of Queen Victoria* at three guineas. In *Murray* v. *Walter* the publisher was able to show that *The Times* and its correspondents had grossly underestimated the costs of publication and completely ignored the advertising expenses. Lord Northcliffe, the new proprietor of *The Times*, then hastened to make peace with the publishers.

The upshot of this curious struggle was to vindicate the Edwardian publishing community, and to show that the net book agreement, so far from being directed against the public, was an act of collective self-control designed, in Charles Morgan's words, to persuade book-sellers 'to abstain from cutting one another's throats by competitive underselling'. For his leadership of the book trade at this time Frederick Macmillan will always be honourably remembered—not least for the quiet and dignified manner in which he accepted his victory. *The Times*, for its part, may be allowed to have acted in what it conceived to be the public interest, though selfish motives had also been involved; the financial pressure which induced this great journal to adopt such an extreme position is a part of the newspaper history of the time.[1]

NEWSPAPERS AND PERIODICALS

At the opening of the new century a revolution in newspaper methods was in full swing. Its beginnings can be traced to the attempts to brighten W. T. Stead's *Pall Mall Gazette* and T. P. O'Connor's *Star* during the late 1880's. Periodicals such as Newnes's *Tit-Bits* (1881), Harmsworth's *Answers* (1888), and *Pearson's Weekly* (1890) had also shown themselves aware of a latent public demand for more readable, enterprising, and entertaining journalism. As early as 1883 crowds thronged to see 'Tit-Bits Villa', Dulwich, the first prize in a competition. In the nineties solid closely-printed columns, which had persisted since Thomas Barnes established editorial responsibility, were increasingly broken by headlines; chatty paragraphs, interviews, and signed articles intruded to relieve the monotony and anonymity of, at least, the halfpenny press. Alfred Harmsworth had a long string of successful periodicals to his credit before he bought and transformed the *Evening News* (1894), and introduced his triumphant *Daily Mail* in 1896, followed, after a false start, by his *Daily Mirror* in 1903. As the *Manchester Guardian* once said, the *Daily Mail* 'made life more pleasant, more exciting, for the average man'. It also made it more interesting for 'the average woman'. This was perhaps Harmsworth's decisive achievement.

In one way or another the ambitious Harmsworth, with his brilliance and charm and his capable brothers, dominated Edwardian journalism. Many newspapermen viewed him, first and last, with dismay. But there were reserves in the character of this undisputed genius which gave him the effect of a dual personality. With one hand he created a whole new popular press, he introduced

---

[1] *The History of The Times*, vol. iii. *The Twentieth Century Test 1884–1912*, 1947; *The House of Macmillan, 1843–1943*, by Charles Morgan, Macmillan, 1943.

the cult of 'personalities' (his own included, which became increasingly arbitrary), he abolished dullness for the multitude; with the other hand he deviously encouraged a higher order of intelligence, he saved *The Times* and he remodelled the *Observer*. His motives were often mixed; but to attempt to disentangle good and bad results in his work is not a rewarding exercise. He must be accepted as a vital force necessary to the time.

In 1901, 2,510 papers were published annually in the British Isles, 516 of them in London. By 1910 the total had increased to 2,785, of which 734 appeared in the capital. (In addition there were published each year throughout the reign of Edward VII between 1,000 and 2,000 magazines.) The majority of the newspapers were weeklies; the seven hundred of these appearing in London in 1910 ranged from *Ally Sloper's Half Holiday* and the *Chauffeur and Garage Gazette* ('the official organ of the National Society of Chauffeurs') to the *Pawnbrokers' Gazette and Trade Circular* and the *Hornsey and Finsbury Park Journal and Muswell Hill Standard*. The list included papers of such varying excellence as the *Spectator*, *Athenaeum*, *Observer*, *John Bull*, *Vanity Fair*, *Punch*—and the *Sporting Times*, otherwise 'The Pink 'Un', which called itself 'the best known twopenny paper in the world' and had as its motto 'High Toryism, High Churchism, High Farming, and Old Port for ever'.

Despite the existence of a large and responsible provincial press, with the *Manchester Guardian* and the *Birmingham Post* among its most distinguished daily representatives, the heart of the newspaper struggle lay in the competition of the London morning and evening newspapers. Strictly speaking, in 1901 there were 19 London morning papers and 10 evening papers: in 1910, 28 'mornings' and 9 'evenings'. Several of these were specialized, however, being concerned with commercial or financial affairs, shipping, sport, or, in the case of the *Morning Advertiser*, the licensed trades. The principal London morning papers in 1901 were the *Daily Chronicle* (1d.), *Daily Express and Morning Herald* ($\frac{1}{2}$d.), *Daily Graphic* (1d.), *Daily Mail* ($\frac{1}{2}$d.), *Daily News* (1d.), *Daily Telegraph* (1d.), *Morning Leader* ($\frac{1}{2}$d.), *Morning Post* (1d.), *Standard* (1d.), and *The Times* (3d.).[1]

Compared with the situation fifty years later, Edwardian newspapers offered a healthy variety of choice and opinion, yet the

[1] *Sell's Dictionary of the World Press* provides these particulars.

situation of many of them was precarious throughout the decade. The shrewd commercial success of Harmsworth's halfpenny papers— he became Lord Northcliffe in 1905—rocked many old-fashioned establishments to their foundations with their emphasis on features designed to attract women readers, their concern for the 'underdog' and the telling small details of daily life, their 'stunts' and gossip and lively treatment of the news, their broad humanity. The penny dailies and even the threepenny *Times* could now appear stodgy as well as serious. In 1901 *The Times* was selling 37,900 copies at three-pence, the penny *Manchester Guardian* 44,300, and the halfpenny *Daily Mail* 836,700 (having nearly reached a million during the South African war a year before). By 1907 *The Times* had advanced to 44,900 while the *Manchester Guardian* had declined to 35,800 and the *Daily Mail* to 720,300. The London *Daily News* sold 151,900 in 1907, its price having been driven down from a penny to a half-penny.[1]

Behind these figures lies the story of a desperate attempt by the more expensive London dailies to face the competition of the Northcliffe press, which bore heavily on 'serious' conservative papers like the *Telegraph* and the *Standard*, the latter destined not long to survive as a morning journal. There were too many Liberal papers about, also; the *Tribune*, which ambitiously set forth to rival *The Times*, had a brief, disappointing career (1906–8), while the *Morning Leader* dropped out of the race in 1912 on its amalgamation with the *Daily News*.

Only by desperate expedients, involving the sponsorship of the ninth edition of the *Encyclopaedia Britannica* at a reduced price, and the precipitation of the 'book war' between its Book Club and the publishers,[2] was *The Times* able to survive the financial storm— until it was acquired in 1908 by Lord Northcliffe, a 'rescue' freely prophesied as a disaster but triumphantly vindicated in the long run by Northcliffe's often exasperatingly expressed but entirely genuine and affectionate respect for the traditions of Printing House Square. Although the editorial quality of *The Times* had been main-tained under G. E. Buckle and C. F. Moberly Bell, it is undeniable that the paper lived largely on its inherited reputation, and that the

---

[1] *Newspaper Circulations 1800–1954*, by A. P. Wadsworth: a paper read to the Manchester Statistical Society, 9 March 1955.
[2] See above, p. 318.

financial position, weakened by the repercussions of the publication
of the forged letter attributed to Parnell in 1887, had been further
undermined by the cumbrous personal rule of the Walter family;
the dissolution of *The Times* partnerships in 1907, which prepared
the way for Northcliffe's take-over, resulted directly from spirited
legal action by small shareholders. Not until 1912, when Geoffrey
Dawson took the editor's chair, was there a real opportunity for a
new broom to sweep. Northcliffe left Dawson in no doubt of what
needed doing: 'I have always said that *The Times* of the last forty
years had as its mottoes "Abandon Scope all ye who enter here" and
"News, like Wine, improves by keeping".'[1]

The lavish and apparently enviable array on the Edwardian
newspaper-stalls was a misleading index to the prosperity of the
newspaper industry. Later journalists have sighed, understandably,
for that rich confusion of reading matter; but in fact many of the
newspapers were barely making ends meet, and a new-comer like
the *Daily Express* lost £60,000 in 1900–6. Only the Northcliffe
papers were really making money.

What has been said about the London morning papers applies
also to the London evenings, though here competition had for some
time been lively; *The Times* and the *Telegraph* may have still
fought stolidly like Tweedledum and Tweedledee, but the evening
papers enjoyed a brisk free-for-all. It will be remembered that
in 'The Adventure of the Blue Carbuncle', which appeared in the
Strand Magazine in January 1892, Sherlock Holmes decided to
insert a newspaper advertisement:

'Here you are, Peterson, run down to the advertising agency, and have
this put in the evening papers.'

'In which, sir?'

'Oh, in the *Globe*, *Star*, *Pall Mall*, *St. James's Gazette*, *Evening News*,
Standard, *Echo*, and any others that occur to you.'

In 1901 the evening papers mentioned by Holmes—all penny papers
except the *Star*, *Evening News*, and *Echo* which sold for a halfpenny—still survived, with the addition of the *Sun* ($\frac{1}{2}d$.) and the
Westminster Gazette (1*d*.), both founded in 1893. By 1910 the *Sun*,
Echo, and *St. James's Gazette* had dropped out (the last-named

---

[1] *The Twentieth Century Test 1884–1912*, vol. iii of *The History of The Times*, and
Northcliffe, by Reginald Pound and Geoffrey Harmsworth, Cassell, 1959, cover much of
the newspaper history of the period in illuminating detail.

amalgamating with the *Evening Standard*). A few commercial papers, technically 'evenings', increased the total; but the principal London evening papers in existence when King Edward died were six—the penny *Globe*, *Pall Mall Gazette*, *Evening Standard*, and *Westminster Gazette*, and the halfpenny *Star* and *Evening News*.

In retrospect the Edwardian evening papers can arouse deep nostalgia, even in those who never knew them. For one thing, they appeared in different colours; it was cheap to print on tinted papers; the *Globe* was pink, the *Westminster* green.[1] They catered for a wide variety of taste, and though they could be trivial, they were rarely dull. The receptive ear still hears their names shouted by newsboys on foggy nights in Baker Street.

Although the halfpenny papers, the *Evening News* and the *Star*— which in 1910 was claiming a circulation exceeding 327,000—paid their way, the penny evening papers consistently tended to lose money. The saddest case was that of the Liberal *Westminster Gazette*, which under the able editorship of J. A. Spender, assisted by the retentive memory of Charles Geake and the cartoons of 'F.C.G.', exerted a political influence out of all proportion to a circulation averaging only 20,000 throughout the Edwardian period (the advent of the first world war raised the sales temporarily to 27,000, their highest figure). The *Westminster*'s losses were sustained first by Sir George Newnes, then by a syndicate of wealthy Liberals, and finally by Lord Cowdray as chief proprietor; but it may seem a sufficient comment on the unhealthy state of the Edwardian newspaper world that this paper, perhaps the most distinguished journal of opinion of the time, which sponsored as an offshoot a memorable literary weekly, the *Saturday Westminster*, should never have been economically viable.[2]

The only sure recipe for success, apparently, was to be backed by Lord Northcliffe. In 1905 the *Observer*, the oldest Sunday newspaper, was in a very bad way, selling less than 5,000 copies a week. Northcliffe, in his search for political power, bought the *Observer* in that year, and after he had spent a lot of money on it and had appointed J. L. Garvin as its editor (1908), the circulation figures climbed rapidly until by 1911 they had reached 60,000. Northcliffe

---

[1] This tradition survived surprisingly; as a small boy, about 1920, I remember my father asking for 'white pepper' at tea-time at the Carlton Hotel and being brought a copy of the *Evening Standard*. (The green *Westminster* was still on sale until 1921.)

[2] See *J. A. Spender*, by Wilson Harris, Cassell, 1946.

and Garvin then quarrelled, and the *Observer* was sold to the Astor family—but not before Northcliffe had established it as a journal of character, a 'newspaper with a soul', and had helped to make Garvin one of the most influential editors in London. In so doing he raised the standard of Sunday journalism to its lasting benefit.[1]

Too much significance must not be attached perhaps to the commercial success or failure of individual newspapers, if one wishes to obtain a true picture of what was—thanks largely to Northcliffe— a generally expanding industry. The first decade of the century saw Reuters's news agency, for example, at the highest point of prosperity it had yet reached; annual revenue rose from £140,000 in 1898 to nearly £200,000 in 1908. Like the newspapers it served, Reuters benefited from the increase in trade, the strengthening of the ties of empire, and the technical advances in communications which followed the close of the South African war. With its service of special missions, interviews, and informed comment, and its privilege (obtained in 1902) of daily calls at government offices, Reuters's work took on more and more the character of that of a newspaper.[2]

Educational progress had stimulated a desire for information of all kinds, and had created a noticeably wider interest in politics and international affairs. This fresh curiosity not only helped Reuters but did much to preserve the balance between the serious and the popular in journalism which was threatened by the bitter competition engendered by the Northcliffe revolution. It serves to explain the relatively happy state of the weekly periodicals and monthly magazines, whose numbers increased considerably within the period. Mr. Polly's cousin, an up-line ticket clerk, read the *British Weekly*; his friend the ironmonger read the *Review of Reviews*. It was also a flourishing period for the better-class illustrated periodicals, of which the doyen was the long-established *Illustrated London News*; others were the *Sketch* and the *Sphere*, both recently founded, and the once-popular *Black and White* (eventually absorbed by the *Sphere*). *Vanity Fair* was still famous for its caricatures, though its days were numbered.

---

[1] See '*The Observer*' *and J. L. Garvin 1908–1914: a Study in a Great Editorship*, by Alfred M. Gollin, O.U.P., 1960.

[2] *Reuters' Century, 1851–1951*, by Graham Storey, Max Parrish, 1951.

A dive into any issue of the *Spectator* in mid-Edwardian days will show that that weekly cannot have given its editor and proprietor St. Loe Strachey too much anxiety (though in weekly journalism there is always some). The paper was fat with advertisements for boys' and girls' schools and improved earth closets and ginger ale, while the numerous announcements of books ranged from *The Law of Churchwardens and Sidesmen in the Twentieth Century* to *If Youth but Knew* by Mr. and Mrs. Egerton Castle; the literary editor, in his long columns of book notices, was able to take the same eclectic view.

The print orders for *Punch* (actual sales were probably about a thousand less) mounted steadily from 58,000 in 1902 to 80,000 in 1908 and to 110,000 in 1913.[1] This was mainly due to the advent of Owen Seaman, who became an effective assistant editor in 1902, during the declining years of F. C. Burnand's editorship, and was himself appointed editor in 1906. He possessed a flair for choosing his staff, recruiting A. A. Milne as his assistant editor, and employing E. V. Lucas, C. L. Graves, and E. V. Knox among his colleagues. Seaman, the urbane classical scholar, was at his best as an Edwardian—shedding some reputation later in a long editorship—and he gave pre-1914 England the *Punch* that it wanted and enjoyed, though without drawing on the wealth of brilliant political writers, from Shaw and Wells to Belloc and Saki, who might have disturbed the golden afternoon.[2]

From the donnish high tables of sedate weekly journalism there was a sharp descent to the cheap snacks provided by Northcliffe's popular journals—*Answers*, which brought him to power, *Comic Cuts, Home Chat*, and the rest. It would be a mistake to disdain them, however; their names are as much a part of Edwardian folk-lore as Marie Lloyd's music-hall songs; they provided innocent entertainment for an awakening people.

Among the popular monthly magazines, the *Strand*, founded by Newnes in 1891, easily held pride of place. The *Strand* was an excellent magazine to the end of its life, but never better than in its Edwardian prime. A glance at the volumes of 1903 and 1904 shows its merit. Besides the Sherlock Holmes stories, classically interpreted in line by Sidney Paget, they contain stories by H. G. Wells, Somerset

[1] Information by courtesy of *Punch*.
[2] *A History of 'Punch'*, by R. G. G. Price, Collins, 1957.

Maugham, and A. E. W. Mason; artists give their opinion as to 'The Finest View in London' and 'The Finest Statue in England'; the engrossing contemporary problem of 'Trousers in Sculpture' is entertainingly discussed and illustrated. The lively *Strand*, combining unusual, informative articles with first-class fiction, deserved its Edwardian sale of 400,000 copies a month.

The *Strand*'s competitors included *Pearson's Magazine, Cassell's Magazine*, and the *Windsor*, each contending vigorously for the best writers and serials; and in this field the public was well served. The firm of Cassell also sponsored a successful 'family' magazine, the *Quiver*, and the best loved of all children's magazines *Little Folks*, which irradiated many a late Victorian and Edwardian nursery. *Little Folks*, the *Quiver, Cassell's*, the *Boy's Own Paper*, the *Girl's Own Paper*, and several other magazines, all produced Christmas annuals, which were greedily anticipated and form a characteristic feature of the age.

A survey of Edwardian reading could be prolonged indefinitely; it is time to bring this attempt to a close. There is a version of the child's game of 'Tinker, tailor . . .' to remind us that the journalistic innovations of the Northcliffe revolution were not universally approved in their day—'Actor, chauffeur, airman, loafer,' it ran, 'undertaker, sausage-maker, inventor-of-shocks-for-a-halfpenny-paper.' But how mild were the shocks compared with what was to come! To look back on the rich diversified book-publishing and journalism that the Edwardians enjoyed is to be assured that it was a blessing to be alive, with a strong pair of eyes, in those peaceful, enterprising, and fiercely competitive years.

8

ART

JOHN RUSSELL

ART

'EDWARDIAN' is one of art-history's unclaimed adjectives. No one name, no particular branch of artistic activity corresponds to it: art has no Elgar or Lutyens to stand beyond question for the full-blown, unhurrying, implicitly proconsular turn of mind which we call Edwardian. Where artistic ambition did relate to this (one might instance Brangwyn's friezes, completed in 1909, for the offices of the Grand Trunk Railway in Cockspur Street) it has failed to retain the interest of a later generation. Where current opinion thinks reasonably well of artists who are in fact Edwardian (Charles Rennie Mackintosh, for instance, Jacob Epstein, Walter Sickert, and Augustus John) their work is often directly opposed to the accepted connotations of 'Edwardian'; like G. E. Moore, 'Baron Corvo', and the James Joyce of *Chamber Music*, they are Edwardian only in so far as no man can altogether escape the characteristics of his own day. Where the adjective is applied to Orpen, or Sargent, or McEvoy, or William Nicholson, it singles out those traits in their work which we tend to deplore. It looks, almost, as if the master-qualities of Edwardian life did not adapt themselves to art, even if a sympathetic eye can glimpse them at their best in Wilson Steer's handling of landscape and Charles Wellington Furse's approach to the well-favoured young. Or is it, also, that our native art, over the years 1901–10, looks feeble and unadventurous when set beside what was going on at that time across the Channel—in Paris, in Dresden, and in Munich?

A first answer is that not 'the times', but the dynasty, was out of joint. Had Queen Victoria died at 70 we should point with pride to the evidence in the 1890's of a youth and vigour altogether appropriate to a new reign: to the great crowds at the Whistler exhibition of 1892, to the apparition of the 'Beggarstaff Brothers' (James Pryde and William Nicholson, not at all outclassed by Chéret, Steinlen, and Toulouse-Lautrec at the poster exhibition at the

Royal Aquarium, Westminster, in 1894), and to the foundation of the International Society in 1898, with Whistler as its president and Degas, Manet, Monet, and Renoir as contributors to its first exhibition. And had King Edward lived to be 75, we could have recorded the first London showings of Picasso (1912) and Brancusi (1913), the formation in 1911 of the Camden Town Group, which was to set one of the main directions of English painting for the next forty years, the development of Gaudier-Brzeska, Wyndham Lewis, Bomberg and C. R. W. Nevinson, the publication of Clive Bell's *Art*, and the establishment in 1914 of the London Group, which was to give Matthew Smith, among others, his first London showing in 1916. Had all this occurred under, and been coextensive with, a single reign, historians could remark on the transformation of English art over the twenty-five years in question, and some part of the credit might well be ascribed to the robust, adventurous, and Frenchy appetites of the monarch himself. As it is, the art and the art-life of the Edwardian era stop where they began: in mid-movement.

It cannot be said that during the Edwardian era living art of the kind which we now admire was supported either by royalty, or by the upper classes, or by the government. In the year 1909, for in-stance, artists must have read with weary resignation of the over-mantel on which Arthur Balfour, then leader of the Opposition, had just spent £1,000. This represented 'The Hesperides' and was carried out by Alexander Fisher in 'gold, silver, bronze, steel and labradorite'. (The commission came, be it noted, from the man who, in the words of an eminent contemporary, 'was of all men the least able to bring his intellect down to what he no doubt considered the low level of the King's'.) From the memoirs of Sir Lionel Cust it is clear that although King Edward did not set out to be a collector on the scale of Charles I, George III, or George IV, or to direct taste in the manner to which his father had aspired, he did none the less take an active interest in the task, then long overdue, of re-distributing the royal collections. In many particulars these had remained undis-turbed since the death of the prince consort, and it was Lionel Cust's duty to put them into presentable order, and get them into present-able condition, after forty or more years of almost total neglect. In this he could count on the active participation of the king. 'King Edward liked to supervise everything himself,' he said later, 'enjoying nothing so much in the intervals of leisure as sitting in a roomful of workmen and giving directions in person. "Offer it up", he would say, "and I will come to see", and when he came he said Yes or No at once. He had a quick, trained instinct for what was right and what pleased him. "I do not know much about Ar-r-r-t", he would say with the characteristic rolling of his R's, "but I think I know something about Ar-r-r-r-angement." '

King Edward's reign was also notable for a practice which, if followed by his successors, would have caused Braque, Bonnard, Dufy, and Matisse to be given the run of Windsor Castle. 'King Edward', Sir Lionel tells us, 'was genuinely proud of his magnificent inheritance in the way of pictures, furniture and works of art, and enjoyed showing them off personally to his friends. In Paris, as Prince of Wales, he had got to know some of the leading spirits in the world of the arts, and, as King, he invited some of them to pay him a visit at Windsor Castle.' Those thus honoured included Rodin, Léon Bonnat, and Edouard Detaille, whose portrait of King Edward at a review of a Highland regiment at Aldershot had been put in the state dining-room at Windsor. Altogether, therefore, it would be a mistake to underrate the king's interventions in matters of art; and one such, unique in its kind, occurred in the first months of his reign.

The Royal Academy: J. S. Sargent

In that early summer of 1901 there was no doubt where art had its headquarters. The summer exhibition of the Royal Academy was still the great event of the year, and the P.R.A., Sir Edward Poynter, was also (till 1904) the director of the National Gallery. A privileged minority might have seen some of the pictures earlier in the year, at one of the half-dozen studios that really counted: but for most people the first week-end in May was the climacteric of the year. Certainly *The Times* left its readers in no doubt of the importance of the occasion. Four articles, totalling in all some 14,000 words, were allocated to the summer exhibition; and in 1901 the critic of the day was able to report a unique instance of royal intervention in the minutiae of the exhibition. The place of honour on the west wall of gallery III was reserved, that year, for a single picture: Benjamin Constant's memorial portrait of Queen Victoria. Readers perhaps gave Constant the benefit of the doubt of his rather cursory acquaintance with the dead queen when they read that the placing and arrangement of the portrait (which was decked out with black and purple hangings) had been 'chosen and directed' by King Edward VII himself.

Benjamin Constant's fame has given way, in our own time, before that of his namesake, the author of *Adolphe*; but in 1901 he was very kindly regarded and no one was heard to complain that a British artist might have been chosen more fittingly to commemorate a British queen. The show as a whole might, in any case, have been designed as a tribute to the painter-queen, for not a room was without some reference to her death. Comment upon these manifestations was of a kind that bore out Lady Eastlake's comment in her diary of nearly half a century earlier. 'The British public', she noted 'has scarcely advanced above the lowest step of the aesthetic ladder— the estimate of a subject.' John Charlton, for instance, had sent in a painstaking account of Queen Victoria's funeral procession, '2nd February, 1901': and *The Times* regretted that in this praiseworthy work the artist had not quite done justice to 'the extraordinary expression, as of one far withdrawn from the actual world, of the German Emperor'. Only one artist was above criticism on this, or any other ground: John Singer Sargent. Such, indeed, was Sargent's prestige in Edwardian times that he might be accorded just that identification with the adjective which I earlier left open. But Sargent was arguably never better than when he painted Madame Gautreau, as early as 1883; he had been A.R.A. since 1894 and R.A. since 1897; and although his portrait-production thinned out very much from 1908 onwards he was a great favourite with the English public up to and after his death in 1925. It would be absurd to rate as Edwardian an artist who lingers in history for pictures dated 1881 (Vernon Lee), 1884 (Robert Louis Stevenson), 1889 (Ellen Terry as Lady Macbeth), and 1913 (Henry James).

And yet it was surely with Sargent in mind that *The Times* wrote in 1902 that 'the finest pictures in the world, since the decline of religious art, have been portraits'. This was the year in which Rodin spoke of Sargent as 'the Van Dyck of our times'; and although Sargent saw himself at that period as afflicted with 'an extreme case of Wertheimerism', his portraits of the Wertheimer family, which were spread over the years 1898–1905, represent a unique contribution to the iconography of Edwardianism. The Sitwell family (1900),

XXIX. 'The Council of the Royal Academy' by Hubert von Herkomer 1907

XXX. 'Homage to Manet' by William Orpen 1909

Lord Ribblesdale (1902), Lord Londonderry with page (1904), Sir Hugh Lane (1906), Lady Astor (1908), are valuable documents; but the Wertheimer portraits could not have been carried out—could indeed, with difficulty have been conceived—at any other period. Earlier, there might have entered into the adventure a satirical note such as marked Trollope's *The Way We Live Now*; later, a generalized flattery would have softened the portrayal. Sargent alone, with his capacity to get close in to the sitter, his vivid but never censorious social sense, his feeling for exuberance and pride, could have produced these paintings. Our own age has shown good judgement in rating high the copies after Velazquez which Sargent produced in 1879; for no painter profited more richly from the enthusiasm for all things Spanish which prompted, among other pertinent productions, R. A. M. Stevenson's book on Velazquez (1899), and William Rothenstein's on Goya (1900).

One of Sargent's greatest charms, for Edwardian society, was his ability to give new money a good opinion of itself. The new rich, in his work, are as good as anyone else and in some ways better: more vivid, one could say, more keenly aware of the excitement of being alive. Quicker than the Home Office, he naturalized those who would otherwise have lingered in a between-world where class, nationality, money, and money's provenance, were matters not to be raised without a qualm. For the reassurance-collector there was no other painter in the country. Success in Edwardian society was measured, after all, in terms of immediate effect and palpable reward; and Laurence Housman made the point when he wrote in 1910 that 'Sargent worships Nature with a tomahawk, and when he returns from the shrine he has the scalp of the goddess hanging at his girdle. If art is merely an expression of the passion to possess, to dominate, to control, then Mr. Sargent is the most complete artist the world has ever seen.'

Galleries, Dealers, and Prices

Those who did not take Sargent at this valuation and were even, perhaps, rather sceptical of the Royal Academy itself had few of the opportunities which they enjoy today. A society like the New English Art Club has an honoured place in the history of art, but it did not break into the general consciousness until, in February 1906, Agnew's had a show of paintings by members of the club and

thus gave them, as it were, the freedom of the west end. Private
galleries were relatively few; and whereas today most galleries are
regarded as half-asleep if they fail to mount a new exhibition every
three weeks the Edwardian was tempted, year in, year out, by a
stock that seems not to have greatly changed from one season to the
next. In May 1901, for instance, you would have had to scour the
west end to find, by way of novelty, an exhibition of water-
colours by Helen Allingham with which to distract yourself from
memories of the Royal Academy. At Colnaghi's there were etchings
by Seymour Haden, at Tooth's paintings by Alma-Tadema, Briton
Rivière, and Dendy Sadler, and etchings (rare plates, however) by
Meissonier. Elsewhere it would have been a long and dusty walk that
revealed anything more startling than a popular biblical painting
('Admission one shilling, including book') or a group of eighteenth-
century English portraits. But in November of that first year of the
reign Robert Ross bought the Carfax Gallery in Bury Street: his
first exhibition was of 'One Hundred Caricatures by Max Beerbohm'.
The Carfax was not, of course, the only gallery in London to have
rewarding exhibitions in Edwardian times, but it had a note of
independence and fine judgement which made it influential out of
all proportion to its size: it was, in fact, the forerunner of the 'little
gallery' which, since the days (1908 onwards) of D.-H. Kahn-
weiler's *boutique* in the rue Vignon, has been the place to look for
what is newest and most stimulating in art. Where earlier generations had called for the apparatus of grandeur before they could be
tempted to buy, settling for nothing less than a staircase hand-
railed with velvet, a frock-coated attendant, and a palm in a pot,
the twentieth century came in with something like today's
delicious dens.

Not that London had ever lacked distinguished dealers. He would
have been a bold man, for instance, who ranked Sir William Agnew,
Bt., as a mere tradesman, or did not feel that when Sir William
bid at Christie's on behalf of the National Gallery he was hardly
less august than that gallery itself. Paul and Dominic Colnaghi
have an honoured place in British art-history—not least for their
encouragement of Constable—and both Parker and Ackermann
have survived, in name at any rate, from the eighteenth century.
But these were dealers with an establishment: premises, exhibitions,
catalogues, archives, auxiliaries, and henchmen. Edwardian times

saw the apotheosis, in the person of Hugh Lane, of the single-handed dealer, the inspired 'eye' whose sole establishment was his own insights. A long life and the arts of biography have made Duveen the most famous of this century's dealers, while Lane is remembered above all for the unhappy ambiguity of his testamentary dispositions; but to the historian there is something distinctly, specifically Edwardian in Lane's character, career, tastes, and way of life.

The people who really count in art are, of course, the people who make it. ('Sir Hugh Lane has been knighted for admiring Manet', said Sickert in 1909. 'Would he have been knighted for merely *being* Manet?') But there is much to be said for a man who took the taste of the day, as Hugh Lane did, and pulled it twenty or thirty years forward with his own hands. Neither Manet nor Renoir was unknown when, in 1905, Lane bought the 'Eva Gonzalez', the 'Musique aux Tuileries', and the 'Parapluies' from Durand-Ruel in Paris. But in England it was still unthinkable that their work should be ranked, as Lane ranked it, with that of the old masters. Orpen's 'Homage to Manet', painted in the rooms which Lane then had next to Orpen's studio in the Boltons, shows Lane with his friends George Moore, Henry Tonks, Wilson Steer, Walter Sickert, and D. S. MacColl; and no document of the times more vividly illustrates both the new acceptance of the French impressionists and the ease with which Lane, then in his middle thirties, had made himself the prized familiar of the superior spirits of the day. The delicate product of an unhappy home, he started at Colnaghi's at a wage of £1 a week, moved in February 1898 to a front room at No. 2 Pall Mall, made £10,000 in two years, shut up shop (in the strict sense) for ever, and lived for the rest of his brief life as the 'gentleman dealer' *par excellence*. Inspired judgement and the gift of persuasion were his assets, but he had not at all the front of brass which some of his successors and emulators have thought necessary to success. His habits were simple (an early visitor to his palace in Cheyne Walk found him dining off bread and Bovril) and his nervosity such that he had often to take a glass of brandy before one of his own tea-parties; but even when, with the advance of his fortunes, he could balance the pictures on his wall with a bookcase designed by Kent for Lord Burlington and an octagonal table designed by Chippendale for Queen Charlotte—even then he remained in all his personal relations *une âme bien née*; nor was there, until the arrival of Samuel Courtauld, anyone comparable to him in the scale and timeliness of his additions to our holdings of modern art.

People were spending, meanwhile, on other sorts of pictures: and spending a great deal of money too. The idea has recently got about that never in the history of the art-market have prices been as high, and as indiscriminately high, as they are today. But the error of this can soon be proved by reference to the auction-prices of Edwardian days. The prices must, of course, be adjusted to real-money values: when we read, for instance, that 7,700 guineas were paid at Christie's in 1908 for a very small oil-painting by Turner we must remember that this was at a time when a decent single room in a London hotel cost 7s. a night and a very passable meal could be got in Soho for 1s. 6d. If we make this indispensable adjustment it will soon be clear that at no subsequent time have pictures of the British school been as expensive or living British artists commanded a comparably high price. Of the European old masters it is harder to speak, partly because modern standards of scholarship are more exacting than those of sixty-five years ago, and partly because auction-prices, then as now, represent only a small proportion of the total volume of trade; but if we consider that the 'Arundel Holbein' cost £72,000 when Colnaghi's sold it to the National Gallery in 1909, and Velazquez's 'Rokeby Venus' £45,000 when the recently formed National Art-Collections Fund secured it from Agnew's in 1906, it will again be clear, given the necessary adjustment, that these are prices not lower than today's. (We should also, in such cases, allow for the very greatly increased rarity, in today's conditions, of pictures of comparable quality.)

Every age had velleities incomprehensible to its successors. The Edwardians loved portraits, as we have already seen—to the extent, indeed, that they were willing to pay almost as much for engravings after the English eighteenth-century masters as ourselves would pay for the originals. Valentine Green's engravings after Sir Joshua more than once fetched over £1,000 at Christie's during the period under review, and among Green's colleagues T. Watson was known to go over £900 at auction. For the portraits themselves, prices were again very high, even if it was only at the end of the period that the name of Duveen began to appear with any regularity in the records of the sale-rooms. A pastel by John

Russell fetched 1,550 guineas in 1901; Romney's 'Miss Sarah Rodbard' 10,500 guineas in June 1902; Gainsborough's 'Maria Walpole' 12,100 guineas in 1904; Raeburn's portrait of Lady Raeburn 8,700 guineas in the following year; and his 'Lady Janet Traill' 14,000 guineas in 1911. Reynolds's prices remained very high even when his subject-pieces were in question: his 'Venus and a Piping Boy' would hardly fetch today the equivalent of 4,600 guineas; and as for Raeburn, if we pursue him into 1912, and find that Duveen was then paying 21,200 guineas at Christie's for the 'Mrs. Hay' from the Charles Wertheimer collection, we may well wonder whether, *mutatis mutandis*, that picture would fetch a tenth of that price today.

At a time when Sickert's top price, for his exhibition at the Carfax Gallery as late as 1912, was 60 guineas, Lavery could ask £1,000 for a landscape; and those who had paid £2,750 for Fred Walker's 'Harbour of Refuge', 1,500 guineas for Dagnan-Bouveret's 'The Vaccination', £3,390 for Van Marcke's 'Cattle by a Stream', 2,250 guineas for Leighton's 'Cymon and Iphigenia', 1,900 guineas for Mason's 'The Gander', and between £2,500 and £3,500 for pictures by Matthew and Jacob Maris, Mauve, Diaz, and l'Hermitte were well pleased with their bargains. No one can doubt that our own time has seen purchases even less well founded; but the point is that the Edwardians were not operating as we are, in an age in which the high-priced work of art is almost the only remaining form of ostentation still sanctioned by society.

Every age needs to feel itself great, and in promoting this feeling may well estimate its own major figures at a level from which posterity will hasten to drag them down. The Edwardian age was no exception to this, and its admiration for Brangwyn has been confirmed in our own day by only a few faithful supporters. Yet Brangwyn had several at least of the attributes of greatness: the colossal output, for instance, the rapid adjustment to whatever scale and subject were demanded of him, the indifference to what other people were doing, the high sense of adventure. One admirer wrote of him that he 'preferred life behind the mast to life behind William Morris', and the phrase does suggest something of Brangwyn's majestic and insubordinate nature.

Brangwyn came, too, at a time when people still believed in the *grande machine* as the supreme test of the artist. This was a belief which, paramount in the nineteenth century, persisted even in the

1920's, when it was taken for granted that Stanley Spencer's 'Resurrection' and Augustus John's huge decorations were those artists' chief claim to enduring fame. First consecrated in the 1840's and 1850's at the time of Dyce's monumental, if fugitive, contribution to the painting of fresco in England, this belief was rampant in Edwardian times and caused Brangwyn to be given commissions which, though now forgotten, were much talked of at the time. These included the four panels illustrative of 'English Industry' which were shown in Venice in 1905 and are now in the Leeds City Art Gallery; a large panel, 'Modern Commerce', for the Royal Exchange; the eleven panels carried out between 1904 and 1909 for the Skinners' Hall on subjects drawn from the history of the Skinners' Company; and 'The Introduction of European Civilization into the Country of the Red Indian', a frieze executed for the offices of the Canadian National Grand Trunk Railway in Cockspur Street, London. Time has not dealt kindly with these works, but the generous instinct behind them can still be deciphered; and to all but a handful of the art-public of the time it would have seemed inconceivable that they would one day be discounted in favour of easel-pictures insignificant in size and unaccompanied by any of the apparatus of 'greatness'.

Outwardly, that apparatus was still intact in Edwardian times. Only now, from a great distance, do we know that it was already meaningless and that what then seemed to be the laurels of immortality were, in fact, so many fateful encumbrances. We remember quite different portents: we remember, for instance, an entry in Charles Ricketts's diary for February 1901: 'We dined with Rothenstein, who showed us the drawings of a Slade student named John. They show, besides the influence of Rothenstein and even Shannon, the study of Rembrandt's drawings, and quite a serious evidence of ability and facility. We bought two.' We also remember the Saturday afternoons in Fitzroy Street, five or six years later, when Sickert and his friends were at home to a small body of sympathizers and their work would be bought for sums so trifling that Lady Cunard was spoken of as a plunger when she spent £40 on a Sickert, and Morton Sands found few to admire his prescience in building up a Sickert collection which was later to be the envy of us all. And we remember, finally, that on 13 March 1905 Bernard Shaw wrote to Robert Ross:

By the way there is a young American sculptor named Jacob Epstein, of 219 Stanhope Street, N.W., who has come to London with amazing drawings of human creatures like withered trees embracing. He has a commendatory letter from Rodin; and when I advised him to get commissions for busts of railway directors he repudiated me with such utter scorn that I relented and promised to ask you to look at his portfolio. It is a bad case of helpless genius in the first blaze of youth: and the drawings are queer and Rodinesque enough to be presentable at this particular moment. . . . There may be something in him.

'There may be something in him' has been, ever since, the phrase that really counts, from the people who really count, in the advancement of any young artist. The days of the grand frontal assault upon the public have gone—had already gone, perhaps, in Edwardian times—and in their place is the semi-clandestine system of recommendation by letter, or by word of mouth, or by the deft planting of one small canvas in a mixed exhibition. But if this was, as it may have been, an Edwardian invention it was well covered by that other Edwardian speciality, the huge miscellaneous exhibition. Strictly speaking, this was an innovation of the 1890's: one should record, for instance, the poster exhibition at the Royal Aquarium, Westminster, in 1894, the International Society's first show at Prince's Skating Rink, Knightsbridge, in 1898, and the Glasgow exhibition of nineteenth-century art in 1900; but in the 1900's the heavy work of breaking through on a broad, as opposed to an individual, front was done by exhibitions conceived and executed *en masse*. Instances of this were the show at Wolverhampton in May 1902 which revealed the 'new English school' as constituted by Steer, Orpen, Tonks, Rothenstein, Conder, William Nicholson, Fry, Clausen, Ricketts, Shannon, John, and Strang; the Durand-Ruel show, in 1905, of modern French painting up to and including Cézanne; the first Allied Artists show at the Albert Hall in 1908, and its successors in 1909 and 1910; and, of course, the first post-impressionist exhibition at the Grafton Gallery in 1910.

These exhibitions were formidable affairs. For the Allied Artists' inaugural show in 1908 there were 3,061 items in the catalogue, not counting the auxiliary section from Russia. The catalogue covered 165 pages and the hanging committee included Sickert, James Pryde, Walter Crane, Augustus John, Lucien Pissarro, and Spencer Gore. The initiator and secretary was Frank Rutter, the art critic of the

Sunday Times. Unexpected exhibitors included Clive Bell and C. H. Collins Baker, and the scale of prices in 1908–9 is an interesting indication of Edwardian prestiges: Lavery, at £1,000, towered above Pryde (£350), J. D. Fergusson (£150), Kandinsky (£50), Gore (£20), and Robert Bevan (£15).

Slade Graduates: Jacob Epstein

Behind much—some would say, behind all—of the best Edwardian art there lay that great forcing-house, the Slade School. Here again, the great generation should be back-dated to the 1890's: perhaps 1894, the year of Augustus John's arrival, would be a point as apt as any at which to announce the Slade's ascendancy among English art-schools. But when we consider that in Edwardian times Matthew Smith, Duncan Grant, Vanessa Bell, C. R. W. Nevinson, Gilbert and Stanley Spencer, William Roberts, and Mark Gertler were among the students of the Slade there is clearly no reason to speak of a decline in its influence. The Slade was predominantly a drawing-school. Nothing can quite counter the notion—to which Stanley Spencer, for one, remained true all his life—that painting, for the Slade, was a matter of tinting the finished drawing as thinly as possible. Augustus John described how the tone was set. 'The student was first introduced to the Antique Room, which is furnished with numerous casts of late Greek, Greco-Roman and Italian Renaissance sculpture; no Archaic Greek, no Oriental, no "Gothic" examples were to be seen. The student was set to draw with a stick of charcoal, a sheet of "Michelet" paper and a chunk of bread for rubbing out.' Not everyone thrived in these conditions. (Matthew Smith, for one, remembered the Slade, and Henry Tonks in particular, with loathing.) But for every super-sensitive student there were a hundred who, in the words of Tonks's biographer, 'felt that they had come to a school where masterpieces *must* be the rule'. Those who arrived in Edwardian times were reminded that the students of the nineties had included Augustus John, Orpen, Ambrose McEvoy, Spencer Gore, J. D. Innes, and Wyndham Lewis. Local patriotism was intense—Tonks later ranked John as 'the greatest draughtsman England had ever produced' and kept a reproduction of his drawing of T. E. Lawrence always in his pocket—and in Edwardian times there was a feeling that the graduates of the Slade were destined by Nature to take over the direction of English

XXXI. 'Gauguins and Connoisseurs' by Spencer F. Gore 1911

XXXII. 'The Café Royal' by Charles Ginner 1911

art. At the time (1905) of Durand-Ruel's show, at the Grafton
Gallery, of French impressionist painting, there were many who
remembered Steer's remark in 1891. 'Impressionism', he had said,
'is of no country and no period; it has been from the beginning; it
bears the same relation to painting that poetry does to journalism.'
Altogether the triumvirate of Tonks, Fred Brown, and Wilson
Steer was by far the most influential in English art-education. It
was, none the less, an 1890-ish influence. 'I cannot teach what I
don't believe in', Tonks said later; 'I shall resign if this talk of
cubism doesn't cease: it is killing me.' That talk did not, of course
spread widely until after the end of the Edwardian era; but there
were signs, long before that, of dissatisfaction with the autocracy
of the Slade. Artistic monopolies are invariably disastrous, and
although the graduates of the Slade were diverse enough in themselves London needed to have one or two startling outsiders to
galvanize its art-life as Picasso, Gris, Chagall, Soutine, and Modigli-
ani were to galvanize the Ecole de Paris. Yet in estimating London
art-life in Edwardian times it should be remembered that Sickert
lived abroad till 1905 and that Epstein might never have come to
London at all. He tells us in his memoirs that he felt that after three
years in Paris he had come to 'a dead end'; and although London
was his first choice his initial sojourn in Camden Town turned out
badly. Discouraged, he began to destroy all the work in his studio
and, again on impulse, took passage to New York. After a stay of
only a week or two he returned to London, took a studio in Fulham,
made friends with Augustus John, Muirhead Bone, Francis Dodd,
and others, studied intensively in the British Museum, and within
two years was offered an immense and fateful commission for the
new British Medical Association building in the Strand. This resulted
in the first of his almost lifelong embroilments with English public
opinion.

A polite sympathy, such as Shaw had already manifested, might
have remained the agreed attitude of those connoisseurs who had
seen Epstein's drawings for Whitman's *Calamus* or his illustrations
for H. Hapgood's *Spirit of the Ghetto*. But nothing so tentative would
do for the eighteen enormous figures which Epstein carved for the
B.M.A. building. Their programme was a simple one: to represent
'man and woman in their various stages from birth to old age'; and
the general intention of the work was well put by C. J. Holmes when

he said that the sculptor 'had turned back from our tired and sweetened adaptations of late Greek ideals to the stern vigour of the pre-Pheidian epoch'. ('Pre-Adamite' was the adjective which Epstein himself preferred.) This interpretation was called forth by a front-page article in the *Evening Standard and St. James's Gazette* for 19 June 1908, in which Epstein's figures were stigmatized as 'a form of statuary which no careful father would wish his daughter, and no discriminating young man his fiancée, to see'. Holmes's defence of the figures was taken up by many qualified persons, among them Sir Charles Holroyd, director of the National Gallery, who said among other things that 'I believe the B.M.A. will be proud of having given him this work to do, in the future when he has made the name for himself which his work promises.' After lengthy controversy of a kind which even today is not extinct the order was given for the work of installation to continue, and the *British Medical Journal* summed up the whole affair when it wrote, 'We are glad that a sculptor of genius awoke one morning to find himself famous, but we are sorry and not a little ashamed that he should owe the foundations of his fame to the hypocrisy with which other countries, and not without reason, reproach the British people.'

Epstein was supported, *una voce*, by all the artists whose opinion he could have valued. But this did not affect either the humiliation which left a lasting mark upon him or the petty exasperations of which Augustus John in a letter to Robert Ross gives us a glimpse. 'Of course the sculptures would stand the *moral* test as triumphantly as the artistic, or even more, if possible. Meanwhile Epstein is in debt and unable to pay the workmen.' These were the conditions which prompted Epstein to believe that the London art-world was infested with 'log-rollers, schemers, sharks, opportunists, profiteers, snobs, parasites, sycophants, camp-followers, social climbers, and "four-flushers"'.

Erroneous as it is to suppose that every artist of consequence must suffer misunderstanding and revilement, many of those who now seem to us to have 'come through' triumphantly were not always given an easy passage in Edwardian times. Sickert, for instance, could take care of himself as well as any painter in history; but even he had to contend with people like Sir William Blake Richmond, who wrote of him (in private, admittedly) as 'an advertiser, who is as pleased by being blamed as praised' and

thought his work 'not worthy of a single drop of ink either one way
or the other'. As for Augustus John, he was the victim, already in
his twenties, of his own legend. George Moore wrote in the *Saturday
Review* in June 1906 that 'John is the wonder of Chelsea, the
lightning draftsman [*sic*], the only man living for whom drawing
presents no difficulty whatever.' Such judgements could only injure
a young artist whose tendency was, in effect, to take things a little
too easily. In 1905 Walter Bayes, in his review of the New English
Art Club's annual exhibition, had said of two of John's large
figure-paintings that they were 'unintelligible through accidents of
drying. John has patched and mended his pictures, repainted them
in bits at all stages of half-dryness, and apparently trusted to luck
to dry them together satisfactorily. . . .' 'Sargent', Bayes went on,
'is the tempter who has lured these men into trying the kind of
painting that is finished at a rush.'

Sargent and the people who liked him did, undoubtedly, make
things difficult for painters of a different persuasion. A modified
version of Stendhal's 'happy few' sympathizers began to be coveted
by those who could not thrive in Sargent's own world. Perhaps, they
thought, it was by fending for oneself that, in the words of one of
Keats's sonnets to Haydon,

> Oft may be found a 'singleness of aim',
> That ought to frighten into hooded shame
> A money-mong'ring, pitiable brood.

And one way of fending for themselves was to show their pictures
privately, as they did at Sickert's Saturday afternoons in Fitzroy
Street. In retrospect these seem to the enthusiast one of the most
important single artistic manifestations of the Edwardian era, but
it would be delusory to suppose that they made much of a mark
at the time. Apart from their other merits—from the individual
stature, that is to say, of the artists involved—they represented
a first attempt at something very close to Sickert's heart: the 'no-
jury' exhibition, at which artists could show what they liked. The
Allied Artists' Association embodied this idea in macrocosm, but it
was in Fitzroy Street that one could find exemplified the converse of
the opinion once advanced by Sickert: that 'a glance round the
walls of any New English Art Club exhibition does certainly not
give us the sensation of a page torn from the book of life'. To give

that sensation, and give it without interference, was a most un-Edwardian ambition: but it was what Sickert intended, and with him were the friends and colleagues who now strike us as the *élite* of their day—Bevan, Gilman, Gore, Lucien Pissarro, Ginner, Drummond. The Camden Town Group, as such, was not founded until after the death of King Edward VII, but in the last months of his reign it was announced in the *New Age* that a 'London Group' had been formed: the artists concerned were Bevan, Gilman, Gore, Pissarro, John, Albert Rutherston, Sickert, and the two marvellous and distinctive ladies who were to be a part of the London, and the Dieppe, art-world for the next half a century: Nan Hudson and Ethel Sands.

Just how this group was metamorphosed into the Camden Town Group is a matter for the historian of a later reign, for the crucial moment was the winter of 1910–11—the period, that is to say, at which the first post-impressionist exhibition was on view and the shortcomings of the New English Art Club (and, for that matter, of Sickert himself) were manifested. Critics have tried to suggest that this period was, chronology notwithstanding, Edwardian in essence; but it seems to me to differ entirely in tone from the one with which we are concerned. The Camden Town Group was composed of men who had travelled and been changed thereby: the true Edwardian painter was the man who, like Steer, had studied in Paris (as long ago, in his case, as 1882–4), but would have regarded Steer's own 'Chepstow Castle' (1905), 'Violet Hammersley' (1907), and 'The End of the Chapter' (1911) as paintings pre-eminently *dans la bonne voie*. There is, in Steer's best pictures, an Elgarian fatness and fullness in the paint which may strike us as the purest Edwardianism. Edwardian art cannot fairly be post-dated '1911' or '1912': it should be allowed to take its chance as it really was, in the oils and water-colours of Steer, the etchings and drawings of Muirhead Bone, the genre-pieces of William Strang, one or two bedazzlements by Orpen, and a rigorous choice of earlyish works by Augustus John. Add to these the enormous body of anecdotal works which was produced, year by year, and discussed as gravely as if it had been by Wilkie or Frith at their best, and you will be nearer to Edwardian art than you would be by reading *Blast* and the *New Age* and thinking piously backwards. There are discoveries to be made, even now, in the art here adumbrated.

The Public Collections

The Edwardian age saw the beginnings of two institutions which have done much to lubricate the otherwise stiff and awkward relationship between private goodwill and our public museums and galleries. These are the National Art-Collections Fund, founded in 1903, and the Contemporary Art Society, founded in 1910. The great public collection, in Europe, was a creation of the late nineteenth century; and nowhere was civic pride more active in such matters than in Berlin, where the growth of the Kaiser-Friedrichs-Museum was a matter for international admiration—and perhaps, a little, for international concern. (Such was the importance of Berlin to the art-trade that Thomas Agnew & Sons opened a branch there in 1910.) The Kaiser-Friedrichs-Museum-Verein was one of the models—the other being the Amis du Louvre—which inspired the formation of the National Art-Collections Fund, whose inaugural committee included Roger Fry, D. S. MacColl, Claude Phillips, M. H. Spielmann, and Robert Witt, under the chairmanship of Lord Crawford. By the end of 1903 it had 308 members, that figure was doubled within two years, and at the third annual general meeting the company was addressed by Bernard Shaw, whose speech remains unique in the annals of the fund. After upbraiding the moneyed section of society for its extravagance in hotels 'where they may be seen from Friday to Tuesday in evening dress, eating dinners in the evening instead of the middle of the day', he went on to say that 'we must continually remind our rich classes not only that we want more money but that they owe it to us'. Church-going, he added, was more amusing than the theatre, and cheaper, and it would leave them with more money to spare for art.

The N.A.C.F. could have done with a good deal of money in its first years, for after a courteous gesture to the memory of Whistler, whose 'Nocturne in Blue and Silver' was purchased in 1905, there began that series of old master crises which, even today, is by no means at an end. In 1906 Velazquez's 'Rokeby Venus' had to be saved for the nation at a cost of £45,000, and three years later Sidney Colvin announced that there was a grave risk that the 'Arundel Holbein', the portrait of Christina, Duchess of Milan, would be sold abroad. The picture was eventually bought from Colnaghi's for £72,000 and was given to the National Gallery on King Edward's birthday, 9 November 1909: an event which made Colvin feel, in his own words, 'like Dante, when having climbed out of the Inferno, he saw before him the stars—*E quindi uscimmo a riveder le stelle*'.

The N.A.C.F. did, in 1906, buy William Strang's portrait of Henry Newbolt, but in general its gaze was directed towards the accepted masterworks of periods already far distant. For living art, the Chantrey Bequest had existed since 1875: 100,000 guineas in consols, the income from which was to be spent on the purchase of paintings and sculptures executed within the shores of Great Britain. The execution of Chantrey's wishes was then entirely in the hands of the Royal Academy, and the results were regarded as unsatisfactory by a great many good judges. 'The moral is plain', wrote D. S. MacColl in the *Saturday Review* in June 1904: 'so long as the Chantrey Bequest is in the hands of a purely academical body, the management will be the same—ignorant, interested, and lazy: either a reforming of the Academy that will make it representative is called for, or the placing of the Trust in disinterested hands.'

When a select committee was appointed to inquire, that same summer, into the administration of the Chantrey trust, MacColl was pressed to define the implications of the words 'interested' and 'disinterested' in the context of his article. But more telling even than his sturdy refusal to climb down was the fact that not since 1891 had the trustees bought a picture outside the Academy. (And, as another witness put it, 'the people in London who never visit exhibitions, with a very few exceptions, are the members of the Royal Academy'.) MacColl's evidence is remarkable also for a question which was put to him by the Earl of Carlisle. 'On your conscience as a man of honour, will you have the hardihood to say that the works of Degas, Monet, Pissarro, and Rodin are things the testator would have looked upon as works of the highest merit and most likely to encourage a School of Art in Great Britain?' To this MacColl replied, 'Certainly. You must suppose the testator to be a continuing being.'

But 'a continuing being' was precisely what most people refused to be, even during their own lifetimes, in relation to living art. The purchases made by the Chantrey trustees were for the most part so ludicrous that no freak of taste, however extreme, has brought them back into favour. Meanwhile those who felt, even confusedly, that an important era in art was at hand began to wonder whether an alternative method of recruitment to our public collections could not be devised. These were the circumstances in which the Contemporary Art Society was founded. As its inaugural meeting was held twelve days after the death of King Edward VII it can be included here only because its momentum was generated some months before, and because its first committee-members included several whose names are by now familiar to readers of this chapter: Roger Fry, Clive Bell, Lady Ottoline Morrell, D. S. MacColl, Robert Ross, C. J. Holmes among them. During its first three years the C.A.S. acquired works by Augustus and Gwen John, Epstein, Sickert, Gill, Conder, William Nicholson, Derwent Lees, and Henry Lamb: we have only to compare these with the work acquired by our museums and galleries under other auspices to recognize that the Edwardian age had produced yet another institution which was to be of great value to British art.

The 'Burlington': Roger Fry

Named after a great connoisseur, and pioneered by two others, the *Burlington Magazine* cannot be left out of a survey of Edwardian art-life. The success of the *Connoisseur*, which was founded in 1902, led a number of people to wonder whether it would not be possible in an age of expanding interest in art to found a magazine mainly concerned with 'the serious and disinterested study of ancient art'. ('Serious' stood, no doubt, for the infant science of connoisseurship: 'disinterested', for a complete freedom from dealers' pressures.) The first issue of the *Burlington* in March 1903 was certainly disinterested, but whether it was entirely serious, by the standards of Morelli and Berenson, could be argued. Its editorial (presumably by Robert Dell, the first editor) harked back to Meredith's ideal of 'an Art at once purgative and tonic, which should work wonders by levigating [*sic*] gross humours and reducing fatty accretions'. Such an art, it was said, would 'reflect with an ordered and purposeful distortion our actual life'. After so stringent an exordium it is disappointing to find along with Berenson's study of Alunno di Domenico, articles on tinder-boxes, oriental carpets, and silver plate. Even the illustrated essay (drawings by F. L. Griggs) on Clifford's Inn can hardly have led to much 'levigation'.

Dated as it looks today, with the cover and lettering that were designed for it by Herbert Horne, the *Burlington* was, for the times, a luxurious publication, and it soon ran into financial difficulties.

One of Roger Fry's solidest, though least publicized, services to art-history was his single-handed resource at this trying period. (As the new editor, C. J. Holmes, said later: 'At every point money seemed to flow out; at none did any seem to come in.') Fry was undeterred: when he went to America he contrived to get substantial support, and by 1909 the magazine was showing a profit. Contributors had included no less a writer than Henry James; the consultative committee, then as now, was almost uncomfortably distinguished; and the *Burlington*'s determination to treat the best new art on an equal footing with the best old art did much to soften opinion which might otherwise have remained obdurate. It was, after all, in the *Burlington* in 1904 that Van Gogh was hailed as 'a great master'; and as the decade proceeded the cause of Cézanne, in particular, was taken up in terms which may well have astonished those who bought the magazine for the sake of the old masters only. In 1906, for instance, Fry said of the Cézannes at the International Society's exhibition that they displayed 'total indifference to those laws of appearance which the scientific theory of the impressionists pronounced to be essential'. And in March 1908 he set Cézanne above Monet, remarking on the 'great advance in intellectual content. It [Cézanne's work] leaves far less to the casual dictation of natural appearance.' And Fry's classic essay on 'Aesthetics', first printed in 1909, was by implication aimed at an art even more 'advanced', for the times, than that which was actually assembled for the first post-impressionist exhibition.

In considering that exhibition it is worth remembering that the Durand-Ruel show of 1905 at the Grafton Gallery was useful in drawing the enemy's fire: the accuracy of its artillery can be judged from *The Times*'s account of the show, where it was said of Degas that 'Never was there a painter who took the road of immortality with so little baggage', of Renoir that 'his faces are often something of a trial', and of Cézanne that his still lifes were a subject 'on which we need not dwell'. And yet this was a major survey of the subject, with 55 Manets, 59 Renoirs, 40 Pissarros, 36 Sisleys, 19 Monets, 13 Morisots, and 10 Cézannes. The battle of 'modern art' was by no means won, and even the Carfax Gallery hedged, some months later, by putting on a show in which B. W. Leader, Alma-Tadema, Macbeth, Sant, Frith, Briton Rivière, Tuke, and Herkomer were represented.

MOTHERHOOD IN EDWARDIAN SCULPTURE

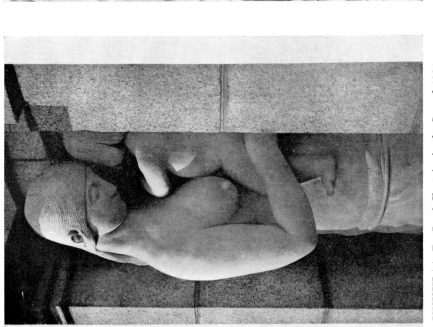

XXXIII (a). By Jacob Epstein, in the Strand 1908

XXXIII (b). By Thomas Brock, on the Victoria Memorial 1911

XXXIV. 'John Singer Sargent' by Max Beerbohm 1907

From our present distance in time it is easy enough to detect the shortcomings and inconsistencies of the first post-impressionist exhibition, which was opened at the Grafton Gallery on 8 November 1910. The art in question was not yet the subject of art-historical inquiry, even if its finest examples were already far beyond the reach of all but a wealthy collector. (One Cézanne was sold in 1910 to Helsinki for £800—the equivalent of about £5,000 in today's money.) The organization of the show had, moreover, none of that unsmiling intensity which we now expect of a major exhibition. (Desmond MacCarthy admitted that Roger Fry invited him to help him with the work, not because he had written a thesis on Cézanne, but 'because we were happy together'.) Roger Fry chose what he liked, or what he could get, and people came to see it: that was what the show amounted to. And, easy as it is to collect the errors of even reputable judges—Laurence Binyon, for instance, thought that the Seurats were 'cold-blooded puerilities' and that nothing anywhere in the show could compare with John's 'Smiling Woman'—it is more to the point to note the instances of shrewd judgement which abounded both among artists and among non-professional visitors. That same Binyon remarked of Picasso's 'Nude with Basket of Flowers', later to become the ornament of Gertrude Stein's Paris apartment, that it was 'painted and modelled with wonderful subtlety'; and from Spencer Gore's painting of the general scene it is clear that artists like John and Steer were absorbed students of the exhibition. And they were not blessed, after all, with half a century's hindsight; when they went along to the Grafton Gallery they were in part conditioned by the hierarchies of the day. Today's scholars reach for Cézanne and Gauguin as they reach for Giotto and Rembrandt, and find a documentation hardly less copious: but in 1910 it remained to be proved that these artists were as good as Aristide Sartorio or Anders Zorn, or their English admirers as gifted as Alfred Drury, author of the panels over the main entrance to the Victoria and Albert Museum, Sir Thomas Brock, sculptor of the Queen Victoria memorial in front of Buckingham Palace, F. H. S. Shepherd, master of the conversation-piece, or Algernon Talmage, poet-painter of the London scene. These, for the general public, were authentic alternatives, and it is to their credit that enough made the right choice for an observant novelist, Ada Leverson, to be able to say of one of her characters, already in 1912, that 'with all his gentle manner, he had in art an extraordinary taste for brutality and violence, and covered his rooms with pictures by futurists and cubists, wild studies by wild men from Tahiti and a curious collection of savage ornaments and weapons'.

Roger Fry's name has so overborne those of his colleagues on the executive committee that it may be worth recalling that they included Lionel Cust, keeper of the King's Pictures and director of the National Portrait Gallery, C. J. Holmes, Lady Ottoline Morrell, and Lord Henry Bentinck: more, here, of Establishment than of *avant-garde*. The legend of its extreme modernity could also be revised in the light of the catalogue which, though incomplete and full of errors, makes it clear that Gauguin, with 37 works, Cézanne with 21, and Van Gogh with 20 were by far the best represented artists. The two Seurat seascapes were works to which even Fry had yet to warm; Toulouse-Lautrec was not represented at all; and Manet's nine paintings, which included 'Un Bar aux Folies-Bergère', were a *point de départ* to which many visitors, armed with Duret's lately-translated *The Impressionist Painters*, would probably have been happy to return. The five Vlamincks, six Rouaults, three pictures apiece by Derain and Othon Friesz, even the two Picassos, would now seem a conservative choice from the production of the past ten years. Still, it was a brave affair: and one which, though not strictly within the Edwardian era, owed its impetus to forces generated within that era and its generous fulfilment to people who had come to the fore since the turn of the century.

9

ARCHITECTURE

JOHN BETJEMAN, C.B.E., HON. A.R.I.B.A.

ARCHITECTURE

In King Edward's reign most British people regarded architecture as an expensive luxury. They liked expensive luxuries. There was a less marked division between builder and architect professionally than there is today. I must draw a line, however, between the big names in the profession with their offices in London and the larger cities and the humbler 'architects and surveyors' who were sometimes employed by the speculative builders. Builders had on the whole more conscience than their forebears, who built back-to-back houses until as late as the 1870's, and their successors, who lined their pockets so well from the hideous private housing-estates that have appeared since 1920. John Burns's Housing and Town Planning Act of 1909 stipulated that houses should not be built more than twelve to the acre and, despite this, the speculators usually built in a solid manner.

Most people today would prefer a pre-1914 house or flat to one built in the between-wars period or later because, though there might be primitive plumbing and wasteful hall space, the walls would be soundproof and the fires would draw. Every city and town has its Railway Terrace and red-brick speculative row put up in Edwardian times. The local materials, whether stone or brick, were thought cheap and old fashioned, except by the sophisticated, and speculators favoured hard glazed red brick from Wales, which came at the end of the century, and blue Welsh slates for the roofs. The design and plan of the speculative villas had changed only in materials from their late-Victorian predecessors. Thus the influence of Norman Shaw's gables and glazing bars was often apparent as a cheap extra. The autumn of English civic building turned the outer fringes of our cities and towns red, a raw red that fifty years have not weathered.

Yet the difference in appearance of Edwardian Britain from Victorian Britain is much less great than the change which has occured since 1910. Roads were still cobbled or dusty; carts and carriages prevailed; motor-cars were rare and wonderful. People went by train and, in the cities, by electric tram. Trains were crowded and branch lines, with frequent services, prospered. Suburbs spread only as far as steam and electric transport could carry their favoured inhabitants. The centres of cities and towns were still thickly populated with poorer people who lived in courts and tenements behind the shops and among the warehouses. Far more houses were lit by gas than by electricity, and all villages were lit by oil, except for the big house whose owner might sometimes make his own electricity or have his acetylene gas plant. Entertainment was largely home-made, with drawing-room concerts or recitals in local halls: local Theatres of Variety were built in the larger towns; they, like the public houses with their polished brass, engraved glass, and enormous hanging outside lamps, were the resort of the poor and less respectable.

Though the industrial towns might be regarded as a painful necessity from which the more prosperous willingly journeyed to large villas in leafy suburbs, the general outlook throughout Great Britain was back toward an agricultural community. People looked back to the safe agricultural symbol of the village as the pattern of society with the squire in the big house, the rector in the next biggest, and the cottagers content with outside sanitation and with framed oleographs of the monarch from *Pears' Annual* and Goss china in the parlour. Most town-dwellers were only one, or at the most two, generations removed from the village. Villages still looked as they had done a century earlier and as they are seen to be depicted in the soft water-colours of 'Black's Colour Book', so popular in the Edwardian period. Lords and ladies were respected and local councils were less powerful and less politically divided. Suburbs were built on the village plan and their middle classes stratified into professional, manufacturer, wholesale, and retail, which not even the church could unite. Nonconformity went with trade, church with the professional and landowning classes. This bred a different type of scenery from the welfare state of today. It was more personal and ostentatious. The superhuman architecture of power conveyed by pylons from gigantic generating stations over the fields to the vast impersonal building estates with their cubes of workers' flats; the poles and the thick wires striding the remote villages; the roaring main roads with their filling stations, neo-Egyptian factories, and road houses and motels, were unimaginable. Architecture was an art, not a branch of economics and psychology, and as such was regarded as a luxury for the rich or the cranky. This attitude to architecture as a luxury survives today in those more retrograde local authorities which still refuse to employ an architect to lay out their estates or even design their houses. If Edwardian building and decoration from the cheapest speculative villa to the most expensive house or office may be summarized it is in the words 'conviction and display'.

Those who could afford the luxury of an architect may be divided into the people with the Kipling and Anthony Hope outlook and the people who admired Wells and Bernard Shaw: that is to say they either liked liners decorated inside in the Adam style by T. E. Collcutt, offices with board-rooms in the manner of Sir Christopher Wren, and country houses which looked as though they had been there for centuries, or they favoured conscious simplicity, the arts and crafts depicted in the *Studio*.

It is hard for us, comparatively near to the period, to appreciate what seems the ostentation of our grandfathers. I think this is best done by considering the architectural moods of the time and the different sorts of buildings erected. Daring experiments in cast iron and glass had been made in the forties and fifties of the previous century—the Coal Exchange, the Crystal Palace, and the great railway stations. The experiments of such men as Victor Horta in Belgium with metal fifty years later were regarded as merely eccentric. The first steel-framed building to be erected in London, the Ritz Hotel (1904) by Mewès & Davis, was speedily covered in Portland stone and made to appear like a French eighteenth-century design—and a very good one too. By King Edward's reign architects and engineers were widely separated, however much later generations may wish to see the gap closed.

Renaissance Styles

There were two sorts of architects: those who worked in the grand manner and employed their own version of the Renaissance style and those who devised a simple architecture of small houses based on the use of local materials and roof-bearing walls. Of both sorts of building there were famous exponents with offices in London and

the big cities. The first group was associated with the Royal
Academy, *Country Life*, and the *Architectural Review*, the second
with the *Studio*, then the *avant-garde* publication with a circulation
beyond England to Europe and America. It was by no means unknown for the exponent of one school to try his hand at another:
Sir Edwin Lutyens, for instance, could design a cottage or a palace
with originality and facility, as could his mighty predecessor Norman
Shaw. In fact there is a parallel in the careers of these two great
architects. Both started as designers of domestic work in the
picturesque style designed to blend in with local scenery, using
gables and half-timber; later Shaw devised his version of Queen
Anne which was really Dutch; while Lutyens employed a classic
domestic style which was akin to Wren's—the vernacular building
in good taste. At the end of their lives both architects were building
large office and administrative blocks in their own widely different
but distinctive Renaissance manners.

A characteristic Edwardian architect of the academic type was
Reginald Blomfield (1856–1942). None of his achievements, except
a manor house for Athelstan Riley in Jersey, may have much appeal
to us today, but he himself is interesting. He was the grandson of a
bishop, the nephew and pupil of a successful and knighted architect
of the Gothic revival, and he belonged to the best clubs, stayed
in country-houses, and mixed with writers and artists at Rye in
Sussex where he had his own country-house. He wrote vigorously,
made delightful pencil sketches of French classical architecture, and
was in advance of the older generation of architects who still held
the Pugin doctrine that the classical style was pagan and to be
avoided. Blomfield, like the volumes of the Royal Commission on
Historical Monuments, stopped at 1714, considering that with
a few exceptions such as George Dance junior, what followed was
decadent. He had no use for Nash and the age of stucco and such
towns as Brighton and Cheltenham. These were not generally
admired until the 1920's, under the influence of Clough Williams-
Ellis, A. Trystan Edwards, and Sir Albert Richardson. Blomfield,
now knighted, was of an older generation. Had he been less of an
Edwardian he would have used stucco for his building in Carlton
House Terrace. .

Foreign Renaissance styles were practised with skill and taste by
several Edwardian architects. The firm of Mewès & Davis was

XXXV. Deptford Town Hall 1902

XXXVI. Hampstead Garden Suburb after twenty years, showing Lutyens's two churches

international. Charles Mewès had his headquarters in Paris, where he designed Ritz Hotels for various parts of the world. The English side of his work was supervised by Arthur J. Davis (1878–1951), whom Mewès had discovered as a student at the Beaux Arts in Paris where he himself had been trained. Mewès was the planner, Davis the decorator, and the Ritz Hotel in Piccadilly is their most admired London work. This building, with its handsome Parisian exterior and colonnade over the pavement, still crowns the approach to the west end of London from the Green Park. Broad, shallow steps lead from its entrance to a magnificent corridor in the Louis Seize style, terminating in the light and vast restaurant with its view over grass and trees, the pleasantest dining-room in London. One detects Mewès's spacious planning in the superb series of public rooms on the main floor, again approached by broad shallow steps, of the Royal Automobile Club (1909) in Pall Mall. Here Davis designed a principal room round a series of Watteau-esque mural paintings that he bought in Paris. Davis designed too all the chairs, desks, and cutlery of the Ritz and the R.A.C. in his own elegant version of Louis Seize. He was also responsible in these years for the redecoration of the interior of Luton Hoo.

Norman Shaw (1831–1912) was an old man by the time King Edward came to the throne: he was too brilliant and experimental an architect to belong to any school, but by no means a spent force. He was called in to devise a decent corner treatment of the Gaiety Theatre (1902, since demolished) on the newly constructed Aldwych part of London's major bit of planning, Kingsway, named after the monarch. Kingsway contains an early commercial building by Lutyens, but it is a cold, official street, Germanic and uncharacteristic of London. In 1905 Shaw designed the exterior of the Piccadilly Hotel, disrupting Nash's low stucco style of Regent Street. Subsequent buildings in that street, though in scale with Norman Shaw's vast Portland stone hotel, lack its imagination and distinguished exterior detail.

There is a good comparison between Victorian and Edwardian work by the Thames at Westminster. Compare Shaw's New Scotland Yard (1888) with Ralph Knott's London County Hall (1908) on the opposite bank of the Thames: note the flimsy chimney-stacks on the latter building and the firm ones by Norman Shaw. Contrast the grim fortress-like quality of the police headquarters with the wide, seemingly purposeless crescent in the County Hall and you will see the difference between Victorian strength and Edwardian display. A provincial equivalent of the work of Mewès & Davis is Frank Atkinson's Adelphi Hotel, Liverpool (1910–12), which still retains its Edwardian furniture.

Equally as distinguished as the work of Mewès & Davis was that of Lanchester, Stewart & Rickards. Lanchester was the planner and Edwin Rickards (1872–1920) the decorator. Rickards was the only English architect of his time—or any other—who could design in a Viennese baroque manner and make it look at home in our climate. This firm's great achievement was in Victoria's reign with Cardiff City Hall and Law Courts (1897) which, with Burges's amazing reconstruction of Cardiff Castle in the 1860's, Dunbar Smith & Brewer's National Museum of Wales (1906), Caroë's rather fussy University College of South Wales (1904), Comper's classic war memorial (1920), and Sir Percy Thomas's more recent additions to the university, forms the finest civic centre anywhere in the kingdom. Despite the varying dates of the buildings, the spacious planning and the grand manner of this whole group is largely Edwardian. Rickards was a superb draughtsman who delighted in detail (he is the author of the famous caricature of Arnold Bennett with the coif of hair on the Penguin editions of his novels). His best work is Deptford Town Hall (1902), with the nautical flavour of its exterior decoration suggesting the dockyard origin of the borough and the golden galleon on its lantern sailing above the drab streets of New Cross. Lanchester and Rickards built Central Hall, Westminster (1905), originally designed to have two steeples either side of the central dome. Here the architects showed imagination by not in any way trying to challenge comparison with the Gothic of Westminster Abbey and Barry's Houses of Parliament. They produced something which subordinates itself in bulk to the older buildings but contrasts in style as strongly and effectively as does the dome of the Radcliffe Camera at Oxford with the spire and pinnacles of St. Mary the Virgin Church. Equally effective in the Westminster group is another Edwardian building—the Middlesex Guildhall (J. S. Gibson, 1905), executed in Portland stone in an *art nouveau* Gothic style of low scale and firm detail, the sculpture on the windows being by H. C. Fehr. Gibson also designed the rich classic municipal buildings at Walsall (1905).

The firm of Warwick & Hall were cultivated exponents of the exuberant Edwardian Renaissance style and specialized in municipal buildings where their plans were practical, their sense of outline and proportion sure, and the general effect expensive and mayoral. The Lambeth municipal buildings in Brixton (1905) and the Shire Hall, Reading (1910), are good examples of their work.

Most Edwardian commercial-Renaissance architects liked to try their hand at a dome. Many are disastrous, notably the awkward one over Harrod's (1901), a strange terra-cotta classic building by C. W. Stevens. No large town in Britain is without an Edwardian dome or two, over a shop, an office, an hotel, or a block of flats. Domes are usually reserved for corner sites.

This was a great age for competitions and it was the custom for a man who wished to win a competition to take into his office a draughtsman who had been trained by the most influential of the assessors. E. W. Mountford was an experienced competition-winner, whose most glittering prize was the Old Bailey (1902) in London. This replaced a Piranesian composition by G. Dance junior, which must have been one of the most awe-inspiring buildings in the country. Mountford caught the craze for domes, and the one over the Old Bailey is a jaunty variation on the theme of Wren's neighbouring St. Paul's, all the poorer by challenging comparison with an adjacent masterpiece. The most successful Edwardian dome is by Sir Brumwell Thomas over the Belfast City Hall (1904). Here the likeness to Wren's St. Paul's dome is further increased by four corner towers to the building which have a certain resemblance to the bell towers of St. Paul's. Sir Brumwell, however, has produced an edifice which could not possibly be mistaken for Wren's work. It is expensive, ostentatious, and full-blooded Edwardian, and the exterior, in a vast square, gathers round it the nonconformist spires and lesser commercial domes, the chimneys and gantries of the city, and forms a splendid copper-green and Portland-stone foreground to the purple-headed mountains beyond. The plan is clear: a wide vaulted entrance hall leads naturally by impressive marble stairs to the principal rooms and galleries on the first floor, the accepted town hall convention dating back to the time when town halls were above an open colonnade over the market.

There was a reaction from the over-florid Edwardian style, a style only successful in a few instances, in favour of a heavy official-looking

classic which looked scholarly and severe. In London Sir John
Burnet's additions to the British Museum (1905) are the best
example, and we see an echo of it in the Oxford Street front of
Selfridge's (1908) by Burnham & Co. of Chicago, supervised by
Frank Atkinson. But here its style is mere façadism. The gigantic
stone columns are supported on a narrow plinth which seems to
rest on a series of plate glass windows, not on solid stone as does
Burnet's addition to the British Museum, and above the columns
and below them the steel frame of the shop is all too apparent.

As H. S. Goodhart-Rendel says: 'In truth the juiciness (there is no
other word for it) of this prosperous period of English architecture
is not very much to our taste today, and the many ambitious works
in which it is displayed should be brought up for judgement 50 years
hence rather than now.'[1] There is, however, one aspect of Edwardian
Renaissance—and indeed all Edwardian building—which we can
appreciate and that is the trouble taken to design doorplates, door
handles, electroliers and brackets, glass shades for bulbs, panelling
and marble pavements and walls, and stained glass for staircase
windows. These are always designed in proportion with the building,
usually by an architect: it is not until they have been removed in the
name of good taste by some recent 'Art committee' that we realize
how integral a part of the design they are, as integral as the colour
schemes that went with the mahogany, satin wood, veined sienna
marble, cut glass, bronze, brass, and red silk and white Adam-style
plaster-work of that age of champagne. The best of the competition
winners of that time was Henry T. Hare whose detailing was always
admirable, whose plans were practical and clear, and whose sense
of proportion never failed him. He essayed many styles, and good
examples of his public work are the county buildings at Stafford
(1907) in early Renaissance, and the University College of North
Wales at Bangor (1907) in the Tudor style. Other respectable buildings in Edwardian classic are Leonard Stokes's King's Road front
to Chelsea Town Hall (1905), Gerald Horsley's St. Paul's School for
Girls (1904), Lloyd's Registry (1901) by T. E. Collcutt—all in
London: Hull Town Hall by Russell & Cooper (1907) and the
Royal Naval College, Dartmouth (1907), by Sir Aston Webb, a
considerably more exciting work than his Admiralty Arch (1905)
and the refacing of Buckingham Palace in London, but less original

[1] *English Architecture since the Regency*, 1953.

than the Birmingham University building, on its huge semicircular plan, which he designed in an individual semi-Renaissance style during his brief partnership with E. Ingress Bell (1907). Nothing in the way of a public building in the classic style approaches in scale and splendour McKim, Mead & White's Pennsylvania Station (1907) in New York. Much of it, like E. Runtz's Anglo-American Oil Company building (1910), ruthlessly clamped to a corner of Queen Anne's Gate, is out of scale with itself and its surroundings, a mere piling up of details like Caroë's extraordinary Ecclesiastical Commissioners' office on Millbank (1903). Much more of it is dull banks, offices, schools, town halls, and libraries. Sometimes magnificence is achieved, perhaps unwittingly, as in Walter A. Thomas's Royal Liver building (1908) in Liverpool which dominates the Mersey with its romantic outline. The most extravagant Edwardian classic work is undoubtedly the Ashton Memorial at Lancaster (1906) by John Belcher, put up by a linoleum peer to the memory of his first wife. The dome and its drum and peristyle are together taller than the sculptured mausoleum on which they stand. No expense has been spared either on this huge Cornish granite and Portland stone building or on the municipal gardening by which it is surrounded. Of all public monuments to Edwardian affluence, this is the chief.

There were some architects who tried to do public buildings in styles other than classic. Marshall Mackenzie at Marischal College, Aberdeen (1903), built in a perpendicular Gothic of his own devising, carrying out its many spires and pinnacles in the local granite, certainly a *tour de force* and a miracle of craftsmanship, as granite is not suited to needle-point sharpness. In its odd way this is an impressive work, though much despised today by purists. They, however, can find consolation in the conscious simplicity, derived from the Tudor manor-houses of the north of England, of Edgar Wood. His design for a club house for the Independent Labour Party (1910) might well be a work of the late twenties in the then modern manner. It was, alas, never built, and most of Wood's work is domestic and nonconformist. In Glasgow George Walton and Charles Rennie Mackintosh, and in London George Jack, originated an even simpler style based on Scottish castles—if the Scottish castles had been drawn by Aubrey Beardsley. The Glasgow School of Art by Mackintosh (1896) is romantic, simple, and thoughtfully detailed. So is his Scotland Street School (1904) in Glasgow. In trying to adapt the native baronial style of Scotland to modern buildings, to introduce large windows into castle-like walls, Mackintosh and his Glasgow friends made a simple manly style which has been wrongly confused with the *art nouveau* of Paris and Belgium. In the south of England Charles Holden, of the firm of Percy Adams, designed the King Edward VII Sanatorium at Midhurst (1903) and the Central Reference Library, Bristol (1906), in an extremely simplified Tudor which owes much to Edgar Wood, Voysey, and Mackintosh, although Holden maintained that he devised the style on his own. In 1908 Adams & Holden designed the British Medical Association's building in the Strand (now Rhodesia House) using Portland stone, as they were building in London in the monumental manner and classical proportions. And although the only sculpture was by Epstein—a frieze in high relief whose figures are now defaced—architects and sculptor worked on the assumption that the sculpture should look as though it had been hewn out of the stone building and not stuck on afterwards. Another, though less obviously experimental, building was Leonard Stokes's National Telephone Exchange (1907) in Gerrard Street, London. The ground floor consisted of four large semicircular arches flanked by entrance doors and supporting walls almost entirely of glass until they reach the heavy cornice which concealed a mansard roof illuminated by portholes with another clerestory above it. Hope's metal casements were a chief feature of the building. One of the earliest exponents of a new art style was Harrison Townsend whose Whitechapel Art Gallery (1897) was damaged by Nazi bombs but whose Horniman Museum (1902) in Forest Hill, London, survives with its frieze of mosaics by Anning Bell.

Big House, Little House, Garden City

The Edwardian was the last age in Britain in which a rich man could afford to build himself a new and enormous country-house with a formal landscape garden and lily ponds and clipped hedges. Many architects specialized in this sort of building, Sir Ernest George and Yeates being the most successful. Lutyens, Lorimer, Guy Dawber, Ernest Newton, Halsey Ricardo, Walter Brierley, and Detmar Blow produced work of high quality, palaces, whether in the Tudor or English Renaissance manner, complete with

A PRINCELY GIFT TO THE PEOPLE.

The Story of the Generous Addition That Has Just Been Made to the Lungs of London.

THE HORNIMAN MUSEUM AND ITS FOUNDER, MR. F. J. HORNIMAN, M.P.

From *The Star* 1901

bathrooms with showers, fireplaces with tiles by William de Morgan, hangings by Morris & Co., paper by Essex & Co., electroliers by the Bromsgrove Guild, and much walnut panelling and plaster-work. Many-gabled, many-windowed, these houses smiled luxuriously down on the chalky slopes of the home counties or within an hour's motor drive of the industrial towns of the north. And if he could employ either C. H. Mallows or T. Mawson to lay out his garden with straight avenues and high beech hedges and sculpture and pavilions, the magnate considered himself lucky—and luckier still if he could persuade King Edward to come and stay. These houses are now at their lowest ebb. Though more than passable imitations and some-times highly original like Ricardo's 8 Addison Road (1906–7) in glazed tiles for the Debenham family, or Lutyens's Temple Dinsley, Herts (1908), Great Maytham, Sussex (1909), Heathcote, Yorks (1906), or Nashdom, Bucks (1905), they are out of favour today except as convalescent homes, government offices, or monasteries because they are not 'genuine': sometimes they are even better than the original. Ernest Newton's Ardenrun Place, Surrey (1909), is so like a work by Sir Christopher Wren as to deceive even an 'art historian' at first glance. The manor-houses in the Cotswold style by Dawber, Forsyth & Maule and by A. N. Prentice, Bateman & Bateman are well built, well planned (generally E- or L shaped), and except that they are better appointed, are indistinguishable from the real thing. Fifty years have given them the texture of three centuries.

There is no doubt, however, that the Edwardian age's greatest contribution to western architecture was the small house for the artistic person of moderate income. It was Baillie Scott's proudest moment when someone told him that he had built more houses which did less harm to the landscape than any living architect. This was no doubt true. He used local materials, and, in the Morris and Voysey tradition, designed the furniture, fabrics, and metal-work of his houses as well as the structure itself. Surrey cottages, Sussex farms, Kentish yeomen's houses, Cornish manor, Cumberland shepherd's cot—he could design them all, giving them that touch of romance which differentiated them from the peasant's humbler abode. He added a few gadgets like oval door-knobs and well-fitting cupboard doors. The most accomplished of all such architects was Ernest Gimson, who later turned to furniture making and smith's work in the Cotswolds, as did other architects such as C. R. Ashbee and the

XXXVII. The Ritz Hotel, Piccadilly 1904

XXXVIII. Christ Church, North Brixton 1902

Barnsley brothers. The mauve and green of the suffragette movement was the popular colour scheme. Pewter shone on Welsh
dressers, warming pans gleamed, rush matting creaked under the
sandal, chintz flowered in the windows, and beyond them the sun
set behind the Berkshire and Surrey pines—for Camberley and
Sunningdale were becoming fashionable places for a small house—
or turned golden the elms and apple orchards of the Cotswolds—
for this was the time when Broadway and Chipping Campden were
rediscovered by those who bicycled through the leafy lanes carrying
Macmillan's 'Highways and Byways' series. And with this new
rustic spirit went the novels of Maurice Hewlett for the romantic,
the plays of Bernard Shaw for the political, the stories of Wells
for the scientific. Socialism was in the air. Everything was getting
better and better. It was the age of the work of each for the weal
of all. England would one day be a huge garden city. C. H. B.
Quennell, W. A. Aikman, Geoffrey Lucas, O. P. Milne, Niven &
Wigglesworth, C. F. A. Voysey, Fred Rowntree, Lancelot Fedden,
E. S. Prior, T. L. Dale, Sydney Caulfield, E. J. May, Arnold
Mitchell, H. R. & B. A. Poulter—their names are many who knew
so well how to build a seemly, practical, small house to fit in with
the landscape, to be warm and comfortable for ladies with Liberty
silk dresses to live in and wait for husbands coming down on the
L.S.W.R. from Waterloo or the Metropolitan from Baker Street
or the Cheshire Lines from Manchester.

And since the village was the ideal unit, as a plan, we find whole
village-like new communities created in this great era of domestic
and rustic architecture. Each garden village had houses graded carefully to income—but no rich man's palace nor poor man's hovel—
a leafy, happy medium instead, with communal grass and clubs and
institutes and a choice of churches. Port Sunlight (1905), Bournville
(1908), Letchworth Garden City (1903), Hampstead Garden Suburb
(1907)—these are all products of the idealism of the Edwardian age.
Raymond Unwin's *Town Planning in Practice* first appeared in
1909 and in ten years' time had influenced local councils to build
their arid imitations of these high-minded experiments. Very
attractive these first garden cities and suburbs were, and attractive
they remain: more individualistic than the housing-estates of later
decades, more 'sentimental' and still popular with the sort of
people for whom they were designed—the middle classes.

Churches

I must conclude this short survey with a mention of churches. Though no daring experiment in church planning was made, except in Beresford Pite's Christ Church, North Brixton (1902), an extremely Protestant building just within the embrace of Canterbury and with a Holy Table far from the east wall, the Church of England was reinvigorated at the expense of nonconformity as people grew more prosperous and church was still regarded as respectable. The later Anglo-Catholic movement produced many fine churches—for example Comper's St. Cyprian's, Clarence Gate (1903). Sir Charles Nicholson, A. Skipworth, F. C. Eden, Fellowes Prynne, Walter Tapper, J. Harold Gibbons, Temple Lushington Moore, W. H. Bidlake, and C. E. Bateman all worked in a continuation of Bodley's style. Comper was the most delicate and original designer and colourist and the most daring planner. Temple Moore simplified his late Gothic into a stalwart Yorkshire style all his own, whose finest example is St. Wilfred's, Harrogate. Sir Thomas Drew designed St. Anne's Cathedral, Belfast (1903), in sturdy Romanesque style. The Anglican men's communities created Mirfield Chapel by Walter Tapper, having rejected an even bolder design by Skipworth, and Caldy Island monastery by Coates Carter. The latter community went over to Rome. Outside the Establishment there was the Central Hall, Westminster, for the Methodists, already mentioned, and St. Anne's Roman Catholic Cathedral, Leeds, in late Gothic, freely treated by J. H. Eastwood (1902), and Buckfast Abbey in Romanesque style by Frederick Walters (1909). If this account seems preoccupied with style, it must be remembered that style was an Edwardian preoccupation.

10

THEATRE

W. BRIDGES-ADAMS, C.B.E.

Formerly Director of Shakespeare Festivals
Stratford-on-Avon

THEATRE

THE VICTORIAN HERITAGE

THEATRICAL history is seldom obliging as to the dates when a given epoch began or ended. The tragedy we call Elizabethan may be traced from the year before the Armada, yet it did not reach its apogee until the reign of James I. The comedy we loosely term Restoration was stirring before the Parliament men abolished the playhouses, and was by no means dead when Queen Anne came to the throne. The English theatre was becoming progressively Edwardian, as was society at large, while the prince was still in residence at Marlborough House. But with the death of Queen Victoria there came a change in the climate of the nation's life that even the stage, a notoriously conservative institution, was not slow to reflect. Still more was this so in August 1914. With the outbreak of war an era in our theatrical history came unmistakably to a close; for convenience we may style it Edwardian, although it out-lasted the reign by four brilliant years. It is no illusion that there was a special radiance in that time. A new sun, it seemed, was rising, and the Victorian afterglow had not yet faded. Indeed the most notable figures of the Edwardian theatre were all Victorians; even young Granville-Barker had emerged in the late nineties. It was as much a time of fruition as of germination. In the few years vouch-safed them the heirs proved worthy to inherit; and the inheritance was a rich one.

Irving: The Actors' Theatre

For half a century or more our drama had been discarding the fetters of traditionalism and striving to come to terms with con-temporary life. Correspondingly, the actor's social standing had improved. It was Irving who had finally compelled acceptance of the view that his art was no less entitled to recognition than the painter's, and that the Lyceum was as respectable an institution

as the Royal Academy. As early as 1883 Gladstone had wondered
whether it would be 'too audacious' to offer him a knighthood, but
Irving was not disposed to accept an honour that might seem to
elevate him in a social sense above his fellow artists. For another
twelve years it remained, as we may suppose, his for the asking.
In 1895 he signified with great dignity that the moment had come,
and accepted the title on behalf of his profession; dubbing him, the
queen said that she was very, very pleased. In due course other
knighthoods followed—Bancroft's in 1897, Wyndham's, Hare's,
and Tree's during King Edward's reign. They ratified society's
admission that the stage was no longer an undesirable calling; the
individual actor was encouraged to think of himself as an artist and
a gentleman.

The men thus honoured were all actor-managers. That was one
day to become a term of opprobrium in certain circles; at the time it
did not seem so ill that the manager of a theatre should be able to
act or that an actor should be responsible enough to shoulder the
cares of management, nor indeed that he should purchase for the
exhibition of his art the kind of play that fitted him. The actor-
manager, particularly if he had established himself in London, was
de facto among the heads of his profession. If he held a long lease
on easy terms and his judgement did not fail him, he could make
himself and his theatre a habit with the playgoing public. The
building became associated with the man; his presence pervaded it
from the box-office to the stage-door. So it was with Irving at the
Lyceum, with Alexander at the St. James's, with Tree at the Haymarket and at the fine new house he had just built across the way,
with Wyndham at the little Criterion and at the theatre which still
bears his name. Two of these four had money-sense, two had not.
Few people knew that the Lyceum's superb display was sustained
by American tours, or how near Her Majesty's had brought Tree to
disaster. In an age that respected property and personality in
equal measure these men and their theatres alike presented a façade
that seemed impregnable.

The economics of west-end management were less daunting than
they are today; the prime distinction being that a play could pay its
way without full houses. For a hundred pounds a week it was possible to rent a theatre of moderate size which had a nightly cash
capacity of more than twice that sum. Normal advertising cost

another hundred a week, and the same amount would cover the wages of the theatre staff and an adequate orchestra. If he drew from the public no more than £800 in a week of eight performances—which was less than half of what his house could hold—a careful actor-manager would have no difficulty in providing also for his company's salaries and his own, his author's percentage on the gross takings, his lighting and heating. He might even hope to recover something of the cost of production, which, for a modest comedy, was not excessive; it is on record that as late as 1911 Alexander mounted one such very handsomely for £145. He could further count on a nightly revenue from his bars and cloakrooms and from the sale of programmes. Moreover, it was a great virtue of the old horseshoe form of construction that a house of two or more tiers, even when it was half empty, did not look so. From the stalls it was possible to notice that the pit was not full, but of the tiers only the front rows were visible. From these tiers only the stalls could be seen, and it was here particularly that the manager could avail himself of the device known as 'papering'. Every west-end box-office had its list of reputable 'deadheads' who could be relied on to occupy the unsold stalls in suitable attire and with an air of having paid for them. Accordingly there was no chill of failure in the house when by these means a successful actor-manager nursed a half-successful play. And if it did not respond to treatment he had time to rehearse another without serious loss.

In the provinces a sharing arrangement was the rule. The touring companies, often carrying their full equipment with them, had well-nigh made an end of the old stock system. They provided, in the words of the contract, all seen and heard upon the stage, and drew a specified share of the week's takings. This averaged fifty per cent., but it varied considerably according to the nature of the attraction and the standing of the theatre. Many of the provincial houses were of great distinction; some for their elegance, like the little Devonshire Park at Eastbourne, some for their size and resources, like the Leeds Opera House, which maintained a notable orchestra and could have mounted the *Ring* as Wagner would have wished to see it done. Many were rich in memories of the famous men and women who had played on their boards; and often this personal touch was still forthcoming from a manager of settled policy who had made himself a respected figure in the town. He, if he assembled his yearly list of fixtures with due regard to his public, could thrive without dishonour. He could even afford to lose on a week of Ibsen during the summer, because the Christmas panto-mime, which was his especial pride and often his own creation, paid for all. Moreover, in a city of the size of Manchester two or more great theatres could co-exist without internecine competition; so long as they kept to their chosen lines of business their only rival was the local music hall, which also pursued a policy of its own. In short, in the last decade of the old century the provincial theatre prospered exceedingly. Even in the first decade of the new one, when the 'kinemas' were springing up everywhere, there were still some 300 true playhouses in the United Kingdom, complete with galleries, pits, circles, stalls, and boxes; the figure excludes innumer-able Palaces of Variety which were theatres in all but name, and also a multitude of halls, pier-pavilions, corn-exchanges, and so forth, all licensed for the performance of stage plays. Not every one of these was flourishing, and often the plays were trash; but they dealt in living drama, of whatever kind or quality.

Rise of the Authors' Theatre

The Victorian theatre was almost to the end an actors' theatre; it was only in its last years that the authors' theatre began seriously to challenge that supremacy. True, certain poets and men of letters had essayed the unfamiliar vein, Bulwer Lytton with more success than Browning was to have; Tennyson had made the grade by submitting his *Becket* to the ruthless blue pencil of Irving; the failure of *Guy Domville* was a lasting discouragement to Henry James. But the practitioners who served the actors' theatre (with increasing profit to themselves under the new system of royalties that they owed to Dion Boucicault) had been in the main concerned to devise effective scenes and situations, to lead up to them with an exciting and sufficiently credible sequence of events, and to find an ending that would surprise and please. These craftsmen had had no hope of achieving another *School for Scandal*, nor had all of them Tom Robertson's perception of the dramatic stuff that may be found in the lives of ordinary people. For help in the mechanical part of their business they had turned, with no qualms as to copy-right, to the French theatre of their day. Scribe had brought his technique to such perfection that for him the well-made play was

XXXIX. Martin-Harvey in *The Only Way*: poster by John Hassall

XL. Train smash in *The Whip* at Drury Lane

almost a matter of geometry; Sardou, with the genius of Sarah Bernhardt at his disposal, had carried it even further.

As a technique it was by no means to be despised. Ibsen drew on it, although he put it to higher uses than the providing of fine players with tremendous scenes. Promoted in the service of a great dramatic poet, it taught him to condense, to compress (only to expand the more explosively), to suggest and foreshadow, to plant clues for us to find, to give us the whole of five lives in one day and one room, with a seeming effortlessness that was beyond the ken of a Sardou or a Scribe. The impact of Ibsen on our theatre in the nineties was fiercely resisted, but for all that a few of our dramatists found this cold wind from the north invigorating; they began to see themselves in a new light. The drama had often preached, seeking to placate the godly; in its lighter manifestations it had not altogether lost its gift of detached, ironic comment. But an irony and detachment that, without any preaching, took all humanity by the scruff of its neck and held it up for judgement: these were something new.

It is interesting to note how the salutary infection spread. Bernard Shaw, an apostle of Ibsen's doctrine (as he pronounced it, for his own ends, to be) rather than his pupil as to method, was hailed as the playwright of the future by certain discerning late Victorians; by some because he refreshingly derided established values, by a few because of his grace and dialectical skill; his earlier plays, from *Widowers' Houses* to *Candida,* were for the coteries, not for the west end, although Germany and America were showing interest in them. But playgoers of average outlook, in whose view *Ghosts* had been rightly banned, were more stimulated than alarmed when the impulse of Ibsen began to work on such middle-of-the-road men as Henry Arthur Jones and Pinero. Jones, of yeoman-farmer stock, had proceeded from his share in that sternly moral melodrama *The Silver King* to his comic masterpiece *The Liars,* in which the follies of rich and lovely women were gently castigated by a golden-voiced *raisonneur* in the person of Charles Wyndham; it is likely that the growing vogue of Ibsenism encouraged him in his bent, which thereafter he freely indulged, toward social comment of a moralistic kind. As to Ibsen's influence on Pinero there can be no doubt. Pinero was a born actor, trained under Irving; he had written several farces which posed with beautiful absurdity the problem of what a man could do in this or that situation and what he ought to do—which is after all the main stuff of drama. Ranging further afield he was drawn to experiment in human dilemmas that invited no farcical treatment, comedic rather, even tragical. Since the first lesson of his calling was that the stage must please to live, it was natural that he, even more than Henry Arthur Jones, should sense the change of wind and set his course accordingly. The hero of *The Profligate* (1889) shot himself; in deference to a general public that had not yet seen Hedda Gabler do the same thing Pinero substituted a happier ending. But by 1893 audiences were ripe for sterner stuff. *The Second Mrs. Tanqueray* was no more Ibsenite than *La Dame aux Camellias*. But it was, and still lives as, an example of the kind of social tragedy (for Paula Tanqueray also shoots herself) that the percolating influence of Ibsen had by that year made acceptable. Pinero's mastery of story-telling won the great public; the actor in him had no difficulty in imparting to the work a faintly Ibsenish flavour that won the intellectuals. It proved itself a perfect play for the St. James's, where Alexander was to flourish for many years by dexterously and most honourably reconciling the claims of his art, his exchequer, and the *Zeitgeist*.

It may therefore be said that the Edwardian age inherited an actors' theatre, dominated by the actor-manager and securely entrenched, and an authors' theatre that was already threatening its fortifications. In January 1901 Irving's tenancy of the Lyceum was nearing its end; Tree was in his fourth year as sole owner of Her Majesty's; Alexander in his tenth as lessee of the St. James's; Wyndham in his seventeenth as lessee of the Criterion and in his second as proprietor of the new house which he had named after himself. Cyril Maude, in partnership with Frederick Harrison, had been settled for some five at the Haymarket; Arthur Bourchier had recently acquired a long lease of the Garrick. Certain others of the breed, equally or less illustrious but each of them resolute to be master in his own house wherever he chose to have one, were not at this juncture committed to the responsibilities of a permanent home in the capital. Charles Hawtrey, cherished by the west end for his amoral comedy, was too habitually embarrassed to stay anywhere for long. It was mainly in the provinces that Edward Compton upheld the standard of old comedy. Mr. and Mrs. Kendal did well in London, but no less well on tour; their old associate John Hare had quitted the Garrick for the United States. Forbes-Robertson was another such; when Irving, his erstwhile chief, was in America he could rent the Lyceum, fill it, and be rid of it when his season was over. The young Martin-Harvey was another: in 1899 *The Only Way* —produced with Irving's blessing at the Lyceum—had brought him fame; but it was his provincial tour of the play in 1901 that restored him to solvency. Wilson Barrett was as welcome at the Adelphi as he had been at the Princess's; but he had freed himself of his English debts by playing *The Sign of the Cross* half-way round the world. To Benson and his Shakespearean company Stratford was as yet a 'date' of two weeks in a forty weeks' tour; their London seasons were few and brief.

Of the non-acting managers, some were long-established, some newcomers but destined to endure. Drury Lane, under Arthur Collins, maintained the traditions of Sir Augustus Harris in spectacular drama and a Christmas pantomime that was exalted by the surrealist genius of Dan Leno and still made a perfunctory acknowledgement of its origins by staging a harlequinade at the end, when most of the children in the audience were dazed by a surfeit of splendour. Daly's was in the hands of George Edwardes, who had built it for Augustin Daly, and now ran it in double harness with the Gaiety as a home of musical comedy. There was a certain distinction between a Gaiety show and a Daly's show, but both could be relied on for catchy tunes, entrancing girls, and adroit comedians. True comic opera, at the Savoy, had been wilting in the face of this competition since Gilbert and Sullivan had parted company. The Duke of York's had become the London outpost of Charles Frohman, an American impresario whose flair for what would 'go' on both sides of the Atlantic was as unquestioned as his personal integrity. The Adelphi and the little Vaudeville, owned but not directed by the brothers Gatti, specialized respectively in melodrama and light comedy; at the latter house young Seymour Hicks and his wife had entered on a long and profitable engagement.

Provincial audiences had been increasingly encouraged, since Irving's majestic tours, to look for productions that approximated to London standards, whether the London star himself appeared or sent a second company on the road. The stock system had had little more to give, even as a training-ground for young actors, since the retirement from the Theatre Royal, Margate, of Sarah Thorne. The repertory movement was not yet in being.

In mounting and lighting the realist convention was almost universally upheld. Telbin and Hawes Craven, who worked for Irving, were acknowledged masters of scene-painting in the great tradition, although for many years William Poel had been crusading for the non-scenic treatment of Shakespeare. The use of electricity was general in London; a number of provincial houses were to depend on gas for some years to come. Yet Tree, at his new theatre, could not achieve the *patina*—it is Mr. Willson Disher's word—that was the hall-mark of the gaslit Lyceum.[1] It was, moreover, at the Lyceum that Mr. Gordon Craig had imbibed those notions of height, space, and luminous shadow that were to revolutionize stage design; he, we must note, had already made his mark (in 1900) with a production of Purcell's *Dido and Æneas* which the observant hailed as something altogether new.

The music hall was thriving. Ballet had been for many years the culminating feature of the bill at the Empire and the Alhambra; although not generally of a quality we should now acclaim it was graced by such individual artists as Adeline Genée. The newly opened London Hippodrome had both a stage and a circus ring which could be submerged for aquatic spectacles. The Palace, redeemed from its failure as an English opera house, was already acquiring an exceptional distinction. But it was at the other halls, the Pavilion, Tivoli, Oxford, Metropolitan, and the rest, that the pure tradition was chiefly maintained. Here were to be seen the stars, as many as twenty of them in one bill, the more opulent driving from house to house in their neat broughams, still wearing the strange insignia they had made their own, and home at last to the Brixton Road. George Lashwood, it is true, affected suitings of an impeccable cut; so did Miss Vesta Tilley, who interpreted with exquisite understanding the joys of the callow but conquering young male; Marie Lloyd relied on handsome gowns and her gift of cheerful and robust salacity. But Albert Chevalier and Gus Elen were ever-faithful to the pearl buttons of the coster, Harry Tate to his incredible moustache, R. G. Knowles to his frock-coat and wildly unsuitable appurtenances, Little Tich to his elongated boots, Wilkie Bard to his dome-like brow, George Robey to his portentous

---

[1] With gas footlights before him, an actor was seen through an imperceptible shimmer of warm air which lent him magic; and the electric arc had not the soft lambency of limelight.

eyebrows; the romantic Eugene Stratton was always a blackamoor. Night after night these abounding personalities plugged songs, which to this hour delight us, in a thick and convivial atmosphere that still recalled the taverns where their immemorial art had been preserved by humbler predecessors.

The Stage Society

The contest between the actors' theatre and the authors'—if we exclude Shaw's frontal attack on Irving—was seldom violent; many playwrights who found themselves in the ascendant were glad to go on writing for the actor-managers, and the actor-managers on their part were glad to observe that they were getting better plays. The task of still further advancing the drama had now devolved upon the Stage Society, pledged from its foundation in 1899 to secure a Sunday-night hearing for works that were not yet marketable but one day might be—as several indeed were. The established playwright's response to these nudges from the left varied, one might almost say, according to the condition of his reflexes. If, like Sydney Grundy, he was irremediably set in his ways, he would shrug them off with a veteran's indifference. If, as was Pinero's case, the man's best work was still to do, he took careful note of them, although he might be guarded in his acknowledgements. But within a few years the mantle of the Stage Society was to be assumed by Granville-Barker at the Court, and a succession of new dramatists emerged who did not seem to know or care what was, or was not, *du théâtre*. They, as it then seemed, hammered the final nails into the coffins of Sardou and Scribe.

The dramatic critics also had kept pace with an advance which a handful of them had done much to promote. Standards of integrity were rising; only a pressman of the baser sort was to be won by making him free of the theatre's bar, although the subtler cajolements which Irving had openly (and in his view quite properly) employed in furtherance of his art were still effective. But while Clement Scott, who understood actors better than he understood the new drama, had become a back-number, Archer and Grein, having fought and won the battle for Ibsen, were now generally respected authorities. Above all it was Bernard Shaw who had transformed dramatic criticism; we must not hold against him the many self-exhibiting men of lighter calibre for whom he paved the way, because in such matters as wit, candour, the quest for whatever seemed true and good, they could not match him. Fortunately, when Shaw's broadsword ceased to flash in the columns of the *Saturday Review*, the stiletto of Max Beerbohm replaced it, and insincerity, smugness, and bombast still went in fear of a deflating prick. Moreover, there were many more newspapers than there are now: each had its critic, and nearly all of them his honoured place, and room in which to speak his mind.

THE ESTABLISHMENT

At the outset of King Edward's reign the Lyceum still enjoyed titular supremacy. But the great productions which constituted, as it were, Irving's insurance against old age had not been themselves sufficiently insured against the disastrous fire which made an end of them, and he himself was for the first time in his life an ailing man. When his Lyceum became the Lyceum Ltd. the heart went out of it and its days, too, were clearly numbered. His last great gesture was a gala performance for the rajahs, sultans, and other potentates of the empire who had come to London for the coronation. In the reception that followed they and their retinues filed before him, some of them wearing jewels of a price that could have endowed his theatre in perpetuity. He was too deeply in debt to accept the viceroy's invitation to the forthcoming durbar in Delhi; he had to earn a living, and that meant touring. But he somehow found the money to pay for the special trains and steamers which enabled his company to appear by command at Sandringham without missing more than one night in Belfast. There were three years of toil and honour still to come before his heart missed a beat in Bradford, and was too tired to go on beating.

Beerbohm Tree

That was in 1905, when Irving's mantle, so far as London was concerned, had already been assumed by Tree. Tree wore it handsomely, if with a difference. The two men were of different generations. Both had intellectual power. But Irving, born just within Victoria's reign and in spirit a Victorian to the last, had put his intellect into his acting; outside his art he seemed to be shockingly oblivious of matters that were agitating contemporary minds.

Tree, a late Victorian who came to full fruition under an Edwardian sun, endeared himself as much to the intelligentsia of his day as to the wider public by dissipating his intellectual gifts as the mood took him; the joy of being himself meant almost as much to him as the vision, which he undoubtedly had, of an exemplary theatre. When he opened Her Majesty's he had been an actor-manager in London for twenty years; nevertheless, by Irving's code he was an amateur who had not been through the mill. But in spirit and body alike he was on the grand scale, presiding as of right over the lordly companies he gathered round him; we did not realize how spacious his Antony in *Julius Caesar* had been until Basil Gill, for many years his Brutus, proved almost too strong for the strongest Antony the post-1914 stage afforded. As Cleopatra's Antony he was undone by a flat tenor-baritone voice that could not (masculine though he undoubtedly was) strike the full male keynote. This deficiency in him was most successfully turned to account in his Richard II, less successfully in his neo-Teutonic Hamlet. It followed that he gave his finest performances in the less great parts, or at moments in the great ones. His Malvolio out-fantasticated Shakespeare's and was gloriously his own. Stung by a malicious paragraph, he embodied as Colonel Newcome a soldierly uprightness that astonished even his friends. In a stage version of *Oliver Twist* his Fagin was a grotesque as horrible as it was delightful. As Beethoven, in the play of that name by René Fauchois, he apparently reduced his natural stature by several inches and showed most poignantly what it means to a musician to become stone-deaf. Only once or twice in this succession of impersonations did he respond to Bernard Shaw's entreaty that he should be himself. *The Van Dyck* began its career as a brief trifle at the Grand Guignol. Tree, with Weedon Grossmith to help him, expanded it from fifteen minutes to fifty by improvisations which varied every night. In Mr. Arthur Blair-Woldingham, the swell crook who robs a mean little collector of all his possessions, there was an echo of Lord Illingworth (in *A Woman of No Importance*); there was the same noble head and faultless bearing, the same air of immoral stability. It is not easy to say whether we gained or lost when this incorrigibly light-hearted man of genius did what the British public expected of him and turned himself into an institution.

His new theatre was now dubbed His Majesty's, with the king's approval. Londoners were soon to be as proud of it as they had been of the Lyceum. The frontage, with great flambeaux between the fluted columns, was noble and exciting; only Lyceumites could object that the stage-door lacked mystery. The foyer was stately, the spring and curve of the tiers were purest theatre, and the proscenium they held in their embrace was full of promise: promise of wonders to be revealed when the great red and gold curtains parted and went hurtling upward. Scenic wonders, of course, were among them; these, with the aid of Herr Adolph Schmidt's considerable orchestra, carried the show to the remotest occupant of the house. Whether he was confronted with Alonzo's galleon yawing in mighty seas, or a Forum whose accuracy as in 44 B.C. had been underwritten by no less an authority than Alma-Tadema, or Flint Castle, or a street in Windsor, this far-away spectator was caught in the play's spell more effectually than experts in what is now called audience-participation might believe. Tree, capable of subtlety enough when his part intrigued him, worked in poster-paint as a *metteur-en-scène*. Consider the street in Windsor aforesaid; this was in *The Merry Wives*. It was streaked by golden sunlight, with Master Page's house in cool blue shadow and the Garter Inn catching the rays, and at the turn of the street there was a smithy where a horse was being shod, with the authentic dull clink of a hammer on hot iron. Tree had taken Shaw's hint that he would never be the Falstaff of *Henry IV*, but in *The Merry Wives*, and in this setting, he triumphed. He made acknowledgements to the Falstaff he could not play by riding through Windsor on a fat white horse, Robin at the bridle, Bardolph, Nym, and Pistol supportant, and an unwashed rabble at his tail. Never before had we seen Shakespeare's great history thus linked with the caprice that his queen, as it is said, commanded of him; the ride from Gloucestershire was in our minds, and the harsh dismissal that ensued. But only for a moment, because laughter at once supervened; and when, at the very end, the reprobate knight went dancing away through Windsor park with the smallest and daintiest of the elves that had walloped him, we experienced the purgation by laughter which is second only to the purgation by pity and awe. We stood up, with tears on our cheeks, clapping in time to the band.

The pictorial representation of Shakespeare had reached its climax with Irving; it is arguable that with Tree it was imperceptibly and

XLI. *Our Miss Gibbs* at the Gaiety: opening chorus in 'Garrods Stores'

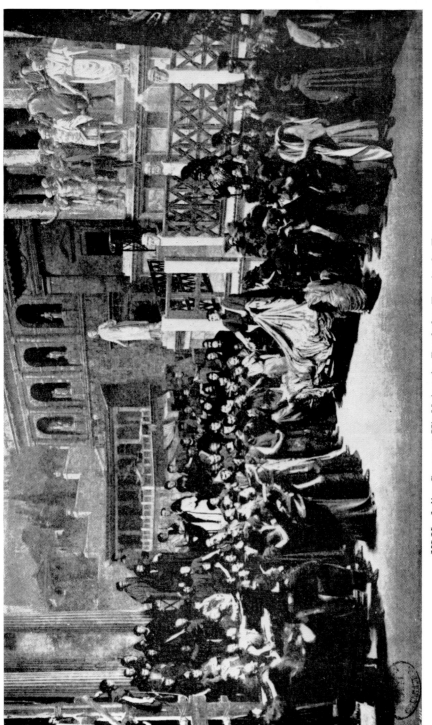

XLII. *Julius Caesar* at His Majesty's: Beerbohm Tree in the Forum scene

ever more gorgeously passing into a decline. The street in Windsor was a delight. It was just possible to forgive a Perdita who, on leaving her childhood's home, tripped back across a running brook to retrieve a bird on which she doted, to a sympathetic accompaniment from Herr Schmidt's strings. Even Tree's real rabbits in a wood near Athens were tolerable compared with the real deer which Mr. Flanagan, of Manchester, introduced into the Forest of Arden. But some felt it was not so good when Tree instructed his designers to reproduce Cleopatra's barge in accordance with the details supplied by Enobarbus—who, when his cue came, could speak only of a thing that had already trundled into our view. Such gildings of refined gold were increasingly a present to the opposition, ineffective as yet, but growing in strength and animosity.

The opposition had in truth a good deal to wear down. Tree not only stood well with his stalls, dress circle, pit, and gallery, he assiduously wooed the middle public of the second tier, who responded warmly when they learned that they could reserve a seat at the back of the upper circle for two shillings. A hard-up young man could take the girl of his choice to dinner in Soho, to Shakespeare at His Majesty's, and even home in a hansom for much less than a sovereign. Moreover, there were no cloakroom charges at Tree's theatre, and the handsome programmes, void of advertising matter, were free. His audience, once they had paid, were encouraged to feel they were his guests. When he took his curtain-call he would survey them with his great, pale eyes and say a few words that seldom lacked pungency and wit. Whatever they thought of his performance, they rejoiced in this final contact with a personality who was manifestly, and on the whole beneficently, doing what he liked.

The Haymarket and the St. James's

Two other houses ranked as highly in the esteem of the playgoing Londoner; both had an advantage over His Majesty's in that they were old, and rich in tradition. The Haymarket is today so old that the most ardent planner would think twice before destroying it; at this time, under the joint command of Cyril Maude and Frederick Harrison, it continued to uphold the standards of polished comedy. But the St. James's, dating only from the reign of William IV, had also accumulated memories enough—of Braham the singer who built it, of Dickens, Rachel, Irving, Hare, and the Kendals—when

George Alexander entered upon his twenty-seven years' tenancy in 1891. If, in the time we are considering, the St. James's took precedence over the Haymarket, this was because through all those years a single artist, not lacking in business sense, shaped its policy.

Alexander, sometime leading juvenile at the Lyceum, was to become that beau-ideal of the civic minded Left, the actor who took an interest in public affairs. If in 1910 one attended a debate of the L.C.C. one might see a grave, elderly man rising from the Moderate benches and contesting, papers in hand, some clause in some amendment; two hours later one might see the same man, young, buoyant, and infinitely desirable to females, on the boards of the St. James's; sometimes, if the debate was prolonged, he might be back in his place at Spring Gardens when the show was over. His life fell into a pattern which in retrospect he had no reason to regret. But he was a far more considerable actor, more versatile, more fiery, than as a rule he permitted himself to be. At heart he was a romantic, as was clear when he played Rassendyll in *The Prisoner of Zenda,* or when, being well over forty, he surpassed himself as the boyish Prince Karl in *Old Heidelberg.* But he was at once too modest and too level-headed to quarrel with his destiny as the administrator of the most fashionable theatre in London; moreover he was genuinely concerned to promote as fine a drama as the public could be induced to support. As he mellowed, the compromise brought its due reward; he excelled in the role of the *raisonneur.*

This was hitherto the acknowledged preserve of Sir Charles Wyndham, who was in such parts the embodiment of grace, wit, and understanding, and whose voice was as rich as old Madeira. But in Alexander's *raisonneurs* there was a harlequin alertness; there was a twinkle in his eye as he watched the comic deployment that might end in tragedy unless he—in the big act—intervened. When, some years ago, a renowned actor of a later generation attempted Hilary Jesson in *His House in Order,* the play did not do well. The *raisonneur,* however wise and mellow, can become a bore if he knows all the answers from the start. Alexander's Hilary, on leave from his legation, was making discoveries from the moment when he perceived that his brother's domestic affairs were heading for catastrophe. So, above the very real drama of a dull and ambitious M.P.'s marriage with a rebellious young wife, there was the further delight, for us, of seeing how a lively and unambitious diplomatist was to straighten things out—as of course he charmingly did. Alexander commanded the play from Pinero, who wrote it for him in full confidence; it ran for fifty-seven weeks, earning a net profit of £23,000.

The St. James's in Alexander's hands struck a happy balance between economy and *ton*. The staging was elegant, and as a rule cost less than one would have supposed. Salaries were not high, because actors of distinction found it as much a pleasure as an honour to play there. Behind the scenes all was ordered to a second, yet there was no hurry; there was always time for Mrs. Evans to give a woman's touch to the flowers and the cushions, time enough to set out in the wings the gilt chairs on which the company awaited their cues. It was a distinguished theatre, in its modest way a national monument; as we know, it has been demolished for gain.

Drury Lane Drama

The most historic house of all must properly take fourth place in the list, because its vast size had enforced on its management a yearly alternation of spectacular melodrama and pantomine, varied by intermittent visits from foreign stars. Drury Lane drama was not yet seriously threatened by the still silent screen. A railway smash in the cinema, once securely captured in celluloid, would endure as long as the film which enshrined it. But a railway smash at Drury Lane was living theatre. It had to be put together again every day, and twice on matinée days, for months on end. It was a planned marvel of stage mechanism, depending for its execution on half a hundred unseen workers who were at that instant under the same roof as ourselves. As the mounting pulse of Mr. James Glover's orchestra heralded the event we prayed not only that the more sympathetic characters might survive it, but for the event itself. Once at least in the long run of *The Whip* the engine of the express rolled over in a cloud of steam before it reached the horse-box (containing the favourite) which the recreant Captain Sartorys had placed in its way. At that dreadful moment it would hardly have done to assure Mr. Arthur Collins that in terms of art his dear smash was not to be compared with his presentment, just before, of a branch line station with paraffin lamps shining tawnily in the murk and someone coughing at the end of the platform: the very station for Holmes and Watson to alight at.

In its quest of the topical, of an outward verisimilitude which by no means excluded creative imagination, Drury Lane drama constituted itself the abstract and brief chronicle of the time as the plain man apprehended it. *The Sins of Society* gave life and colour to his doubts about the Smart Set and their bridge-clubs: there was a passable stage-replica of Father Vaughan, who was at that time denouncing both from his west-end pulpit; it revived, to King Edward's displeasure, an ingenious jewel fraud for which a real nobleman had recently been sent to prison. Yet these matters were but contributory to the evening's sensations, notably a weir on the upper Thames, by moonlight, and the sinking of a troopship.

Sometimes Drury Lane got things a little wrong; its attempt at Oxford University did not satisfy Max Beerbohm. And in *The Price of Peace* the Earl of Derwent (or was he an Irish peer?) died of a sudden seizure while addressing the House of Commons. Yet great value for money was to be had from *The Price of Peace*: the accident ward in St. Thomas's Hospital, where the story began; the Terrace at Westminster, with real tugs and barges going up and down the river and real traffic passing over the bridge; the garden of the heroine's convent school, rich in appropriate blossom; Prince's Rink with real skaters; Palace Yard after an all-night sitting; the sands at Somewhere-on-Sea—complete with photographers and nigger-minstrels—in the constituency of Mr. Tulk, the comic M.P.; an inner room in Downing Street where Lord Derwent, intent on peace, shot a foreign scoundrel through the heart; the House in session as aforesaid; a sectional view of the yacht of the wicked M.P., having the abducted heroine aboard and (since ships seldom appeared at Drury Lane unless they were to be sunk) a collision, in which the wicked M.P. went down with his Chinese servant at his throat while the heroine climbed the rigging; a road above the cliffs where a young man on a bicycle roused up the coast-guards; a cove between them where the rocket apparatus brought the intrepid and still chaste girl into the arms of her affianced: at which juncture a clergyman appeared and affirmed without fear of contradiction that the Price of Peace was Love. All for a shilling, in the ample and well-sighted gallery of Wyatt's Drury Lane.

D'Artagnanism and Tushery

Romantic, or 'costume', drama died with the men who knew how to play it; it bequeathed its treasure to the cinema. The persistence

XLIII. *Julius Caesar*: design for the Forum scene by Gordon Craig

XLIV. Programme cover by Albert Rutherston

of the kind of film we call 'western' is proof enough that in the public heart there is still a certain D'Artagnanism, an urge to mount,
vicariously, a gallant steed and ride with might and main in some
cause that is ethically defensible. The thing was there before Dumas
gave it a new name; it may be found in Dryden, in Beaumont and
Fletcher, in the Arthurian legend. For its essence is knightliness, perfect as to manners, splendid and terrible when confronting heavy
odds: chivalrous, in short—which brings us back to horses. In
romantic drama there was to the last a whiff of saddle-leather.

Women flocked to it because in a time of sartorial conformity it
gave them man as they craved to see him, in plumage he had long
ceased to wear. It made them no other concessions; its tone and
code were uncompromisingly male, not to say boyish. Women were
here to be fought for, won, and cherished; one never hit a girl. A
rough and ready casuistry was sometimes needed in the romantic
drama we acquired from France. In Lewis Waller's version of *Les
Trois Mousquetaires* there was a scene, too exciting to omit, in
which D'Artagnan had to engage Miladi in single combat. A solution
of the problem was quickly found. 'Fiends have no sex!' cried Mr.
Waller, and promptly set about her, with the entire approval of the
gallery.

This drama evolved for its purpose a language of its own, deriving
in part from the basic stage-English of the early nineteenth century
yet seldom excessively absurd. It was a fustian language, but terse
and to the point. At its best it acknowledged the influence of
Browning in his Cavalier vein; more often it drew on Bulwer Lytton.
Its purpose was to put the audience on terms with 'period' as pain-
lessly as might be. In some periods one swore by one's halidom; in
others one said zounds and egad; in nearly all it was permitted to
say tush; otherwise the words used were very much the same. This
excellent actors' language eluded precise designation until someone
remembered Stevenson's word for it: Tushery.

In quality it ranged from high to low. The purest form was perhaps the French, as imported and acclimatized by Charles Kean. But
The Lyons Mail, in the hands of a romantic realist like Irving (whose
son revived it in these years with others of his father's plays), was
not chivalresque; it came as near to Stendhal as to Dumas. Of finer, if
softer, texture was *The Only Way*, which Martin-Harvey and his
wife devotedly built out of *A Tale of Two Cities* and passed to

a couple of pseudonymous writers who supplied the dialogue to measure; it was small wonder that the part of Sidney Carton fitted the actor like a glove. Romantic drama was for actors; in *The Breed of the Treshams* Lieutenant Reresby and Martin-Harvey positively ran away with each other, to such effect that very soon the American ladies who had written the play were protesting that this was not at all the sort of hero they had had in mind. Wilson Barrett, on the other hand, had avoided any risk of that trouble by turning author on his own account. With *The Sign of the Cross* he had opened up a field for romantic drama of a strongly religious bent which he was now exploiting with great honour and profit. There were other and equally rewarding deviations from the perfect norm. The inter-action of Mayfair and Ruritania was, to the secular-minded, as exciting as the conflict between Rome and Galilee as seen by Mr. Barrett. In *The Prisoner of Zenda* Anthony Hope and George Alexander had united in giving D'Artagnanism a new look, and had discovered romance in the continental Bradshaw: one left for Strelsau by the boat-train from Victoria. Mr. Walter Howard embraced this *fin-de-siècle* conception, and for many years sent his company round the provinces in Ruritanian melodrama, well played, handsomely mounted, and of a strictly moral tone.

But the quintessential D'Artagnanism remained in Lewis Waller's keeping. An unsurpassed Brutus and Henry the Fifth, he brought the same integrity, vigour, stance, and bell-mouthed utterance to countless heroes, from the great Musketeer downwards (or upwards) to Monsieur Beaucaire, who won his lady like all the rest because it was part of Waller's understanding with his public that beauty must always be the reward of valour. Humour was not his strongest point; but just as we were becoming aware of this there emerged Fred Terry, the first and most urbane of Scarlet Pimpernels, who faced the direst peril with a snuff-box and a smile.

Musical Comedy and Music Hall

These were years of growth for the musical play. At the turn of the century Gilbert and Sullivan opera was dating but was not yet a classic, and there were those who claimed that Edward German's *Merrie England* and *Tom Jones* entitled him to rank as Sullivan's successor and superior. In this favouring time it was musical comedy that came into its own. Impenitently English, it had not taken much infection from *The Belle of New York*, but pursued its own insouciant and sprightly way. Less shapely or coherent than *The Mikado*, it afforded scope to comedians who were more self-assertive than Gilbert would have found tolerable, and to chorus ladies who, while performing their evolutions, were encouraged to exert their individual charm. It attracted a public devoid of connoisseurship which sought only as good a time as was to be had from fun, tunes worth whistling, and pretty legs and faces. The plot, a mere device for the display of such delights, turned almost always on the lawful pursuit of a virgin; the word 'Girl' continually recurs in the titles of these pieces. But that was so much groundbait. It was the particular girl, notably Miss Gertie Millar in *Our Miss Gibbs*, who drew the *cognoscenti* in, George Grossmith and Edmund Payne abetting.

Nevertheless, as comic opera began to show signs that it was not yet dead, musical comedy now entered on the slow metamorphosis that was to culminate in the 'musical' which today we can nearly equate with opera. At the beginning Paul Rubens had some hand in this. His eponymous Miss Hook of Holland was a girl, but she lyrically embodied an idea; his King of Cadonia, of Ruritanian stock, had a purposeful marching song to sing. The notion slowly grew that a musical play could be, seriously if lightly, about things that mattered. *The Duchess of Dantzig*, a native product, gave us more than a whiff of the revolution and the first empire; *Véronique*, a fragrant importation from France, was steeped in nostalgia for the second; both had tunes that still charm us, and in both there was a view of life as something more than fun. In *The Arcadians* hedonism assumed, for one act, its less metropolitan and more pastoral aspect, and bare-legged nymphs proclaimed that

> In Arcady life flows along
> As careless as the shepherd's song,
> But Strephon pipes along the lea
> In Arcady, in Arcady. . . .

A corrective to this guilelessness came from Vienna with *The Merry Widow*, in which sex unmistakably reared its half-ugly, half-alluring head with the aid of a score that has now won the work a place beside *Fledermaus*. Indeed it is from Vienna as much as from New York that we may trace, through the over-orchestrated banalities of *The Dollar Princess* and the lilt and vigour of *The Chocolate Soldier*, a line of descent that brings us at last to *Rose Marie*, to

No, No, Nanette!, to *Oklahoma!*, and to *My Fair Lady* and *West Side Story*. It must be remarked that from first to last not one of these is, as to the music, of English derivation.

Music hall was as strong as ever in its own domain. But as an institution it was already threatened by forces that were seeking to organize it, sober it up, to a degree that old *habitués* deplored. Under Moss Empires Ltd. a chain of Empires began to extend throughout the provinces and suburbs. They opened their doors twice nightly, they had plush seats and no bars, and a respectable matron could enjoy the show without fear of impropriety. The art of Yvette Guilbert was made accessible to thousands who had never heard of her. But the immemorial reek of the stag-party was fading, save in those long-established (and licensed) halls which still tended the lamp of Dionysus. Ballet continued to flourish at the Alhambra and the Empire; but in 1910 the Palace brought us Pavlova and Mordkin. In 1904 the Coliseum opened over-ambitiously with a double bill and four performances daily; a deft reconstruction of its finances and policy ensured for it the success it enjoys to this day.

In retrospect the dramatic renaissance of these years owes very little to poetic drama. But it should be remembered that Tree and Alexander strove to foster it, and not without reward. As throughout the eighteenth and nineteenth centuries, the hand of the Elizabethans lay heavily on any conscientious poet who aspired to tragedy, and Stephen Phillips, although he did not always obey the five-act rule, conformed so far as to write his plays in decasyllabics. A parson's son who had opted for Benson's Shakespeareans rather than the civil service, he emerged as an actor-poet of truly Elizabethan bent who would have been an ornament to the sodality of the Mermaid if he had had a stronger head. It was Alexander who had caught him for the stage. *Paolo and Francesca* at the St. James's in 1899 had evoked comparisons with Sophocles, Dante, Racine, Sardou, and Tennyson. *Herod*, produced by Tree a few months before the queen's death, had confirmed him as an acceptable alternative to Shakespeare at Her Majesty's. In the new reign came *Ulysses*, then *Nero*, then *Faust* (Comyns Carr collaborating): we can now perceive in these substantial successes the decline that was to end in *Armageddon*, which he wrote for Martin-Harvey in the year of his death. He was accomplished not only in the rhetoric that

comes easily over the footlights but in the revealing phrase at the
right moment. 'Mother, I am thy son', says the guilty Nero to the
guilty Agrippina across the body of the dead Britannicus—a telling
curtain-line. If Phillips is today as remote as his early nineteenth-
century predecessors in the same vein, the reason may be that the
true life-stream of the drama flows through other channels.

The Social Code

The social drama of this time, already impelled by Ibsen to
widen its choice of theme, was now further enfranchised by a
perceptible slackening of the social code. There was surely evidence
of slipping standards when *Raffles* (1906) invited applause for a
public school man who played cricket by day and stole by night.
But the code of sexual morality was still rigid enough to afford the
serious dramatist a moral frame. To the satisfaction of stalls and
gallery alike, the creatures of his fancy did the done things in the
right clothes and changed for dinner. They were seldom fettered by
economic considerations; based on Mayfair and the shires, they
could be sent abroad when the action called for this, to Biarritz, to
Monte Carlo, or (when crossed in love) to the Rockies. Within the
frame aforesaid they were as free to be themselves as Shakespeare's
young lords and ladies. But scandal of a sexual kind meant ruin.
When a young wife fled abroad with her lover there was no trouble
over passports and reservations: they could be in Vienna in twenty-
four hours. But she knew that in Vienna she would not be received,
and that when she came home she would be cut by her friends; at
the moment of decision she had a formidable choice to make. In
short, the current sexual code was of immense service to the
Edwardian playwright, even when he challenged it; in his view a
drama which acknowledged none would have been on a fair way
back to the jungle.

Accordingly, when Pinero's correct but comfort-loving Iris availed
herself of the cheque-book which an admirer had put at her disposal, she signed not only the cheque but her death-warrant as well.
When his honest Letty discovered that the man who had won her
love was already married, the whole house took the shock as she did,
and her gentle comment was long remembered by old playgoers.
When Filmer Jesson, M.P., warned his defiant young Nina that she
might compel him to seek the best advice he could procure, those

characteristically pompous words had meaning: separation, to say nothing of divorce, was a dreadful thing. *The Walls of Jericho*, a best-seller in which Alfred Sutro can have taken no great pride, made us excitingly free of the looser Edwardian set; we were put right with our better selves when Jack Frobisher, as rough as he was rich, persuaded his nobly born but skittish wife to go back with him to Queensland; we approved, even if we could not picture Lady Alethea among the sheep. Pinero, on the other hand, always saw his people through to their end, even if the end was death; there was a morally conceivable future for Filmer and Nina Jesson.

If *His House in Order* is not Pinero's finest work, it is a jewel of Edwardian comedy *comme il fallait*. But he explored other social strata, not always scoring a box-office success. *The 'Mind-the-Paint' Girl* was so just a satire on the musical-comedy world that it did not recover from its first-night booing. *The Thunderbolt*, a study of provincial life in its more Balzacian aspects, failed at the St. James's. So did *Mid-Channel*, a tragedy in which the childless marriage of a stockbroker falls in ruin. All these plays were implicitly critical of the tenets that we now call bourgeois: if they had found their way to the Court under Granville-Barker's rule they would have made even less money, but their fame might be greater than it is. Unhappily Pinero's style was not Barker's, nor was his view of men and things, and he on his part may have been reasonably disinclined, at his years, to seek adventure with the Left.

The rising star was Barrie's. Having proceeded with native caution from the farce of *Walker, London* and the comedy of *The Professor's Love Story* to his own stage version of *The Little Minister*, he was now persuading a hard-headed but soft-hearted public to accept nothing less than his own most marketable philosophy of life. In *Quality Street* (1902) he gave his Edwardian audience an expertly calculated dose of Jane Austen and Mrs. Gaskell with a measure of whimsy as an adjuvant; the little play was pronounced sweet—as indeed it was—and everyone was much the better for having seen it. In *The Admirable Crichton* he at once brought up, as it were, his intellectual rearguard and consolidated his advance. Here was a lively, impish mind at work; the butler who in altered circumstances becomes his master's boss is a figure deriving from Beaumarchais—who was equally applauded by the choicer spirits of a doomed régime. From then on, within the period we are considering, his slightest play (*Little Mary*, for example) relied securely on 'the Barrie touch'. In 1904 Tree read *Peter Pan* and thought the author had gone mad; but Charles Frohman believed in it, and the out- come is a familiar story. In *What Every Woman Knows* (1908) his fantasy, his tenderness for small brave souls, were sustained by a stagecraft that was not given its due. It was thirty years before his appropriate Nemesis caught up with him; our theatre would be vastly the poorer without him.

But in 1908 London was confronted with a new young dramatist, who after ten years of writing and waiting found himself with four plays running in the west end at the same time. In *The Summing Up* Mr. Maugham has told with as much charm as candour how and why, after *A Man of Honour* had had its brief success with the Stage Society, he took leave of the coteries and addressed himself to a wider public whose intelligence-quota lay somewhere, as he puts it, midway between A and Z. Estimating their requirements as coolly as Congreve had done, he delighted their palates with a dry wine which had the faintest possible flavour of the Restoration. Students of dramatic literature may one day find significance in *Lady Frederick*, *Mrs. Dot*, and *Penelope*, if only as forerunners of that perfectly amoral comedy *The Circle*—which is beyond the range of our survey. Like Barrie, indeed like Shakespeare, Somerset Maugham wrote with an eye to the stalls, circle, pit, and gallery of the Establish- ment; yet the students aforesaid may decide that in fact both were smoothing the way for the *avant-garde*. Barrie set our fancy free, Maugham pleased, and never ignobly lulled, our minds; both had made themselves masters of the art of dramatic story-telling.

Reflection of an Age

The established Edwardian theatre, then, still drew strength from its Victorian past; but it exulted in its present and did not by any means close its mind to a future that as yet seemed to hold no menace. With less than its habitual time-lag it faithfully reflected the age. It cautiously fostered a progressive drama, insisting only that the progress must not be of an abrupt kind that might spell ruin. But it was still very much an actors' theatre; and it is in the quality of acting it achieved that it stands justified before posterity: not, save in rare instances, acting on a disturbingly heroic scale, but acting so adequate to an unheroic theme, so sure and deft, so confident within its own limitations, that from the moment of the player's first appearance the spectator shared that confidence, and knew that whatever the play might amount to he would see it impeccably played. It was said with some justice that the actor-managers had between them turned the west-end stage into a club which young actors found hard to join. But there they were, in their respective strongholds: Cyril Maude was reputed to favour public-school men; Arthur Bourchier, himself a founder of the O.U.D.S., offered an opening to university men; Hawtrey, the most debonair of stage sinners, had to have men of good *ton* about him. So, as he rose to command, had du Maurier, whose light but exquisite art would have suffered against a background of assumed gentility; so had Marie Tempest and Graham Browne in the social comedy that Maugham supplied. There was, as indeed there had been from the days of the Bancrofts, an unabated demand for competent and personable small-part players who could *behave*, and the training afforded them was as sound as it was limited. This was not enough for the exacting art of melodrama or of farce—*Charley's Aunt* was still running; they called for an older, tougher technique. It was not enough for Sir Charles Wyndham, whose voice and scale seemed to transform a trifling play into a classic, and needed riper support. It would not do for Shakespeare or romantic drama: for Tree, Alexander, Waller, Martin-Harvey, or Fred Terry, for Oscar Asche and Lily Brayton. These last, newcomers in management, had almost eclipsed the memory of John Drew and Ada Rehan with their robust and jolly *Taming of the Shrew*, and soon were heading, by way of the oriental spectacle of *Kismet*, for *Chu Chin Chow*. They were old Bensonians. Mr. Benson's young company, robust, ardent, and of unmistakable distinction, were neither (as we might now say) behaviourists nor (as we might now say) 'ham'. If, after a year with Benson and another year under the benevolent despotism of Fred Terry, one had the luck to emerge as one of Tree's or Alexander's young men, one's foot was firmly on the ladder. It was only when long runs palled, or the lure of adventure became irresistible, that one turned one's eyes toward the Left.

THE AVANT-GARDE

There was one characteristic of the age which we must rather wistfully acknowledge: its confidence. The Establishment was still

confident in its security, the Left no less so in its hope. Little had
yet happened to shake the citadel of English humanism; the reddest
of our revolutionaries had no ardent wish for a Feast of Pikes. All
that the liberal-minded majority asked and expected was that freedom should broaden down from precedent to precedent, with mind
and soul in Tennysonian accord. Tennyson, to be sure, was dating,
and that orderly sequence did not exclude any manifestations of
obstreperousness that might hasten the millennium, particularly in
the domain of art.

Throughout Europe, indeed, artists were imbued with a new
spirit; in retrospect it is as though they were making the most of the
few easy years that were left them. Everywhere there was a gay
resolve to challenge the old rules—to spread beyond the frame. The
continental theatre did not escape the contagion. In Germany
Adolphe Appia had long been striving to liberate Wagner from his
self-imposed subjection to the stage machinist, while on the other
hand the Prinzregenten-Theater in Munich was beginning to outclass
Bayreuth with Rhine-maidens who dived and frolicked on wires
instead of rotating on a turntable. The Meiningen way with Shakespeare was giving place to semi-permanent settings that were
satisfyingly scenic but did not hold up the play while scenes were
changed. Max Reinhardt, an eclectic of genius who borrowed where
he chose, staged within this decade a scenic *Midsummer Night's
Dream* with a revolving wood, a monolithic but still scenic *Lear*, a
Jedermann (our *Everyman*) on a platform stage with access from the
auditorium, and an *Oedipus* in the round of a circus in Vienna.
Meanwhile the Imperial Russian Ballet had revealed that within
the limitations of orthodox stage-carpentry it was possible to
achieve effects that were equally new and thrilling. Stanislavski and
the Moscow Art Theatre were already names to conjure with.

Dionysians and Puritans

It was not long before the English stage was caught up in this
happy ferment of ideas. The *avant-garde* embraced them all, in a
confusion which the historian must try to unravel. If in that time
we sought to rank with the theatrically forward-looking, it was not
only required of us that we should swear fealty to Appia, Reinhardt,
and the Russians. On the home ground we were expected to avow
our disapproval of Tree's Shakespeare, of actor-managers in general,

and of plays that the public paid to see, and our belief in Elizabethan staging, in a people's theatre, and in the drama of ideas; finally most of us agreed that we were disciples of Gordon Craig. Here was, as we now see, a pretty complication. Certainly Mr. Craig was so brimful of ideas that Reinhardt found him good to steal from; but as his philosophy of art enchantingly took shape he made it clear that his ideas were by no means those of the drama of ideas, which he disliked and derided. He thought the Elizabethan reconstructors silly; the Old Vic, when it emerged, reminded him of the Salvation Army; and he claimed as his master the greatest actor-manager of all, and Irving's Lyceum as his *Alma Mater*. Not for the first time in history the prophet was to prove something of a puzzle to the faithful.

Meredith, in his *Essay on Comedy*, reduced mankind to two types: those who are prone to laughter and those who are not. Without going as far as that, we might broadly classify the reformers of the Edwardian stage as Dionysians and Puritans; there was some intermarrying, but the strains can still be distinguished. Ever since Irving had made the stage respectable the Puritans had been steadily (as we now say) infiltrating; they were fortified when Matthew Arnold decided that the theatre, since the people would have it, must be organized. Art in the service of social progress was one thing, art for its own sake was another; the eager Left of the theatre did not bother to resolve a perpetually troublesome antagonism, they were too keen to get going. But we, looking back, can detect in this seething time two movements, sometimes in temporary alliance under a single leader but fundamentally divergent. One, which was rational, saw in the theatre a force making for civic fulfilment; even emotionally arid drama was to be deemed worthy if it impelled the plain citizen to think. The other, in which Mr. Craig was the dominant figure, was not rational at all. The theatre was a temple administered by a high priest who was henceforward to be known as the Producer; to its rites all other arts were tributary. Although Mr. Craig was understood to be a pagan, this was in essence a religious concept, commending itself more to enthusiasts than to the hard-headed. His *On the Art of the Theatre* was in no sense a practical book, but it was beautiful, fanciful, and stimulating; above all it evoked the immemorial magic of the stage. It appeared in 1905, and within a very few years it had captivated Europe.

The *avant-garde* owed something to the Establishment. From the nineties onward Tree had mitigated the boredom of an 'obstinate success' by staging matinée productions of more limited appeal, Ibsen's *An Enemy of the People* among them. Martin-Harvey, Fred Terry, and Oscar Asche had lost money by venturing too far ahead of the general taste; Forbes-Robertson was by no means the poorer for Shaw's *Caesar and Cleopatra*. A dramatic renascence was clearly on the way. But it found its focal point at the little Court Theatre in Sloane Square, and under a younger management.

Granville-Barker and Shaw

In 1904 Harley Granville-Barker was 27. He had been on the stage for fourteen years, had served in Shakespeare with Ben Greet, and had emerged as a notable Richard II under Poel. In 1900 his grace of body, mind, and spirit had qualified him for the poet in the Stage Society's production of *Candida*, and it was with six experimental matinées of this play that, four years later, the Vedrenne–Barker régime at the Court was inaugurated. Only when the history of that adventure came to be written was it revealed how slender its resources were, or by what desperate shifts it was maintained until, thanks to the ardour and optimism of Barker, the prudent pessimism of Vedrenne, who had charge of the finance, and the unfailing productivity of Shaw, it had left an indelible mark on our stage. From the first the object was clearly not to make money but to enjoy life, fully and strenuously, while life lasted. There was so much to be done, so many fine or promising playwrights to be given a hearing, that the run of a play which filled the house was determined by the time needed to rehearse its successor: Shaw, Euripides (in Gilbert Murray's renderings), Maeterlinck, Ibsen, Hauptmann, Yeats, St. John Hankin, Galsworthy, Laurence Housman, Masefield, Barker himself; and after every three of these we may repeat the name of Shaw, whose reputation mounted from celebrity to fame with that of the little theatre he indefatigably supplied. *Candida* was followed by a definitive *You Never Can Tell*, by *Man and Superman*, by *John Bull's Other Island*, *Major Barbara*, and *The Doctor's Dilemma*. Originally presented for a few weeks at most, these plays have now a secure place in the international repertoire, yet scarcely one of them would have had a chance on the west-end stage of the time.

It was quickly apparent that a new school of acting and production was coming into being. Barker was the ideal complement to
Shaw, as in some parts—Marchbanks in *Candida* for instance—he
was his ideal exponent. A perfectionist and something of a precisian,
he might well have found himself antipathetic to the robustness and
resonance which Shaw's art derived from Italian opera. But Barker
had Italian blood in his veins and his genius, submitting almost un-
reservedly to the genius of the elder man, achieved a fusion that
from the other side of the footlights appeared to be complete. Shaw,
however ascetic in his life, cried for red blood in the theatre;
Barker responded, but with the due regard he felt bound to pay to
style. To Barker in those days style connoted a faithful naturalism,
devoid of plumage: it was a notion that served excellently in Galsworthy's *The Silver Box*. The settings at the Court were as realistic
as the convention of the day required. The round tower of Roscullen
in *John Bull's Other Island* was a real tower, in no way stylized: the
Trafalgar Square scene in *Votes for Women!* gave us the authentic
Nelson column, complete with lions and plinth. The suspension of
disbelief was never attained by the elaborate pretence of 'let's
pretend' with which we are now familiar. Even in *Prunella*,
a dainty pastiche in which the rational Barker, aided by Laurence
Housman, made his first acknowledgement to the irrational, the
setting was (in Max Beerbohm's view) too much the real thing.

No one, however, found that the acting at the Court was too much
the real thing. Barker was manifestly dedicated. A light shone
through him, and his resolve and intellectual power amply made
good his lack of experience. It was commonly said that under his
stage-management—the grander word was not yet used—even
well-known players seemed to do themselves more justice than elsewhere. This was true; many such were lured into service at the
Court, at salaries which they would have disdained in the west end,
by the hope of adding a cubit to their stature, as not a few of them
did. Nor was the advantage on their side only. For the new drama,
particularly when it was of Shaw's kind, relied heavily on actors
who had learned their business in the old. An outstanding case was
that of Louis Calvert, a seasoned Shakespearian whom we might
today style 'ham'. His Broadbent and his Undershaft were virtually
classic creations, embodying eternal types, eternal ideas, in the
persons of everyday men. His successors in these parts could no

doubt explain them better than he ever could, but they seem unable to *be* them, on anything like his scale. The pressure of personality at the Court was, in fact, part of the Victorian heritage.

Even to those of the Left who were not theatre-minded the Court offered a platform for the exposition and dissemination of their views. Shaw had fought his way through the stage door less as an artist than as an iconoclast and reformer; and on the boards of the Court the economic, social, and even imperial problems of the day were set spinning in eddies of dialectic that recalled the *Fabian Essays*. The uneasy, brooding conscience of Galsworthy impelled him to write a tract on social inequality which is still disturbing. Even St. John Hankin, who was inclined to dismiss the scheme of things entire with a cheerful shrug, had some kind of message for his time. The fact remains that *John Bull's Other Island*, *The Silver Box*, and *The Return of the Prodigal* are all, in their varying degrees, dramatic works of the quality which endures. At the Court Theatre the drama of ideas was supported in part by an intelligentsia who were avid of ideas, but largely also by those who were keen on fine drama finely played.

Barker himself wrote plays, and there was much speculation as to his future in this vein. *The Marrying of Ann Leete*—such was the faintly precious title of his first work—was so sedulously Meredithian that William Archer himself could not make head or tail of it; the young man was all too clearly concerned to show that he had style. But in *The Voysey Inheritance* he shook himself free of his nonage, and drew from the life. The righteous young solicitor who receives from his seemingly righteous father a legacy of irredeemable fraud— there is a theme indeed; and Barker's handling of it is a masterpiece of sustained irony, marred only by one brief concession to the feminism of the day. For Barker had not yet liberated himself entirely from Fabian tutelage: the reformer and the artist in him were not yet perfectly on terms. Concerned though he was for a rational and orderly social system, he was none the less fascinated by the irrationalism and disorder of humankind. The intrusion of lawlessness into the domain of social and moral law became one of his chief preoccupations: we may remember that it was one of Shakespeare's, too. In *Prunella* it was no more than an intrusion of disorderly players; in *The Madras House* it became the universal intrusion of sex; in *Waste* it was crystallized in one woman's intrusion on the career of an incorruptible politician.

The pace at the Court proved too hot to last. An attempt was made to transfer the venture to the west end in the hope of attracting a larger public; but after four years of precarious life it was wound up, honourably and without loss save to the promoters; and even they had gained in reputation immeasurably more than they had lost in cash. Moreover they were soon to be consoled by the reflection that they, by their example, had set the English repertory movement on its way. It was in 1908 that Miss Horniman, having done all she could for the Abbey Theatre in Dublin, opened the Gaiety in Manchester. This institution, with the help of Iden Payne, Lewis Casson, and Sybil Thorndike, became the Court Theatre of the midlands. In 1911 Basil Dean, one of Miss Horniman's young men, founded the Liverpool Repertory Theatre, still thriving as the Playhouse. There is hardly a repertory theatre in existence today that does not, knowingly or unknowingly, acknowledge its debt to Granville-Barker and the Court.

But to Barker in 1908 the salient fact was that a very small subsidy would have kept his head above water. He had to have money, and as a good Fabian he believed that the state must foster the arts. What could be more natural than that his thoughts, and the thoughts of all who hailed him as their leader, should incline toward the notion of a national theatre?

A National Theatre?

To many people of liberal and orderly mind it had seemed a reproach that the capital of the empire possessed no institution comparable with the *Comédie Française*. From the days of the Globe our theatre had been content to live dangerously, unsupported by monetary aid from the state: the patents conferred on Davenant and Killigrew by Charles II had carried no subvention with them. Its survival through centuries of fine acting in bad plays had now culminated in a rebirth of fine drama that seemed to herald a second golden age. Now was surely the time to press for an English national theatre, free from the tyranny of the box-office, which should at once preserve tradition, set and maintain a standard, and foster new developments in the art. Early in King Edward's reign a committee was formed with this end in view. The tercentenary of Shakespeare's death was approaching, and another body was concerned with the erection of a suitable memorial in London. The two movements merged, and in 1908 the Committee of the Shakespeare Memorial National Theatre came into being. An anonymous donation of £70,000 set the ball rolling, the donor (Mr. Carl Meyer) was rewarded with a baronetcy, and by the outbreak of the first world war the committee had acquired a site. It was to be the first of several.

The enthusiasm of its advocates was real enough, but their approach was not entirely realistic. They embarked confidently, in a climate of opinion that seemed to favour planning, government by committee, and a conception of the state as an enlightened and beneficent patron of the arts. The Liberal government of the day was not unsympathetic, and they believed that if the cost of the building could be met by public subscription the Treasury would be persuaded to endow it. It is easy for us to see where they were wrong. They thought too much in terms of bricks and mortar: enduring institutions do not begin so. They planned too much. By way of showing how practical the project was, William Archer collaborated with Barker in *The National Theatre: A Scheme and Estimates*, which set forth in detail the running of the great machine; it was too perfectly thought out to be perfectly convincing. They greatly overestimated their expectations from a London public that was well enough pleased with His Majesty's and the St. James's, and from a provincial public that was not interested in London. They were too rigidly committed to principle. With the funds at their disposal they might have emerged from the first world war, had the terms of their trust permitted, as the owners of His Majesty's, earning through normal channels the money that the public had failed to subscribe. But that would have involved them in commercial speculation, which was forbidden; moreover the Shakespearians on the committee, William Poel among them, would as soon have come to terms with the devil as with Sir Herbert Tree. The national theatre must be, from the outset, its pure self or nothing: in consequence it was, for many years, nothing.

When, in 1909, the executive of the Shakespeare Memorial National Theatre produced its report, Max Beerbohm pronounced it a monumentally ridiculous document and put forward, as the modern drama's chiefest need, 'a quite small theatre, decently endowed, with one enlightened despot to govern it'. He instanced the

Court, as it had been under the rule of Granville-Barker; and it was incontestable that during that brief reign more had been accomplished than a cautious, democratically administered and state-subsidized institution would have dared even to envisage. It was a characteristically impish suggestion, and to the serious, authoritarian Barker who was now deeply committed it must have seemed wantonly subversive. But Max delighted in coaxing public men to be their true selves: the artist in Barker cannot have been altogether displeased.

Censorship of Plays

Another agitation drew strength from the experiment at the Court, and that was for the abolition of the censorship. This dated as an office from the latter half of the sixteenth century, when its main function was to suppress matter injurious to church or state. The same ruling held, roughly speaking, to the end of the seventeenth, and this is why we are still free to savour the bawdry of Shakespeare, Fletcher, Wycherley, and Congreve. Under Queen Anne the moral reins were tightened. In 1737 Walpole, chafing under persistent lampoons, enacted that all matter played upon the stage must have the prior sanction of his own Lord Chamberlain; this drove Fielding from the Haymarket and left it to the wilier devilries of Foote. By the Theatres Act of 1843 the previous legislation was consolidated. The Lord Chamberlain became the licensing authority for all London theatres save the patent houses of Drury Lane and Covent Garden, and for all stage plays whatsoever if they were publicly played for gain within the United Kingdom. His retrospective powers entitled him to ban any play which in his judgement was not conducive to the preservation of good manners, decorum, or the public peace. Incest, for example, was not a permitted theme—and that ruling disposed of Shelley's *The Cenci*, as it was to dispose of D'Annunzio's *La Città Morta*.

The thing had worked tolerably well until the advent of the new drama. But the new dramatists, as their field widened, began to clamour for the freedom that was granted to novelists; it was intolerable that even the works they were allowed to print could not be played. In Maeterlinck's *Monna Vanna* the heroine came, like Judith, to a conqueror's tent; she was wearing nothing but a cloak, and said as much: the play was banned. In Granville-Barker's

XLV. *Oedipus Rex* at Covent Garden: Max Reinhardt's Theban chorus

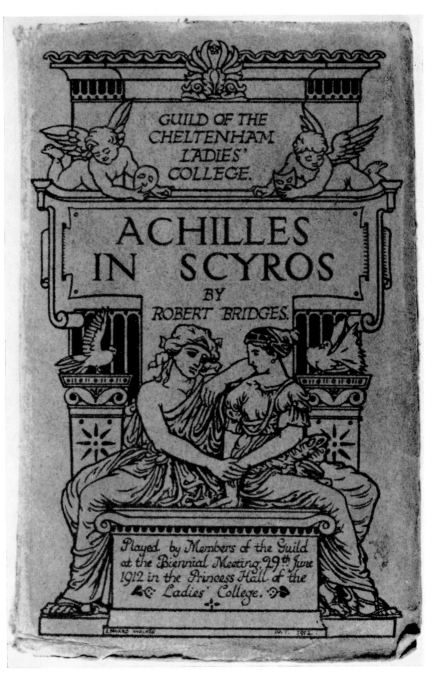

XLVI. Amateur theatricals: programme cover by Edward Walker

Waste, conjecturably written as a test case, the catalytic event was an abortion which proved fatal; this—to us—almost heavily moral tragedy was banned. The same fate befell Shaw's *Blanco Posnet*, in which a sinner finds his way to God.

There was another view of the matter. The Lord Chamberlain's licence was, after all, a guarantee which protected author, manager, and company from molestation at the bidding of local authority; the police could not march them and their audience off to prison, as might happen in the United States. And a profounder question loomed. The censor was reputed to have a 'down' on plays which treated sex seriously and to favour Mr. Hawtrey's salacious farces. Which, then, was the more healthful: to laugh one's head off at a comedy of light love, or to sit for three hours brooding over the consequences of lust? When *Les Avariés* was given privately in London as *Damaged Goods* M. Brieux's bombinating doctor was discovered to be a bore, and his syphilitic patients (who were in no position to moralize) stole the evening.

Be that as it may, the pressure of opinion grew until in 1909 a joint committee of both houses of parliament was set up by the prime minister to inquire into the working of the censorship. Many celebrated persons testified before it, some of whom were perhaps thinking as much of the showing they made as of the question at issue. The outcome was a characteristically British compromise. The institution was upheld, its severities were a little relaxed, and the Lord Chamberlain was left free to reconsider his ban at any time in individual cases.

Repertory

We can now return to the *avant-garde* as represented by Barker and by the new repertory movement which the Court had inspired. It must be stressed that only a few of the so-called repertory theatres were in fact anything of the kind. The ideal aimed at was a stock company, qualified for classical and modern drama alike, that would draw a sufficient audience by a nightly change of bill. That was the continental way and, with the help of state or municipal subsidies and the *abonnement* system of which a theatre-minded public willingly availed itself, it worked. In England, without these two advantages, it did not. The subsidy was limited by the resources of a private backer, and the unschooled British playgoer would not

readily commit himself, even at reduced prices, to a series of plays
that had been chosen for him in advance; he liked to see whatever he
had a mind to see on any evening when he had a mind to see it. In
Manchester Miss Horniman was for a long time compelled, at some
cost to the nerves of her distinguished company, to put on a new
play every week; only when they travelled could they present a
repertoire of plays. It was vexing that the true repertory system had
been made to work by Covent Garden, by the Carl Rosa, Moody–
Manners, and Savoy opera companies in the provinces, by Tree in
his Shakespeare festivals, by Benson's Shakespearians throughout
the year, and by the actor-manager who did excellently on tour in
a round of his most famous parts. But these after all were not
manifestations of the *new* drama. There was a brief moment of hope
that, pending the national theatre, the new drama would achieve its
Covent Garden at the Duke of York's. Here, in 1910, Charles
Frohman was persuaded—some say by Barrie, under pressure from
Barker and Shaw—to give the thing a chance, on the grand scale.

It was customary to dub Frohman a 'commercial' manager, in that
he habitually inclined to good plays that other people would like
and would come to see. But he was as true an enthusiast on his own
plane as any of the Left, and it was shabby in some of them to hint,
afterwards, that he had not really wanted this venture to succeed.
In terms of accountancy it was foredoomed. There were no stars,
yet the salary list alone, with three well-cast plays simultaneously in
the bill, was enough to make the financial structure top-heavy.
Administrative costs were minimal by present standards, but even
here repertory proved more exigent than the long run. Perhaps the
prime cause of failure was that the London public, like Miss Horniman's in Manchester, preferred a sound play which stayed steadily
in the bill to any alternating masterpieces. When the brief season
ended, Frohman was the poorer by some thousands and we were the
richer by Galsworthy's *Justice*, Barker's *The Madras House*, Shaw's
Misalliance, all works of lasting quality. Barker, having again
risen in stature through a set-back, was partly comforted by finding
a winner in *Fanny's First Play*, and bided his time.

From Poel to Reinhardt

So far we have been concerned with that aspect of the new movement which may be broadly styled rational. Here was the authors'

theatre triumphant, supplanting the actors' theatre and more intent on fine plays and the ideas behind them than on fine parts.
But it had little fault to find with the *playhouse* that the twentieth
century had evolved from the nineteenth, eighteenth, and seventeenth: the consummation of the picture-frame seemed final and
hardly to be improved upon. Players had found their effective place
within it; playwrights, from Robertson to the great Ibsen himself,
had conformed to its discipline. The lure of curtain and footlights—
'Aurora's harbingers'—was as potent as in Charles Lamb's day:
even in the strenuously forward-looking Court under Barker's rule
there was a band in the usual place. But the other, less rational,
wing of the *avant-garde* was now to challenge such set notions; it
was to challenge above all the restraint of the proscenium frame.
And it is here that we have to salute the lonely figure of William
Poel.

Lonely, because he is impossible to place, save on the bleak
eminence he chose. He was at once a mystic and, on rationalistic
grounds, an anti-clerical: the finest fruit of his extreme dissent was
his resuscitation of *Everyman*, a more austerely soul-searching
affair than the profuse *Jedermann* of von Hofmannsthal and Reinhardt which still draws easy tears at Salzburg. But the end to which
he consecrated his life and his meagre resources was the restoration
of Shakespeare to the theatre for which he wrote. We now know, or
think we know, better than he did what that theatre was really like;
but in certain vital matters Poel and his Elizabethan Stage Society
were undoubtedly on the right track. Shakespeare can be, and must
be, spoken trippingly on the tongue; his action must be continuous;
he responds to the freedom of an open stage. These last were, for the
other wing of the *avant-garde*, the operative words. Poel, whom it
would be hard to describe otherwise than as a Puritan, did in fact
help to make the way smooth for those Dionysians who were
seeking to escape from the proscenium frame. A professed ration-
alist, he made a present of his apron stage to men who claimed that
the theatre was dying of its rationalism.

In its lighter mood playgoing London had long cherished the
irrational, as is testified by its addiction to the burlesques of
Planché and Burnand, to farces galore, to Savoy opera. During our
period the lamp was tended by The Follies, a concert-party of wits
led by the illustrious Pélissier, who charmed Edwardians for

several years by 'potting' their favourite plays and generally reminding them that man was as ridiculous as he was sublime. But as the new century entered its second decade there was a heady sparkle of irrationalism in the very air we breathed, premonitory, a social historian might feel, of a day not now far distant when all Europe was to do a staggeringly irrational thing. Labour, with the millennium supposedly in sight under Liberal rule, was even more restive than it had been under the Tories; women were demonstrating their fitness for the vote in the oddest ways; certain statesmen were lightheartedly fomenting civil war in Ireland. In the coteries that fostered the arts there was a growing perception that to be truly vital one might have to be a little mad. It was through the ballet that the infection of a *serious* irrationalism reached our stage. Our ballet was not at that time very good; it was orthodox and in no way imperilled our reason. Then came Maud Allan, bare-legged, in *The Vision of Salome*; there came also Pavlova and Mordkin in their *Bacchanal*, a riot of the senses; then came the Russians in full force: was there not something exhilaratingly savage in *Schéhérazade*? Meanwhile a grosser public was succumbing to the African beat of ragtime, the forerunner of jazz. And then came Max Reinhardt, from Berlin.

Gordon Craig had sketched the image of the great producer; Reinhardt, with his train of players, authors, composers, designers, *unterregisseurs*, technicians, and aides-de-camp, gave us the undoubted thing. There was seemingly no limit to his range or style. He could be elegant, he could be farouche or even coarse, as the play and its period required; always he was *kolossal*. In 1910 he impacted on London with *Sumurun*, a mimed Arabian Night which in movement and colour rivalled the art of the Russians. In 1911, at Charles Cochran's prompting, he gave us *The Miracle*, flooding the arena of Olympia with some 1,500 priests, nuns, barons, knights, pikemen, and rabble, all as authentically of the middle ages as in any early Flemish painting; by way of creating the necessary atmosphere of faith Reinhardt's first great stroke was a miraculous healing which no one who saw it is likely to forget. In 1912 he brought his massive *Oedipus Rex* to London, with Martin-Harvey as the king; Covent Garden could not accommodate more than 400 Thebans, but they, as wave after wave of them came surging through the auditorium, were among the sensations of the evening. By now the greater public had taken the man to its bosom. Here, one felt, was no half-Tartar stuff but thoroughbred German art (Reinhardt was in fact an Austrian Jew) asserting in a cousinly way its right to dominate the Nordic stage.

The Establishment was the first to respond. Within a year of *Sumurun* Oscar Asche was embarked on *Kismet*, another Arabian Night in which, thanks to the painting of Joseph Harker and to German costumes and methods of lighting, the plain playgoer enjoyed his Gorgeous East as never before. *The Miracle*, defying imitation, nevertheless left its mark on the many pageants that were then in vogue. But a few months after *Oedipus* Granville-Barker presented the *Iphigenia in Tauris* in a blood-red setting quite out of his accustomed vein, and that autumn (1912) he opened a season of Shakespeare at the Savoy.

Barker at the Savoy

It is from Savoy Shakespeare that we derive nearly everything that is of worth in our treatment of the plays to this day. In its own day it burst out of the blue, unheralded by any assignable English precedent, and detonated with effects that were both revolutionary and lasting. It was Barker's child, but it was also the child of the time. There was nothing phrenetic or Dionysian in Barker's make-up; his strength and his weakness alike lay in his cool, clear head; but he caught the Reinhardt tide, and whatever other tides were running his way, at the flood.

In the trial scene of *Justice*, still remembered, he had touched the pinnacle of naturalism. Now, in *The Winter's Tale*, he spread his wings. What followed was a masterpiece of temperate planning; not until all the elements were carefully assembled did Barker fuse them into gold (or something very like) with a flame that was whiter than Reinhardt's. In putting Shakespeare on the stage he must first of all be true to his master, William Poel: the speech must be deft and brisk and the action must flow from scene to scene; this meant an apron stage. But his master's reconstruction of the Globe was too sombre for the west end—it had put Max Beerbohm in mind of owls; moreover, he was flinging down the gauntlet to Tree and at the same time was wooing the formidable public of the Russian ballet: his non-scenic Shakespeare must be exciting and delightful to the eye. He was bound to shock: he must charm as well. His old

Court following must be induced to accept actuality without realism. He had the devotees of Craig and Reinhardt to think of; them also he must woo, the Craigites by a setting of tall, bare pylons and vast expanses, the Reinhardtites by a discreet touch of the farouche every now and then, and by his undisguised indebtedness to Reinhardt's production of the play in Berlin. He won the suffrage of the morris dance and folk-song fraternity, even of the select few who preferred a consort of Elizabethan viols to Herr Schmidt's band at His Majesty's. His hygienically white staging and his egalitarian lighting, which shone alike on principals and supers, were not, as someone wickedly alleged, a sop to Fabian planners; they were part of his attempt to recapture in the London of 1912 the daylight and open air of the Globe.

To those who ask whether all this does not mean that Barker was 'stealing', the answer is that Shakespeare himself stole unblushingly, as great creative artists do. What matters is the authentic touch that warrants the stealing, and because of the white-hot passion afore-said Barker stood abundantly justified. He wove together a dozen strands that any man was free to use, and the tapestry was lifelike, beautiful, and his own. But above all their other merits these shows were strong. He did indeed replace the masculine art of the scene-painter with a new thing called *décor*, and the dainty work of Albert Rutherston and Norman Wilkinson appealed more to the women in the audience, perhaps, than to the men; old Lyceumites, shocked by Noah's Ark trees and such levities, foretold an era of decadence. But he drew on Tree and Benson for his actors; there was no lack of manhood on the stage of the Savoy—nor, in consequence, of woman-hood either. Next year came *Twelfth Night* and then *A Midsummer Night's Dream*. These brought the same sense of freshness, alertness, enfranchisement to many who felt they were seeing Shakespeare for the first time. It was, as a leading critic observed, post-impressionist Shakespeare. If the challenge to tradition sounded in some ears a little stridently, it was at least full and clear. As for the moments— and more than moments—of dramatically significant beauty, they linger in the recollection of all who were there to hear and see. Leontes (Henry Ainley) pacing up and down beside the flaming brazier; Perdita (Cathleen Nesbitt) footing it with her lover in the sheepshearers' dance; the golden voice of Paulina (Esmé Beringer) bidding Hermione come down, and the grace of the descent as

Lillah McCarthy made it; a very old Feste (Hayden Coffin) winning nostalgic tears from two drunken gentlemen (Arthur Whitby and Leon Quartermaine) with his thin, sweet voice: these are ineffaceable memories.

Barker was no Reinhardt. He lacked the common touch of the impresario who can force the public to accept a first-rate thing, and this venture did not pay its way. But he was now acknowledged as the English leader of a theatrical revolution that was in progress all over Europe; his future seemed rosy. Confidently he staked everything on his faith in a national theatre (surely just round the corner?) of which he had now proved himself the predestined head. He set about forming a classical repertory company as a nucleus of the grander thing that was soon to be; like others he had to face the ineluctable fact that actors of quality needed more time to ripen in their parts than the conditions of English repertory afforded. There was still that absurdly narrow gap, which an absurdly small subsidy could have bridged, between what he wanted to do and what the paying public wanted to see. It was a tired and harassed Barker who staged Shaw's *Androcles* at the St. James's in September 1913. Within twelve months the stronghold he was building fell in ruins.

Even his cloud-castle dissolved; there was little talk of a national theatre after August 1914. The war made an end of him as a dominant figure on the English stage; it is a queer proof of his quality that this disaster was also, in a sense, the remaking of him. America was not ready for his Shakespeare; he returned to England, put on Hardy's *Dynasts* as an appropriate gesture to the time, and joined the Red Cross in France. His marriage with his beautiful leading lady was dissolved, and he made a fresh start with a new wife who devotedly aided and abetted him in giving to literature what he had sought to give to the theatre. Those who reproach him should remember that the debased standards and soaring costs of the post-war stage offered no inducement to a perfectionist; also that his *Prefaces to Shakespeare*, a record of what he would have liked to do, will long outlast the legend of what he did.

Conclusion

A final survey. In the summer of 1914 the Establishment was in rude health; its arteries, if hardening at all, were not yet too hard to suffer an infusion of new blood. It was not seriously threatened by the men of the *avant-garde*, because they after all were planting the flag further afield, and trade, given time, must follow the flag. Indeed the higher theatre of commerce was already profiting by this extension of the drama's frontiers. Traditionally a laggard, it could now claim to be catching up with the times. The unrest in the Welsh coalfields found an echo in Galsworthy's *Strife*; this noble play did well. Feminism was in the ascendant; the heroine of *Hindle Wakes* opted for unmarried motherhood and independence, and the Kingsway Theatre flourished under Miss Lena Ashwell with a series of domestic comedies which upheld the rights of women and wives. Youth was demanding its latchkey, and at the Haymarket *The Younger Generation* put parents in their place, to the delight of packed houses. The actor-managers continued to revel in the warmth of a sun that showed no sign of setting. Tree suffered not a whit from Barker's Shakespeare, although in his *Henry VIII* (1910) a tentative forestage had suggested that he was not above taking a hint from Poel. In 1913 Alexander, taking more than a hint from Reinhardt, had lost heavily on *Turandot*, a Chinese spectacle in the German manner, but the St. James's was now its prosperous English self again. Some great figures of the time (these two among them) were not to outlive the war; few were to emerge from it as masters in their own houses. But in this last radiant summer their tradition was still unbroken. Charles Wyndham and Mary Moore, Alexander and Irene Vanbrugh, Marie Tempest, Cyril Maude, Charles Hawtrey and Gerald du Maurier; Martin-Harvey, Lewis Waller, Matheson Lang, Fred Terry and Julia Neilson, Oscar Asche and Lily Brayton: here are some of the names on the roll. Musical comedy, if not all that it had been, was aboundingly alive: the splendours of Drury Lane were not diminished. Much of this wealth was available to the provinces when the London companies took the road. But there were also the repertory theatres in Manchester, Liverpool, and Glasgow, and, since 1913, thanks to the munificence of Barry Jackson, its founder and accomplished director, in Birmingham; a new venture was feeling its way at the old Theatre Royal, Bristol. Everywhere the amateurs were taking themselves with unwonted seriousness; the O.U.D.S. was breaking free from the statutory alternation of Shakespeare and the Greeks; in Cambridge the new Marlowe Society was tackling the

Elizabethans: in Norwich Nugent Monck had laid the foundations of the Maddermarket Theatre, a unique institution in which highly trained young people played for love, not money. Half England was going mad about plays and acting; pageants were everywhere, and ancient Britons, crusaders, cavaliers and roundheads, became common objects of the countryside. Still more significant was our growing awareness of the theatre as a bond between nations: Bernhardt and Duse, Sardou and Ibsen, were no longer the only great foreign names we knew; it was not only to Paris but to Moscow, Berlin, Munich, Prague, and even Budapest that we turned in search of an art that would revivify our own. All in all, the Edwardian era was a good era for our drama and our stage, and in 1914 both of them sustained as hard a knock as they had had since 1642.

11

MUSIC

FRANK HOWES, C.B.E.

Formerly Music Critic of The Times

MUSIC

I n musical history changes, revolutions even, have a convenient way of occurring at the turn of a century, so that it is not putting events into a strait-jacket to docket them by centuries, as it would be in political history. Even that elusive abstraction, the Spirit of the Age, is unusually tidy when it attends to the art of music. The change from single-line monody to polyphony can be put at the end of the tenth century, the emergence of individual composers in *ars nova* at the beginning of the fourteenth, and the monodic revolution, associated with the name of Monteverdi and the beginning of opera, can be dated at 1600 with less than the usual amount of qualification.

The years 1600 to 1900 hang together as the period in musical history in which major–minor tonality by key is the structural principle that enabled a whole literature of music, our current repertory, in fact, and all that is half-submerged beneath it, to be written. The present century has seen European music disintegrate, and while some of the fissiparated successors of the key system have already produced masterpieces in their several styles, the unity and coherence of music as the ordinary man knows it, embracing as it does Purcell, Bach, Mozart, Beethoven, Wagner, and Brahms, is no more, and other systems, polytonality, serialism, neo-classicism, and other such solemnly-named heirs of nine centuries of harmonic evolution compete for the future. Brahms died in 1897 and Debussy published his first book of preludes in 1903, wherein the solvents of the key system, consecutive fifths and octaves, the whole-tone scale, and the interval of the augmented fourth, banished since the middle ages as the very devil of music, reappeared in respectable society.

But England, usually behind the musical practice of the continent by about a generation, started its own movement of reform a quarter of a century earlier: Victorian music began to show signs of change to something more vigorous in 1880. Edward Dent, writing in the companion volume on Victorian England, speaks, as most other historians (e.g. Walker and Colles) have done, of the 'renaissance which began in 1880'. Its chief architect was Hubert Parry, its most important composer Charles Stanford, and its adherents numbered Arthur Sullivan and Alexander Mackenzie among them. This renaissance was one of spirit and standards rather than of technical advance or revolution. It was a revolt against the persistent sentimentality of Victorian music, an attempt to get away from German domination, a prospecting for an English style, a search for something more original than the copies of Handel and Mendelssohn which dominated our festivals, a more acutely critical awareness of quality, strength, and sincerity. There is a paradox somewhere in the fact that the vigorous Victorian society, whose enterprise increased wealth, whose philanthropy showed moral insight, whose politics devised a workable system of democracy, which produced great writers as well as great engineers, for its music was content with the weakest in its churches of any period in the long history of Anglicanism, for its serious enjoyment with imports of Italian opera, German conductors, and internationally celebrated pianists. But there it was, and as late as 1921 a German writer was still found to be speaking of *das Land ohne Musik*—though what he and the originators of the phrase probably had in mind was the dearth of composers who could even with indulgence be compared with the continental giants, among whom were Brahms, Wagner, and Verdi. At any rate what Parry and Stanford set before them was a more sincere, a less facile art with higher standards of performance, the possibility of obtaining a decent musical education in England— the Royal College of Music was established in 1883—and a proper national pride.

They only partially succeeded in their pioneering and it was left for the next generation to reap their sowing. When Queen Victoria died in January 1901 the feeling of change in society coincided with the emergence of the first great English composer, great in his undoubted mastery and in individuality of imagination. Edward Elgar declared himself as such with the *Enigma Variations* in 1899 and *The Dream of Gerontius* in 1900, and when Richard Strauss proposed his famous toast, 'I drink to the welfare and success of the first English progressivist musician, Meister Elgar' at the Lower Rhine Festival, the implied recognition startled England. The first decade of the twentieth century, extended up to the outbreak of war in

1914, was the Edwardian age and Elgar was recognized as its musical laureate; and, though there were many other forces at work which changed the picture of English music after the war, no one has ever really challenged the aptitude of that somewhat sententious title. Elgar is the biggest single figure in Edwardian music, for it was he who put back English music on the map of Europe. England once more, after centuries of continental charity, was contributing something distinctive to the world's output of music.

Elgar and Bantock

Edward Elgar was born at Worcester in 1857. For the first forty years of his life he was a provincial musician working in comparatively humble capacities and outside the movements stirring for the renaissance of English music. He played the organ at the local Roman Catholic church, he played the violin in Mr. Stockley's Birmingham orchestra, he conducted Worcester amateurs and the asylum band, he composed salon music, and struck out more ambitiously on cantatas for choral societies in the midlands. Suddenly he produced a masterpiece, the *Enigma Variations*; and not content with one, a second, *The Dream of Gerontius*, in the following year. At a stroke he stepped from the local to the national stage and to an international reputation. The Time Spirit took a hand in his career. King Edward's England was exuberant, opulent, maybe vulgar, but expansive, confident, and charged with a gusto of living that war extinguished for our succeeding generations. Elgar, once having tasted success, found that the new *Zeitgeist* released a flood in him, and there poured from him two symphonies, a violin concerto, and a symphonic poem, the like of which neither Parry nor Stanford nor their predecessors had been able to conceive. Inspiration was lavish, invention gushed out without inhibition to fill orchestral music of the largest scale. He planned a trilogy of oratorios, following the predominant English tradition of vocal music and encouraged by the success of *Gerontius*. But the impulse did flag here, and after the completion of *The Apostles* and *The Kingdom* his idea for a sequence of sacred oratorios on the subject of the early church was allowed to lapse, for his mind had bitten on to the orchestra as the real and proper outlet for his genius.

It is possible in the presence of too uninhibited a performance to feel that the symphonies are too much of a good thing. The flood of golden sound, the rhapsodic flow, and the sheer copiousness of richly wrought invention of the second symphony, which was written avowedly as a loyal tribute and subsequently dedicated to the memory of the king who died between its conception and its completion, does not accord with the puritan streak in the English character, and in the fluctuations of taste and in the varieties of emphasis in interpretation it may cause some offence to those who believe that restraint is desirable in the expression of feeling. But if music is not passionate in its conviction, unforced in its inspiration, and masterly in expression, what is the good of it? The second symphony in E flat, in spite of an elegiac note in it, is a reflection of that secure and happy decade. It has been thought that, though it is not a programme symphony like Beethoven's 'Pastoral', it might, like Beethoven's 'Eroica', with which it shares the distinction of employing a funeral march for slow movement, be an expression of a quasi-political ideal. Besides being a loyal tribute to the king, might it not also be a comment on the state of his nation? But other programmes have been suggested for it—St. Mark's in Venice for one—and it would not be well to pin too specific a meaning to it, for indeed there is no need. However regarded, and whatever else it is, it is also an epitome in music of the Edwardian age.

When the war came Elgar turned away from these lavish orchestral masterpieces to the composition of chamber music, and wrote the violin sonata, the string quartet, and the piano quintet, as well as some occasional music. When he returned to large-scale instrumental composition in the 'cello concerto (1919) the exuberance was chastened, the feeling mellowed. After his wife died in the following year the mainspring of his genius was broken and he felt out of sympathy with the post-war spirit, so that the last fifteen years of his life—he died in 1934—were unproductive of anything more than a couple of suites and sketches for an opera and for a symphony, neither of which came to anything. Thus negatively he showed himself an Edwardian genius, although the twenty years which produced all his great works and his best music enveloped the reign of King Edward with a year of Queen Victoria, several years of King George V, and a world-wide war. What was new in Elgar was not idiom or style, though the historian can now in retrospect see that the three-century cycle had revolved once more to the point of major change at the turn of the century and that Debussy, the

XLVII (*a*). Piano by Edwin Lutyens 1900

XLVII (*b*). Piano by C. R. Ashbee 1904

XLVIII. Mr. Henry Wood 1907

arch revolutionary of the century, Schönberg the iconoclast, and Stravinsky the irreverent radical, had punctually begun the movements which we now lump together as modernism. There was nothing revolutionary about Elgar and his music. His idiom is eclectic and the expression is late romantic. To a foreigner ignorant of English music it is most easily described as like Richard Strauss. Texture, harmony, orchestration belong to the end of the German hegemony. In feeling it is free from the interest in morbid psychology, in the portrayal of which the eupeptic Strauss excelled—his Salome, Electra, Don Juan, Don Quixote were all dotty. Although there is moodiness—a curious wistfulness and an exuberance which has been stigmatized as vulgarity jostle each other—it is all as healthy as can be in its coverage of normal emotions. Some of it, e.g. the 'Cockaigne' Overture, is extrovert, as befits a programmatic description of Edwardian London. *Falstaff*, a symphonic poem with an even more detailed programme, shows the other side of the composer, sympathetic to, and percipient of, humanity. The Introduction and Allegro for strings, a splendid work that travels more easily abroad than the symphonies, combines the conscious nobility, which has been criticized as of too frequent occurrence in Elgar's music, with the tenderness, the open-air feeling, and the *genius loci* of the west country. Form was not Elgar's strong point. His method of composition was that of fitting mosaic together, and the sheer quantity of material in the symphonies and the violin concerto would present a problem of formal organization to any composer. Conceived in an age of leisure and expansion they can seem too long to a more impatient, more austere generation. Yet there are formal felicities in abundance: the self-generating theme out of a one-bar phrase in the finale of the second symphony, the accompanied cadenza of the violin concerto, and the use of a motto theme for the 'cello concerto are instances. His orchestration has been universally admired, but no one got down to analysing it till Miss McVeagh found that its secret was the way he underlined his themes with constantly changing instrumental doubling. It was, moreover, the orchestration which proclaimed Elgar's mastery to the English public, for whom Brahms's restrained and undemonstrative scoring was all that was expected from an English composer. Elgar scored, as Berlioz and Rimsky-Korsakov scored, with an acute and subtle sense of tone-colour and a resulting sound-web that was his own.

This frank embrace of the sensuous medium which had been growing out of Wagner, Strauss, and Mahler on the continent, was suspect by Parry, who was a puritan, and by Stanford, whose artistic ideal was economy—both Brahmsian virtues and in their contexts right enough—but it was surely invading English musical life. Henry Wood, the great popularizer of orchestral music for the fifty years on from 1890, liked fully saturated timbres and thick textures, and the vogue for Wagner grew steadily from 1880 till a slight reaction set in about the time of the second world war. Granville Bantock (1868–1946), who had a fertile but chameleon-like talent, was of the same way of thinking as Elgar about the use of the orchestra. As he was a product of the Royal Academy of Music and not of the Royal College where Parry and Stanford reigned, he too went in for Edwardian luxury, and was a progressive not only in the sense applied by Strauss to Elgar but in his zeal for establishing a distinctive English music within the European comity. This missionary work he pursued by different methods at different times, by a magazine, by promoting concerts, notably when he was conductor at New Brighton near Liverpool, and when he became principal of the Birmingham and Midland Institute School of Music and subsequently, as successor to Elgar (who could not endure even the modest academic duties of the chair) as professor of music in Birmingham University. He certainly wrote too much, but his tone poem *Fifine at the Fair* was kept in the repertory by Beecham and his 'Hebridean' Symphony and his comedy overtures to Greek plays have life in them. *Fifine at the Fair* is elaborately scored with sub-divided strings (six firsts, five seconds, four violas, and 'cello), and an impressionistic use of triple wood-wind and much percussion. This is the Straussian tone-poem transplanted none too securely to English soil. For the Orient was tempting Bantock with its rich imagery and strong colours. He set Fitzgerald's *Omar Khayyám* in three huge cantatas with soloists, chorus, and orchestra between 1906 and 1909, as well as six cycles of *Songs of the East* and some ballet scores. This did not prevent him from time-travelling to ancient Greece, taking up his English heritage of Elizabethan music and Browning's poetry, and exploring the Celtic twilight. It was all skilfully done and generally conveyed the atmosphere of whatever locality he had reached. He was a big man with a generous mind, but a greater concentration on finding an idiom for himself and hammering his ideas into shape with less discursiveness in word-painting or programmatic illustration would have given his works a greater durability. He could evoke the sensuous paganism of *Omar Khayyám* but not cope with its easy pessimism: he was more tone-painter than tone-poet. Furthermore, its size was self-defeating since it made frequent performance impossible. His *Atalanta in Calydon* was another choral work on a large scale to a text of luscious imagery by Swinburne. True, the scale was less colossal than the Persian trilogy and the orchestra was eliminated, but the choral writing is enormously elaborated into as many as twenty parts, and the work is described as a choral symphony in four movements. It was written at a time when Bantock was also composing much choral music as test pieces for the competition festivals in which north-country choirs attained a high degree of virtuosity in their tournaments of song. This kind of choralism was important in the general musical life of the country and if it only produced a few masterpieces it served its generation. But Bantock's facility was his undoing.

Like Elgar and Bantock, Frederick Delius (1862–1934) handled the orchestra with a natural facility and with an idiosyncratic ear for its sonorities. But he was a solitary figure who played little part in English musical life during the early years of the century beyond securing, or sometimes himself conducting, one or two first performances in London and the provinces. Of cosmopolitan origin, French domicile and Nordic sympathies, he was English only by his birth and boyhood in Bradford. Some of his most characteristic music was written before the war and before he became generally known, through Beecham's persuasive advocacy, to British audiences. Thus the idylls, *In a Summer Garden, Summer Night on the River*, and *On hearing the first cuckoo in spring*, all belong to these years and show him as essentially a nature-poet in music. The more robust side of his epicurean personality appears in his Nietzschean oratorio, *A Mass of Life*, which had its first performance in London in 1909. *Brigg Fair*, however, a curious by-product of the folk-song movement, was first heard abroad (in 1907), as were most of his earlier compositions.

It thus looked before 1914 as though music in England was going the way of the continent, importing less and making more of better quality at home certainly, but cultivating size, programme music, and the orchestra to an extent never before accepted in Britain. The centre of the movement was in the midlands; Elgar and Bantock were its ablest exponents, but Julius Harrison and Rutland Boughton were other adherents. Distinct from it were the academic worlds of Oxford and Cambridge and South Kensington which embraced Donald Tovey, Ernest Walker, Charles Wood, T. F. Dunhill, Walford Davies, as well as Parry and Stanford, and the incipient nationalists Holst, Vaughan Williams, and George Butterworth, who, though alumni of the Royal College, were to be the emancipators of English music from the German and Italian tutelage which had lasted since the arrival of Handel in England. Both these groups were less characteristic of the Edwardian age than Elgar, and their composing lives covered a larger span, but they were active in the first decade and a half of the century and some of the ferments, like the folk-song revival which had far-reaching effects later on, were at work round 1905.

The Folk-song Revival

All the nationalist movements of the last half of the nineteenth century which enriched the European repertory had found national legend and native folk-music the most valuable instruments of emancipation from the central European international language of music. The harmonic language of music was developed through the seventeenth and eighteenth centuries by Italian, Austrian, and German composers, and their lingua franca was used almost without modification or extension by Mozart and by his contemporaries such as Cimarosa and Cherubini. What sufficed for Mozart's huge output was good enough basis for Beethoven and for Rossini's more personal idioms. Central Europe's greatest achievement was the invention of sonata form, which has proved one of the most fertile discoveries of the human mind. But the romantic movement, which turned artists' minds to anything mysterious or wonderful, such as ballads about old unhappy things, legends of battles long ago, folk-tales of magic, almost accidentally directed their attention to the traditional literature of their own language, thence to songs and dances embodying the national characteristics of each language group. Thus Hungary adjoined Austria, but apart from race—which in spite of its abuse is a term with a minimum meaning of blood relationship—its language was differently accented, so that while German has anacrusis, with weak accent leading to strong,

Hungarian avoids anacrusis, begins with a strong accent even on a short syllable and so produces Scotch snap. These peculiarities are reproduced in the folk tunes to which the poems are sung. Similar differentials are to be found in the various branches of the Slavonic peoples in eastern Europe. Differences of compass, phrase-length, and interval mark out boundaries between the peoples who, by the time their artists had become conscious of them, had become modern nation-states. Nationalism is thus regarded by most musical historians as a consequence of romanticism, though it is possible in the case of peoples living under foreign domination, Czechs and Finns for instance, to see a political motive at work. But whatever touched off nationalism in Russia, Poland, Bohemia, Hungary, Spain, and Scandinavia, the result was a break-away from the idiom of Italian opera and German sonata. Russia produced its Kuchka, the 'mighty handful' of Balakirev, Rimsky-Korsakov, Cui, Borodin, and Moussorgsky; Bohemia Smetana and Dvořák, Hungary Bartók and Kodály, Spain Albéniz, Granados, and Falla, Scandinavia Grieg and Sibelius. France, having been distinctively French in its music in spite of constant refertilization by Italians such as Lully and Cherubini and by Belgians such as Grétry and Franck, had no need of musical nationalism in the nineteenth century.

But England had. Here, as elsewhere, the way forward was achieved by a step backwards. England had had a flourishing school of composers in Tudor and Stuart times which had certain national characteristics, e.g. a liking for the harmonic feature known as false relation, as well as a more general pastoral feeling. It also had, though none of the educated class seemed to know it, a vigorous folk-music of its peasantry somehow obscured by the industrial revolution. It was the tapping of these two sources that led to the emancipation from the central European idiom and tradition. Both Parry and Stanford supported the folk-song movement—Stanford, for instance, edited and arranged the famous Petrie collection of Irish folk-songs—but they were too much convinced of the superiority of the German and Italian models provided by Brahms and Verdi to anything homespun, so that they never took the next step to found their own styles on the idiom of folk-song—they were in fact a generation too soon to recognize its necessity. The next generation of composers, Vaughan Williams and Holst, both men of radical mind, did recognize the necessity and took the step. They went back to the Elizabethans, to Purcell, and to folk-song.

English folk-song, however, had only just been discovered at the turn of the century. Back in the sixties Carl Engel, an expatriate German musicologist who specialized in musical instruments, had written an *Introduction to the Study of National Music*, in which he had expressed surprise that he could find no authentic examples of English folk-song comparable to what was available from Scotland and Ireland, and had ventured the extraordinarily shrewd prophecy that if a search was made 'in districts somewhat remote from any large towns' something would be found handed down from the forefathers of the rural population. This was in fact exactly what happened. In 1894 was published a collection of *English County Songs*, compiled and provided with piano accompaniments by Lucy Broadwood and J. A. Fuller-Maitland, the music critic of *The Times*. This set in motion the impulse towards a more systematic search in the English countryside for songs other than those culled from literary sources by William Chappell and published by him in his *Popular Music of the Olden Time* (1855). In 1898 the Folk Song Society was founded. In 1903 Cecil Sharp collected the first of his thousands of folk-songs. The place was Hambridge in Somerset; the singer was the vicar's gardener, by a significant symbolism named John England; the song was 'The Seeds of Love', of which the tune is an organic whole without repetition of phrase and the words are an allegory of love presented in the symbolism of flowers. The song was a portent.

THE SEEDS OF LOVE

Collected by Cecil Sharp

I sowed the seeds of love, I sowed them in the spring : I

gathered them up in the morning so soon, While small birds did sweet-ly

sing, While small birds did sweet - ly sing.

So equally was 'Bushes and Briars', collected by Vaughan Williams in Essex a month or two later.

BUSHES AND BRIARS

Collected by R. Vaughan Williams

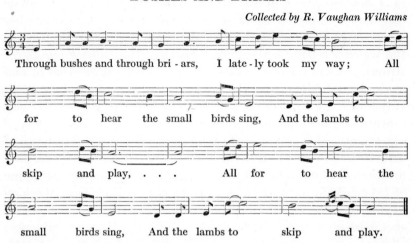

Through bushes and through bri - ars, I late - ly took my way; All for to hear the small birds sing, And the lambs to skip and play, . . . All for to hear the small birds sing, And the lambs to skip and play.

For this was for him not so much discovery as recognition, according to Vaughan Williams's own account of the way in which he found the clue to a problem of style that had been impeding his development. He had turned thirty, and seemed to his Cambridge friends and the musical world in general to be something of a fumbler. Certainly technical assurance came late simply because he was not sure how to discover himself and was dissatisfied with what he was writing. He had tried English training at the Royal College in London and at Cambridge between 1890 and 1894; he then went to Berlin and worked with Max Bruch (1897); later still (1908) he went to Ravel in the hope of refining his technique. But he recognized what he needed in the folk-songs of East Anglia. This was a pure stream of English melody that still preserved what were known as the church modes and had avoided the square phrases and the restraints of major–minor tonality. In technical terms the old modes were his salvation and to them he applied three centuries of harmonic experience. The effect is perhaps seen most clearly in his Mass in G minor.

He had, of course, a strong personality of his own, one which combined feeling for tradition and the past with a radical outlook and singular directness of expression. When he had found his technique and his style the personality found free play. The new voice in English music was heard at the Leeds festival of 1907 in the Whitman cantata *Toward the Unknown Region,* and three years later in *A Sea Symphony,* words also by Walt Whitman. Previously he had been working on *The English Hymnal,* which opened another source of English melody to him. He discovered Purcell by editing the *Welcome Songs* for the Purcell Society. The *Tallis Fantasia* for strings, given at the Gloucester festival of 1910, showed that he had made the acquaintance of the Elizabethans. The fruits of the cultivation of these English roots were to be gathered in the next half century in nine symphonies, cantatas, masques, a fine corpus of solo songs, and a crop of works written *ad hoc* which had the stuff of permanence in them. But the only works, besides those already mentioned, to mark him out as a coming man before the guillotine of 1914 descended, were the song cycle *On Wenlock Edge,* the incidental music to *The Wasps,* the *Songs of Travel,* and the *Fantasia on Christmas Carols.* None of these reflected German influence: all were a declaration of hard-won English independence and they were exactly contemporary with Elgar's achievement in writing a personal kind of music engendered in quite other ways.

The only other nationalist in the continental sense was George Butterworth, who was killed in the war. Holst nourished himself on folk-song and Purcell to some extent: he made a number of folk-song arrangements and wrote *A Somerset Rhapsody*—the rhapsody being the accepted solution of the formal problem presented by thematic material that will not develop in the symphonic sense because the folk-tune is already an organic whole. But the impulse to write extended compositions based on the splendid melodies of folk-music was very strong, and every nationalist movement in Europe adopted it. Holst turned away to the Orient for inspiration and wrote a distinctive and characteristic music; his mind was even more radical than Vaughan Williams's, since it had less regard for the values of tradition; but he was not so great a composer, nor did he live so long.

Butterworth, on the other hand, took part in the collection of folk-songs and founded his own style on them. Housman was the poet of this decade—there must be a dozen composers who have made songs out of Housman's strophic elegies—and Butterworth set a number of songs from *A Shropshire Lad* and called by that name his first orchestral rhapsody. The second was called after a folk-song,

The Banks of Green Willow. No one knows what he would have done had he not been killed in the battle of the Somme at the age of 31. But the significant thing is that when the smoke of battle had cleared it became apparent that the way forward for English music was not along the trail blazed by Elgar and Bantock but by the retroactive folk-song school.

The folk-song revival flourished in Edwardian England, although it seemed at odds with the ethos of the period. Cecil Sharp discovered the English folk-dance—morris, sword, and country—surviving in much the same way as folk-song had survived and been discovered. Percy Grainger, an Australian who wrote some very agreeable and in those pre-radio days very useful songs and salon pieces for piano or chamber combinations, collected 300 songs in Lincolnshire before turning his attention to Denmark and going to live in America. Dorset was combed by H. E. D. Hammond. The north of England was similarly served by Frank Kidson of Leeds and Anne Gilchrist of Lancaster, both of whom became scholars in the lore of tunes. Northumbrian songs and tunes for the local instrument, the small-pipe, had already attracted the attention of the Society of Anti-quaries of Newcastle upon Tyne, but it was W. G. Whittaker who made a collection (of which the publication was delayed by the war till 1921) during this period of maximum activity, when two not subsequently justified assumptions were made, that the songs were regional and should be collected by counties, and that they would finally disappear if not rescued 'just in time' from the lips of the aged.

Another piece of folk-song policy that was right in the circum-stances but had boomerang consequences was the decision, taken by Arthur Somervell in his capacity as chief inspector of music for the Board of Education, to make folk-song the material for singing classes in schools. Sharp approved, and indeed the knowledge of our unexpected heritage was disseminated in this way, but it did not escape the cussedness of human nature which makes children turn away in reaction from their educational literature alike in poetry and music, and the result has been that many English people, including some who should know better, while acclaiming the folk-songs and dances of other countries with enthusiasm (of Scotland, to go no further, but also of Russia and other such exotics) treat their own with embarrassed condescension and even sarcasm. The gains, however, were immense. Apart from what it has contributed to the English musical renaissance, the movement has made available a huge corpus of fine tunes, and has presented the historian with a sociological document of great interest and the humblest amateur with music he can manage to perform himself.

Concurrently with the discovery of English folk-song was the discovery that we still had surviving in practice some English dances, though the waltz and the polka had driven out of the ball-room at every social level all the social dances 'longways for as many as will' that had been current in the 1830's, as incidentally is attested by Mendelssohn's friends, the Horsley girls of Kensington. Cecil Sharp, even before he went looking for folk-songs in Somerset, had been a chance witness of the Headington morris on Boxing Day 1899, and fired by what he saw took down the tunes the next day from the concertina player, William Kimber (who continued to play them for the next sixty years). Circumstances caused this seed to germinate underground during the first flush of Sharp's folk-song collecting, but after 1905 he began practising the morris, first of all and not wholly satisfactorily with a girls' club run by Miss Mary Neal. Between 1910 and 1912 Sharp had enlarged his knowledge of the morris in the midlands, investigated the sword dances of the north, worked at the traditional country dances in the light of Playford's *The Dancing Master* (1661), published books of tunes and dance description and founded, in 1911, the English Folk Dance Society to do for the dance what the Folk Song Society had been doing since 1898 for song and a little more besides. Songs can be sung by an individual and as long as tune and text are available the song is safe even if its audience is small, but a team dance can only be preserved by being danced, so that the English Folk Dance Society was both a propagandist and callisthenic body. The two societies amalgamated in 1932 into the English Folk Dance and Song Society, which has its headquarters in the house built (in 1930) to commemorate Cecil Sharp, who died in 1924. On its foundation stone are truthfully inscribed the words: 'This building is erected in memory of Cecil Sharp who restored to the English people the songs and dances of their country.'

Social and Academic Status

The folk-song revival was not the only movement that contributed to a general awakening to the need for higher standards and deeper roots in our musical life. It is easy to underestimate what the Victorians did through concentrating attention on what they did *not* achieve in the field of composition. At the end of the nineteenth century there was always opera in London during the season. Permanent orchestras were established in Manchester and Bournemouth; the promenade concerts, which provided for the wider dissemination of knowledge of the classics of music, were begun by Henry Wood in 1894 and continued annually without a break up to the war. Choral singing flourished, the competition festival movement had begun its healthy activities. Chamber music was cultivated in private by amateurs and the St. James's Hall was the centre of both orchestral and chamber public concerts. But somehow the general standing of the art in official, academic, and popular esteem was below that of literature and painting—there was no musical equivalent of the Royal Academy and no body comparable to the B.B.C. for providing music—and below the position it occupied in Germany and Italy, where at least the opera houses and the orchestras were to some extent subsidized by the state. Government was wholly indifferent to it, though a musician's name sometimes appeared in the honours list—there were five knighthoods conferred by King Edward. At the universities degrees in music were post-graduate awards open to non-residents, although Sir Frederick Gore Ouseley, during his Oxford professorship after 1855, had done something to improve their status. Of research there was none till E. J. Dent became active at Cambridge. The cathedral organist was still a person of some importance in his locality, since the direction of the local choral society and the most advanced teaching usually came from him. In the public schools the music masters were a depressed minority, though here again an improvement had begun following the lead of Thring and David at Uppingham; Clifton had established a scholarship in music and Peppin made music respectable at Rugby. It was one of Sir Hubert Parry's services to music that he, an aristocrat, an intellectual, a magistrate as well as a composer, changed the attitude of the upper classes, the universities, and the public schools to music by bringing it into the company of the humaner letters. Colleges at Oxford and Cambridge were chary of making their musicians fellows of the college. Sir Hugh Allen ultimately achieved it at New College in 1908, but Stanford, brilliant as he was in the combination room of Trinity, Cambridge, was never offered a fellowship, and it only became a regular practice to make the university music staff and the college organists fellows when proper faculties of music, conferring ordinary arts degrees, were established after the second world war, so that only then those who taught music belatedly received parity of esteem with classical and mathematical dons.

Scholarship and criticism shared in the renaissance and began to show signs of life. Bernard Shaw's criticism in the nineties, which has since been accepted as literature of permanent worth, was a unique phenomenon without parallel in the daily and weekly journalism of the time. W. H. Hadow, who was the chief advocate of music as one of the humaner letters though himself a classical don, castigated London newspaper criticism in one of the prefatory essays of his *Studies in Modern Music* (1892). Even Shaw was not exempt from his strictures for his blind spot about Brahms. His essay 'broke through the prejudices created by a narrow ring of professed music critics and opened the door to a wider treatment of the subject'. Fuller-Maitland, who pronounced this verdict in Grove's *Dictionary of Music and Musicians*, in the second edition (1911) for which he was responsible, was himself one of the new school of more enlightened critics. From 1890 to 1911 he was music critic of *The Times* but managed to do a great deal of musicological work, of which the chief was his joint editorship with his brother-in-law, W. Barclay Squire of the British Museum, of the *Fitzwilliam Virginal Book*. He was a pioneer of the folk-song revival, as already recorded, an editor for the Purcell Society, a considerable pianist and harpsichordist. He rather unjustly came to be regarded as a conservative because he did not get on with the music of Richard Strauss, but he was in fact actively associated with every progressive movement of his generation, if the antiquarian researches which have fertilized the English renaissance can be called progressive, as they certainly were at the time. In 1911 he retired from *The Times* and was succeeded by H. C. Colles, who very largely shared his tastes and interests but being younger was saved from getting out of touch with the music of the new century.

Ernest Newman was another newspaper critic who wielded considerable influence on English music for sixty years, though during the Edwardian era it was exercised not from London but from the provinces, where he was on the *Birmingham Post* (and for a short interval on the *Manchester Guardian*). He taught for Bantock at the Midland Institute and produced his *Musical Studies* in 1905, a volume of essays which dealt with the aesthetic issues that occupied him all his life, and studies of individual composers, Wagner, Strauss, Elgar, and Hugo Wolf, the last an important monograph. In 1914 came *Wagner as Man and Artist*, which was a preliminary but substantial study for the four-volume life of Wagner which he was to publish twenty years later. Newman was self-trained and no more a respecter of the leaders of English musical life than Shaw had been ten years earlier. His journalism was incisive and witty, his style urbane, his scholarship careful and acute. He was to make an international reputation as an English music critic and in these early years marked out the nineteenth century, with its special aesthetic problems of programme music and music-drama, as his chosen field of operations.

The Tudor revival which accompanied the folk-song revival and helped in the process of refertilizing native composition also goes back before the first decade of the twentieth century to the last decade of the nineteenth. Arnold Dolmetsch, a versatile Swiss musician, whose life-work was the study of obsolete instruments, clavichord, harpsichord, lute, and recorder, and how to play them— an art, incidentally, which includes the intricate business of the interpretation of the ornaments and graces essential to stylish performance—settled in England in 1885 and began the concert-giving which culminated in the Haslemere festivals still carried on by his son, Carl. But from 1905 to 1909 he was in Boston, U.S.A. and from 1911 to 1914 in Paris, working respectively for Chickering and Gaveau. However, he published his important book, *The Interpretation of the Music of the XVII and XVIII Centuries* in this country in 1915, and in his pioneer work, though not limited to English music, he was marching in the same direction as were Squire, Fuller-Maitland, George Arkwright, editor of an old English music series, and W. H. Cummings, who was prominent in the foundation of the Purcell Society.

To this company was added Edmund Fellowes, who single-handed produced the *English Madrigal School*, the complete corpus of the Elizabethan madrigal, the *English School of Lutenist Song Writers*, and the complete works of Byrd, simultaneously writing books to expound and explain them. Fellowes had nibbled at musical

antiquarianism before going down from Oxford; in 1897 he was appointed precentor of Bristol Cathedral; in 1900 he became a minor
canon at St. George's, Windsor, and spent the remaining fifty-one
years of his life in that office and place. It was while he was at Bristol
that the direction of his scholarship was determined, for the Bristol
Madrigal Society, which Fellowes joined, still kept alive the practice of singing madrigals in such editions as they could obtain.
Fellowes perceived that there was something wrong in the rhythm,
pace, and pitch at which both the sacred and secular music of the
Elizabethan period was sung. He was moved to action first on the
sacred side of the problem, which led him by stages along with
P. C. Buck, John Stainer, Hadow, and Parry to the foundation of
the Church Music Society, the first aim of which was to raise the
standard of cathedral music by the elimination of the feebler Victorian services and anthems. The church music of Byrd and Gibbons
was in due course to take its place. But it was not till 1911 that the
radical solution of curing the malpractices by providing correct
editions occurred to him—at a tennis tournament, according to his
own account. He set about the task of producing an edition that
would serve the double purpose of being at once cheap, practical, and
correct for singers, and complete for the library when the sheets were
bound up in the sets as their composers had assembled and published them. He began on Morley, whose four volumes he covered
financially by subscription, and proceeded to Gibbons and Wilbye,
whose hitherto unknown life history he unearthed as a by-product.
The war threatened to disrupt the plan but ultimately Stainer and
Bell agreed to undertake the publication of the rest, which finally
amounted to thirty-six volumes, completed in 1924.

Meantime Richard Terry, on appointment as organist and choirmaster of the newly built Westminster Cathedral in 1901, began to
revive the English liturgical music of the great period and use it
along with continental settings of the mass. The Pope's *Motu
Proprio* of 1903 encouraged the use of unaccompanied polyphony,
and though its austerity was too much for the contentment of some
Roman Catholics, Terry did, for more than twenty years, make
Westminster Cathedral a centre from which influence radiated
throughout the Catholic church in Europe and America as a model
of the way the liturgies could be sung. Out of Terry's work at
Westminster, editorial and executive, arose the project financed by

the Carnegie Trust of producing the ten volumes of *Tudor Church Music* completed in 1929. Terry was appointed the first general editor in 1916, but in 1922 he left the editorial committee basically because the performer in him undermined the patience necessary for the drudgery of editing, so that the need for punctuality and proof correction began to irk him. But publication was the natural outcome of his Westminster performances.

This interaction of performance and publication—in Fellowes's case publication being the motive for performance and in Terry's performance being the starting point of publication—has been the distinguishing feature of English musicology, which is pragmatic. The German ideals of pure scholarship and completeness without discrimination, which prevail also in America, have never been accepted in Britain. Editorial scrupulousness has been no less exacting in all the research that the folk-song, the Tudor, and the Purcell revivals have involved, but the written note is to be understood all the better for having to be sounded, and not all the products of the past are equally good as works of art. Edward Dent, who was our first professional musicologist operating from the base of a university, was just as much a pragmatist as the parsons Fellowes and F. W. Galpin, who collected, studied, and played old instruments, and Terry the choirmaster. Dent's operatic researches led him to, and were fertilized by, the sequence of performances of Mozart at Cambridge before 1914 and of the masque of *Cupid and Death* (by Matthew Locke and Christopher Gibbons, 1659) in 1915. His books, the classic *Mozart's Operas* (1913) and *The Foundations of English Opera* (begun in 1914 and published in 1928), are the outcome of his faith in the combination of exact scholarship with the hazards of performance. In the revival of the madrigal Fellowes was not alone: Arkwright's edition of miscellaneous old English music has been mentioned; Charles Kennedy Scott founded his Oriana Madrigal Society for the practice of it in 1904. Arkwright had also edited a periodical, *The Musical Antiquary*, from 1909 to 1913. Such digging about the roots of English music has proved in the event to have had three values: first, its intrinsic historical interest; second, the discovery of a vast amount of music enjoyable by a broadened taste; and third, as has subsequently appeared, the stimulation of new music by composers who were nourished on the revival of the old from Vaughan Williams to Benjamin Britten.

It is hard to generalize about the taste of a nation or an epoch, or even of a nation during an epoch, but it is clear now, if it was not then, that underneath the exuberance and gaudy show of Edwardian life, musically depicted by Elgar, there was stirring a fairly wide-spread impulse towards a strengthening and purifying of taste. The Bach revival, pioneered in Britain by Sterndale Bennett in the fifties, helped on by the foundation of the Bach Choir in the seventies, and spread like an evangel by Hugh Allen after he went to Oxford in 1901, was one such factor. But maybe most significant was the creation of *The English Hymnal*, of which Vaughan Williams was musical editor. The 1904 revision of *Hymns Ancient and Modern* seemed to the more ardent spirits, mostly high churchmen of the progressive party in the Church of England whose book it was, not to have gone far enough in purging it of sentimentality, flabby tunes, and chromatic harmony. Led by Percy Dearmer they proposed a new book which, if it was not to displace *Hymns Ancient and Modern*, was at any rate to supplement it with 'the worthiest expressions of all that lies within the Christian creed from those "Ancient Fathers" who were the earliest hymn-writers down to contemporary exponents of modern aspirations and ideals', coupled with fine tunes in place of some that were popular 'but quite unsuitable to their purpose' and 'worthy neither of the congregations who sing them, the occasions on which they are sung, nor the composers who wrote them'. It took two years' work by Vaughan Williams to produce what he and Dr. Dearmer wanted, and he had sometimes to convert a folk tune into a hymn (e.g. for 'O little town of Bethlehem') or compose one himself (e.g. *Sine nomine* for 'For all the Saints'). *The English Hymnal*, which came out in 1906, steadily spread a healthy influence, penetrating ultimately the denominational hymn-books of the free churches, and producing an offspring in *Songs of Praise* (1925) which was national instead of Anglican in its aim. In the Church of England itself a *Historical Edition of Hymns Ancient and Modern* was issued with a long introduction by W. H. Frere, afterwards Bishop of Truro, a liturgiologist who was also a scholar and a musician (1909).

Other Composers

While Elgar was emerging as a great composer and the forces that moulded Vaughan Williams into one were at work, along with

Mlle. ADELINE GENEE.

XLIX

L. Dan Godfrey's Band at the Bournemouth Winter Garden Theatre

the other fructifying influences of the Bach and Elizabethan revivals, the old German dominance still persisted. Anglo-German music continued to be written by composers so widely different as Cyril Scott and Donald Tovey. Scott was one of the small band of Englishmen who went, not to Leipzig any more but to Frankfurt, to study with Ivan Knorr. The group consisted of Scott, Balfour Gardiner, Roger Quilter, and Norman O'Neill, to which the name of the Australian Percy Grainger may be added, who studied with Kwast and Busoni. Their music, though individually different, sounded English compared with the denser textures and late romantic feeling of Strauss and Reger but not as Butterworth and Vaughan Williams sounded English. Tovey was soaked in Teutonism through his upbringing under the formidable Sophie Weisse, who in her zeal for his good did him irreparable damage by impregnating him with German ideals, German methods, German axioms (e.g. that the best music is German music)—this at the very time when it was emerging that English roses would not bloom on German pines, however careful the grafting, but might take root with a little cultivation in their native soil.

Tovey's tragedy was like Busoni's. Both were men of powerful intellect and native musicality, and so placed in time that they might well have helped to usher in the newer music which the twentieth century was bound to throw up from the natural decline of nineteenth-century romance. Busoni was torn in pieces by the clash of his Italian birth and temperament with his German domicile and mental sympathy, and Tovey was stultified by being out of touch alike with his fellow countrymen and the times he lived in. For Miss Weisse had encased him in a shell of Bach, Beethoven, and Brahms from which he never even tried to break out. He wrote a piano concerto (1903), a symphony (1913), and later (1935) a 'cello concerto, of which Casals became the exponent; he wrote an opera, *The Bride of Dionysus*, which was like a resurrection of Gluck in its classicism. The breath of life fluttered in them all, but they could not inhale the air of the twentieth century. The chamber music is more successful—the *Elegiac Variations* for 'cello and piano, written in 1909, can still convince with their eloquence and sincerity. But Tovey only lives in his critical writings, which were by-products of the professorship at Edinburgh to which he was appointed in 1914. His personal idiosyncracies must not be overlooked in

computing the might-have-beens for English music and English
scholarship, but the story of what he did not do is of significance
for the historian. He was not the only composer to miss the
Zeitgeist of the new century—his fellow Balliol man, F. S. Kelly,
famous also as record breaker in the Diamond Sculls at Henley,
had begun to write music in the same sort of idiom, but as he
was killed in the war in 1916 the argument illumined by Tovey's
subsequent career cannot be pressed with anything like the same
rigour.

The Frankfurt-trained Englishmen, on the other hand, did succeed
in writing a distinctive and appreciably English music, perhaps
because Knorr was a teacher whose creed was to respect the indivi-
dualities of his pupils, perhaps because they chose to work in the
smaller forms, Scott and Grainger in piano pieces, Quilter in songs,
O'Neill in incidental music for the theatre, and Gardiner in part-
songs and short orchestral pieces. Cyril Scott actually wrote in all
forms, large and small, and made an impression in Germany such
that before 1913 he was the only English composer at all well known
there. But attractive piano pieces that superficially seemed to have
some resemblance to Debussy's in harmony, scale, and evocative
titles, and a large number of sensitively turned songs, won him
renown and performances at home in the first decade of the century.
The war, however, and the change of direction in English music
caused all his quite extensive corpus of later works to be practically
ignored. Quilter's songs, though also strongly perfumed, have proved
tougher in fibre, perhaps because the harmony, though full, is less
encrusted with chromaticisms than Scott's and the vocal line is
more diatonic. He set poems of all periods from Shakespeare onwards but Herrick seemed to match his peculiarly jewelled and
gracious urbanity, a quality that suited Edwardian tastes. Gardiner
was more robust and the English open air more immediately dis-
cernible in, for instance, *Shepherd Fennel's Dance*, which came out
of Hardy in 1911, than in either Scott or Quilter. Something might
have come of his talent, at once distinctive and representative, but
he gave up composition for other forms of Englishry, the land and
the restoration of old houses. This gifted group was not, however,
appointed by destiny to lead English composition out of the wilderness, but only to cause some flowers to bloom in it and show that
the soil was not incurably barren. At the time they appeared to be

part of the renaissance in which Stanford, Elgar, and Bantock were the leaders.

There is one other figure, though his stature twenty years after his death seems to have diminished, who more successfully crossed the breach in styles opened by the first world war, Frank Bridge. Like John Jenkins, who similarly accommodated himself to a change of style accelerated by war in the seventeenth century, Bridge mainly wrote chamber music. He composed several songs that have defied the ravages of time, and supplied Britten with a theme for a set of variations. He was both performer on, and composer for, strings. His personal idiom was firmly rooted in the classics but it did develop a greater harmonic freedom in his later years. Even in 1905, when he won one of the prizes instituted by W. W. Cobbett, a wealthy amateur with a lifelong—and his life was ninety years long—interest in chamber music, he showed aptitude for a new form, to which the name 'fantasy' was given. The Jacobean implications of the title were brevity and congruity of different sections, though not fugal texture. The modern fantasy was a single movement work in which the development and recapitulation sections of a sonata movement were so reduced and modified as to admit features from the four movements of a normal string quartet. Bridge and an impressive list of English composers then in their twenties and thirties, of whom John Ireland was one, wrote a number of these fantasies, as well as more orthodox works, which consolidated the renaissance, for without chamber music, the purest and most abstruse kind of composition, English music could hardly be worthy of its own past or look the continental classics in the face. Cobbett's public spirit bore fruit.

In song England has a long tradition, never interrupted as the tradition of church music was interrupted by the puritans, but in late Victorian times debased and sentimentalized, like the church music, by some quirk of taste by which it was hoped that the weaker brethren might be made more musical. The infection manifested itself in the virulent symptom of the drawing-room ballad. This was an odd phenomenon. It was not the equivalent of what is now called popular music, neither was it a true narrative ballad. It consisted of some sentimental verses, usually three in number, which invoked God in the last of them to make an apotheosis-like climax. The piano part was within the scope of an amateur who was not defeated by an occasional accidental to create chromatic pathos—'the accompaniment not too difficult, the voice part not too high', as one of the comic songs of the period truly put it with gentle satire. These 'royalty ballads' were destined for the amateur market but they were launched by professionals at special London ballad concerts, and the singers kept them in their repertories for use as encores at Saturday night concerts in Bournemouth Winter Gardens and similar places of musical resort and in the second part of the promenade concerts at Queen's Hall. The two things about them were that they were easy and they were sentimental. The coming of the radio, which killed off the humbler efforts of amateur performers, was the death of them.

Composers like Cowen and Sullivan, who wrote specimens like 'The Better Land' and 'The Lost Chord', were not insensitive to the need for something better, and composers who followed them had as their ideal a sort of English *Lied*. Some like Stanford and Hadow actually set German poems, others like Cowen published their songs in sets with German translations beneath their English texts. The powerful influence of Parry and Stanford was directed at making songs worthy to stand beside German *Lieder* on programmes of the recently invented song recital. Parry's 'The Lover's Garland' from his fifth set (1902) of English lyrics is an exquisite setting of a text from the Greek anthology that is indeed an English song that could, as has been remarked, pass for Brahms, and Stanford could invoke the atmosphere of Ireland in what came to be known, hideously but usefully, as the art-song.

The new century saw much well-directed and successful effort to retrieve the English song to a standard worthy of the tradition that stretched back to Dowland and Purcell. The work of Scott and Quilter has already been mentioned. Arthur Somervell wrote cycles based on Tennyson's 'Maud', on Housman, and on various poets (in 'Love in Spring Time') at the turn of the century. John Ireland began with 'Hope the Hornblower' a serious career of song composition which was to include sets and cycles by Housman and Hardy and many individual songs by contemporary poets, among which was Masefield's 'Sea Fever', composed in 1913 and destined to go round the English-speaking world. Butterworth wrote a Housman cycle; Ivor Gurney, another victim of the war, had a true lyrical gift which he harnessed to poems of the Georgian group who came together about 1912 and of which he was a poet member. Vaughan Williams's 'Songs of Travel' (words by R. L. Stevenson) were a landmark, a sign that German ideals, having effected their purpose, were to give place to a new and more English harmony.

These songs are not beyond the capacities of the better amateur singers and pianists. Before the days of gramophone and radio there was much domestic music-making, not all of it good enough to be listened to with pleasure but affording intimate knowledge of song literature to the performers not otherwise obtainable and not so common today. Society hostesses paid professionals to sing at their parties, so that songs played an active part in social life outside the public recital, which singers like George Henschel, H. Plunket Greene, and Gervase Elwes were steadily making into an artistic experience not only of the highest worth but of immense and immediate pleasure. The royalty ballad, then, did not have everything its own way, though some curious hybrids were produced when the two strains, ballad and art-song, were crossed, as in Amy Woodforde-Finden's ubiquitous set of four 'Indian Love Lyrics'.

Performers, Opera, and Ballet

Music is only fully alive in performance. Histories of music can do very little to record what performances were like, how music sounded to its audiences, what standards were attained, what conventions were taken for granted at any given period. To discover these things, however sketchily, one must turn to the files of journalism rather than to the history books. Indeed, the only permanent value of musical criticism, beyond the shaping of current taste and opinion, is that it records and describes music as it lives in performance. Burney is the only historian who tried to combine the functions of journalist and historian—and succeeded—since he noted what he heard on his famous travels through France, Germany, and Italy in search of material and so was able to record 'the state of music' in those countries. Now we have the gramophone record to help the historian of the future, but even so we may doubt whether it will ever be very easy to form a picture of 'the musical life of the country', as the phrase goes for that addition sum of the amateur, professional, educational, and ecclesiastical effort which is recalcitrant to simple arithmetic.

Certainly in Edward VII's reign the gramophone was only at the

beginning of its epoch-making career. Caruso, who sang at Covent
Garden between 1902 and 1914, was the first to make gramophone
history by demonstrating its possibilities for disseminating knowledge of the individual musician's art among his contemporaries and,
as it proved, for posterity. We know today what his singing sounded
like and there are available in gramophone archives husky acoustic
recordings of other musicians' performances. All the same it is
difficult to evoke the ethos of the provincial festivals when motor-
car and radio had not begun to change their pattern, to imagine the
atmosphere of a royal gala during the reign of H. V. Higgins at
Covent Garden, or to think back to the impermanent orchestras
of those days.

However, we have Hadow's word for it that things were improving. On the other hand, to read the annals of opera at Covent
Garden is to make the mouth water, even while we know quite well
that production was non-existent, scenery shabby, and the repertory
under-rehearsed. But great singing was certainly to be heard there
in those days, though that is not the whole story of opera in Edwardian England. Hadow had more in mind orchestral and chamber
music, piano playing, and *Lieder* singing, though the royalty ballad
persisted.

In the sphere of orchestral music the appetite was growing, an
appetite that was to continue to grow in spite of financial difficulty
through the present century, manifesting itself in the gradual establishment of permanent orchestras based on long-term contracts for
the players in London and the great provincial cities. At the turn of
the century the Hallé Orchestra was firmly established in Manchester; Sir Dan Godfrey had begun his work with a municipal
orchestra in Bournemouth; the Scottish Orchestra had been founded
in Glasgow and Elgar's friend, Alfred Rodewald, had recruited an
orchestra which played regularly for the venerable Liverpool Philharmonic Society. In London the Philharmonic Society, which was
dubbed Royal at its centenary in 1912, began to feel the rivalry of
other orchestras that were springing up to expand the work which had
been begun by Manns at the Crystal Palace. Of these other orchestras one was formed by Henry Wood for his promenade and week-
end concerts at Queen's Hall, whose name it bore; another was the
result of a secession from it, the London Symphony Orchestra,
which broke away on the not very creditable issue of the employment

of deputies which made anything like polished performances impossible. However, the outcome was better than the motive that prompted it, for the new orchestra was established on a self-governing basis in 1904 and has served not only London faithfully and well ever since but also the big provincial festivals. The new orchestra decided on a policy of visiting conductors and the Philharmonic Society followed suit soon after as well as inviting composers to conduct their own works. In this way Sibelius was brought over to conduct his third symphony and most of the English composers, including Delius, also obliged with their services. Nikisch was the chief of the visiting conductors, the first of the international virtuosi conductors of the modern globe-ranging type to appear on the English scene in the concert hall. Richter conducted regularly and does not fit the description. While Henry Wood and Landon Ronald were making their reputations there was an incursion by Thomas Beecham, who appeared on the scene in 1905. A little later he was to impinge on London opera with dynamic effects that in spite of apparent eclipses still reverberate happily more than fifty years later.

Beecham is the greatest, perhaps the only, executant genius ever thrown up by music in Britain. Dowland in his day had an international reputation as a lutenist and added to it immortality as a composer, but with this single exception no Englishman among the many who have at one time or another over the centuries pursued honourable careers as singers and players of instruments and won fame abroad as well as at home has had such an unmistakable stamp of genius as Beecham. He had astonished Berlin in 1912, which was itself an astonishing thing to do in the state of German opinion about English music and musicians. When he died in 1961 he was known the world over as one of the supreme orchestral conductors in the same class as Mahler, Nikisch, and Toscanini. The basis of this sort of genius is an ear finely sensitive to blend, gradation, and balance of tone—musicianship can be taken for granted—combined with fire in the belly, fire in the eyes, and rhythm in the blood. Catholicity of taste is less important than penetration of understanding in the music that is liked. Beecham's taste declared itself quite early—it was Latin rather than Teutonic—but he went on enlarging his sympathies all through life, and though they soon embraced Handel they never were whole-hearted towards Bach. There was a streak of Mediterranean man in this Lancashire-born,

orthodoxly educated Englishman, whose wit was like a rapier in
repartee. He was a man of intelligence, business experience, wide
reading, and sufficient wealth to enable him to undertake any projects that his active brain and mercurial character suggested to him.
He was thus impresario as well as musician and his factual biography is a list of projects for the foundation of orchestral and
operatic organizations. Individually they collapsed, but taken together they have changed the face of English music in half a
century. Some great interpreters get on without conspicuous intellectual ability. With Beecham, while the sheer magic of his playing,
notably of the music of Delius, who without him would have foundered into oblivion, was due to his sensibility, the strength of his
interpretations, even when they seemed questionable, was based
on good intellectual foundations. It was the combination of
the unusual ear with the quick wits, sound intelligence, and a
streak of quicksilver in his make-up that spelled out the word
'genius'.

Beecham began his orchestral activities in 1905 and his operatic
in 1909. In 1911 he brought over Diaghilev's Russian ballet and in
1913 a Russian opera company that gave London for the first time
Boris Godunov with Chaliapin. Nothing has been the same since
that Russian invasion. The brilliant quasi-oriental exoticism of the
décor affected women's clothes and household decoration. The
dramatic force called attention to the need for stage production
in operatic performances. The ballet, which was rated as a poor form
of art if a moderate kind of entertainment in a music-hall programme,
became at once a matter for connoisseurs and in due time produced
our own Royal Ballet. Beecham had, moreover, been giving seasons
of opera in English at His Majesty's including a Mozart cycle,
specimens of French *opéra comique*, and native opera in the shape
of Stanford's *Shamus O'Brien*. In 1910 he mounted in twenty-eight
weeks some thirty operas. These included Strauss's *Elektra* and
Salome, which were introduced to the British public after some difficulties with the Lord Chamberlain. *Der Rosenkavalier* similarly enjoyed this functionary's attentions when Beecham, at the time a
member of the Covent Garden Opera Syndicate, gave its first London
performance in 1911. In *Salome* it was the head of the Baptist, in
Rosenkavalier the bed in the third act—the first act apparently escaped
—that gave offence. But whatever the difficulties Beecham rode

undaunted over them, though the public reception of his offerings was capricious. At the end of his 1910 season he was still learning the incalculable reactions of the British public. 'Something was wrong somewhere', he wrote in his autobiography, 'and I was not at all sure where the fault lay, with the public or myself.' What was wrong was the attempt to do too much at once, a fault on the right side.

The grand seasons at the Royal Opera House ran for two or at most three months in the early summer of the London season. They were promoted by a syndicate that took over the lease of the house from Augustus Harris. They were committed to a policy of star singers and to the use of any language but English—there was one case of an English opera by an English composer, Herbert Bunning's *The Princess Osra*, being sung in French. Even after the successful production of *The Ring* in English in 1908 and 1909, when Richter proposed that the practice might be extended he met with opposition from Higgins in a letter that expressed his conviction 'that there is very little demand for opera at all outside the season, and that outside the small circle of those who have an axe to grind, the idea that a craving exists for opera to be given in English is an absolute delusion'.[1] It was true that the demand was not as great as it might have been if England had had the same traditions and organizations for opera as were accepted as axiomatic and normal in Italy and Germany—Beecham's experience proved so much. On the other hand the first decade of the century showed an increase in the supply if not in the demand for opera. The Carl Rosa Company toured the provinces and gave occasional London seasons. There was another touring company, the Moody–Manners, run by two singers. There was an incursion by Oscar Hammerstein, who in 1911 built what was afterwards called the Stoll Opera House in Kingsway. Then came the Russians. Mozart's operas, of which the production was to flower into perfection a quarter of a century later at Glyndebourne, were restudied not only by Beecham but by amateurs at Cambridge under the inspiration and instruction of Edward Dent. There were winter and spring seasons at Covent Garden as well as grand seasons. The taste for opera was growing, though there was still a powerful opposition to it as a meretricious art-form. Parry thought it a fraud; lesser musicians called it a bad

[1] Quoted by H. Rosenthal in *Two Centuries of Opera at Covent Garden.*

mixture of two good things; this attitude remained after 1918 and
only disappeared with the death of its last spokesman, Sir Walford
Davies, and the discovery of what opera was really like as a going
concern by a British army in Italy in 1945. The belief that opera
is so much an Italian phenomenon that anything is preferable to
English on the stage is still alive in both high and low places, but
it stands on a slightly more reasonable aesthetic basis than formerly
in that the plea is now for opera in the original language. It is
doubtful, for instance, if there would now be a call for a performance
of *Il Flauto Magico* at the Royal Opera House, though a lady was
heard to disapprove of the Glyndebourne *Rosenkavalier* because it
was sung in German, not Italian.

Still, a more rational approach to the whole art of opera was
attempted in the heyday of the international seasons at Covent
Garden. Richter's English *Ring* is the first landmark; Beecham's
season at His Majesty's, his encouragement of native composers
(Smyth, Delius, de Lara, Clutsam, Holbrooke), and the touring
companies all did something to acclimatize this Italian art to our
northern culture, to lay the foundations of a native tradition in
opera, to provide something that England had lacked ever since the
arrival of Handel with *Rinaldo* in 1711. The blame for our failure to
do what the French and the Germans had done with music-drama
has been laid with a certain plausibility at Shakespeare's door: the
poetic drama of the Elizabethan age dealt with the heroic subjects
that in Italy were made into operas. We had composers then equal
to Monteverdi in genius but Monteverdi had no Shakespeare to
wrest the drama from him. Anyhow, from Handel onward through
the centuries opera was regarded in Britain as an imported luxury
and enjoyed as such. At the time of the crash in 1914 all of the
strenuous efforts to make opera an integral part of our musical life,
as was done everywhere outside the Anglo-Saxon world, seemed to
have reached the same sort of failure after promising beginnings as
had occurred all through the chequered history of opera in this
country. But with the benefit of hindsight we can see that they were
not all waste but bore later fruit. Mr. Rosenthal remarks that 1913
was one of the most exciting years that London had ever experienced
in opera. It was never forgotten and the memory of it played a part
after the passage of a generation in the less hazardous attempt, now
for the first time supported by a government subsidy comparable to,

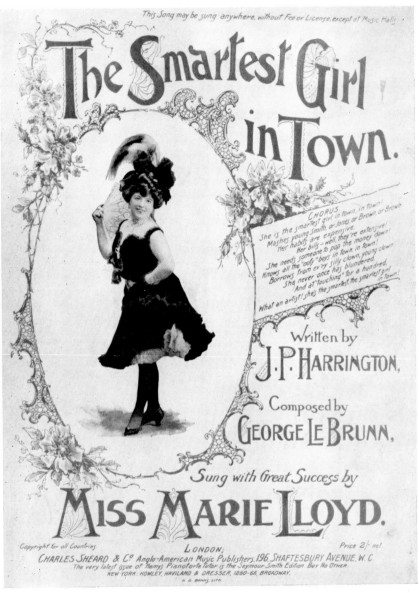

LI. A song-sheet of 1902

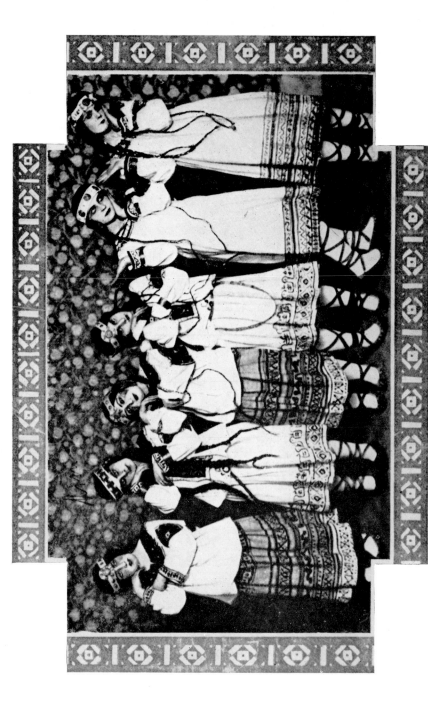

LII. Diaghilev's Russian Ballet 1913: chorus in *Le Sacre du Printemps*
Marie Rambert second from left

though smaller than, those enjoyed by continental opera houses, to create a national opera.

Ballet in England hardly existed in its own right till after Diaghilev's revolution. There had been seasons at His Majesty's (then called the King's) Theatre in the eighteenth century when Noverre came to London, and up to the middle of the nineteenth century London was visited by the great dancers, Grisi, Elssler, Taglioni, and even Lola Montez, but after Lumley, who finished his management in 1858, ballet became either an appendage of the opera or part of a music-hall show. In 1900 its home was the Empire, where it was the principal part of a variety entertainment. Adeline Genée, the Danish ballerina, came to the Empire Palace of Varieties in 1897 at the age of nineteen and she soon became its principal dancer. There she remained till 1914, with intervals for appearances in America and Australia, having in the meantime been joined by Lydia Kyasht and Phyllis Bedells. She gave her official farewell at the Coliseum on 2 March 1914. The Empire ballets had not been without their splendours, but apart from classics like *Giselle* and *Coppélia*, they had mostly been ephemeral productions of a light-hearted character—*The Dancing Doll, Round The Town Again, The Milliner Duchess* being characteristic titles—with plenty of *divertissements* to portray Genée's quality as a soloist. Ballet excels at this sort of thing and can rarely cope with tragedy, and there is no doubt that Genée's art was of a high order: she was an excellent mime, could encompass national and *demi-caractère* styles as well as pure ballet. But the Empire was not the Royal Opera at Copenhagen nor the Maryinsky at St. Petersburg nor even Covent Garden, and the standing of ballet as an art, which it now enjoys on terms of equality with its operatic partner at the Royal Opera House, was not then its portion.

The story of Diaghilev's recruiting a company from St. Petersburg with Pavlova, Karsavina, Fokine, Bolm, and Nijinsky and bringing it first to Paris and then to London has often been told. The reason why it made such a terrific impact on western Europe was that Diaghilev was a connoisseur of all the arts and so produced a *Gesamtkunstwerk* the like of which was hitherto unknown either in Russia or the west. Curiously enough, though the Diaghilev company visited Berlin and Vienna, the impression it created in the German countries, where it might have been supposed that the Wagnerian ideal of a union of the arts of the theatre would have been hailed with enthusiastic recognition, was slighter and impermanent, the Germans preferring the barefoot technique of Isadora Duncan and the dance-mime of Rudolf Laban. Diaghilev came to ballet not from music but from the visual arts. During his student days in St. Petersburg he made friends with a group of young, high-spirited intellectuals and aesthetes who called themselves the Pickwick Club. Its leading spirits were Alexander Benois, son of an architect, a balletomane and draughtsman who was to design *Le Pavillon d'Armide*, Leon Bakst the painter, Nouvel, a good amateur pianist, and the aristocrat Dima Filosofov. Diaghilev, who came from Perm in the Urals, was a cousin of Filosofov and he was a man of action. In 1899 he founded the art periodical *Mir Isskoustva* and received an official appointment at the Imperial Theatre of brief duration. After arranging an exhibition of Russian portraits in St. Petersburg he took it to Paris in 1906. In the following year he took Russian music to Paris in a series of concerts in which Rachmaninov played and Chaliapin sang. In 1908 he took Russian opera, namely Moussorgsky's *Boris Godunov*, again with Chaliapin, to which in 1909 he added Borodin's *Prince Igor*, Rimsky-Korsakov's *Ivan the Terrible* (*Pskovitianka*), Glinka's *Russlan and Ludmilla*, and the ballet *Le Pavillon d'Armide*, which Benois had managed to get produced at the Maryinsky with Pavlova in the title part. This production decisively added ballet to Diaghilev's other interests. In Paris he showed along with it Fokine's *Les Sylphides* and *Cléopâtre*, which gave Bakst his chance for luxuriously oriental décor. In 1910 the repertory was enlarged to contain *The Firebird*, *Scheherazade*, *Carnaval*, and *Giselle*; in 1911 *Petrushka*, *Daphnis et Chloé*, and *Le Spectre de la Rose* for Nijinsky. With seven of these dances Diaghilev conquered London in Coronation year. He came again in 1912, 1913, and 1914, when *Prince Igor* with Chaliapin and the ballet in the Polovtsian dances produced a new climax of enthusiasm. Meanwhile a person destined to make a decisive contribution to the English ballet, which was to emerge after Diaghilev's death, had joined Diaghilev's company in a special capacity. Marie Rambert, a pupil of Dalcroze, was given the task of disentangling the rhythms of Stravinsky's *Le Sacre du printemps* for Nijinsky by eurhythmics. She adopted England as her country. Two British girls joined Diaghilev's troupe, Ninette de Valois in 1923, Alicia Markova in 1925, following a youth calling himself Anton Dolin who had joined in 1921. Out of the ferment of Diaghilev's four London seasons has come a whole chapter of artistic history.

Conclusion

Music is not an art wholly detached from public affairs and the spirit of the age, but it is recalcitrant to politics and moves at a different tempo from public events. On the other hand composers do not live in ivory towers, and Elgar at any rate reflected without any conscious attention to fashion something of the exuberance of life in the reigns of Edward VII and George V. But its major currents run below the surface and the changes of direction in its course tend to take half a century rather than a decade to establish themselves clearly enough for the public to perceive them. Thus the years between the death of Queen Victoria and the outbreak of the first world war saw two musical phenomena evolving side by side, the reaping of the first fruits of the renaissance of 1880 and the initiation of trends that were going to take another generation to produce in their turn another harvest. In composition the first phase was completed by Parry, Stanford, Elgar, and Delius, but a new school arose in Holst and Vaughan Williams which was to lead on to Walton and Britten. In performance the process of the democratization of music had begun, but a new awareness of the need for finer discrimination based on scholarship in some cases, on a sharper critical sense in others, and much more imagination everywhere, began to emerge. In scholarship itself and education we began to be more self-reliant. In opera initiative and tradition reached a stalemate. What came after the war was not quite what was expected, for here, as in Europe, there was a realization that the romantic period was over. We were in for neo-classicism and experiment, for radio diffusion and the gramophone record, for a redistribution of wealth that affected patronage. But fifty years ago sunset and dawn were curiously blended in the golden light of Edwardian England's afternoon.

12

SPORT

JOHN ARLOTT

SPORT

THE Edwardian period has been called 'the Golden Age' of English sport. Indeed, had it been less it would have fallen short of its inheritance and disrupted the pattern of English social history. Nostalgia can make unwitting liars of us all, and later generations have tended to become wearied and doubtful of the superlatives of those who saw that age with the impressionable eyes of youth and now look back on it through the magnifying glass of memory. Yet even in 1890 any observer must have noted a steady building up, everywhere in Britain, towards a standard of sporting performance and participation never known before in the world. We can see now that it resulted in such an all-round supremacy as no country can enjoy again. It was the birth of modern, organized sport, common now in most countries, but then a new concept, originating in Britain.

Sport remains more deeply engraved on popular memory than almost any other facet of the history of Edwardian times through the names of men who were heroes in a society sufficiently remote from the realities of war to regard games as serious matters. In every sport the Edwardian names remain nostalgic and heroic. Even outside their own fields they still have an evocative, epic quality—C. B. Fry, 'Peerless' Jim Driscoll, Bombardier Billy Wells; John Roberts and Tom Reece; Gilbert Jessop, the young Jack Hobbs, S. F. Barnes, 'Ranji', Hirst, and Rhodes; Applegarth and Shrubb; Taylor, Braid, and Vardon; Billy Meredith, Steve Bloomer, Sam Hardy, Crompton, and Pennington; Otto Madden and young Steve Donoghue; John Daniell, Poulton-Palmer, Adrian Stoop, and the Welsh backs; the Dohertys and Mrs. Lambert Chambers; Paul Radmilovic; Leon Meredith; Yorkshire; Swansea, Llanelly; Newcastle, Sunderland, Aston Villa, and the Corinthians. Looking back it is possible to appreciate, more clearly than their own generation could do, how justly these men were esteemed. They were the outstanding athletes of a generation unique because it was the first ever to come of age in a society where sport could be accepted as part of the domestic setting. They grew up in an unselfconscious consciousness of their particular games, familiar with them from the earliest days of impression, using a cricket ball or football, golf club or billiard cue, as a toy.

These sports, except perhaps cricket and boxing, had hitherto been played more or less haphazardly, at least without great study. The outstanding performers of the Edwardian age, however, represented the transition from light-hearted to expert play. It is hard to find amongst them a common denominator. They were amateur or professional, spectacular or meticulous, muscular or cerebral. But they all had ingrained, if not inborn, aptitude so that, with a degree of gaiety—or at least contentment—and almost spontaneously, they evolved, as if by instinct, modern techniques. Their innovations could be regarded by their successors of twenty years and more later as basically, even classically, sound methods upon which play might studiously be founded. Another fifty years of more scientific approach has done little more than confirm the playing methods evolved in these first dozen or so years of the century. Such unorthodoxy as appeared at the time to reside in the methods of the Edwardian sportsmen—with the possible exception of Jessop—has become the orthodoxy of subsequent generations. Indeed these men furnished such a concentration of aptitude and perception, brilliance in execution, and innovation in the practice of games, as can never be paralleled again. Their performances have been exceeded by statistical yardsticks, through concentration, harder training, and specialization. But theirs was the new concept and the elevation; their successors cannot create, for the creating was done by the Edwardians. The survivors among their contemporaries often argue, too, that higher levels of performance have not given players or spectators greater pleasure than in those first fourteen years of the century.

By 1900 conditions were favourable for several English sports— most of them team games, such as Association football, Rugby football, water-polo, cricket, and hockey, but also lawn tennis, badminton, swimming, and boxing—to reach new high standards which placed Britain appreciably ahead of any other country on an all-round basis. In boxing and some sections of athletics the United States was superior; but no other country had been developing sports long enough or thoroughly enough to provide serious competition to the best British athletes. Nevertheless the standing of sport within a nation should not be measured solely by the technical yardstick of top-level performance; its true greatness is the stature of its public image. That image had never been so large nor so real to so many people in England as it was in the era that began in 1900: it was never to appear quite so flawless after 1919.

Sporting reports in the newspapers of the time—as true a mirror as we can wish of public feeling—are essentially friendly. The reader cannot help but feel that the reporter himself enjoyed watching the game and assumed his readers wanted to enjoy it at second hand. There is criticism of technical errors, but the entire feeling implies, beyond the need to state it, general contentment that sport should be, and that it should be as it was. The overriding impression of these reports, even of the most ordinary day's cricket or run-of-the-mill football match, is that the reporter happily and easily found pleasures, humours, and dramas, however minor, to share with his readers. Outstanding players emerge as amiable giants, upon whom the occasional—unmalicious—funny story hangs warmly, detracting nothing from their dignity. British sport was followed, enjoyed, and supported by the public.

Modern sport, organized on a nation-wide basis in the form the mid-twentieth century knows it, began in Britain in about 1850. Until then it had been largely upper-class so far as participation was concerned, and its control was entirely in aristocratic, and autocratic, hands. In the second half of the nineteenth century, however, the increasing and flourishing middle class—far more what is now called 'Victorian' than the sections of the community on either side of it—turned its competent attention to sport. The early founders, administrators, and organizers of the multi-class sports—most of them active, or recently active, participants— were of nonconformist origins and outlook and much more democratically inclined than the noblemen who, by patronage and wagering, had controlled hunting, shooting, horse racing, cricket, and boxing. Other sports fell into two categories. The first, including rackets, real tennis, Rugby and Eton fives, yachting, were limited to the public schools and the upper classes. The second type, which could be played without expensive equipment—primitive forms of football, handball, highland games, wrestling, bowls—had been essentially local, uncoordinated cottage games, recreations for the scanty spare time of a population still largely rural in character despite the drift to the towns since the industrial revolution. As Britain became preponderantly urbanized, its people's sports changed. In place of parochial inter-village occasions, there grew up a network of matches and competitions within national organizations based on units for which the British counties proved ideal in size. These national associations provided the essential shape for any sport which is to flourish, ladders of incentive and opportunity by which players of ability could climb from the village club to national or international championship.

The urge to play competitive games is natural enough. Hitherto the playing had been geographically limited, poorly equipped, largely uninstructed and undirected; restricted by the sheer lack of leisure of people often reduced, by their hours and conditions of work, to a state of exhaustion too advanced to leave strength for strenuous games. Over the second half of the nineteenth century these difficulties were gradually reduced. More widely spread wealth, growing literacy, improving transport, and better working conditions led up to the consolidating Factory Act of 1867 which created *la semaine anglaise* by giving factory employees Saturday afternoons free from work. In the years between 1863 and 1873 were founded the Football Association, the County Cricket Championship, the National Hunt Committee, and the Rugby Union, and the Queensberry rules were introduced into boxing. By 1890 the Amateur Athletic Association, the Amateur Boxing Association, the Lawn Tennis Association, the Amateur Rowing Association, the Swimming Association, the Hockey Association, and the Football League were all established; and the last two boxers had fought a title contest with bare knuckles. In 1896 the classic Olympic Games were revived at Athens in the first modern Olympiad.

The Amateur Rowing Association ruled that no 'menial or manual worker' came within its definition of an amateur—a ruling which, despite the contrary attitude of the N.A.R.A. (1890), debarred an American Olympic sculling champion, J. B. Kelly, from competing at Henley as late as 1920. But, for the rest, the new associations cut determinedly and completely across all class boundaries. For working-class people who did not play themselves there were rapidly expanding terraces from which they could watch. The spread of most games was limited only by lack of grounds. But plenty of inexpensive land was available for football and cricket, and only lawn tennis and golf were seriously handicapped by shortage of suitable playing accommodation.

Game fishing—though a number of trout-streams, vast by the standards of 1960, could still be fished without payment—hunting, riding, and shooting remained, from their economic structures, the prerogative of the rich. In the setting of Edwardian country-house society they flourished richly. On 18 December 1913, at Hall Barn in Buckinghamshire, seven guns killed 3,937 pheasants, which is still a record. In the following year, the Scarteen Hunt in County Limerick set up an Irish record run of 24 miles from scent to kill. Essentially, however, the packs and the guns were enjoying an Indian summer, the more glorious in retrospect for the nearness of the war which was to change their society beyond recognition or reclaim.

Horse Racing

Meanwhile the coinciding economic, physical, social, historic, and administrative elements of sport were fused by the accession of a 'sporting monarch'. King Edward VII was 'sporting' in outlook—widely so—rather than a practising sportsman. But his attitude made sport respectable in his realm. His own major interests were horse-racing and yachting. The huntsman Charles Payne once said of him to Lord Spencer, 'He'll make a capital king, my lord—sits a horse so well.' He developed a sound knowledge of thoroughbred horses during his long career as a racehorse owner, which began in 1871. In 1896, as Prince of Wales, he led in the Derby winner, Persimmon, and the first telegram of congratulation came from Queen Victoria. Then, in the first year of the new century, that flawlessly formed but unruly colt, Diamond Jubilee, ridden by Herbert Jones, won the 'triple crown'—the Two Thousand Guineas, St. Leger, and Derby—to place the prince at the head of that year's winning owners with £29,585. For several subsequent years he met with less success; but in 1909 his colt Minoru became, by a short head from Louviers, the first horse to win the Derby for a reigning monarch. The scene when the king went to lead in his horse was never forgotten by those who saw it. The vast crowd surged down the course, sweeping aside the police barrier, and stood cheering until, at the cue of a single voice, many thousands, in an enthusiastic unity, sang 'God Save the King'. Less than a year later, when King Edward was dying, his filly Witch of the Air won a race at Kempton Park. The Prince of Wales brought the news to the deathbed, and the king's last words were of delight at his success.

Royal patronage gave horse racing much of the 'respectability' it had been struggling for over many years. The Jockey Club, with the Earl of Durham an uncompromising first steward, took complete control of the sport. In 1900 it introduced the use of the starting gate, in 1902 assumed ownership of the *Racing Calendar*, and in 1903 took the right to 'warn off' offenders from all courses. Improved legislation, coincidentally or not, was reflected in considerable benefits to the sport. Bloodstock breeding took strong strides forward. Notably, in 1902, Colonel Hall Walker (later Lord Wavertree) founded, on the edge of the Curragh, the Tully stud which in 1915 became by his gift the national stud and which has had an immense and healthy effect on British breeding. Among the outstanding horses of the time, Diamond Jubilee was followed as a maker of racing history by those two remarkable fillies, Sceptre— still only the second horse to win four 'classic' races (1902)—and Pretty Polly, and by that remarkable sprinter The Tetrarch, known as 'the spotted wonder'.

In this period, too, the modern school of race-riding was founded. The traditional English style, established over centuries, was of riding long, with a seat halfway down the horse's back; tactics consisted of little more than a slow approach to a final sprint, often of less than a furlong. In 1897 the American jockey Tod Sloan had his first mount in England. In 1900 the Jockey Club, under its newly acquired powers, terminated Sloan's licence for the offence of betting. But in the intervening three years his 'monkey crouch' up on the horse's neck, short leathers, pace-forcing tactics, and ruthless determination to win had revolutionized English race-riding. Mornington Cannon, champion jockey for six years before Sloan's arrival, clung to the older method, but in the new century he was behind the times. True, slim stylish Otto Madden was champion jockey in 1901, 1903, and 1904. But from 1906 to 1913 the title was held by the American Danny Maher or the Australian Frank Wootton. Not until 1914 did the young Steve Donoghue supplant them to demonstrate that Sloan's methods had been successfully absorbed and modified by a new school of English riders.

English racing of the Edwardian period—'very plebeian and very patrician', as a journal of the period described Epsom Downs on Derby Day—made a colourful scene. Lord Lonsdale with his yellow phaeton and long cigar, Bob Sievier—gambler, trainer-owner of Sceptre—and the Aga Khan, who sent his first horse to training in 1900, were far from being alone as personalities. But over them all stood the figure of the king, enthusiastic, autocratic yet generous, and appearing to the race-goer—from owner to tout—a benevolent patron.

The king's yachting made much less impact on the life of the country: Cowes Week was Cowes Week, picturesque but exclusive and extremely limited in appeal. But the installation of pigeon lofts at Sandringham—incidentally, one of the prince's birds won the National Flying Club's Lerwick race in 1899—was royal patronage in a form which meant much to the devotees of a sport particularly strong in the working class of the north and midlands.

Boxing

There was only one sport of any importance from which the royal approval was pointedly withheld. In 1901 the case *Rex* v. *The National Sporting Club* on a charge of manslaughter followed the death in the ring of a certain Billy Smith, who boxed under the name of Murray Livingstone. Leading counsel for the Crown stated that the prosecution was brought 'rather with a view of putting a stop to future competitions than to get any punishment inflicted upon the defendants'. The defence was presented by Marshall Hall and the jury found that 'Smith met his death in a boxing contest, therefore the defendants are not guilty'. Thus, negatively, boxing was made legal in Britain. But, although Marshall Hall worked with the N.S.C. on a code of rules which excluded, as they still do, any mention of a knock-out, boxing continued to be regarded, especially by a middle class drilled in Victorian morality, as disreputable. The National Sporting Club had been founded in 1891 and, with Lord Lonsdale, Lord Tweedmouth, and John Douglas as prominent members of the committee and Mr. 'Peggy' Bettinson as manager, it gradually assumed control of British boxing. The N.S.C. was autocratic; but it is doubtful whether it could have made effective progress had it been anything less. It ruled, characteristically, that a British championship could only be won on its premises, a decision strengthened by the inauguration in 1909 of the Lord Lonsdale belts for British champions as recognized by the N.S.C.

The boxing booths, of which there was one in every fair, turned out a race of boxers hardened by at least a dozen bouts a day. The major 'bills' were at the National Sporting Club, Premierland, and Wonderland. But swimming baths all over London, and especially in the east end, were emptied to stage ten or more fights an evening. Six, or even eight, full professional bills a week in London alone was commonplace, and dozens of provincial halls provided their weekly evenings, with Liverpool stadium—'the graveyard of champions'—and the Cosmopolitan gymnasium at Plymouth the most important. Nor were the promoters ever short of boxers to fill the bill, with another half-dozen of assorted weights standing by in hope of the chance to substitute for an absent boxer. The pinched bellies and tightened belts of the east end and the poorer immigrants provided a steady stream of young men prepared to fight like savages for the price of a few meals. It was a hard world. On one side stood those who esteemed the sport and sought to lift it socially. Ranged against them, in far greater numbers, were men always ready to exploit, for a few pounds, a boy's half-promise or the mere need to fight for food. The National Sporting Club attained control over the sport in Britain and retained it until it handed over to the British Boxing Board of Control in 1929. But there was not, and still is not, any effective world authority. So, although some nine British boxers came near to—or were steered away from—world titles between 1900 and 1914, only three or four of them were universally recognized. Nevertheless, while Americans and the British-born Bob Fitzsimmons kept tight hold on the titles in the heavier weights, Britain produced some of the finest welter-, feather-, and fly-weight boxers of the period.

Outstanding and characteristic of the period were Bombardier Billy Wells and 'Peerless' Jim Driscoll. Both boxed in the English style, with upright stance and employing the classic straight left. Wells, a man of strikingly handsome physique and one of the rare heavy-weights who could both box and punch, was heavyweight champion of Great Britain for nine years—longer than anyone else has ever held that title. One of the most perceptive sporting writers of the time described Wells as 'the very best sort of "new" boxer', but, nervous and a poor starter, Wells fell short, in that tough world, of the heights good judges believed he might have reached. To the end of a career more successful than tradition recalls, he was an admired figure in British sport. 'Peerless' Jim Driscoll—the nick-name reveals the age and its attitude to its sportsmen—was a Welsh-born feather-weight as skilful and stylish as Wells, but an altogether harder fighter. He was an effective boxer against the American style and was unlucky that the manœuvrings of those who controlled boxers in America steered him away from a match for the world title. But, before the first world war, two new and greater boxers, both to become world champions within two years, held British titles. By 1914 Jimmy Wilde had fought over two hun-dred fights without being beaten. Underweight even as a fly-weight, he was a phenomenon: apparently fragile, he was a master of ring-craft with a punching power far beyond his size. Indeed it is argu-able that, ounce for ounce, Wilde was the most effective boxer Britain has ever known. Ted ('Kid') Lewis boxed at every weight from bantam to heavy, held British and European titles at three different weights, and was welter-weight champion of the world. British boxing has never since produced the peers of these two.

If the number of participants in proportion to the population is the criterion of health in a sport, British boxing was never healthier. If there was an embarrassment of professionals, there was also a huge, and very separate, number of amateurs in the public schools, at the universities, and in clubs all over the country. Great Britain won all five boxing competitions in the 1908 Olympic Games in London, but only in the absence of any opposition from the United States, whose entrants had won at every weight in the 1904 games. Nevertheless, J. W. H. T. Douglas, who won the middle-weight class, was described as the finest amateur at that weight ever seen in Britain. Douglas was one of the many fine all-rounders produced in the period: he also captained England at cricket and won an amateur cap for Association football.

Athletics

The 1908 Olympics were peculiarly British in character. They were truly international in that the 2,647 entries came from 22 different countries; but of the twenty types of competition, more than half were of British origin or revival and they included such specifically English-centred sports as archery, association and rugby football, rackets, lawn tennis, hockey, water-polo, and even the tug-of-war. Despite the hints of deepening study of technique, the Olympics of 1908 were genuinely amateur at heart. The disqualification of the American J. C. Carpenter for 'boring' in the 400 metres gave rise to the only ill-feeling of the gathering. Many of the best performers took part in two or three events, and the large number of athletes who entered for eight or more indicates that it was still the day of the gifted all-rounder with a natural aptitude for sport, and that strict specialization still lay ahead.

The United States held all the world records of the time for running up to 800 metres, hurdles at all distances, and all but one of the field events: and they proved, as expected, more successful than the United Kingdom in athletics, but only by a comparatively narrow margin, far outweighed in the complete results by the British strength elsewhere. Moreover, while the American runners were prominent over shorter distances, an Englishman, Albert Shrubb, set up a remarkably long-lived series of records in the years 1903 and 1904—for the two miles (not broken until 1926), three miles (1923), six miles (1930), ten miles (1928), and one hour (1913). Shrubb undoubtedly would have been outstanding by world standards in any period. The sprint records of W. R. Applegarth endured in Britain for equally impressive periods: his 9·8 seconds for 100 yards (1913) was not beaten until 1923 while his 21·2 for both 200 metres and 220 yards (1914) remained British records until 1958.

The overall Olympic result was a galloping win for Great Britain, as indicated by these aggregate figures for the first three nations— United Kingdom, United States, and Sweden:

Country	First places	Second places	Third places
United Kingdom	56	$43\frac{2}{3}$	$30\frac{1}{2}$
United States	22	$11\frac{1}{2}$	$11\frac{5}{8}$
Sweden	8	6	$9\frac{1}{3}$

Britain had never known quite such supremacy in world competition before, and has never approached it since. Certainly the United States entered fewer competitors (159 to the British 614) but they seem to have picked on events which they could expect to win.

Nevertheless British standards at the time were so high that they mustered 69 points to America's 108 even in the field of athletics.

In most events there was clear dawning of the modern approach, but still there could arise such a pure comedy situation as that of the tug-of-war. There were five entries for the event—the United Kingdom with three teams (City Police, Liverpool Police, and K Division Police), Sweden, and the United States. Sweden withdrew, allowing K Division to walk over for third place—an attitude of mind unthinkable in the modern Olympics. Something of the spirit of the games at the time can be gathered from the fact that the American tug-of-war team, composed entirely of athletes chosen for other parts of the competition—such as the discus, weight, javelin, hammer—clearly entered for fun without even understanding the event. The official account of their first round heat with Liverpool police remarks 'The police team at the word "heave" pulled their opponents over with a rush. The Americans then withdrew.' The Olympic Council's report ends with the passage:

A few words of explanation are necessary as to a protest raised by certain members of the American Committee in the first round. The Tug-of-War is a game in which the English teams had carefully specialised, and they knew their business well. The Americans were magnificent athletes but were not aware how to tie an anchor or how to place their men. They were, in fact, not used to the game at all, and were very naturally surprised to find how little their strength availed against skilful combination. The English policemen wore their ordinary duty boots as it is their invariable custom to pull in these contests in such boots which have become too shabby for street duty. When they heard that remarks had been made as to the nature of their footwear, they offered to pull in their socks. It is right to add that the American team did not support the protest made, and it was ruled out.

These games are remembered now chiefly for the collapse of the Italian, Dorando, as he came into the stadium to complete the marathon, his disqualification because he was helped to finish, and the sympathetic presentation of a gold cup to him by Queen Alexandra. Yet, in terms of social history, the most important aspect was public reaction. The king declared the games open and the queen presented the prizes; the official report noted that 'The English contingents were led by an Oxford blue, a Cambridge blue, and a former member of the Eton eight.' The general public relished, discussed, and

attended the games in great numbers. It was conservatively estimated that 90,000 people were inside the White City on the day of
the marathon and that altogether over 300,000 people paid to watch
the events. No figures could be given for the huge crowds that
lined the course of the marathon, all the way from Windsor to the
stadium. It is certain, however, that the proportion of the population
that watched some part of the games provided a new conception of
'spectator potential'. Contemporary photographs show the large
crowds not only in the White City but along the route of the marathon. There the runners passed through narrow, but completely
clear, passages maintained by dense crowds which seem barely to
have been marshalled at all.

Rowing

Great Britain won all five events in the rowing section of the
games, held at Henley, against competition stern enough to prove
them genuine world champions. Reports of the four-oar race show,
pleasantly and nostalgically, that when the Dutch crew ran into
the booms their opponents, Leander (rowing as United Kingdom),
waited for them to get clear before taking up the race again:
Leander won. The closest challenge to the British oarsmen lay in the
eights. The Belgian Royal Club Nautique de Gand had won the
Grand Challenge Cup at Henley in 1907 and the same crew, as
Belgium, seemed likely to win the Olympic event. The British
selectors, anxious to produce the best possible crew, approached
Guy Nickalls and asked him if he was available for the trials.
Nickalls, the most successful oarsman Henley had ever known—
winner of the Diamond, Pairs, Stewards', and the Grand, as well
as the Wingfields and four blues—was by then over forty and had
retired from rowing. His response to the invitation was 'I have
never yet been beaten by either a colonial or a foreigner.' He went
into training and rowed number four in the Leander crew which
beat the Belgians in the Olympic final.

In general public consciousness, however, rowing meant the
University Boat Race, a free show which drew its tens of thousands
of spectators to the Thames every year, wearing favours and calling
encouragement on extremely flimsy bases of loyalty. Between 1900
and 1914 Cambridge won eight times and Oxford seven. Cambridge
had won in 1899 after nine consecutive defeats and they won again

in 1900, 1902, 1903 (when the starter's pistol stuck at half-cock on 'Are you Ready?' and Cambridge took a flying start), and 1904. Oxford won in 1901, in the 'Brocas' boat designed by Dr. Warre, and again in 1905, when there were ten Etonians in the two boats. Then, in 1906, as so often in Edwardian sport, the personality of an outstanding performer dominated the event. D. C. R. Stuart became the Cambridge stroke. Stuart's 'sculling style' came in for considerable criticism from knowledgeable students of rowing. Nevertheless, he had great influence on his crew and stroked Cambridge to win in 1906, 1907, and 1908. In 1909 he approached the distinction —unsurpassable under modern rulings—of four consecutive wins in a university match: the Oxford stroke opposing him was a freshman, R. C. Bourne. Oxford won and a new 'star' was made in Bourne—slightly built, not particularly strong, and an unattractive oarsman, but with the power to rally a tired crew and the reputation of being 'never so dangerous as when behind'. Bourne went on to gain the distinction of which he had robbed Stuart—stroking four winning boat race crews. In his last year, 1912, both boats sank in the first race and, though Oxford refloated their boat and finished the course, it was ruled 'no race': Oxford won the re-rowed race.

Something of the changing nature of the times so far as sport was concerned can be gathered from two aspects of an event assumed to be as disinterestedly amateur as the University Boat Race. The *Sunday Times* in 1906 commented on a letter from a reader:

A jarring note is struck by Mr. E. V. S. Hayman (St. Malo) who regrets that even the Boat Race is contaminated by betting. Such an insinuation is ungracious to put it mildly. Some people bet over anything and everything, and certainly if betting is countenanced at all, to wager about the speed and endurance of two such crews is about the noblest form of gambling in existence.

But two years later the race showed up in a very different light. Oxford rowed a 'secret' full-course trial on the ebb just before the day of the race. Several of the Oxford crew were at the time writing or commenting for the press: thus the trial was secret to some newspapers and not to others. The consequent recriminations led to the ruling, which still exists, that no member of a crew or coach in the boat race may write for the press.

Lawn Tennis

One of the least successful, and least necessary, of the Olympic competitions was lawn tennis. With no entrants from the United States or Australia—the other two major tennis-playing countries —and at least six of the best British players absent, the United Kingdom won all three events—men's singles, men's doubles, and women's singles. The event was unnecessary because international competition, both individual and team, already existed. The Wimbledon championships had been held since 1877, and in 1900 the Davis Cup was first contested—in a match between U.S.A. and Great Britain at the Longwood Cricket Club, Boston. The U.S.A. held the cup from 1900 to 1902, Great Britain from 1903 to 1906, Australasia from 1907 to 1911, and each of the three won it once more up to 1914.

Lawn tennis had been invented in Britain; the first known game, under the name of 'sphairistike', was played in Wales in 1873. It was established as a major sport with the rise of the brothers R. F. and H. L. Doherty, who first won at Wimbledon in 1897. Stylishly and genuinely gifted players, widely popular, handsome in appearance, faithfully Westminster and Cambridge in manner and manners, they, more than any others, caused the rapid spread and popularity of lawn tennis and the world-wide importance of the Wimbledon championships from about 1900 onwards. R.F., the elder of the two, was the more subtle, H.L. the faster. They were never happy to oppose one another; but as a doubles pair they were superb, and one or the other won the men's singles at Wimbledon for all but one year from 1897 to their retirement at the end of the season of 1906. Between them, in singles or doubles, they won seventeen championships and they were largely responsible for the British successes in the Davis Cup in the middle of the decade. The two were extremely likeable figures, successful as well as attractive: tragically enough, they both died in their thirties. The outstanding member of the vast and fast-increasing number of women tennis players in the period was Mrs. Lambert Chambers, steady, determined, and a shrewd tactician who, first as Miss Douglass, won the women's singles at Wimbledon seven times, and twice was the losing finalist, between 1903 and 1914.

These players set a high standard of consistency and brought about complete change in the character of lawn tennis in England.

Hitherto it had been almost entirely a middle- and upper-class game played on private courts rather than in clubs, and social rather than competitive. Shortage of courts and price of equipment were to impose limitations on its spread for many years. In Edwardian times, however, clubs grew more numerous, public courts —few but significant—began to be opened, and the game spread widely. In many cases the clubs remained social in feeling, their members content with a low standard of play, but the game was taking firm hold in fresh strata of the community. The club at Wimbledon had originally been known as 'The All-England Croquet and Lawn Tennis Club': in 1882 the word 'croquet' was dropped, but in 1902 for sentimental and traditional reasons it was restored, in changed order, with 'croquet' following 'lawn tennis'. Croquet was still played only in restricted circles but in 1905 Mrs. R. J. C. Beaton became the first woman to win the croquet championship; she and her husband were known as the 'Unbeatons'.

Meanwhile, lawn tennis, so far as the solid body of the game was concerned, had set up an unofficial, but nevertheless wide, link with badminton, in which British players were vastly superior to any others in the world. Miss M. Lucas set up a record with six wins in the women's singles of the All-England championships, while in 1903 G. A. (later Sir George) Thomas, the father-figure of the game, began his remarkable, and surely unsurpassable, record run of twenty-eight All-England (virtually world) titles. Thomas created modern badminton with his varied all-round game and intelligent court-craft, though in his early days the game tended, in line with lawn tennis, to be played for its social rather than its athletic attractions.

Golf

Golf, too, was limited in its spread by economic factors—less seriously in its native Scotland than elsewhere, though even there the cost of equipment presented a barrier. Nevertheless the Edwardian period saw the growth of golf to a world sport. The foundations had been laid in the previous century when it ceased to be a solely Scottish game and came to England for the second time. The Royal North Devon Club at Westward Ho! was founded in 1864. There had been clubs in England much earlier—Blackheath, Manchester, and Wimbledon—but they had been founded by Scotsmen for Scotsmen and the game had not spread outwards from them. Westward Ho! was begun by Englishmen, and their example was followed by others in England and in the United States.

The game in England developed along two channels. The first was dictated by the enthusiasm of Arthur Balfour, a personable young Conservative politician, clearly destined to become a prime minister, who was, for golf, the finest public relations officer any sport ever had. Although he came of a golfing family, he took up the game late and was never a particularly good player. He destroyed the idea previously and widely held in England that golf was an old man's game, presenting it instead as the recreation to which a busy man might escape, finding mild exercise and enjoyment not limited by scanty ability. Thus he set in motion what was to become the major part of the game of golf—recreational play of a standard lifted by professional instruction and compensated by handicap.

The other channel was that of expert performance. The skill of the great Scottish players had spread out, partly through Oxford and Cambridge—the university match is the oldest first-class amateur competition in golf—and then through clubs all over England, Wales, and America. Their Scottish methods were learnt and applied so that in 1890 and 1892 two English amateurs, John Ball and H. H. Hilton, interrupted the hitherto unbroken run of Scottish professional winners of the open championship: and when, in 1894, the Open was for the first time played over a course outside Scotland, it was won for the first time by an English professional, J. H. Taylor.

With the beginning of the new century, both lines of development were accelerated by two technical innovations. The first was the discovery that satisfactory courses, apart from the littoral, sand-dune links, could be created inland from otherwise useless heath or scrub-land. The Sunningdale course, seeded in 1900, was ready for play inside a year; Walton Heath was prepared in four months less. The second factor was the introduction, in 1902, of the rubber-cored and wound 'Haskell' ball which, after a brief period of costing 30s., soon settled at 2s. 6d. in ample, uniform supply. So the business man in search of recreation had more and more courses available within easy reach of the great towns, and, to encourage him out of his rabbithood, there was this new, mass-produced, responsive, liftable ball in place of the recalcitrant 'gutty'.

In senior competition play it was the legendary, and technically important, period of the 'Great Triumvirate'—J. H. Taylor, an Englishman; James Braid, a Scot; and Harry Vardon, a Channel Islander. One or other of these three won the open championship in sixteen of the twenty-one years between 1894 and 1914. Another Scot, Sandy Herd, so often Braid's partner in international matches for Scotland, was only just behind the three as a professional; while the remarkable amateur, John Ball, in addition to the Open in 1890, won the amateur championship six times over the remarkably wide period of 1888 to 1912, and H. H. Hilton, as well as two Opens, won the Amateur four times and was thrice losing finalist. The three great professionals—setting the tune for such slightly lesser but extremely competent players as Herd, White, Ray, Duncan, Robson, Tom Ball, Ayton, and Sherlock—lifted tournament play to what seemed inhuman levels. With an all-round consistency which appeared unnatural to the golfers of earlier generations, they reduced temperament and loss of touch to minor irritations with year after year of low figures. Until 1914 this triumvirate and British golf were virtually supreme, although the Frenchman Arnaud Massy won the open championship in 1907 and W. J. Travis, a New Zealander by birth but an American as a golfer, beat Blackwell in the Amateur of 1904. The clear portent of the levelling of the field came in 1913 at Brookline, Massachusetts, when an American amateur, Francis Ouimet, won the American open championship in a replay—after a triple tie—against Vardon and Ray.

By 1914 the almost entirely Scottish game of thirty years earlier was an enthusiasm in England which reigned from the Prince of Wales to members of the early artisan clubs and municipal courses. It had even its own uniform. In the nineteenth century the 'tiger' was identifiable by his frayed, shabby jacket; but in the decade before the first world war, good and bad golfers uniformly wore neat, sober Norfolk jackets, breeches and stockings, and the very English cloth cap. One record from Edwardian golf endures: in August 1913 at the ninth hole of the old Herne Bay course E. C. Bliss sent his ball a surveyed and measured 445 yards—the only independently authenticated drive of over a quarter of a mile in golfing history.

The earliest women's golf was played in Scotland but it spread more rapidly in England and it was in London, in 1893, that the Ladies Golf Union was formed. The best women golfers at the beginning of the century were in Northern Ireland, chief among them Miss May Hazlet and Miss Rhona Adair, winners of five English and nine Irish championships between 1900 and 1908. Miss Dorothy Campbell (later Mrs. Hurd) won the Scottish women's championship three times, the British twice, then went to live in America and won the American National twice and the Canadian Open three times. But the two most important Edwardian women golfers were Miss Charlotte Dod and Miss Cecil Leitch. Lottie Dod, who held both the British and Canadian championships in 1913, had been five times women's singles lawn tennis champion at Wimbledon up to 1893 before she turned her attention to golf. A hockey international and the finest woman archer in Britain, she was a natural all-rounder and the pioneer figure of British women's sport. Cecil Leitch, who reached the semi-final of the British championship when she was only seventeen (1908), had played golf from childhood on the nine-hole course her father laid out at their home in Silloth. Thus bred up in the game, she hit with a cleanness, power, and control which set a new standard of iron play for women. Miss Leitch continued as an outstanding player for long after the first world war, far into the new era of play that she had introduced.

The figures for most of the pre-1914 women's competitions are not, in isolation, impressive. But it should be remembered that they were achieved by players balancing straw boaters on their heads, and wrapped about in heavy tweed skirts which reached to the ground and concealed their thick, sprigged boots. We may wonder, too, the extent to which golf helped women's emancipation. As one of their writers put it: 'None of the pre-golf pastimes led their devotees so far afield or brought them together in such numbers as golf has done.'

Rugby Football

In a period of such prosperity and expansion in almost every sport, it is surprising to find one—rugby football—which, in England at least, fell back. On the other hand it might be argued that it had become two games instead of one—Rugby Union and Northern Union (later Rugby League)—so that rugby in general had gained. As a result of a dispute in 1893 over 'broken time' (compensation for earnings lost through playing rugby) a group of strong and well-supported Lancashire, Yorkshire, and Cheshire clubs

broke away and founded the Northern Union, legalizing the payment to players which, they claimed, already went on in the Rugby
Union. Many outstanding English players of the time came from
the north, so the quality of play in England declined over a considerable period. It was considered remarkable that so few of the
Welsh players were tempted by the prospect of payment.

Edwardian rugby was dominated by Wales, strong in its clubs
and international sides. Of the thirteen outright championship
wins, Wales achieved six—and one of the two ties. In assessing
Welsh teams it is easy to overlook the high competence of the pack
because of the brilliance of the backs—such men as Gabe, Llewellyn,
E. T. Morgan, Gwyn Nicholls, Trew, R. M. Owen, and Bush, whose
names are still luminous in Welsh rugby talk. None who saw them
ever forgot the fire, fluidity, and cohesion of the Welsh club sides
of the period and if Swansea, Llanelly, and Cardiff made the deepest
impact, there were some fine teams at their heels. Only Wales
succeeded in beating the New Zealand All-Blacks of 1905, the first
touring side to visit England since the Maoris in 1888–9. The New
Zealanders had a fantastically successful tour. They ran away with
their first game, against Devon, by 55–4 (which many British rugby
followers, when they read it in their newspapers, took to be a mis-
print for 5–4), won 31 of their 32 matches, and scored 830 points
against 39. Their effect was as impressive as their figures: they
brought crowds back to watch rugby, and they revolutionized
British methods. Employing a seven-man scrum (packing 2–3–2)
with a 'spare' man (usually their captain, D. Gallaher) acting as an
extra scrum-half or a wing-forward, they played extremely fast
football and used their backs with an imaginative variety far beyond
anything existing in Britain. In the following season the first South
African touring side, captained by Paul Roos, emphasized the New
Zealand lessons of pace, passing, and back-play.

English football, meanwhile, was slowly climbing back to something of its old eminence. H. T. Gamlin (a full-back, the 'Octopus'
of many classic rugby anecdotes) and John Daniell, an inspiring
forward and captain, had given gleams of hope in some spirited
performances, while Adrian Stoop, a Harlequin half-back, had done
much to improve the standard of passing among the backs in his
club and in the English team. In 1908 the ambitious ground at
Twickenham was opened as the headquarters of the Rugby Union

and in 1910 the English revival was marked by the winning of the
international championship. In that fine team, Dai Gent and Adrian
Stoop were the half-backs; J. G. Birkett was at centre; the legendary runner R. W. Poulton (later Poulton-Palmer) played his first
international at three-quarter and C. H. Pillman was outstanding
as a wing-forward. By 1913, when England won for the first time
at Cardiff Arms Park, their fifteen included such famous players
as W. J. A. Davies, C. N. Lowe, and V. H. M. Coates, and they won
the championship three times and shared it once in the five seasons
up to the beginning of the war.

Scotland won the championship in 1901, 1903, 1904, and 1907.
The keynote of the Scottish play was the drilled efficiency of the
forwards in scrummaging and dribbling. Outstanding among those
established forwards were Mark Morrison (with 23 caps and the
unmatched record of having five times captained the winning side
in the Calcutta Cup match with England), D. R. Bedell-Sivright (27
caps), J. C. McCallum (23 caps), W. P. Scott, and A. G. Cairns.
Ireland, effective through less precise but even more fierce forward
play, shared the championship twice: G. T. Hamlet, A. Tedford,
and the brothers J. and M. Ryan were outstanding among their
rampaging forwards; the English-born Basil Maclear was a back
with a terrific hand-off, and Louis Magee a fine half-back.

Rugby has strong social significance in Britain. In southern
England it has always been a middle-class sport: in Wales it covers
all sections of the community, but its great tradition is largely
working-class: in the north the division was very sharp: Rugby
Union was middle and upper class, Rugby League the working-class
sport. By 1914 the visits of touring sides, with consequent improvement in British play, and the opening of Twickenham had brought
the game back to general health. Of all the major sports of Britain,
however, Rugby Union was—except in Wales—the one most
affected, within and without, by class-consciousness. Meanwhile
Northern Union rugby, later to be known as Rugby League, went
on its warm, localized way, played with varying degrees of public
support by both professionals (paid strictly on a match basis) and
amateurs, in Yorkshire, Lancashire, and Cumberland. At first it had
been played exactly as Rugby Union but, to the end of making it
a more attractive spectacle, constant changes have been made in
the rules and in 1906–7 the number of players in a team was reduced

from fifteen to thirteen. To the original knock-out Challenge Cup competition of 1896–7 were added, after the reconstruction of 1905, the Yorkshire Cup and the Lancashire Cup; and separate Lancashire and Yorkshire Leagues came in 1907. Huddersfield, the home of the game—indeed, for many years the hub of northern sport—had between 1909 and 1915 the famous 'Empire team', and other powerful clubs of the time were Hunslet (who won all four cups in 1907–8), Hull, Halifax, Oldham, Wigan, Salford, Leeds, and Wakefield. In 1905 G. H. West scored 53 points (10 goals and 11 tries)—still a record—for Hull Kingston Rovers when they beat Brooklands Rovers by 73–5 in the first round of the Challenge Cup.

Hockey

Hockey, with fewer ambitions, had no such troubles as rugby. Strong in the public schools and the services, it went healthily along, contentedly and unquestionably amateur, essentially a players' rather than a spectators' game. England was the strongest hockey country in the world and won the 1908 Olympic event quite easily. The players who were eventually to replace England as the model of successful hockey were then only learning the game, in India and Pakistan, and no overseas team could present a worth-while challenge to the English team. Women's hockey, too, was sturdily established in its own particular niche. With netball—introduced from America and gaining a hold in schools—and figure-skating, it offered the best opportunities, after lawn tennis and golf, for the growing number of women who were struggling under the handicap of long skirts to master an increasing number of games. Moving towards emancipation and suffrage, they did not seek to compete with men but were determined to play their own games in their own clubs and, where no such opportunity existed, a 'spin' on a bicycle was at least a gesture.

Association Football

Meanwhile, in spite of a proliferation of minor activities,[1] the

[1] The sporting 'rage' of the time was roller-skating: in 1911 at Olympia, A. R. Eglington set a paced amateur mile record of 2 minutes 48·4 seconds. Two records by amateur cyclists are still unbeaten: W. J. Bailey won the sprint title three times (1909, 1911, and 1913), and Leon Meredith was the amateur 100-kilometre champion seven times between 1904 and 1913. R. Montgomerie's performance in winning the Amateur Fencing Association épée title five times is also unequalled. In billiards Tom

British people's vast and rapidly increasing hunger for sport was most fully satisfied by the huge mushroom-growth of Association football in winter and the long-established and all-embracing cricket in summer.

The cricket grounds of most towns and villages had the air of rightness, as if they had grown into the landscape. But the new football fences and grandstands, raw, tall, gaunt, and bare, were harsh new features of the urban fringe. Football had come far since the days of the leadership of the public schools' old boys' teams. The professional clubs which had broken away and, in 1888, formed the Football League were the dominant power in the game, so strong that for the last sixteen years of the nineteenth century no team from south of Birmingham reached the cup final. The clubs of Yorkshire, Lancashire, and the midlands were powerful playing combinations, well supported and wealthy, meeting a huge, hungry demand for football as Saturday afternoon excitement for the workers in industry. A similar situation existed in Scotland and Northern Ireland but, although there were Welsh soccer centres, in Wales the word 'football' meant Rugby Union.

The Football Association postponed its arranged cup ties of January 1901 for one month 'to give expression to the profound grief which is felt by its members on account of the death of Her Majesty Queen Victoria'. A year later King Edward became the patron of the Football Association, which in 1903 registered under the Joint Stock Companies Act. The first cup final, played at the Oval in 1872, was watched by fewer than 2,000 people: at the 1901 Crystal Palace final there were 110,820 spectators. These were the cloth-capped hordes which caught the imagination—favourably or unfavourably —of so many observers of the time, invading London in their northern-voiced, thick-suited, and heavy-booted thousands on cup final day. There were some stormy scenes in Glasgow at matches between Glasgow Rangers and Glasgow Celtic —in 1909 the Scottish

Reece in 1907, by use of the 'anchor' cannon, made a break of 499,135: it took five weeks (85 hours 40 minutes) but was not recognized as a record because the press and public were not present throughout.

Motor-cycling and motor-car and motor-boat racing were minority sports with a growing following, but, while all three were restricted by their cost, the first two were additionally handicapped by the fact that racing on road circuits was illegal in England: so, in 1907, the inaugural tourist trophy (T.T.) race was held in the Isle of Man. The United Kingdom was first, in the 1908 Olympics, in two events in archery, five in cycling, four in swimming, three in wrestling, and in water-polo.

cup was withheld because of rioting—but these were out of character. The Edwardian football follower regarded booing of players
or referee as his right: the Millwall and Barnsley crowds were good
examples of the southern and northern manifestations of that
attitude. Yet the players of the time recall crowds as generous and
essentially good mannered: certainly their reactions included nothing
so studiedly cruel as the slow handclap of later years. Perhaps the
fairest and clearest definition of these very masculine hordes is that
they were supporters rather than spectators. Many of them had
watched their local clubs grow up from waste-land play to the
heights of success and they felt themselves passionately involved
in the fortunes of their team.

The dominant northern and midland professional sides were
concerned with the Football League (which then consisted of two
divisions) and the F.A. Cup. But the concentration and regionaliza-
tion of their matches is indicated by the other competitions with
which they were concerned—the Manchester Cup, the Lancashire
Cup, the Lancashire League, the Midland League, the Staffordshire
Cup, the Birmingham Cup, and the Birmingham Charity Cup. So the
original league clubs and those few they had allowed to join them
hung together in an all but exclusive group. But it would be wrong to
assume that they were in anything like a majority. Of the 8,000 clubs
registered with the F.A. in 1900, 300 were professional, with 4,500
paid players: but there were 200,000 amateur footballers in England.

English football had tended to fall into five compartments. Outside the two major leagues, yet inevitably increasing in strength,
were the professional competitions of the south—notably the
Southern League (in two divisions) and the Western League. At
the opposite pole there were the original founders of the game in
England, the old boys' clubs. (Association football was firmly established in a number of major public schools such as Westminster,
Harrow, Charterhouse, Eton, Winchester, Shrewsbury, Malvern, and
Repton, as well as in the universities.) In twenty years they had
waned as playing forces from cup winners to minor powers indeed—
except in the case of the unique Corinthians. The remainder now
confined themselves to matches with one another, and in 1902 began
their own competition, the Arthur Dunn Cup. They refused to
recognize the penalty kick, which they regarded as a necessary
penal weapon in professional football but a reflection on the moral

standards of amateur play—an attitude which incurred them a sharp reprimand from the Football Association. In 1907 a number of them, feeling that they were neglected by the F.A., decided, on the issue of including professional clubs in county associations, that it was 'essential for the good of the game of Association Football' for them to form a separate body, the Amateur Football Defence Association: the split continued until 1914. The other important section of amateur football included the vast majority of players—in a working-class game embracing minor village, small-town, and sectional clubs. The play, as the records of the Amateur Cup show, was dominated by the north-east—Bishop Auckland, West Hartlepool, Stockton, Crook Town, and South Bank—with, however, close challenge from the London area, outstandingly from Clapton, but also Bromley and Ealing.

In 1900, the thirty-six clubs of the two football leagues included only one from the south—Woolwich Arsenal—although Luton Town had spent three undistinguished seasons in the second division during the nineties. But the south, particularly London, if only because of its resources of finance and population, was bound, once it accepted professionalism, to challenge the domination of the north. Surely enough, Southampton reached the first cup final of the new century—the first time a southern club had done so since the Old Etonians in 1883. Southampton were beaten by Bury, but in the following year Tottenham Hotspur followed them to a final at the Crystal Palace—and won. By 1914 six clubs from the south and west had entered the Football League.

The problems of professionalism had by no means been solved by its legalization in 1885. The differing standards of wealth between the league clubs meant that some were in a position to offer greater inducement to players. As a result, the F.A. ruled in 1901 that no player might receive more than £10 for signing on as a professional, or be paid more than £208 a year, or any bonus dependent upon the result of a match. The league clubs undoubtedly resented the Football Association legislating on what they regarded as their domestic affairs. The F.A., for its part, was again disturbed in 1905 when Alf Common, the Sunderland forward, was transferred to Middlesbrough for a fee of £1,000. Within a few weeks the Football Association had countered with a ruling that, after a three-year period of grace, no club should pay or receive more than £350 for the transfer of a player. Within three months that unworkable ruling was rescinded, and in 1912, in the King's Bench division, the transfer system was upheld. The action brought by a footballer named Kingaby against the Aston Villa club, for maliciously preventing him from earning his living as a footballer, was closed on the ground that there was no case to go to the jury.

The rapid rise of professional football, spectacular in its main outlines, contained, nevertheless, the evils associated with any boom. A F.A. commission of 1900 found a Burnley player guilty of attempting to bribe the Nottingham Forest team and in 1913, after a civil action, a man was sent to prison for five months for offering a bribe to the West Bromwich Albion captain. Even nearer the bone were malpractices in club administration: over the period, the F.A. council held inquiries into the affairs of eight or nine clubs and—what makes odd reading—the trainer of Stoke City was fined £1 for opening the bags of the Sheffield Wednesday players. A professional Players' Union was formed in 1908 with the consent, if not the enthusiastic blessing, of the Football Association. But all semblance of official approval was withdrawn a year later when the union affiliated with the Federation of Trades Unions and, once its members had proved insufficiently united to carry out a threat to strike, it sacrificed all real power for another forty years.

On the field, however, British football was more than merely healthy—it dominated the world, so that, although the F.A. sent a touring team to Germany in 1899–1900, there was, in fact, no worthwhile opposition outside the British Isles for even one of its average elevens. The Fédération International de Football Associations was founded in Paris in 1904, but while the F.A. adopted a fatherly attitude towards it, the rest of British football was far too involved with its own immediate domestic results to be concerned with such an apparently unpromising and unimportant offshoot of its play.

This was a period of great clubs. Aston Villa, already outstanding in the last decade of the nineteenth century, continued on their majestic way, collecting players of marked ability in the traditional English style. The north-east, however, was the new rising power. Newcastle and Sunderland blended—sometimes, their opponents felt, overstressed—the Scottish methods with English. Sunderland had earlier produced their 'team of all the talents'. In the fifteen seasons between 1900 and 1914 they built another side of

similar brilliance with its famous international 'triangle' of Cuggy–
Mordue–Buchan, powerful half-backs, and lively forwards. They did
not quite achieve, in results, all that their exciting football promised: even so, they were twice champions of the Football League,
once runners-up, and four times third, as well as reaching the cup
final of 1913. Sheffield Wednesday, Liverpool, Manchester United,
Everton, Blackburn Rovers, Bury, Sheffield United, and Derby
County all had considerable successes in the period, while Bristol
City made a sharp rise to—and in—the first division. But the outstanding football club of the Edwardian period was Newcastle
United—three times league champions and twice third: five times
cup finalists in seven seasons. Yet in those five appearances they
only won the cup once: it was said that the Crystal Palace ground
was unlucky for them and certainly they only won (1910) in a replay
at Everton after the first match had been drawn at the Crystal
Palace. The rapid rise of Middlesbrough completed such a picture
of football in the north-east as pushed the traditional handball and
even the whippets into the background of public enthusiasm.

Yet, respected and admired as the professional clubs were, they
did not fire the national imagination so warmly or so romantically
as the Corinthians. The Corinthian club, originally founded in 1882
to play friendly matches outside any competition, was open to any
amateur. But its eventual playing strength came largely from
Oxford, Cambridge, and the public schools, with occasional support
from the services and the training hospitals. Its founder, N. A. Lane
Jackson, saw that, if he avoided entering his side for any competition, he could recruit the cream of amateur talent; and he did so.
Indeed in 1895 the English team against Scotland was composed
of nine Corinthians and two Blackburn Rovers players.

With the new century a fresh and picturesque generation of
Corinthians made its impact on the sporting imagination. If Edwardian sport is to have one exemplar—which is not truly possible
—it must be the Corinthians. They seemed to personify, in their
dashing, dilettante brilliance, the gay gallantry which a world war
pillaged. Even in the twenties they were a nostalgically faithful echo
of that earlier time. Simply to see them saunter on to a football
field, scorning shin-guards, in fresh white cricket shirts, hands deep
in the pockets of their uniquely shaped, dark-blue shorts, was to
feel a difference—deep, however outdated—between their patrician

negligence and the professional football of the industrial towns. Even their style of play was peculiarly their own, a blend of the artistic and the robust; in attack, keeping the ball closely along the ground with fast dribbling and short passing: defending with racing tackles and lusty shoulder-charging.

The rules of the club had to be changed to allow the Corinthians to play for the Sheriff of London Shield—a single annual match between the leading amateur club and the leading professional club in the country. In that competition for the 1899–1900 season the Corinthians beat the remarkable Aston Villa side, in the middle of the six- or eight-year period when the Villa dominated English professional football. The players themselves, however, considered the Corinthians' most striking triumph was in the Charity Shield match of 1904 against Bury, who had won the cup without conceding a goal and the final by a still enduring record score of 6–0 against Derby County. Early in the match Bury led by 2–0 but brilliant bursts of Corinthian-style football took the amateurs first to a 4–2 lead at half-time and then swept the Bury defence spectacularly aside to a win by 10–3.

It is difficult to rank the twentieth-century Corinthians, but most would put first G. O. Smith, a Carthusian and Oxford blue who played twenty times in full internationals for England between 1893 and 1901 and might well have done so more often: certainly he refused two 'caps' in 1900 while he was in mourning for his mother. Smith was a true Corinthian in style: he played strictly on the ground, and was said never to have scored a headed goal. Almost frail in physique, with a slight stoop and a pale, delicate face, Smith led, as well as pointed, his forward lines, a superb stylist with a strong, accurate shot. He was once described by James Catton as 'the quietest, mildest man who ever deceived a pair of heavy backs and crashed the ball in to the net'. Like so many of his Corinthian contemporaries, he was a natural games player (he scored a century for Oxford against Cambridge at Lords in 1896). Like them, too, he was a genuine amateur; he might have continued longer, even at international level, but he played football solely for amusement.

This Corinthian club produced eighteen footballers good enough to win full international caps, in competition with professionals, between 1900 and 1914. Norman Creek has described M. M. Morgan-

Owen as the greatest of the Edwardian Corinthians (rating G. O. Smith as having been at his best before 1900), but the decision must be hard to make between W. J. Oakley, the two test cricketers— C. B. Fry and R. E. Foster—the Rev. K. R. G. Hunt, S. S. Harris, B. O. Corbett, and S. H. Day. Another amateur, Vivian Woodward, who played for Chelsea and Tottenham Hotspur, succeeded G. O. Smith in the English team: he played in 'full' and amateur international matches. Like Smith slight in physique, Woodward was an all-round footballer, poised, shrewd, stylish, and deadly in finishing.

The quality of these players is made apparent by their standing and success in comparison with the professionals of the time, who were the founder-giants of the modern game, many of whom returned to first-class play after the first world war and demonstrated their mastery to a new generation. Sam Hardy, of Liverpool and Aston Villa, continued for many years as the ideal goalkeeper, graceful, unhurried, superb in judgment, positioning, and handling. Steve Bloomer played alongside G. O. Smith for England: he was an inside forward, neatly built and amazingly fast to sense or create an opening for his cold, fierce shooting. His aggregate of 352 goals in league football has been beaten: but his 28 goals in only 23 internationals (over 12 years) is unapproached in terms of goals-per-match. English football had to wait fifty years for another such goal-producer in Greaves. Bloomer's club, Derby County, came near to winning both cup and league but, so it was popularly believed at the time, a gipsy's curse kept them from achieving either.

Athersmith, the Aston Villa outside-right, until 1961 the last player to win a league championship medal, a cup-winner's medal, and an England cap in the same season—and who once played on the wing holding up an umbrella against the rain—continued his lithe way into the new century. But he was succeeded in the English team by two of the finest of all right-wing men—Billy Bassett of West Bromwich Albion, and Jock Simpson of Blackburn Rovers—who could consider themselves vastly unfortunate to be contemporaries, competing for a place which either, but for the other, might have filled more than adequately for many years.

Among the half-backs, the great days of Crabtree and the tough, tireless 'Nudger' Needham extended only a little into the new century, but Andrew Ducat was their true successor, and for five years England looked no further than that powerfully complete footballer,

'Fatty' Wedlock of Bristol City, for a centre-half. The greatest of all English full-back pairings—Crompton (Blackburn Rovers) and Pennington (West Bromwich Albion)—lasted even longer: otherwise those two majestic backs Howard Spencer and Herbert Smith might have reigned as long and as successfully.

Of the eleven home countries international championships clearly decided in the period, England won six and Scotland three and those two shared the four tied competitions—once, in a triple tie, with Ireland also. The Scottish teams of the time, too, were impressively regular, with two rare, and closely successive, flowerings of master ball-players, mostly from the Glasgow clubs or Anglo-Scots playing with north-eastern teams. Among them were such great names as the first Bobby Walker (probably the noblest forward who ever set boot to field), Alex Raisbeck, Peter McWilliam, Brownlie, Aitken, Templeton, Quinn, R. S. McColl, Robertson, Thompson Hay, and McMenemy. Wales won the championship for the first time in 1907 with a curiously irregular team selection, which did not regularly include all of their chief players of the period—L. R. Roose, A. G. Morris, M. M. Morgan-Owen, W. Lot Jones, W. H. Blew, E. Lloyd-Davies, and R. E. Evans. In their side, too, was Billy Meredith from Chirk, who played in his forty-eighth international at outside right for Wales when he was 45 years old and for Manchester City in the cup final in his fiftieth year. Meredith was originally a traditional-style, run-and-cross winger but he was also the first to hint at 'cutting in', with far more goals (470) than Stanley Matthews, with whom he has often been compared for the guile of his wing-running. Meredith was so relaxed a footballer that he would play through the hardest match with a toothpick held nonchalantly between his lips.

Ireland, most of whose players came originally from Ulster, beat England for the first time in 1913 and were first champions in 1914. J. Darling, of Linfield, had finished his long stint in internationals a few seasons before and now there were Gillespie, Hamill, Rollo, V. Harris, and F. W. Thompson in the finest team Ireland produced until the later 1950's. Their outstanding personality was Billy McCracken, whose astute exploitation of what was called 'the one-back game' eventually brought about the revision of the offside law.

When war began in 1914, only England of the four home countries had played a full international match against a country outside

Great Britain. That gesture consisted of six matches: a visiting
German team of 1901 was beaten 12–0 and 10–0, and in 1908 a
touring English side won against Austria by 6–1, 11–1, and 8–1,
and against Bohemia by 4–0. There had been no playing contact
between Britain and Europe on representative level in the subsequent six years. British footballers, deeply immersed in their own
domestic play, gave little more than a condescendingly distant nod
to the game beyond the Channel. They were not to know, and
would not have believed, when Great Britain won the Olympic
football tournament at Stockholm in 1912, that none of them
would live to see that victory repeated.

All this football was, by its essential method, an entertainment.
The keynote of the game was attack. Safety first, spoiling, the
'stopper' centre-half, and the entire defensive approach, lay far in
the future. Wing half-backs played wide to the wings: the full-backs
towards the centre, and the inside forwards lay upfield so that the
forwards played in a line-of-five. Thus the centre-half—cast as
the major figure on the field—became a sixth defender, or ranged the
midfield, or made a sixth forward, according to the run of the game.

Cricket

Edwardian Association football, its play and its following, was a
warm, strong, little world of its own. But that world had recognized
limits. In England the season began on the first Saturday in September and ended on the last Saturday of April. The popular sporting year of the Edwardians was divided precisely, without thought
of quibble or rivalry, into the (rugby or association) football season,
and the (summer) cricket season. There was virtually no other
summer spectator sport: long columns in the press, green squares
in every town and village, country-house weeks, and the talk of the
clubs and pubs declared that cricket came into its kingdom with
the first warmth of the English sun.

A popular print of England v. Australia dated 1887 showed the
then Prince of Wales standing with Princess Alexandra in front of
the old Rover stand at Lord's, while Miss Lily Langtry and several
other ladies averted their heads from the royal visitors. The year
of King Edward's accession saw cricket suffer its greatest single
personal loss, yet enter upon its richest, most varied, and popular
period. Dr. W. G. Grace, the most dominating figure any sport has

ever known, ceased to play cricket for Gloucestershire in 1900.
A jubilee Gentlemen *v.* Players match at Lord's had celebrated his
fiftieth birthday in 1898; and a year later he played his last Test
Match. He had become a legend in his own time, but even that time
had to end. Henceforward, for a few years, small boys might be
taken to see him, like some Eiffel Tower or historic monument,
playing in *quasi*-first-class matches for his London Counties eleven
at the Crystal Palace. But the sterner game knew him no more.

No single man could replace him. But even if there had been one
of his quality, he would not have been sufficient. First-class cricket
had grown and spread: between 1891 and 1905 the number of 'first-
class' counties was doubled by the entry of eight new teams to the
championship. Crowds at forty grounds in sixteen counties wanted
to watch great cricketers in every match. The period from 1900 to
1914 met that demand with such prodigality as, surely, can never
be repeated. The entertainment they offered was the unfailing delight of the cricket watcher—a profusion of runs, handsomely
scored. Once more, the circumstances were ideal. The rough grounds
of fifty years earlier had given way to strips marled to perfection,
defying the skill of all but a few bowlers to wrest pace or turn from
them. In such a setting stroke-players flourished through what
appears, in the recollection of those who played in it and from the
records of the time, to have been an age of sunshine and true, fast
pitches. Of course there were sticky wickets, and of course bowlers
had their days, but the main picture is of batsmen lording it in
a summertime of runs.

True, every county had a genuine fast bowler; but they made little
impact. Spectators went to Hove to watch C. B. Fry and Ranjitsinhji, the Jam Sahib of Nawanagar, score centuries in their con-
trastingly beautiful styles. At Old Trafford the majesty of A. C.
MacLaren and the savage square-cutting of that bad-wicket master,
J. T. Tyldesley, linked with the wristy ease of R. H. Spooner. On
the flawless turf of the Oval Tom Hayward and Bobby Abel were
joined, and then outshone, by the magnificent hitting of the young
Crawford and then by the greatest of all professional batsmen—the
man who came, perhaps, nearest to completeness in batting—the
modest master, Jack Hobbs. Somerset had the princely stylist
Lionel Palairet; Nottingham, the mischievously dextrous George
Gunn and his obdurate brother John. It was for Nottingham, one

bleak day of May 1911, at Hove, that a muscular man by the name of Alletson scored the only century of his career. Few people saw it, for the overnight score promised that Sussex would coast to a win by lunch. So it appeared when Alletson came in, eighth man, to score 50 in the hour up to lunch. After lunch he launched the fiercest sustained onslaught any bowlers have ever suffered—149 in 30 minutes. He hit 34 from a single over by Killick; a square cut wrecked the pavilion bar; and at one time ten balls struck by him were 'lost' outside the ground. Gloucestershire's captain, in place of W. G., was the unique Gilbert Jessop, the 'Croucher', who by his glorious eye, power, and speed in movement achieved such a level of consistency in fast scoring as no other cricketer has ever approached, mixing the unorthodox with the orthodox as he willed so that, on his day, no bowler in the world could be sure of bowling him a ball which would not be hit for six. R. E. Foster—'Tip' Foster—of the family which caused Worcestershire to be called 'Fostershire', was a true period piece: a handsome driver in the Malvern manner and a graceful cutter; his 287 against Australia in 1903 remained the highest score made in a Test Match until 1929. Early and late in the period Yorkshire developed two of their ruthless champion teams, both based on the prodigious labours of the two matchless all-rounders from Cleckheaton, George Hirst and Wilfred Rhodes, but with the weighty batting of 'Long John' Tunnicliffe, David Denton, J. T. Brown, and that patrician figure, F. S. Jackson (who excused his century for Harrow against Eton with the words 'It will give the guv'nor a leg-up'). For all the Yorkshire successes, Kent maintained a higher average championship position over these years, when their batting held the grace of Woolley, K. L. Hutchings, J. R. Mason, James Seymour, and S. H. Day. At need, of course, all these batsmen could play effectively to the on side: C. B. Fry's main strength lay there and 'Ranji's' leg-glance was one of the delights of the cricket field. But the true battle-ground of the struggle between the Edwardian batsman and bowler was along, and just outside, the line of the off stump. Thus the batsman, with every successful blow, played an attractive stroke. It is playing regally to the off side—driving and cutting—that memory and history picture these batsmen.

As always in cricket, however, and even in this blaze of batting, there were influences at work to adjust the balance between bat and

LIII. Two England cricket captains: W. G. Grace and F. S. Jackson

LIV (c). Over-arm Service

LIV (b). Four Open Champions: White, Braid, Vardon, Taylor

LIV (a). Full Swing

ball. B. J. T. Bosanquet had been an Oxford blue of the late nineties as a strong but rough batsman and a fast-medium bowler. In 1901, after some experiment, he became the first man to bowl—deliberately, in county cricket—the delivery which was to be known as the 'googly' or, to Australians, in honour of its inventor, 'the bosey'. The googly is, in terms of a right-arm bowler and a right-handed batsman, an off-break bowled with a leg-break action. Within three years Bosanquet had decided a Test rubber with his invention; while R. O. Schwarz, who played with Bosanquet for Middlesex, carried the trick back to South Africa, and the South Africans employed it as their main attacking method to win the 1909–10 Test series against England.

Until George Hirst began to bowl his left-arm swing, bowlers had habitually rubbed the new ball in the dirt to gain greater finger purchase. But now it was not always so. J. B. King, an experienced baseball pitcher, touring with the Gentlemen of Philadelphia cricket team in 1897 and 1903 had shown that there were possibilities of a controlled swing and swerve of which cricket had barely scratched the surface. Duly on his historic cue, in 1908, W. T. Greswell came straight from the remarkable Repton School team to the Somerset side and was instantly successful with his right-arm inswing bowling. From 1913 until the war in which he was killed, the Hampshire player Arthur Jacques bowled fast-medium inswing to a massed leg trap. This was the tactic bowlers were to employ increasingly over the next forty years, to confine, dismiss, and finally change the entire method of the batsmen who had so haughtily and expensively thrashed them through the off side of the cricket field in the golden age of batting.

The bowler who could have caused these batsmen most discomfort cared little for county cricket. Of all the cricket superlatives, the least debatable is that which calls S. F. Barnes the greatest bowler the game of cricket has known. Indeed the point is made by his record in Test cricket alone. After three scattered matches with Warwickshire and two seasons with Lancashire, he withdrew to minor counties and league cricket where he played until he was 64 years old with immense and unbroken success. He appeared in only 27 Test Matches, spread over a period of thirteen years and in three different countries: yet he took the amazing number of 189 test wickets, at an average of 16·53—and that in an age of perfect pitches and dominant batting. Tall, with a high action, commanding swing and cut in both directions, of an impeccable length and with snarling lift from the pitch, he came as near to perfection in bowling as may be imagined. Even in his sixties he was a hostile bowler for the best of batsmen to face, confirming, beyond argument, his own legend to generations after his own.

But the age had, also, two of the classical slow left-arm bowlers of artful flight: Wilfred Rhodes, the tactician, and Blythe, dealing gracefully in vicious spin. The pace of Lockwood and Fielder and—left-arm—F. R. Foster; the off-spin of Schofield Haigh and J. N. Crawford (described as the greatest of all schoolboy cricketers); the leg-spin of that fine athlete and all-rounder, Len Braund; the controlled fast-medium of Albert Relf, J. W. H. T. Douglas, and E. G. Arnold: all, with hard work, won wickets and respect, even in that batsman's heyday.

English first-class cricket meant the county championship, the long established—home and out—Test Matches with Australia, and the newer series with South Africa. The first home Test rubber of the reign, in 1902, was quite memorable, fit to be a showpiece for the sport of the period. The Australian side was unquestionably strong, with Victor Trumper (that consummate, happy artist of batting), Clem Hill, Hugh Trumble, M. A. Noble, Joe Darling, S. E. Gregory, J. J. Kelly, Warwick Armstrong, and J. V. Saunders. The team that met them in the first test—at Birmingham—has been described as the finest England ever put into the field: A. C. MacLaren, C. B. Fry, K. S. Ranjitsinhji, F. S. Jackson, J. T. Tyldesley, A. A. Lilley, G. H. Hirst, G. L. Jessop, L. C. Braund, W. H. Lockwood, and W. Rhodes. We may notice that, of the six main batsmen, all but one—Tyldesley—were amateurs. England scored 376 for nine wickets, bowled out Australia for 36 and made them follow on: but heavy rain prevented a finish. The series, however, was won by Australia, after two historic finishes. In the story-book match on a rain-damaged wicket at Old Trafford, Trumper scored a century before lunch: England collapsed but were rescued by a remarkable stand of Jackson and Braund. When Fred Tate—who had dropped an important catch earlier in this, his only Test Match—came in as the last batsman, England wanted only eight runs to win. As Tate reached the wicket rain began to fall and he had to go back to the pavilion and wait, contemplating the crisis, for three-quarters of

an hour before he could begin his innings. He edged the first ball
for four but the fourth bowled him and Australia had won by three
runs. It seemed impossible that there could be another such finish
in the same series. Yet in the final Test, at the Oval, when England
were set 263 to win and were on the verge of defeat with five wickets
down for 48, Jessop, in one of the immortal innings, scored 104 in
an hour and a quarter. Still when Rhodes, last man in, joined Hirst,
England wanted 15 to win and, in forty-five long, tense minutes, the
two Yorkshiremen made them.

Until this time English cricket tours of Australia had been
unofficial ventures, sponsored sometimes by Australian clubs but
usually promoted for private gain. It was not until 1903, after
Australia had beaten England in four consecutive rubbers, that
the M.C.C. undertook the responsibility for arranging future overseas Test tours. 1911–12 was probably England's best series in
Australia, when they won by four matches to one chiefly through
the batting of Hobbs, Rhodes—who had played his way up from
last man in to first—and Gunn, and the pace bowling of Barnes and
R. E. Foster. At Melbourne in that rubber S. F. Barnes, in the finest
opening spell of Test Match history, bowled out the first four Australian batsmen for one run on a perfect batting wicket. The 'trian-
gular tournament' of 1912, in which England, Australia, and South
Africa met each other in three 3-match rubbers, was the ambitious,
but eventually disappointing, scheme of Sir Abe Bailey. After a
domestic dispute, five of the leading Australian players refused to
make the tour and, since the South African side too was weak,
England, captained by C. B. Fry, won the tournament—but all too
easily: the series proved, both financially and in public esteem,
one of the period's rare sporting failures.

Crowds at first-class cricket matches were relatively large, but
the game's real health and strength lay in its local roots. Not a town
or village but had its club, while churches, institutes, schools,
factories, collieries, and the most fortuitous groupings of young men
had their teams. Never, before or since, were there so many active
cricketers in England. There was, too, one uniquely Edwardian
aspect of the game, the social phenomenon of country-house
cricket. An entire eleven—and more, for reserves—often with their
wives and fiancées would be invited to stay as guests at the mansion
to play a week or more of cricket on their host's private cricket

ground. The pavilions they used may still be seen on some of the large country-estates, often relatively elaborate buildings, with the groundsman's stores and rooms, dressing-rooms and dining-room— the latter often large and elaborate enough to be used as a ball-room in the evening—and sometimes a balcony above for spectators. Country-house cricket could not survive the war of 1914–18; but the rest of British sport also changed. In method, character, standing, and atmosphere the clean-shaven sport of the twenties declared that the day of the moustached Edwardians was now romantic past history.

It may be said that post-war realism reduced the sportsman-hero to his true stature as an ordinary human being, subject to, even deserving, criticism more irreverent than he had received from the Edwardians. Yet nostalgia, the romantic view, and a firm stratum of unassailable fact argue that the Edwardian era produced—or by coincidence included the lifetimes of—an unusually large number of outstandingly gifted men who, encouraged by the circumstances and temper of the time, applied their gifts to sport, lifting it to new heights and making themselves the first generation of sporting idols. The first and obvious example for such an argument is, of course, Charles Burgess Fry. At Oxford he was president of athletics, captain of soccer and cricket, and almost certainly missed a rugby blue through injury. He made centuries for Oxford against Cambridge, for the Gentlemen against the Players (232 not out, the highest score for the Gentlemen at Lord's), and for England against Australia. England never lost a Test Match under his captaincy and his sequence of six consecutive innings of over a hundred, though equalled by Bradman, has never been surpassed. He won a full cap for association football and played as an amateur in the F.A. cup final. He was a freshman at Oxford when, in 1892 at Iffley Road, with the inter-university long-jump event already started, he put down the cigar he was smoking in the dressing-room, ran out, set a world record for the long jump which remained unbroken for twenty-one years and went back and finished the cigar. He was a fine boxer and capable at swimming, sculling, golf, lawn tennis, and the javelin, a good shot, salmon-fisherman, and horseman. It remains only to add that he was as handsome and superbly made as a Greek god; won a scholarship to Wadham ahead of John Simon and F. E. Smith; wrote a novel, an autobiography, a history of the League of Nations, and three fine technical studies of cricket; and was offered the throne of Albania—to complete the picture of an Edwardian sportsman more than life size. If C. B. Fry was a phenomenon, he was also characteristic of the sport of his age in two of its main aspects. He was one of the Edwardian pioneers of the examination of sporting techniques: his cricket books remain the finest analytical studies of batting and bowling. He represented, too, the tendency—quite new in association football and partly so in golf and cricket—for the pure amateur to play side by side with professionals. Yet while, in play, he made unqualified common cause with them, he was as socially conscious as any Victorian, and remained the 'aristocratic' amateur and autocratic captain.

Conclusion

The greatest of the Edwardian sportsmen fell into three definite, though sometimes overlapping, categories. The first two—the all-rounders who found the widest field that had ever existed for their diversity, and the men with utter and unmistakable genius given a new range of opportunity—belong inside their period: the third, those who reduced the element of chance to a minimum by evolving constant and communicable methods, created, or at least clarified and handed down, the techniques which endure as the canons of their sports. Fry was the supreme example of the first class, a highly and variously gifted games player. R. E. Foster, Corinthian and full soccer international, whose 287 against Australia in 1903 long stood as the highest Test innings; J. W. H. T. Douglas, international cricketer, boxer, and footballer; R. P. Keigwin, with blues for cricket, soccer, hockey, and rackets, a county tennis player, and an international at hockey; G. N. Foster, S. H. Day, C. J. Burnup, L. J. Moon, J. S. F. Morrison, John Daniell, and R. A. Young, were amateurs who excelled in two or more sports. Meanwhile, the professionals, J. Sharp, H. Makepeace, A. Ducat, and H. T. W. Hardinge played for England at both cricket and football: Makepeace, indeed, won all the major honours at both games. All-rounders were to be found in greater profusion in Edwardian times than at any other, on all levels from international competition to the village green. In the second group, Jessop—pre-eminently—G. O. Smith, Woodward, F. S. Jackson, Shrubb, Nickalls, Applegarth, the

Dohertys, and Poulton-Palmer were some of the vintage crop of athletes who, playing their sports purely for pleasure, did so with such a quality of genius as to put it beyond doubt that they must have been great in any age. The third important section of Edwardian sportsmen, numerically the smallest but historically the most significant, was that of the professional master, developing his own particular craft to a standard of completeness so near perfection that it might be said that it could never be done better. Such were J. B. Hobbs—about whom A. C. MacLaren, in fact, wrote a book called *The Perfect Batsman*—S. F. Barnes, Wilfred Rhodes, J. H. Taylor, Harry Vardon, John Roberts, Sam Hardy, 'Fatty' Wedlock, Billy Meredith, Steve Donoghue, and 'Kid' Lewis. Their manner of play was not simply *their* style—it was *style*.

If sport is unimportant, then Edwardian sport was unimportant: but it was heartily idealistic, virtually untouched by decadence or cynicism. No graver matters weighed on the minds of any majority of the British public of that day to argue that a Test Match—or their village cricket match—was trivial. The dominant of Edwardian sport was pleasure: but it was also characterized by versatility, gallantry, brilliance, and enthusiasm. All these qualities were lodged in varying degrees in the men who have become its mythology. They encouraged the hundreds of thousands of lesser performers in their happily serious endeavours, and warmed the hearts of a nation of supporters. If these sporting idols had feet of clay, the public did not see, and was not told. Social, economic, and athletic history dictated that the Edwardian period should be the Golden Age of British sport. It was so—and the more richly and satisfyingly so because it was seen through the eyes of enthusiasm.

13

THE ROYAL NAVY

LIEUTENANT-COMMANDER P. K. KEMP, R.N. (RETD.)

Head of Naval Historical Branch, Ministry of Defence

THE ROYAL NAVY

T H E Edwardian navy was dominated by the towering figure of one man, Admiral Sir John Arbuthnot Fisher. He had already made his mark in the later years of Victoria's reign, partly as a specialist in gunnery and torpedoes and partly as a naval administrator, crowning that period of his service with the appointment, in 1899, as commander-in-chief, Mediterranean fleet. His years in the Mediterranean gave final proof of his quality as a leader, thinker, and innovator. He had also the opportunity, during a visit to the fleet of Lord Selborne, first lord of the Admiralty, in 1901, of expounding his view on the future development of the navy in a series of private discussions. Few men could resist Fisher's animated charm when he exerted himself to please, and Selborne was not one of them. Even more important was the evidence that he could see all around him of the impressive improvement in efficiency and morale in the Mediterranean fleet since Fisher had taken command of it. By the time Selborne left Malta, his mind was made up and Fisher's future was assured. The whole pattern of the Royal Navy was to be changed, during the years of Edward's reign, under the dynamic influence of one man.

To understand Fisher's work at the Admiralty it is necessary to take a quick look at the development of the navy throughout Victoria's reign. Since 1815 and the final overthrow of the Napoleonic threat to the classic European balance of power, the Royal Navy had been resting on its laurels. No sea power had emerged to challenge it, no stimulus to creative design or experiment operated to force it into a more progressive state of mind. Behind the impressive façade of its numerical strength there was little of real value either in the design of its ships or in the training of its senior admirals. Progress, both material and intellectual, proceeded at a snail's pace, occasionally stimulated by the appearance in a foreign navy of a ship of advanced design, or a weapon of novel potentiality.

Resistance to change spread its tentacles through every aspect of the naval service, and not only in the design of ships. It was not until more than half-way through the nineteenth century that seamen were granted the dignity of a naval uniform or that a true naval career was opened to them in the form of continuous service. Not until 1860 was the penalty of hanging a man from the yard-arm by sentence of court-martial abolished in favour of a more humane method of capital punishment; not until 1880 did flogging with a cat-o'-nine-tails finally disappear from her majesty's ships. But although these two extreme disciplinary measures had gone by the time of Edward's accession, the Naval Discipline Act of his day was still a ferocious document, and much of the arbitrary day-to-day discipline in the navy was still largely based on the Nelsonic pattern. The general conditions of service under which the seaman lived on board, and even his rates of pay, still bore more than a passing resemblance to those which operated in the days of the sailing man-of-war. It was the same with strategy and tactics. There was no training or instruction beyond the annual manœuvres, in which admirals were given a reasonably free hand to move their ships and fleets as they wished within the confines of the fixed exercises. There was little attempt to study and analyse the outcome of the exercises after their completion, and no attempt at all to award praise or blame to the participants. Discussion of these subjects was almost entirely confined to the columns of the more erudite service journals, and no junior officer could take part without temerity and risk of reprimand. Seniority was all-powerful and all-pervading.

In the dying years of Victoria's reign a new naval power was emerging in Europe. In 1898 and 1900 Germany passed two laws designed to provide her with a fleet of such power that, in the words of the German official statement of 1900, 'if the strongest naval power engaged it, it would endanger its own supremacy'. These laws were clear evidence of a decision to engage in *Weltpolitik*, a remarkably rapid development, both political and material, in a country which had only reached true nationhood thirty years earlier. Not that there had been lacking earlier signs of this emergent ambition; the Kruger telegram of 1896, the partition of the Portuguese colonies in Africa in 1898, the occupation of Samoa in 1899, and the extreme German anglophobia during the South African war had all indicated the road along which Germany was determined to march. But the building of a fleet was a direct threat aimed at Great Britain in her most vulnerable spot, and it aroused a violent reaction not only in British naval circles but throughout the whole fabric of British national life.

The normal political reaction in past years to any threatened change in the European balance of power had been the creation of a system of compensating alliances designed to restore the *status quo*. In the course of her long history of European entanglements Britain had found herself with many different bedfellows, each chosen to satisfy the exigencies of the moment. Lord Palmerston had perhaps best summed up the national policy when he remarked that England had no eternal friendships and no eternal enmities, but only eternal interests. In 1900, however, Britain had no friends with whom to form a counterbalancing alliance against the German threat. The Franco-Russian alliance of 1894 was still active, and moreover hostile to Britain, and a possible new ally across the Atlantic, in the shape of the United States, was still resentful of the British stand in the Venezuelan boundary disputes. Spain, Italy, and the Netherlands were of too little account in the maritime field for consideration, and an emergent Japan was geographically unsuitable in any European context. Britain found herself isolated, and so forced to take refuge in a greatly accelerated naval building programme, a fact of considerable political unpopularity in the economic climate of the day.

This then was the naval pattern when Edward VII ascended the throne. On paper the Royal Navy was still by far the most powerful maritime force in the world, but it was becoming more and more difficult to disguise the fact that the fighting value of the ships so bravely set out in long lists on paper was no more than a fraction of their face value. Apathy, ineptitude, and sterility of thought were partly to blame, poor ship design was another factor, but beyond these there was no body of war experience from which to draw either precept or practice. Ships and weapons had changed out of all recognition since Britain had last been engaged in a naval war, and the long soporific years of peace had done much to stifle the experiment and enterprise which alone could stimulate the evolution of a tactical doctrine fitted to the new era of steam and the long-range gun.

No one appreciated this more than Fisher, who was coming to the end of his time in the Mediterranean when the old queen died in 1901. His restless energy there had produced a miraculous change in the fleet and he exerted all his enthusiasm and charm to instil a spirit of rejuvenation and to force it downwards until it reached into every corner of the ships under his command and animated even the most junior rating in the fleet. He taught the younger officers how to think for themselves and encouraged them in this novel doctrine by instituting prizes for essays on every aspect of modern naval warfare, setting aside time to meet them and discuss their essays with them. He was tireless in giving lectures to his officers on any subject connected with professional skill or technical improvement, and he practised what he preached in far-ranging and vigorous fleet exercises. His spirited unconventionality and his explosive style of speech delighted all who served under him during these notable years.

He was one of the few admirals of the period who realized the great importance to the navy of a happy, contented, and well-treated personnel. 'We are the one Navy', he wrote to Lord Selborne from the Mediterranean, 'where man is so valuable and so scarce (our most valuable asset), as we have no conscription. . . . ' In the Mediterranean he took it upon himself to interpret with a new liberality the conditions under which the lower deck was granted shore leave. Under the existing regulations seamen not actually under punishment were entitled when serving on a foreign station to a minimum of forty-eight hours' general leave ashore every three months. Most commanders-in-chief and captains of ships interpreted the regulation literally, with the not unnatural result that these brief periods of leave degenerated into drunken orgies ashore with a majority of seamen attempting to crowd into their short grant of liberty enough riotous living to last them through the next three months on board. Indeed, so far as most of the senior officers were concerned, this was the easiest way of dealing with the men under their command, concentrating into only two days all the temptations ashore to which seamen were prone, and maintaining strict control of them on board for the rest of the three months. Heavily swollen lists of defaulters were the common experience after a period of general leave, with punishments ranging from imprisonment in the ship's cells to extra drills and deprivations of pay. It did not take Fisher long to change this short-sighted regulation when he found himself in chief command in the Mediterranean. Seizing on the word 'minimum' in the order, he instituted short leave ashore when ships were in harbour, each watch on board taking it in turns to enjoy a few hours of liberty from ship's discipline. He did much to increase the number of playing fields available to the ships' companies, promoted inter-ship competitions in all forms of sport, and even took the trouble to be present himself when important matches were played. This was not all. He interested himself in the preparation of food, inspecting ships' galleys and suggesting ways of making victuals more palatable for the men on the messdecks. He improved the supply of fresh meat, bread, fruit, and vegetables as far as was within his power, even to the extent of installing bakeries in some of the larger ships. It was no wonder that the seamen adored him.

Changes such as these, which cut across the whole pattern of naval lower-deck life as it was lived at the turn of the century, could hardly be introduced without opposition from older and more conservative admirals. Admirable as they were in intent, and inevitable as they were in the growing national consciousness of social change, they had the unhappy effect of dividing the navy into two distinct camps, the 'Fisherites' and the 'antis'. This was the beginning of what became known as the 'Fishpond', and all officers who hesitated to take the plunge into its exhilarating waters were liable to find their prospects of promotion seriously endangered as Fisher continued his inexorable march to supreme naval power.

From the Mediterranean, as his term of service there came to an end, Selborne brought Fisher to the Board of Admiralty as second naval lord. At the time Fisher was high in the seniority list of vice-admirals, and in this alone was a portent of coming reforms. The post of second naval lord was normally filled by a rear-admiral, and to appoint so senior an officer, particularly one of so forceful a character, gave rise to fears among many senior admirals that the old order was indeed about to change.

Training Officers

As second naval lord Fisher found himself responsible for naval personnel in all its aspects. He concentrated first on improving the training of the young gentlemen who were to be the navy's future officers. The accepted pattern of training was the *Britannia* system, under which boys entered at the age of 14–15½ for three terms on board the wooden ships *Britannia* and *Hindustan*, permanently moored in the river off Dartmouth, and one term in the training cruiser *Isis*. After their fifteen months of training they passed out into the fleet as midshipmen, at which period of their career virtually all theoretical instruction came to an end. The new scheme, or the 'Selborne scheme' as it came to be called, was closely modelled on the public school system of education. The training ships disappeared, their place being taken by two new colleges, a junior one at Osborne and a senior at Dartmouth. Age of entry was brought into line with normal public school practice at about 12½–13 years, and the two colleges provided four years of education, of which one-third was mainly professional and technical and two-thirds general. By this means, the cadets' theoretical education would be satisfactorily completed by the time they joined the fleet at the age of 17½. Two main objectives were to be realized by this reform. First, the boys would become available for naval training at the normal time of leaving their preparatory schools and while still full of youthful enthusiasm for a life at sea. Secondly it short-circuited the prevailing system of cramming, which boys entering at 14 or 15 had found necessary to pass the examination into the *Britannia*. The new entry into Osborne was to be entirely by selection at an interview board, those selected later taking a written examination based on the Common Entrance and designed to eradicate those few who, although selected at their interview, were hopelessly backward educationally. Fisher pressed hard for the abolition of all fees at the two colleges, on the ground that a career as a naval officer should not be denied to any youth merely because his parents could not afford to pay for the necessary four years of further education before joining the fleet. He was, however, unsuccessful in this, and it was not until many years later that the reform was made.

With this new scheme of entry was devised a new theory of common training. Under the *Britannia* system only the executive, or seaman, class were received on board: those who were to become engineers or Royal Marines were separately entered and trained. Now they were all to enter as cadets and to follow their chosen specialization only after the completion of their time as cadets at college and as midshipmen in the fleet. The real reason underlying this decision was the difference in social status which had grown up on board between the seaman and the engineer, originally bred in the old days when a conservative navy had deplored the introduction of steam as something both dirty and undignified, and fostered by the entirely separate courses of instruction which the engineer officer underwent in his training. This social difference was obviously inimical to efficiency at sea, and the new scheme of a common training was designed to eliminate it at one blow. With some seven or eight years of uniform training before the engineers departed for their specialist course, it was thought that a unity of sentiment would be engendered throughout the whole officer corps during their formative years and would continue throughout their career. So sanguine a hope was not entirely fulfilled, for the old prejudices died hard, but the reform certainly helped towards removing many of the social injustices which had hitherto attached themselves to engineer officers. Nor was it only the training of young officers which engaged Fisher's attention. In place of the crowded and insanitary hulks in which boy seamen and artificers had undergone their training new schools were built ashore and an enlightened curriculum devised in place of the outdated syllabus which no one had had the energy or inclination to investigate or change for a great many years.

Radical reforms such as these could not, of course, be introduced without rousing considerable opposition. Fisher and Selborne between them were strong enough to brush aside the objections of such elderly admirals—'pre-historic' in Fisher's scathing language —as Sir Frederick Richards, Charles Penrose Fitzgerald, and Sir Vesey Hamilton; but when these were backed up by Lord Goschen, Selborne's immediate predecessor as first lord, more definite measures were necessary to protect the scheme. Fortunately for its protagonists, the opposition took some months to get fully under way and become really vociferous, and by that time Selborne's protective measures had at least ensured that the new scheme got away to a good start. The first interviews for the new entry were held in July 1903. The Royal Naval College at Osborne—Queen Victoria's Isle of Wight estate, presented to the nation by Edward VII—had been built and equipped in the record time of seven months and was completed in August. Its doors opened for the first of the new entry in September. And there, as commander-in-chief,

Portsmouth, and charged by Selborne to superintend and administer this new establishment, was Fisher. No one could meddle with it except through him.

Reshaping the Navy

When Fisher hoisted his flag as commander-in-chief at the end of August 1903 he knew that, barring accidents, he would be returning to the Admiralty in a year's time. Lord Walter Kerr, at that time the first naval lord, would reach the end of his term of office in October 1904. With this glittering prize virtually within his grasp Fisher's days at Portsmouth were spent in designing the new fleet which he was convinced that Britain needed in order to maintain her security and her position in the world. He worked in virtual secrecy, well knowing the renewed storm of opposition which his proposals were bound to raise, and he worked to such purpose that he was able to present to Selborne, on the day after entering the Admiralty as first sea lord (it was on his representations that the title was changed from first naval lord), a complete print of his proposals worked out to the minutest details. The print was headed *Naval Necessities*, vol. i, foreshadowing yet more to come, and its sub-heading, printed in bold italic, read: *The Scheme, the Whole Scheme, and Nothing but the Scheme.*

Looking back at these new proposals from our present vantage point of sixty years on, it appears almost unbelievable that they could have caused an upheaval that split the navy into two opposing camps. The new pattern of naval power which the proposals postulated seems to us today eminently satisfactory for the times in which they took place; and with that knowledge of the real state of the navy which could have been no secret to any officer who took the trouble to look around him, it is strange that they did not appear in the same light then. No doubt part of the reason for resentment was mistrust of Fisher's methods in making certain that the plans would go through. He persuaded Selborne on his first day in office to refer the proposals as a whole to a committee, which he then packed with his friends. Opponents of the scheme, who included men of such recognized ability as Admiral Sir Reginald Custance and Admiral Sir Cyprian Bridge, found themselves in the wilderness and the target of bitter calumny and ridicule, engineered by Fisher through the many friends he had in the press whom he

assiduously cultivated: indeed, using a pseudonym which at times
only faintly disguised his authorship, Fisher himself addressed
letters to the newspapers when he considered that it would further
his aims. That he completely remodelled the navy in the five and
a half years of his reign as first sea lord, and did so with a considerable financial saving on the annual naval estimates, is the real
measure of the brilliance of his reforming zeal. He realized from the
start that if he was to succeed in getting his reforms implemented
he would need to change the whole mental outlook of the navy in
its acceptance of technological change. He succeeded in this partly
through the example of his own sublime faith in the inevitability
and desirability of change and partly through the manipulation of
promotions and appointments in order to bring his own protégés
and adherents into positions of power.

Four major schemes were put into operation in this radical reshaping of the navy: the wholesale scrapping of obsolete warships,
the reorganization of the reserve fleet, the strategical redistribution
of fleets and squadrons, and the introduction of a completely new
conception of a capital ship. They were carried through simultaneously and with ruthless expedition.

For many years already there had been apparent a good deal of
stagnation in ship design and much muddled thinking about
armament and armour. Every battleship then in commission had
a mixed armament of large, medium, and small guns, which necessitated a multiplicity of shellrooms, magazines, and spare parts.
Nor had much strategical thought been given to determining the
types of ships best suited to the needs of British sea power, resulting
in a collection of miscellaneous vessels whose value in war was
problematical. The lack of homogeneity not only multiplied the
difficulties and cost of efficient storekeeping, but also locked up
large numbers of trained seamen in trying to keep inefficient ships
at sea and added to the burden of repair work carried out in the
royal dockyards. Fisher's solution was to divide the nominal list
of the navy into three groups, which he headed 'sheep', 'llamas', and
'goats'. The sheep were retained as battleworthy ships; the llamas
came up again for reconsideration whether they might have some
further use as lesser sheep, or depot ships, or should be downgraded
to goats; the goats were to be disposed of by sale or by breaking-up.
'Scrap the lot', wrote Fisher in his own bold handwriting at the

bottom of this list, which comprised no fewer than 154 ships and included 17 battleships.

With this drastic pruning of the navy's existing ships the first sea lord laid down a guiding principle for new construction.

The new navy [he wrote], excepting a very few special local vessels, is to be absolutely restricted to four types of vessels, being all that modern fighting necessitates.

    I. Battleships of 15,900 tons. 21 knots speed.
    II. Armoured cruisers of 15,900 tons. $25\frac{1}{2}$ knots speed.
    III. Destroyers of 900 tons and 4-inch guns. 36 knots speed.
    IV. Submarines of 350 tons. 14 knots surface speed.

This, of course, was vast oversimplification, for it entirely ignored the smaller cruisers which not only served the main fleets as scouts but were also the most economical ships for a variety of purposes on foreign stations, such as imperial policing and showing the flag. Yet any diminution in types was a step in the right direction, and although Fisher's dictum certainly went much too far, and was in fact impossible of achievement, it did serve to bring home to the design staff at the Admiralty the need to concentrate their enthusiasm upon a minimum of types. Simultaneously a committee of designs was set up to consider the new ships which were to be built. Like the committee which was to debate the new scheme as a whole, this design committee was also packed with Fisher's nominees. Its findings, of course, were a foregone conclusion, but they were so important that they merit examination.

In the summer of 1903 Fred Jane, the editor of *Fighting Ships*, commissioned from the well-known Italian ship designer, Colonel Cuniberti, an article to be entitled 'An Ideal Battleship for Great Britain'. The article appeared in *Fighting Ships* at the end of that year. The desirable features of such a ship, suggested Cuniberti, were a uniform main armament of ten 12-inch guns, in place of the mixed 12-inch and 9·2-inch which was the standard battleship armament in almost every navy in the world; good, but not too good, armour protection to cover all magazines and boiler and engine rooms; and a speed of at least 20 knots produced by main turbine machinery. There can be no doubt that Fisher had read this article while he was at Portsmouth, for the description of Cuniberti's ideal battleship fits almost exactly the battleship design recommended by the committee of designs. Only in one point was it altered: the speed was raised from 20 to 21 knots. In the face of all opposition, Fisher insisted on turbine propulsion. The first battleship ever to use this form of propulsion, the *Dreadnought*, was Fisher's (or Cuniberti's) masterpiece. She was completed in the record time of eleven months, and she proved a world-beater. At one stroke every other battleship in the world was outdated and Britain had gained a lead in ship design, if not yet in ship numbers, that would enable her to keep ahead of all other nations in sea power. Against all the rumblings and criticisms of other admirals who argued that the *Dreadnought*, as well as rendering every foreign battleship obsolete, performed the same service for every British battleship and so reduced the British lead in numbers to nil, the *Dreadnought* on her trials proved herself a triumphant success. Her superiority lay not only in the huge increase in hitting power of her broadside compared with the former mixed armament ships but also in the ease of tactical handling with which her high speed endowed her. Fisher crowed with delight. 'A new name for the *Dreadnought*', he wrote in his vast, flowing script: 'The Hard-Boiled Egg. Why? Because she can't be beat!' Yet even the acknowledged success of her trials failed to stifle criticism. It was in vain for the Board of Admiralty to point out that technical development could not be halted merely because of a temporary preponderance of obsolete ships. The real reasons could not be made public, for they were based on information that was still confidential—the analysis of battle practices carried out by the fleet and the reports of officers who were on board the Japanese battleships in the Russo-Japanese war.

Fisher's committee of designs did not, however, stop at the *Dreadnought*. There was still his other dream of the great armoured cruiser to be brought to reality. Thus was the *Invincible* born, the world's first battle-cruiser, although in fact a sister ship, the *Indomitable*, was the first to be commissioned. She had a designed speed, unheard of in those days for a ship of her size, of $25\frac{1}{2}$ knots, and her armament consisted of eight 12-inch guns. She too was a world-beater at the time, and she set a fashion that was to endure for the next twenty years. The term 'battle-cruiser' was an unfortunate misnomer introduced in 1912, for in Fisher's appreciation of her tactical tasks lying in the line of battle was not included. Her main duty was to act as a scouting cruiser able by reason of her speed and heavy armament to push home a reconnaissance of the enemy's fleet in the face of any opposition by the opposing cruisers. A second was to catch and destroy armed merchant raiders, particularly the German 23-knot Atlantic liners which, the Admiralty knew, all carried guns that could be quickly mounted for commerce destruction in war. A third potentiality was that they could, when required, act as a fast wing in a fleet action to reinforce the van or the rear of the battle fleet, but this was always to be subsidiary to their other duties. The fact that, at the battle of Jutland in 1916, British battle-cruisers suffered heavily was due in the main to their use in a role not envisaged by Fisher when he called for the original design, or more accurately, by pushing home their reconnaissance against an opposition stronger than Fisher ever intended. It may be, too, that their actual use in this role was stimulated by the change in nomenclature.

In Fisher's original brief from Selborne in which the tasks facing the new first sea lord were discussed was the stipulation that, although the fleet was to be modernized and brought up to full fighting efficiency, it was to be done with a substantial saving on the annual naval estimates. These had risen steadily, from £23,778,400 in 1898–9 to £36,889,000 in 1904–5, and both parliament and public were growing restive at the annual increases. The *Dreadnought* and the *Invincible*, and the follow-up ships of those types, were relatively expensive. The disposal of the 'goats', and those of the 'llamas' which were later reclassified as goats, provided fairly substantial savings, though not sufficient. Something more was necessary, and it had to be something that would combine a considerable saving in cost with an equally considerable addition to naval efficiency. In considering the role and the state of the reserve fleet, Fisher found what he wanted.

In general the reserve fleet in 1904 was divided into two classes, the fleet reserve and the dockyard reserve, the latter being ships out of commission or undergoing major refits. The fleet reserve consisted of ships which were nominally ready for active service in an emergency, retaining on board a proportion of their normal complement, mainly in the engineering department. On mobilization officers and men were drafted to them to bring them up to full complement, and they were supposed then to be ready in all respects for war. Experience in the annual manœuvres, however, demonstrated that they invariably fell far short of what was expected of them. Manned as they were in emergency by a great majority of men who had probably never even seen the ship before, it was hardly surprising that each successive annual exercise should produce a dismal tale of breakdown and inefficiency. It could hardly be otherwise. In the case of the dockyard reserve, each ship carried a care and maintenance party of active service seamen and engineers on board, even though there were virtually no ship's duties which they could perform while their vessels were in dockyard hands. The navy was thus getting the worst of all worlds on every count, for no admiral at sea could rely on any useful reinforcement from the reserve fleet, and yet they were expensive in upkeep both in personnel and in money. Though the reason for their sorry performance was not far to seek, no one at the Admiralty or in the dockyards had yet managed to pin it down; or if they did, they took no steps to eradicate the nuisance or even to try to alleviate it.

Fisher's approach to the problem was direct. The 'sheep' and 'goats' policy was applied to the reserve fleet. Sixty ancient ships were recommended for sale or scrapping, while the care and maintenance parties from the dockyard reserve ships were withdrawn permanently and replaced by dockyard men under the administrative control of the captain of the dockyard. These measures provided a useful total of trained, active service seamen and engineers, sufficient to man every ship which had been retained with a nucleus crew of two-fifths of her full war-time engine-room complement, the whole of her gun-turret crews, gunlayers and sightsetters for all guns, two-fifths of her normal seamen complement, and her captain and all important officers. With this nucleus of trained men permanently on board, the ship was expected to be able to proceed to sea and exercise with the active service fleet at least once a quarter. For the annual manœuvres, lasting from two to three weeks, she was brought up to full complement by a draft from the royal fleet or royal naval reserve. At the same time the fleet reserve system itself was abolished and replaced by a system of reserve squadrons at the home ports, thus substituting for a collection of individual ships a homogeneous squadron trained to work together as a whole during its quarterly exercises. Each reserve squadron was placed under the command of a rear-admiral. The gain was considerable,

and not only in operational efficiency. Administratively and financially the new arrangement also paid handsome dividends, and it
concentrated effort into those reserve ships which could still play
a useful part in war.

The final reform of the navy, as set out in Fisher's plan, was the
reorganization of fleets and squadrons on a sounder strategical
basis. He had always been critical of the plans which stationed small
squadrons of ships at various centres all over the world as part of
the imperial policing policy of the government. Most of these squadrons consisted of small second-class cruisers which were too weak
to fight and too slow to run away: the 'Snail' and 'Tortoise' classes,
Fisher called them. In a classic memorandum to Selborne, he painted
the scene as follows:

> *Venus* approaching her fleet at full speed.
> Admiral signals: 'What have you seen?'
> *Venus* replies: 'Four funnels hull down.'
> Admiral: 'Well, what was behind?'
> *Venus* replies: 'Cannot say; she must have four knots more speed than
> I had and would have caught me in three hours, so I had to close you
> at full speed.'
> Admiral's logical reply: 'You had better pay off and turn over to some-
> thing that is some good; you are simply a device for wasting 400 men.'

There was no answer to such evident good sense, and one by one the
small squadrons were recalled. At the same time, on the presumption that the building up of the German navy represented the real
menace, the strategical disposition of British fleets and squadrons
was reorganized to concentrate the main strength in the North Sea
and the Channel, instead of in the Mediterranean, which had been
for so long the main focus of British sea power. The new plan
reduced the Mediterranean fleet from twelve battleships to eight,
and instituted a new Atlantic fleet of eight battleships based on Gib-
raltar and available to reinforce either the Mediterranean fleet or
the Channel fleet, which was based on Dover and consisted of ten
of the most modern battleships. Independent squadrons of armoured
cruisers, available to reinforce the main fleets when required, were
allocated to the Atlantic, East Indies, Australia, and Pacific. Joint
manœuvres were held twice a year between the Atlantic and
Mediterranean fleets, and once a year between the Atlantic and
Channel fleets. This interlocking policy served two purposes: the

rapid reinforcement of any fleet which might find itself in the centre of war operations, and a considerable economy in the number of ships required to maintain British sea supremacy. It also made certain that the main concentration of sea power was always within easy reach of the North Sea, though not so obviously as to cause legitimate alarm in Germany.

It was on these lines that the new Edwardian navy took shape under Fisher's forceful direction. Throughout the whole period of these reforms he had the enthusiastic support of the king who, while remaining very much in the background, yet did much in a quiet way to ease the passage of naval reform. Left to Fisher alone the great scheme might well have foundered, owing to the violence of his spoken and written words, on the rocks of personal antipathy and the suspicion, not entirely ill-founded, that he was being carried away by an enthusiasm bordering on *folie de grandeur*. The king softened some of Fisher's explosive impact on the cabinet and, by setting the seal of his approval on the scheme, worked effectively to get it implemented.

'Blue Water' versus 'Blue Funk'

In the navy itself, Fisher's reforms met a mixed reception. A majority of officers, particularly in the more junior ranks, became his fervent admirers. Led by such enlightened men as Prince Louis of Battenberg, Percy Scott, Henry Jackson, John Jellicoe, Reginald Bacon, and Charles Madden, all of whom later reached the highest ranks in the service, the bulk of the personnel of the navy found themselves willingly engulfed in the 'Fishpond', as his enemies called it, or the 'Blue Water school', which was Fisher's own collective name for his friends. The opposition, led by Admirals Sir Reginald Custance, Sir Edmund Fremantle, Sir Cyprian Bridge, and Charles Penrose Fitzgerald, and ably seconded by Commander Carlyon Bellairs, who had retired from the navy to become a member of parliament, lost no chance of pouring scorn on the scheme, even attempting to stir up a campaign in the press against naval reform. Fisher had his own pet names for this opposition party, varying from the 'Blue Funk school' and the 'Syndicate of Discontent' to the 'Yellow Admirals'. On one recrudescence of their campaign he wrote to a friend: 'The Yellow Admirals seem to have taken fresh heart. Yellow, I suppose, with suppressed jaundice at the unalloyed success of the Admiralty policy from the *Dreadnought* down to bread-baking.'

While the quarrel between the two opposing groups, largely aired in public, caused a good deal of merriment among the general public it divided the navy into two hostile camps, between which non-co-operation gradually became the rule. That such a state of affairs had been allowed to grow up was bad enough; that it was permitted to continue unchecked was a grave reflection both on the good sense and the duty of responsibility which the nation had a right to expect from its senior naval officers. Much of the blame for this must be laid at Fisher's door, for he had a genius (if that be the word) for tactlessness in his dealings with other men. A favourite saying of his was: 'I entered the Navy penniless, friendless, and forlorn. I have had to fight like hell, and fighting like hell has made me what I am.' There can be little doubt, on reading his official letters and memoranda, that he gloried in battle and that fighting like hell was a far more congenial exercise to him than the gentler arts of reason or persuasion. It did the navy much harm. At one period it looked as though all the really good work that Fisher was doing in reforming the navy and bringing it up to date might be scattered almost beyond recall by the winds of dissension.

Besides his new *Dreadnought* and his new *Invincible* Fisher championed the development of the submarine. (In his later years he claimed also to have fostered the adoption of the aircraft as a naval weapon, but contemporary records do not bear this out.) In a letter to the controller of the navy, he wrote:

It's astounding to me, *perfectly astounding*, how the very best amongst us absolutely fail to realize the vast impending revolution in naval warfare and naval strategy that the submarine will accomplish. I have just written a paper on this, but it's so violent that I am keeping it! . . . I have not disguised my opinion, in season and out of season, as to the essential, imperative, immediate, vital, pressing, urgent (I can't think of any more adjectives) necessity for more submarines at once, at the very least 25 in addition to those now ordered and building, and a hundred more as soon as practicable, or we shall be caught with our breeches down. And then, my dear Friend, you have the astounding audacity to say to me, 'I presume you only think they (the submarines) can act on the *defensive*!' Why, my dear fellow, not take the offensive? Good Lord! if our Admiral is worth his salt, he will tow his submarines at 18 knots speed and put them into the hostile port (like ferrets after the rabbits!) before war is officially declared, just as the Japanese acted before the Russian naval officers knew that war was declared. In all seriousness, I don't think it is even *faintly* realized—*The immense impending revolution which the submarines will effect as offensive weapons of War.*

Written in 1904, at a time when the universal concept of the submarine was as a weapon of coastal defence, this note shows a remarkable grasp of possibilities which lay no more than a decade in the future. By 1914 both British and German submarines were acting entirely on the offensive, and the revolution which they effected on naval thought and strategy was certainly immense. More than to any other man, it was due to Fisher's foresight and enthusiasm that, when the testing time came, British submarines had reached a pitch of development advanced enough to enable them to carry their war against the enemy in waters as far distant from their bases as the Baltic and the sea of Marmara.

As Fisher's many plans came to fruition through the years of Edward's reign the shape of the navy settled down to a new and modern pattern. The ponderous monsters of the late Victorian navy disappeared from the scene—ships such as the *Trafalgar* and the *Sans Pareil*, with two guns so vast that it was dangerous to fire them with full charges of powder, and the hideous *Devastation*, which squatted so low in the water that she was covered with sheets of spray if the sea was anything more than a flat calm. The small unarmoured cruisers, expensive both in men and in upkeep, such as the 'Odins', 'Fantômes', 'Scyllas', 'Hyacinths', and 'Katoombas', were withdrawn from the oceans and condemned to the breakers' yards. In their places were built the *Dreadnought* and the follow-up battleship classes, the 'Superbs', 'St. Vincents', and 'Orions'; the 'Invincibles' and the later battle-cruiser classes, 'Indefatigables' and 'Lions'; lighter cruisers of the 'Boadicea', 'Blanche', and 'Amphion' classes; the 'River' class destroyers, followed by the 'E', 'F', 'G', and 'H' classes; and the 'B', 'C', and 'D' class submarines. As the new ships came into commission and the old ships disappeared a completely revitalized navy began to face up to the growing menace on the other side of the North Sea, and, with the start afforded by the radical change in design introduced by the *Dreadnought* and *Invincible*, kept ahead of it in numbers of ships and gun-power.

Another of Fisher's dreams was the substitution of oil fuel for coal. He first put the suggestion forward in a memorandum to the first lord in 1904, which received from Selborne the chilling reply: 'The substitution of oil for coal is impossible, because the oil does not exist in this world in sufficient quantities. It must be reckoned only as a most valuable adjunct.' Yet Fisher saw at least some of his dream come true. The thirty-six torpedo-boats launched in 1906–8, known as the 'oily wads', burned only oil; the 'Tribal' class destroyers of 1906–7, and the 'Acorns' of 1909–10, were all designed for oil fuel only ; and by the time his work at the Admiralty was done, plans were well advanced for the 'Arethusa' class cruisers to be oil-fired only.

These reforms were not achieved without cost. The reforms of 1904–7 had produced a considerable saving in the annual estimates, reducing them by substantial stages from £36,889,000 in 1904–5 to £30,442,409 in 1907–8. But as the full impact of the shipbuilding race with Germany came to bear, the estimates inevitably began to rise, by some £2,000,000 in 1908, a further £3,000,000 in 1909, and £4,500,000 in 1910, reaching a total of £40,603,700 in that year. Lloyd George, the chancellor of the exchequer, wrote angry notes to the first lord and enlisted the active support of Winston Churchill at the Home Office in his battle against the mounting cost of the navy, but the implied menace of the German dreadnoughts being built on the other side of the North Sea was too strong for their argument. The public, whipped up by the 'big navy' press, applauded every demand by the admiralty for more ships.

Not all the increase in the estimates was spent on ships. As far back as 1903 the Admiralty had bought land at Rosyth for the creation of a new naval dockyard. In the days when France was the traditional enemy Chatham and the two Channel dockyards of Portsmouth and Devonport had amply covered the waters in which a naval war was most likely to be fought, but the emergence of Germany as a first-class naval power drew attention to the North Sea as a more likely battleground and the consequent need of a dockyard in northern waters. Rosyth was an obvious choice. Yet in the economic climate of the early years of Edward's reign expenditure on the development of Rosyth was hard to justify. The German fleet, especially after the appearance of the *Dreadnought*, was in no shape to risk a naval war with Britain. So the Rosyth project was pigeon-holed, to be brought out again in 1909 when the threat of the rapidly growing German sea power could be blinked at no longer. Provision for the start of work at Rosyth was included in the 1909–10 estimates, and the barren land on the banks of the Forth estuary began to take shape as a modern naval dockyard. It was completed only just in time. In the other home dockyards, and in some in the colonies abroad, new docks large enough to take the bigger ships being built were constructed, and a world-wide network of coaling stations was set up to serve the fleets and squadrons on distant stations.

Victuals and Pay

With the changes in *matériel* came changes in the amenities of life as lived on board. The new ships provided more spacious and airy messdecks for seamen and stokers, with more plentiful bath-rooms and washing places. Canteens on board were reorganized to provide a wider choice of additional food to supplement the official ration, and the provision of cutlery for the men was taken over from the canteens, which had hired it to the messes, and made an article of ship's stores for free issue. The ship's biscuit, which generations of officers and men had tapped smartly on the mess tables to dislodge the black-headed weevils before eating it, was largely replaced by fresh bread baked on board in modern bakeries. The seaman and the stoker, enjoying for the first time a degree of comfort which, if still austere when judged by today's standards, was far advanced of anything he had known before, attributed it all to 'Jacky' Fisher, as he was universally known on the lower deck. Officers might be disgruntled and divide themselves into two mutually antagonistic camps, but the seamen and stokers were behind Fisher to a man. They were behind him even more solidly when they discovered that he had been instrumental in getting foreign commissions reduced from three to two years, and had followed this by ordering the relaxation of some of the more repressive severities of the Naval Discipline Act.

Yet the rates of pay in the navy, and particularly lower-deck pay, still lagged far behind all these new amenities. They were low by any standard of the times. The pay of seamen, which ranged from 1*s*. 3*d*. a day for an ordinary seaman to 3*s*. 2*d*. a day for the top-rate chief petty officer, had not been altered since the introduction of continuous service in 1853. A committee on lower-deck pay, under the chairmanship of Captain Montague Browning, reported in 1905 with proposals for modest increases, ranging from 1*d*. extra a day for leading seamen (1*s*. 9*d*. to 1*s*. 10*d*.) to 10*d*. a day for the top-rate chief petty officers. Able and ordinary seamen were to remain unchanged. But in order to keep the total of service pay to the same figure as appeared in the annual estimates, the rates of non-substantive pay, with which seamen generally were able quite materially to augment their wages, were to be reduced. Thus the qualifications of seaman gunner or seaman torpedoman, the most widely held non-substantive rate, was to be reduced in daily value from 4*d*. to 3*d*., while the rating of trained man, worth 1*d*. a day to every able seaman and above, was to be completely withdrawn. The main purpose of these proposals was to improve the status of the petty officer. An able seaman qualifying for the maximum available non-substantive pay could add 1*s*. 9*d*. a day to his basic 1*s*. 7*d*., making a total of 3*s*. 4*d*., or 2*d*. a day more than the top-rate chief petty officer, who had probably earned his promotion through character and leadership rather than any particular trade skill. The committee held, quite rightly, that this state of affairs was conducive to a lowering of disciplinary standards, and pointed to the big increase in crime in the navy, particularly in cases of striking a superior officer, as evidence for this belief. Indeed, they reported having come across several cases of petty officers being forced to augment their income by undertaking tailoring and repairs of clothing for seamen. There was, of course, no marriage allowance in the Edwardian navy, but all men, and even boys under training whose rate of pay was 7*d*. a day, were encouraged to allot a proportion of their pay, up to seven-eighths as the maximum, to their families: even with the maximum allotment, one wonders how some of the wives and families managed. The recommendations of Captain Browning's committee were accepted by the Admiralty with a few minor amendments, generally downwards, except that the old rates of non-substantive pay were not to be changed at once but were to die out as the present holders either qualified for an advanced rate or left the service.

The pay of officers was hardly more generous. Midshipmen received 1*s*. 9*d*. daily, lieutenants on promotion 10*s*., commanders £1, captains £1. 2*s*. 6*d*. to £1. 13*s*. according to seniority, rear-admirals £3, and admirals of the fleet, of whom the establishment permitted a maximum of five only, £6 a day. It is true that, as for the seamen, there were non-substantive additions in the form of command and table money for senior ranks, and allowances for navigation and gunnery duties for junior, but unlike the seamen only a very small proportion of officers qualified for these.

Victualling in the fleet, as it had been for well over a century, was as generous as the pay was meagre. The basic daily ration for both officers and men was $1\frac{1}{4}$ lb. biscuit or $1\frac{1}{2}$ lb. bread, 2 oz. jam, $\frac{1}{2}$ oz. coffee, 3 oz. sugar, 4 oz. preserved meat, $\frac{3}{4}$ oz. chocolate or cocoa, $\frac{3}{4}$ oz. preserved milk, and $\frac{3}{8}$ oz. tea. When procurable, $\frac{3}{4}$ lb. fresh meat and 1 lb. fresh vegetables were issued daily in addition; when not, $\frac{3}{4}$ lb. salt beef or pork, $\frac{1}{3}$ lb. split peas, and 1 oz. compressed vegetables was the daily issue, with 9 oz. flour, $\frac{3}{4}$ oz. suet, and 2 oz. raisins issued every second day. All ships except the smallest, which could rely on their depot ships, had a canteen on board, and a small *per capita* messing allowance could be spent in the purchase of such extras as butter, eggs, bacon, sausages, and the like. If the navy was ill paid, it was certainly not ill fed, and the quality of the victuals matched the quantity. It is, however, true to say that some of the naval cooks were not as well trained in their jobs as could have been desired.

The Home Fleet Controversy

By 1906 the transformation of the navy was already remarkable. Its outlook had changed from a lethargic peacetime navy to a fighting machine geared to a state of instant readiness for war. Fisher's new ships were beginning to commission into the fleet, his new officers produced under the Osborne and Dartmouth scheme were beginning to go to sea. Ships which, before 1904, missed the battle practice targets with their big guns at 2,000 yards range, were now hitting them at 7,000 yards. A 15-knot navy was becoming a 20-knot navy. It is true that all this was not achieved without friction and a good deal of vehement opposition, but to a majority of officers the good results distinctly outweighed those drawbacks. And as each month passed and showed a continuing improvement in the state of the navy, the great feud of 'Fisherite' and 'anti-Fisherite' began to lose some of its virulence. There were many who even believed that it would die a natural death as continued evidence of ordered progress came to hand.

These hopes were shattered when, in the 1907–8 estimates, only two new battleships were announced instead of the normal four. In fact it was a reasonable reduction since no European power had as yet laid down a single dreadnought and there was no evidence of any unusual shipbuilding activity on the part of any potential enemy, but the big-navy press, supported by the Navy League, attacked the Board of Admiralty for not standing up to the government and insisting on the laying-down of four dreadnoughts. Worse was to follow when the Admiralty, carrying to its logical conclusion the redistribution of fleets made in 1905, announced the constitution of a new Home fleet. With the object of strengthening still further the concentration of power in the North Sea, the three reserve fleet squadrons at the Nore, Portsmouth, and Devonport, which had previously been independent commands, were now amalgamated to form a Home fleet under the command of one admiral. The Nore division, of six battleships, was kept fully manned: the Portsmouth and Devonport divisions, a total of seven battleships, were to be manned with three-fifths complements. To provide this new Home fleet with ships the Channel, Atlantic, and Mediterranean fleets were all proportionately reduced. The Admiralty's reasoning for this change in organization was perfectly sound, though it could not be stated in public. The growing evidence of anglophobia in Germany, the implied menace of her increased naval building, pointed inexorably towards her as the enemy in the war which many men could already see was coming. To reinforce the Channel fleet, already well publicized as an active fleet, was likely to act as an irritant on Germany and possibly stimulate her to further naval building. But to constitute a new Home fleet (the new dreadnoughts were sent to the Chatham division for the ostensible reason that they could not adequately exercise with older battleships) was thought likely to produce no obvious provocation in German eyes, since it was announced that the Home fleet was to be essentially a reserve fleet. It may not have been very profound reasoning, but at least it made sense in the prevailing climate of Anglo-German relations.

It was this new Home fleet, made up from what were until then known as the reserve squadrons, which refanned the flames of controversy. According to the critics the Admiralty (by which they meant the first sea lord) was jeopardizing the safety of the nation by weakening the Channel fleet, which was fully commissioned and operational, in favour of a new fleet which was not only semi-reserve but also was divided geographically between the Nore, Portsmouth, and Devonport. Moreover, while in peacetime the Home fleet was under its own commander-in-chief, in the event of war it would come under the direct orders of the commander-in-chief, Channel fleet, who would be the supreme naval commander at home in a war against Germany. Later, in the summer of 1908, the 'Invincible' class ships, together with a second squadron of battleships, were added to the Nore division of the Home fleet, making it more powerful, even without the Portsmouth and Devonport divisions, than the entire German fleet; and finally, in March 1909, the Channel fleet itself was added to the Home fleet to become its second division. These developments, however, were still in the future when the original plan was announced: no inkling of them emerged at the time from a silent Admiralty. It was this silence on future plans, or the apparent lack of them, which aroused the anger of the anti-Fisher party. Admirals Sir Hedworth Meux and Sir Gerard Noel joined the 'Syndicate of Discontent', which found a new leader in the popular and engaging figure of Lord Charles Beresford. Beresford had been Fisher's second-in-command in the Mediterranean and the two had been close friends, but the Admiralty's fleet redistribution scheme was made the cause of a break between the two which was never to heal, and which eventually resulted in the retirement of both of them from the navy.

In April 1907 Beresford took up the appointment of commander-in-chief, Channel fleet. In May he publicly denounced the formation of the Home fleet as 'a fraud upon the public and a danger to the Empire'. On the receipt in July of the Admiralty's war orders, on the basis of which he should draw up his own war plans for approval by the Admiralty, he took no action for over a year, and in fact never produced any war plans at all. In November occurred the famous 'paintwork' incident. On the fourth of that month Beresford ordered the Channel fleet to curtail its exercises and to paint ship in preparation for a forthcoming inspection by the German emperor. The cruiser *Roxburgh,* engaged in gunnery practice, sent a signal to the rear-admiral, first cruiser squadron, Percy Scott, requesting permission to continue her practice. Scott, who was well known to be in the 'Fishpond', replied by signal: 'Paintwork appears to be more in demand than gunnery, so you had better come in in time to make yourself look pretty by the 8th.' Beresford was furious, sent for Scott, and publicly reprimanded him on the flagship's quarterdeck in front of all the officers. The Admiralty refused his demand for Scott to be superseded. The incident quickly became public property—a godsend to agitators and journalists of every political hue. Thus the *Bystander*:

> Percy Scott
> Thought it rot
> All his shot
> Gone to pot
> While he got
> Like a yacht
> Pretty for the Kaiser.
> Beresford
> Simply roared,
> 'Have that scored
> Off the board,
> By the Lord
> You'll be floored
> If you are not wiser.'

On the whole the public hugely enjoyed the free spectacle of public men at daggers drawn. But the rift between Fisher and Beresford quickly began to reach proportions beyond all limits of decency, and to an extent that it became a public scandal. Beresford demanded an official inquiry into Admiralty policy; Fisher demanded Beresford's dismissal. The matter came to a head when a letter was printed in *The Times* which stated 'It can no longer be denied that the Commander-in-Chief of the Channel Fleet (who is presumably the Admiralissimo designate in the event of war) is not on speaking terms with the admiral commanding his cruiser squadron on the one hand, or with the First Sea Lord of the Admiralty on the other.' After a good deal of argument in the cabinet, which was reluctant to take sides one way or the other, McKenna, the first lord of the Admiralty, at last got approval to terminate Beresford's command. He was ordered to haul down his flag early in 1909, the reason given being the absorption of the Channel fleet into the Home fleet. Beresford took the decision hard, for it was difficult to disguise the fact that instead of serving a normal period of three years as a commander-in-chief, he had served only two.

LV. 'Admiral Fisher' by William Nicholson 1905

LVI. H.M.S. Dreadnought

The Fisher–Beresford Inquiry

Fisher celebrated his victory with a spate of letters to his friends, flamboyant and boastful. His success, however, was short-lived. In 1909 there occurred a German naval scare. On evidence which the Admiralty had accumulated, coupled with the supplementary navy law passed in Germany in 1908, it looked as though there could be a parity in battleships as between Britain and Germany by 1912. As a result the Admiralty asked for six battleships, instead of the usual four, in the 1909–10 estimates.

This demand met violent opposition in the cabinet, mainly from Lloyd George and Winston Churchill, who refused to believe the Admiralty's case. They were adamant that four battleships were sufficient to retain superiority over Germany. The sea lords threatened to resign in a body unless they got their six in the current estimates. Again they brought forward their evidence on the rate of building in Germany, and on re-examining it, and with the receipt of even more alarming intelligence from Germany, actually increased their demand from six to eight. There was complete deadlock in the cabinet for over a month while the arguments swayed backwards and forwards. It was solved by an ingenious compromise, that four battleships be laid down during the financial year 1909–10, and four more on the first day of the financial year 1910–11 provided the need for them was still proved to exist. This compromise, debated in parliament, raised a storm throughout the country. The Conservatives, in opposition, produced a rallying cry that echoed through the nation—'We want eight, and we won't wait.' The argument raged for the next three months, and was only finally stilled when McKenna announced that the four contingent ships would become part of the 1909 programme, although their keels would not be laid until 1910, and without prejudice to the navy's needs in 1910.

Fisher of course came in for much criticism. He was accused of having been caught napping by the German acceleration in their building plans. He was widely criticized for not standing out for the eight ships from the start of the agitation. A great press campaign began to build up against him. 'We arraign Sir John Fisher', wrote the *Daily Express*, 'at the bar of public opinion, and with the imminent possibility of national disaster before the country, we say again to him, "Thou art the man!" ' Beresford, quick to scent his chance, once again demanded from the prime minister an official inquiry into Admiralty administration and policy. With the state of public opinion as it was, Asquith could not refuse. He appointed a sub-committee of the committee of imperial defence to investigate the charges, with himself as chairman and four other cabinet ministers, Crewe, Morley, Grey, and Haldane, as members.

The committee began their sittings on 27 April 1909, and issued their report on 12 August. They found that no danger to the country arose from the Admiralty's handling of the situation in the case of the German building scare or from the organization and distribution of the fleets, which was Beresford's main charge against the Admiralty. They blamed the Admiralty for not taking Beresford sufficiently into their confidence when he commanded the Channel fleet, and they blamed Beresford for not acting in the spirit of the board's instructions which he received and for failing to recognize the board's paramount authority. But the real sting came in the tail. 'The committee have been impressed with the differences of opinion amongst officers of high rank and professional attainments regarding important principles of naval strategy and tactics, and they look forward with much confidence to the further development of a Naval War Staff, from which the naval members of the board and flag officers and their staffs at sea may be expected to derive common benefit.' Thus, although Fisher had been virtually vindicated of Beresford's charges against him, at the same time the committee, though probably unwittingly, signed his death warrant as first sea lord. Throughout his term at the Admiralty Fisher had always resisted all attempts to set up a naval staff. 'A Naval War Staff', he wrote, 'is a very excellent organization for cutting out and arranging foreign newspaper clippings. . . . So far as the Navy is concerned, the tendency of these "thinking establishments" on shore is to convert splendid sea officers into very indifferent clerks.'

This was, probably, the greatest weakness of the whole Fisher administration. He may have made war plans, but if he did so he kept them securely locked up in his own brain. It is certain that, even if they were preserved in his brain, no attempt was ever made to bring them into any state of reality in terms of ships and movements. Such war plans as he was known to favour were the seizure of Heligoland on the outbreak of a war with Germany and a great amphibious assault on the German coast, preferably inside the

Baltic. But no details of these were ever revealed, and even the army, which was to be landed on the Baltic shore, was never informed of the role which Fisher had in store for it. No naval war plan ever came to the committee of imperial defence for discussion, in spite of repeated requests for a statement of Admiralty policy in the event of a war with Germany.

Belatedly, in view of the Fisher–Beresford inquiry, the Admiralty had set up a navy war council, which consisted of the first sea lord as its president, the director of naval intelligence, the director of the naval mobilization department, and the assistant secretary of the Admiralty. But even the Admiralty could not pretend that it was a naval staff; it met only on the initiative of the first sea lord and its function was purely advisory.

It had always been a tenet of Fisher's faith that plans for war must be prepared by the first sea lord alone and in the greatest secrecy. The essence of this belief was that modern war could only be won by the 'suddenness and unexpectedness' of major operations. Even though all his plans, nebulous as they were, embraced a large measure of amphibious assault, the army was not to be informed of them until war had actually broken out. Fixed rigidly in his mind was the belief that the role of the army was to be 'a bullet fired by the navy', and allied to that was a profound contempt for the War Office and the army as a whole. He even extended that contempt to the Royal Marines, whose sympathies and loyalties, he firmly believed, lay far more in the direction of the War Office than the Admiralty.

Conclusion

Fisher was elevated to the peerage as Baron Fisher of Kilverstone on the king's birthday, 9 November 1909, and though he never paid much attention to political honours, he was aggrieved that it was not a viscountcy. His resignation as first sea lord took effect from 25 January 1910. By that time his work for the navy was finished. The five and a half years during which he had held the reins of naval power had witnessed vast and important changes. The old lethargy had been swept away, the outworn customs and traditions had been assaulted, the innate conservatism of a naval administration which had slumbered on unchallenged for a century was violently and even brutally assailed. From the ashes of the Victorian navy had arisen the glittering reality of an Edwardian navy, newer, stronger, progressive, and imbued with the spirit of efficiency and technological change. Fisher's reforming zeal, his vision, and his ruthless energy left behind him a navy so revitalized and so alive to change that it could face the coming war with confidence. During those years of power he *was* the navy, and it was his work which laid so surely the foundations of the British victory at sea which in 1918 brought the German empire down to ruin.

Yet it would be unrealistic not to recognize that this revolution in technical efficiency had cost the navy, and the country, dear. The spirit of unity, which Nelson had epitomized a century earlier with his 'band of brothers', had been torn and shattered, and the wounds lingered on until the common perils of war with Germany healed them in 1914. The growing and evident needs, during those restless years, of understanding and co-operation between navy and army had been sacrificed on the altar of Fisher's hate and distrust of the entire military machine. That, too, was a grievous burden which also lingered on for many years after its architect had disappeared from the scene.

Yet if the cost was heavy, the gains to the navy were enormous. At the start of King Edward's reign, the navy desperately needed a man of Fisher's stamp, a man impatient of the settled somnolent order, a man who could shake it and beat it into a shape designed for modern war. Probably no one but Fisher could have done it, for there was then no other officer who combined the necessary vision and courage with the tempestuous energy to force reform on to a reluctant navy. By the end of the king's reign the consummation of his vision was there for all to see, nurtured perhaps through unnecessary turmoil and strife, yet alive, virile, confident, and ready. Fisher's monument will stand, intangible perhaps but none the less real, in that sombre scene on 21 November 1918 when a defeated German fleet steamed into captivity through the lines of the British grand fleet. He was not himself present to witness these sweets of victory, but none the less it was on the solid foundations which he had laid down that the navy's great triumph was constructed.

14

THE ARMY

CYRIL FALLS

*Chichele Professor (emeritus) of the History of War
in the University of Oxford*

THE ARMY

After the Boer War

T H E Royal Navy of the Edwardian age was dominated by one admiral. No general officer dominated the army. The greatest figures, Wolseley and Roberts, were time-worn. Roberts remained commander-in-chief until the office was abolished, but it would have been happier had he departed sooner. There was no one to replace him in fame: Nicholson, able though he was, seemed by comparison merely a bureaucrat. No serving general, no victorious general, aroused love and enthusiasm such as greeted a victim of adversity in retirement. It was not Roberts who, driving to a private business appointment in London, stopped the traffic; not even he who, arriving at a rural railway station to stay at a friend's mansion, found the horses removed from the carriage and was drawn by men, through a cheering crowd, to his destination. These honours were paid to Redvers Buller.

The void was partly filled by a civilian, the secretary of state for war of 1906. Haldane dominated the army because he remade it from top to bottom. He was popular with all who understood his effort. One should, however, scrutinize conventional assessments such as 'the army likes and trusts Lieutenant-General Bangs': perhaps 20 per cent. of officers and 80 per cent. of rank-and-file have never heard of this worthy. To the private soldier Haldane was less well known than Hore-Belisha a generation later. To the men at the top, however, he was a tremendous figure.

The Edwardian army lived under two influences which overlapped. The first was that of the South African war, which was concluded after the accession of King Edward VII. The second was that of the threat from Germany and of measures to meet it. The army had emerged from the war with diminished credit at home and in disrepute abroad. Yet condemnation had been exaggerated, largely owing to misapprehension of the difficulties of the task.

Bed-rock qualities, discipline, musketry, movement under fire, were good. The junior officers were lively and quick learners. The column leaders of the later phases included Plumer, Allenby, Byng, and others, who showed skill and initiative and rose high in a greater war.

However the deficiencies were glaring. To begin with, the staff work was haphazard and there existed nothing comparable to the general staff system then well established in continental armies. Roberts sent out his senior staff officer, Kitchener, to fight a battle; Kitchener, who succeeded Roberts in the chief command, did the same thing with his senior staff officer, Ian Hamilton; in fact, the two chiefs-of-staff were treated very much as seconds-in-command. They should not have been able to spare the time for such diversions. Manœuvre and marches were slow and clumsy. Kipling has immortalized them at their slowest and most obvious in 'The Captive' where they are observed through the eyes of an American adventurer showing off to the Boers his version of the quick-firing pom-pom, in hopes of selling them the patent. Ambushes by wily and mobile foes were inevitable, but too many were successful. The military machine was ponderous. Its armament was obsolescent, though this was not the fault of the authorities responsible during the war: they had no time to produce new weapons, but they were working out the lessons to embody them when this could be done. The time had been lost before the war. At all events, while it lasted the artillery remained unable to shoot effectively from cover, mainly because there was no well-thought-out systematic observation of fire. This was perturbing to those who realized what would happen if our gunners had to face, with this lack of preparedness, troops of a great European power.

Finally, good as were the bulk of the regular rank-and-file, little was done to stimulate their intelligence or initiative. 'We make the private soldier in many cases a fool', wrote an officer, 'because we start with the assumption that he is a fool.' A familiar, but to the imaginative a pathetic, sight was that of three or four soldiers being marched across a square by a non-commissioned officer, presumably incapable of doing some little job otherwise. Sir Alfred Milner's verdict on the post-war army and its organization was 'an avalanche of military incompetence'. He went on to show what he considered to be the virtues that were being neglected, and why.

'And what is the disease really? Do you know? Splendid men, splendid officers—and so many things, mobilization, sea and railway transport, commissariat, admirably done. . . . But the *central machinery* and the *chosen leaders* ——'

The German Menace

The second influence, that of Germany, did not affect the army as much as the navy, because the army could not hope to face the German army or much more than a tenth part of it. The biggest role it could aspire to in a continental war was that of a junior partner to a European power possessing a mass conscript army. Such a prospect appeared distant when the South African war ended in 1902, though the unfriendliness of Germany during the conflict was naturally taken into account. In the years that followed senior officers who were invited to German manœuvres were deeply impressed. They might have to hide a smile at the finale, a great assault launched by order of the emperor and headed by the cavalry, which inevitably routed the opposing side; but they were shrewd enough to recognize that this was a trimming, a perquisite of the kaiser's and a tribute to the imperial régime. They did not allow it to divert their attention from more favourable factors. One of these was the competence and ease with which commanders and staffs moved and manœuvred large troop formations. Another was the appearance and behaviour of the reservists, fine-looking men, well disciplined and good marchers, who seemed to fit smoothly into their role. The visitors were well received.

The British and German armies had earlier experienced a closer, small-scale contact, which the former had found less agreeable. This was in the suppression of the Boxer rising of 1900 in China. The polished commander of the international force, Field-Marshal Graf von Waldersee, and a soft-spoken staff officer, Erich von Falkenhayn, who was to be better known to the British army a decade later, were affable. Other officers were not. They showed scorn for the British because their land forces were so small, with a certain jealousy for one asset represented in the contingent, the Indian army. British sea power and colonial possessions obviously excited their anger. When the Anglo-Japanese alliance appeared on the horizon they commented on it with mingled rage and sneers. All the worst riots—and one was extremely savage—occurred between

German and British (or Indian) rank-and-file. The latter were certainly not complete innocents, but they got on well with the American, Japanese, and Italian troops and the Austrian naval detachment, if not quite so well with the French. All this was not a very grave matter in view of the international tensions which could not be excluded from the force, but it made a bad impression on the British officers.

Much more serious was the situation brought about by the swashbuckling attitude of Germany over Morocco and the emperor's challenge to France at Tangier on 31 March 1905. From then on matters began to go from bad to worse. Evidence, not conclusive but which could not be disregarded, reached England that Germany was contemplating a sudden declaration of war and attack on France. It came at the time of a general election in which the Conservative government was swept out of office. The nominated Liberal secretary of state for foreign affairs, Sir Edward Grey, and the secretary of state for war, R. B. Haldane, actually discussed it after speaking from the same platform at Berwick on 12 January 1906. The result was that the new prime minister, Sir Henry Campbell-Bannerman, authorized Anglo-French staff talks, while explicitly laying down that they must involve no commitments on the British side.

This action has since been criticized, but, whether or not the business was mishandled, there was nothing sinister about it. The subject had already been approached by Grey's predecessor, Lord Lansdowne, in his last days at the Foreign Office. The conversations did not, in fact, create any definite commitment, though Grey's personal view, like Haldane's, was that if Germany forced a war upon France, Britain ought to go to France's aid. The War Office talks were distinctly less binding than those of the Admiralty because the latter led to a redistribution of the British and French fleets, which denuded the Channel and North Sea of French battleship strength and thus created something like an obligation of honour, as was to appear. Apart from the principle, the fact that the decision was not submitted to and approved by the cabinet was strongly condemned by those who in 1914 strove to prevent Britain's entry into the war. Grey himself afterwards wrote that if he had had more experience he would have 'asked for a cabinet', but that Campbell-Bannerman never suggested that he should. No one seems to have thought of conducting the talks under the control of the new committee of imperial defence. It is interesting to find that Field-Marshal Lord Kitchener knew nothing about the talks until 1910, though he had been for seven years commander-in-chief in India, and that he learnt of them only because his former staff officer, Henry Rawlinson, came out to join him on a tour of the Manchurian battlefields.

The chief representatives of the British army in the talks were Spencer Ewart, who became director of military operations in October 1906, and Henry Wilson, who succeeded him in this appointment in 1910, that is, shortly after the death of King Edward. The earlier director's conduct was cautious; that of Wilson, a strong Francophil, rather less so. By 1911 it had been decided that, if Britain intervened, an expeditionary force of six divisions should be sent to France.

Reorganization and Rearmament

Before we come to the conception of the British expeditionary force we must see how it was made conceivable and could be created out of the hotchpotch of an army existing after the South African war. And this calls for a brief survey of the progress made before Haldane took office. The Conservative government has seldom received due credit for what was accomplished. This is particularly true of the prime minister, Arthur Balfour, whose part was even greater than that of the successive secretaries of state for war, St. John Brodrick and H. O. Arnold-Forster. It was Balfour who created the committee of imperial defence—though evidence exists that Brodrick had put up a plea for it—the seed from which the Ministry of Defence grew after the second world war. Without the prime minister's encouragement and political initiative the findings of the Esher committee could not possibly have been brought into force. The report was also warmly backed by the king. Lord Esher records that on 30 January 1904 he had two sessions of work on it with the king, from 11 till 1 and 2.30 till 4, and finally received his approval of the whole thing as it stood. He had been in frequent consultation with Edward VII throughout.

The long-lived dualism of a War Office represented in the government and a commander-in-chief in the Horse Guards was at last abolished, together with the appointment. A general staff was formed. This was based on continental practice but did not follow it exactly, since it was set up within the War Office, whereas the general pattern was a war ministry mainly concerned with administration and a separate general staff. In the British organization there was also established an army council, including a civil side, to oversee administration, personnel, and armament, and to handle finance and 'non-effective' votes such as pensions. Major-General Douglas Haig wrote to Esher: 'I feel sure that no one appreciates *what you have done for the Army* more than I do. I never believed it possible to get such a thorough reorganization without undergoing first of all some military disaster.'

No serious reorganization below the top was achieved under this government; Brodrick and Arnold-Forster both announced schemes —diametrically opposed—but they remained on paper. However, good progress was made with training and armament. Brodrick established Salisbury Plain as a manœuvre area and artillery centre because increased ranges had made the Aldershot area too small. In order to accustom commanders to handle large bodies of troops, so far as this was possible in the small British army, corps districts were established. How closely Edward VII followed the work is shown by the following communication to the secretary of state:

The King understands that at Aldershot, where the First Army Corps is supposed to be training with a view to being ready at any moment to be sent on active service, nearly all the Brigades have no Brigadiers and will only receive them on mobilization. . . . The appointment of the senior Battalion Commander as Brigadier the king considers a great mistake. . . . The fact of his being Senior Battalion Commander in no way implies that he is a suitable Brigadier.

He also pointed out that this officer ought to lead his own battalion on manœuvres. Like many monarchs, the king was apt to become unduly absorbed in ornamental detail, especially full-dress and mess uniform. His grandson, the Duke of Windsor, relates that King Edward caught him wearing the uniform of one regiment of Foot Guards, with the spurs belonging to another, and for long afterwards used to say over and over again how lucky it was they had met that morning. This pleasant story does not alter the fact that the king could hit the right nail on the head with certainty. Above all he backed the right schemes and the right men.

Rearmament followed rapidly upon the close of the South African war. The field artillery was equipped with the quick-firing 18-pounder, and the horse artillery with the 13-pounder. After deep research to find the best possible gun and equipment for army mobile heavy batteries, one was produced in the 60-pounder, tough, handy, hard-hitting, and with a range of 10,000 yards. It was an army-corps gun, but a section could be attached to divisional artillery. A 4·5 inch quick-firing field howitzer came later. Little attention was, however, paid to heavy artillery because the general opinion was that the next war would be one of rapid movement throughout. The infantry received the short Lee-Enfield rifle, which had the great advantage that it could also be used as a cavalry weapon, carried in a bucket on the off side, and was far superior to the various carbines with which continental cavalry was armed. Brodrick introduced a uniform for training at home which would be used on active service. In India also an advance took place, but precious time was wasted in conflict over the reorganization and control of the army between the viceroy, Lord Curzon, and the commander-in-chief, Lord Kitchener. The latter achieved a good deal in establishing the divisional system effectively for the first time, forming nine divisions instead of four by cutting down garrisons, and replacing a number of southern regiments which had for long seen no active service by others from martial northern stock. General Sir O'Moore Creagh, who succeeded Kitchener in 1909, after acting as secretary to the military department at the India Office under Morley, declared that neither the Indian government nor the India Office contemplated the use of the Indian army to fight a European foe. As one proof he pointed out that they left it seriously under-gunned for this sort of warfare. At least it can be said that it had become more readily adaptable to the needs of a great war.

The lot of the private soldier was bettered, if only by minor measures hedged by pressure for economies. The men got rather better bathing facilities, better cookery, a number of new dining-halls, a certain amount of new housing. When Smith-Dorrien commanded at Aldershot he decreed that soldiers should be put on their honour to behave well; he withdrew from the streets the pickets hitherto sent out at night in garrison towns to herd the tipsy into barracks and frog-march those who were fighting drunk. From this

period dates the first sign of appreciation of 'soft' drinks by the
private soldier which has grown so strikingly since.

One dreadful scourge afflicting the rank-and-file had been the
lack of any provision for marriage except for a select few. If a
soldier obtained his commanding officer's permission to marry, his
wife was henceforth 'on the strength', was moved with the unit,
obtained fair quarters abroad or, if she had to be left behind, a small
allowance. But the commanding officer was not his own master in
the matter. He had only a handful of tickets to wedded bliss. The
fate of the wife married 'off the strength' was grisly. Even if she
and her children could be kept alive while her husband remained
on one station, what was to happen when the unit moved? Theoretically there was one answer only: they must starve. In practice
this did not occur, but the sufferings of soldiers' families in this
plight were often atrocious.

The memory of the writer of these lines goes back to the days of
the South African war, when his mother was the local honorary
treasurer of the Soldiers' and Sailors' Families Association. As
a small boy he occasionally accompanied her when, with a roll of
names as check, she handed out food vouchers to women in the
situation described. (Vouchers were used because of a not unreasonable fear that some at least of the recipients would convert cash into
alcohol; also because they had to be directed to respectable shops
which would not be likely to connive at this transaction.) The
squalor, the dirt, and the misery of the scene left on the observer's
mind an impression which has endured for sixty years. The quota
for marriage 'on the strength' was now increased, but the sore was
not yet healed. It is not an easy problem; the tough-minded might
maintain that modern armies of democratic states are cluttered up
with too many prosperous and exigent wives of young soldiers. Nor
must it be forgotten that the British soldier, trifling as his pay in
the first decade of the century now looks, was affluent beside the
conscript. At this time the aim of most far-sighted German privates
was to be accepted by a girl in a shop or domestic service for walking
out, when she paid.

What was done amounted to something, but it had not gone very
far because structurally the army was virtually unchanged except
at the very top, that is, the general staff at the War Office. Brodrick
had during the war drafted a scheme which was to produce six corps,

three entirely of regular troops, which would be available to serve as an expeditionary force in Europe; of the other three, one was to be half regular and the remaining two to be formed almost completely from auxiliary forces. The merit of this draft was that it found a role for a large proportion of the amorphous forces—militia, volunteers, and yeomanry—which hitherto possessed no administrative services. It certainly provided Haldane with pointers when he became secretary of state. However, the war dragged on longer than Brodrick had expected and in the immediate post-war period equipment could not be found. When he passed on to the India Office, his successor, Arnold-Forster, put everything into the melting-pot. He thought the time had come to end the Cardwell principle[1] of two linked infantry battalions, carrying out alternately foreign and home service, and decided to establish 'general service' and 'home service' armies, the former on long engagements, nine years with the colours. He shared the fate of his predecessor in being overtaken by events, in his case the fall of the Conservative government. Both secretaries of state were above the average. Brodrick's weaknesses were that he was unbusinesslike and aroused political hostility; Arnold-Forster's that he came to the War Office with a cut-and-dried plan, without knowledge of the background.

Let us take a passing glance at Arnold-Forster's capable private secretary—naturally not retained by Haldane—because it illustrates the frustrations of an officer living beyond his means. Stanley Maude came of an ancient family, but his father had to make heavy sacrifices to send him to Eton. He was commissioned in the Coldstream Guards. As a young adjutant he was something of a martinet and made what was known as an 'adjutant's battalion', the significance of which term should be obvious. He was a good brigade-major in South Africa. However, after 1905, with a family to keep, he could not afford to accept good opportunities open in the brigade. Early in 1914 he entered the directorate of military training. The outbreak of war found him a colonel, low on the list, aged 50, and with few prospects. Exactly two years later he became

[1] As secretary of state for war Edward (later Viscount) Cardwell introduced multiple reforms between 1868 and 1873. He is best remembered by a minor one, abolition of the purchase by officers of commissions and steps in rank. The linking of battalions was preceded by the assignment to regiments of local (nearly always county) titles, association with the county militia, and the establishment of a local regimental depot.

commander-in-chief in Mesopotamia. When he died in Baghdad he had become a national hero.

Haldane at the War Office

When Haldane took office at the beginning of 1906 he found himself with at least the beginnings of an effective machinery at the summit and—for a country without conscription—an impressive-looking total of whole-time and part-time soldiers. His experts did not take long, however, to make him realize how largely the picture was fictitious. The regular forces numbered well over a quarter of a million, but with a quite inadequate reserve. The militia numbered about 100,000, varying in quality but seldom seriously trained, and not available for foreign service except by individual transfer and re-enlistment to regular units. Yeomanry and volunteers together amounted to 280,000 men, but this big force of amateur cavalry and infantry was all flesh without backbone, ribs, or limbs. It was not organized in formations and included no field artillery, no engineers, no medical or veterinary services, and no transport.

The regular army by now had made long strides in reform. The great majority of the officers were taking the profession of arms much more seriously than in the past. A high proportion of the army was, however, permanently abroad in time of peace. Critics, and Arnold-Forster himself, talked airily of 'getting rid of the Cardwell system', but troops had to be found for foreign service, particularly for India. Now recruiting, though not disastrously bad, was never quite as good as was needed, and this shortage had an important effect upon the strength available for an expeditionary force and upon mobilization. It was desirable, in India essential, to keep units abroad up to establishment or near it. The immature could not be sent because they would not have stood the climate. Even as it was, drafts in the trooping season included soldiers who were too young. Kipling had noted some consequences.

> When the 'arf-made recruit goes out to the East
> 'E acts like a babe an' 'e drinks like a beast,
> An' 'e wonders because 'e is frequent deceased
> Ere 'e's fit for to serve as a soldier.

The result was that infantry battalions in India and generally on foreign stations contained the pick—and the bigger half—of the

LVII (*a*). Portland Place 1906

LVII (*b*). Officers of the Dragoon Guards on a 10-h.p. Wolseley 1902

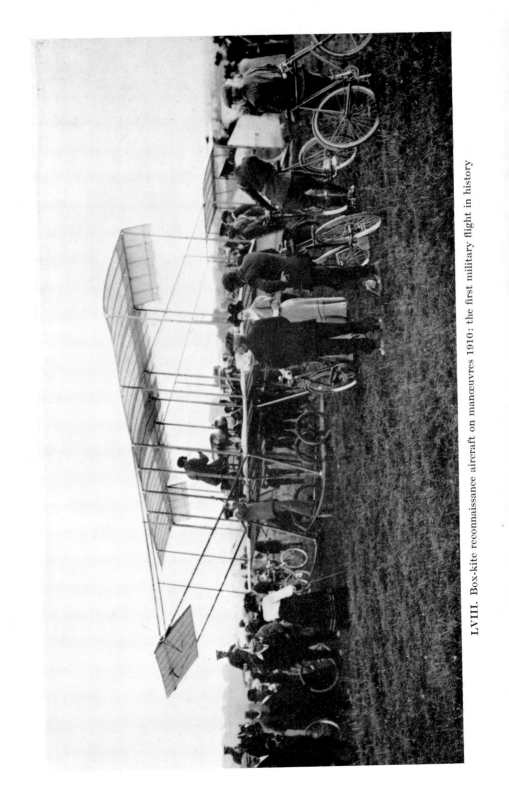

LVIII. Box-kite reconnaissance aircraft on manœuvres 1910: the first military flight in history

regiments, and that their sister-battalions at home were for the most part weak in numbers and at the same time largely made up of recruits. A proportion of these were so young that they could not be included in any expeditionary force, though they would be available as drafts within a few months. If left behind they would have to be replaced by reservists, of whom, as has been pointed out, there was a shortage. So when Haldane asked his chief of the general staff who would be available to form an expeditionary force from the grand total of nearly 650,000 (regulars, militia, yeomanry, and volunteers), he was told 80,000 men, providing three infantry divisions and a strong cavalry division, *at the end of two months*. The war between Prussia and Austria in 1866 had been concluded within a shorter time.

Haldane, a Liberal imperialist, aroused in the army none of the reservations or anxieties which it would have felt had it fallen into the hands of certain of his colleagues in the new cabinet. Their accusations of inhumanity and worse in the South African war had not ceased to smart. His appointment was greeted with relief, and the effect of his good send-off was heightened by his friendliness, enthusiasm, and modesty. He could hardly have known less than he did about the army, whereas a man like Brodrick (now Earl of Midleton) knew it through and through. Haldane did not disguise the fact that he was learning from elementary facts upward, but professionals discovered that he grasped profundities with astonishing speed. He was pleased with his chief of the general staff, Sir William Nicholson, whom he described as one of the ablest men he had ever met, shrewdly adding that he was not the man to make a first-class commander.[1] The secretary of state had one minor but appreciable slice of luck. Early in his period of office he moved out of the old building in Pall Mall, demolished and replaced by the Royal Automobile Club, to the new War Office in Whitehall, a more commodious and of course up-to-date building.

We may say he began with four simple principles. The defence of Britain rested on the navy, and the army's role must be a secondary one to meet emergencies. The role of the army at home should be to provide, in a European war, an expeditionary force as large as there

---

[1] The title 'Chief of the Imperial General Staff' was introduced by Haldane later. It was based on the prospect of a general staff for the whole empire, which did not come about. The title is therefore, strictly speaking, a misnomer.

was a reasonable prospect of maintaining, ready to be shipped abroad in the shortest possible time. The militia must be reshaped to fill the deficiency of the reserve. The yeomanry and volunteers must be in some way reorganized so that they should be better prepared for war if required, though he was clear in his mind that they would need a considerable spell of formation training—he thought six months, an underestimate, though in 1914 the first division considered to be ready reached France just within that time. All this would have to be done economically because economy was in the air. In fact, Haldane's hardest battles were fought against his colleagues, Winston Churchill, Lloyd George, and Lewis Harcourt, who strove to cut his estimates. Economy involved ruthless disbandments.

He found he could make available enough troops to fix the strength of an expeditionary force at six divisions, within three corps commands. With a certain number of regiments it was possible to increase their strength, and later their reserves, by disbanding the third battalions which some possessed. Once or twice Haldane aimed too high, as when he held out his shears over the 3rd Coldstream Guards, and the well-informed were highly amused when he had to abandon his prey. By careful planning the time needed for mobilization and the movement to the theatre of war was cut down to an extent not before considered possible.[1] The speedy formation of a seventh division from troops in relatively near stations and surplus at home, including battalions of the Brigade of Guards, was also envisaged. It may be added that Haldane steadfastly opposed the conscription campaign led by Lord Roberts. His motive was practical politics rather than theory: indeed he afterwards drafted a conscription bill.

The militia was turned into the special reserve to provide drafts for the British expeditionary force. The force had to be radically altered in its functions and made fully liable for active service. It has in fact been argued that, though the special reserve units retained the regimental titles borne by the militia, in practice the

---

[1] The move of the 1st battalion the Gordon Highlanders in 1914 may be given because, at Crownhill, Plymouth, it was stationed 400 miles as the crow flies from the depot. It received the mobilization order at 5.20 p.m. on 4 August. On the 6th 235 reservists arrived from Aberdeen, next day 296 more. The battalion reached Boulogne on 14 August and billeted in the zone of concentration, near Avesnes, on the 15th. It fought in the battle of Mons on the 23rd.

old militia, proving unco-operative, was abolished and the special reserve built on its ruins. At all events this asset was secured.

The creation of the territorial force, later known as the territorial army, was the most spectacular of the reforms. The material was the yeomanry and the volunteers, but some minor elements, cadet corps and rifle clubs, played a small part. It consisted of fourteen mounted brigades and fourteen infantry divisions, on the same basis as those of the regular army. Its local administration Haldane confided to bodies known as 'County Associations'—a look back to Oliver Cromwell. One useful result was that it did something to placate the landed magnates who had been offended by the treatment of the militia. Funds did not stretch to the fine new field artillery which the regular army had received or was receiving. The scheme itself was in a critical situation; 'L. G., Winston, and Lulu Harcourt challenged the whole thing as an extravagance.' So as good a job as possible had to be made with the field artillery used in the South African war, improvising a check to the recoil and thus, though not entitling the weapon to be called a quick-firer, at least somewhat increasing its rapidity of fire. It was the king who showed most open disquietude about this artillery. Needless to say, someone had discussed it with him, but he had found a weak point. His comments on major questions as well as on detail were shrewd. Haig wrote hopefully about the reconditioned guns in March 1908, when the king took the opposite view—and the king proved right.

The relations between Edward VII and Haldane were remarkable. Rarely can they have been as close between the monarch and any minister except the prime minister of the day, and it was in the setting up of the territorial force most of all that Haldane required royal support. Claims having been made for some men who ought not to rank as parents of the scheme, they can be tested by his own evidence; if any witness on this point is reliable, he surely must be. He names two civilians and three officers: himself, Sir William Nicholson, Spencer Ewart (director of military operations), Douglas Haig (director of military training), and Sir Charles Harris (head of the financial department of the War Office). The adjutant-general, Sir Charles Douglas, is not included, but he had the formidable task of putting the plans into action. It is naturally less easy to name the principal backers, but perhaps not invidious to mention five here also, putting the king first. Two prime ministers, Campbell-Bannerman

and Asquith, gave their support when Haldane was under fire
simultaneously from colleagues, Liberal back-benchers, and Lord
Midleton; Lord Crewe piloted the Territorial and Reserve Forces
Bill through the House of Lords with skill and tact; from his seclu-
ded tower of anonymity Lord Esher was always ready to help. In
June 1909 the king presented colours to 108 territorial battalions
at Windsor.

It was a curious experience [Haldane writes] to stand beside the King
and watch the outcome of three years of strenuous days and nights of
missionary enterprise; and of long hours of work in the War Office and in
Parliament. I have had splendid backing and from no one more than from
the King.

Haig had a first-rate General Staff mind [he recorded later]. When he
arrived in London [from India] he grasped the situation completely and
gave invaluable guidance in the fashioning of both the Regular first line
and the Territorial second line.

Next month Haldane accompanied the king to Knowsley and
Worsley Park, for the presentation of colours to the West and East
Lancashire Divisions. On 6 May 1910 King Edward died. Haldane's
tribute deserves to be remembered:

The relation between my king and myself was not a usual one as
between minister and sovereign and something personal is snapped. He
was one of the few outside the professional soldiers who understood
what I was trying to do for his army, and without his constant support
and advice I could not have done what I have done.

Little space can be found for detail, but another quick look at
the artillery may serve as an example of the ingenuity with which
gaps were filled and financial chasms were bridged. Haldane had to
provide bigger ammunition columns because the new guns would
expend far more shell than those of the South African war. As almost
always, he had to make a saving somewhere to set against increased
expenditure. He found that he could afford to reduce the number of
field artillery batteries and save both money and trained men for
his purpose. He also made use of the personnel of unnecessary
garrison artillery militia to help fill the ammunition columns on the
outbreak of war. Over this measure he fought a spirited duel with
Midleton, the one in the Commons, the other in the Lords.

The expeditionary force, the special reserve, and the territorial
force were the main features of the reforms, but far from the only

ones. The general staff system was introduced throughout the army as a whole, whereas it had so far existed only within the War Office. Another simple but useful measure was that of co-ordinating home and colonial forces. Haig, soon after having been brought back from India by Haldane, drew up in April 1907 for the 'Colonial Premiers'—the prime ministers of what have become the self-governing commonwealth states of European origin—a memorandum pointing out the need for uniformity between the British army and their forces in organization, tactics, administration, and equipment. The prime ministers agreed unanimously. As already indicated, a proposal to establish a general staff for the whole empire, which they at first sight seemed to favour, went no further, but what had been done was of substantial, if secondary, importance. The committee of railway managers was formed to control the rail traffic of mobilization, and proved highly successful when its labours were put to the test.

The existing reserve of officers would obviously prove insufficient in war. An interesting experiment was carried out, the creation of officers' training corps, a senior in the universities, a junior in public schools. It is fair to say that the results were valuable without being far-reaching. The training received, especially that of the public schoolboys, carried possible candidates for commissions only a short way, but was not wasted.

A 'War Book' was compiled and kept up to date. In it was laid down every action to be taken on mobilization by every ministry and branch. Here the committee of imperial defence functioned as had been intended when it was formed. Another literary effort was equally important. In 1902 Colonel G. R. Henderson, a celebrated writer and teacher, whose life of Stonewall Jackson is still read in Britain and the United States, had brought out a textbook entitled *Combined Training*. In 1905 this became Part I of *Field Service Regulations*. It was superseded in 1909 by *Field Service Regulations* Part I (Operations), and Part II (Organization and Administration). Haldane's role was significant in a matter in which secretaries of state are not commonly active movers. Haig, his protégé, was much to the fore in this business and compiled Part II himself. The adjutant-general and quartermaster-general, both his seniors by a good deal, resented what they considered his dictation, and his fund of tact was not big enough to placate them. Haldane saw to it that he got a free hand.

Staff training became more practical. A cavalryman, Hubert Gough—who celebrated his ninetieth birthday on 12 August 1960, the day these words were written—delighting in foxhunting, pig-sticking, and steeplechasing, but gifted, energetic, and devoted to his profession, has described the change he witnessed on returning after the South African war as an instructor to the staff college, which he had earlier attended as a student. Rawlinson was now commandant, supported by Capper, Haking, and Du Cane.

Capper revolutionized the teaching of staff duties. He never discussed the details of the duties of a junior staff officer in peace at Aldershot, which had been my sole study in this subject. . . . On the contrary, he went thoroughly into the plans, orders, and arrangements which might be required for the success of some definite operations in war.

Towards a British Expeditionary Force

Severer critics, notably Major-General J. F. C. Fuller, have pointed out that, despite study of the Russo-Japanese war, virtually no one grasped the significance of an essential factor: the devastating effect of small-arms fire from entrenchments, which was to bring the defensive into the ascendant. They have also shown that few realized the power of musketry in defence even when entrenchment was at its most primitive or there had been time for none, and that the possibilities of machine-guns were underrated. These errors were to be found on the continent also. We may also argue that the staff college lived too closely up to its name. It was not in a true sense a 'school of war', and there was none.

For the army at large training culminated in interdivisional exercises and army manœuvres. They, as well as earlier basic training, at least showed that Boer musketry had not been forgotten. *Combined* fire and movement was the ideal inculcated for attack. A senior commander of the next war, Charles Monro, advocated it so persistently that it became known as the 'Monro doctrine'. The essence of this theory was that in attack the whole force, and even a single battalion, would be unable to advance simultaneously in face of a defence capable of bringing to bear on it effective rifle and machine-gun fire and would suffer crippling loss if it tried to; the only means of keeping down the weight of this fire would be to hold the defence under fire while the movement was taking place; so ground must be gained by rushes carried out by part of the battalion, covered by the fire of the remainder and of the artillery. The latter would normally divide its fire, engaging the hostile infantry and the covering artillery simultaneously—this form of preparation being known as 'counter-battery fire'.

The final assault would be made by all troops who had by these means been brought into sufficiently close contact with the enemy, but supports and reserves were still kept in hand. The object became the building-up of a heavy line roughly 200 yards short of the hostile front. If this line could first beat down resistance by sheer fire-power it would postpone its advance until it had done so. If that were not completely achieved but the prospects of a charge looked good, the signal would be given by whistles and by hand, and the whole line would dash forward.

Such was the method of the attacks of the early phase of open warfare up to the winter of 1914. It did not differ essentially from that of the Germans and was more prudent than that practised by the French at the outset. It was often found over-optimistic, though with superior numbers—for instance, in the German attacks at Le Cateau—it was effective. The strength of the defensive actually began to appear before trench warfare started. From the first it was found that insufficient account had been taken of the power of the machine-gun firing in enfilade. However, few troops can ever have been better capable of looking after themselves on the defensive than the original B.E.F.

The training of all arms in concealment from view reached a high standard. Night operations were practised. British doctrine was more enlightened here than German. In the pursuit from Mons some German detachments gained successes under cover of darkness, but, fortunately for the British, they were few and small. As darkness gathered over the battlefield of Mons, the British were astonished to hear German bugles sounding the cease-fire all along the front and then to see a tracery of flames, indicating that supper was being cooked.

In the artillery practice camps which played a notable role in the training the counter-battery fire was often 'indirect'. That is, it was ranged by a forward-observing-officer with a telephone because the gun detachments, serving their pieces from pits or from behind epaulements, for the sake of protection and concealment, could not see their targets. However, when the war came the F.O.O. did not play a great part until the autumn of 1914. On the strategic side manœuvres were valuable in remedying the handicap which lack of experience in handling large bodies of troops imposed on senior commanders. Manœuvres did not go far enough to remove the handicap altogether.

The achievement was highly creditable. In most respects, and especially in that of the British expeditionary force, Britain went to war in 1914 better prepared than for earlier continental wars or indeed for any of her wars.

The debit side of the ledger was, however, closely filled, and it is fair to add that Haldane's writings are not the place where the items are to be found. Deficiencies in artillery have been mentioned. Genuine heavy artillery scarcely existed and what is now called 'medium' artillery, a distinction not then used, was inadequate. The guns of the territorial field artillery remained bad guns, even though renovated. The supply of reserve ammunition was woefully small, even taking into account the surprises which the war was to bring. The layman hearing of such a state of affairs attributes it wholly to parsimony in manufacture; more intimate knowledge is required to realize that the authorities are more likely to shy off their task owing to the cost and difficulty of storage. Even provision for the expansion of the artillery and ammunition supply was trifling. Though telephone apparatus was issued, it was insufficient, and was in some cases supplemented by artillery officers from their own pockets.

There was no battalion mortar for close support; no practical hand grenade for close fighting. A third machine-gun for infantry battalions was refused. The lack of motor ambulance wagons led to the abandonment of many British wounded during the retreat from Mons. In some cases even when equipment had been authorized and issued it did not reach all the hands for which it was intended. Thus two of the six divisions of the B.E.F. went to war without the mobile kitchens known as 'cookers', which could cook food on the march, with the consequence that the process could not be begun until the march was over. All these and other shortages were due to lack of money. Haldane sometimes pleaded with those who pointed out their gravity not to press him too hard. He would speak of the difficulties he had to overcome in inducing his colleagues to agree to the expenditure already sanctioned and the risk of souring them by asking for more. This was undeniable, but a deficiency such as that in ambulance vehicles, which had already been well tried and were as reliable as any car of those days, was inexcusable.[1]

Another weakness of the expeditionary force could not have been remedied by Haldane or the adjutant-general unless they had been able to stimulate recruiting by higher pay. The contrast between infantry battalions on home service and abroad has been described. Now the expeditionary force was of course made up of the former. In consequence, the proportion of reservists was high. Their training had been so sound that they had seldom grown rusty and did not represent a weakness from that point of view. From another they did in the early stage, when the force had to endure gruelling marches in the retreat and heavy rearguard duties when halted. A considerable proportion of the reservists were not fit enough for the test, into which they were pitchforked without a second hardening. It was they who formed the bulk of the stragglers, and these were numerous. This criticism may seem redundant because it applies to a period of from two to three weeks at the beginning of a war lasting four and a quarter years. It is none the less worth making because the B.E.F might have been annihilated; indeed possibly would have been but for the changes in direction of the German pursuit.

Yet the B.E.F. was a fine force. One accessory of training, the small-arms cartridge, cheap in a small army, had never been stinted, and off the range soldiers had spent much time simply working their bolts. Reservists and young soldiers alike could shoot steadily and accurately at a relatively slow rate for long periods, or in emergency fire what they called their 'mad minute'. A good man fired eighteen rounds in the period; supreme experts, often non-commissioned officers, claimed so many that one hesitates to set down the figures for fear of perpetuating a legend. The blast of fire produced was paralysing. No such rapid fire, due to the skill of a man's hands without the aid of automatic devices, has since been witnessed outside schools of musketry. It never will be, because human skill in producing speed has by now been completely replaced by these devices in well-equipped armies. It was without a parallel in the contemporary continental armies. The composition and training of the

[1] The three field ambulances of the 36th (Ulster) Division, formed very early in the war as one of Kitchener's 'new army' divisions, were provided with exceptionally good motor ambulance cars by the subscriptions of the people of Ulster, and these units were the first in the division to be equipped.

B.E.F. had throughout been distinguished by forethought and the result was remarkably good in view of the narrow resources of the army.

The cavalry, artillery, engineers, and services were all good horse-masters and outshone both allies and foes in keeping their animals fit. The cavalry in the retreat from Mons were to dismount and lead their horses over long distances. Whenever practicable they unsaddled at halts. The French cavalry corps which supported the British loyally in that emergency seldom did either, with the consequence that large numbers of horses were foundered and the majority suffered from sore backs. Some regiments of the enter-prising German cavalry divisions rode their horses into the ground.

Officers in Undress

One of the effects of the South African war had been an increase in the attention officers were called on to pay to professional duties, whether in staff appointments, with their units, as students at the staff college and specialist teaching centres such as the school of musketry, or even reading for examinations. Yet leave, especially for sporting occasions, remained liberal and for those with what would appear to us trifling bank balances life could not have been more pleasant. By no means all possessed such balances and many had overdrafts. Few infantry officers and none in the cavalry could live on their pay, though in some infantry line regiments a parental allowance of as little as £150 or even £100 just sufficed. In India the situation was different because prices were lower. Yet Creagh tells us he had seen junior officers in India 'almost in a state of starvation' and points out that officers of the Indian army had to engage language tutors. The fact remains that, whereas in England few infantry officers could play polo, in India many did. The out-standing feat of infantrymen, not yet forgotten, is that of the Durham Light Infantry, shortly before the South African war. Mounted on relatively cheap ponies, but wonderfully trained and coached in tactics by Beauvoir de Lisle—a corps commander of the first world war—this team beat all the best, British cavalry or Indian, for three seasons.

In the Edwardian period England was represented chiefly by cavalry officers in international polo, which meant in effect conflict with the Americans, becoming superbly efficient and possessing the best ponies in the world. The English team of 1914 which brought back, for the last time and on the eve of the war, the Westchester Cup was made up of cavalrymen: Major Barrett and Captains Tomkinson, Cheape, and Lockett. There was however, another side to pride in success in regimental polo. An officer, himself a keen player, attached for duty to one of the famous polo regiments, records that he found something rather disagreeable in the means lavished on the team and in its privileges, which were largely at the expense of the rest of the mess, and put them at a disadvantage in the enjoyment of sport and relaxation.

Foxhunting, steeplechasing, shooting, fishing, sailing, and in India pigsticking were the other most favoured diversions, and some of these could be enjoyed by men with, to our eyes, infinitesimally small incomes. On the other hand, there were young officers like Archibald Wavell and Bernard Montgomery whose main sporting interest lay in hockey, and Basil Maclear, the great Rugby three-quarter.

One subject which cannot well be omitted is that of ragging. All young male communities go in for it on occasion and it is unpleasant only when it gets out of hand. Cases where it did became known to the public and were not made to appear any prettier in the telling. Early in 1906 one in which the Scots Guards were concerned came to light, and the popular press treated it all the more sensationally because a battalion of the Guards was in question. Next year there was another case. King Edward was all against what he called washing dirty linen in public. Haldane favoured full publicity, and most people today will hold that he was right. These incidents were not unimportant because they created a good deal of prejudice against the army and especially against officers of what were considered to be aristocratic regiments, but in fact it was rare for them to take a serious form.

The austerely democratic found the aristocratic element too large. Some went so far as to say that the army was 'run by the aristocracy'. It is true that the aristocratic element was large in the Household Brigade and in a number of cavalry regiments. (This had one advantage in that, whereas promotion was often unduly slow, heirs usually sent in their papers on succeeding their fathers, above all when they inherited considerable landed estates.) If, however, any particular type can be said to have 'run the army' it was upper-middle-class officers who called each other by their Christian names. These were less bandied about then than now and implied close links. 'Johnny' (Ian Hamilton), 'Archie' (Murray), and 'Henry' (Wilson) were men who knew each other's minds and who counted in the development of the army. The aristocracy played no such part in the British army as it did in the German.

The British officer's appearance in plain clothes was scrutinized almost as carefully as when he was wearing uniform, and in his days as a subaltern he might be reproved either for looking too flashy or for turning out too casually. Before the South African war officers coming up on a visit to London wore top hats and tail coats. Those whose people lived in London might travel in simpler garb, but they would take a hansom at the station, drive home, and change before setting out for their clubs or elsewhere. It is the writer's impression that this rule had been greatly relaxed before 1914, and he cannot have created out of his imagination the memory of seeing an officer, who had been riding later than usual in the park, arriving on foot for luncheon at a club, wearing breeches and top boots. Regimental ties were worn, though still frowned on here and there and not approaching the popularity which was to follow the first world war: they had scarcely been noticed before the Edwardian era, but were in fact then half a century old.[1]

Army officers probably interested themselves in the arts and letters less than the average of their social orders and education. One notable exception was painting, especially water-colour because the appliances were more portable than those of oil painting. This is an old and honourable tradition, happily unbroken today. A great deal of what we know of campaigns and battles, even of landscapes, in distant and inaccessible lands comes to us from the artistry of officers who were often excellent draughtsmen and delightful colourists.

'A Shillin' a Day'

The rank-and-file had improved in health. The majority of the recruits, though by no means all, were not of the best physique and their education was on average wretched. Better food and perhaps

[1] Mr. G. J. Lewin, director of a firm closely associated with regimental and club colours, was kind enough to investigate this historical by-path seriously. By questioning long-established weavers he traced such neckties—or rather the scarves and cravats of the time—for the R.A. and H.A.C. to approximately 1850.

most of all more rational physical training, into which Swedish theory now entered, built them up to a litheness unattained by their fathers, who had been stiff in posture and gait. Some county regiments had always recruited fine men off the land. Education was hammered into them by not very highly certificated schoolmasters, who often got astonishingly good results. Drunkenness had declined, but drink was still a curse of the army, naturally prominent in units recruited in the spirit-drinking towns of Scotland and Ireland: three days' pay would buy a bottle of whisky. Games were encouraged. Cricket especially reached a high standard, and most regiments included a couple of veteran rank-and-file stock bowlers, who could stay on for hours and remain dangerous. Association football (and rugby in Welsh regiments) flourished. Hockey, always popular with officers, was extending its appeal. 'Other ranks' walked out in uniform still. The sight of a guardsman in scarlet escorting a young nurse while she wheeled her charge in a perambulator in Hyde Park was impressive, and the nurse was clearly a proud young woman.

The highly complex subjects of pay and allowances may be reduced to a few examples from a single year.[1] Let us base them on rock bottom, the private soldier and second-lieutenant of the infantry. Kipling characterized the pay of the former as

> Shillin' a day,
> Bloomin' good pay—
> Lucky to touch it, a shillin' a day!

The latter, engaged in the restoration of law and order, was on an historic occasion described by an Irish patriot as 'a five-and-thruppenny assassin'. The Royal Engineer sapper started with 1s. 1¼d. and the Royal Artillery gunner with 1s. 4d., the latter reaching 2s. as a sergeant. Officers of the two learned arms started level at 6s. 10d., but as lieutenant-colonel the gunner went ahead, with £1. 3s. to the engineer's 18s. The most important allowances were: one ration for each soldier on the effective strength at home and abroad, a half ration for each soldier's wife on the married establishment, a quarter for each child over the age of fourteen. The separation allowance to a wife with quarters or lodging allowance amounted to 4d., and without to from 1s. 4d. to 2s. 3d. Though the

---

[1] *Royal Warrant for the Pay, &c., of the Army,* 1907; *Regulations for the Allowances of the Army,* 1907.

officer did not draw rations at home, he did when abroad. In certain circumstances when seconded he drew a messing allowance. The most generous aid of this kind was not individual but an issue to the mess, based on the size of the depot, and earmarked for the younger officers.

Reviewing these details of the life of officers and men—some of which have gone in mainly because they are likely to be novel to most readers of today—a fear arises that they may be thought too idyllic. The intention has been to bring out the advances made in fitness for war by all ranks, to describe the officers' background, and sketch the general welfare of non-commissioned officers and men. In neither the first nor third was the improvement as big as it might have been, but it was striking in both. To ridicule the efforts and deny the substantial success is proof of ignorance, unfairness, or both. Probably the efficiency of the army as a whole increased to a greater extent than the comfort and happiness of the rank-and-file; if so, it was because the smallest demands made for this purpose were regarded as financially profligate. A good deal of the money that was raised came from profits from tattoos, gate money for games, and the generosity of officers.

Punishment was still altogether too severe, at its severest verging on the brutal in units containing a large element intractable in character. It was difficult for the most enthusiastic commanding officer or adjutant to make much progress in humanizing the boorish because accommodation was still inadequate. There remained waste of time by doing what was needless, doing what was required without the appliances which were a commonplace in civil life, or doing nothing.

Yet even while we contemplate the cavalry officer applying every few days for hunting leave or Thomas Atkins twiddling his thumbs, we should bear in mind a factor often forgotten by critics. On home service and quite often when stationed abroad, soldiers are among those who also serve though they only stand and wait. Their role is to be prepared for emergencies. They have no other professional occupation; any other activity must be some sort of diversion. Now troops cannot be trained all the time. That would lead only to staleness, boredom, and resentment, however ingeniously the programme were tricked out with variety. A proportion of wasted, or anyhow of unorganized, time is inevitable. It is a far less serious matter than training on the wrong lines in accordance with a faulty doctrine. In the profession of arms there are no time limits for work. Troops are called upon to perform night duties following straight upon day duties. Heavy and prolonged exertion is demanded of them, especially on manœuvres, and they could not be prepared for the rigours of active service without it. We have been considering here mainly those in training in the home country, who know that their next foreign station may involve an austere and laborious existence, perhaps in a trying climate.

The compensations are an allowance of leave greatly in excess of the holidays of civil life, breaks when in barracks or in camp, ample opportunities for sport and games. Ideally, leisure should be spent to the greatest possible advantage, but soldiers may not welcome dictation in this field any more than other men. They can be encouraged to use their leisure sanely, and a good proportion of them will respond to such efforts. A streak of wildness among the best-disciplined units may often be regarded as a positive advantage and asset when boldness and a defiant spirit are most needed.

Conclusion

Much credit has been given and is due to Haldane for the transformation of the army carried out while he was at the War Office, which was virtually complete when he left in 1912. It was indeed a remarkable achievement, most of the shortcomings of which were due to the sentiments of the cabinet, the parliament, and the political party to which he belonged. The whole scheme, or succession of linked schemes, is a mingling of the maximum simplicity, involving the least possible disturbance, when simple measures were practicable, and radical improvisation of the most ingenious kind when they were not. Coming to work on material of which he was entirely ignorant, he mastered it so quickly that he was able to form his programme and put it through within an astonishingly short time. His lucid mind rejected inessentials but at the same time realized the possibilities of items which to others seemed unimportant. Haldane wielded a power such as no secretary of state for war can hope for today, and exploited it freely, determinedly, but without rashness, arrogance, or obstinacy.

The process was, however, above all a feat of team-work, outstanding of its kind. The notion which we are sometimes asked to credit, that Haldane bustled and badgered a band of myopic reactionaries into activity, is an absurd perversion of the facts and would have been impossible anyhow. Minister and advisers moved together and in harmony; in a wider sense the army proved itself his collaborator. There is no reason to take these statements on trust from the hand that sets them down. The minister was capable of assessing the value of the advice and the loyalty of the service he received. It was Haldane himself who wrote gaily: 'My generals are like angels.'

15

COUNTRY CHILDHOOD

EDMUND BLUNDEN, C.B.E.

Late Professor of English in the University of Hong Kong

COUNTRY CHILDHOOD

I HEARD a tune an evening or two ago, which made more impression on me than all the other programmes. It was a composition for the pianoforte; I had not happened to hear it for years; and now that it came my way it seemed to transfer me all at once to summer evenings when, in bed upstairs, I listened to enchanting notes from our modest drawing-room. The tune was given us by my father practising, before he went out for a little secretarial duty, officially, at the working men's club in the village of Yalding in Kent; and I wished the music would last for ever.

That was nearly sixty years ago. The resurgence of the music enlivened an old intention. I would recapture even fragments of the tunes which life played in my young hearing through that period.

My sister Lottie, who was always a quick observer, may agree with me that the sunshine was truly golden, the convolvulus bell really white and miraculous sixty years ago. She and I were great companions—we were the eldest children—within the limits of a garden hedge and a school playground. My complaint against her was that she was inclined to fall thinking without telling what she was thinking; she had a round, clear-complexioned, quiet face, and at one time possessed a musical hoop, or rather an imitation garden roller which played tunes. Both of us were deeply affected by the discovery of a dead mouse, whom we enclosed in a tin together with some sort of written epicedium and buried on the east side of a cooking-apple tree. Both, in our room or rooms upstairs, were troubled by a queer terror when it was not yet dark, and set up a united moaning which brought our mother to our aid; but she could discover no reason for this outcry. Neither could we, then. Both watched with intentness the gardener at his mysteries, and persuaded beans of our own to start growing, but could not leave them at peace. Sometimes in the evening our parents would walk up and down the garden path, so neatly edged, followed by ourselves and the tabby cat, who did not object to our joining the procession. We shared feelings of worship and of disapproval for our father, of whose greatness we were quite sure—not only was he the tallest of men, our mother said he was the cleverest—but who menaced our liberty in a very Victorian and dogmatic manner.

The twelfth-century church with its multitude of graves and grave-stones, its strong tower and far-resounding ring of bells, stood only a few steps from our garden gate. It did things to our imagination. I had to have bells of my own, and with Lottie's help I contrived them. She got me at need one of the dress-weights which lived with my mother's reels of thread and collection of buttons and beads; this became the clapper of my mighty bell, that is to say some carefully chosen tin can, lashed to a stick. The stick was fixed across twigs in a tree-top, so that the bell would swing correctly and could be pulled and rung; but what pleased me more was to wake in a night of gale and rain, and hear my bell clanking with odd rhythm though no hand was ringing it, except that of the wind. One such stormy night it was not that beloved tinkling noise I heard. The deep and ominous thumping of drums was in my ears as I started up on my pillow; it went on, and I was sure it came from the churchyard, from opening graves. My father was disturbed by my cry, but he made nothing of this dreadful drumming—indeed he declared he could not hear it—and told me indignantly to go to sleep again.

Naturally the churchyard so near our gate was among the first parts of the parish that we of the schoolhouse explored. It was rather wild in appearance then, the grass and flowers running high in the summer season about the ancient mossy tombs, some of which time had cleft and tilted; there were vast chestnut trees, an immense yew, many shrubs of moody dark-green foliage. The memorials were not all simple. One of them recorded a young soldier, our neighbour once, who had been killed by falling over a khud at a strangely named place in India. Another was the memorial of Georgiana König, who died in the Victorian sixties, and I suppose was a German governess at our old rectory. I took my time looking at the china immortelles and tablets within sphere-shaped glass covers protected with wire on many graves. The sexton, old rosy-cheeked Mr. Longley, presently allowed me to help him chime the treble bell for morning or evening service, which still happened every day, though only one or two ladies attended. And one day for the first time he took me with him up the church tower stairs to the clock-room, to wind the clock—a performance of dignity and unearthly noise. He had to go up a small wooden stairway from the clock room floor to turn the huge key. The world was far, far away. He was the mystery man and I was his audience.

It must have been quite early in my life that a vision or hallucination found me, beyond my explaining. The drumming which I mentioned before might have been the consequence of having stood behind Mr. Longley at the verge of some new grave—my friend Maggie Parham's, for instance—while the grave-digger 'stomped' the earth down upon the coffin. But one evening, lying wide awake although I had been packed off to sleep, I was gazing southward at the window and then at the infinite blue beyond 'The Elms'. Without any particular notion of anything out of the common, I saw there in the glowing sky a range of architecture; not quite

A rose-red city, half as old as time,

for the fabric all looked new, but a series of tall, many-windowed brick buildings. Some years afterwards, on first approaching the extensive buildings of the great school in Sussex to which I had the good luck to go, I was oddly aware that the scene was not quite unknown to me. It had been mine by some mysterious order at our old home.

Still thinking of almost sixty years ago, I will not arrange too methodically what comes to light. Ours was a world of wonder, mixed with dull and common things. The older poets of England speak with some regard of the motes in the sunbeams. Well did I observe that marvel too. Playing with my ball on the stairs of our small house, I could often see the ray of light stream through the keyhole of the front door, and in it such populous throngs of tiny atoms tingling and dancing, bright to the eye but ever free of the catching hand. Icicles, fallen feathers, shed snake-skins, young birds, earwigs hiding in droves under the coil of rope at the end of the clothes-line, robins tapping the pane and many other things were hailed as wonders. A vast storm, one of those which even in England can do plenty of mischief to the farmer's year in one hour, remains in my memory because of a mistake on my mother's part. She was upstairs in the afternoon, putting on her new dress no doubt, and she called out to me to stop throwing stones on the iron roof of the coalshed. But I was not throwing. It was a sudden down-pour of 'hailstones big as hen's eggs' that made the clatter.

So important were the small things in the Edwardian childhood village.

My mother! so well known to me and so mysterious. I had the suspicion that Lottie was much nearer to her, behind the scenes. My portrait of her was: not so tall as my father, especially when he put on his tall hat for Sunday morning service, and usually more benevolent in small allowances, yet well able to deal with our various mutinies. When I was still an infant, I sat on her knees pulling her nose, and was thoroughly alarmed when she suggested that I had loosened it and that it might fall off. One day I was made to wait in her room with her, from a doubt of what wrong I might do elsewhere if left to it, and then it was that a picture of woman's grace was first impressed on me. How lovely she was as she took off her bodice and washed her white shoulders, and stood (not long, poor busy darling) at her mirror! Probably this was in preparation for one of our trips to Maidstone, the great city! which included a famous treat, tea and fancy cakes at a little shop more like a private house, then and to this day called Herbert's. My mother's bene-volence before long aroused our criticism. She would go to the door of our schoolhouse and hear the set speeches of poor rogues with results that even we saw were not to her advantage. Old fuddled creatures would call, offering (for instance) to repair broken china, dishes, saucers, egg-cups which they took round the corner and brought back apparently made whole. For this she and even they seemed to think half a crown a fair payment. She enjoyed the threshold talk, at least, and often quoted gaily one dreary old dodger who announced 'I *reside* at Tonbridge, mum.' His invention for sticking together bits of glass was as bad as the rest. In fact he was a traditional rural knave.

The Misses Lewis, whose semi-detached villa bore some such name as Clovercombe or Sunnyside, had opened a private school. Into that I was propelled. The nature of the instruction, though I must have forgotten parts of it, was not elaborate: the infants read aloud from a large Bible. I could read, and yet I did not avoid trouble, for I remember being stood in a corner. This little school was not so lively as the national one which my mother ruled (I dare say she thought sometimes of a song and dance in *Ruddigore*). There we had blocks of many colours to teach the alphabet, we operated tambourines, and received visits from gigantic beings—the vicar and other managers, as well as an attendance officer, with mutton-chop whiskers, whose name we accepted as Mr. Horrible. In the ceiling of the schoolroom there was an area of distracting interest. It was a sheet of whitewashed canvas under the cupola, and as the draughts passed it swagged out or pulled back. It made life worth living, as did the occasional mouse or butterfly which came in, and, outside, the playground with its sycamore and the seat round its young trunk. There was a great deal of singing at the school, and I think the book which my mother used for us was that compiled by Mrs. Carey Brock. Earnestly we sang, and without aspirates to the last,

> Honey bee, honey bee, why do you hum?
> —I am so happy the summer has come.

The moral lyric was frequent:

> O how brightly shines the sun,
> Other lads are having fun,
> For it is an holy-day;
> Jacky cannot join their play.
> Ill he is, and so instead
> Is compelled to stay in bed.
> Sneezing makes his face quite red,
> Tishoo, *Tishoo*, TISHOO.

This boy had disobeyed orders, gone sliding, fallen into the icy water—and such was his punishment.

Religious instruction at the infant school, though assiduous, left some points doubtful; and in particular I remember that one or two were puzzled about the meaning of 'mercy', which they fancied had something to do with red india-rubber. About us floated the equally strange term 'kindergarten', and we had our share of instruction in the form of pastime, with the abacus, and coloured straws and strings. The reading books in use were not agreeable to me because they were illustrated in a complicated pseudo-Dürer fashion, which did not correspond to anything I could see or fancy in the outside world. Equally, at home the numbers of a periodical called *Punch* baffled me; the drawings of footmen and statesmen did not look like people, nor did they look beautiful. The earliest enjoyment of pictures I can recall came from a brightly tinted Japanese piece of finches on a bough, a grey, gleaming view of Sonning-on-Thames, and a proud, dark sketch of Irving as Hamlet.

When we were droning away in school on a fine morning, it was paradise to hear all round the crowing of cocks and clucking of hens, mooing of cows and cawing of rooks, and many other country voices of content from yard and pasture. But there was also now and then the painful screeching of some unfortunate pig aware of his doom. Great excitements occurred once or twice, to the cry 'Runaway Horse', and after school some were afraid of Noble Diprose's herd of cows going their way along the road, with horns lowered as though they might 'pook' you.

A little girl with the rosiest of cheeks and quick eyes of blue was one of the celebrities at the infant school; she was called Hetty, and already occasioned some adverse criticism ('she's as artful as she's high'). Hetty, I heard Mrs. Cheesman tell my mother, at Mr. Young's shop, held out the coins with which she was to pay for some article with the audacious observation, 'Will you have it now, or wait till you get it?' Yet I believe she eventually became a valued member of the Band of Hope.

Out of school a little party of us, including Alfred and Alice Cheesman from Church Cottages, used to plan and perform important journeys into the Kintons. This was a wide stretch of meadow sloping down to a pretty river called the Beult. In it more than one place was famous. An old hawthorn at the top had roots like chairs, almost polished by sheep rubbing their fleeces against them. Towards the river, a big oak was sometimes accompanied by horse-mushrooms, all seeming of similar bigness. A shallow of the river with a steep little headland over it was The Sands. This green region became my private elysium for some years. Here I came upon things which everyone knows but which, first encountered, changed the world: the glorious yellow flag-flower in the swampy hollow, the rabbits playing and racing by their sandy buries, the sorrel and dewberry and oak-apple (the little boys in those days did not miss celebrating Oak-Apple Day), and of course the minnow and fresh-water mussel and wasp-nest and war-painted dragon-fly. Mostly the children went in a party, and with the air of conspirators. It was an age of daisy-chains, and the buttercup game ('do you like butter?'), and sand-castles, and paddling—sometimes more. A great scandal was brought to light one evening when we had all gone in for a bathe. It would have remained unsuspected (perhaps) but Mrs. Cheesman, putting Alice to bed, discovered that her knickers were back to front. The greatest crimes are detected by such little oversights.

Sometimes I went to the river alone, and one day when the weather was too dull for the others I almost failed to return. My ambition was to trap a minnow or two with my jam-jar, and a deeper part of the stream seemed promising. But I lost my foothold and down I went; it was alarming under the high banks; I snatched at the only possible tuft of reeds and so escaped. The moral was to keep jam-jars for better use, namely sale or exchange. A huckster often wheeled a cart through the village and would give one of his gaudy 'windmills' or a halfpenny for one jar.

But my course did not run smooth. At the town bridge one evening some boys were playing in the twinkling stream and though I could have gone through the shoemaker's garden to join them they told me to keep away. Such was the passion I had for the waterside that I answered by jumping down at once from the parapet. It is quite a height above the stream. The jump landed me in a hateful thicket of stinging-nettles, and the surprised big boys had to drag me out, so thoroughly stung that I was hurried home and put into a hot bath. Mrs. Freeman, the landlady of the Anchor inn, was then one of my school-teachers; long after, she would remind me of the incident, as something of historical importance in our 'town'.

Through my first recollections river and stream flow much and mightily; and even the parish rejoicings upon the accession of King Edward VII have to do with them as I look back. The Medway at Twyford Bridge was the chief scene, in a blaze of sunshine. Among the competitions, the best was this: a greasy pole was projected from the bridge over the pool with a leg of mutton at the far end. There was good sport and a sailor who was home on leave was the easy and amusing winner. What vast buns and mugs of tea there were that afternoon! Every child was given a little volume called *King Edward's Realm*, bound in imitation crimson leather, which I found slow going. The fate of books is strange. Perhaps it would be hard to get a copy of it now though an immense number must have been distributed throughout infant Britain. As for reading, there was *Little Folks*, the *Boy's Own Paper*, *The Children of the New Forest*, *Fighting the Flames*, and plenty besides; but the book appetite grew later.

Lottie and I became aware that new brothers and sisters were part of life's plan. First arrived Gilbert, who quite soon showed an engaging willingness to be forgiven for some originality in behaviour. He was still, I think, in the pinafore stage when (on a Sunday moreover) he absented himself from morning to evening. This was naturally the topic of the day. Stationing myself at the window, I observed the young fellow late in the afternoon scampering past the garden gate with several bad characters, heading for the Kintons without the least sign of coming home. In the manner of the look-out roaring 'There she blows' to a whaler's crew, I sounded the alarm, and presently the truant was overtaken. To my surprise and, I am sorry to say, to my disappointment, no punishment was awarded. In fact he could always get away with it. Not so I, whom even my mother might address as a 'perfect little demon'. Forbidden to go to the Kintons one evening, I watched my father start out that way with his rod and landing-net, and I followed at a safe interval; but so merry was the foolery that evening that when at last the thought of him rose again, there he was returning from his fishing. I slid out for the clap-gate, but in those days he could run; he took me prisoner, and at home gave me a formal beating which he preceded with the traditional expression—I swear to it—'This is going to hurt me more than it hurts you.'

Phyllis, a pretty little girl, rather podgy and very very good, was the next addition to the family circle. When she was quite young an amateur uncle, Mr. Marsh, used to offend her by warbling at her 'Phyllis is my only joy'. She strengthened the feminist faction which I already saw working in our midst. And then there was Lancelot. I believe he has abandoned that idyllic name in his riper age. He disturbed the peace very early by having a fit, and my mother, holding him in deathly stillness, was afraid that all was over. The rest of us shed tears, and I thought I had better get on with my sums until the doctor came. The baby recovered, though one evening while my mother was at the piano he again had some convulsion, and it was a long time before he was as strong as the others. This brings me to the year 1904 or so.

The church then and for years afterwards was probably the greatest thing in the life of young villagers—or the chapel, for those who were shepherded that way. But except for one or two dubious visits I did not count that part of the village. The church with its bell-ringing, organ, and choir, and outside activities was quite a glorious presence. Its morning service was full of dignity, its even-song of cheerfulness. The boys of the grammar school attended in neat short jackets and faultless white collars; even the doctor never missed unless something really frightful kept him away. Apart from solemn and splendid occasions, the church at evening used to fill up in a remarkable way. You supposed that old So-and-So would never come into such a place; but there, as the single bell was ringing 'hurry', there he came, to sit in a side aisle with the rest. Excitement grew as the pews filled, and similarly in the vestry there was eager speculation over the strength of the choir that night. We could muster forty and more, though some might be rather social than musical contributors. The little boys saw with exclamations one and another old-timer come in, and hunt for a cassock and surplice, till with all the host assembled the vicar appeared with beaming countenance and a little joke, then the prayer; thereupon the choir marched up the aisle with lusty tune and all was happy.

Or perhaps not quite all. There were artistic rivalries, it could be discerned, among the choirmen. But I will not rake them up. It was enough to see so many personages joining in so insistently. Mr. Waters, who had had a famous voice once, was now difficult to hear, and sang in gulps, but mostly the singers were audible, and well deserved the vicar's 'Thank you for a nice service' afterwards. The main danger in the musical part of the service was the tendency of the blower to sleep during the sermon and not wake when needed, but usually his snores gave my father warning. Some of the boys listened to the sermon, and I did, but I had a little practice with the golden letter and other curious matters included in the prayer book when it got tiresome. The choir went to Linton once to sing in that church, and the vicar, whose name was Leveson-Gower, feasted us in his study afterwards. He slung out buns to the small boys all seated on the carpet; every boy took the catch, and he said 'Cricket-ers to a man.' How we liked him for that! Actually our cricket team was rather mixed, but we played an annual game against the public schoolboys of the village. It depended mainly for us on Fred Latter, who had made about sixty runs when I came last in, for my first innings in a match. The bowlers treated me kindly and Fred had his century before my stumps were knocked down. He was a youth of great promise, athletic and personal; some time later he died of consumption, which was not an uncommon tragedy in the place. His bright face (and when I see pictures of Keats I think of him) will not yet be utterly forgotten in the village.

The practical rewards of being a choirboy were not many, but the excursion to the seaside was looked for with huge delight. We went to the station in chilly early morning by brake, and each boy had ninepence allowed for his luxury at Hastings or Margate or some other place of piers and esplanades, besides tea at some melancholy hotel. The difficulty I found was to keep something out of my ninepence for buying a souvenir for my mother. On the whole, she did not complain on our return if I referred to my wish to have bought one. The family went one or two summers to the seaside, where I found an axiom: Marine Parade does not ordinarily command a view of the sea. The food on these holidays was worse than at home, and the curtains and quilts grubbier, and though I watched many gentlemen holding out lines over jetty and rock I seldom saw a catch. My mother's anxiety over the landladies' cutlery and furniture made an undersong which has survived that of the waves.

No, one was best off in the village, for all the tasks (fetching the milk, lessons, home-work, choir practice, taking notes to the vicar and the curate, polishing the silver, putting out the choir music). I welcomed the winter because my friends became exceedingly sociable. Alf Cheesman would persuade me to stay the night though it was only a moment's walk home, and his father was wonderfully good at dominoes, halma, ludo, snakes-and-ladders. His mother's cake and cocoa were beyond all praise. That admirable woman was able too to make us a cricket ball out of rags which had quite a pace off the pitch (till smitten over Captain Reid's high wall). In that home the reading was *Pearson's Weekly*, *Answers*, *Tit-Bits*, and the *Daily Chronicle*, with of course the *Kent Messenger* and 'Old Moore'. Another house where I have passed hours of lamp-lit bliss was that of Mr. Zachariah Cozens, gardener. He was a choirman and a wit; his boys were great at a hook-it board; and Mrs. Cozens too could make such a cake as modern dreams cannot guess at. It did not occur to me then that 'Kent and Christendom' was one of the parts of Europe in which an old civilization of skill and energy was most fruitful; where the 'peasant' had long ago become the yeoman.

But for some years the house which lured me most was that at Cheveney where Will and George Baldock lived. It was the dwelling attached to a water-mill which had lately been converted into an electrical power-house, as well as a village institute where concerts and flower-shows were given. This may sound very commonplace, but the scene all round the house was wonderfully free and unspoiled. The river Beult came deep and slow, with borders of willow and a kind of bamboo one side and meadow and maybush the other, to the mill-dam. There one stream was sent through a tunnel to the big mill-wheel, and plunged into a dark shade whitened with its splashing, foaming life. The other stream, the real river, went through a tall floodgate over a weir into a pool which could not be seen from any road, but lay deep and round and broad with a thick copse and oak-trees sheltering its banks. Mill-tail and main stream joined after a short travel and between them formed an island of wilderness where thistles and tansies and ox-eye daisies flourished without correction. There was room for our play with bat and ball, but it was the waterside which we haunted most, and though the bullfinch and the dove often made music there it was the sound of the falling and the rippling waters which we chiefly heard.

About the pool itself fear and mystery dwelt; we had ideas of the tremendous depth of the abyss below the weir, and even Mr. Baldock, who looked after the floodgates and the penstocks, spoke of that on a winter's night with a tone of awe. Besides, one day two well-known youths were drowned as they swam there. We fished in this pool and stared at the shoals of bream and roach and the occasional pike like an alligator who lay on the top in the summer sun. But we preferred to be down stream, among the tiny pebbly inlets and clay channels and where the forget-me-not crowded the dewy shore. The water was pure and we drank it often. We caught stone-fishes (I wonder what these brilliant little people really were— I have not seen them for years), gudgeon with such violet colours when just taken, minnows, and sometimes a dace or roach. The names of other fishes were often in our talk, as rudd, tench, perch (there was a perch, that striped fellow flashing into the weed-bed), chub, and even salmon-trout, legendary monsters. Will Baldock seemed to know all that could be known of these watery personages, as indeed he appeared never in difficulties about our equipment, from 'indian-grass' hooks to spare top-joints for the rods. But his talk altogether was good, and our friendship was eternal.

There was and is a comfortable house over the road from Cheveney mill, and one day Will informed me that a countess was coming to live in it. I had not seen any countesses, and so I kept a good look out for this one. Presently I saw her, and was not disappointed. My Aunt Maude, who now and then visited us, was hitherto my example of the well-dressed, elegant woman, but I meanly transferred my vote to this vision from Riverside—the details of her hat and costume I do not remember, but the lightness of her step in those tiny shoes, the softness of the colours of her clothes, the delicate glance and smile with which she noticed our salute, are still in my mind. I think of her sometimes when I am trying to see Katherine Mansfield as she looked in the year 1920.

How richly dressed was my mother's old companion (as it were, sister, for they had had one home together), who had become Frau Haas! There she was on a visit from far-away Kassel, taking off her marvellous veil, and at once asking me how I was behaving nowadays. When she sent us a great Christmas cake from Germany it was declared by my mother to be far too rich, but I was ready to hold the heresy that such cakes ought to be, and so were we all; Aunt 'Lyd' was distinctly popular. My mother was jealous, that was what it was. Her own cakes were certainly good, but had a moral tendency—plain living and high thinking.

Her friend Miss Kett from Hunton called on summer evenings for talk and music. They played and sang devotedly. The songs were selected by Miss Kett, and probably the words were mostly by Fred E. Weatherley. 'The Children's Home' I think moved us most, and there was one of a romantic turn, 'Come, Cara Mia' or thereabouts, in which I thought I might assist; but, Miss Kett pointed out, it was not a duet. Mr. Kett, the Hunton schoolmaster, was a grand personality, and my mother, who was always prowling about genealogical trees in enchantment, was none the worse pleased with him for being descended from Kett the Tanner. Herself she might be of the line of Wat Tyler, but she had some other notions on the ancestral question which, though sparkling with honour, might not accord with that.

But let me go on with my musical recollections, for the village and our home were productive of these. About the new organ. The old one, made by Walker, had its peculiarities, and the day came when its doom was pronounced. In its place a new one, of which my father made the specification, was provided by subscription. It was to be blown by hydraulic pressure, and the laying of the tubes required the digging up of the floor of the church—a most attractive unearthing of bones and skulls. The digging was the more extensive because the new organ had a 'detached console', and the pulpit changed sides to give it room. At last the builders had done their job, the pavements were replaced, and the organ was opened with due magnificence. The music was played partly by the organist of Tonbridge School, the sermon on 'Church Music' (and I have seldom heard a better) was preached by the vicar's brother. For some time afterwards my father gave displays on this organ after evening service and the congregation was willing to hear all he would offer. It would not have been well in those days to suggest in our village that he was not the finest organist in existence, or that the organ was not equally fine. For my part, though it had a handsome supply of combination stops and other improvements (indeed, keys instead of the old pull-out stops), my readings in his *Musical Times* and *Organist and Choirmaster* made me faintly sceptical. I thought a few more manuals and 64-foot stops would have been reasonable, and drew up my own specifications, which amused the tuner when next I helped him. That was one of my sources of income—my fee, I fancy, was eightpence a visit.

The private concerts associated with Miss Kett's tall form and fair hair were much surpassed by public performances. One of those, given in the boys' school under the oil lamps, was a winner. I suppose that in a spirit of universal brotherhood all the choirmen were invited to appear in the programme, 'one by one'. A good many did. Even Mr. Waters stumped on to the platform, and he was to sing 'Three Cheers for the Red, White and Blue'. Every little while, phrases of it came forth loud and bold from his good old face, but there were omissions. Bill Longley came forward, dressed in a kind of ex-Khartoum uniform, to deliver 'Be British was the Cry, as the Ship went down'. Albert Cheeseman (his branch of the Cheesemans held to that spelling of the name) had signed on to sing 'Alice, where art thou?' and the till-ready was played while he looked at his music, but there was a technical hitch. He sounded notes, but was not satisfied. He walked to the piano protesting, 'I can't pitch her, Charlie.' 'Well, you start and I'll come in.' After a bit he started, and very wistfully he sang. He followed with 'The old rustic bridge by the mill', increasing the popular sadness.

These and some part-songs and glees ('We all have a very bad cold') made up the high-brow part of the entertainment, but something else was provided. Taking a seat near the school door, I was impressed by a sudden burst of giggling from the decidedly respectable housemaids in the next seats. They were being signalled at from the glooms of the porch by an illuminated figure with a battered straw hat and a cane, whom I recognized as Mr. Thredgold. In ordinary life he conducted (it was a recent development) a fish-and-chips business somewhere behind Mr. Tippen the watchmaker's. This evening he was the comedian. I should have thought him the success of the evening with his check trousers and his red nose, in such numbers as 'As soon as I looked at my seaweed' and 'You would think that I was her old man', but in spite of all the applause and my own approval I found later that he had really been the blot. Why this was correct opinion I could not quite catch, but it was official that Mr. Thredgold was not recommended for future concerts.

The boys' school saw many village functions in those days. Occasionally a conjurer was allowed to give a show after lessons, admission one penny, and as if that was not cheap enough he distributed toys afterwards. As for lessons, they were endured and even liked, but not the poetry part; my father relied on such works as H. W. Longfellow's 'Building of the Ship'. I regret to say that one afternoon when something like that was being droned out a boy next to me tried to alleviate the boredom of his neighbours by showing his nakedness. In the playground there was plenty of 'driving horses' still, and 'Buck, buck, how many fingers do I hold up?' (frowned upon), nip-cat, and 'Touch-you-last'. Some boys were almost like farm products to the rest of us, already working part-time with their fathers on the land.

I was not very sure of my hold on my brother Gilbert. Now and then he would obligingly make one of some expeditionary force, but he was provokingly apt to be somewhere else. He was an explorer by himself, and was first to interview Miss Cahill's parrot, which he described as a green chicken. He already chose the life of the village as his real school, and one day I passed him outside Mr. Hards's shop, with its loaves and buns, and Mr. Gabriel Hards in his bowler hat, having a sparring match with a lad of giant size. 'A comical young devil', the boys began to call him, by 'comical' meaning odd and daring. At all events he got to know things which I could not manage, and if a 'mad dog' appeared or a cuckoo laid in a chaffinch's nest he would have the full story at once. Lottie at the girls' school was also receding from my command. She learned other songs ('Catch the sunshine'), and hop-scotch, and cookery; but she still played cricket if I had nobody else. She borrowed books at the parish room, served out by Miss Warde from the old rectory, a lady of invincible breeding and faultless sympathy with young people. I have not seen a copy of *The Star of the House of David* lately.

Lottie's kind of reading, though I could manage it, was not mine; it was usually fiction conducive of the domestic virtues. At the club, my father discovered a number of volumes which to me were very heaven. The author was Jules Verne. I was quite convinced that he told the truth, and in *The Mysterious Island* (with an organ on a submarine) I lived in perfect joy and felicity. Perhaps the best moment of all in that new, but inevitable, world was when the one thing needful on the submarine was a supply of quinine—and, without fuss or bother, the quinine was lying on the table. It makes me feel a trifle uncomfortable that at this moment I have no other book by Jules Verne among the thousands of volumes I house than his illustrated geography of France; what was even France to this mage's Atlantis? He eclipsed Marryat and Ballantyne and Kingston for me; and Henty never fully caught my imagination.

Another child, Geoffrey, came along; it was this visitor who got me into trouble with Dr. Wood. For I was sent to his surgery at dead of night with injunction to knock as loud as I could and call him forth. I obeyed so thoroughly that when he came to the door thrusting his arms into his jacket as he walked, he was not at all pleased with me; and he seemed to be quite unconcerned at the news of my mother wanting his attendance. With Geoffrey's arrival, the schoolhouse proved too small for us all, and as they were taking a part of the garden filled with currant bushes and gooseberries for a new cemetery I was not sorry to hear that we were going to move. For the last time I heard as a familiar sound Mr. Honess sawing wood for coffins in his yard just above the little orchard, and called at Mrs. Giles's shop, hitherto the handiest, for some of her home-made black toffee. The cricket-pitch in the alley with its stone wicket would perhaps know Alfred Cheesman, Harry Excell, and me no more. I found that small stone with dusty grass again canopying it, but no play in progress, last summer.

CONGELOW

A mile, if so much, out of the village there was a hamlet consisting of a few cottages, an inn hardly better than an alehouse, a farm or two, and several hop-kilns. The biggest house, called Old Congelow, happened to be no longer wanted by the farmer for himself and we went as tenants; it was a complete and a fascinating change. The building was ancient and various, containing even a brewhouse and a dairy. The kitchen had a tiled floor, the scullery a brick floor; some of the windows had diamond panes; there were cupboards as big as rooms, and attics big enough to be playgrounds (which they quickly became). Steps up and down amused the young if not the old, and the way to get to the attic was by ladder. Everywhere old timber met the eye. The kitchen garden was walled round on every side; the yard was shaded by yews and a walnut-tree, and beyond it were stables and straw-yards, wagon-sheds, apple-lofts, tar-tanks, hop-kilns, granaries, and all else that a Kentish farm comprises. Even the pump (which was working perfectly) was centuries old. We danced about the new-found place in high spirits, which were not entirely in keeping with its sleepy, shadowy presence and the sense that its great days of farm importance were past.

It retorted by frightening us in the night season. Everybody knew that Congelow was haunted. We heard sounds. The attics in daylight were not sinister, but perhaps even then there was a question mark; and when I dislodged from a crevice a bottle of pills labelled Belladonna the name alone seemed strange. At night more than once a violent thump startled us; it thumped from the attic. The attempted explanation was rats, dislodging brick or tile. Then there arose in fits and starts a dull, whirring, buzzing noise. This was found to be the work of the wind in a loose pane of glass up there. Any night, you heard stony knockings. Gilbert investigated these; they were, he said, caused by a restless old horse stamping in the farm stables. But what was it that made the child Geoffrey leave his bed once or twice and walk towards the attic door? Filled with imaginary terrors I came into the courtyard one November dusk and saw a grey motionless figure, making me shriek, but making her laugh. It was

Miss Bell, waiting for our maid Lizzie Perrin to come out. Still, with the yew trees' darkness just got through, my mistake was pardonable.

In time I grew accustomed to this rambling old house and liked nothing better than to have it to myself, as sometimes happened on an afternoon. By this time I was going to the grammar school, and Wednesday was a half-holiday, when I might run off to the river and catch a fish or two and come back and pretend to cook them. The art of angling had grown on me, and I even kept a little book with dates, weights, and other records of my victims. It was my feeling and it still is that fishing with too fine killing tackle is no sport, and I commonly got an old willow stem from the tangled wood at New Bridges and fished with that and the simplest of watercord, corks, and hooks. This style was in part enforced by penury. It had its own tantalizations. One day Will Baldock was with me, he being let off for an hour or two from his mild houseboy duties at Dr. Pout's, and the game was slow. Cheveney chimes warned us home already. My line was some of that coloured wax thread which was or ought to have been used at the infants' school for some improving minor art. Looking into a deep hole which we seldom bothered about, under a knobbly willow stump, I saw what looked like a length of hop-pole in the shadows. I had a gudgeon ready as a bait and quietly put him in the water; the pike, for that was the pole-like shape beneath, swallowed him at once. I ventured to pull, and the pike at once snapped my line and moved. But he had to pass a shallow either way. By this time Will occupied one end and I waded into the other, but the pike shot past me still trailing a bit of pink cord and a float. We watched him by these along the stream, till we met two grown-ups fishing, and while we reported our adventure the pike appeared. 'So help me God he is a bloody fine fish', said one of the anglers. It was like a bit of the Benedicite: in spite of the swear-word.

Another day, with yellow leaves tumbling from every bough, I left my rod with a bait for a jack in the weir pool at Cheveney. The hour was such as Crabbe might enjoy describing, God-forsaken, and I wandered for a little relief. On my return no cork to be seen! I pulled up, and a slow weight moved at the end of the line—a foul-hooked branch I supposed. Then I saw, past the wooden stakes over which my rod had been laid, that I had something else on the line. A really huge pike's head came slowly above the surface. I could not stop myself shrieking, but my alarm was unnecessary; the hook had not pierced the pike's inside and he sank back from the line as if asleep. Big pike are fearsome visions in English streams: I once went under an arch over the Arun in Sussex, to see the ancient stonework, and there in the silent dark water was one of them, a gross giant with murder in his eye and jaw. Still, if caught younger, they eat very well; and my mother used to cook them very well under Waltonian rules.

The water-world around us seemed endless. Every farm had its ponds and dykes, every winter brought its floods, which were watched by the boys with a sort of pride. 'She's highering!' The floods over the Leas made the way to the station difficult except in a cart. At New Bridges an innocent summer stream was metamorphosed into a loud, brown-lathered, glutting race of water to the top of the arch and over. Once the floods were out when a sharp frost came on; the water drained away and left a glassy lid of ice for many an acre, through which we found a pleasure in crashing a way. The swamp ponds in the shaws were the homes of marsh marigolds innumerable, and on their bank the celandine, wood anemone, primrose, bluebell bloomed as though all the children in the world might fill their baskets and make no difference to the throng. I was willing to go primrosing, though it might be a little undignified, for a pretty reason: Lavinia Pattenden was going with the girls. Her face was as beautifully clear as a primrose, and I liked all she did; she passed the house every day and on Sundays wore bright clothes and carried a prayer-book and hymn-book and even a little walking-stick. Her grandmother brought her up in a cottage at Benover, the next hamlet—the cottage was tiny but exquisite, and has been utterly demolished with its neighbours in the progress of England. 'Lavinia'—but she was called Vina by everyone. Her sense of flowers was charming, and she enjoyed poetry, especially (or so my memory has it)

> It was the time when lilies blow
> And clouds are highest up in air . . . .

The master of the grammar school suggested to my father that I might become a pupil. Cleave's School, established 1665, to give it its full title, stood on a high site looking down at the church and high street; a building ornamented in local style with rich red half-moon tiles, and guarded with a line of chestnut-trees. The village green sloped down from its gate to the cross-roads, and just at the corner of its wall was the primitive lock-up with iron-studded door. This school, though its history was one of gaps and mis-managements, had long been held in honour. Many farmers in the district had had their schooling at Cleave's, especially since Mr. Samuel Williams had been headmaster. In my day about sixty boys attended, half of them boarders, and of those one or two came from France or Germany. The curriculum printed on the terminal reports might impress even a German parent, for I fancy that it included (mensuration was one of the simpler items) callisthenics and astronomy. There was an usher; he had one classroom and Mr. Williams the other.

So in the spring of 1907 I was committed to the charge of the junior schoolmaster, in the long classroom with the leaded window running its entire length; and after the diligent work of my father's school I was rather surprised at the amiable leisure here. Under the desks the boys kept stacks of private reading—magazines and serial adventures of Sexton Blake and Jack, Sam, and Pete; and the young master was urged to give opinions on matters far removed from even algebra. But algebra there was; and parsing and analysis; and Euclid. Why? Nobody stopped for that, and I wandered along with the rest—*omnes eodem cogimur*. One thing was sure: Mr. Williams himself was a learned man and learning was a desirable state rather than a number of things memorized. But we were given much to remember.

The school day began with a general assembly in the senior classroom for prayers. Mr. Williams, marching in fresh and puffing importantly, read these with little melodies at phrases like 'neither run into any kind of danger'. Then he would select a hymn, and very often it was one with angels in it. Seated at the harmonium, he would brush back his scarecrow gown and execute the tune with flying fingers; the boys were well used to his system, which was to take the first three lines of a stanza at a gallop and the fourth with solemn delay.

full speed	Around the throne of God a band Of glorious angels ever stand, Bright things they see, bright harps they hold,
dead slow	And On Their Heads Are Crowns . . . Of . . . Gold.

When the music was over the lesser boys receded into their school-room, the others heard an address or exhortation from Mr. Williams, usually on character. Behind him as he spoke we saw the gilded names of former scholars who, presumably possessing character, had passed several public examinations; and on the notice board he had perhaps pinned a column out of a newspaper concerning some old boy who was now on the frontiers as a mounted policeman, or otherwise making his way in the world. Character, that was what mattered, it was something each boy must take out to his future mission, now was the time to develop character. Now, boys, if you cut your finger, is that worse than losing your cap? No. Your finger will heal up again; but you won't get a cap so easily. Character. Sometimes Mr. Williams would resume the music with a song which might almost be called our school song, and which was poured out with energy:

> Whatsoe'er you find your duty,
>   Do it, Boys, with all your Might;
> Never be a little truthy,
>   Or a little in the right.
> Trifles even lead to heaven,
>   Trifles make the life of man;
> So in all things, great and small things,
>   Be as thorough as you can.

How he loved his boys! We had some difficulty to perceive this at the time. He liked to be thought a bit of an ogre. As we filed in still chattering from the playground, he suddenly appeared with large eyes at a window, and then we were expected to give an 'eyes left', which he acknowledged with a military salute. How curiously he smiled as this happened! Cleave's was all a little state, himself the president of it, and no other state at war with it. Sometimes he dealt out justice, which was always betokened by his setting up a violent clatter with his new cane on his desk, and sometimes by his repeating loudly 'The Lord hath spoken unto Samuel.' It was not at me that he was looking one day as he said this, but he meant me. I had absented myself the Saturday morning before, and thought I had escaped notice altogether; but he had found out by his uncanny power where I had been, and he thrashed me without appeal.

The homework on which he insisted was considerable. He would write up on blackboards a table, thus:

City	*On what river*	*Country*	*What famous for*

and add a great string of place-names, for which we were to get the required information that evening. At Congelow I had a private corner for my work, not far from the family's barrel of beer, which I tried in very modest samples for the good of the grammar school. Mr. Williams taught us French so well that when I reached a great school I was much in advance of almost all competitors; he had the grammar and the spoken language. A time was given for writing our diaries, contained in thick books of abominable paper which nevertheless had the shield of Cleave's School on their cardboard covers, and cost only twopence each. Each entry had to be begun with a weather report ('Beastly weather' was often enough), and Mr. Williams read and marked all we wrote. In my time I suppose the cleverest boy in the school was Tom Singyard, who was a born mathematician and, generally, understood whatever was put before him. He lived some way beyond Congelow in a house near a disused brickworks, which had become a chain of ponds hidden in thickets and sagbeds, full of carp and tench and water lilies and moorhens. He kept me in a state of misery all the road home by pulling my hair and swinging me round and using me as a butt for his wit; but I was devoted to him. One day I appeared at school wearing some knickers of a certain breadth hurriedly made by my mother. Tom Singyard raised his eyebrows, and, to the boys round, he uttered the sufficient description 'Bells'. Thereafter, when he would torment me, he merely uttered this word in a lovely tunable voice, 'Bells', and it became my nickname, which he does not live to use. He and his promising young mind were not to survive the first world war. Everything that we could do at all he could do well, including cricket and football. I envied him this superior gift, but perhaps even more his home in that lonely place with the old kiln overgrown with ivy and ash, the pools only separated by narrow paths, the swans winging to and fro out of the forests of reeds.

One advantage I had—some say it was not an advantage—even over clever Tom Singyard. At Congelow there was a good-sized cupboard off the sitting-room and into it my father bundled (for it had good shelves) a number of his books. Either I had not had access to them before or I had not been interested, but now I was. They were miscellaneous, but they included some old literature—sets of the *Tatler* and the *Spectator*, a few eighteenth-century plays like *Oroonoko* bound together, the works of Paley, of Josephus, *British Battles by Land and Sea*, an early Victorian Encyclopaedia, Bacon's essays, *New Atlantis*, and other pieces, apocryphal plays of Shakespeare, two quarto Bibles with copper engravings, and much else. One tall book, which had been deposited on my father in acknowledgement of a loan, had my attention for years: it was Thomas Stanley's *History of Philosophy*, a seventeenth-century masterpiece, with alleged portraits of the Greek philosophers. These were not the best books in the house, but such as they were they aroused in me some sense of bygone tastes, studies, and feelings.

Boys came from the remoter parts of the parish and from other villages to Cleave's School. The two Readers from Laddingford way, the Featherstones from East Peckham were among my special friends. The Readers had, in their fathers' farms, a lovely little river, all twists and turns, called the Teise, and we had afternoons with rod and line there. The Teise runs into the Medway at last round a place called the Ring, an ancient cricket ground, which at that time was girdled with many splendid trees and one or two white pillars that had been trees but had been struck by lightning. This circle of greensward, invaded by coarse tussocks of swamp grass, was the school's cricket ground, and sometimes we played a match against a Maidstone school. Cricket was a great thing in the village, and I had the honour of being scorer often and sometimes last man in for the second eleven. The away matches might mean a delightful ride in a horse brake, and songs on the way home under skies of golden glow, past unknown parks and orchards, yet at last down our own familiar hill with its spring-well and stacks of fruit baskets by the farm gates. Sometimes Jack Cheeseman would inspect a little book in which scores of our private contests (Alf Cheesman, Harry Excell, and me) were kept if creditable enough. Alas, going in last for the men's eleven was not always without responsibility. I once did so when Herbert Cheeseman (and he is still a batsman to be reckoned with) had gone all through the innings and was within sight of his century. My orders were to stay, naturally, and I was being wary, when the grandly moustached enemy bowler had an idea and sent me down a lob on the leg side. I saw an obvious gift and took a bang—just where he wanted, for the ball sailed straight into somebody's safe hands in the distance, and poor Herbert Cheeseman was not out 92, no more. He was scoring well forty years after that.

Mr. Williams had no special affection for cricket, which he knew was a menace to common sense and useful knowledge, but he sent the school off to afternoons at Tonbridge when the county side was playing, and he obtained very cheap tickets for the railway journey and the ground. As for the play, I cannot now recall much. Kent certainly disappointed us once by being overwhelmed by lunch time, and a fine attacking innings by K. G. MacLeod of Lancashire placed him among my heroes. All who figured in county cricket were indeed heroes to me, and when my father pointed out to me (after some such match) Mr. E. W. Dillon actually standing on the railway platform I gazed as on 'the herald Mercury, new-lighted on a heaven-kissing hill'. My father took me to Chichester among other scenes of the summer game, and sweetly still I hear the words 'the Priory ground', which that day lay bathed in sunshine and Sussex serenity.

The village cricketers of the Edwardian period were not so learned and assiduous in the game as those of today. A few were skilful, the others turned out for friendly reasons. Should they score a run or catch a ball there was wit and delight. But the stock bowlers were born to their business. Albert Cheeseman at one end and my father at the other were accurate and had resources. Bowling at me on our Congelow pitch, C. E. B. one evening hit the single stump I was defending three times in succession with big leg breaks, and next match on the Kintons he bowled down the wickets of three batsmen similarly in three balls. He had formerly defeated K. S. Ranjitsinhji so in the nets at Brighton; and he was the stamp of bowler who still gets the day, even in international cricket. He played for several sides, and sometimes when he was teaching in school the vicar would dash in to collect him and we would see no more of him till the late evening unless his game was on the village ground. The ground was a perfect piece of green, the darling study of Dr. Pout, a retired army surgeon who was little pleased one day to come along when Excell, Cheesman, and I were enjoying the unauthorized use of his very best pitch. We fled with our tackle to the river to hide but the little Doctor trotted along as one with a grievance and standing on the top of the bank addressed us below, 'You are the worst boys in the whole village.' This was not all. Striking a ball into the gutter of his pavilion roof I had to recover it, whereupon a section of the gutter came off in my hand. In this dreadful situation I decided on boldness and went straight to Dr. Pout's Georgian front door. He heard my confession and saw the evidence with a grin, then said, 'I dare say it can be mended.' We once even managed to pitch our stumps on the county ground at Hastings (it was a choir excursion day, and we had got sick of drifting about promenades and had come prepared). But the groundsman was soon aware of the enormity and again we had to go like the wind.

A recurrent difficulty was to get enough money for cricket and other expenses. At home the family was growing—Geoffrey and Anne were now of the flock—and we could not expect much. My receipts from the choir were very irregular; weddings and funerals of a wealthy kind were all too few; and organ-tuning was rare too. The scorer, if somebody remembered it, had a penny or twopence at the end of the afternoon; and I imposed myself upon visiting cricketers of the many-coloured blazer class, to carry their bags to the ground, which made something. One Christmas Will Baldock encouraged me to sing carols outside the French windows at Cheveney: result, 6d. apiece, of which I spent a halfpenny on the way home. Hanging up my trousers in my bedroom I was rash enough to jingle the remaining 5½d. and boast about it to my brother; this was overheard and the cash confiscated by my father with the advice that it was disgraceful to get it in such a way and it would be returned to the donor. Next, an advertisement in a *Union Jack* caught my fancy. If I would send for 50 Beautiful Coloured Postcards, it appeared that I could sell them for 2d. each and receive a commission. I wrote, and the cards came, but even to my eye they were all too purple, and it was obvious that I should stand no chance of selling them in competition with the charming coloured views to be had at half the price from Mr. Hards next the bridge. While the postcard plan was in preparation I had hopefully entered my name at Mr. Butler's as a subscriber for a new and all-eclipsing boy's paper, entitled *The Marvel*. But on the collapse of the scheme, I saw that this was a liability beyond my prospects, and I could no longer call for the paper. Instead, I used to start running about a hundred yards from Butler's Shop and slow down only when well past it.

Meanwhile, it was mortifying that young Gilbert, who was not among the prize-winners for reading and writing acclaimed at the flower show, was able to command a certain income. Either in money or in kind he was passing rich, and from the very start he had been quite clear about his tactics. These were, 'to make himself general useful'. If he saw somebody doing a job of work, he at once showed sympathy and suggested that he might lighten that labour. Peter Jones, for example, had plenty to do round about Captain Reid's garden, sheds, and lofts. Gilbert was ready to save him steps and errands. This produced a remuneration in apples, or even in medlars, besides a kind of freedom, so that Gilbert could go in and out where others were not expected. If he was rebuffed at first, he still insisted on his handsome, disinterested offer of help, and generally he had his way. His biggest capture was Sid Mercer, who for so many years drove the baker's van on a tour extending miles round the district. The boy became his perpetual companion, and was remarkably handy with every item of the business, from proving dough to dosing the horse; and kind Sid Mercer saw to it that he had lots of windfalls. If Gilbert was too confident, Mercer would point out to him that his father was set on making a parson of him—most hateful thought, and revolved with some moral advantage. The most expressive moment in Gilbert's career as we saw it came a little later when he was officially confined at home with measles. Mercer's van drew up outside, and the boy Lancelot meeting our old friend said that as Gilbert was not at liberty he would like to come out for the day in his place. Mercer, opening his eyes comically, agreed; and Lancelot climbed up into the front seat of the van. But suspicion had arisen in Gilbert's room at the back of our house and in the nick of time he danced forth in his nightshirt, out into the road, and hauled the dejected Lancelot out of the seat sacred to himself.

Through Gilbert it was that we heard of makes of cars and motor-bicycles, and his eye for business combined with pleasure was useful in getting home a modest machine of our own. His Threepenny Bicycle was not very new, naturally, but it went. It had, or once had, solid tyres; otherwise it had only essentials. With this bicycle I went off, a little unwilling to be observed by too many acquaintances, into parishes around, where I never was till then; these rides were delightful, for every crooked lane and smithy and timber-yard and country-box came before me in its individuality. That sense is gone nowadays. It stayed with me some years, even in the battle-fields of Flanders, where generally I saw and felt every communica-tion trench and every sandbagged ruin as a personal, separate figure, quite distinct from every other one. But of battlefields, except some required to be memorized for examinations, my world was free in the Congelow days.

The trouble of examinations was becoming serious. I sat many hours in the little brick-floored room by the street door with my desk and selection of textbooks, trying to get all the prescribed subjects into my tidiest writing. These efforts, on which the western sunbeam looked gently and kindly, won me a prize or two inscribed by Samuel Williams—but he was getting me ready for an outside test, with that queer name on it, 'The College of Preceptors', which shone in gold letters from the walls of his classroom, and beneath it the names of old pupils who had been found worthy. I was one day sent off to take this examination at Rochester, where Uncle Hubert looked after me. He was a schoolmaster, a witty, merry man with a light beard, and Aunt was pretty and ever on the move, and they loved their little new house on the side of the river valley, and all was gay—even the examination. Great games were played by their son and me and some little girl whom we had collected with the trolleys in the old cement quarries near there. I later returned for another examination, also held in the Mathematical School at Rochester, the object of which was to get me admission to Christ's Hospital. My expectations were not high, and I thought nothing much of the matter, being more interested in the fact that I was suddenly a man of the world, ordering my own lunch ('dinner') at a restaurant in one of the county's finest towns. Sixpence!

The College of Preceptors decided in due course that I had done well enough, but it appeared that the other examination was the more important one. I was called to my father's room one morning and told that I had been successful, and would be given a place at Christ's Hospital. It was good and bad news too. For I did not see how I could leave our old home, with all its faults, and the village, with all its happy scenes and pastimes. Still, I should very shortly be going. Farewell the bread-and-butter pudding and toasted cheese round Cleave's fume-emitting stove, farewell the hours as volunteer teacher in my mother's school, farewell the solos in St. Peter and

St. Paul, and those midnights on the frozen ponds in naked hop-gardens under bobbetty-topped pollards and tingling stars!

Parents of boys to be admitted to Christ's Hospital were required to bring them up to London for medical examination and an address by the headmaster; this solemnity took place at a solemn hotel in Aldersgate. The headmaster, the great Dr. A. W. Upcott, in a friendly speech, though to my eye he looked formidable with his thick beard and strong shoulders, put the parents at their ease, and then asked them one by one whether their boys were to be included in the classical side or the modern. My father had agreed with me already on this, and he confirmed it in a whisper before he replied 'classical'. There was time for us afterwards to hasten to the Oval cricket ground and watch a little of the last game of the season. 'Perhaps we shall see you playing for Oxford yet', said C.E.B. It was as though Jules Verne had got me in a tale. My recent performances for the grammar school had not been quite up to this standard, though I had discovered how to remain at the wickets for ages without anything much happening. Meanwhile, A. E. Relf was 'doing a little hitting'. Yes, the immortals were all there. But I felt curiously lonely and out of my road.

With hair newly cut, and equipped with a blue 'fisherman's' jersey, a pair of rubber shoes, a Revised Version of the Bible, and so on according to Christ's Hospital instructions, I duly joined the boys who were now to follow Edmund Campion and Charles Lamb. Mrs. Allen, the wife of our former curate, had given me a small book of selections from Lamb, some of them delightful though devious. The reign of King Edward seemed, in spite of some occasional nonsense (my German cousin, not altogether gently, had said there was to be a war between our nations), a golden security. Everything did: the *Daily Telegraph*, the fishmonger on his due hour once a week with his basket on his quite imperial head (Mr. Goodwin), the flower show, and the never-delayed 2.23 to Maidstone on Saturday afternoon. The ripened apple-orchards and the light smoke from the September hop-kilns were always there. Perhaps the innovation of a magic lantern service in our old church did not please everybody, but Mr. Brooker and his bell-ringers did. Now I think of it, Mr. Brooker and our Brigadier-General later on the old Western Front had much the same gift of leadership.

INDEX

Compiled by R. E. Thompson

PRINTED IN GREAT BRITAIN
AT THE UNIVERSITY PRESS, OXFORD
BY VIVIAN RIDLER
PRINTER TO THE UNIVERSITY